FOR LACHLAN

DEAD ENDIA

- THE BROKEN HALO -

NOBROW

LONDON | NEW YORK

⨍ ⚊ ⚏ ⚌ ᵚ ⟋⟍ THE MULTI-PLANE ⨶ ⟍ ⬥ ⊡ ᵘᵘ ⟍

THE UNIVERSE IS DIVIDED INTO 13 PLANES. TRAVEL BETWEEN THE DEMONIC PLANES IS PERMITTED ONLY TO THOSE WITH AN OFFICIAL PLANE TICKET FROM AN EMBASSY OF THE ANGELIC HORDE. TRAVEL BETWEEN THE ANGELIC PLANES IS PERMITTED ONLY TO ANGELS AND GUESTS OF THE DIVINE. THE SEVENTH PLANE IS TO REMAIN A NEUTRAL PLANE BETWEEN THE SIX DEMONIC PLANES AND THE SIX ANGELIC PLANES AND THE EXISTENCE OF EITHER SIDE MUST REMAIN A SECRET TO THE NATIVE CREATURES KNOWN AS HUMANS.

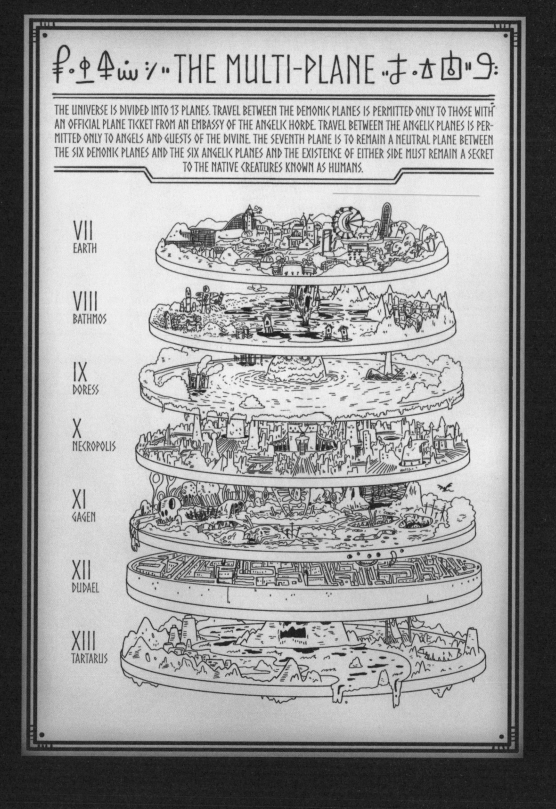

VII
EARTH

VIII
BATHMOS

IX
DORESS

X
NECROPOLIS

XI
GAGEN

XII
DUDAEL

XIII
TARTARUS

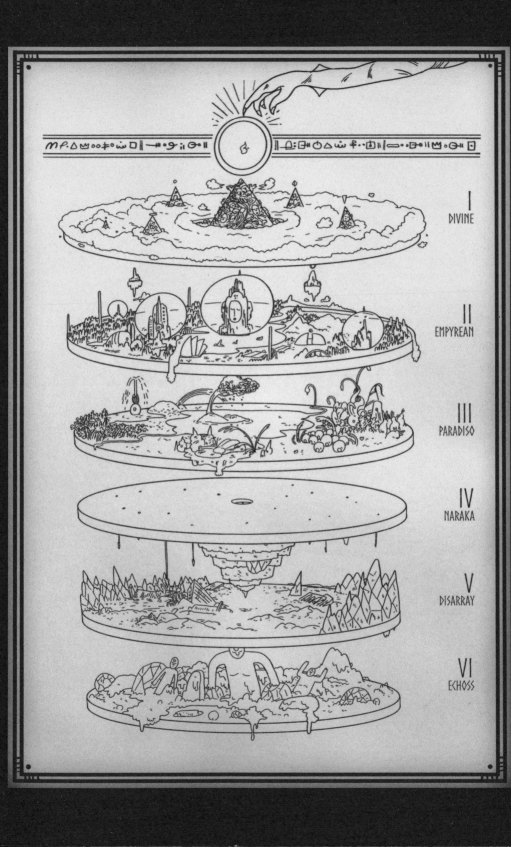

I
DIVINE

II
EMPYREAN

III
PARADISO

IV
NARAKA

V
DISARRAY

VI
ECHOSS

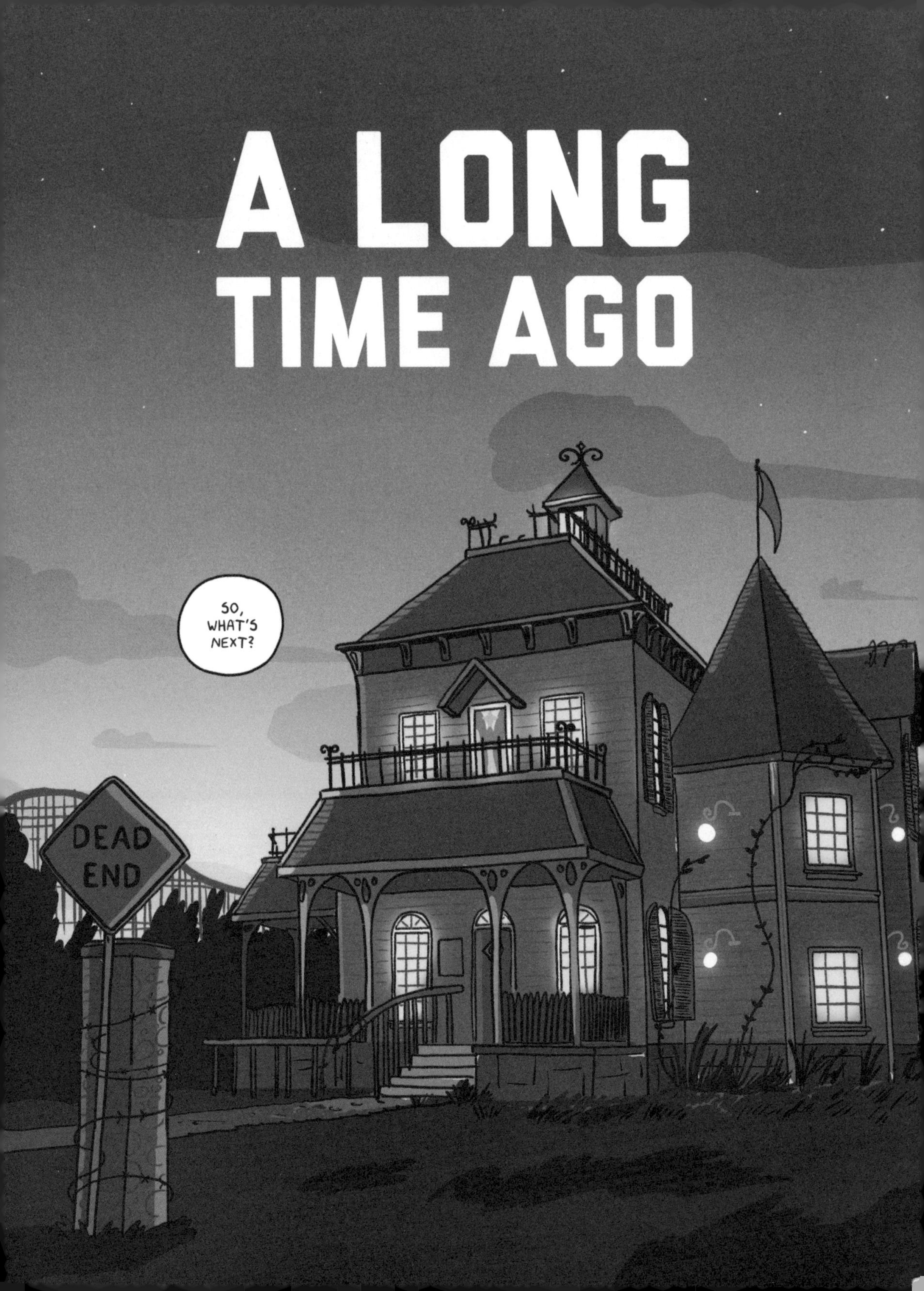
A LONG TIME AGO
SO, WHAT'S NEXT?
DEAD END

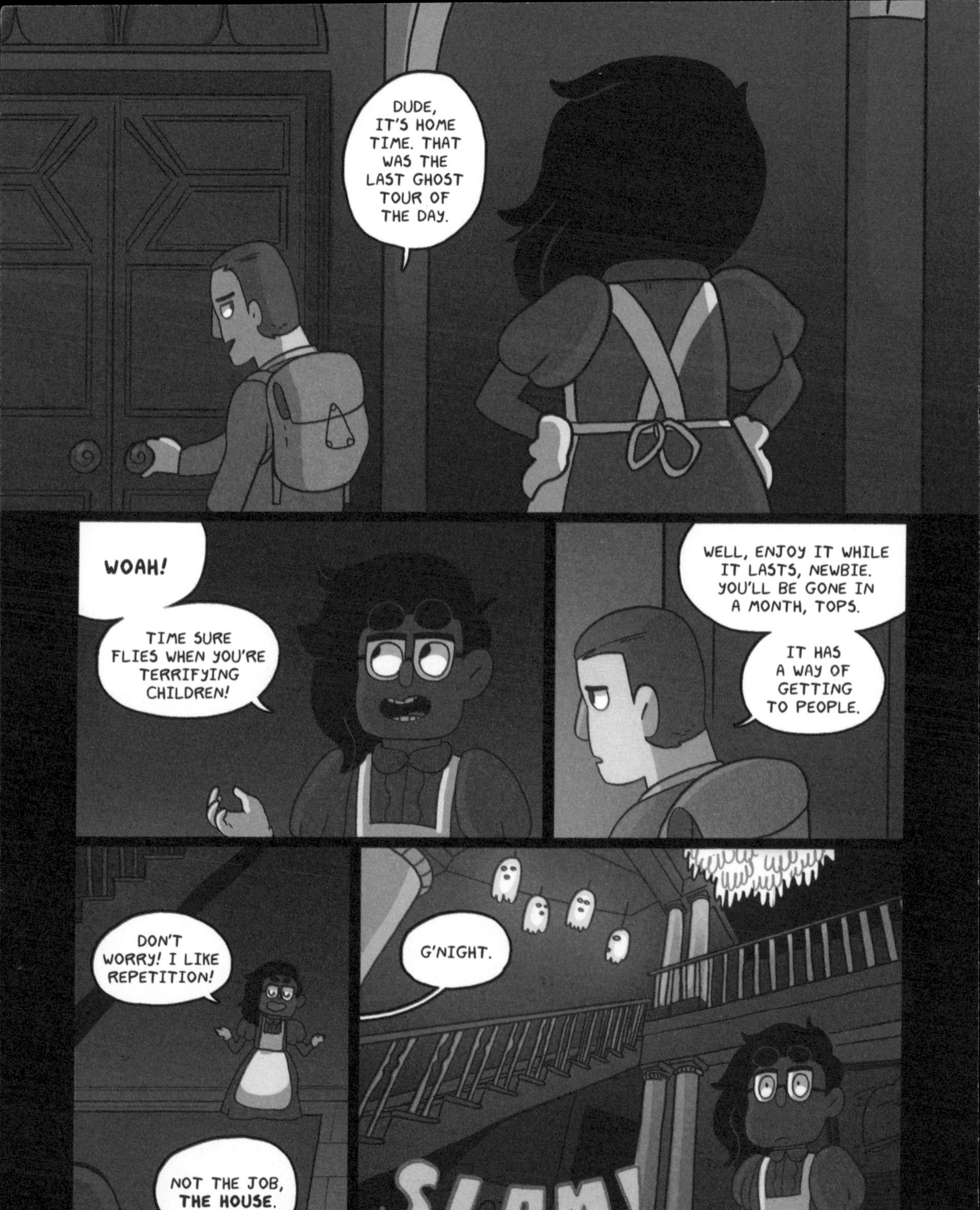
DUDE, IT'S HOME TIME. THAT WAS THE LAST GHOST TOUR OF THE DAY.
WOAH!
TIME SURE FLIES WHEN YOU'RE TERRIFYING CHILDREN!
WELL, ENJOY IT WHILE IT LASTS, NEWBIE. YOU'LL BE GONE IN A MONTH, TOPS.
IT HAS A WAY OF GETTING TO PEOPLE.
DON'T WORRY! I LIKE REPETITION!
NOT THE JOB, **THE HOUSE**.
G'NIGHT.
SLAM!

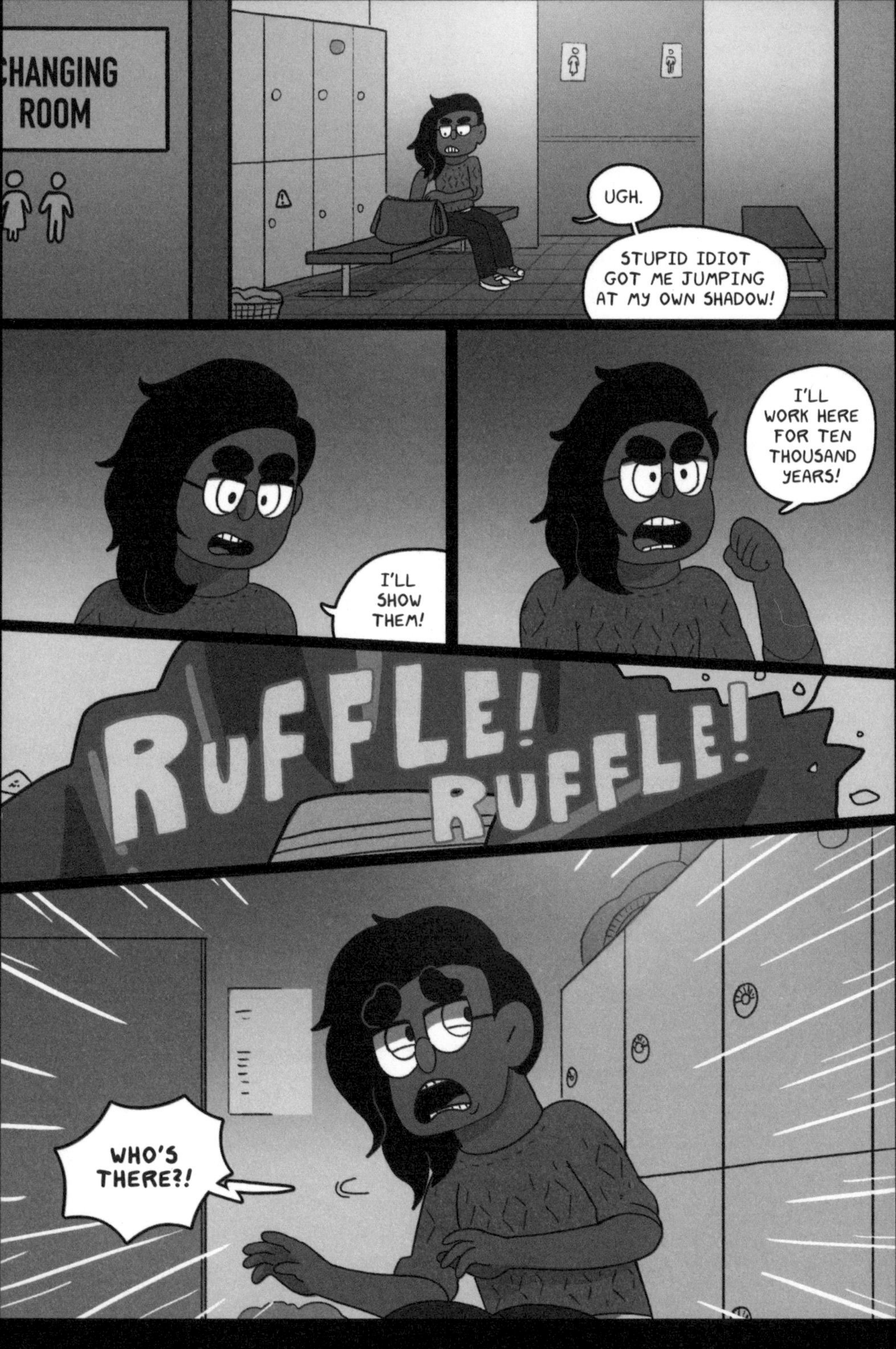
CHANGING ROOM
UGH.
STUPID IDIOT GOT ME JUMPING AT MY OWN SHADOW!
I'LL SHOW THEM!
I'LL WORK HERE FOR TEN THOUSAND YEARS!
RUFFLE! RUFFLE!
WHO'S THERE?!

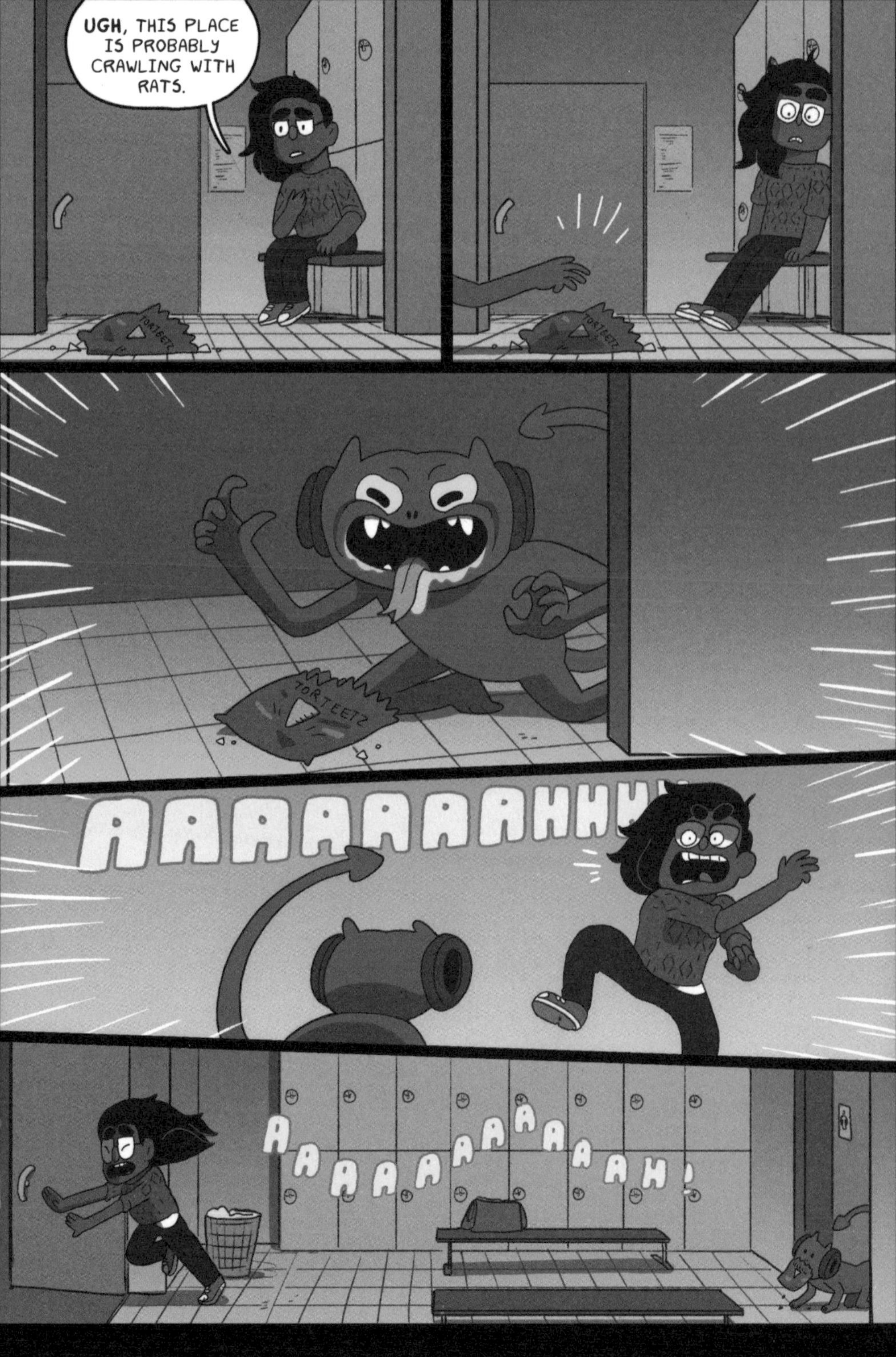

UGH, THIS PLACE IS PROBABLY CRAWLING WITH RATS.
TORTEETZ
AAAAAAAHHH
AAAAAAAAAAAH!

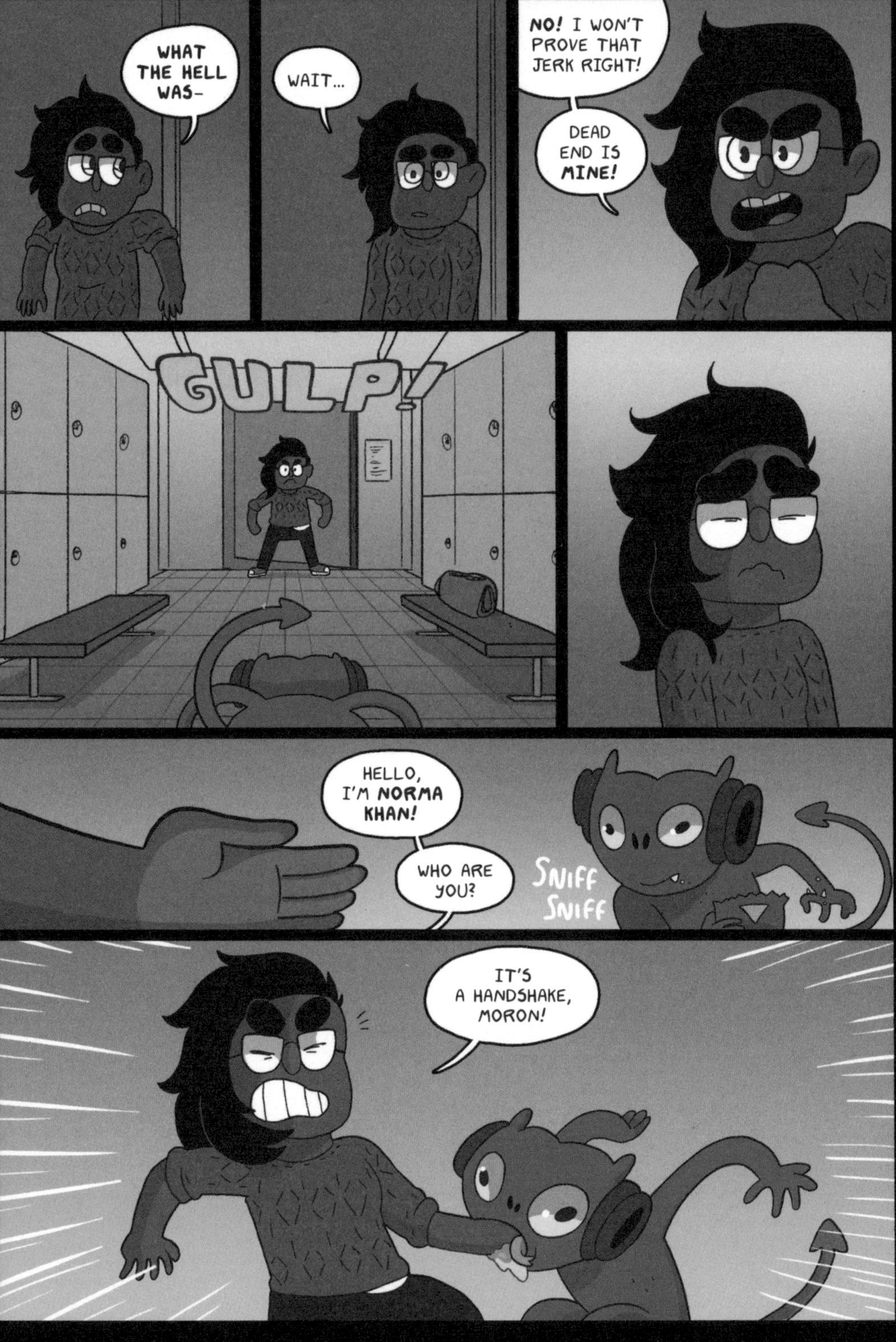
WHAT THE HELL WAS-
WAIT...
NO! I WON'T PROVE THAT JERK RIGHT!
DEAD END IS MINE!
GULP!
HELLO, I'M NORMA KHAN!
WHO ARE YOU?
SNIFF SNIFF
IT'S A HANDSHAKE, MORON!

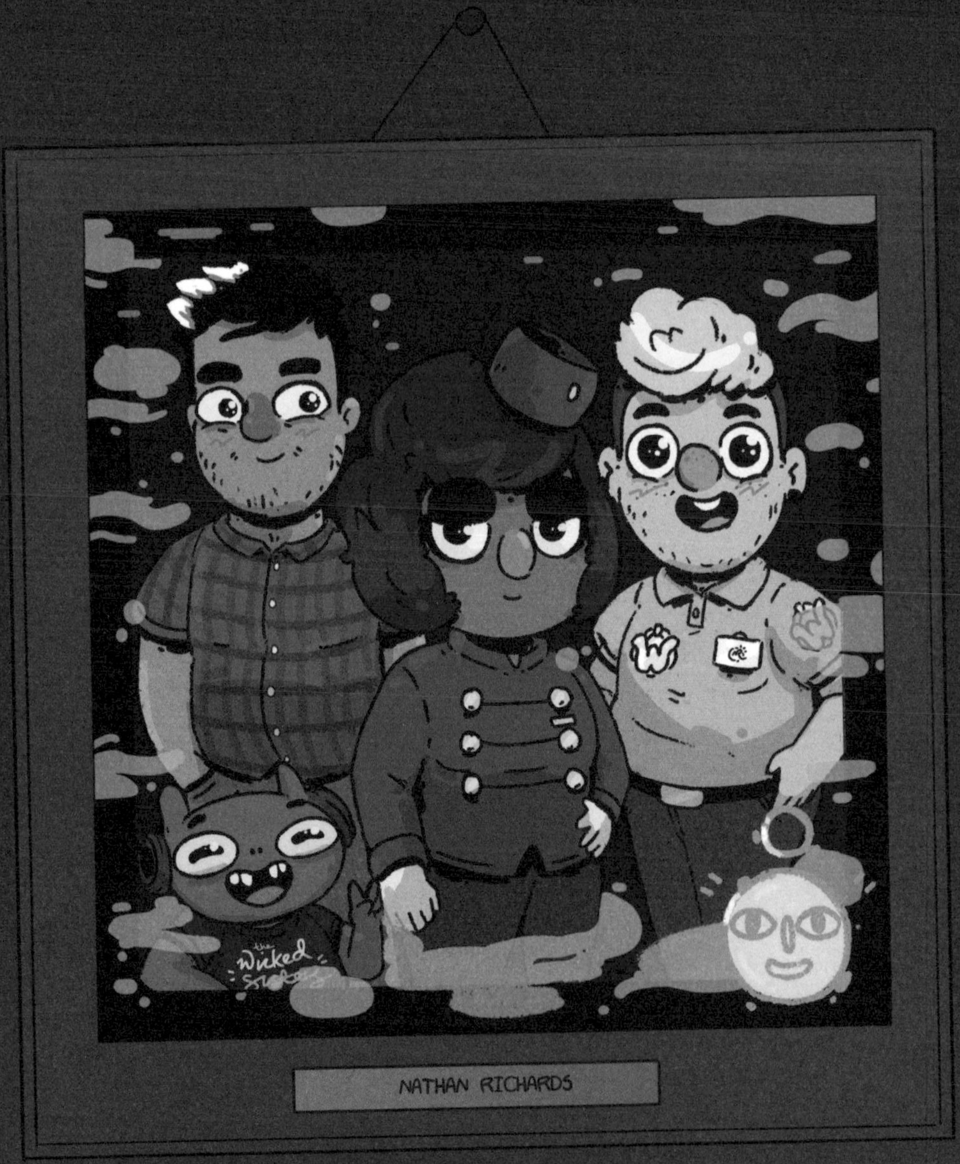
NATHAN RICHARDS

CHAPTER 1
A VERY SPECIAL GUEST

NORMA

TOUGH ●●●●●○○○
SMART ●●●●○○○○
WEIRD ●●●●●○○○
STYLE ●●●○○○○○

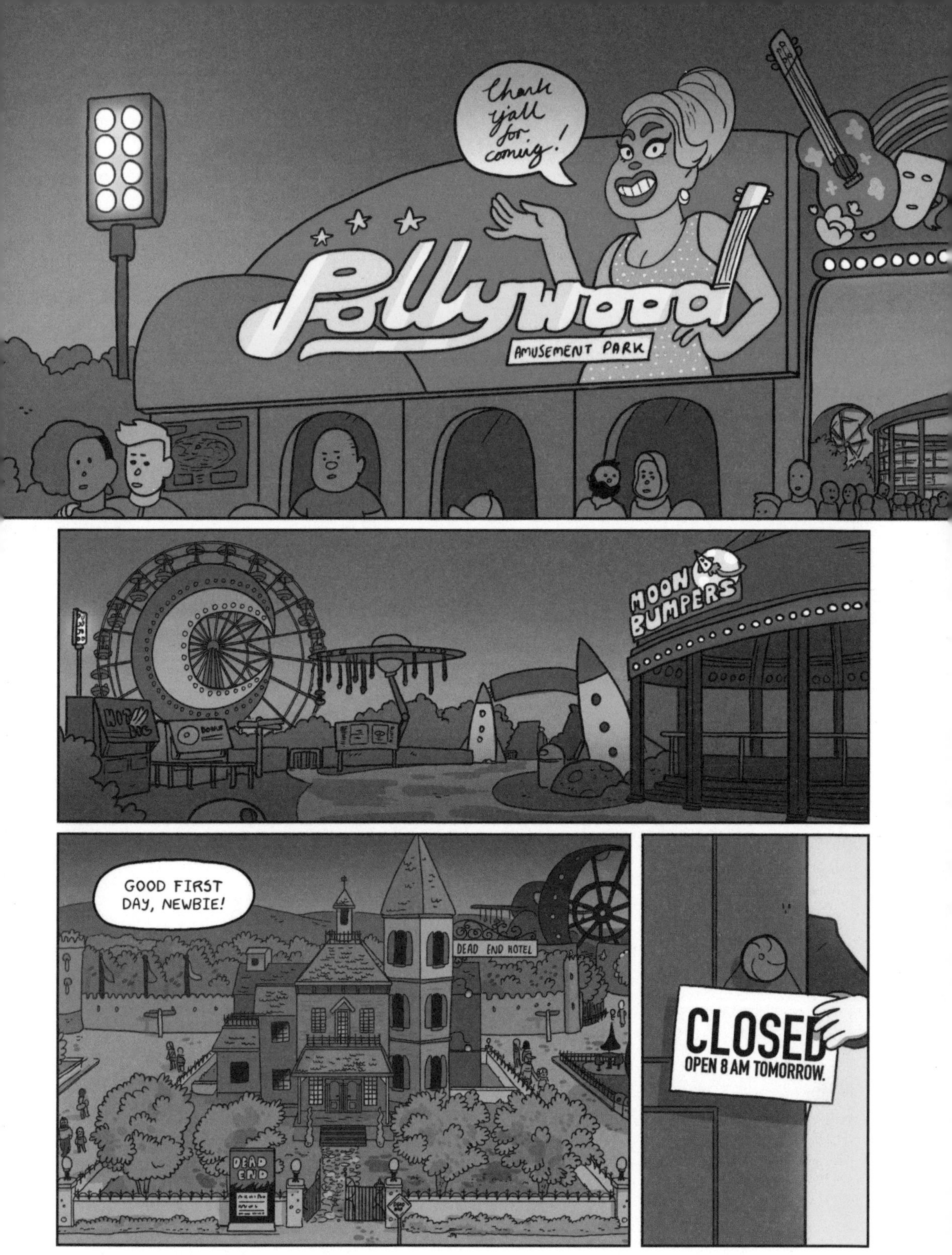
Thank y'all for coming!
Pollywood
AMUSEMENT PARK
MOON BUMPERS
GOOD FIRST DAY, NEWBIE!
DEAD END HOTEL
DEAD END
CLOSED
OPEN 8 AM TOMORROW.

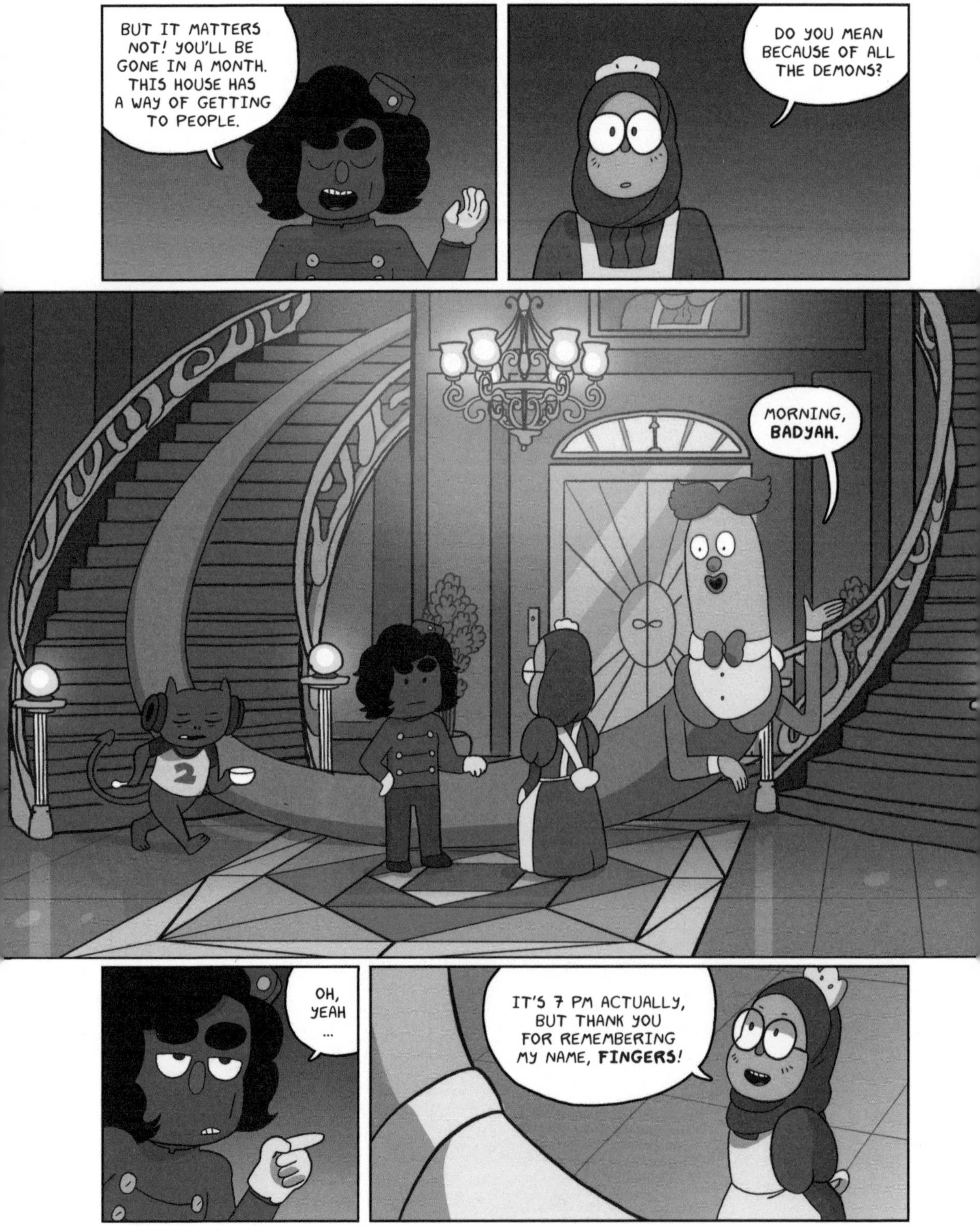

BUT IT MATTERS NOT! YOU'LL BE GONE IN A MONTH. THIS HOUSE HAS A WAY OF GETTING TO PEOPLE.
DO YOU MEAN BECAUSE OF ALL THE DEMONS?
MORNING, BADYAH.
OH, YEAH ...
IT'S 7 PM ACTUALLY, BUT THANK YOU FOR REMEMBERING MY NAME, FINGERS!

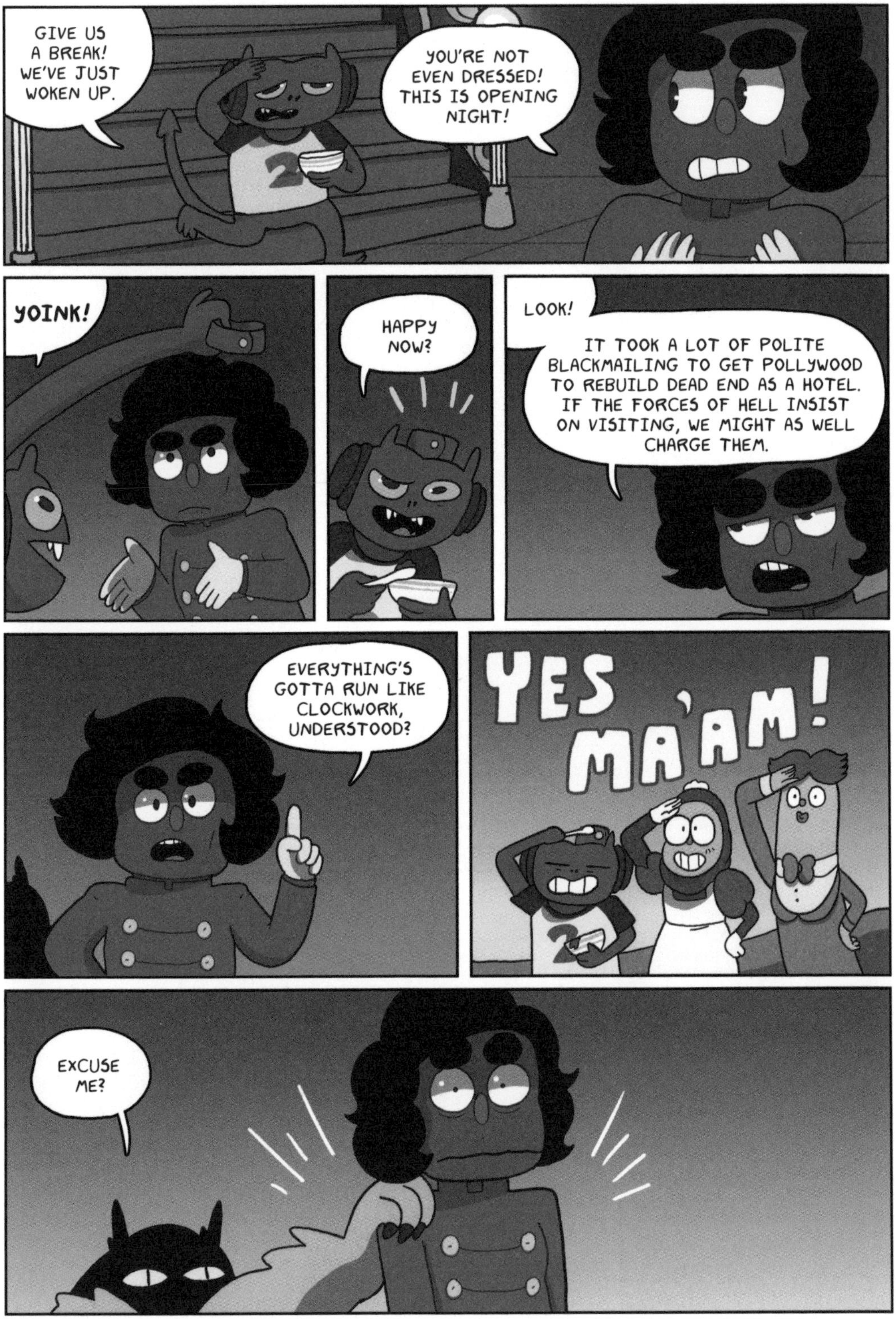
GIVE US A BREAK! WE'VE JUST WOKEN UP.
YOU'RE NOT EVEN DRESSED! THIS IS OPENING NIGHT!
YOINK!
HAPPY NOW?
LOOK!
IT TOOK A LOT OF POLITE BLACKMAILING TO GET POLLYWOOD TO REBUILD DEAD END AS A HOTEL. IF THE FORCES OF HELL INSIST ON VISITING, WE MIGHT AS WELL CHARGE THEM.
EVERYTHING'S GOTTA RUN LIKE CLOCKWORK, UNDERSTOOD?
YES MA'AM!
EXCUSE ME?

MAY I CHECK IN YET?

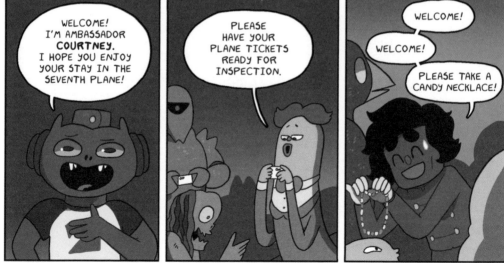

WELCOME! I'M AMBASSADOR **COURTNEY.** I HOPE YOU ENJOY YOUR STAY IN THE SEVENTH PLANE!

PLEASE HAVE YOUR PLANE TICKETS READY FOR INSPECTION.

WELCOME!

WELCOME!

PLEASE TAKE A CANDY NECKLACE!

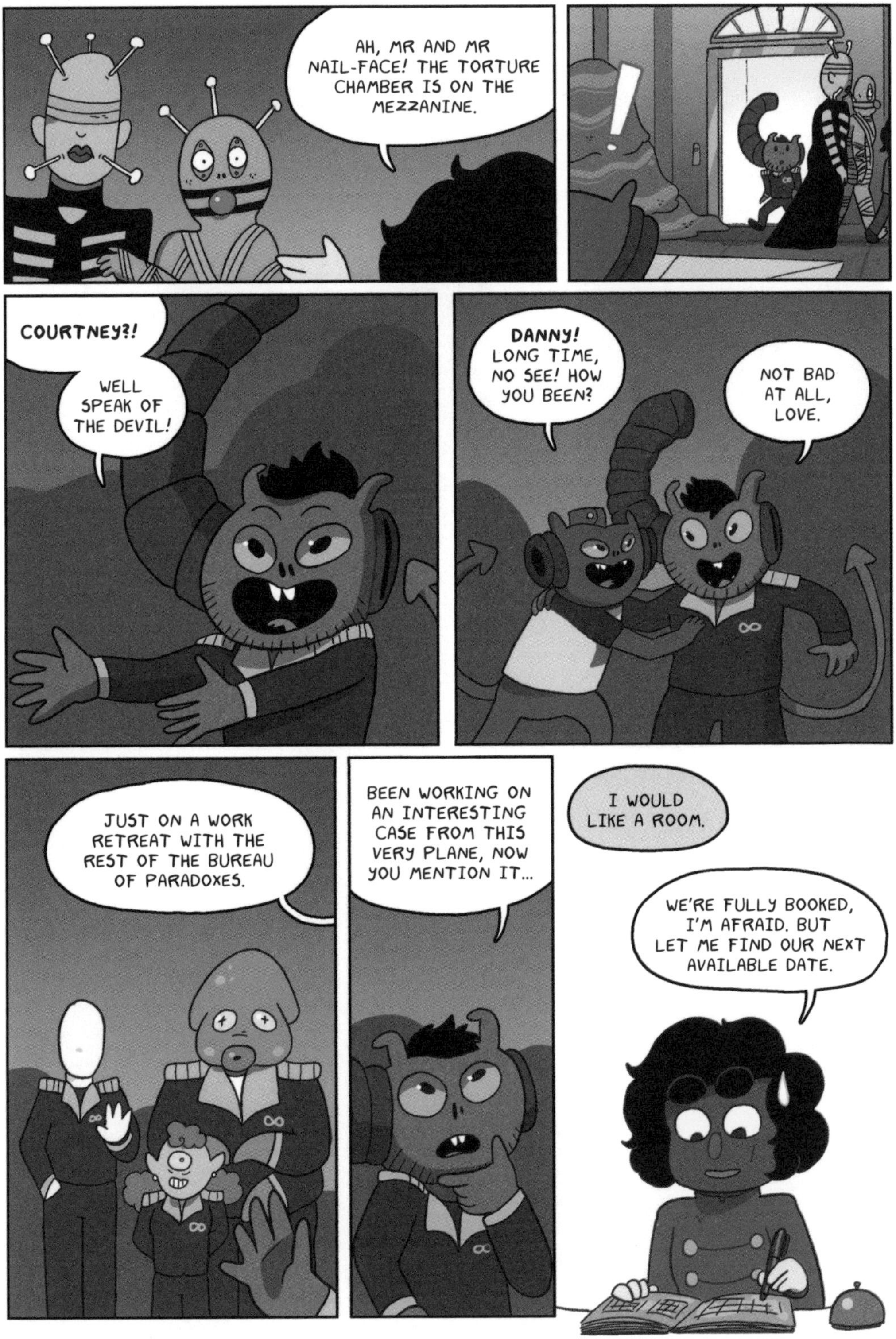
AH, MR AND MR NAIL-FACE! THE TORTURE CHAMBER IS ON THE MEZZANINE.
!
COURTNEY?!
WELL SPEAK OF THE DEVIL!
DANNY! LONG TIME, NO SEE! HOW YOU BEEN?
NOT BAD AT ALL, LOVE.
JUST ON A WORK RETREAT WITH THE REST OF THE BUREAU OF PARADOXES.
BEEN WORKING ON AN INTERESTING CASE FROM THIS VERY PLANE, NOW YOU MENTION IT...
I WOULD LIKE A ROOM.
WE'RE FULLY BOOKED, I'M AFRAID. BUT LET ME FIND OUR NEXT AVAILABLE DATE.

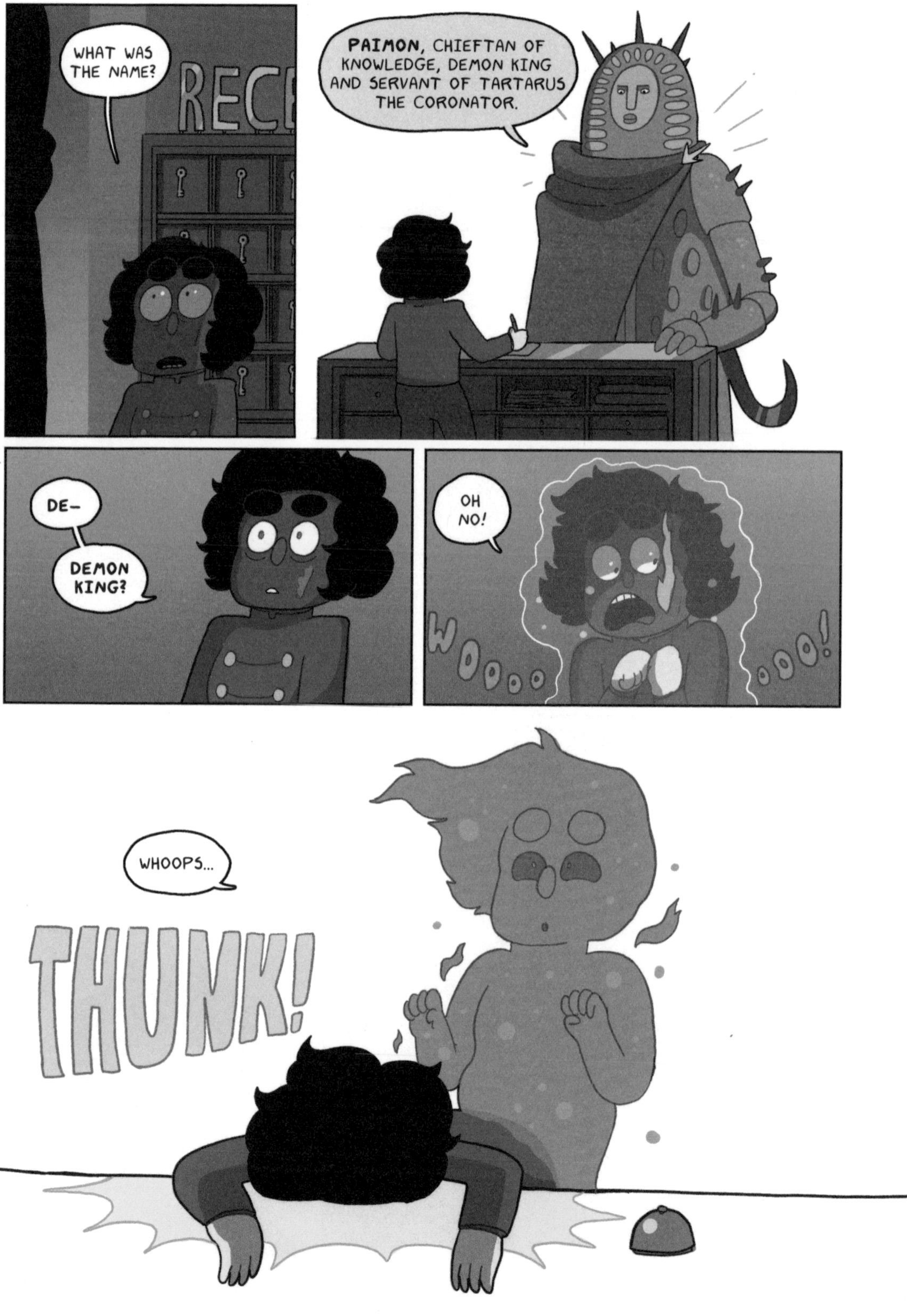
WHAT WAS THE NAME?
RECE
PAIMON, CHIEFTAN OF KNOWLEDGE, DEMON KING AND SERVANT OF TARTARUS THE CORONATOR.
DE–
DEMON KING?
OH NO!
WOOOOO...OOO!
WHOOPS...
THUNK!

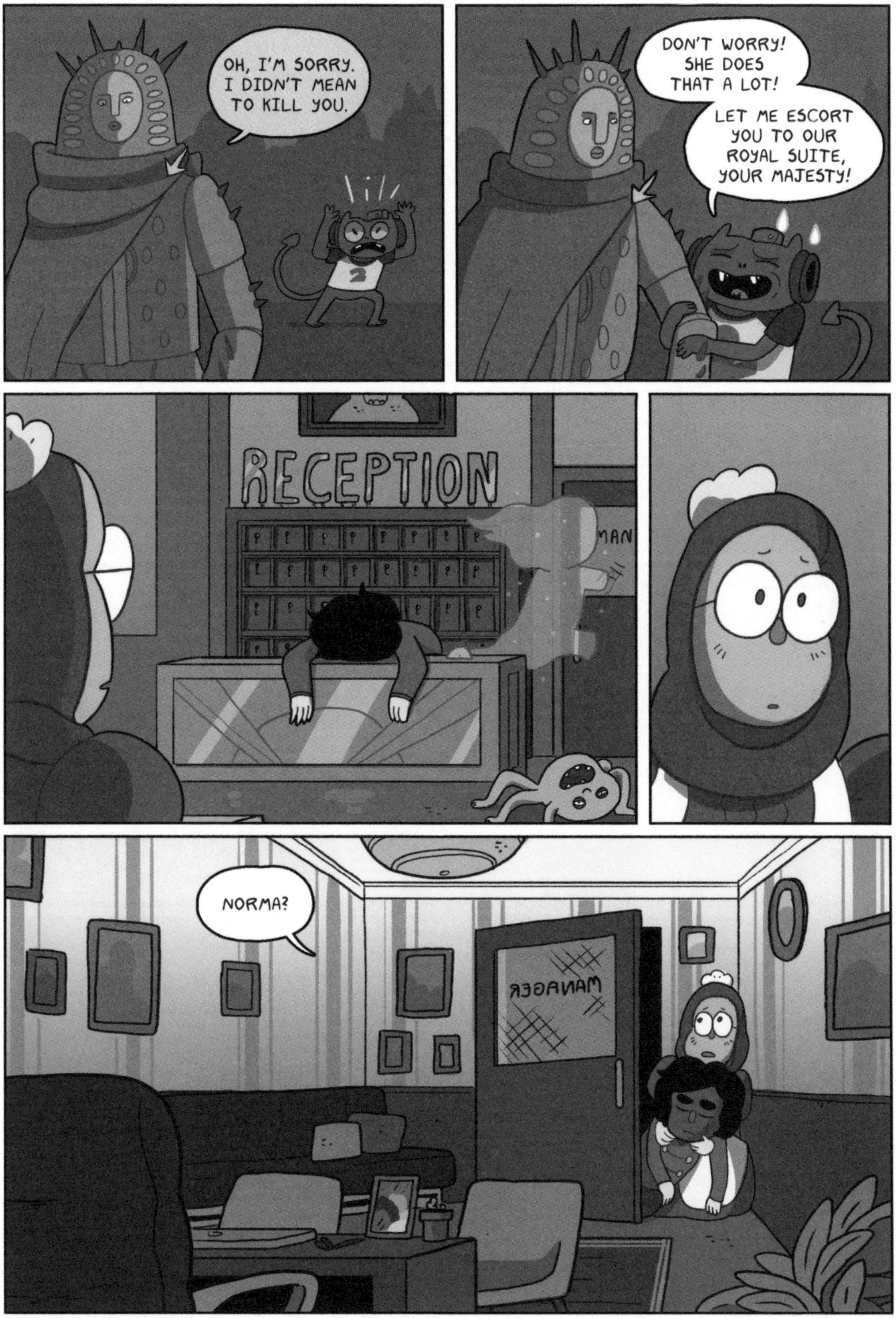
OH, I'M SORRY. I DIDN'T MEAN TO KILL YOU.
DON'T WORRY! SHE DOES THAT A LOT!
LET ME ESCORT YOU TO OUR ROYAL SUITE, YOUR MAJESTY!
RECEPTION
NORMA?
MANAGER

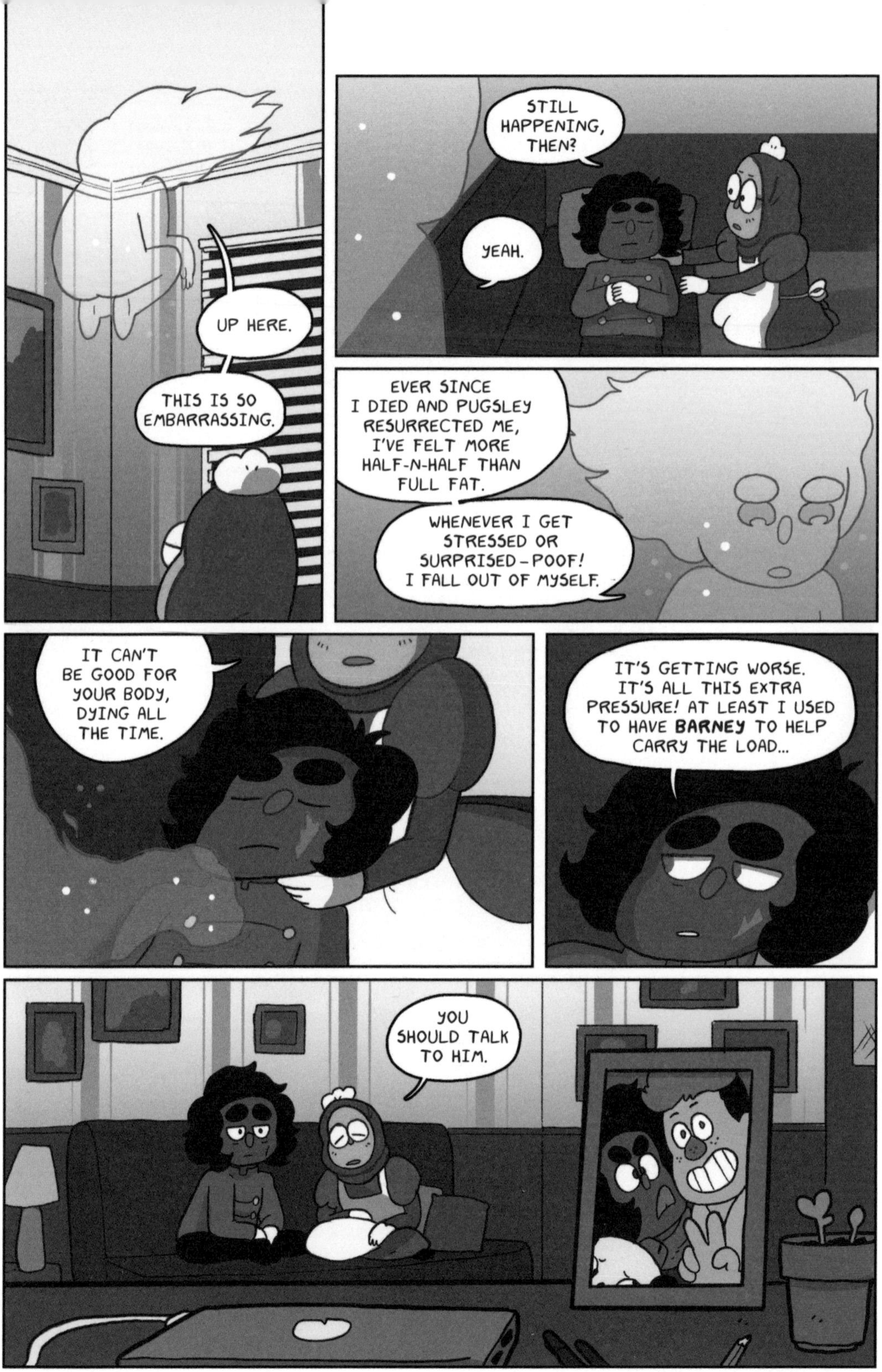
UP HERE.
THIS IS SO EMBARRASSING.
STILL HAPPENING, THEN?
YEAH.
EVER SINCE I DIED AND PUGSLEY RESURRECTED ME, I'VE FELT MORE HALF-N-HALF THAN FULL FAT.
WHENEVER I GET STRESSED OR SURPRISED - POOF! I FALL OUT OF MYSELF.
IT CAN'T BE GOOD FOR YOUR BODY, DYING ALL THE TIME.
IT'S GETTING WORSE. IT'S ALL THIS EXTRA PRESSURE! AT LEAST I USED TO HAVE BARNEY TO HELP CARRY THE LOAD...
YOU SHOULD TALK TO HIM.

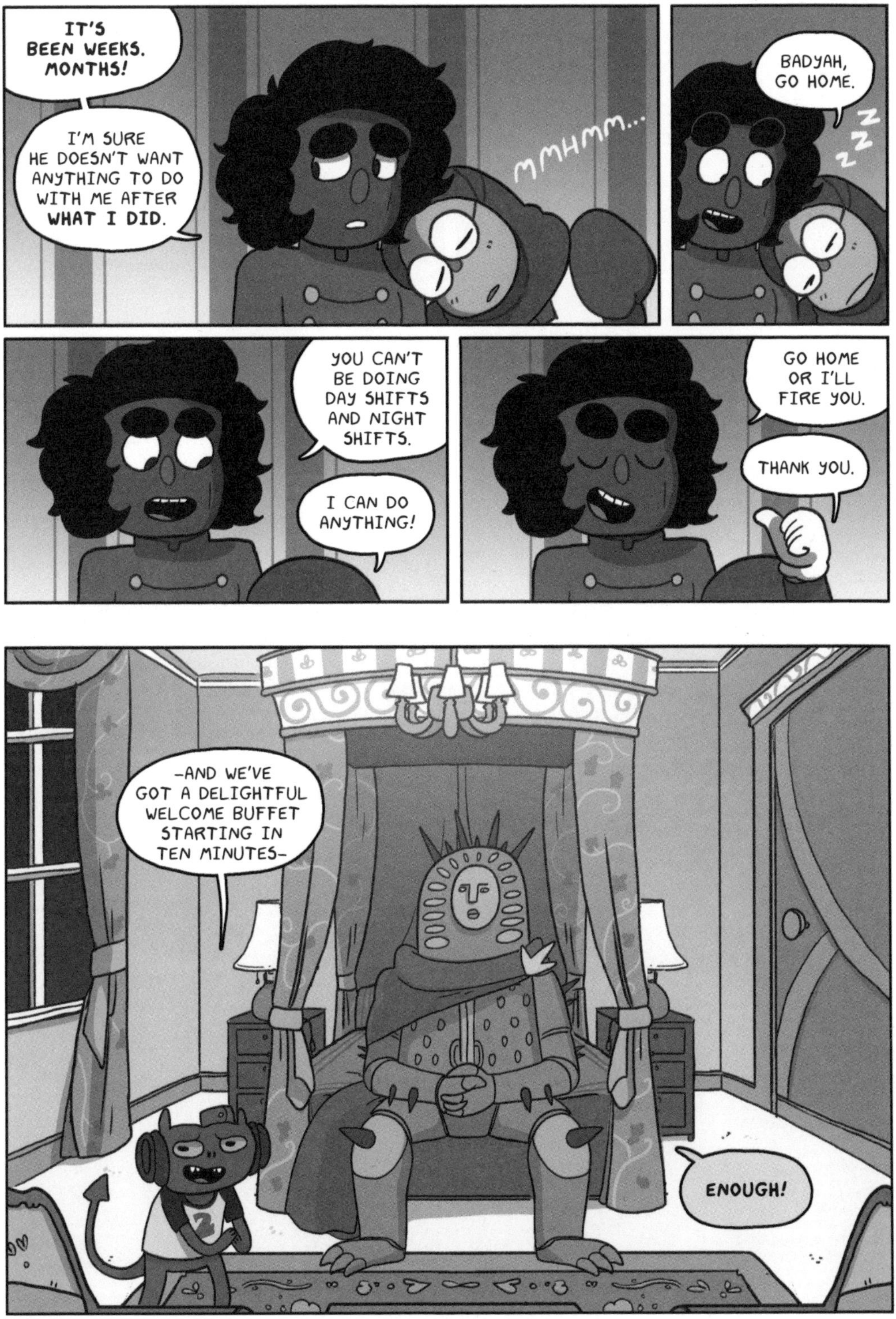
IT'S BEEN WEEKS. MONTHS!
I'M SURE HE DOESN'T WANT ANYTHING TO DO WITH ME AFTER WHAT I DID.
MMHMM...
BADYAH, GO HOME.
Z Z Z
YOU CAN'T BE DOING DAY SHIFTS AND NIGHT SHIFTS.
I CAN DO ANYTHING!
GO HOME OR I'LL FIRE YOU.
THANK YOU.
-AND WE'VE GOT A DELIGHTFUL WELCOME BUFFET STARTING IN TEN MINUTES-
ENOUGH!

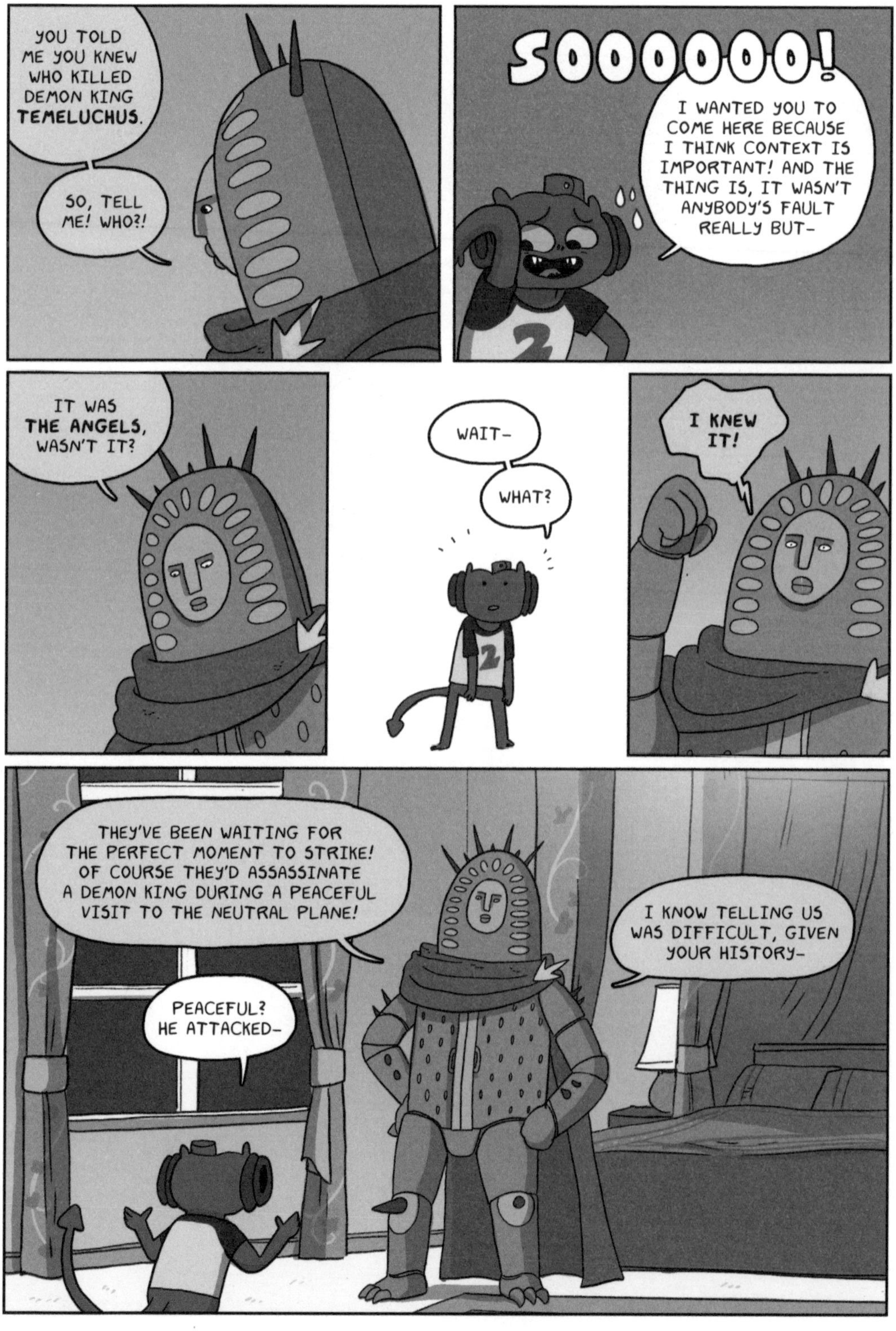
YOU TOLD ME YOU KNEW WHO KILLED DEMON KING **TEMELUCHUS**.
SO, TELL ME! WHO?!
SOOOOOO!
I WANTED YOU TO COME HERE BECAUSE I THINK CONTEXT IS IMPORTANT! AND THE THING IS, IT WASN'T ANYBODY'S FAULT REALLY BUT-
IT WAS **THE ANGELS**, WASN'T IT?
WAIT-
WHAT?
I KNEW IT!
THEY'VE BEEN WAITING FOR THE PERFECT MOMENT TO STRIKE! OF COURSE THEY'D ASSASSINATE A DEMON KING DURING A PEACEFUL VISIT TO THE NEUTRAL PLANE!
I KNOW TELLING US WAS DIFFICULT, GIVEN YOUR HISTORY-
PEACEFUL? HE ATTACKED-

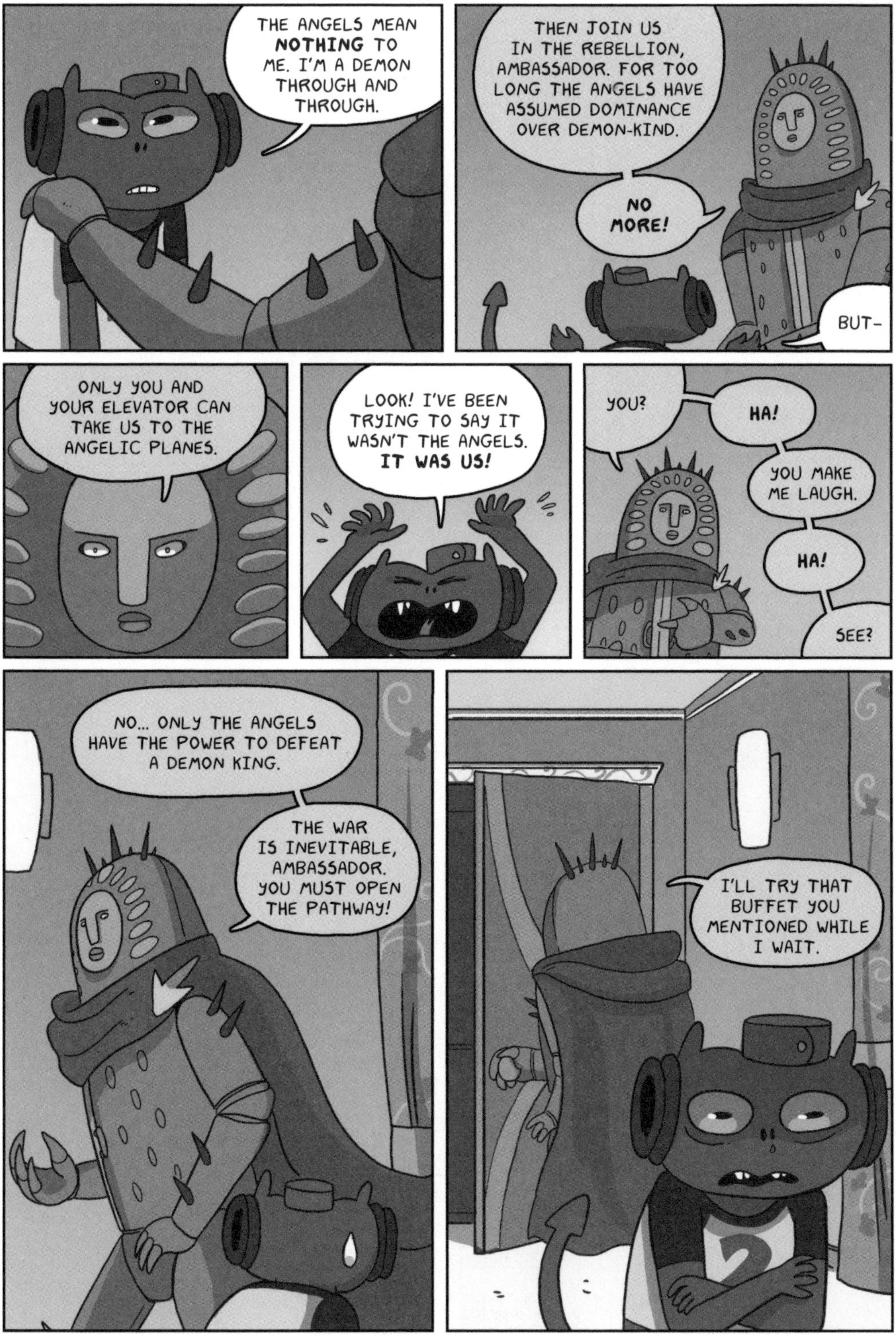
THE ANGELS MEAN **NOTHING** TO ME. I'M A DEMON THROUGH AND THROUGH.
THEN JOIN US IN THE REBELLION, AMBASSADOR. FOR TOO LONG THE ANGELS HAVE ASSUMED DOMINANCE OVER DEMON-KIND.
NO MORE!
BUT-
ONLY YOU AND YOUR ELEVATOR CAN TAKE US TO THE ANGELIC PLANES.
LOOK! I'VE BEEN TRYING TO SAY IT WASN'T THE ANGELS. **IT WAS US!**
YOU?
HA!
YOU MAKE ME LAUGH.
HA!
SEE?
NO... ONLY THE ANGELS HAVE THE POWER TO DEFEAT A DEMON KING.
THE WAR IS INEVITABLE, AMBASSADOR. YOU MUST OPEN THE PATHWAY!
I'LL TRY THAT BUFFET YOU MENTIONED WHILE I WAIT.

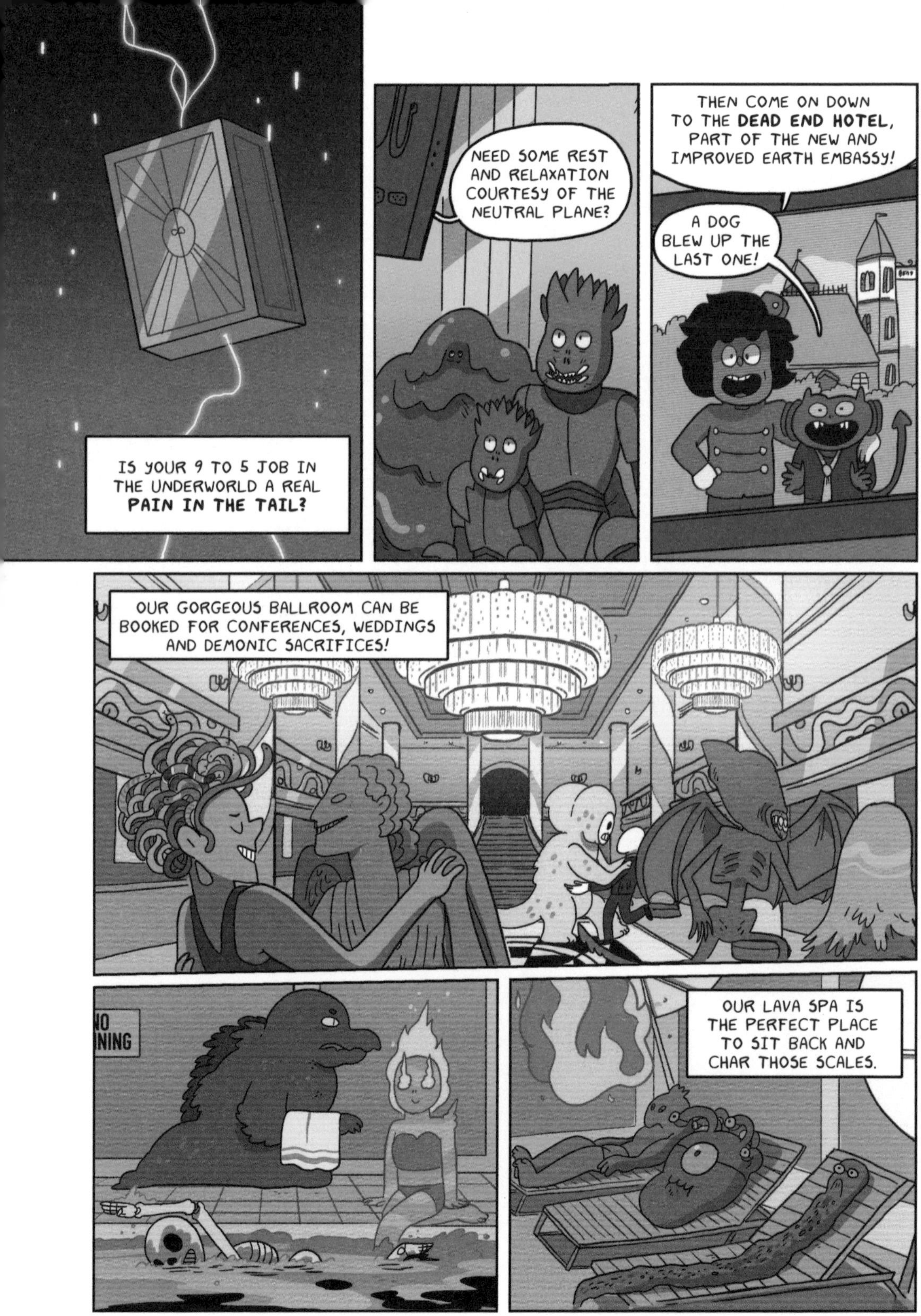
IS YOUR 9 TO 5 JOB IN THE UNDERWORLD A REAL **PAIN IN THE TAIL?**
NEED SOME REST AND RELAXATION COURTESY OF THE NEUTRAL PLANE?
THEN COME ON DOWN TO THE **DEAD END HOTEL**, PART OF THE NEW AND IMPROVED EARTH EMBASSY!
A DOG BLEW UP THE LAST ONE!
OUR GORGEOUS BALLROOM CAN BE BOOKED FOR CONFERENCES, WEDDINGS AND DEMONIC SACRIFICES!
OUR LAVA SPA IS THE PERFECT PLACE TO SIT BACK AND CHAR THOSE SCALES.

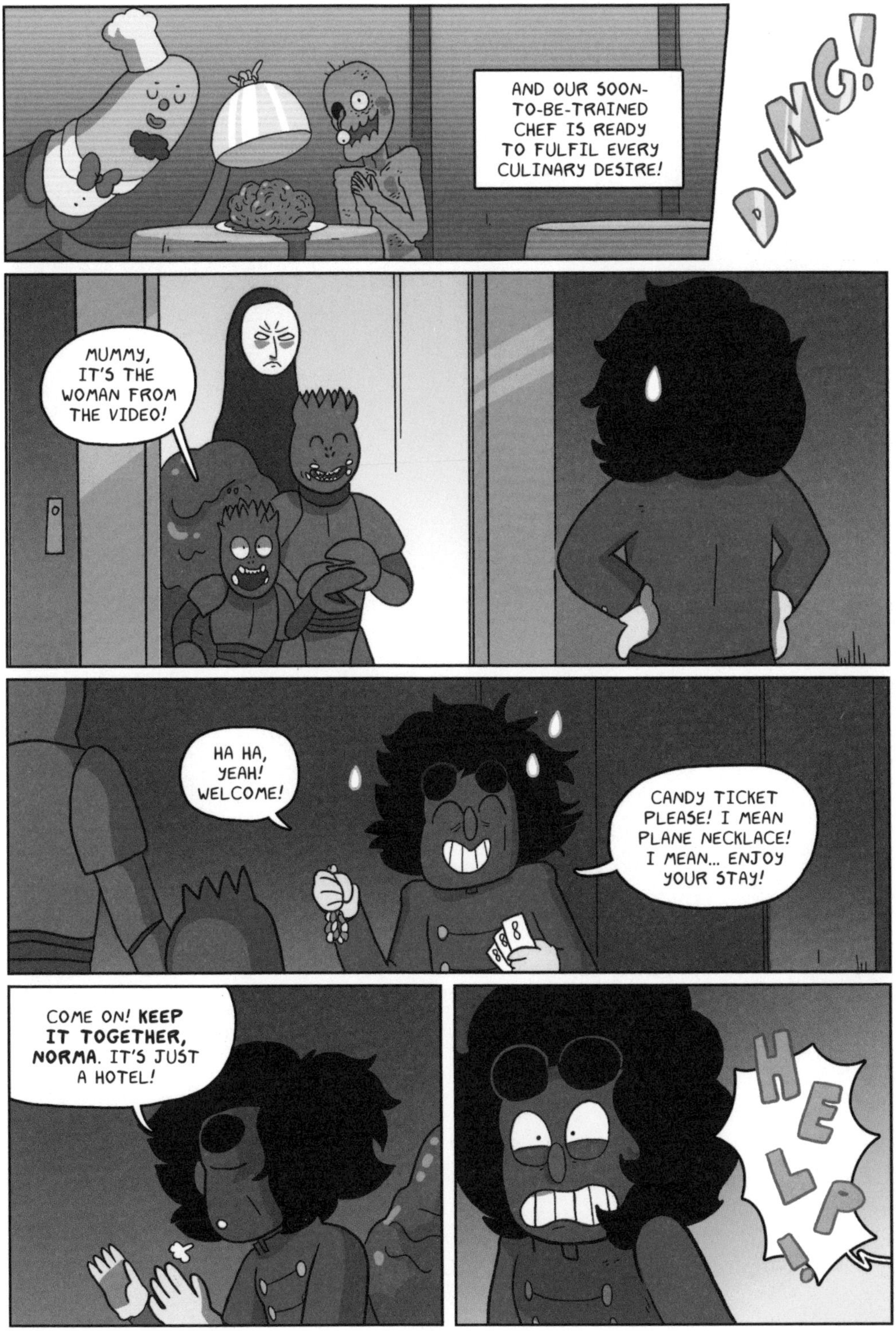
AND OUR SOON-TO-BE-TRAINED CHEF IS READY TO FULFIL EVERY CULINARY DESIRE!
DING!
MUMMY, IT'S THE WOMAN FROM THE VIDEO!
HA HA, YEAH! WELCOME!
CANDY TICKET PLEASE! I MEAN PLANE NECKLACE! I MEAN... ENJOY YOUR STAY!
COME ON! **KEEP IT TOGETHER, NORMA**. IT'S JUST A HOTEL!
HELP!

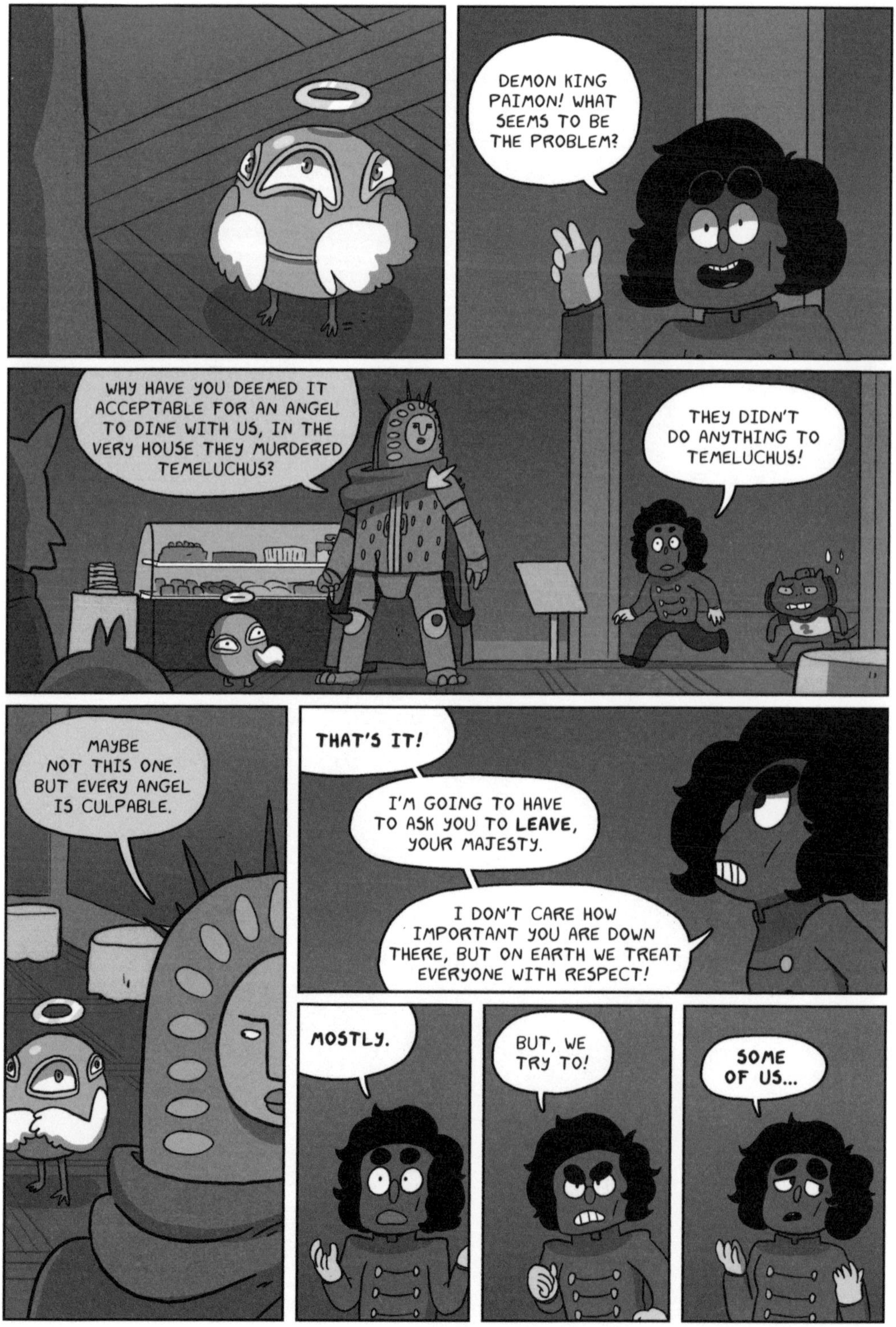
DEMON KING PAIMON! WHAT SEEMS TO BE THE PROBLEM?
WHY HAVE YOU DEEMED IT ACCEPTABLE FOR AN ANGEL TO DINE WITH US, IN THE VERY HOUSE THEY MURDERED TEMELUCHUS?
THEY DIDN'T DO ANYTHING TO TEMELUCHUS!
MAYBE NOT THIS ONE. BUT EVERY ANGEL IS CULPABLE.
THAT'S IT!
I'M GOING TO HAVE TO ASK YOU TO **LEAVE**, YOUR MAJESTY.
I DON'T CARE HOW IMPORTANT YOU ARE DOWN THERE, BUT ON EARTH WE TREAT EVERYONE WITH RESPECT!
MOSTLY.
BUT, WE TRY TO!
SOME OF US...

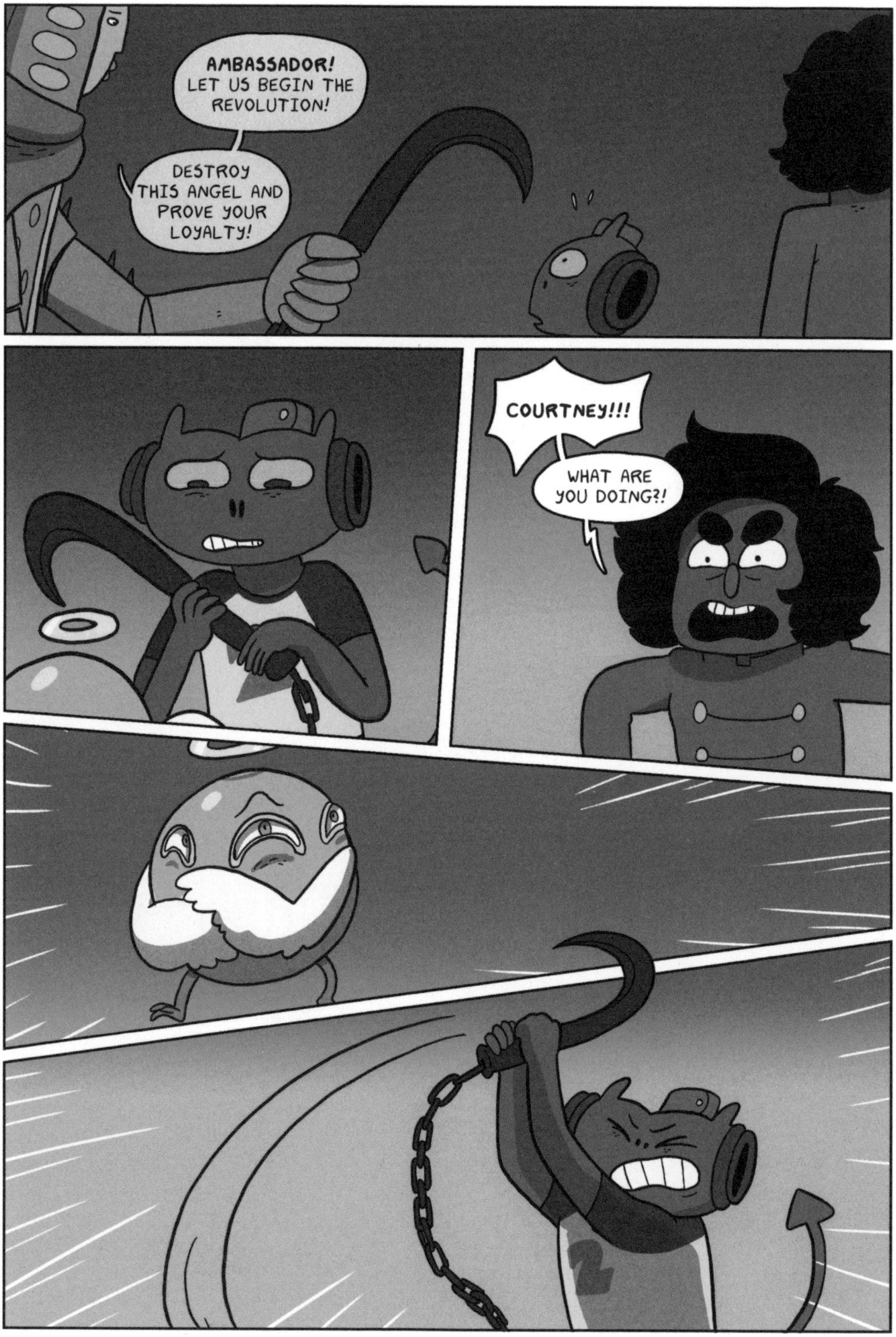
AMBASSADOR! LET US BEGIN THE REVOLUTION!
DESTROY THIS ANGEL AND PROVE YOUR LOYALTY!
COURTNEY!!!
WHAT ARE YOU DOING?!

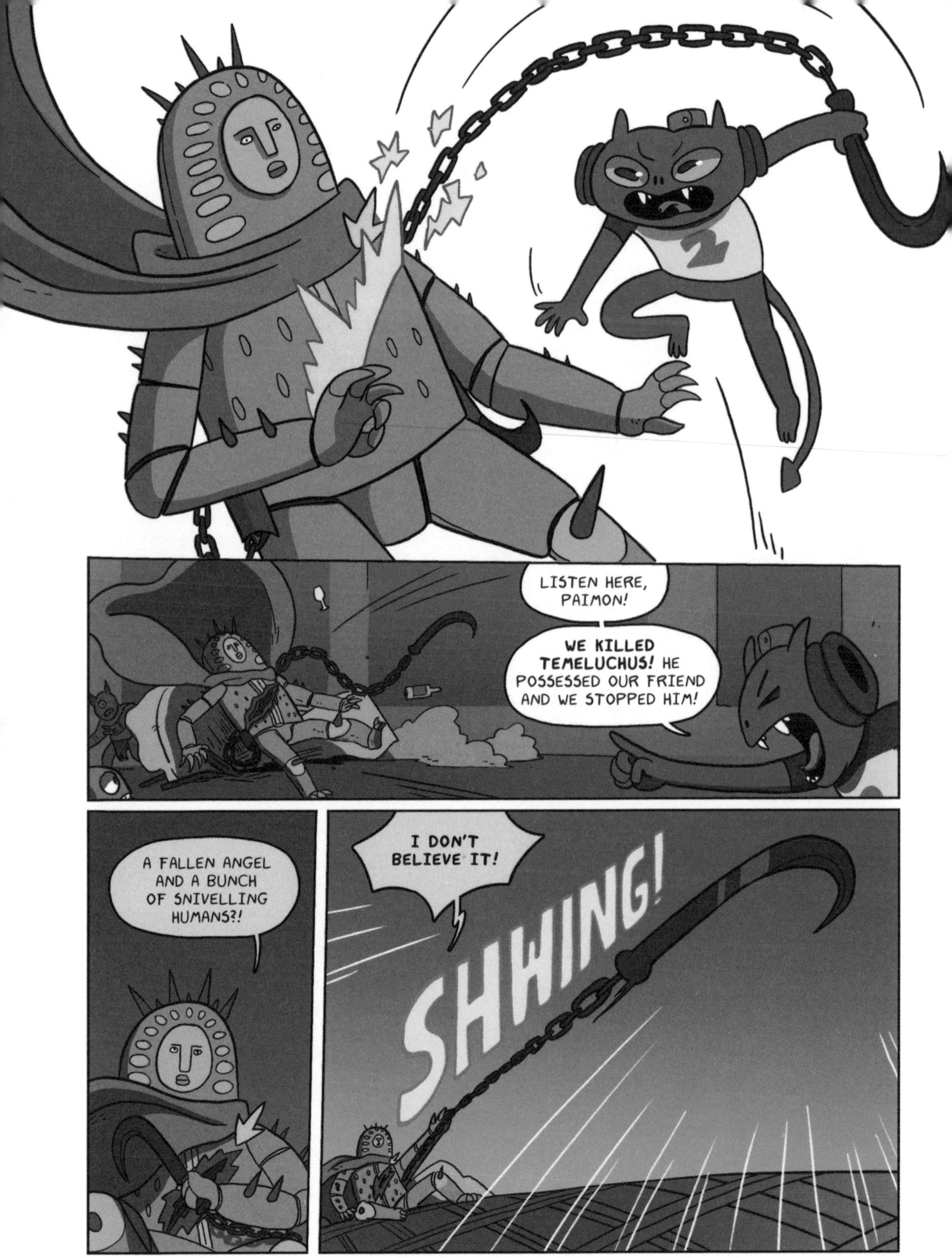
LISTEN HERE, PAIMON!
WE KILLED TEMELUCHUS! HE POSSESSED OUR FRIEND AND WE STOPPED HIM!
A FALLEN ANGEL AND A BUNCH OF SNIVELLING HUMANS?!
I DON'T BELIEVE IT!
SHWING!

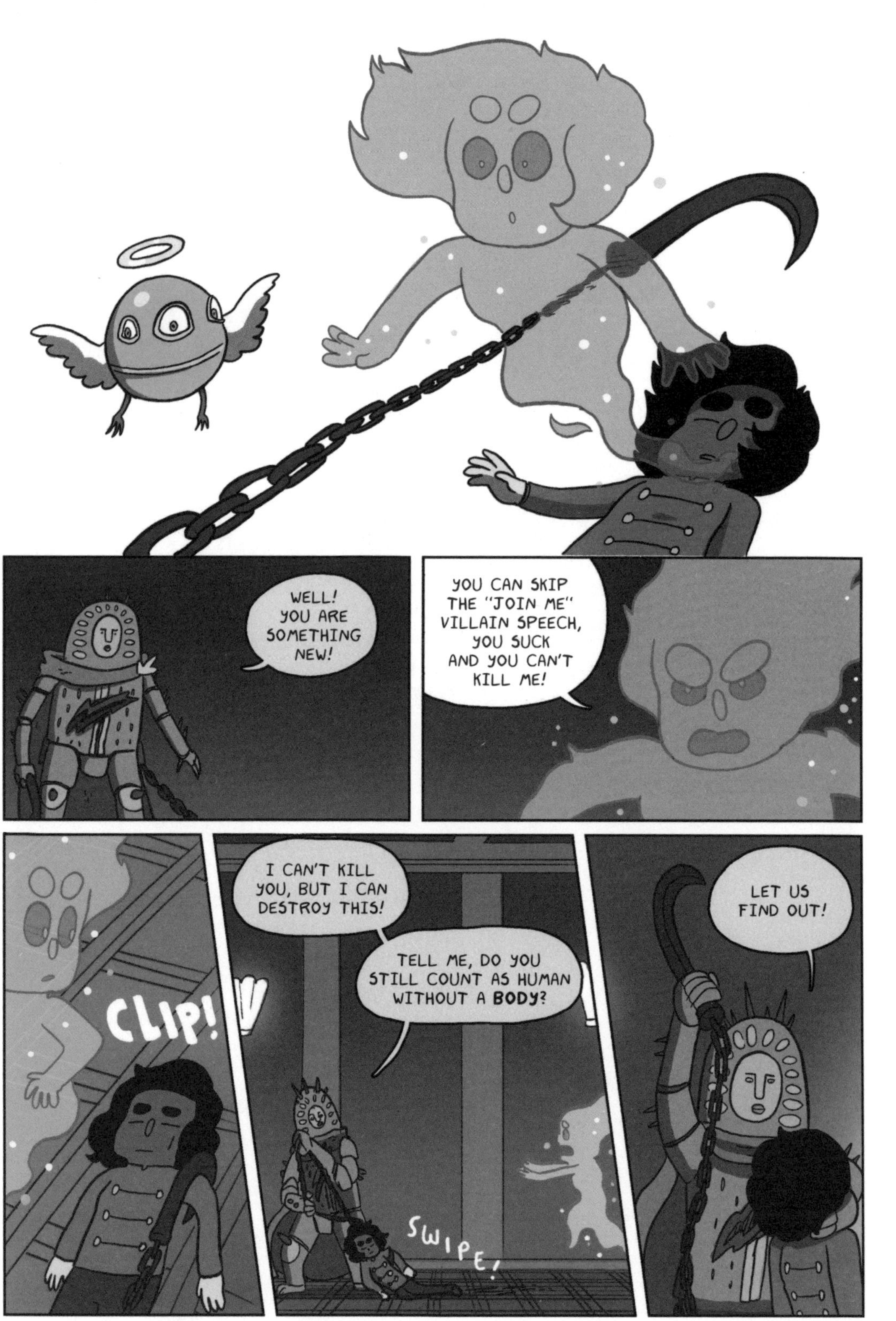
WELL! YOU ARE SOMETHING NEW!
YOU CAN SKIP THE "JOIN ME" VILLAIN SPEECH, YOU SUCK AND YOU CAN'T KILL ME!
CLIP!
I CAN'T KILL YOU, BUT I CAN DESTROY THIS!
TELL ME, DO YOU STILL COUNT AS HUMAN WITHOUT A **BODY**?
SWIPE!
LET US FIND OUT!

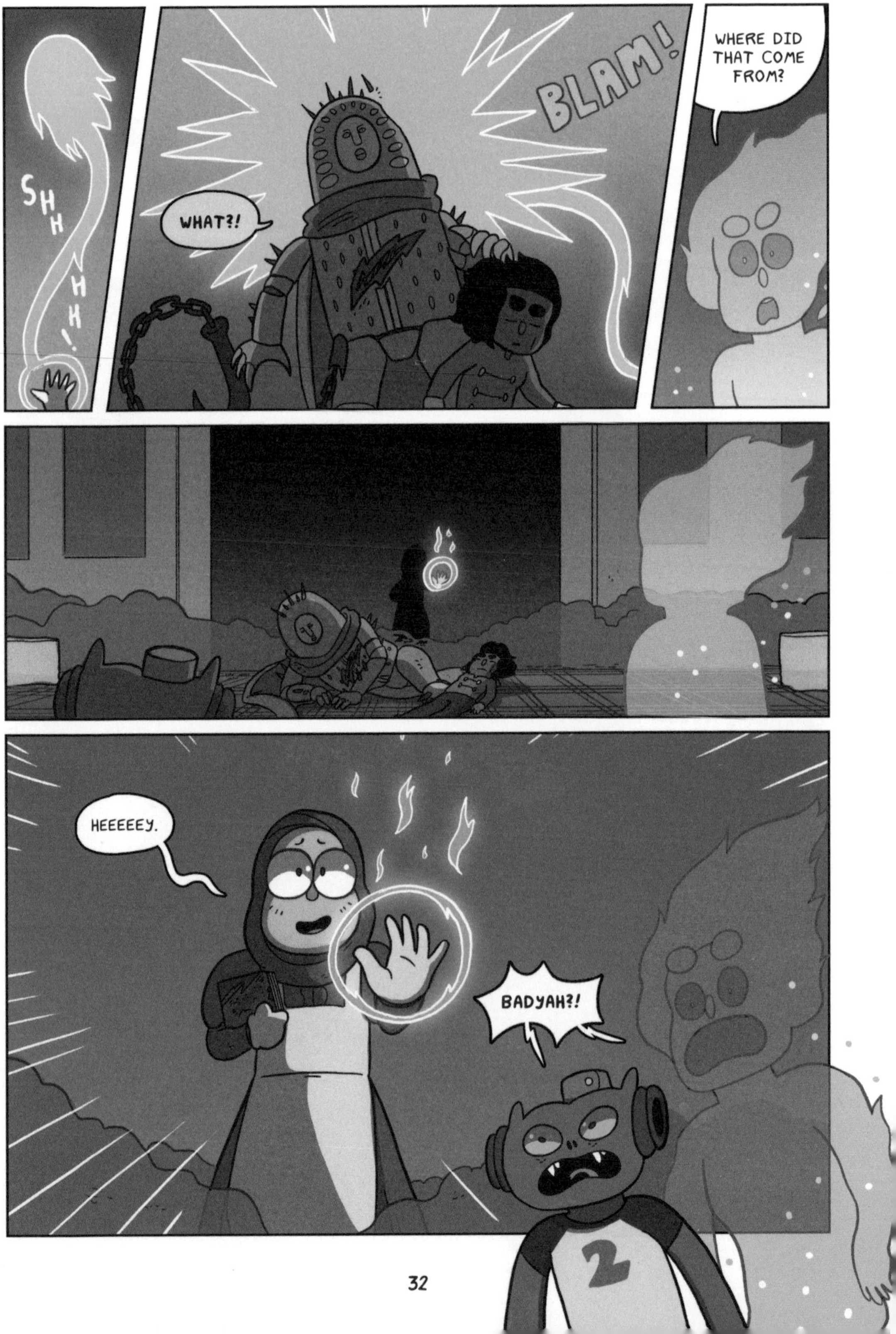
SHHHHH!
WHAT?!
BLAM!
WHERE DID THAT COME FROM?
HEEEEEY.
BADYAH?!

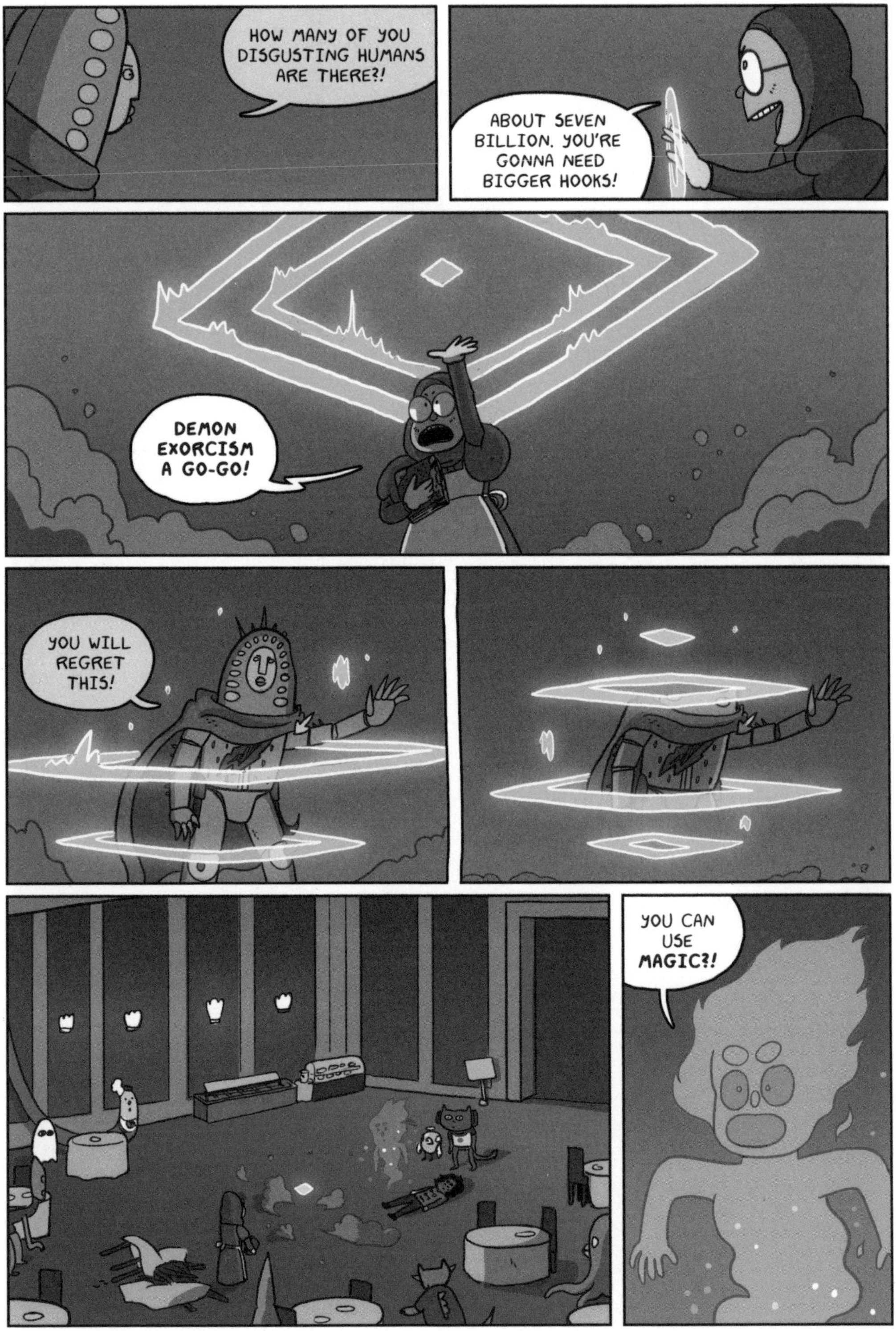

HOW MANY OF YOU DISGUSTING HUMANS ARE THERE?!
ABOUT SEVEN BILLION. YOU'RE GONNA NEED BIGGER HOOKS!
DEMON EXORCISM A GO-GO!
YOU WILL REGRET THIS!
YOU CAN USE **MAGIC**?!

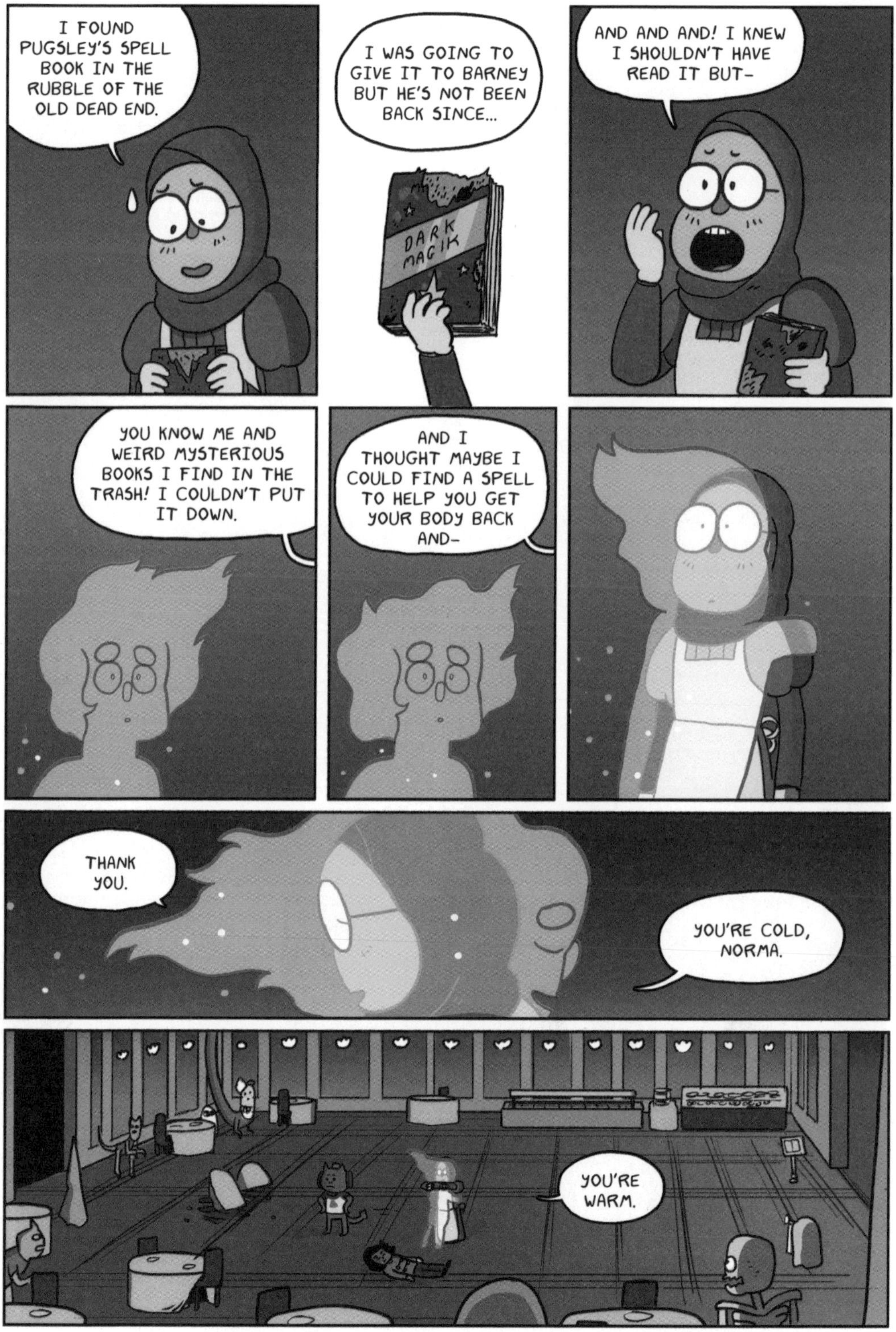
I FOUND PUGSLEY'S SPELL BOOK IN THE RUBBLE OF THE OLD DEAD END.
I WAS GOING TO GIVE IT TO BARNEY BUT HE'S NOT BEEN BACK SINCE...
DARK MAGIK
AND AND AND! I KNEW I SHOULDN'T HAVE READ IT BUT-
YOU KNOW ME AND WEIRD MYSTERIOUS BOOKS I FIND IN THE TRASH! I COULDN'T PUT IT DOWN.
AND I THOUGHT MAYBE I COULD FIND A SPELL TO HELP YOU GET YOUR BODY BACK AND-
THANK YOU.
YOU'RE COLD, NORMA.
YOU'RE WARM.

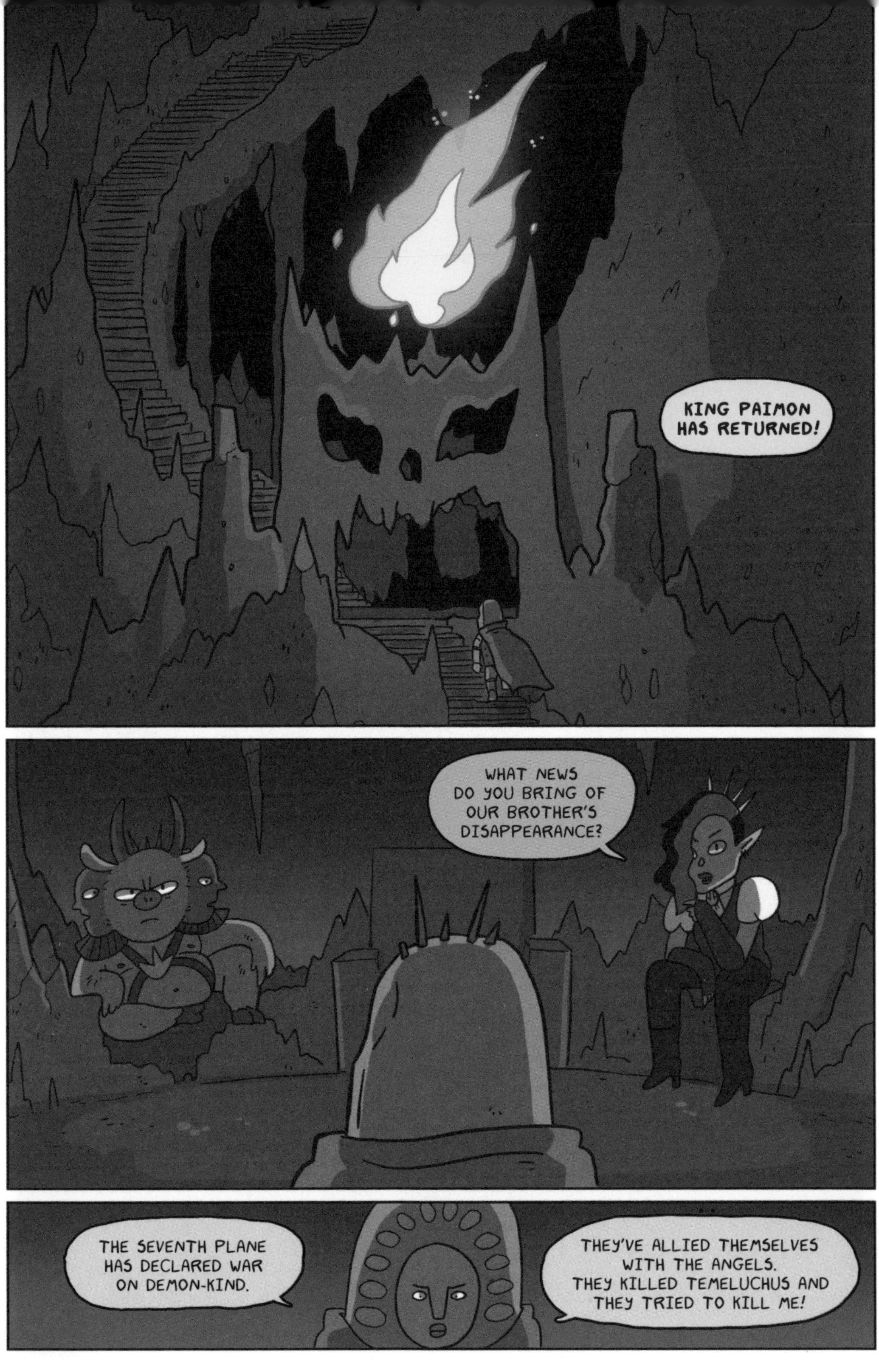
KING PAIMON HAS RETURNED!
WHAT NEWS DO YOU BRING OF OUR BROTHER'S DISAPPEARANCE?
THE SEVENTH PLANE HAS DECLARED WAR ON DEMON-KIND.
THEY'VE ALLIED THEMSELVES WITH THE ANGELS. THEY KILLED TEMELUCHUS AND THEY TRIED TO KILL ME!

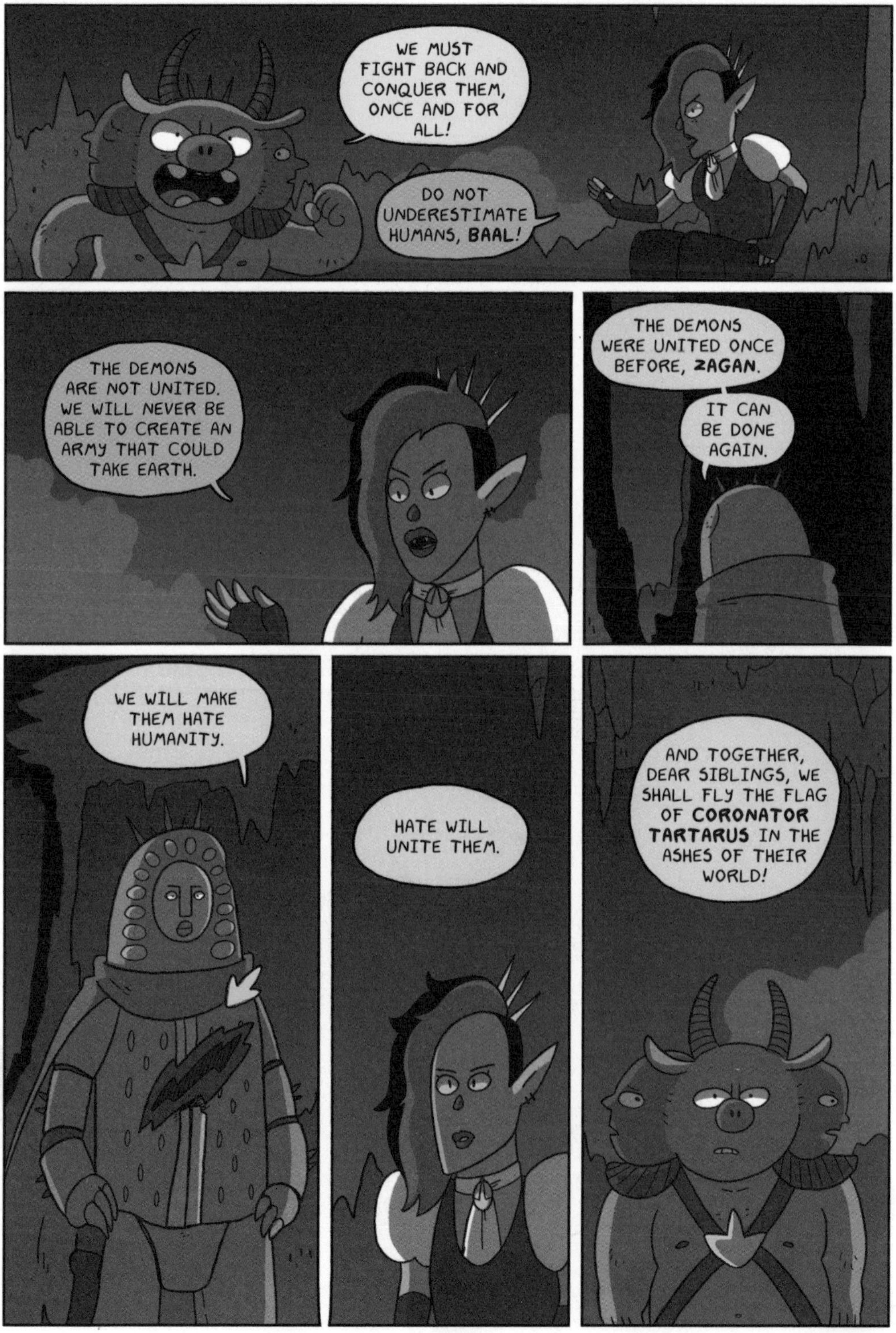
WE MUST FIGHT BACK AND CONQUER THEM, ONCE AND FOR ALL!
DO NOT UNDERESTIMATE HUMANS, BAAL!
THE DEMONS ARE NOT UNITED. WE WILL NEVER BE ABLE TO CREATE AN ARMY THAT COULD TAKE EARTH.
THE DEMONS WERE UNITED ONCE BEFORE, ZAGAN.
IT CAN BE DONE AGAIN.
WE WILL MAKE THEM HATE HUMANITY.
HATE WILL UNITE THEM.
AND TOGETHER, DEAR SIBLINGS, WE SHALL FLY THE FLAG OF CORONATOR TARTARUS IN THE ASHES OF THEIR WORLD!

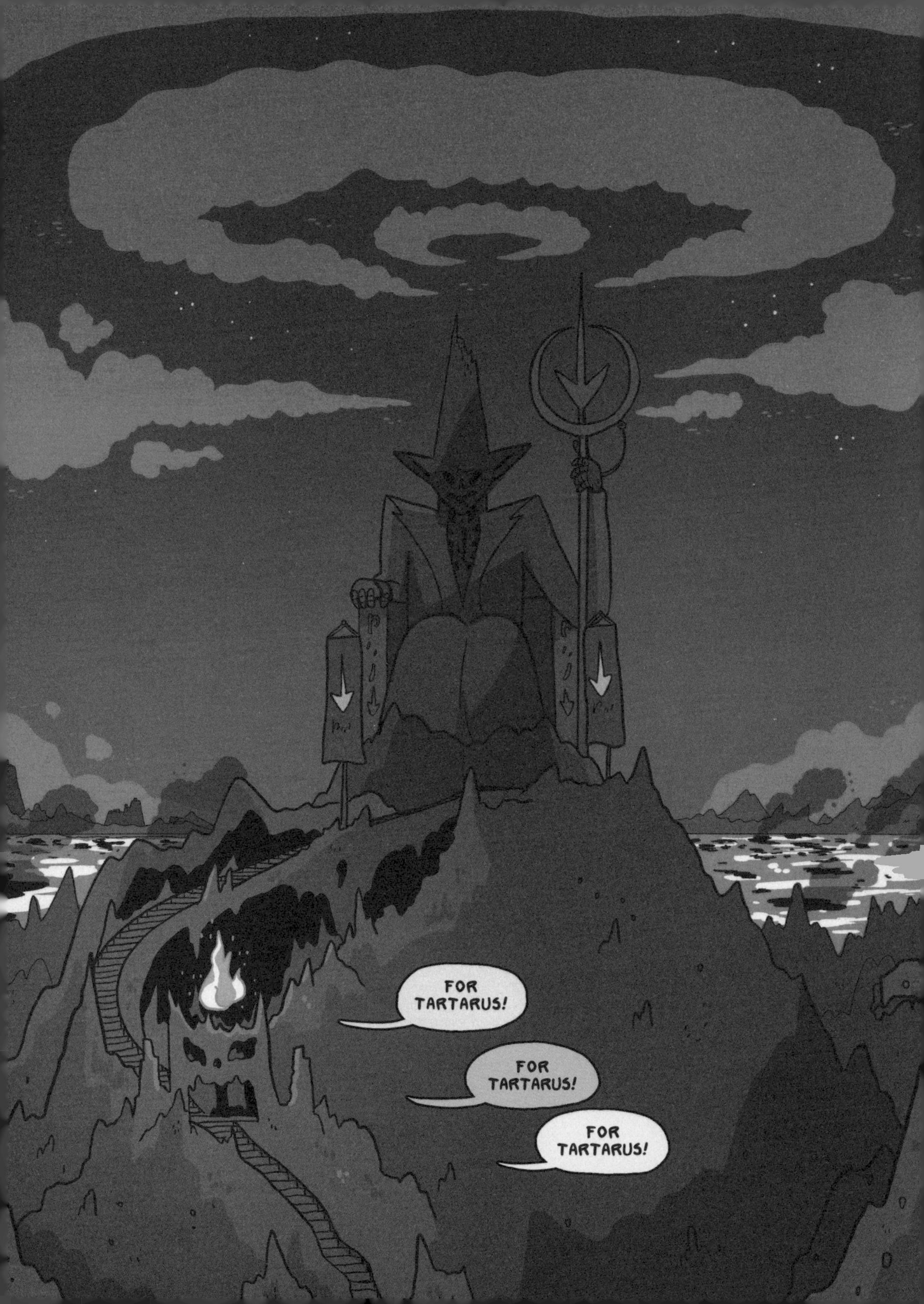
FOR TARTARUS!
FOR TARTARUS!
FOR TARTARUS!

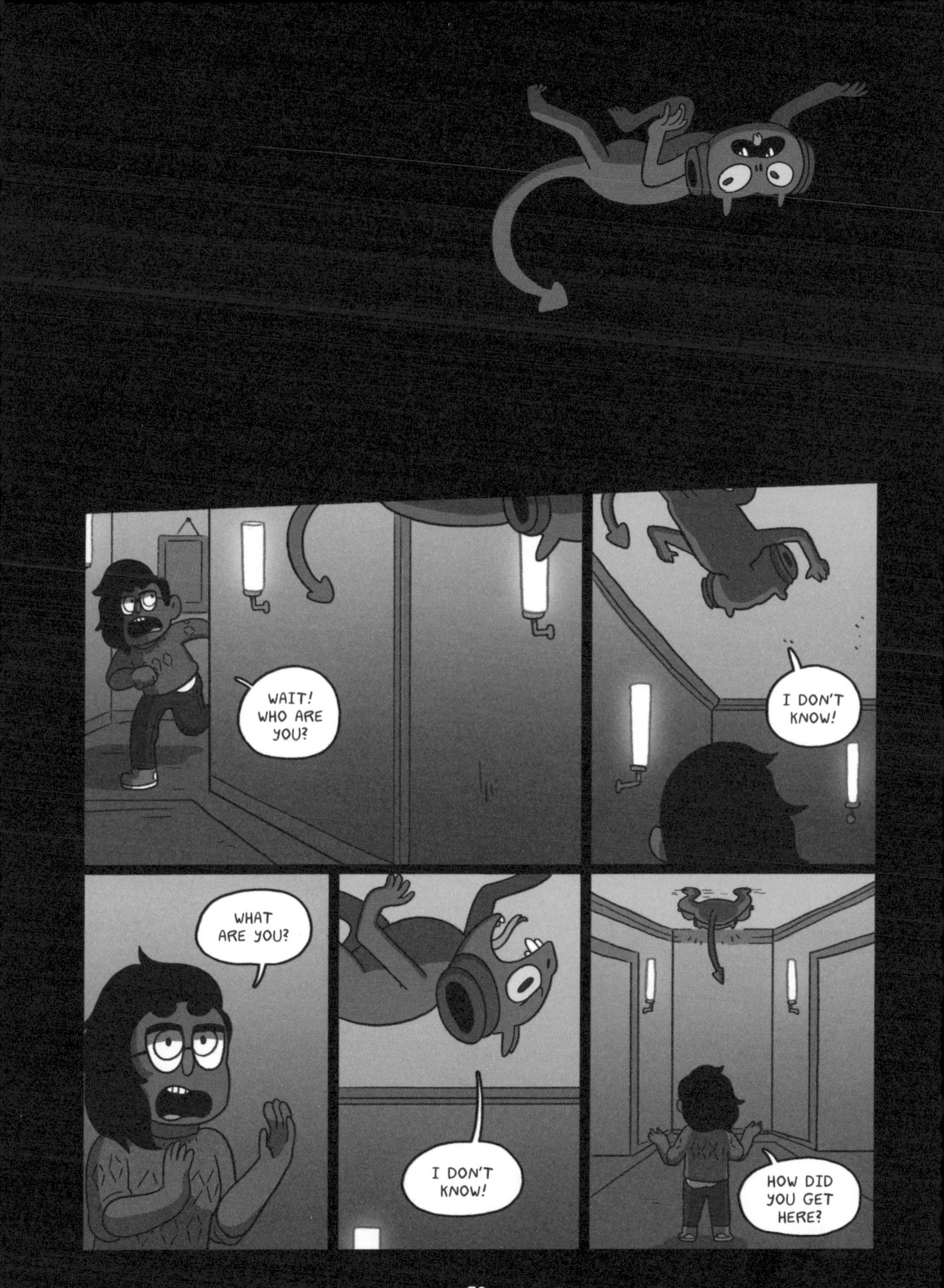
WAIT! WHO ARE YOU?
I DON'T KNOW!
WHAT ARE YOU?
I DON'T KNOW!
HOW DID YOU GET HERE?

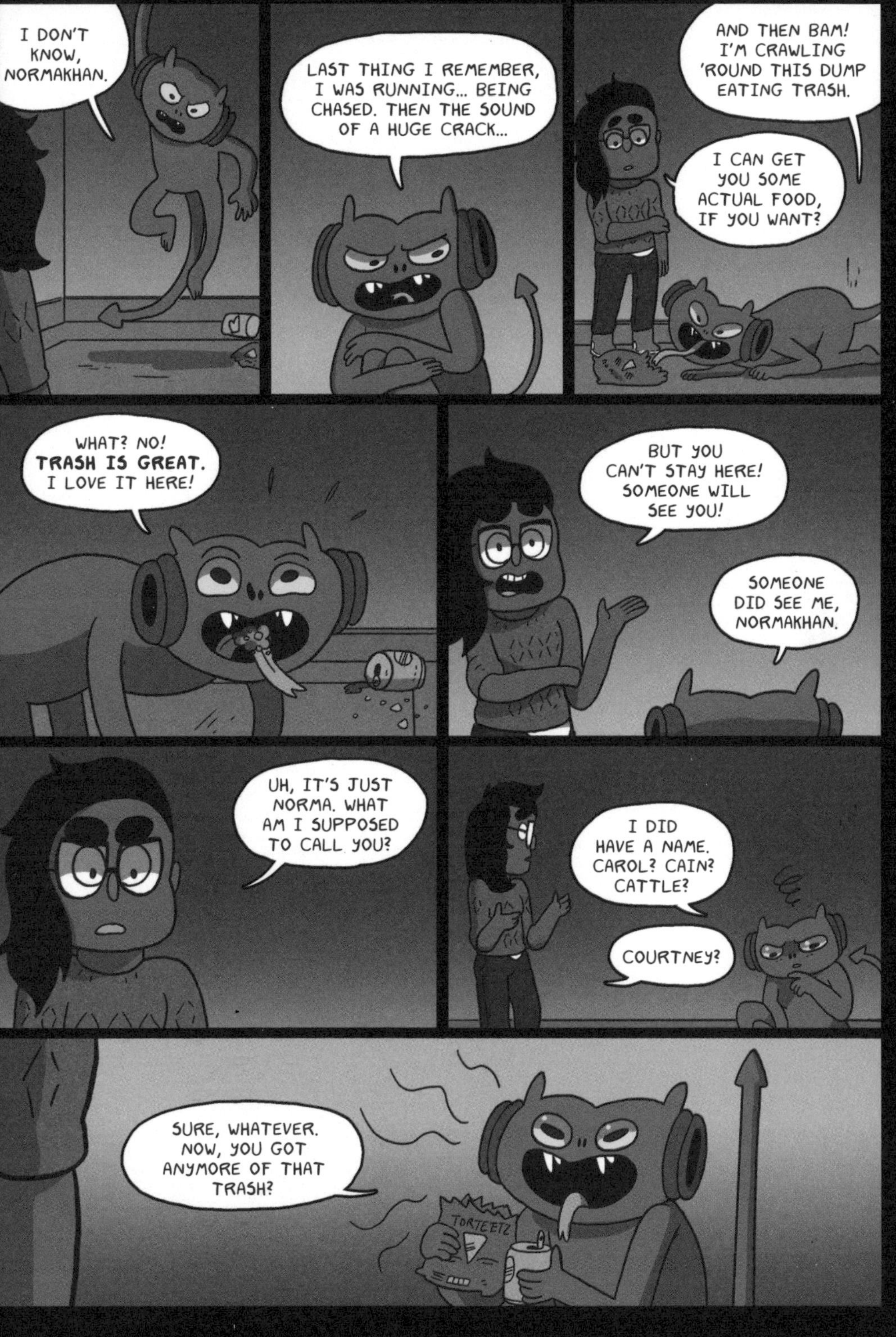

I DON'T KNOW, NORMAKHAN.
LAST THING I REMEMBER, I WAS RUNNING... BEING CHASED. THEN THE SOUND OF A HUGE CRACK...
AND THEN BAM! I'M CRAWLING 'ROUND THIS DUMP EATING TRASH.
I CAN GET YOU SOME ACTUAL FOOD, IF YOU WANT?
WHAT? NO! **TRASH IS GREAT.** I LOVE IT HERE!
BUT YOU CAN'T STAY HERE! SOMEONE WILL SEE YOU!
SOMEONE DID SEE ME, NORMAKHAN.
UH, IT'S JUST NORMA. WHAT AM I SUPPOSED TO CALL YOU?
I DID HAVE A NAME. CAROL? CAIN? CATTLE?
COURTNEY?
SURE, WHATEVER. NOW, YOU GOT ANYMORE OF THAT TRASH?
TORTEETZ

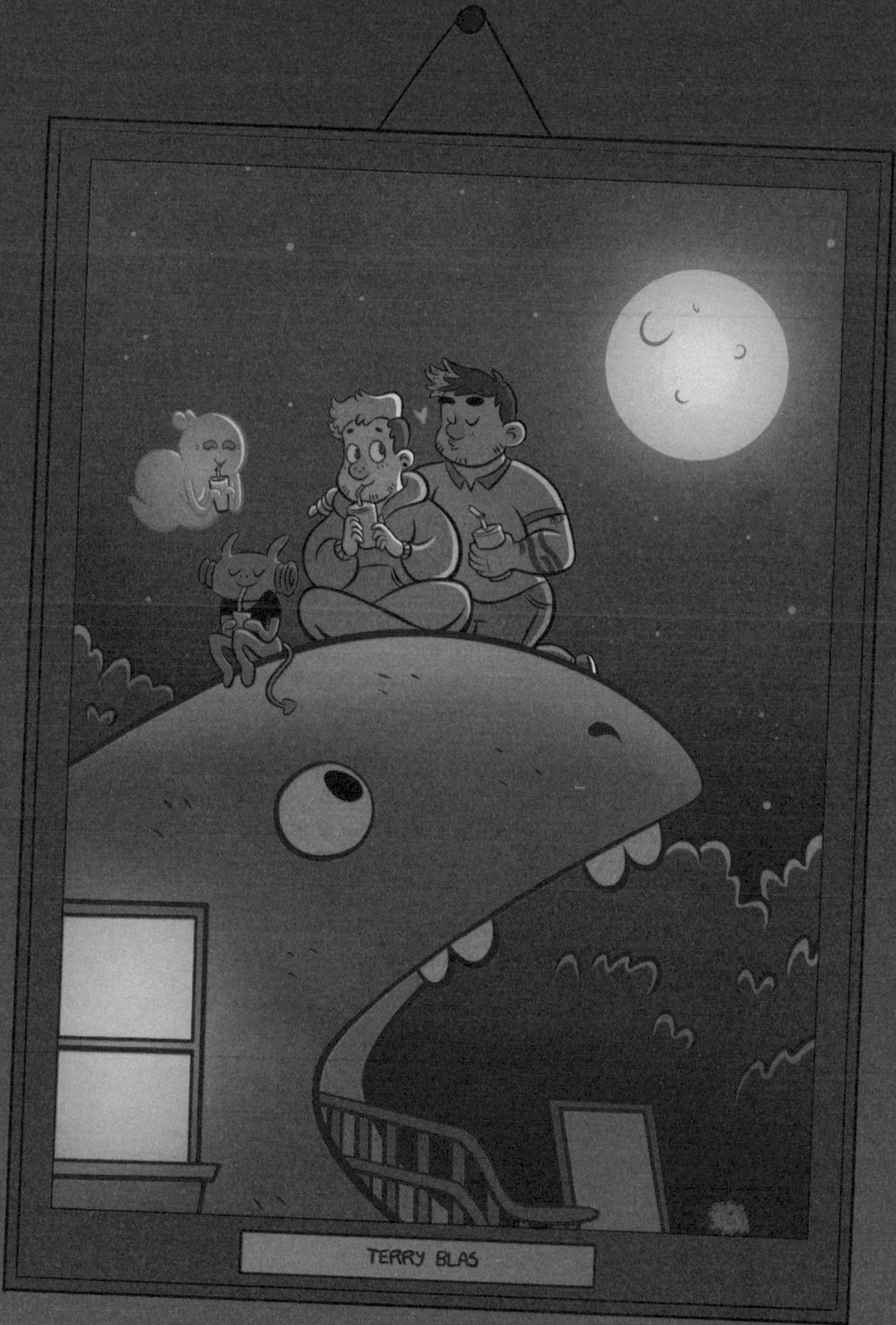
TERRY BLAS

CHAPTER 2
ALL STAR BARNEY

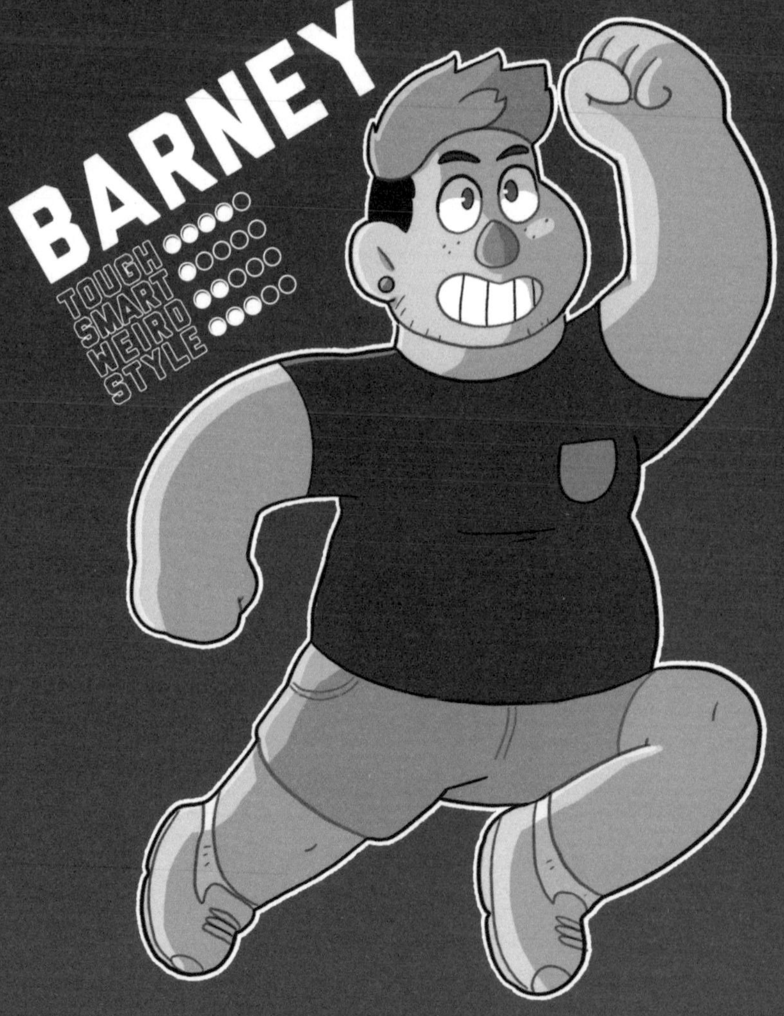
BARNEY
TOUGH
SMART
WEIRD
STYLE

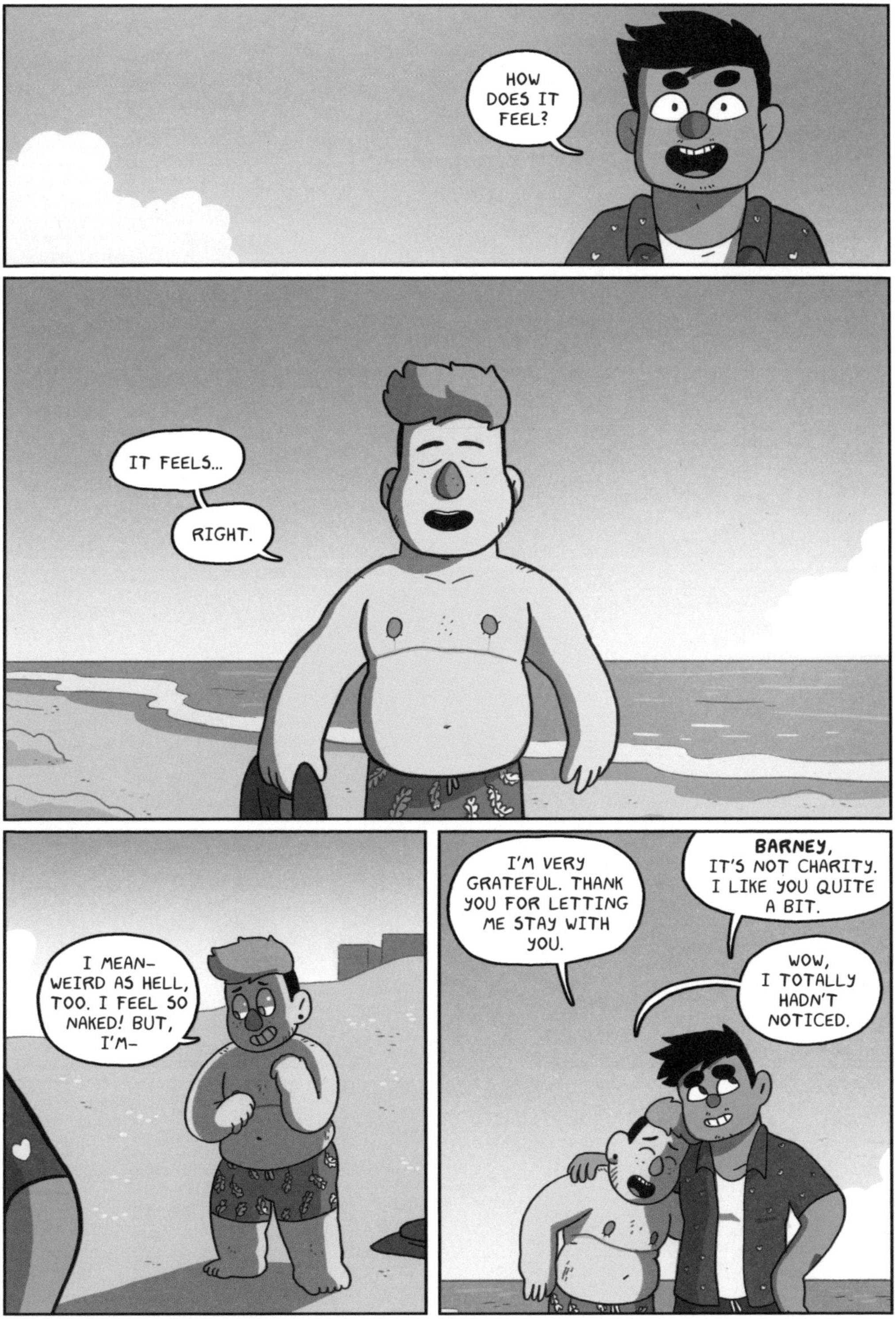
HOW DOES IT FEEL?
IT FEELS...
RIGHT.
I MEAN- WEIRD AS HELL, TOO. I FEEL SO NAKED! BUT, I'M-
I'M VERY GRATEFUL. THANK YOU FOR LETTING ME STAY WITH YOU.
BARNEY, IT'S NOT CHARITY. I LIKE YOU QUITE A BIT.
WOW, I TOTALLY HADN'T NOTICED.

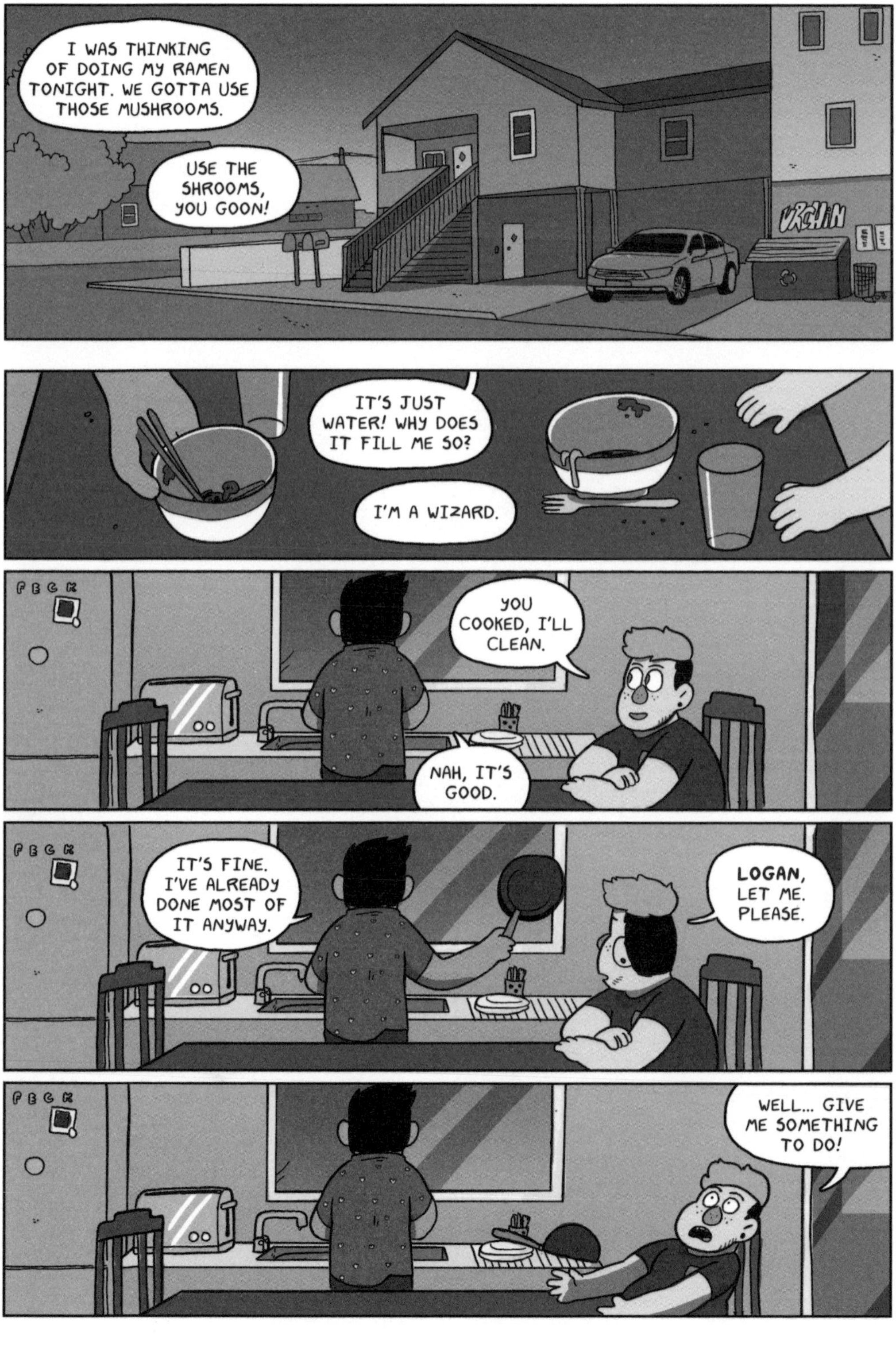
I WAS THINKING OF DOING MY RAMEN TONIGHT. WE GOTTA USE THOSE MUSHROOMS.
USE THE SHROOMS, YOU GOON!
URCHIN
IT'S JUST WATER! WHY DOES IT FILL ME SO?
I'M A WIZARD.
YOU COOKED, I'LL CLEAN.
NAH, IT'S GOOD.
IT'S FINE. I'VE ALREADY DONE MOST OF IT ANYWAY.
LOGAN, LET ME. PLEASE.
WELL... GIVE ME SOMETHING TO DO!

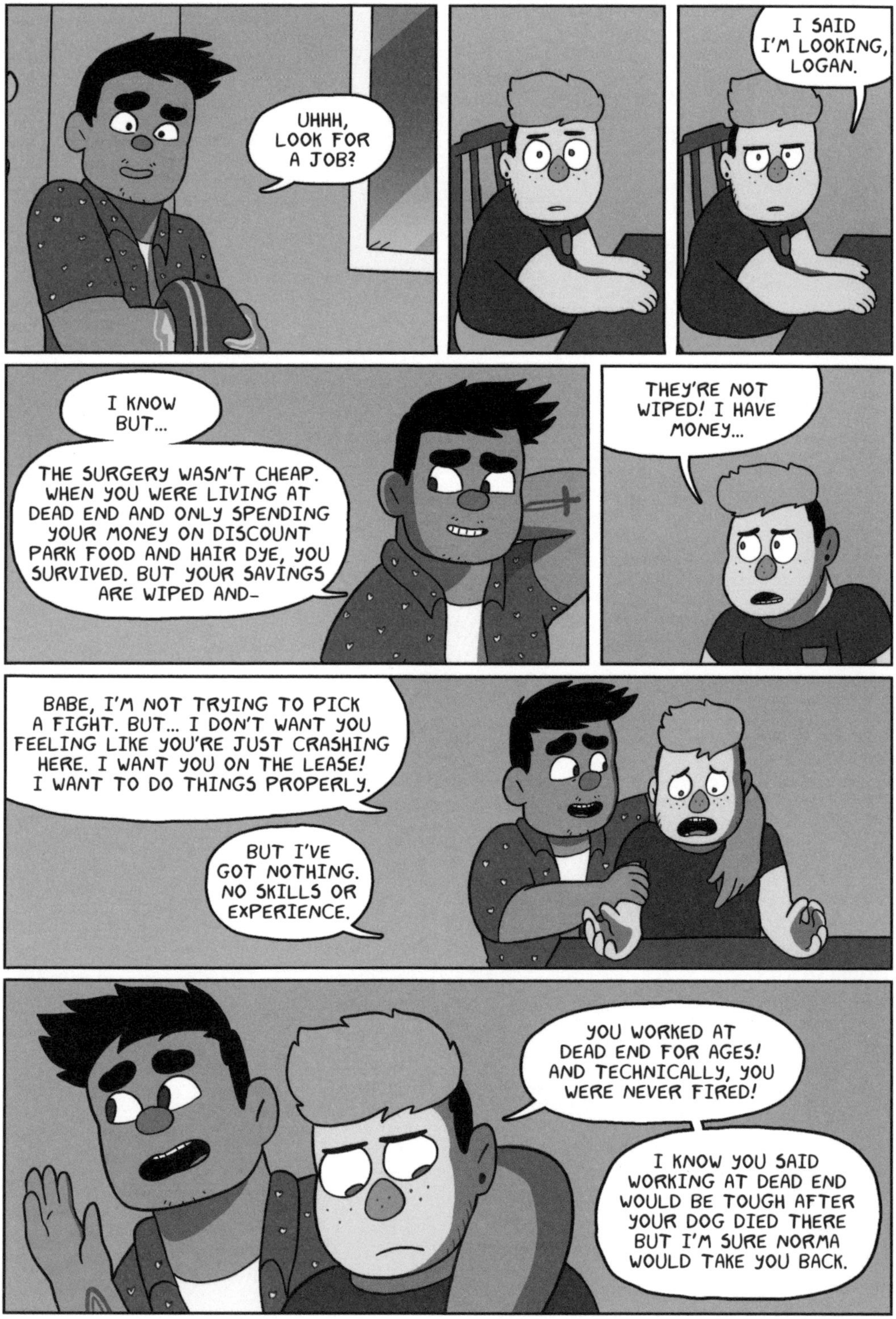

UHHH, LOOK FOR A JOB?
I SAID I'M LOOKING, LOGAN.
I KNOW BUT...
THE SURGERY WASN'T CHEAP. WHEN YOU WERE LIVING AT DEAD END AND ONLY SPENDING YOUR MONEY ON DISCOUNT PARK FOOD AND HAIR DYE, YOU SURVIVED. BUT YOUR SAVINGS ARE WIPED AND-
THEY'RE NOT WIPED! I HAVE MONEY...
BABE, I'M NOT TRYING TO PICK A FIGHT. BUT... I DON'T WANT YOU FEELING LIKE YOU'RE JUST CRASHING HERE. I WANT YOU ON THE LEASE! I WANT TO DO THINGS PROPERLY.
BUT I'VE GOT NOTHING. NO SKILLS OR EXPERIENCE.
YOU WORKED AT DEAD END FOR AGES! AND TECHNICALLY, YOU WERE NEVER FIRED!
I KNOW YOU SAID WORKING AT DEAD END WOULD BE TOUGH AFTER YOUR DOG DIED THERE BUT I'M SURE NORMA WOULD TAKE YOU BACK.

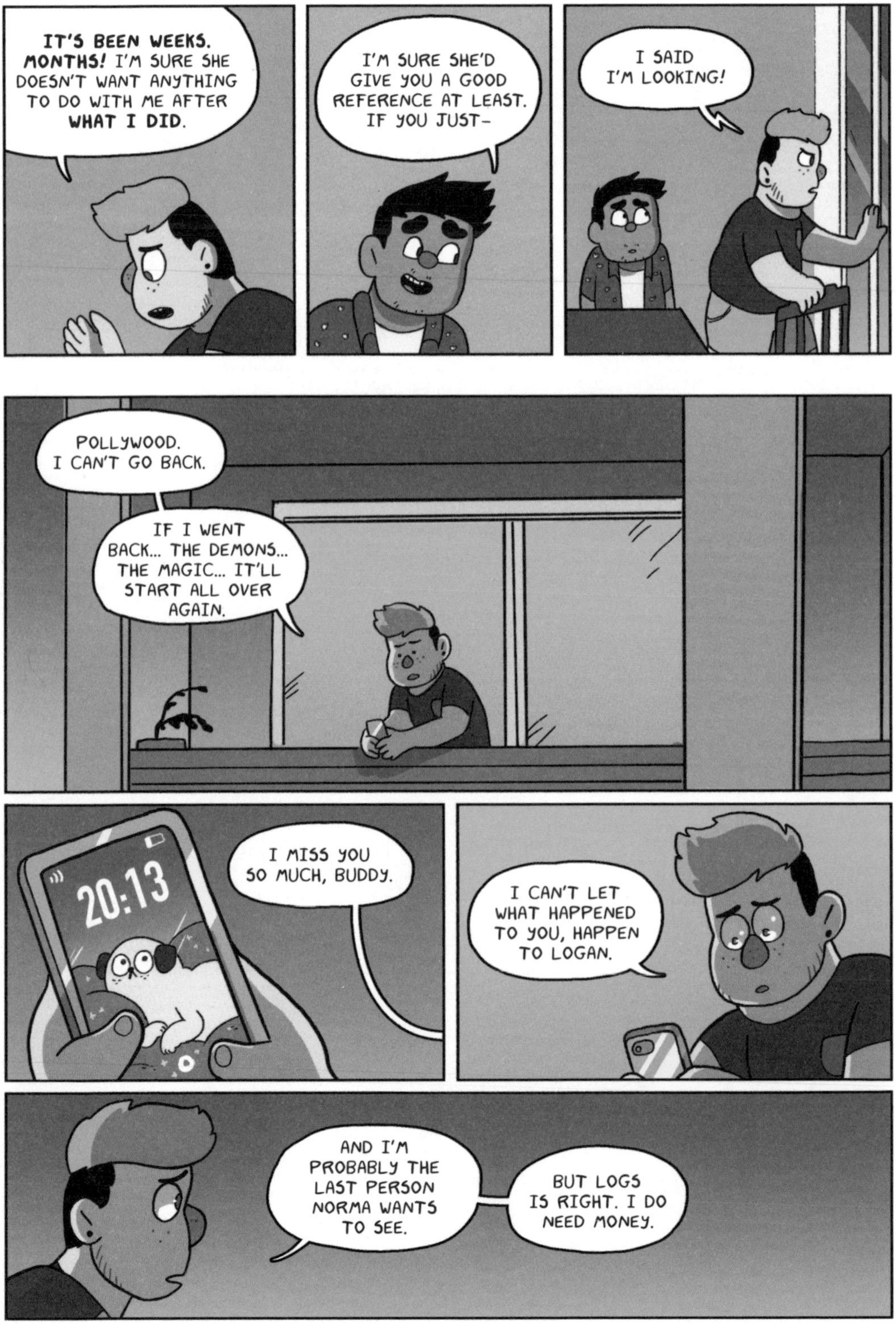
IT'S BEEN WEEKS. MONTHS! I'M SURE SHE DOESN'T WANT ANYTHING TO DO WITH ME AFTER WHAT I DID.
I'M SURE SHE'D GIVE YOU A GOOD REFERENCE AT LEAST. IF YOU JUST-
I SAID I'M LOOKING!
POLLYWOOD. I CAN'T GO BACK.
IF I WENT BACK... THE DEMONS... THE MAGIC... IT'LL START ALL OVER AGAIN.
20:13
I MISS YOU SO MUCH, BUDDY.
I CAN'T LET WHAT HAPPENED TO YOU, HAPPEN TO LOGAN.
AND I'M PROBABLY THE LAST PERSON NORMA WANTS TO SEE.
BUT LOGS IS RIGHT. I DO NEED MONEY.

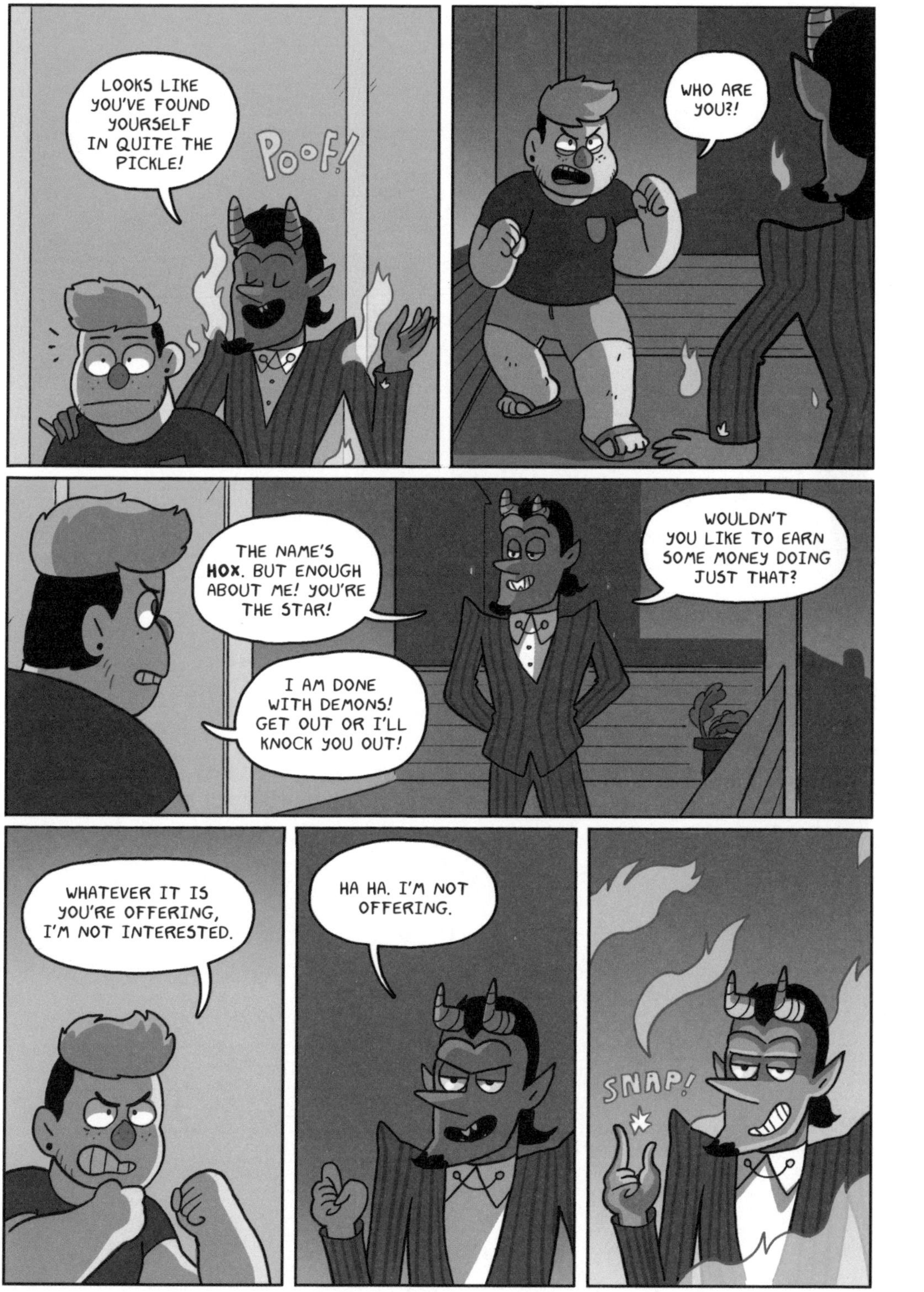
LOOKS LIKE YOU'VE FOUND YOURSELF IN QUITE THE PICKLE!
POOF!
WHO ARE YOU?!
THE NAME'S **HOX**. BUT ENOUGH ABOUT ME! YOU'RE THE STAR!
WOULDN'T YOU LIKE TO EARN SOME MONEY DOING JUST THAT?
I AM DONE WITH DEMONS! GET OUT OR I'LL KNOCK YOU OUT!
WHATEVER IT IS YOU'RE OFFERING, I'M NOT INTERESTED.
HA HA. I'M NOT OFFERING.
SNAP!

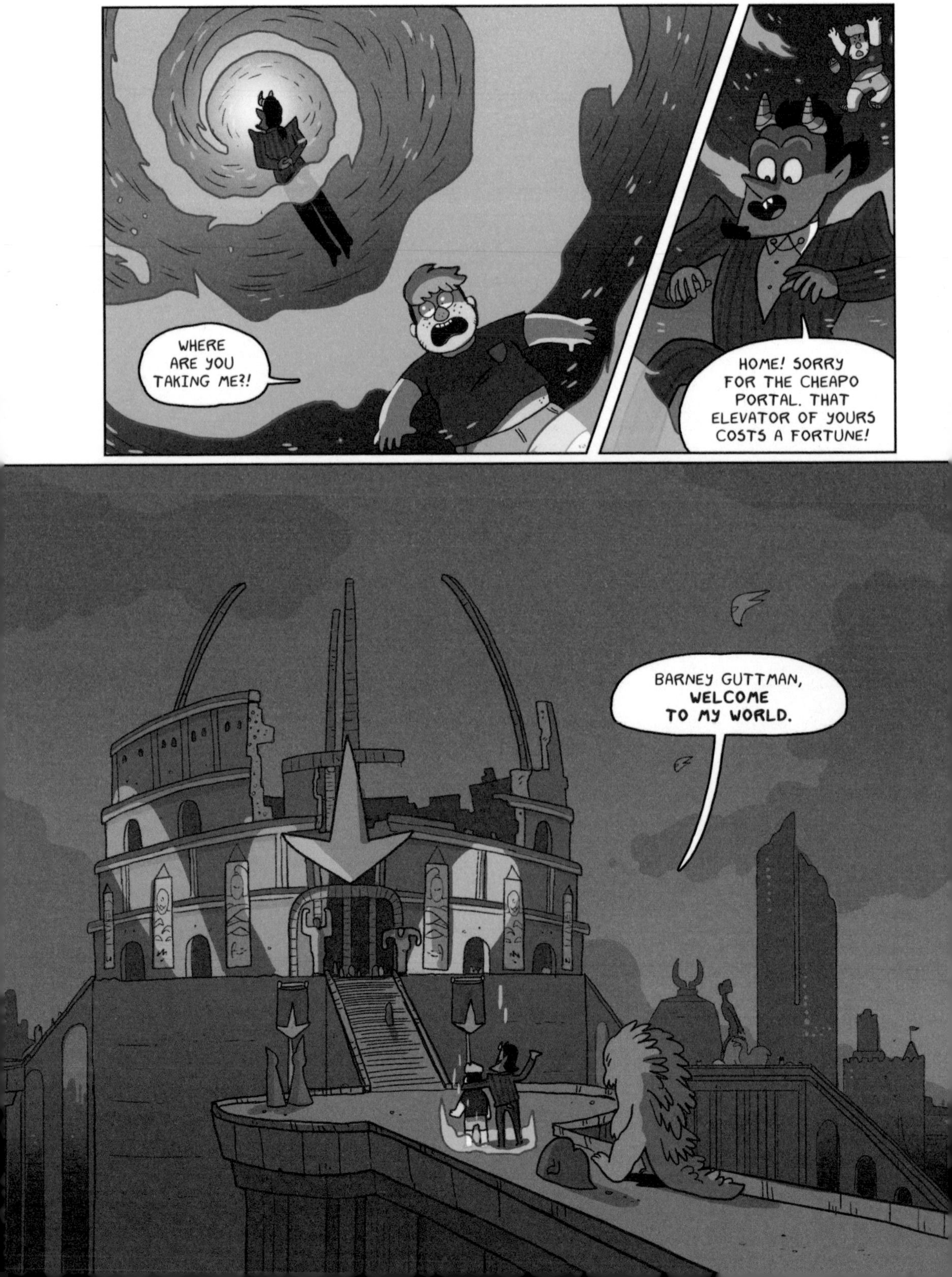
WHERE ARE YOU TAKING ME?!
HOME! SORRY FOR THE CHEAPO PORTAL. THAT ELEVATOR OF YOURS COSTS A FORTUNE!
BARNEY GUTTMAN, **WELCOME TO MY WORLD.**

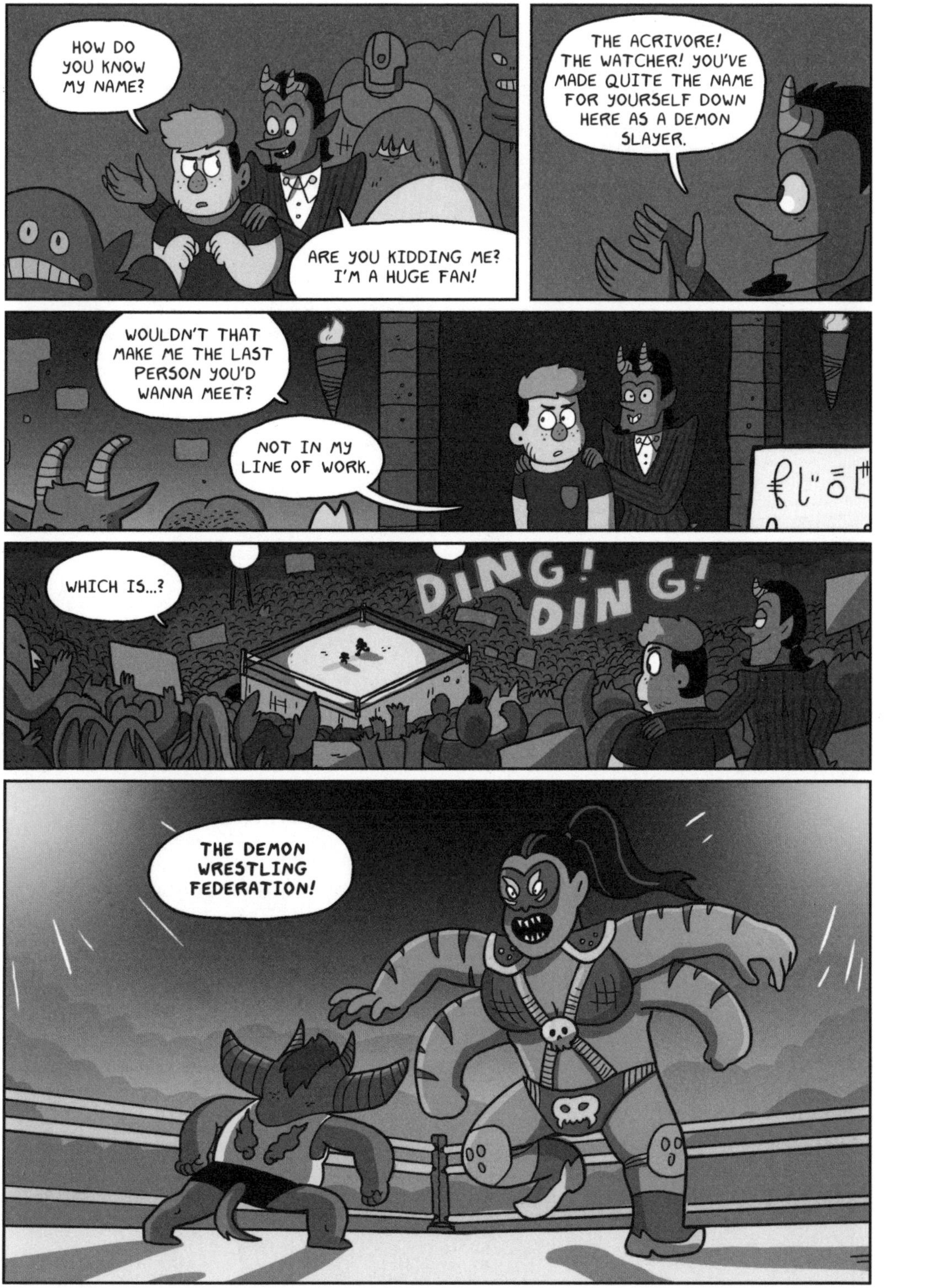
HOW DO YOU KNOW MY NAME?
ARE YOU KIDDING ME? I'M A HUGE FAN!
THE ACRIVORE! THE WATCHER! YOU'VE MADE QUITE THE NAME FOR YOURSELF DOWN HERE AS A DEMON SLAYER.
WOULDN'T THAT MAKE ME THE LAST PERSON YOU'D WANNA MEET?
NOT IN MY LINE OF WORK.
WHICH IS...?
DING! DING!
THE DEMON WRESTLING FEDERATION!

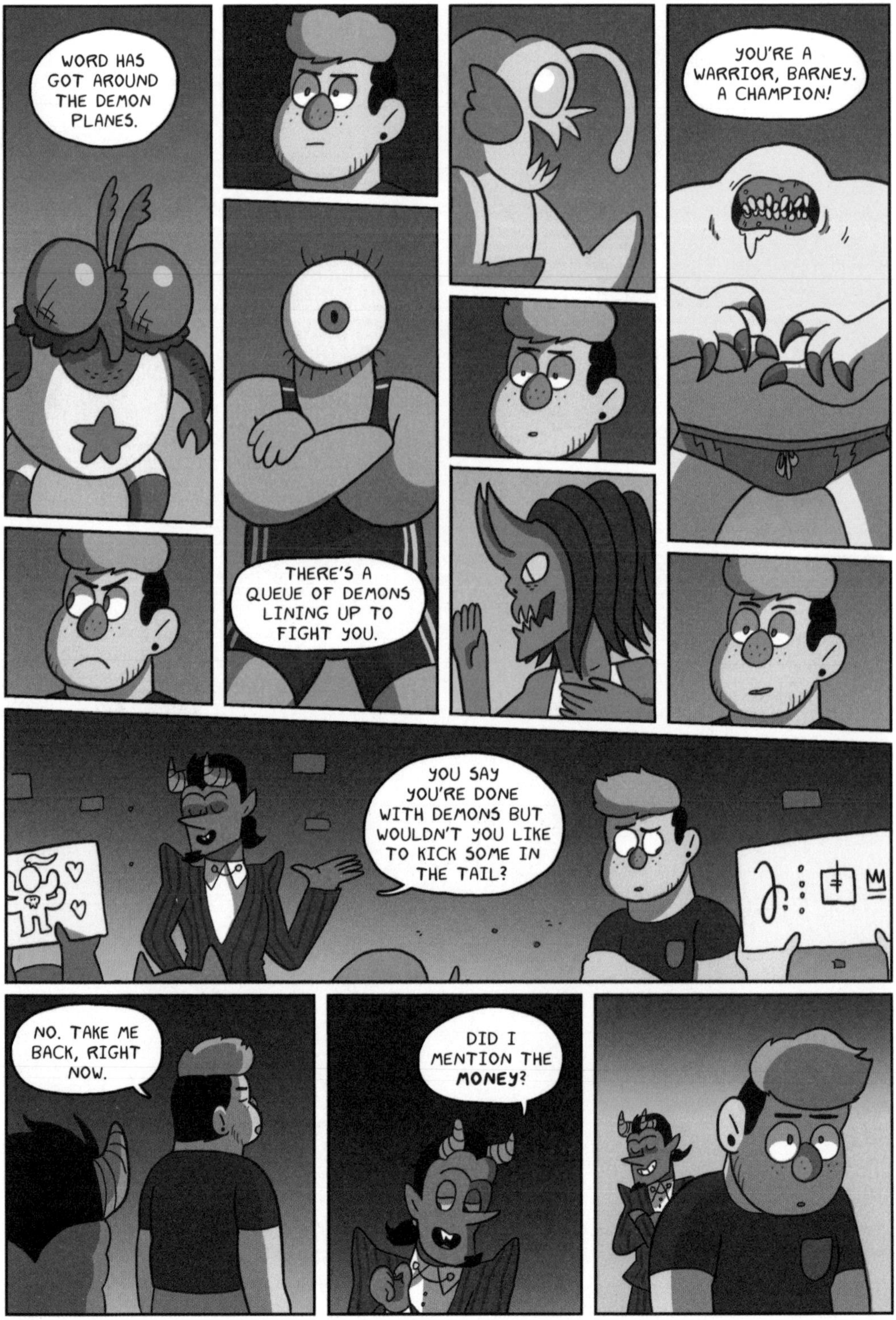
WORD HAS GOT AROUND THE DEMON PLANES.
YOU'RE A WARRIOR, BARNEY. A CHAMPION!
THERE'S A QUEUE OF DEMONS LINING UP TO FIGHT YOU.
YOU SAY YOU'RE DONE WITH DEMONS BUT WOULDN'T YOU LIKE TO KICK SOME IN THE TAIL?
NO. TAKE ME BACK, RIGHT NOW.
DID I MENTION THE MONEY?

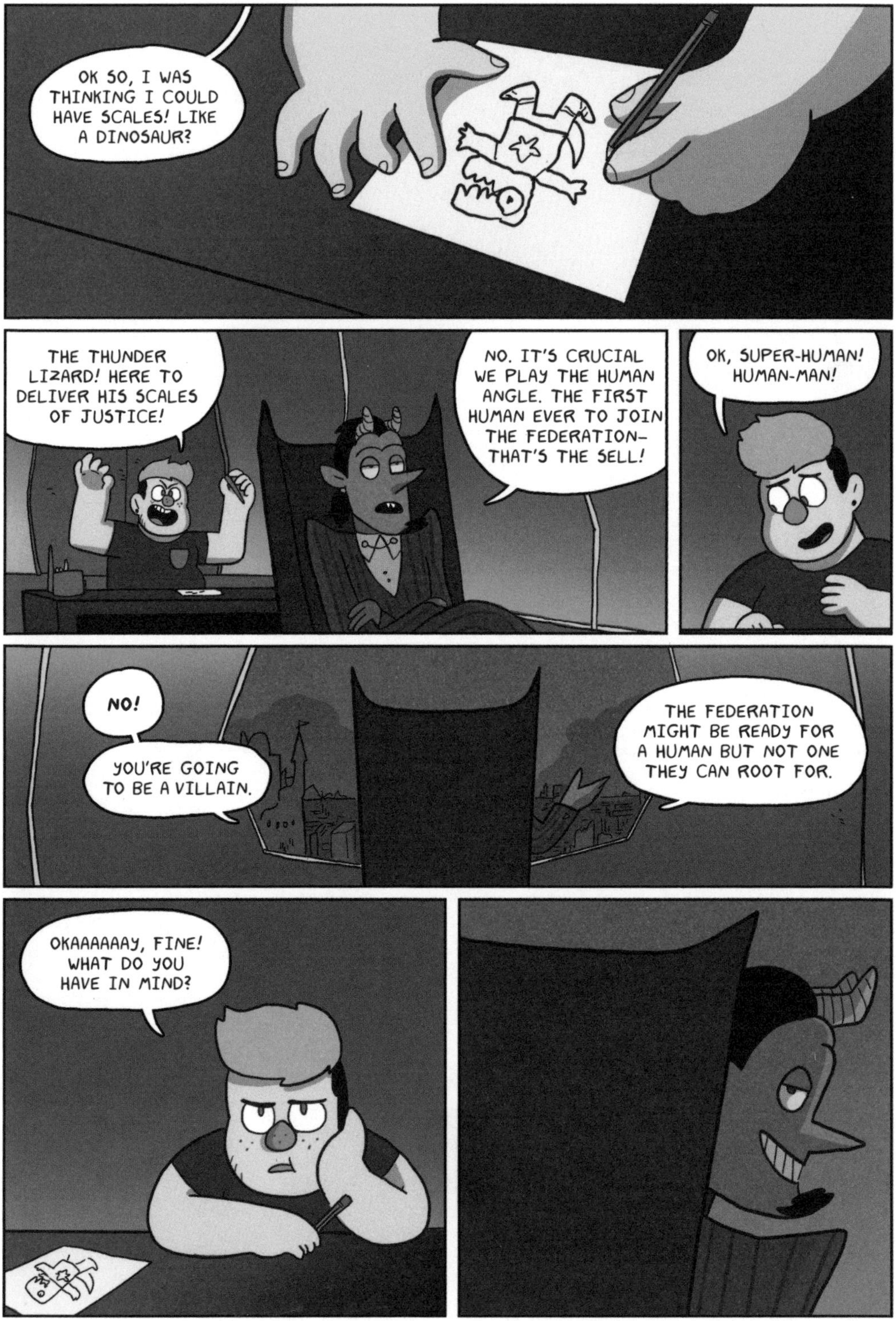
OK SO, I WAS THINKING I COULD HAVE SCALES! LIKE A DINOSAUR?
THE THUNDER LIZARD! HERE TO DELIVER HIS SCALES OF JUSTICE!
NO. IT'S CRUCIAL WE PLAY THE HUMAN ANGLE. THE FIRST HUMAN EVER TO JOIN THE FEDERATION– THAT'S THE SELL!
OK, SUPER-HUMAN! HUMAN-MAN!
NO!
YOU'RE GOING TO BE A VILLAIN.
THE FEDERATION MIGHT BE READY FOR A HUMAN BUT NOT ONE THEY CAN ROOT FOR.
OKAAAAAAY, FINE! WHAT DO YOU HAVE IN MIND?

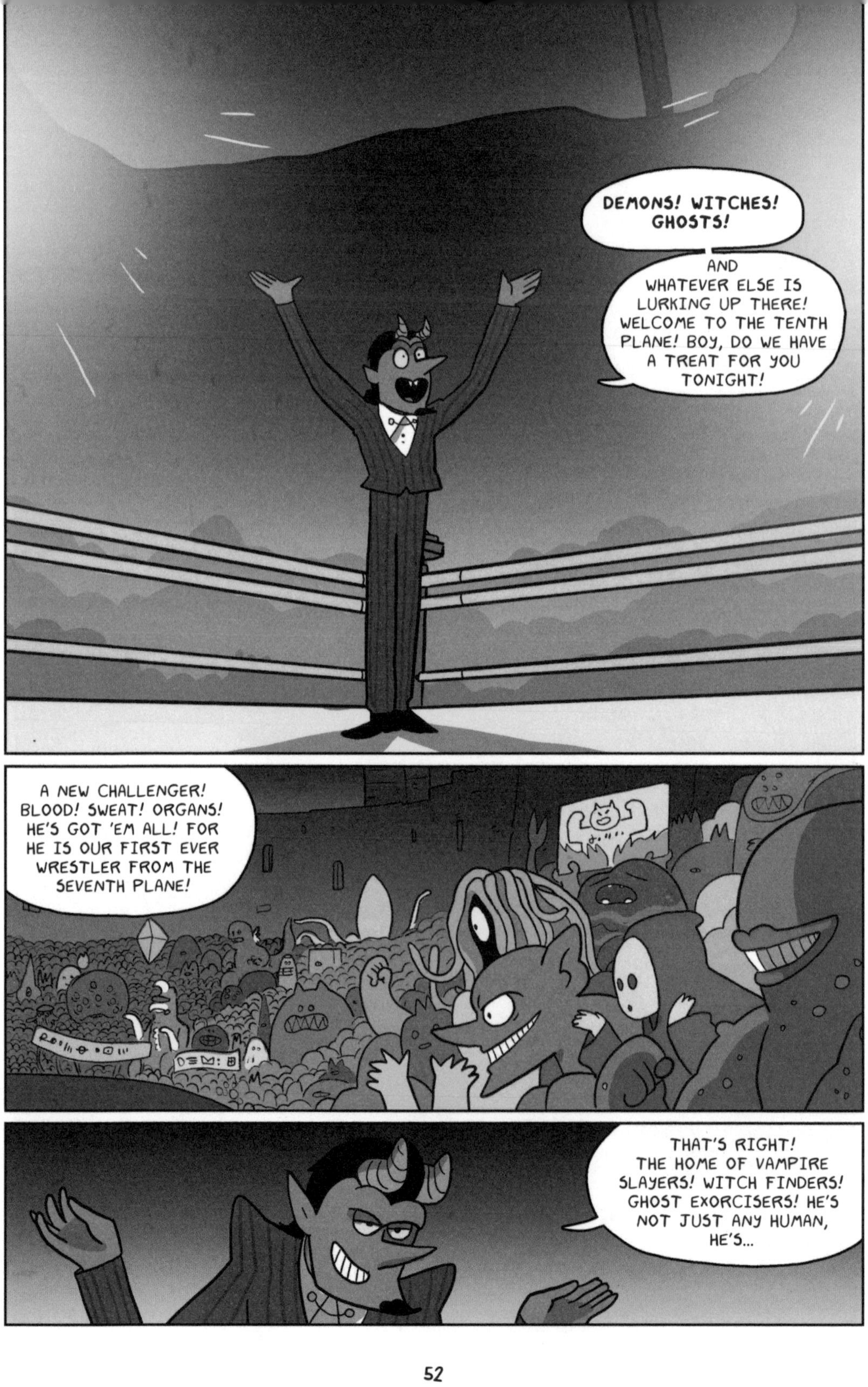
DEMONS! WITCHES! GHOSTS!
AND WHATEVER ELSE IS LURKING UP THERE! WELCOME TO THE TENTH PLANE! BOY, DO WE HAVE A TREAT FOR YOU TONIGHT!
A NEW CHALLENGER! BLOOD! SWEAT! ORGANS! HE'S GOT 'EM ALL! FOR HE IS OUR FIRST EVER WRESTLER FROM THE SEVENTH PLANE!
THAT'S RIGHT! THE HOME OF VAMPIRE SLAYERS! WITCH FINDERS! GHOST EXORCISERS! HE'S NOT JUST ANY HUMAN, HE'S...

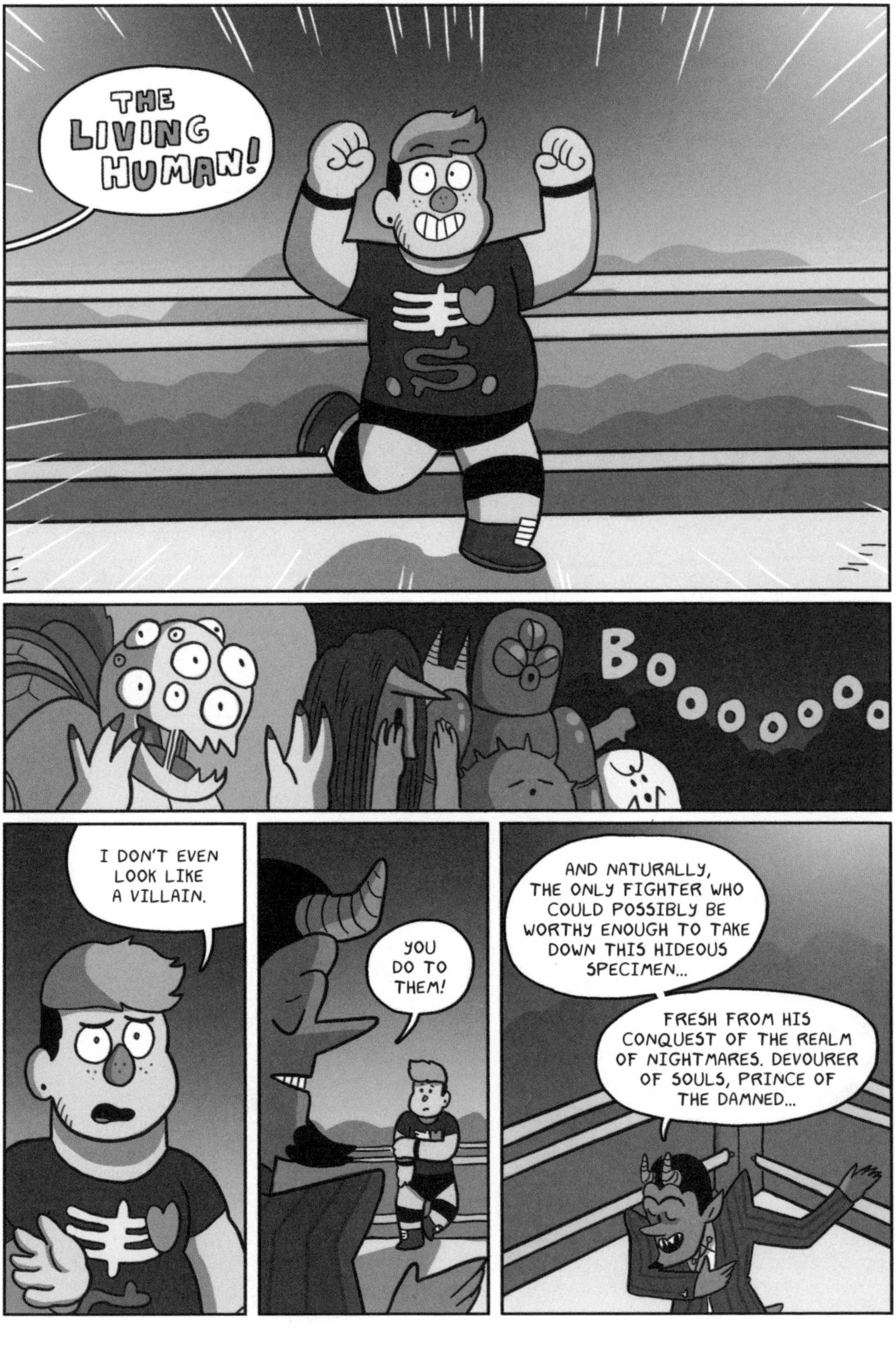
THE LIVING HUMAN!
BOOOOOOOO
I DON'T EVEN LOOK LIKE A VILLAIN.
YOU DO TO THEM!
AND NATURALLY, THE ONLY FIGHTER WHO COULD POSSIBLY BE WORTHY ENOUGH TO TAKE DOWN THIS HIDEOUS SPECIMEN...
FRESH FROM HIS CONQUEST OF THE REALM OF NIGHTMARES. DEVOURER OF SOULS, PRINCE OF THE DAMNED...

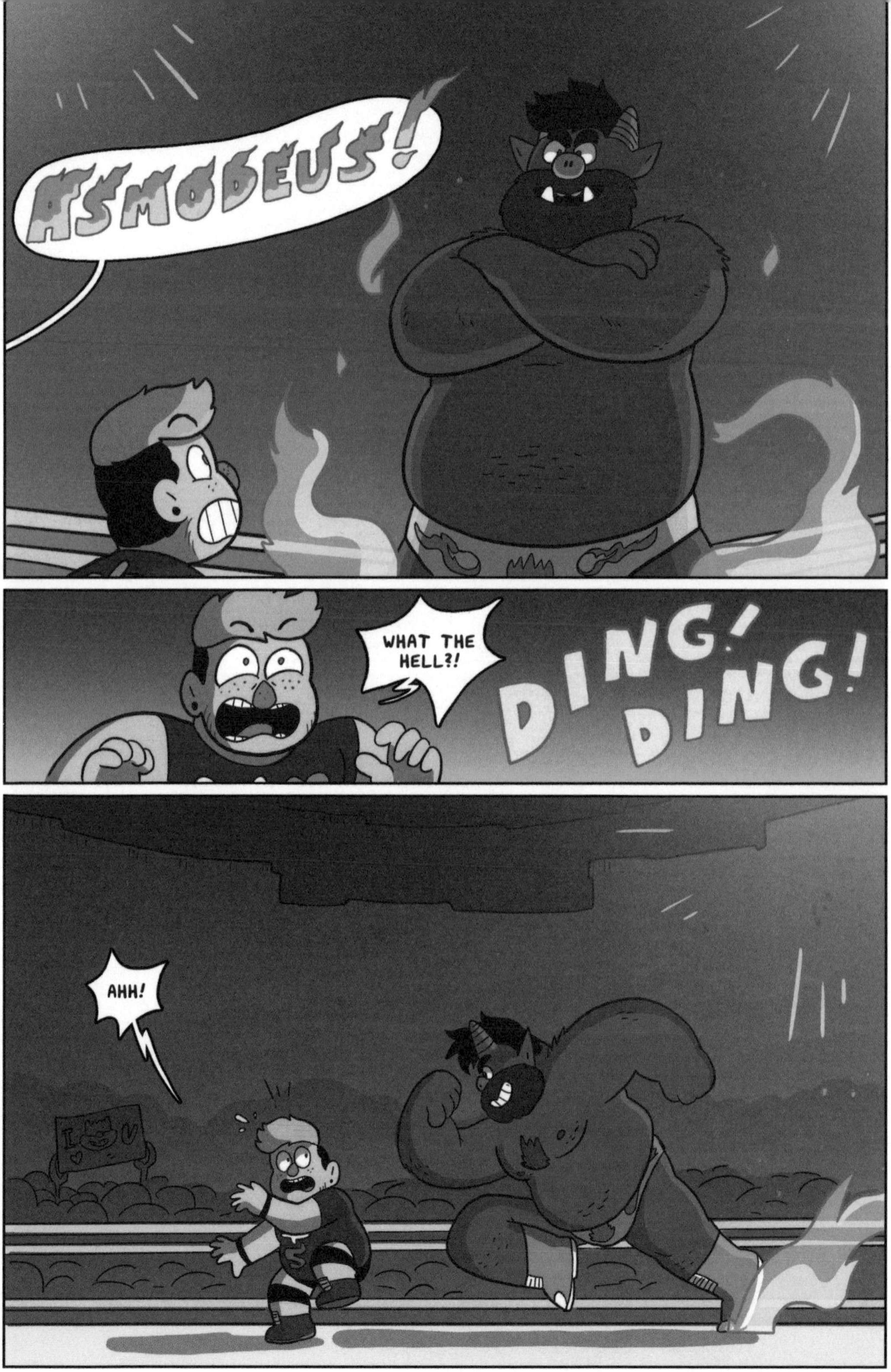
ASMODEUS!
WHAT THE HELL?!
DING! DING!
AHH!

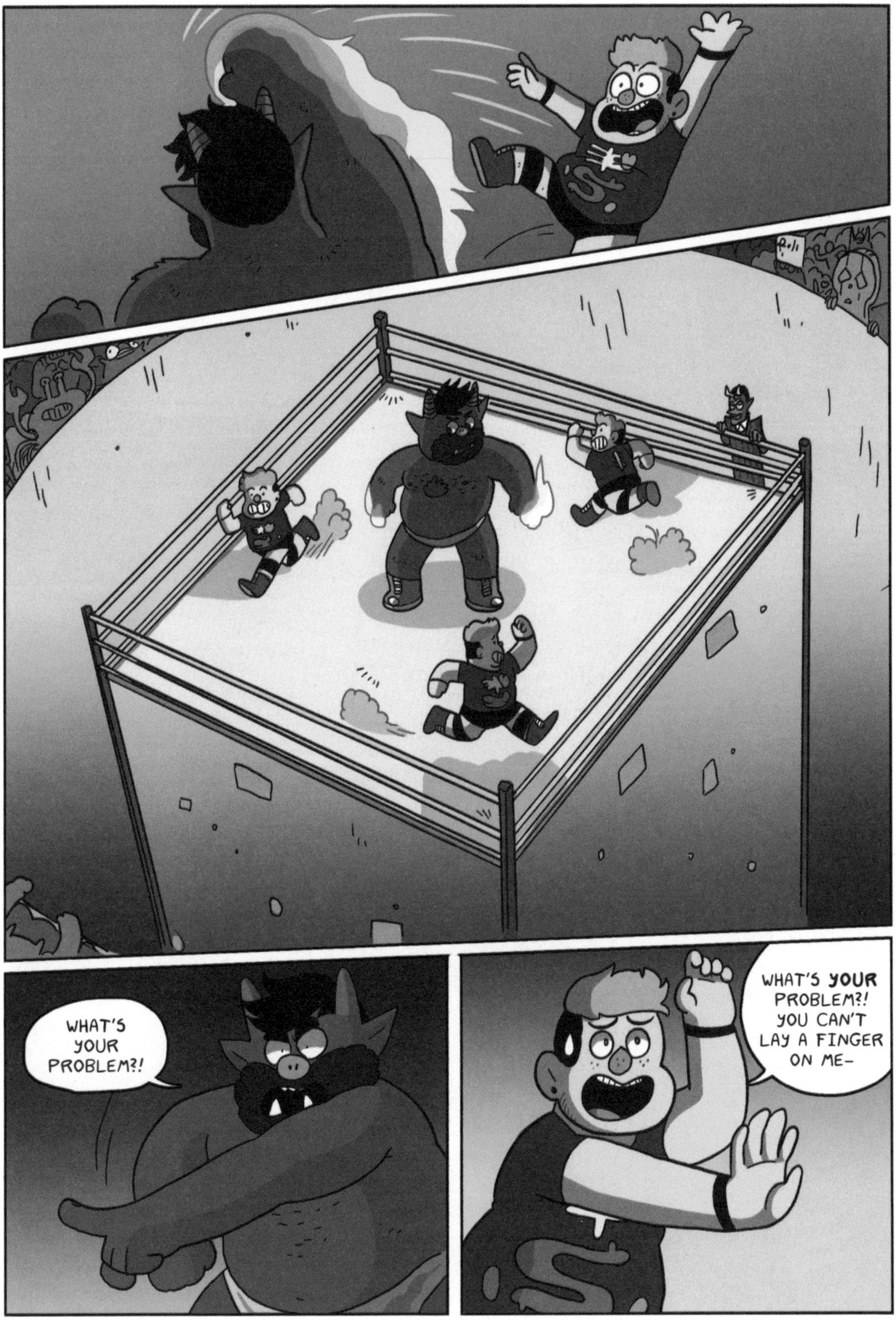
WHAT'S YOUR PROBLEM?!
WHAT'S YOUR PROBLEM?! YOU CAN'T LAY A FINGER ON ME–

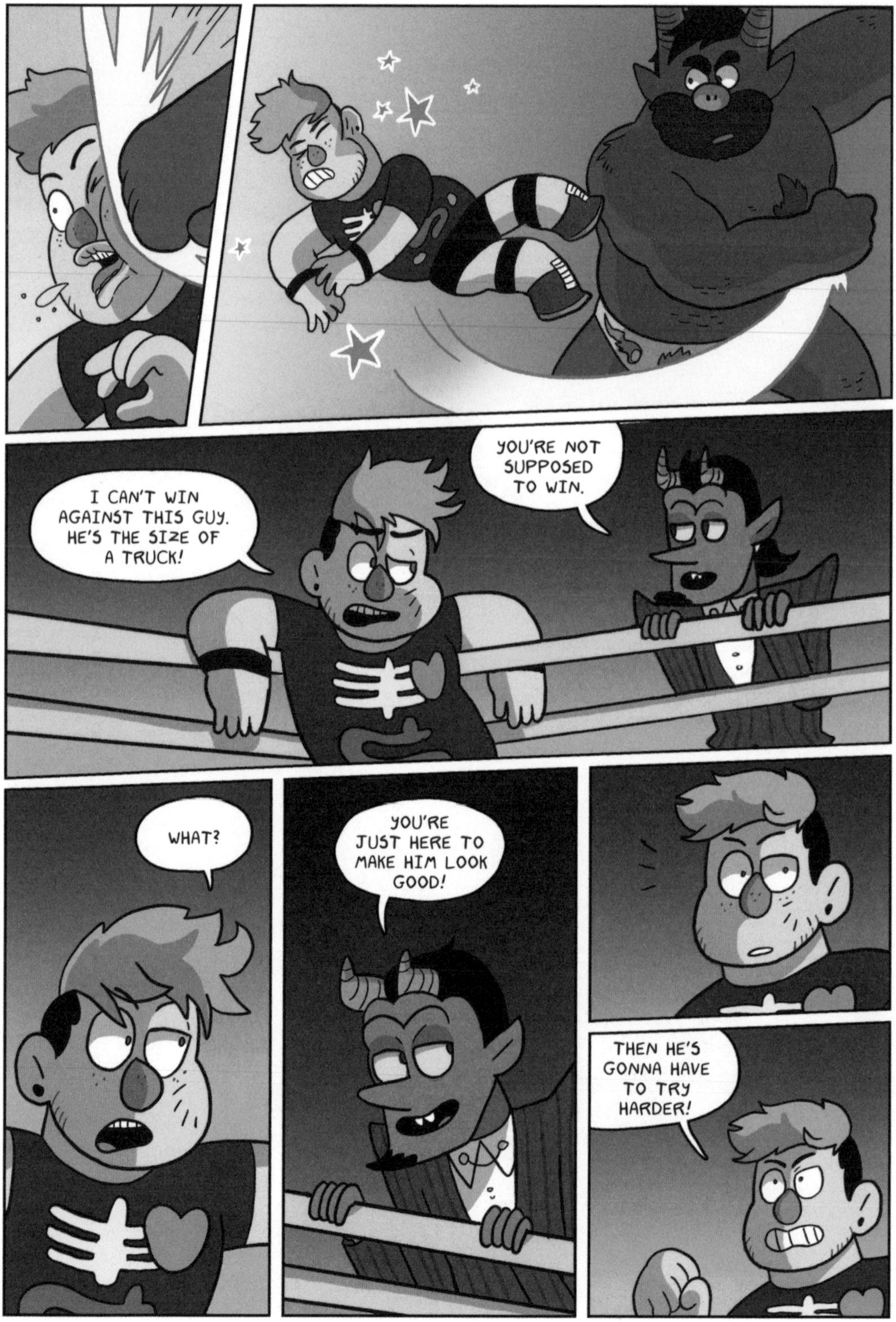
I CAN'T WIN AGAINST THIS GUY. HE'S THE SIZE OF A TRUCK!
YOU'RE NOT SUPPOSED TO WIN.
WHAT?
YOU'RE JUST HERE TO MAKE HIM LOOK GOOD!
THEN HE'S GONNA HAVE TO TRY HARDER!

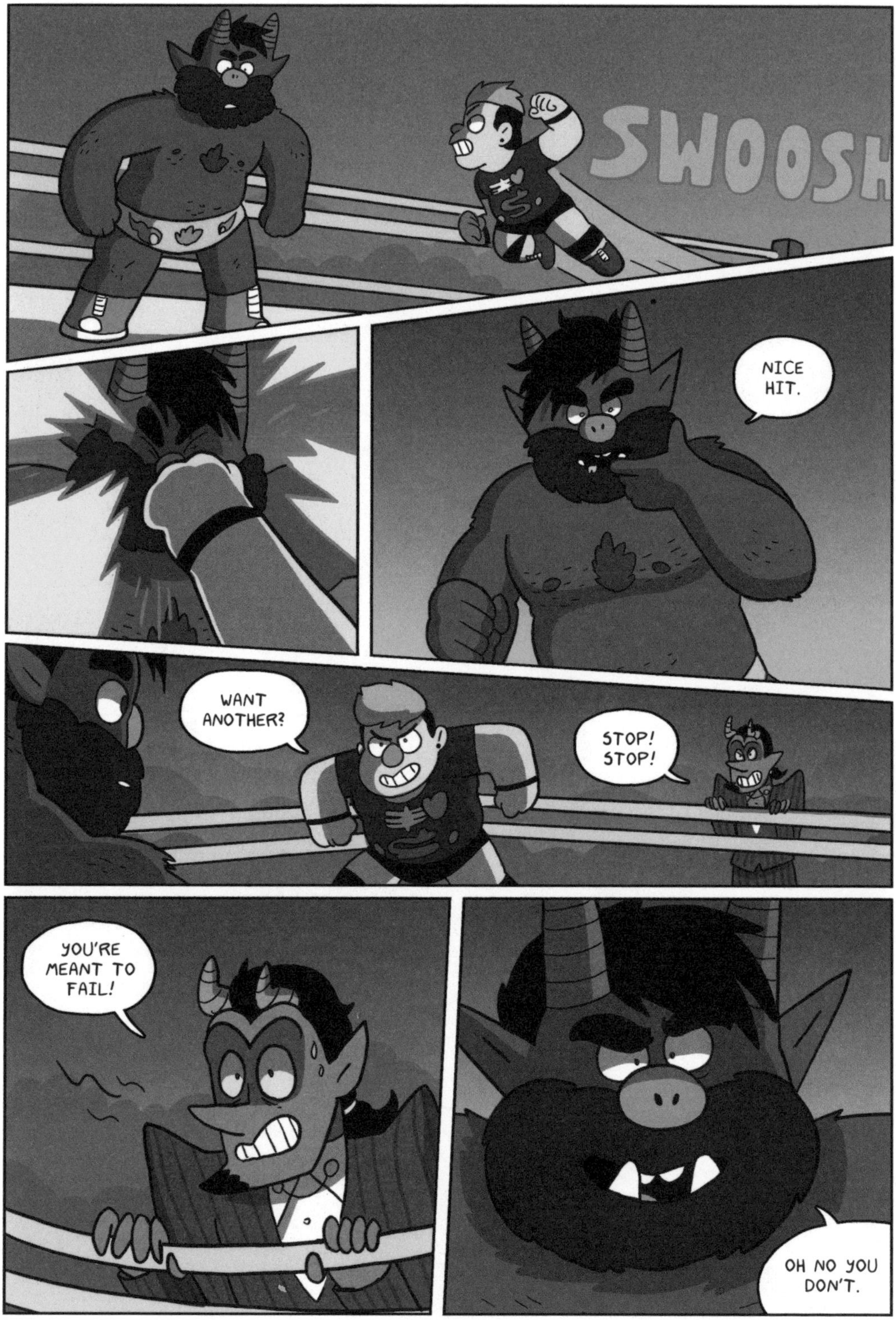
SWOOSH
NICE HIT.
WANT ANOTHER?
STOP! STOP!
YOU'RE MEANT TO FAIL!
OH NO YOU DON'T.

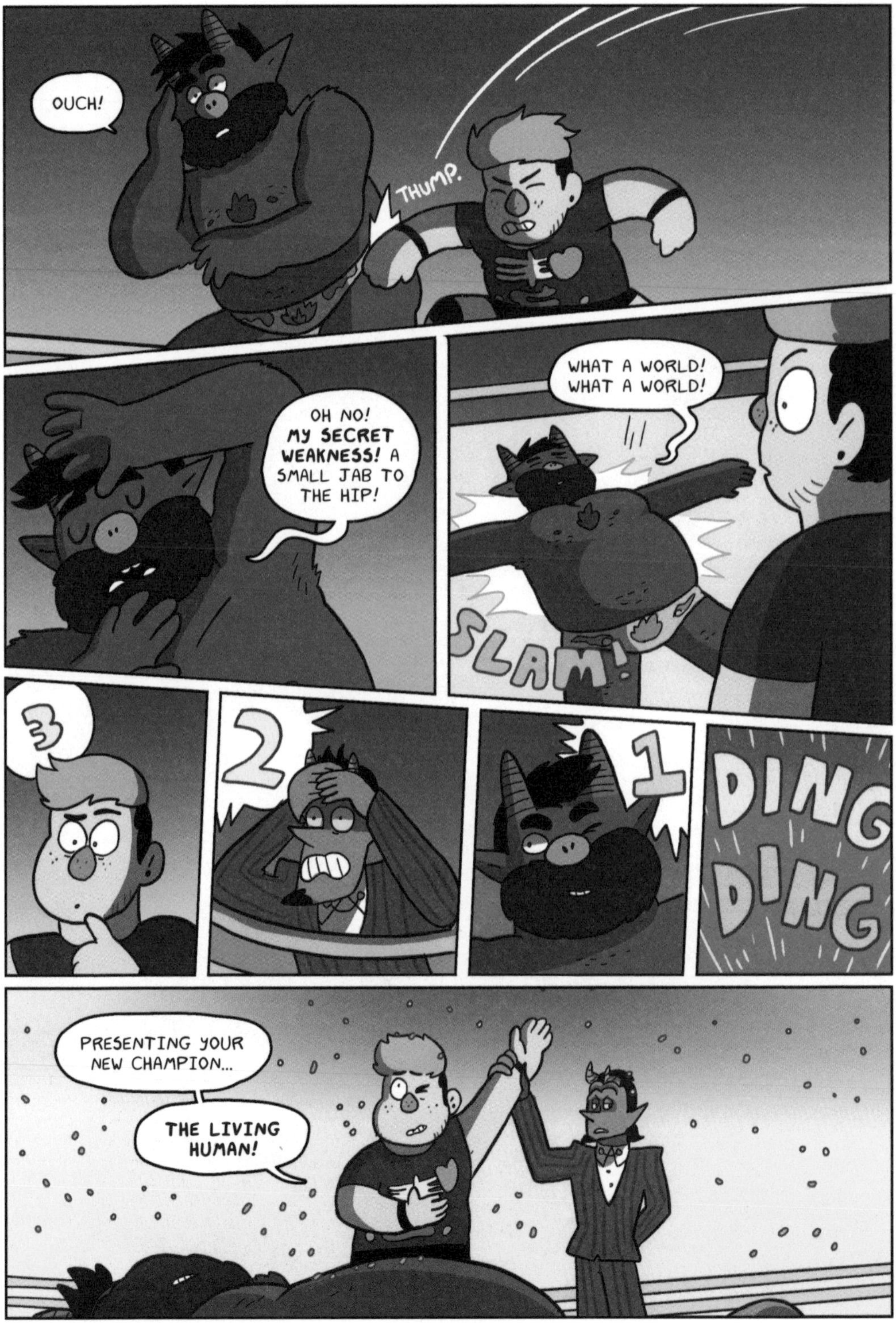
OUCH!
THUMP.
OH NO! MY SECRET WEAKNESS! A SMALL JAB TO THE HIP!
WHAT A WORLD! WHAT A WORLD!
SLAM!
3
2
1
DING DING
PRESENTING YOUR NEW CHAMPION...
THE LIVING HUMAN!

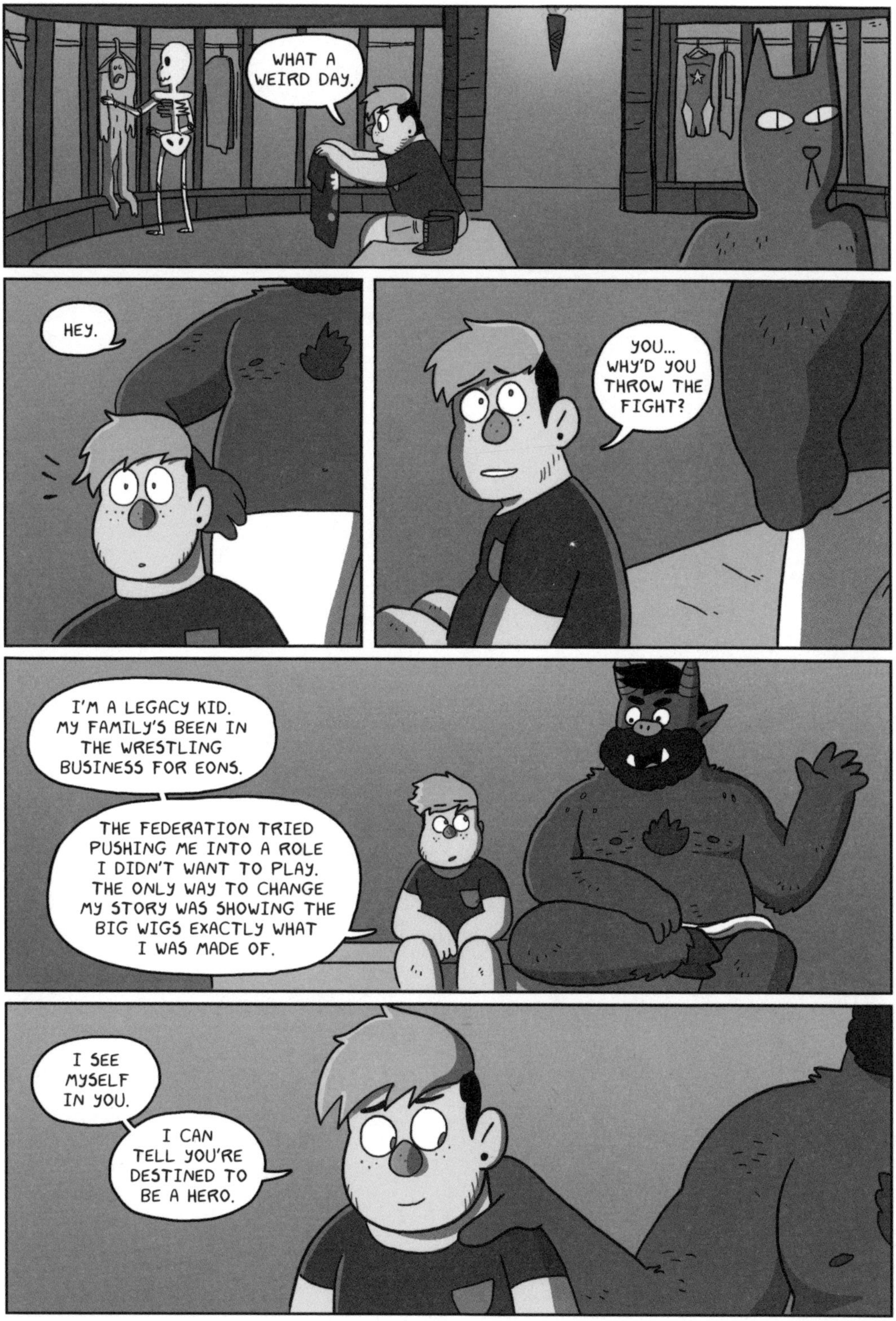
WHAT A WEIRD DAY.
HEY.
YOU... WHY'D YOU THROW THE FIGHT?
I'M A LEGACY KID. MY FAMILY'S BEEN IN THE WRESTLING BUSINESS FOR EONS.
THE FEDERATION TRIED PUSHING ME INTO A ROLE I DIDN'T WANT TO PLAY. THE ONLY WAY TO CHANGE MY STORY WAS SHOWING THE BIG WIGS EXACTLY WHAT I WAS MADE OF.
I SEE MYSELF IN YOU.
I CAN TELL YOU'RE DESTINED TO BE A HERO.

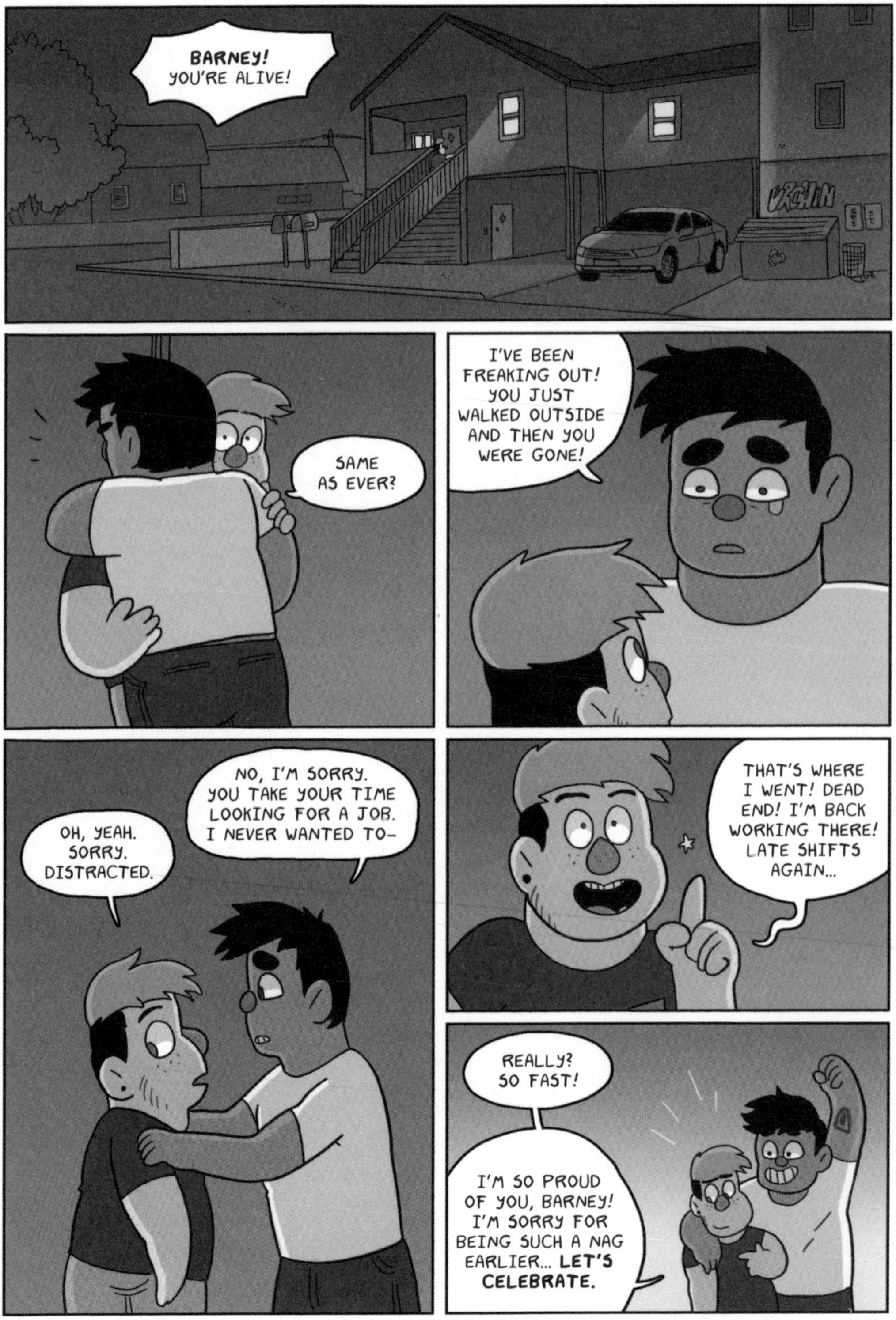
BARNEY! YOU'RE ALIVE!
SAME AS EVER?
I'VE BEEN FREAKING OUT! YOU JUST WALKED OUTSIDE AND THEN YOU WERE GONE!
OH, YEAH. SORRY. DISTRACTED.
NO, I'M SORRY. YOU TAKE YOUR TIME LOOKING FOR A JOB. I NEVER WANTED TO-
THAT'S WHERE I WENT! DEAD END! I'M BACK WORKING THERE! LATE SHIFTS AGAIN...
REALLY? SO FAST!
I'M SO PROUD OF YOU, BARNEY! I'M SORRY FOR BEING SUCH A NAG EARLIER... **LET'S CELEBRATE.**

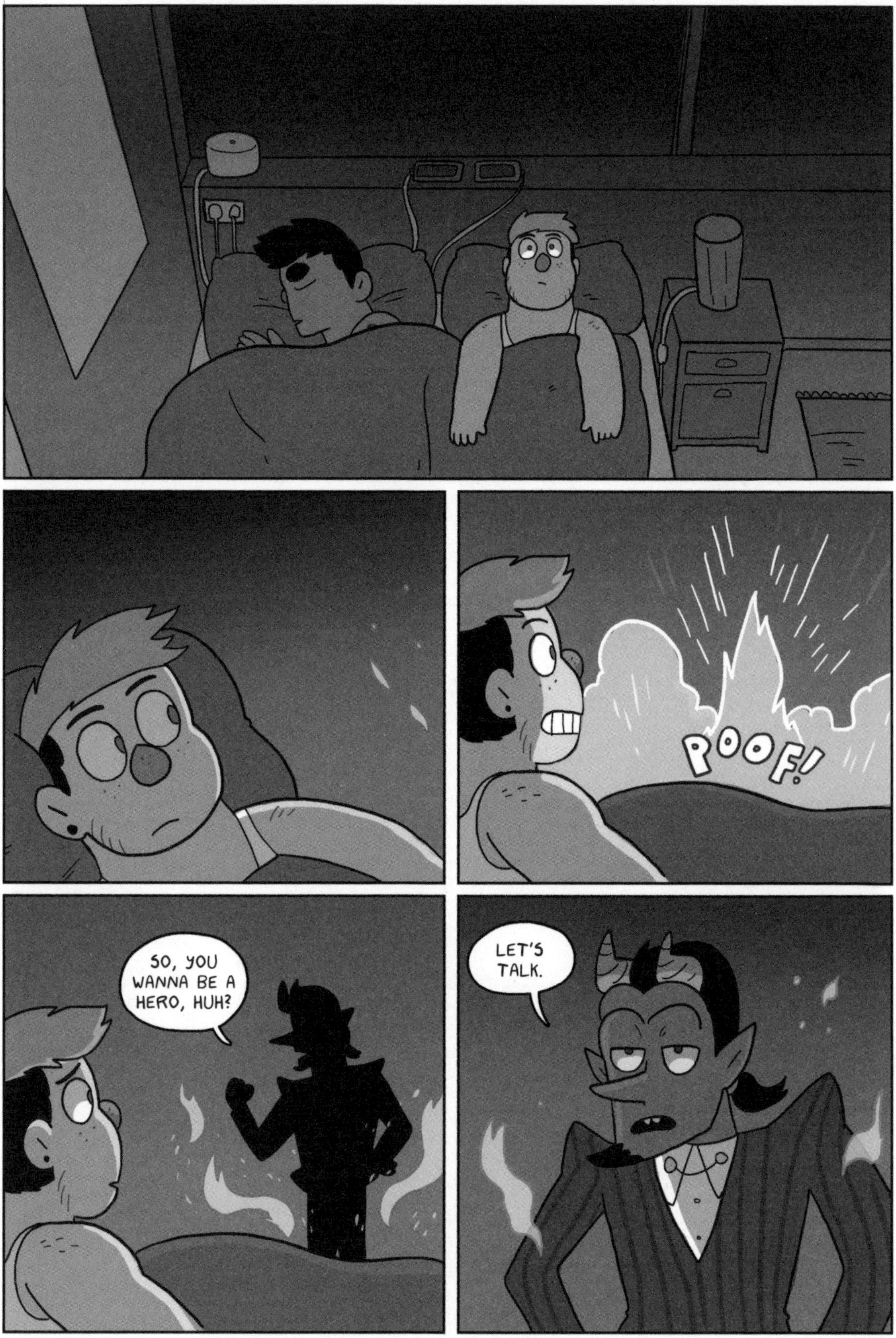
POOF!
SO, YOU WANNA BE A HERO, HUH?
LET'S TALK.

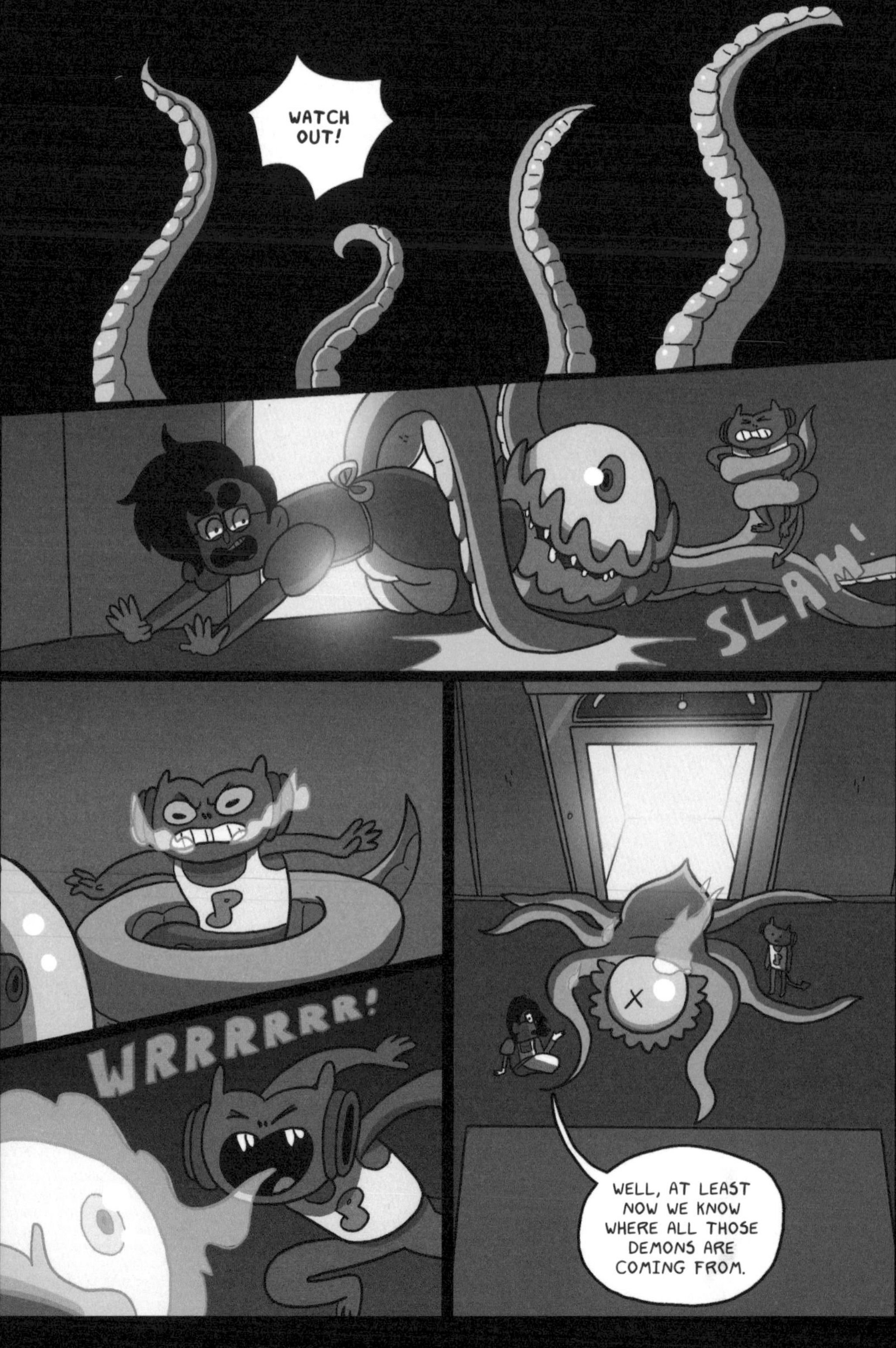
WATCH OUT!
SLAM!
WRRRRRR!
WELL, AT LEAST NOW WE KNOW WHERE ALL THOSE DEMONS ARE COMING FROM.

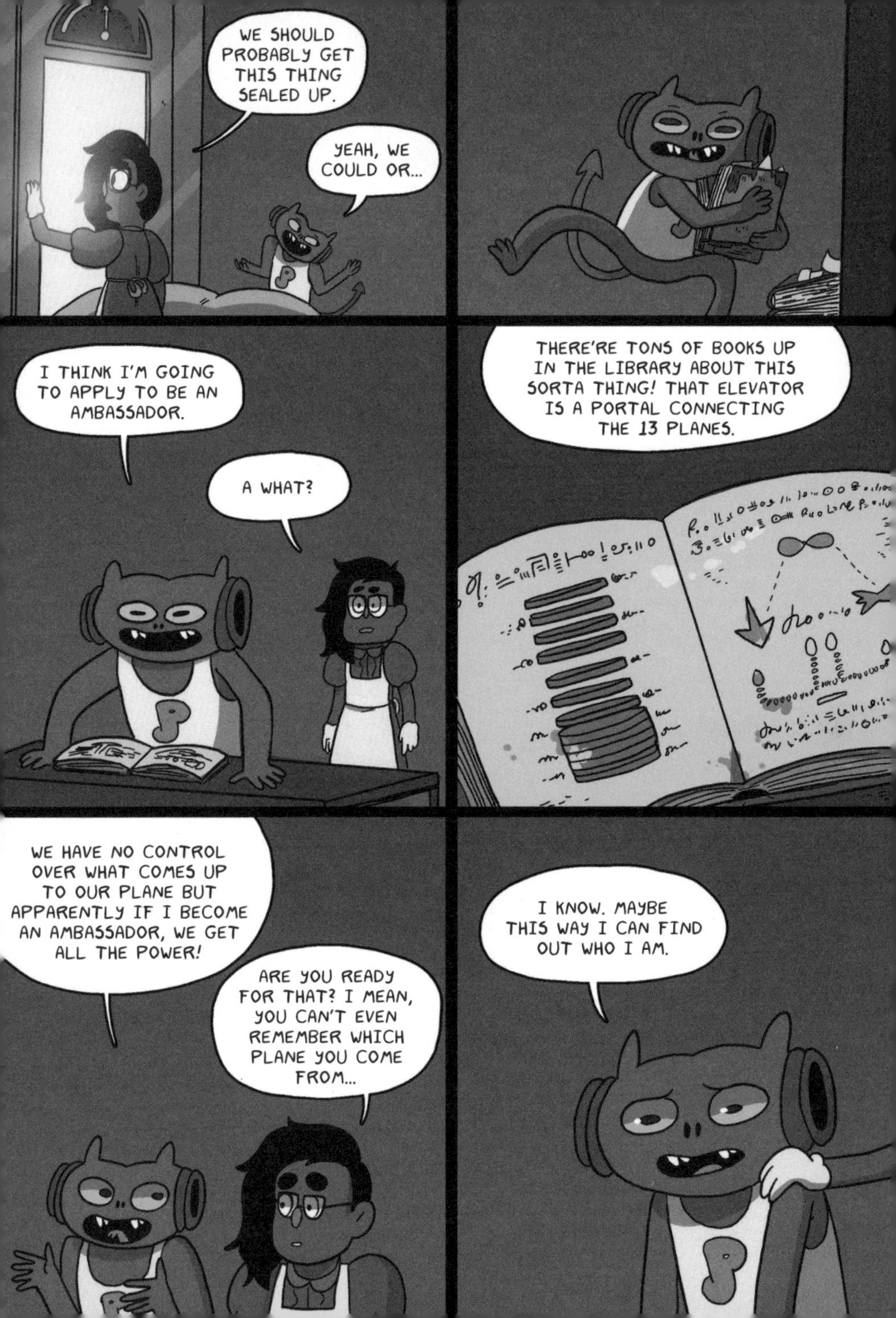
WE SHOULD PROBABLY GET THIS THING SEALED UP.
YEAH, WE COULD OR...
I THINK I'M GOING TO APPLY TO BE AN AMBASSADOR.
A WHAT?
THERE'RE TONS OF BOOKS UP IN THE LIBRARY ABOUT THIS SORTA THING! THAT ELEVATOR IS A PORTAL CONNECTING THE 13 PLANES.
WE HAVE NO CONTROL OVER WHAT COMES UP TO OUR PLANE BUT APPARENTLY IF I BECOME AN AMBASSADOR, WE GET ALL THE POWER!
ARE YOU READY FOR THAT? I MEAN, YOU CAN'T EVEN REMEMBER WHICH PLANE YOU COME FROM...
I KNOW. MAYBE THIS WAY I CAN FIND OUT WHO I AM.

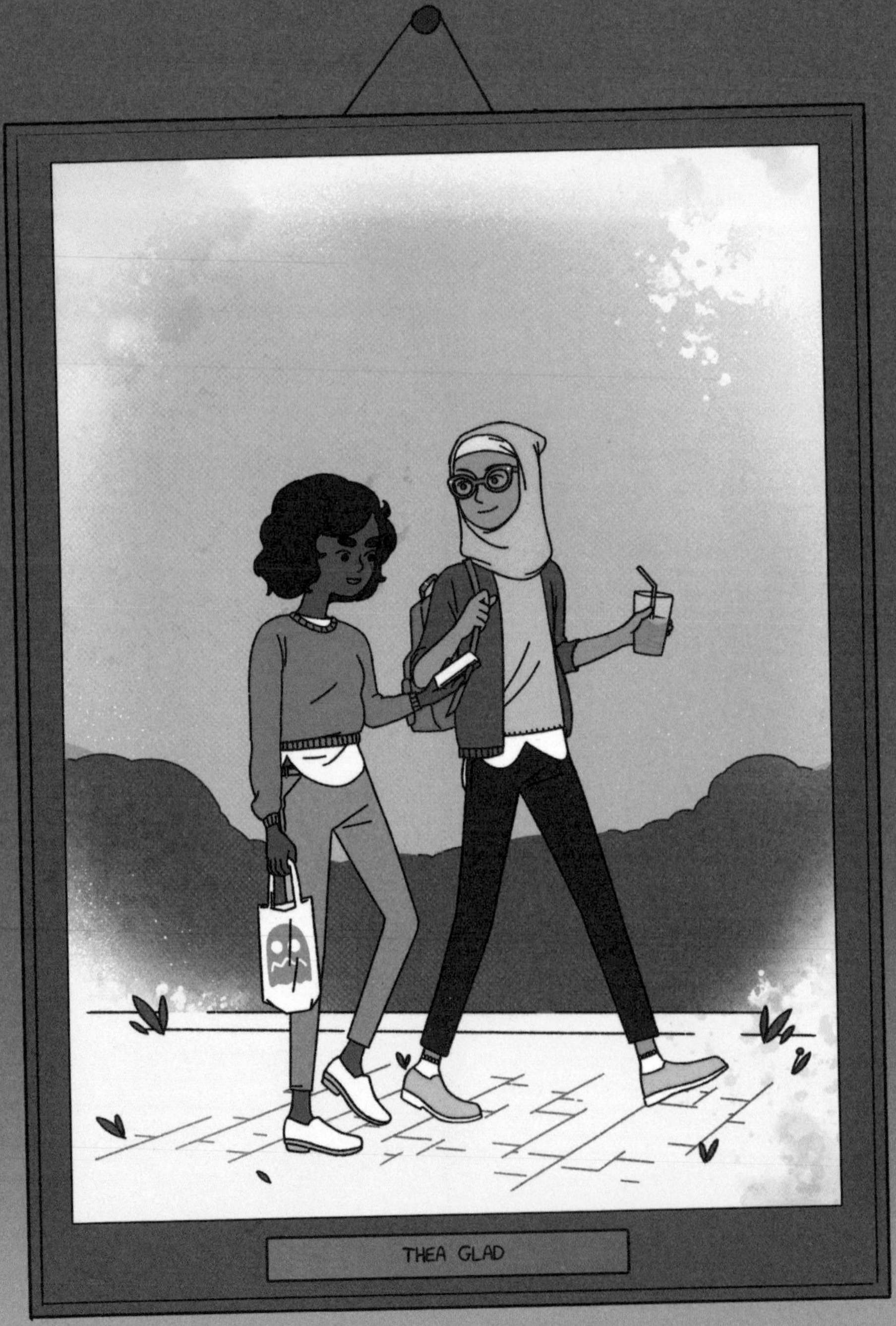
THEA GLAD

CHAPTER 3
HEAD TO HEAD

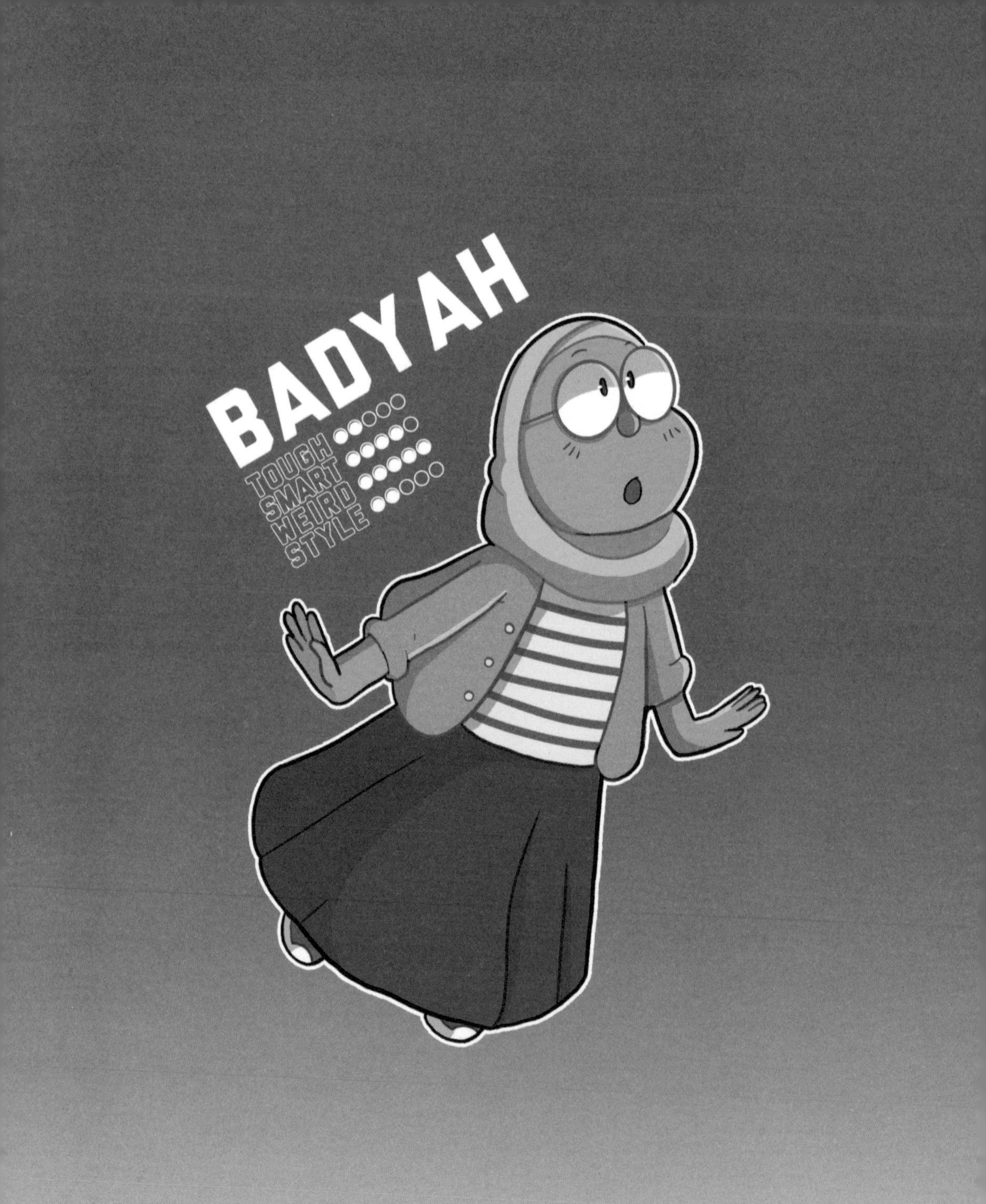
BADYAH
TOUGH
SMART
WEIRD
STYLE

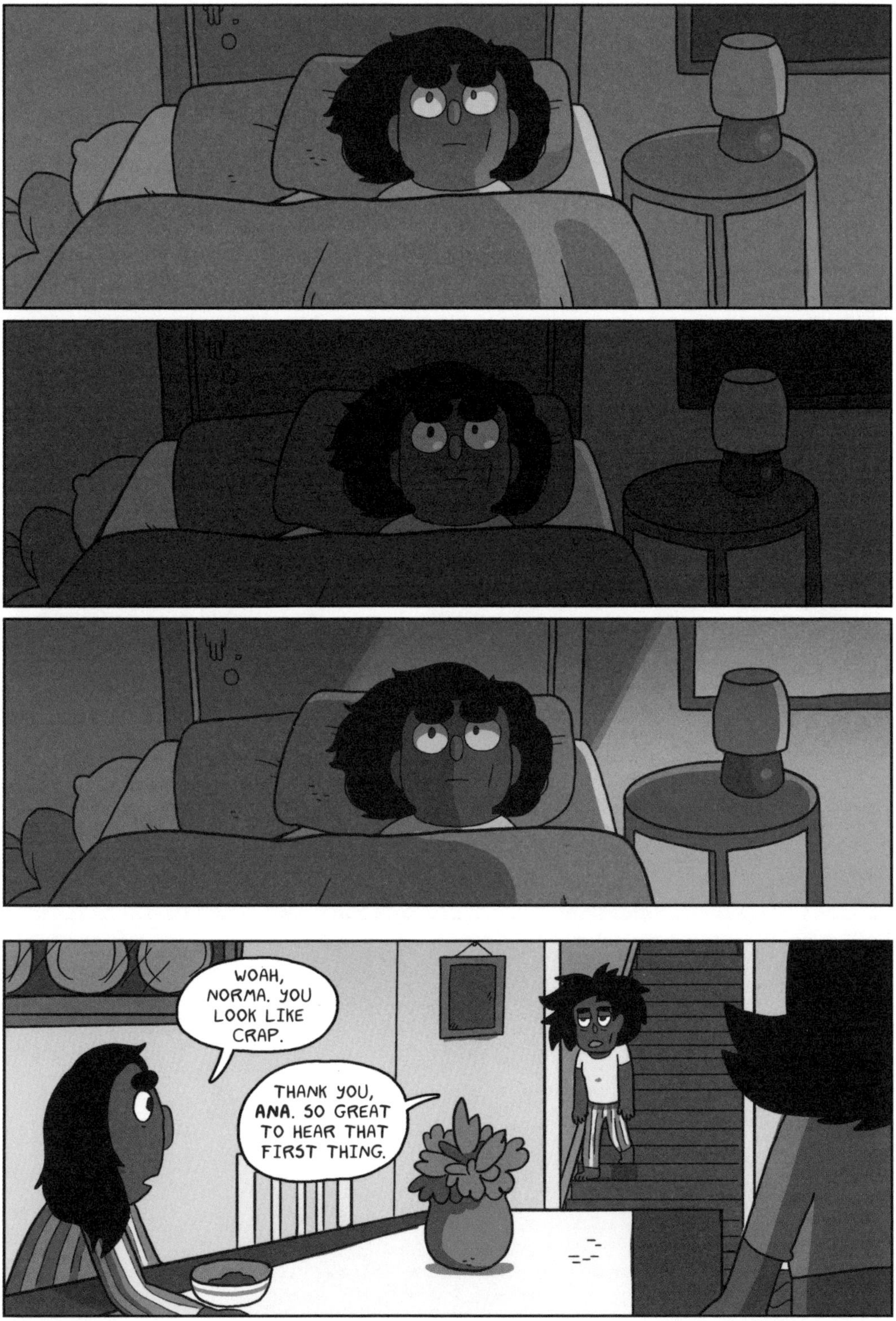
WOAH, NORMA. YOU LOOK LIKE CRAP.
THANK YOU, ANA. SO GREAT TO HEAR THAT FIRST THING.

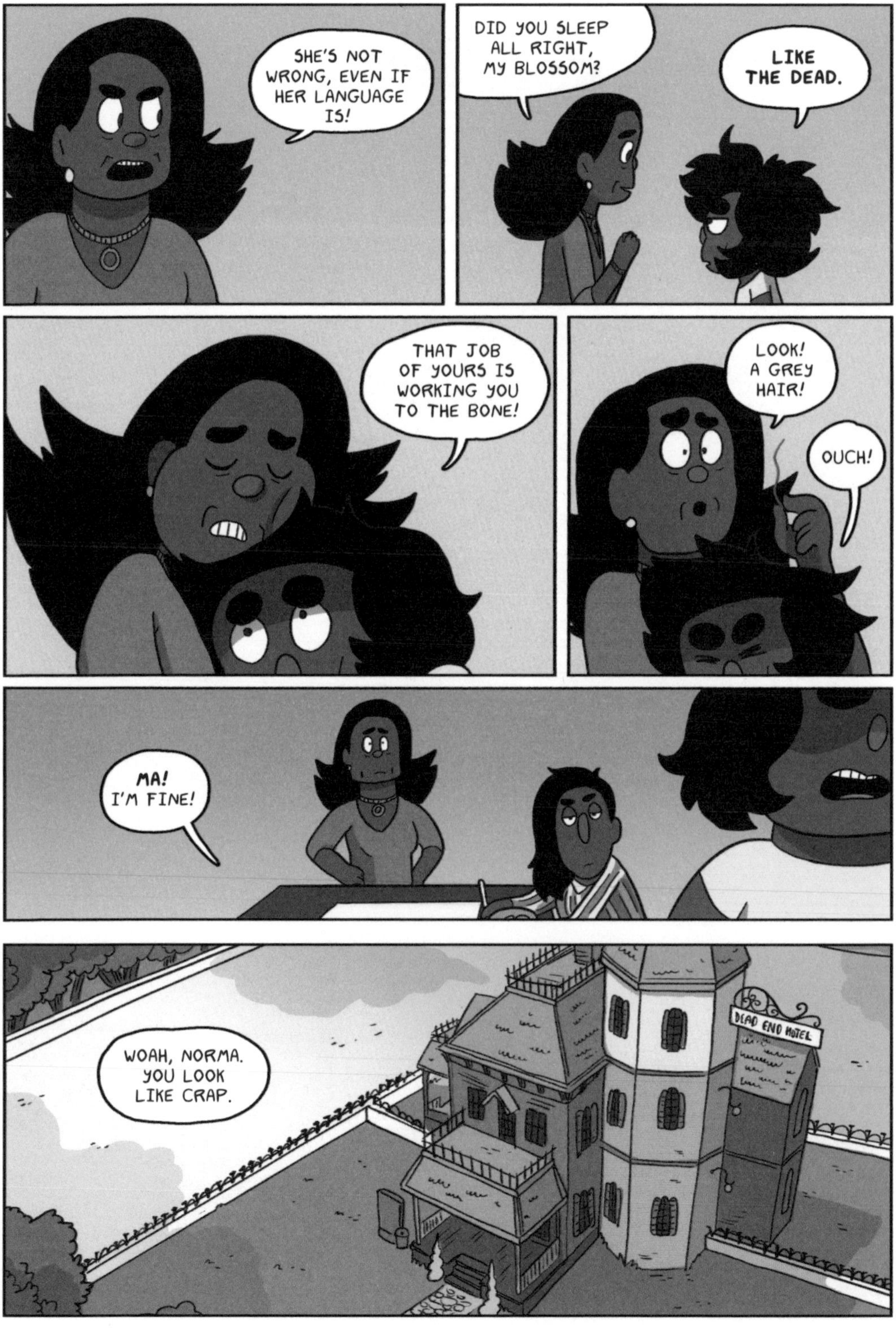
SHE'S NOT WRONG, EVEN IF HER LANGUAGE IS!
DID YOU SLEEP ALL RIGHT, MY BLOSSOM?
LIKE THE DEAD.
THAT JOB OF YOURS IS WORKING YOU TO THE BONE!
LOOK! A GREY HAIR!
OUCH!
MA! I'M FINE!
WOAH, NORMA. YOU LOOK LIKE CRAP.
DEAD END HOTEL

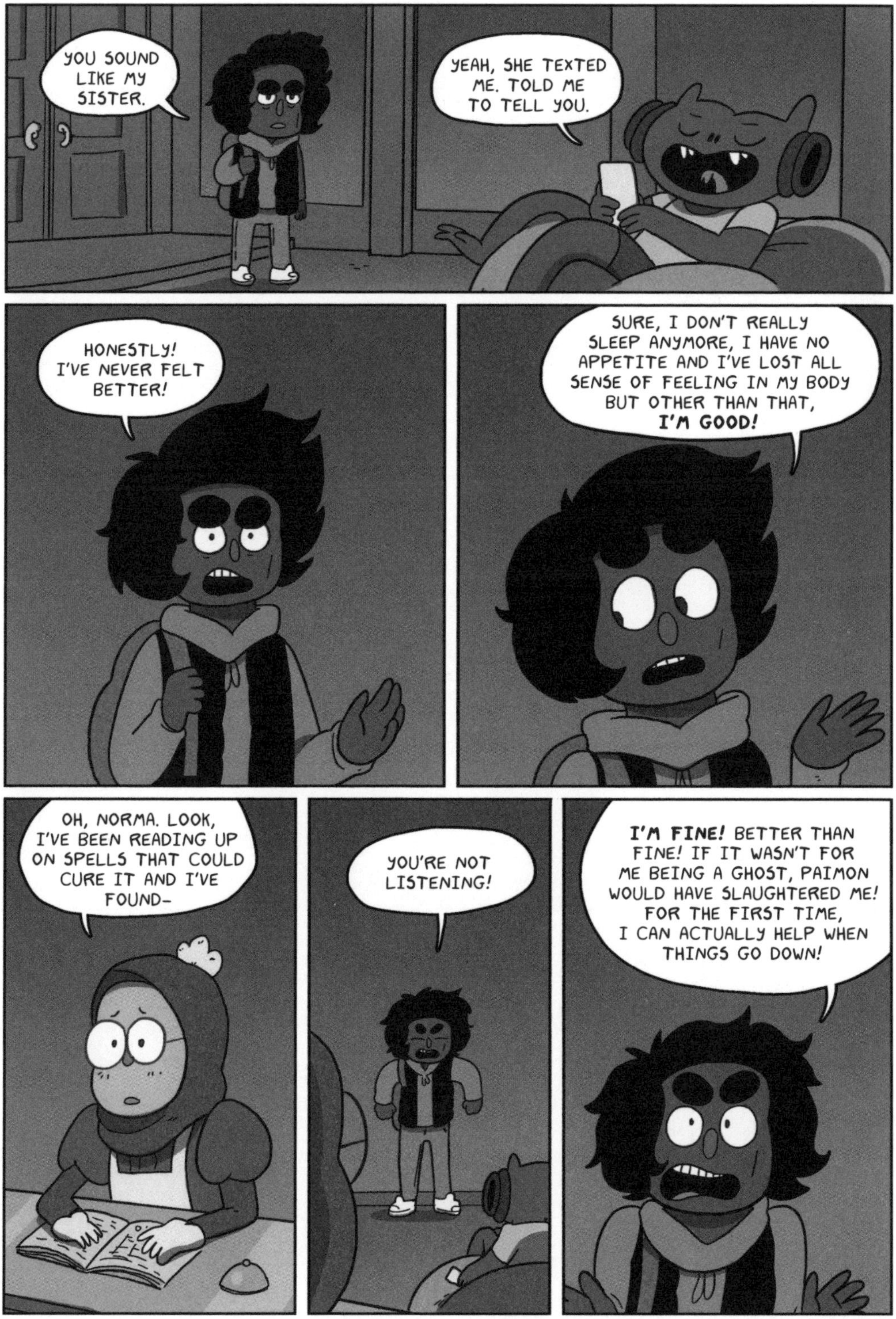

YOU SOUND LIKE MY SISTER.
YEAH, SHE TEXTED ME. TOLD ME TO TELL YOU.
HONESTLY! I'VE NEVER FELT BETTER!
SURE, I DON'T REALLY SLEEP ANYMORE, I HAVE NO APPETITE AND I'VE LOST ALL SENSE OF FEELING IN MY BODY BUT OTHER THAN THAT, **I'M GOOD!**
OH, NORMA. LOOK, I'VE BEEN READING UP ON SPELLS THAT COULD CURE IT AND I'VE FOUND–
YOU'RE NOT LISTENING!
I'M FINE! BETTER THAN FINE! IF IT WASN'T FOR ME BEING A GHOST, PAIMON WOULD HAVE SLAUGHTERED ME! FOR THE FIRST TIME, I CAN ACTUALLY HELP WHEN THINGS GO DOWN!

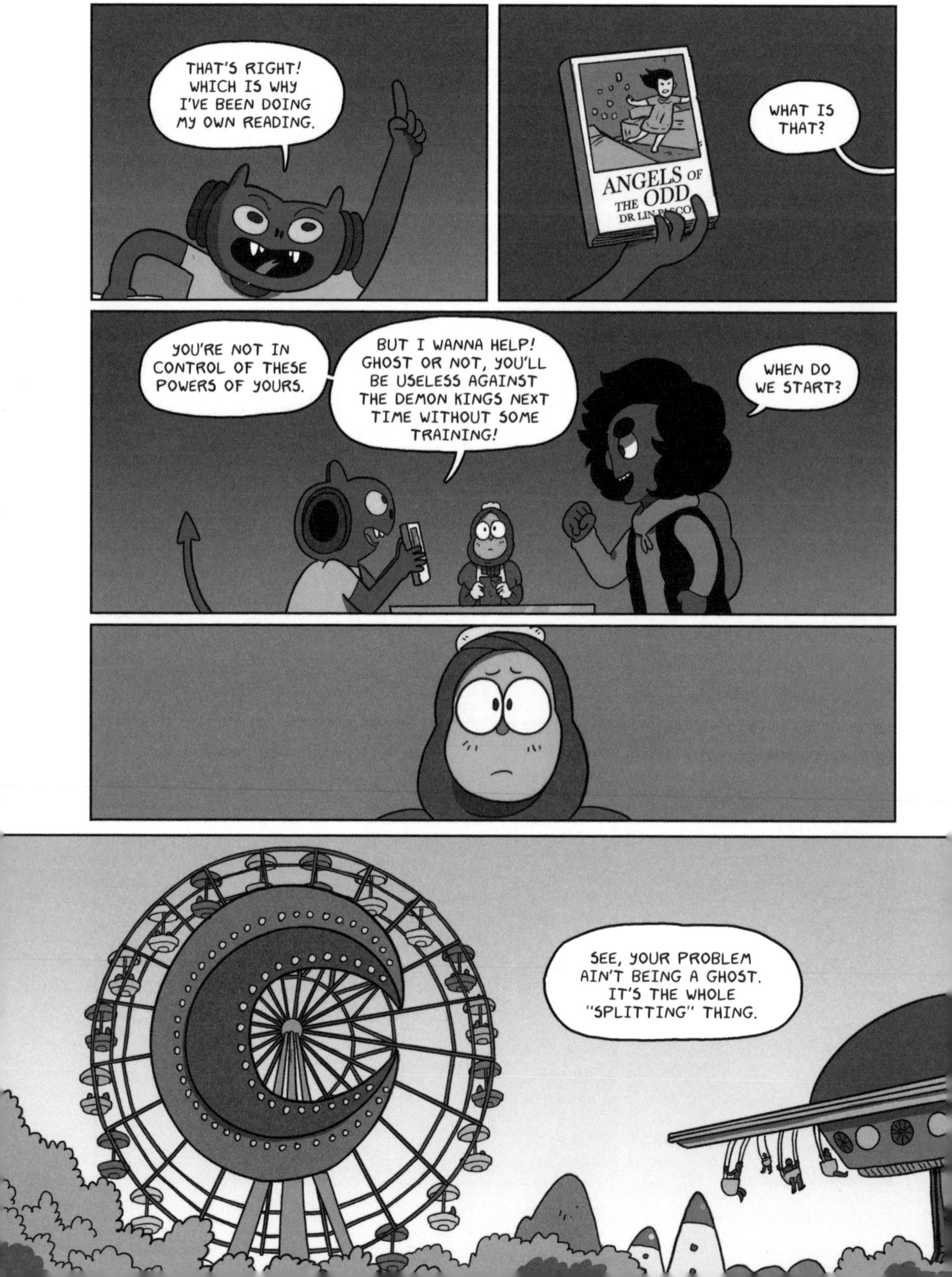
THAT'S RIGHT! WHICH IS WHY I'VE BEEN DOING MY OWN READING.
ANGELS OF THE ODD
WHAT IS THAT?
YOU'RE NOT IN CONTROL OF THESE POWERS OF YOURS.
BUT I WANNA HELP! GHOST OR NOT, YOU'LL BE USELESS AGAINST THE DEMON KINGS NEXT TIME WITHOUT SOME TRAINING!
WHEN DO WE START?
SEE, YOUR PROBLEM AIN'T BEING A GHOST. IT'S THE WHOLE "SPLITTING" THING.

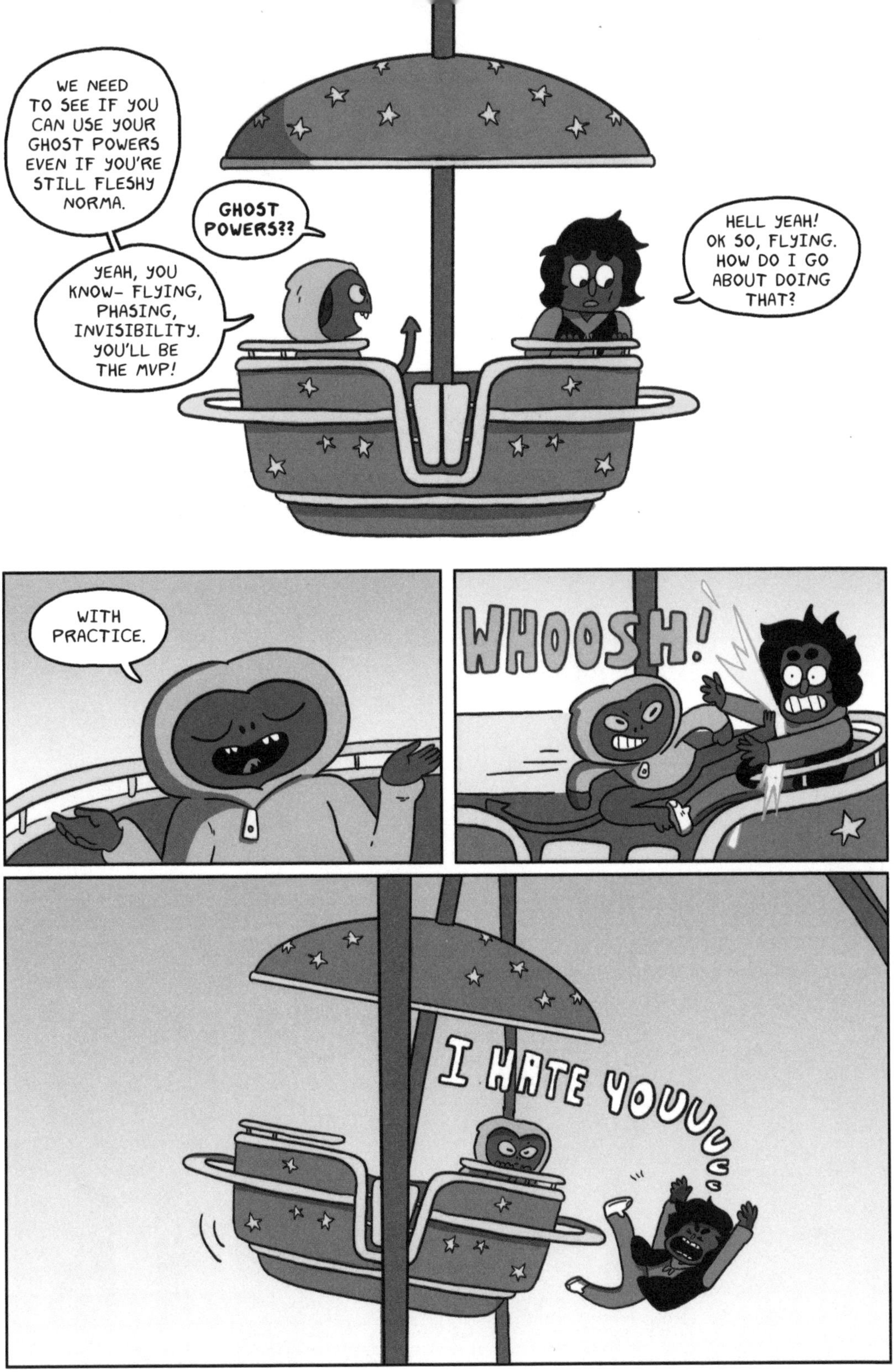

WE NEED TO SEE IF YOU CAN USE YOUR GHOST POWERS EVEN IF YOU'RE STILL FLESHY NORMA.
GHOST POWERS??
YEAH, YOU KNOW- FLYING, PHASING, INVISIBILITY. YOU'LL BE THE MVP!
HELL YEAH! OK SO, FLYING. HOW DO I GO ABOUT DOING THAT?
WITH PRACTICE.
WHOOSH!
I HATE YOUUU

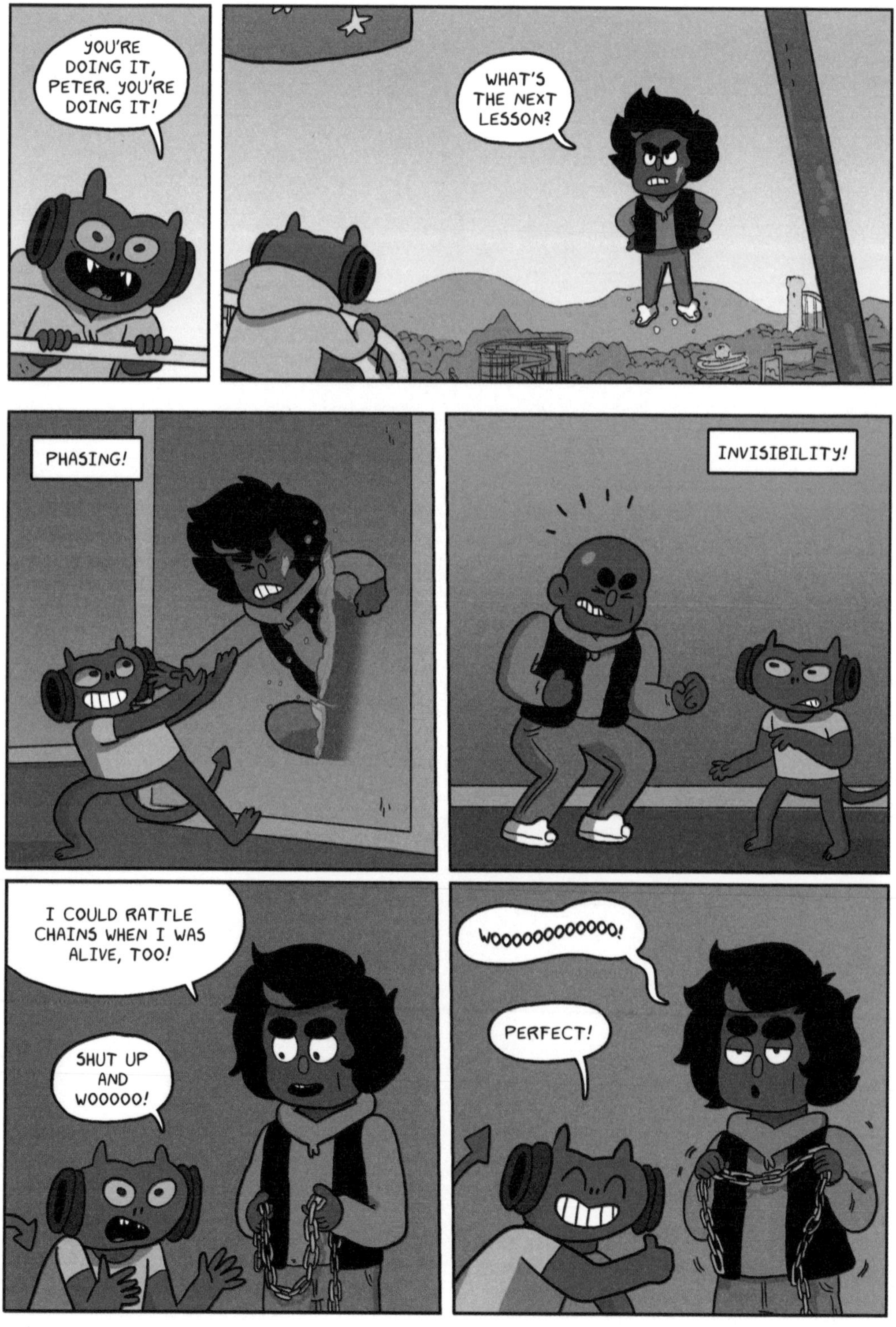
YOU'RE DOING IT, PETER. YOU'RE DOING IT!
WHAT'S THE NEXT LESSON?
PHASING!
INVISIBILITY!
I COULD RATTLE CHAINS WHEN I WAS ALIVE, TOO!
SHUT UP AND WOOOOO!
WOOOOOOOOOOOO!
PERFECT!

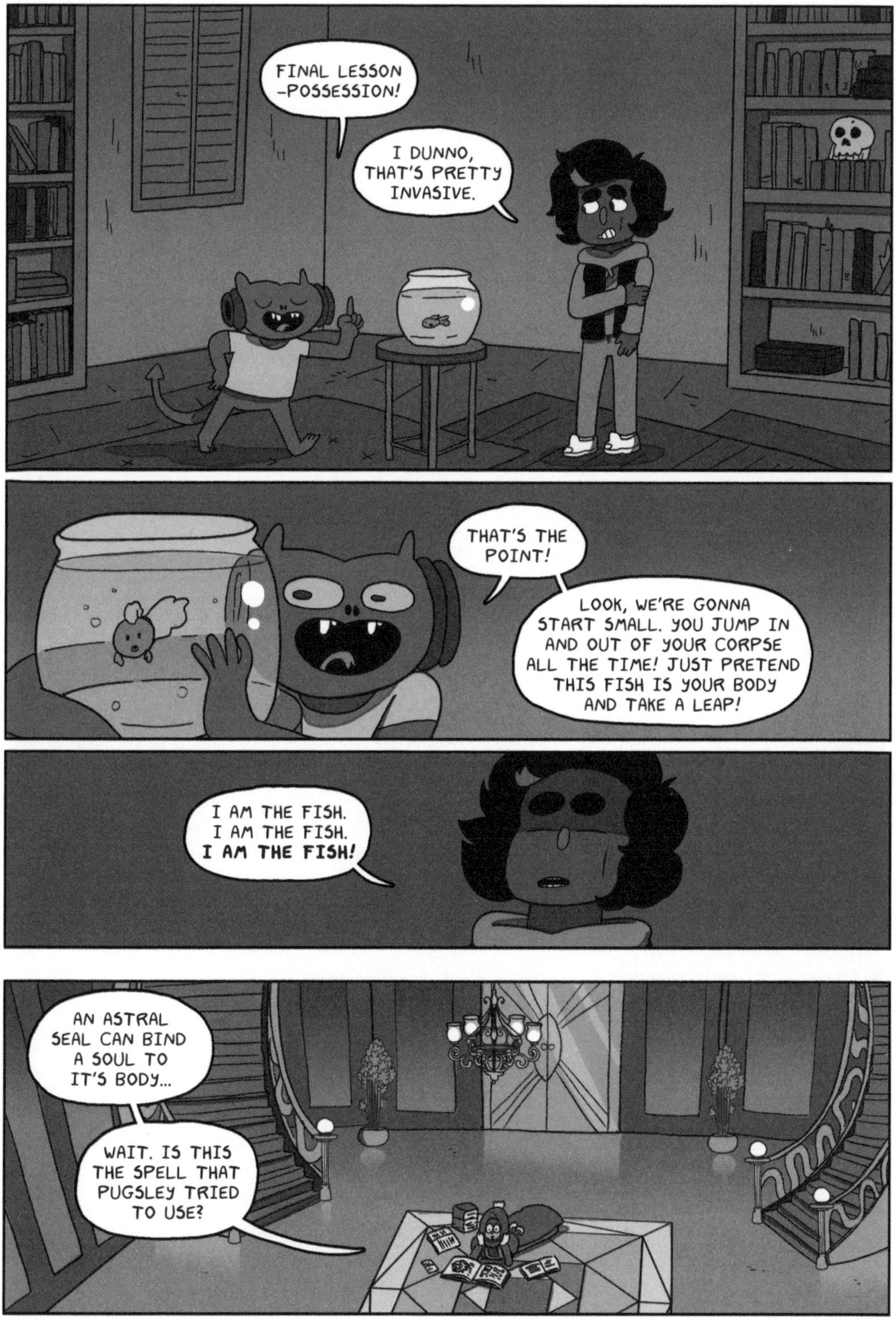

FINAL LESSON -POSSESSION!
I DUNNO, THAT'S PRETTY INVASIVE.
THAT'S THE POINT!
LOOK, WE'RE GONNA START SMALL. YOU JUMP IN AND OUT OF YOUR CORPSE ALL THE TIME! JUST PRETEND THIS FISH IS YOUR BODY AND TAKE A LEAP!
I AM THE FISH. I AM THE FISH. **I AM THE FISH!**
AN ASTRAL SEAL CAN BIND A SOUL TO IT'S BODY...
WAIT. IS THIS THE SPELL THAT PUGSLEY TRIED TO USE?

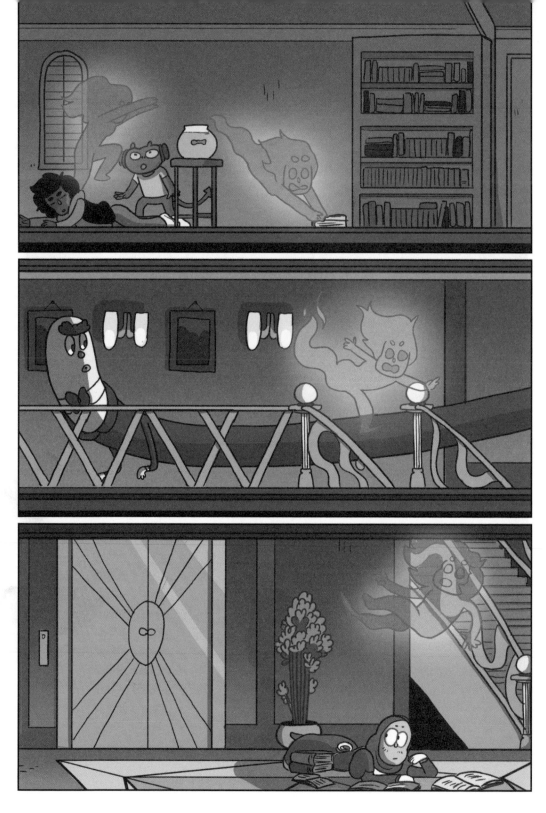

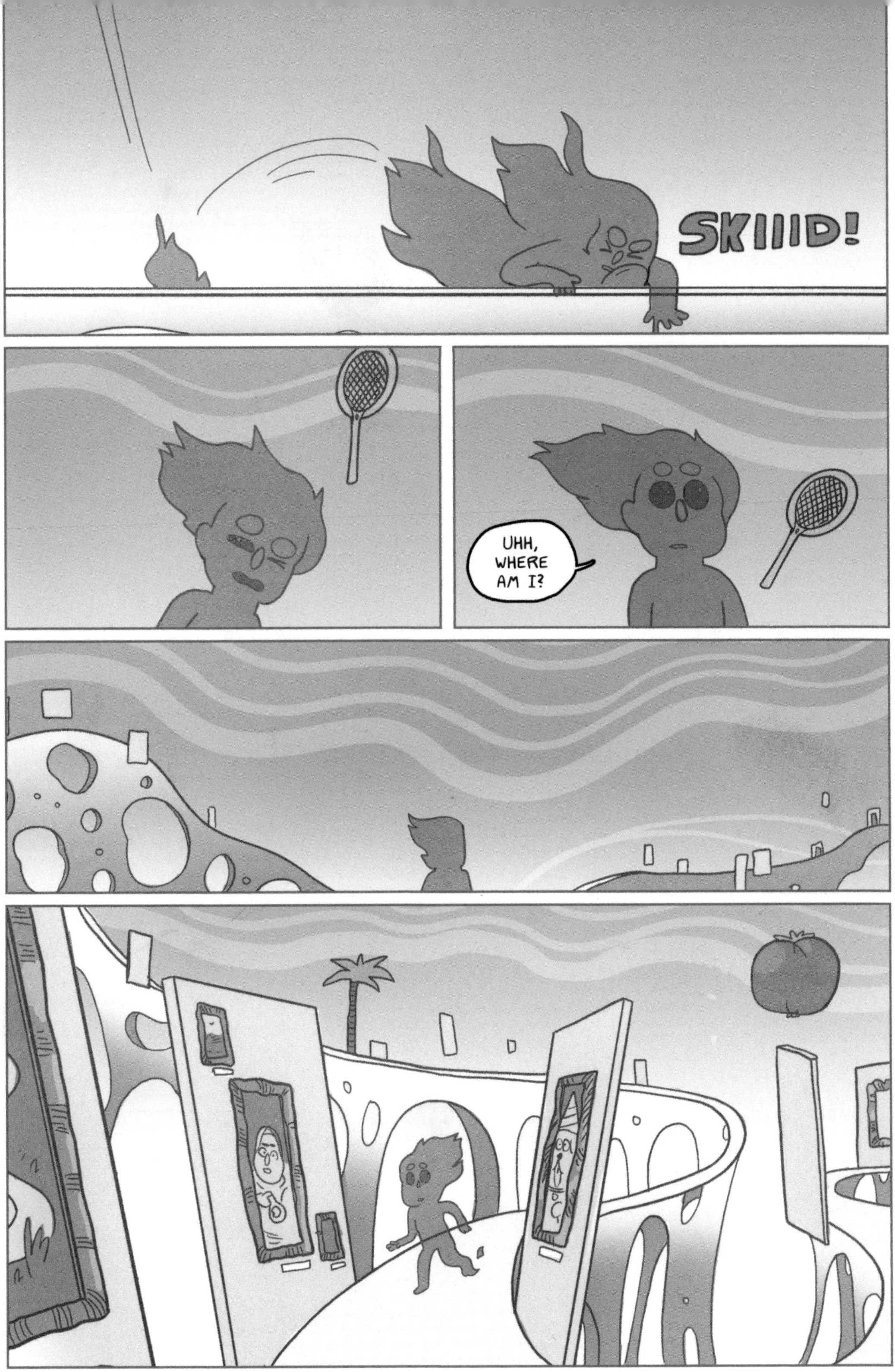
SKIIID!
UHH, WHERE AM I?

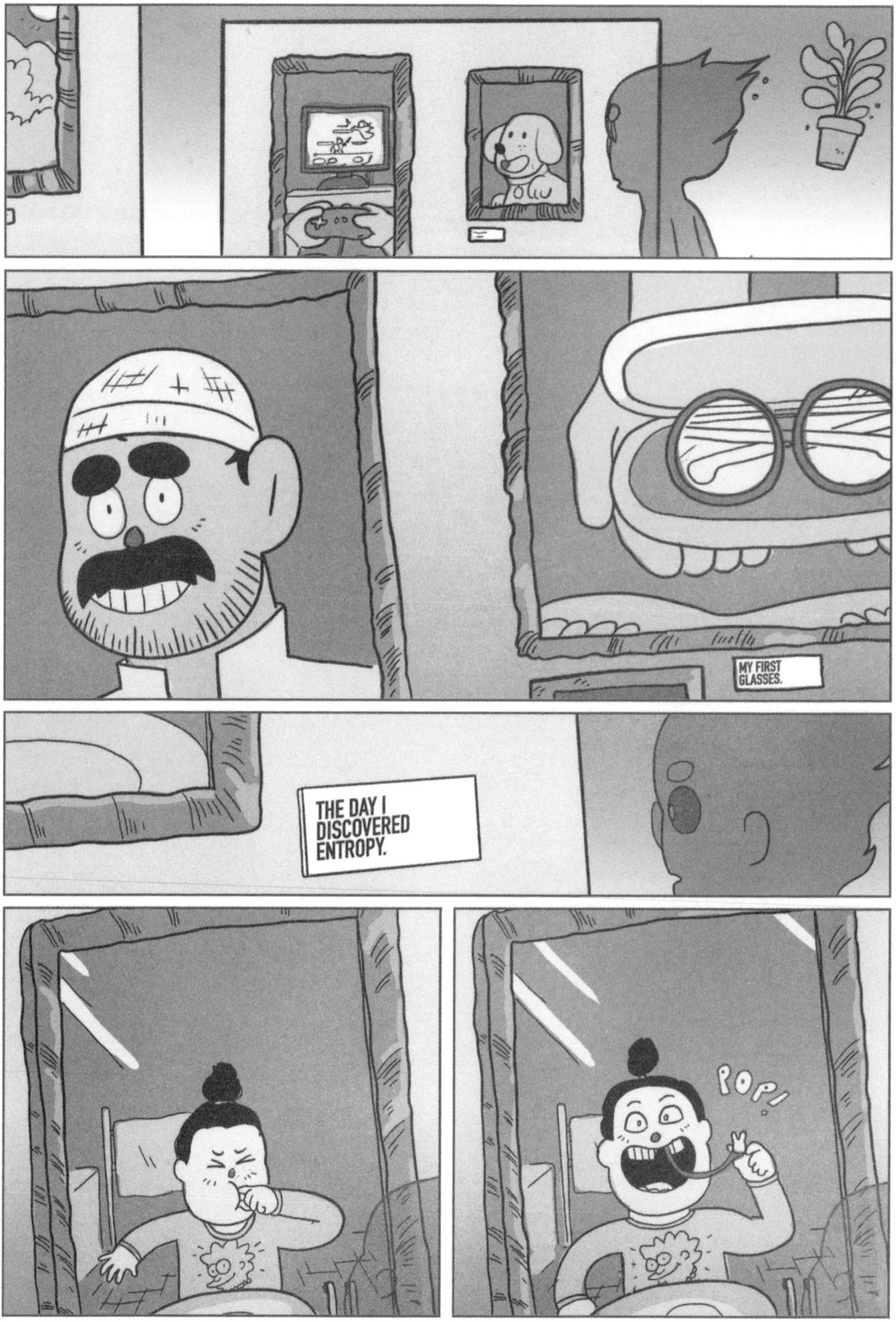
MY FIRST GLASSES.
THE DAY I DISCOVERED ENTROPY.
POP!

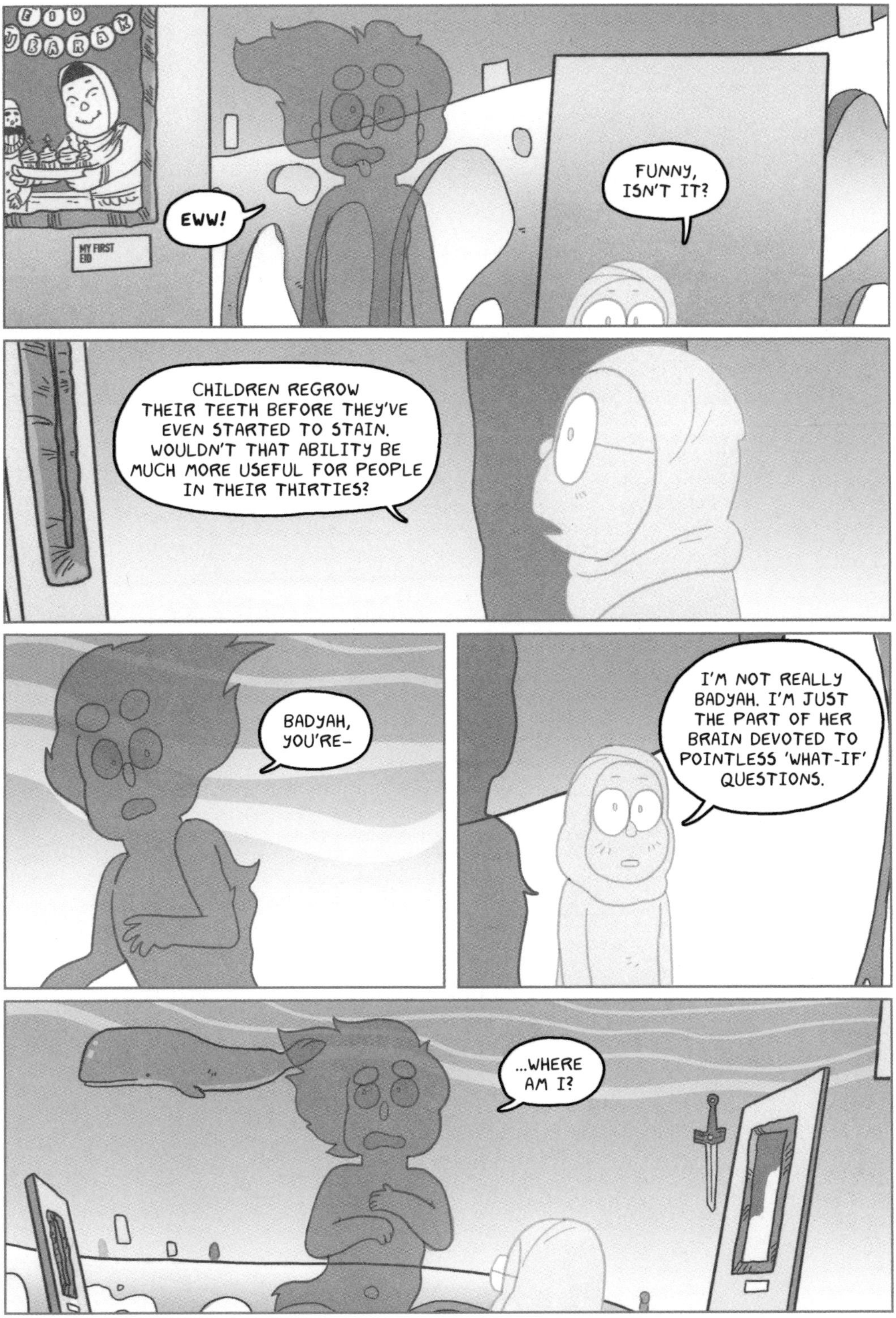
EID MUBARAK
MY FIRST EID
EWW!
FUNNY, ISN'T IT?
CHILDREN REGROW THEIR TEETH BEFORE THEY'VE EVEN STARTED TO STAIN. WOULDN'T THAT ABILITY BE MUCH MORE USEFUL FOR PEOPLE IN THEIR THIRTIES?
BADYAH, YOU'RE-
I'M NOT REALLY BADYAH. I'M JUST THE PART OF HER BRAIN DEVOTED TO POINTLESS 'WHAT-IF' QUESTIONS.
...WHERE AM I?

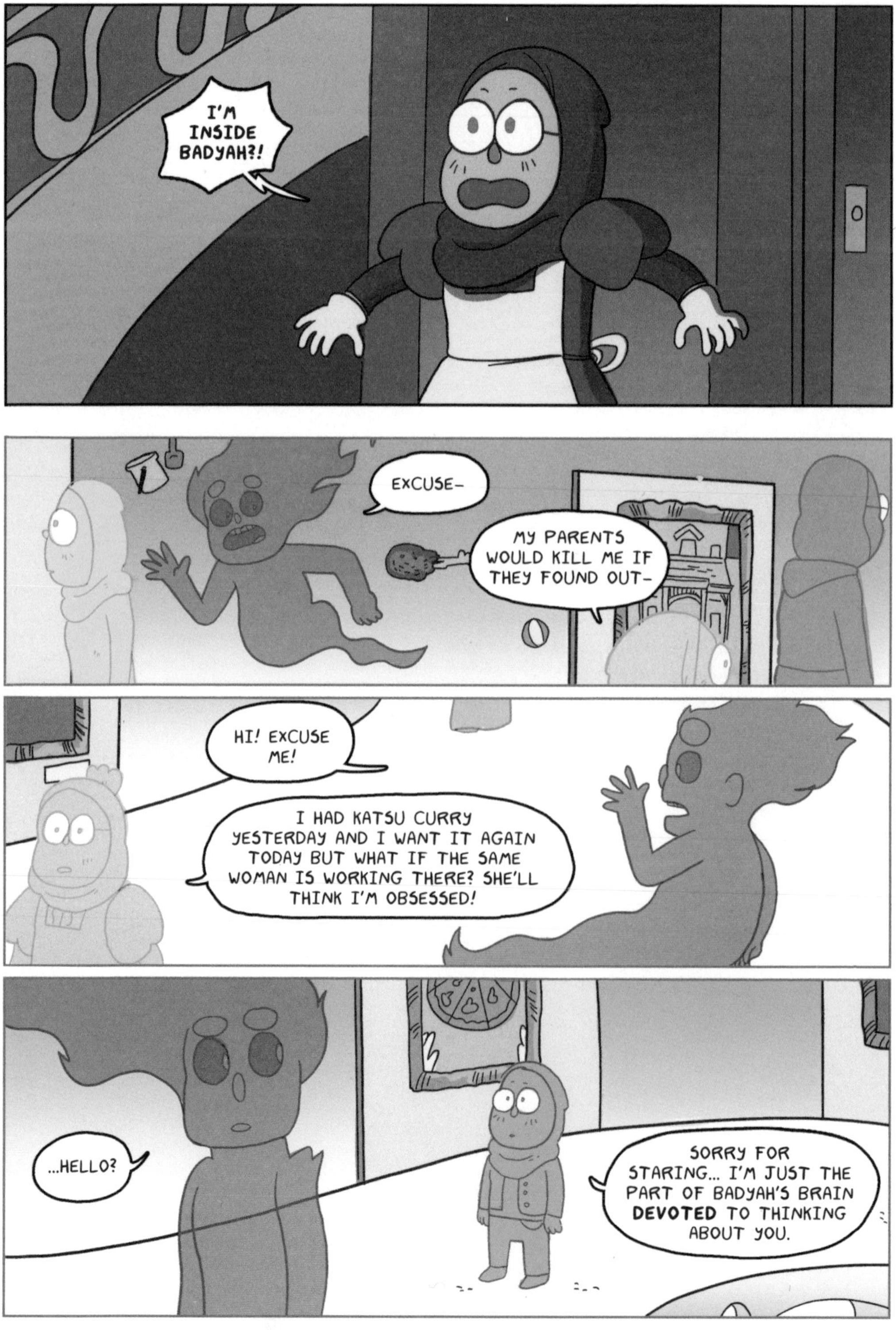

I'M INSIDE BADYAH?!
EXCUSE-
MY PARENTS WOULD KILL ME IF THEY FOUND OUT-
HI! EXCUSE ME!
I HAD KATSU CURRY YESTERDAY AND I WANT IT AGAIN TODAY BUT WHAT IF THE SAME WOMAN IS WORKING THERE? SHE'LL THINK I'M OBSESSED!
...HELLO?
SORRY FOR STARING... I'M JUST THE PART OF BADYAH'S BRAIN **DEVOTED** TO THINKING ABOUT YOU.

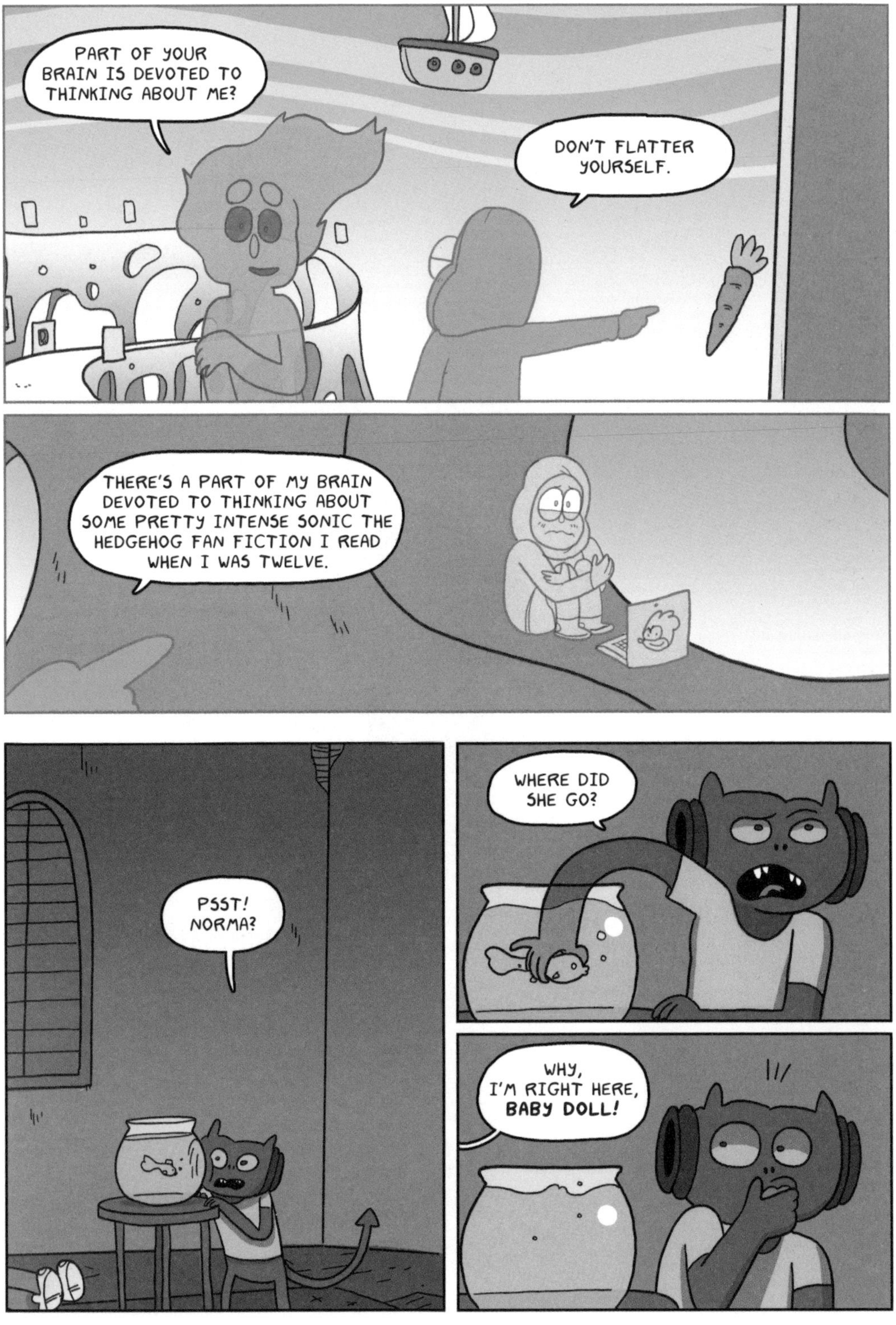
PART OF YOUR BRAIN IS DEVOTED TO THINKING ABOUT ME?
DON'T FLATTER YOURSELF.
THERE'S A PART OF MY BRAIN DEVOTED TO THINKING ABOUT SOME PRETTY INTENSE SONIC THE HEDGEHOG FAN FICTION I READ WHEN I WAS TWELVE.
PSST! NORMA?
WHERE DID SHE GO?
WHY, I'M RIGHT HERE, **BABY DOLL!**

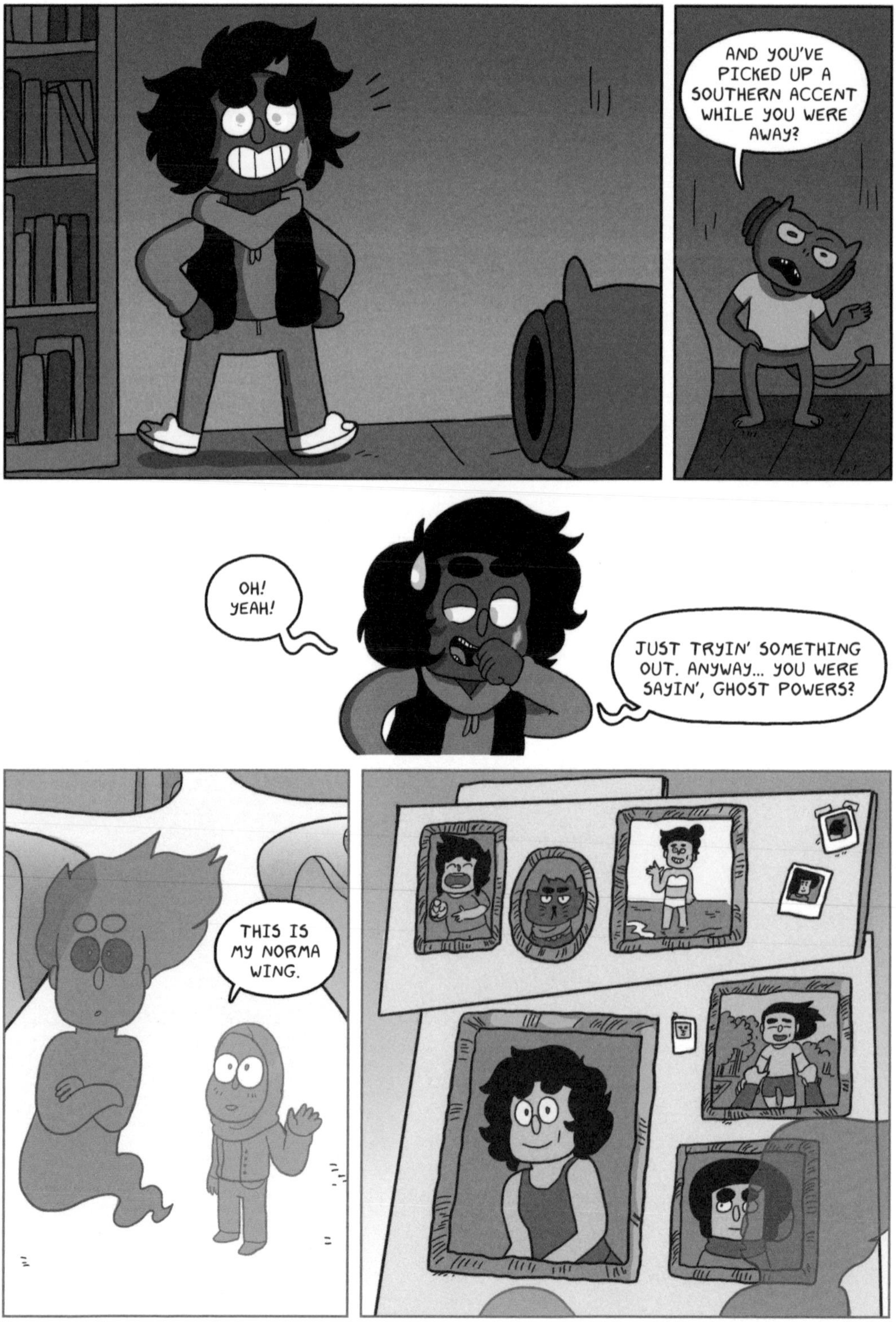
AND YOU'VE PICKED UP A SOUTHERN ACCENT WHILE YOU WERE AWAY?
OH! YEAH!
JUST TRYIN' SOMETHING OUT. ANYWAY... YOU WERE SAYIN', GHOST POWERS?
THIS IS MY NORMA WING.

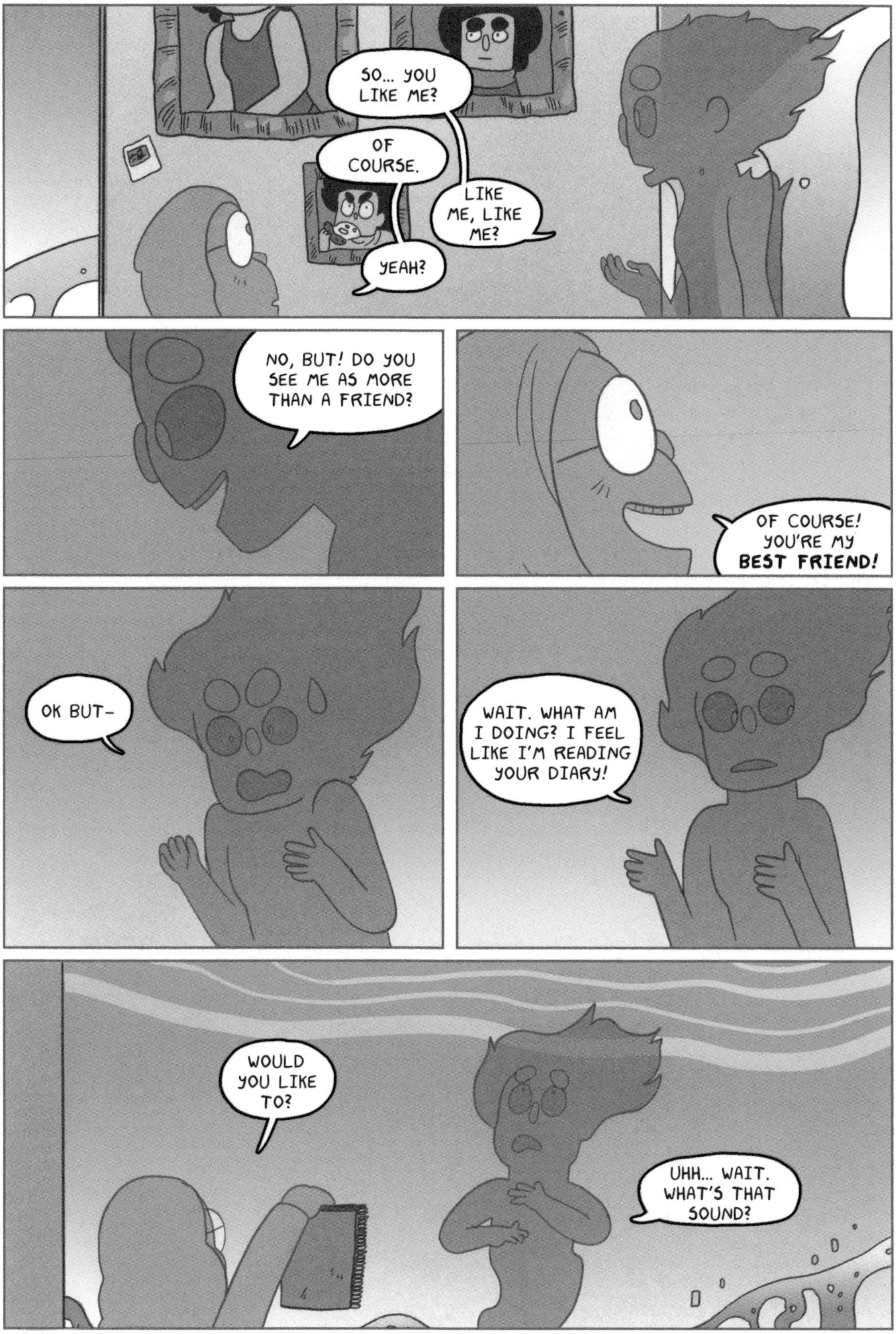
SO... YOU LIKE ME?
OF COURSE.
LIKE ME, LIKE ME?
YEAH?
NO, BUT! DO YOU SEE ME AS MORE THAN A FRIEND?
OF COURSE! YOU'RE MY **BEST FRIEND!**
OK BUT-
WAIT. WHAT AM I DOING? I FEEL LIKE I'M READING YOUR DIARY!
WOULD YOU LIKE TO?
UHH... WAIT. WHAT'S THAT SOUND?

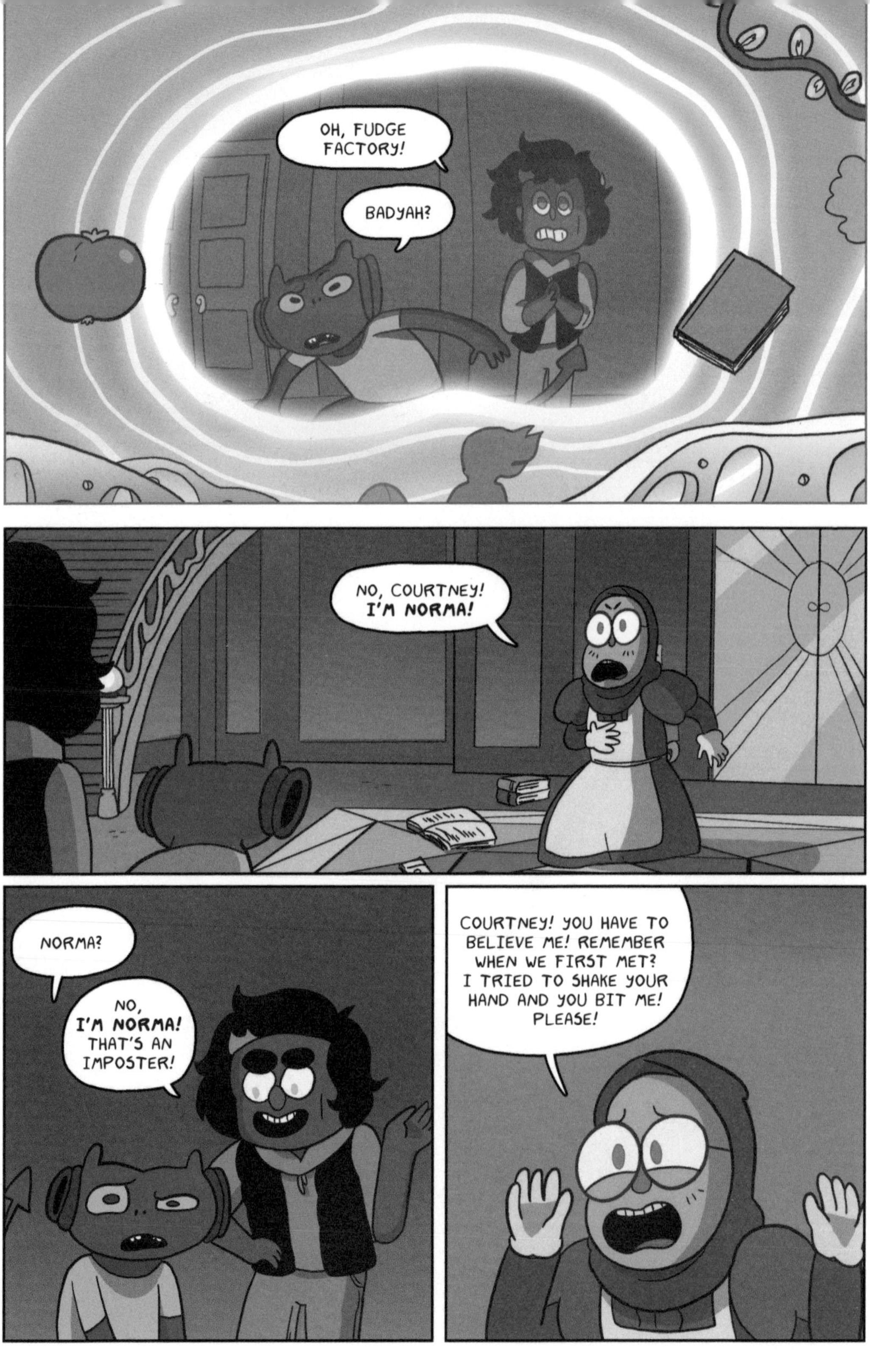

OH, FUDGE FACTORY!
BADYAH?
NO, COURTNEY! **I'M NORMA!**
NORMA?
NO, **I'M NORMA!** THAT'S AN IMPOSTER!
COURTNEY! YOU HAVE TO BELIEVE ME! REMEMBER WHEN WE FIRST MET? I TRIED TO SHAKE YOUR HAND AND YOU BIT ME! PLEASE!

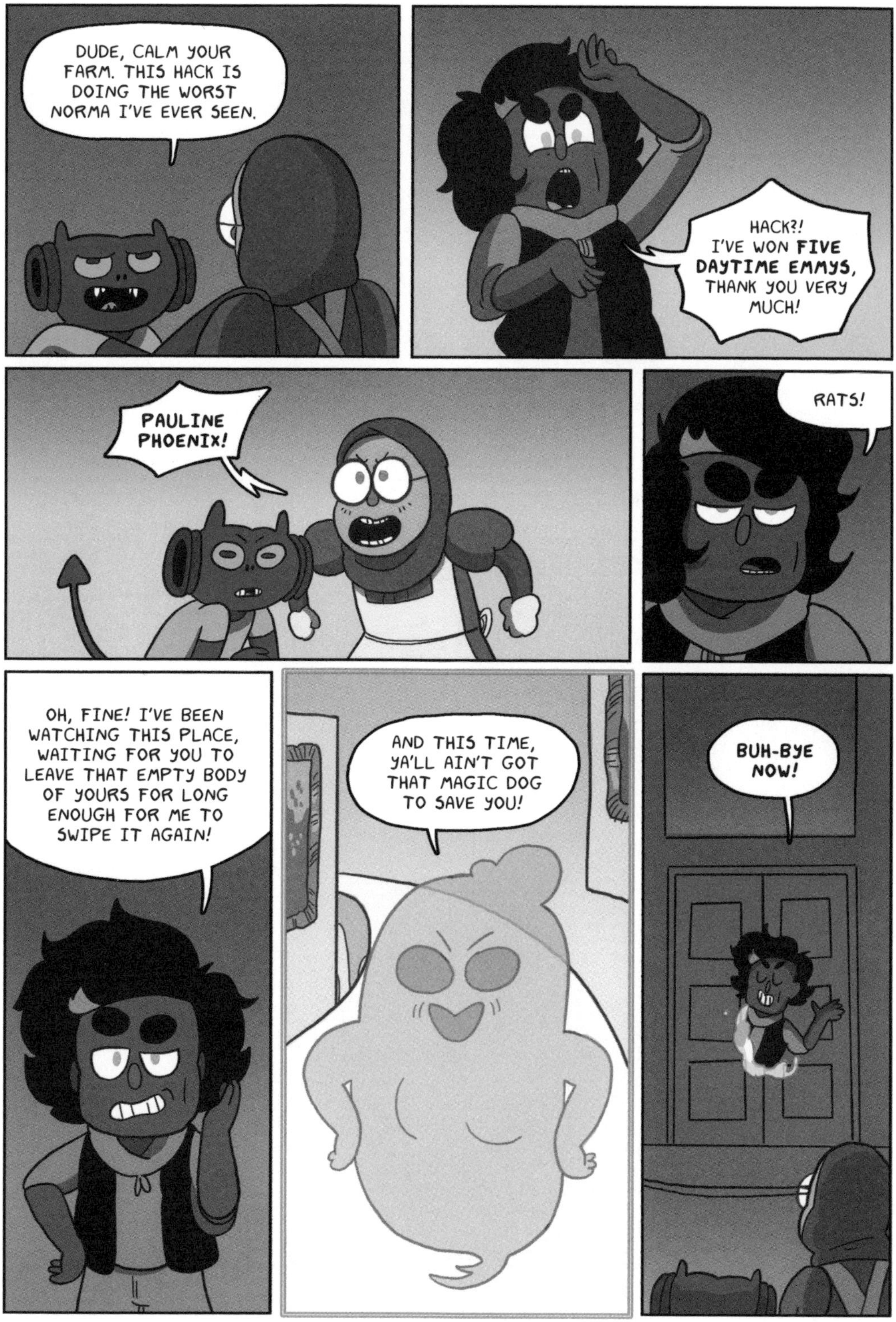
DUDE, CALM YOUR FARM. THIS HACK IS DOING THE WORST NORMA I'VE EVER SEEN.
HACK?! I'VE WON FIVE DAYTIME EMMYS, THANK YOU VERY MUCH!
PAULINE PHOENIX!
RATS!
OH, FINE! I'VE BEEN WATCHING THIS PLACE, WAITING FOR YOU TO LEAVE THAT EMPTY BODY OF YOURS FOR LONG ENOUGH FOR ME TO SWIPE IT AGAIN!
AND THIS TIME, YA'LL AIN'T GOT THAT MAGIC DOG TO SAVE YOU!
BUH-BYE NOW!

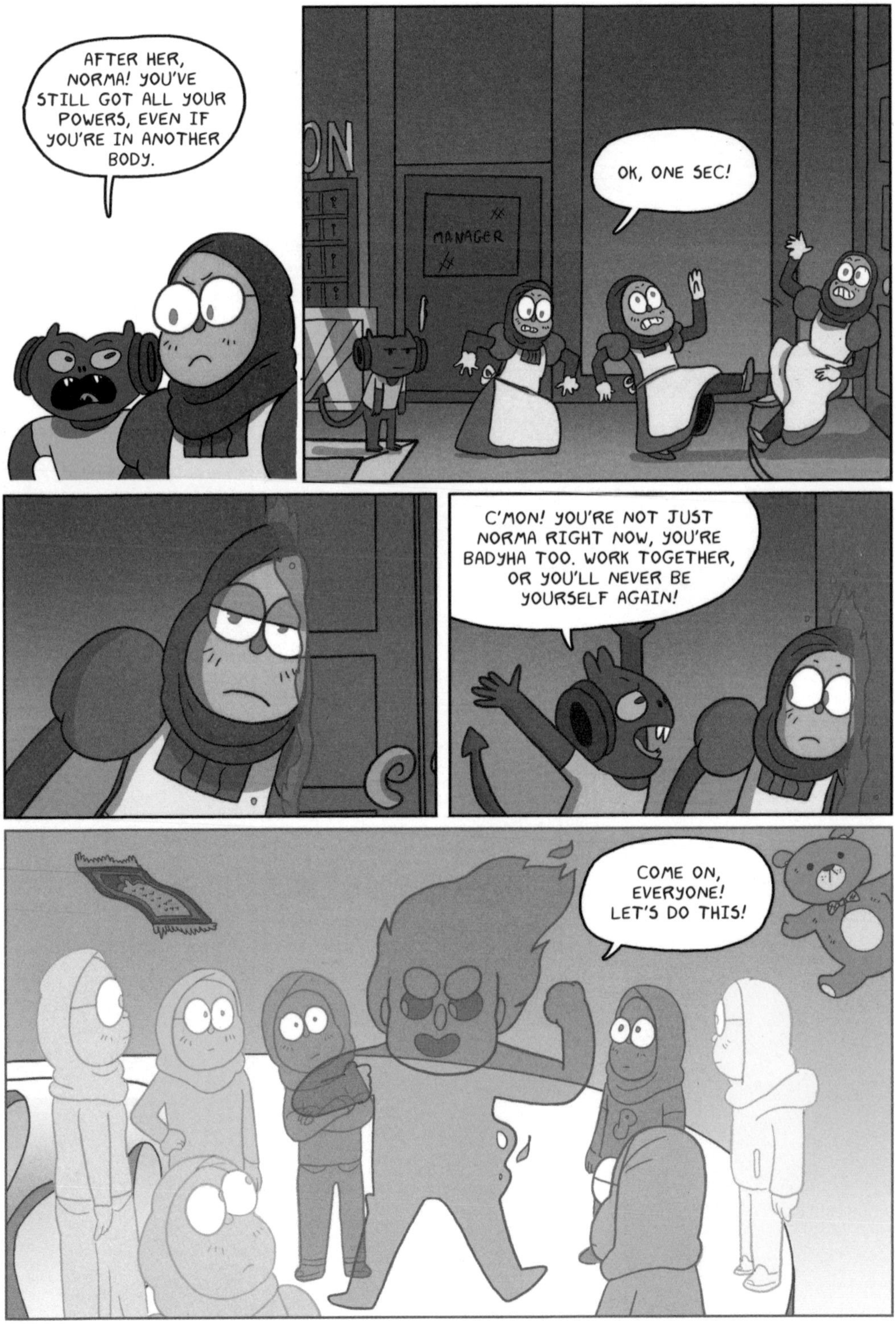
AFTER HER, NORMA! YOU'VE STILL GOT ALL YOUR POWERS, EVEN IF YOU'RE IN ANOTHER BODY.
OK, ONE SEC!
MANAGER
C'MON! YOU'RE NOT JUST NORMA RIGHT NOW, YOU'RE BADYHA TOO. WORK TOGETHER, OR YOU'LL NEVER BE YOURSELF AGAIN!
COME ON, EVERYONE! LET'S DO THIS!

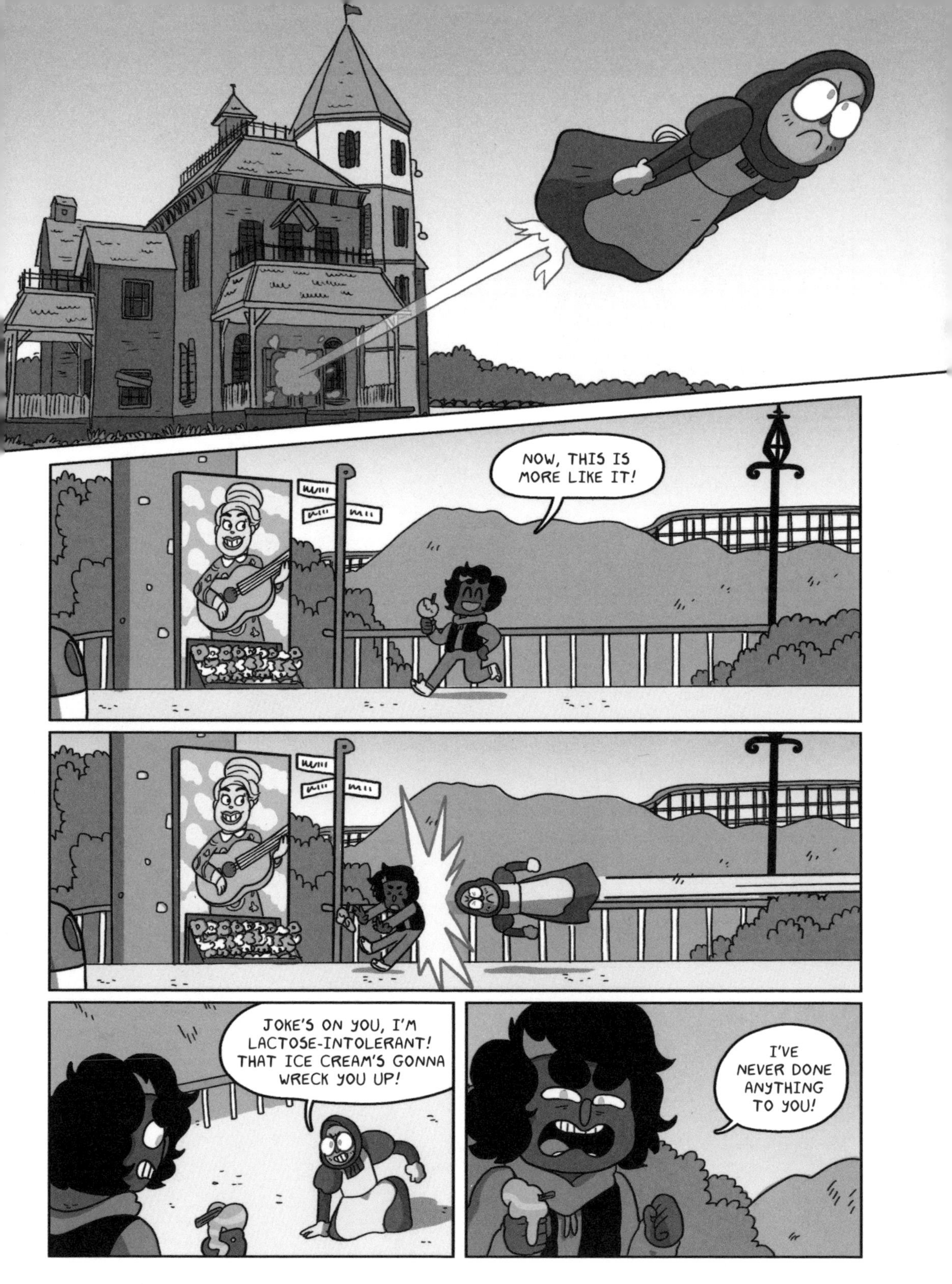

NOW, THIS IS MORE LIKE IT!
JOKE'S ON YOU, I'M LACTOSE-INTOLERANT! THAT ICE CREAM'S GONNA WRECK YOU UP!
I'VE NEVER DONE ANYTHING TO YOU!

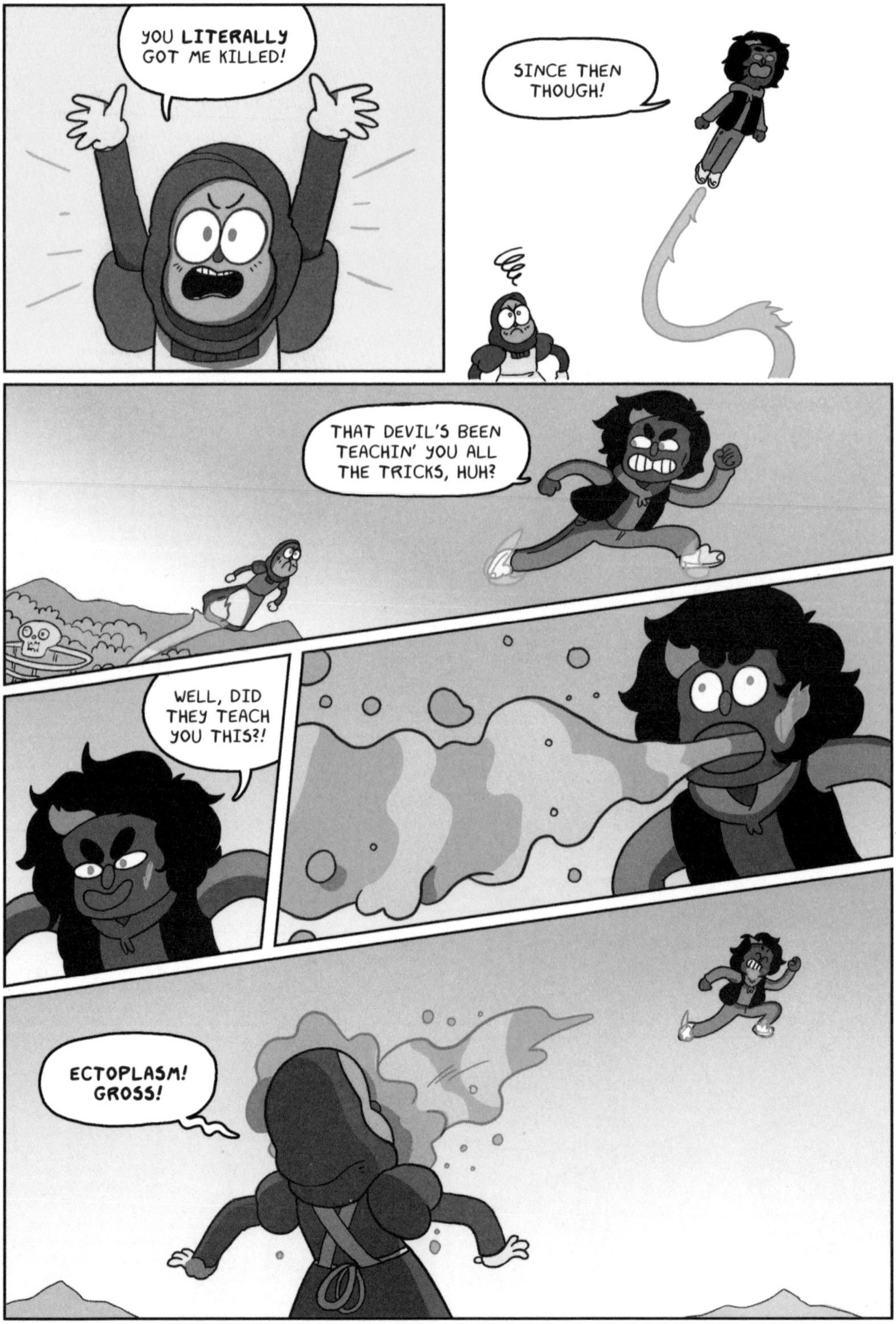
YOU LITERALLY GOT ME KILLED!
SINCE THEN THOUGH!
THAT DEVIL'S BEEN TEACHIN' YOU ALL THE TRICKS, HUH?
WELL, DID THEY TEACH YOU THIS?!
ECTOPLASM! GROSS!

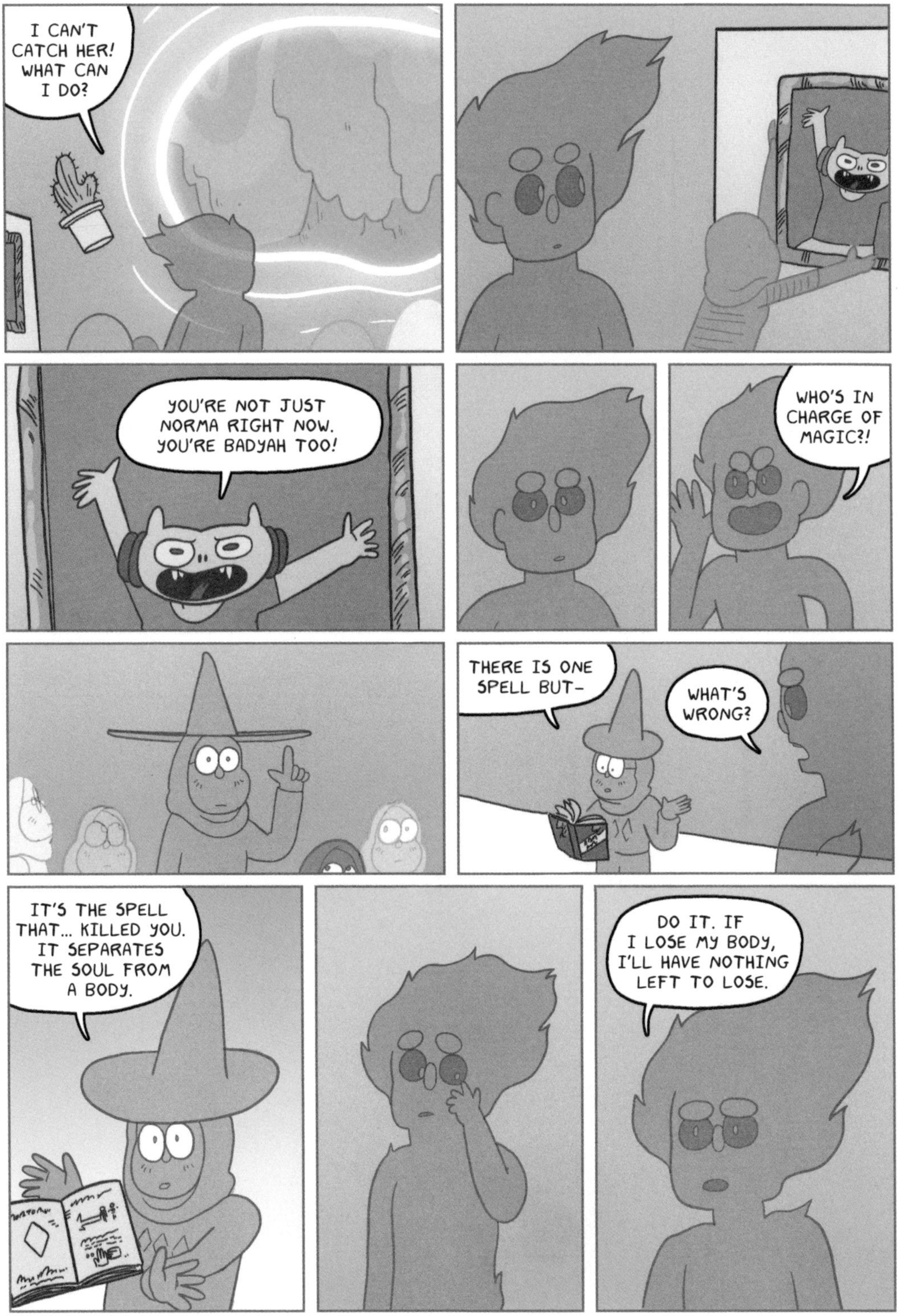
I CAN'T CATCH HER! WHAT CAN I DO?
YOU'RE NOT JUST NORMA RIGHT NOW. YOU'RE BADYAH TOO!
WHO'S IN CHARGE OF MAGIC?!
THERE IS ONE SPELL BUT-
WHAT'S WRONG?
IT'S THE SPELL THAT... KILLED YOU. IT SEPARATES THE SOUL FROM A BODY.
DO IT. IF I LOSE MY BODY, I'LL HAVE NOTHING LEFT TO LOSE.

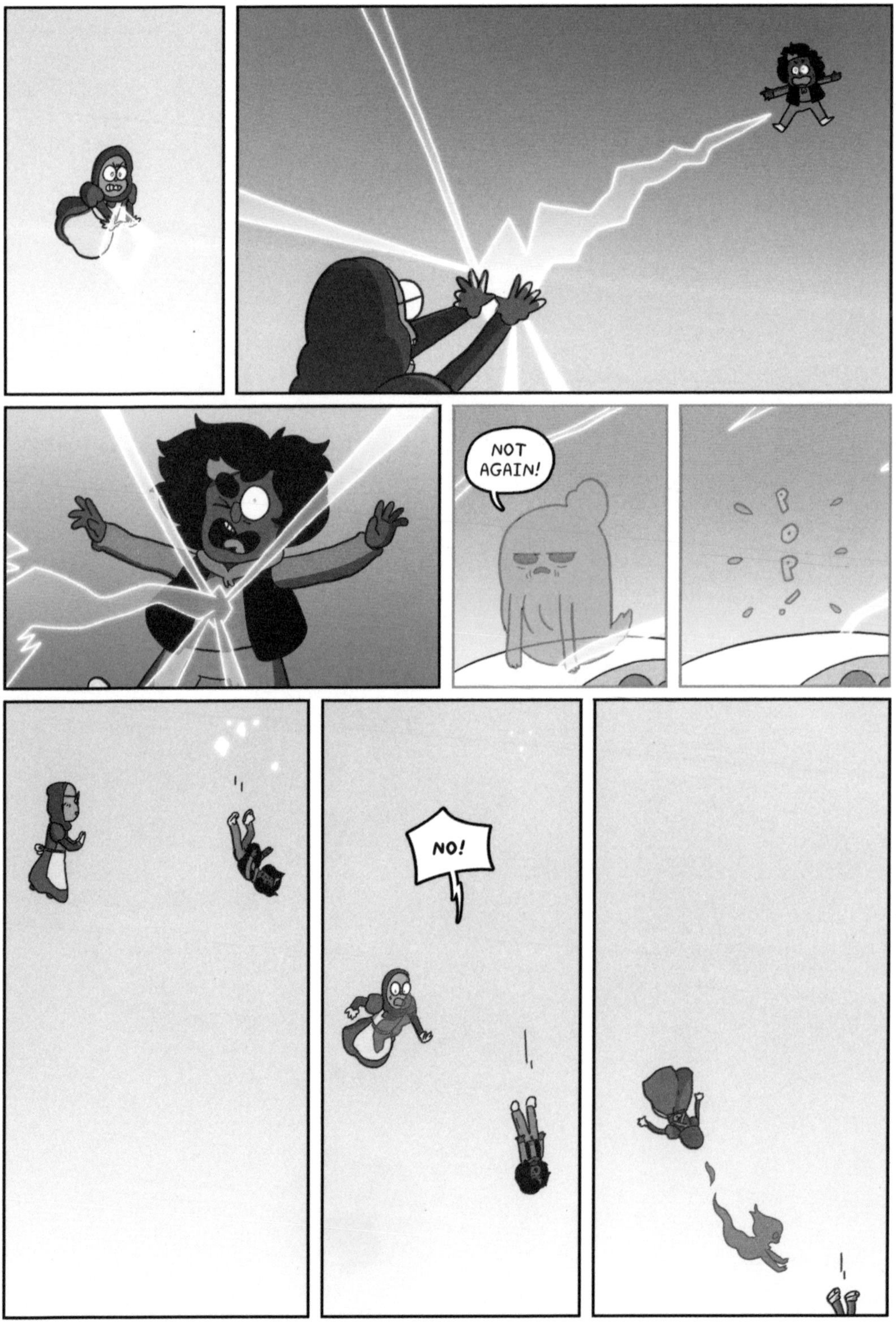
NOT AGAIN!
POP!
NO!

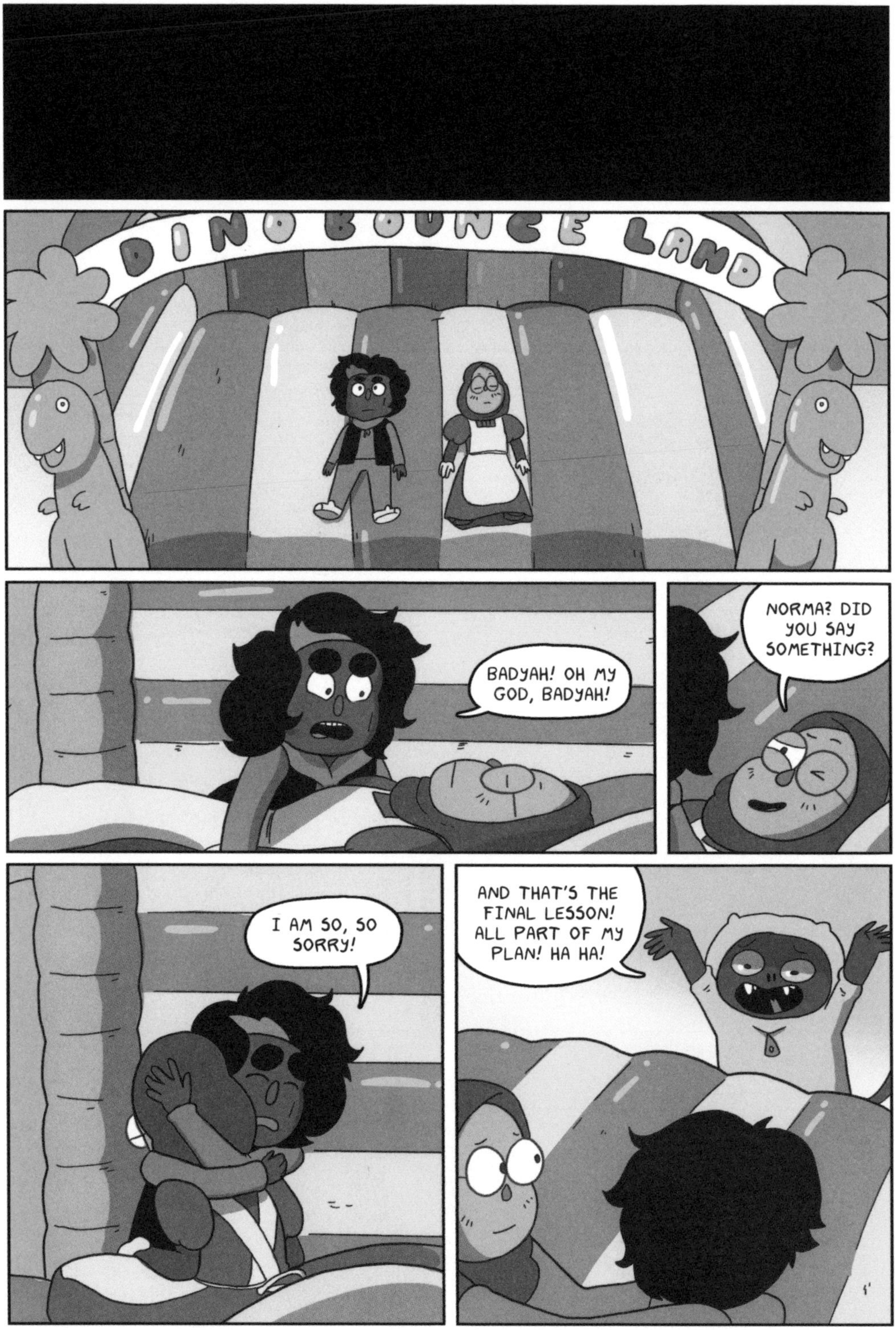
DINO BOUNCE LAND
BADYAH! OH MY GOD, BADYAH!
NORMA? DID YOU SAY SOMETHING?
I AM SO, SO SORRY!
AND THAT'S THE FINAL LESSON! ALL PART OF MY PLAN! HA HA!

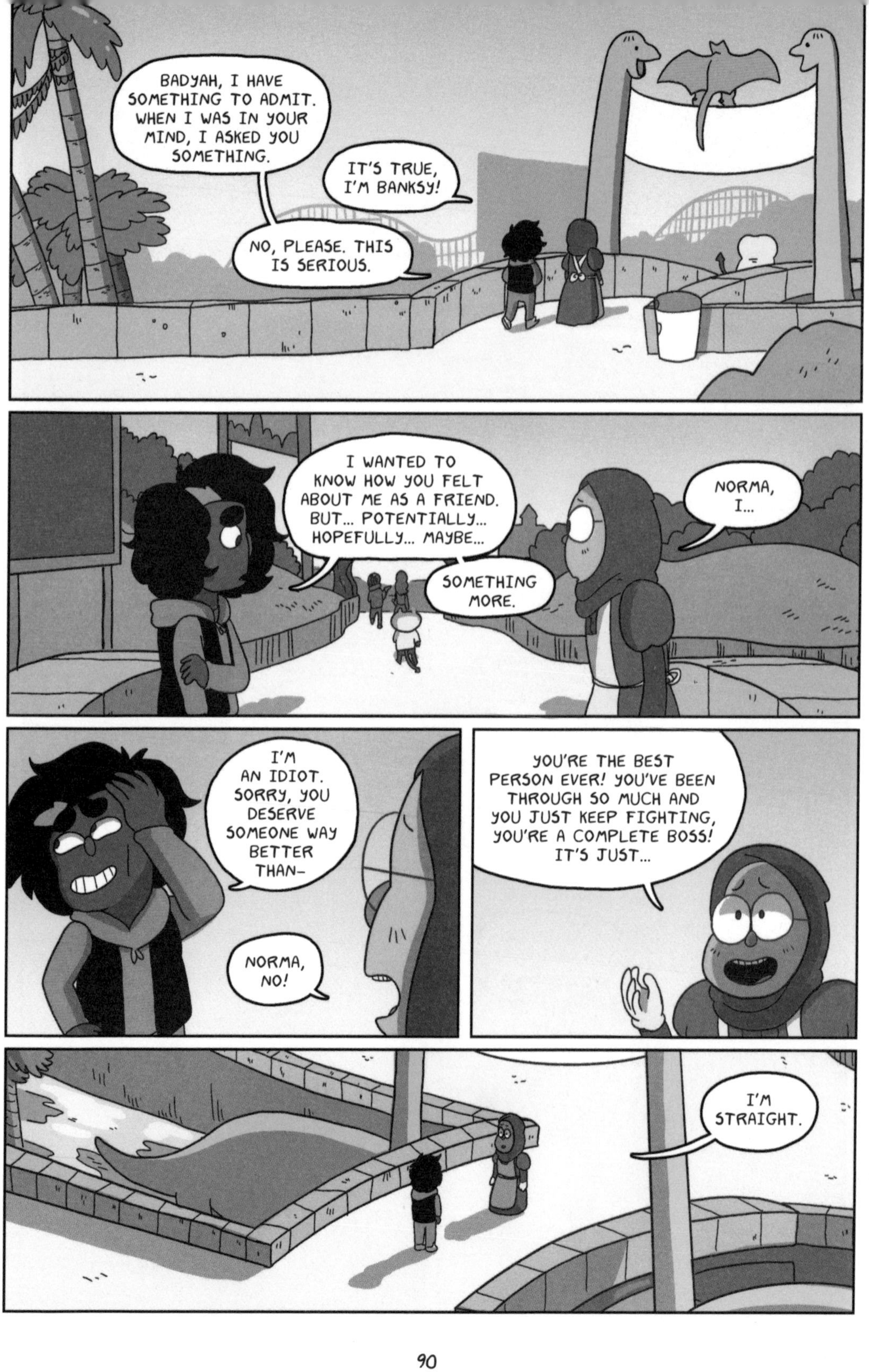
BADYAH, I HAVE SOMETHING TO ADMIT. WHEN I WAS IN YOUR MIND, I ASKED YOU SOMETHING.
IT'S TRUE, I'M BANKSY!
NO, PLEASE. THIS IS SERIOUS.
I WANTED TO KNOW HOW YOU FELT ABOUT ME AS A FRIEND. BUT... POTENTIALLY... HOPEFULLY... MAYBE...
SOMETHING MORE.
NORMA, I...
I'M AN IDIOT. SORRY, YOU DESERVE SOMEONE WAY BETTER THAN-
NORMA, NO!
YOU'RE THE BEST PERSON EVER! YOU'VE BEEN THROUGH SO MUCH AND YOU JUST KEEP FIGHTING, YOU'RE A COMPLETE BOSS! IT'S JUST...
I'M STRAIGHT.

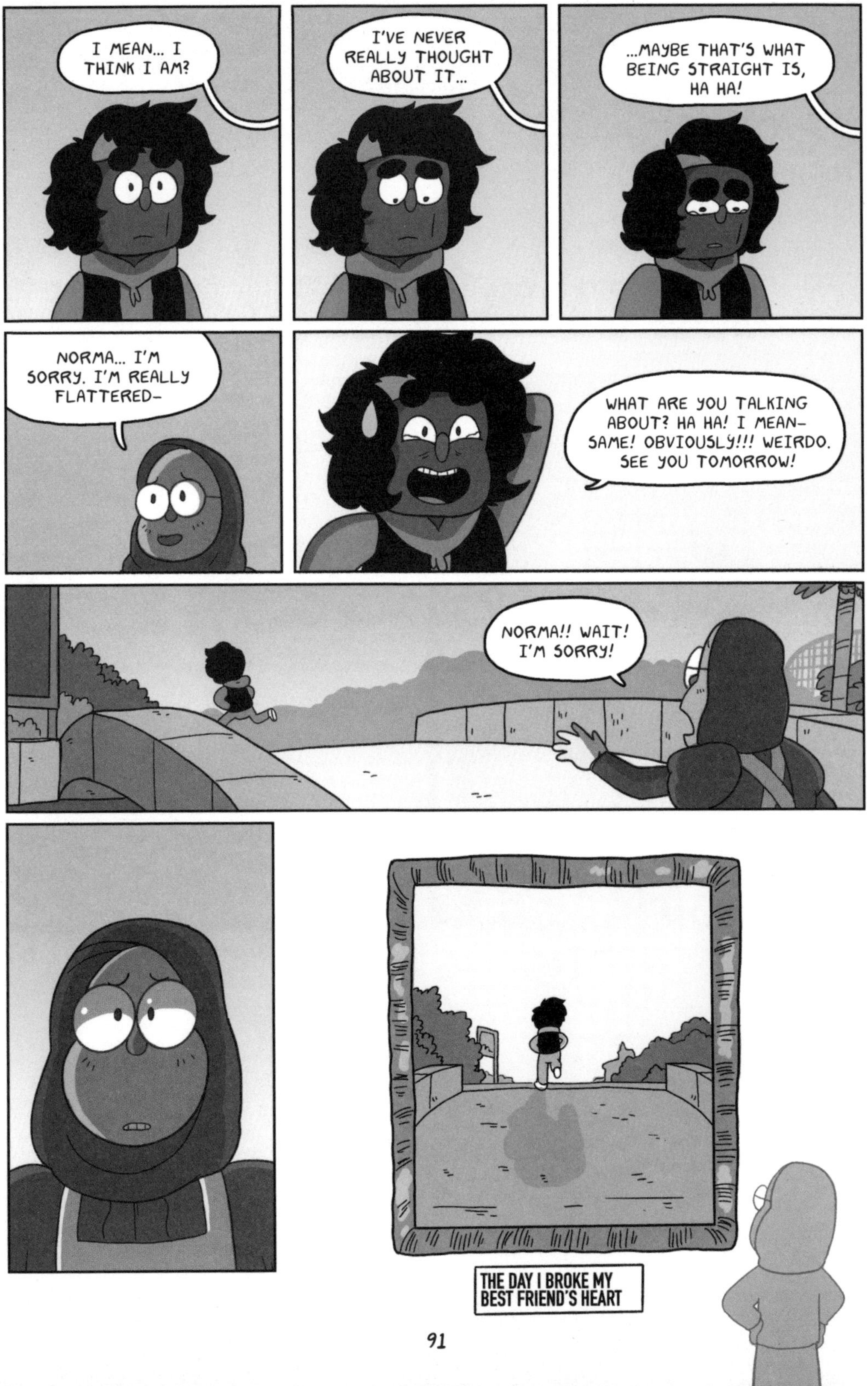
I MEAN... I THINK I AM?
I'VE NEVER REALLY THOUGHT ABOUT IT...
...MAYBE THAT'S WHAT BEING STRAIGHT IS, HA HA!
NORMA... I'M SORRY. I'M REALLY FLATTERED-
WHAT ARE YOU TALKING ABOUT? HA HA! I MEAN-SAME! OBVIOUSLY!!! WEIRDO. SEE YOU TOMORROW!
NORMA!! WAIT! I'M SORRY!
THE DAY I BROKE MY BEST FRIEND'S HEART

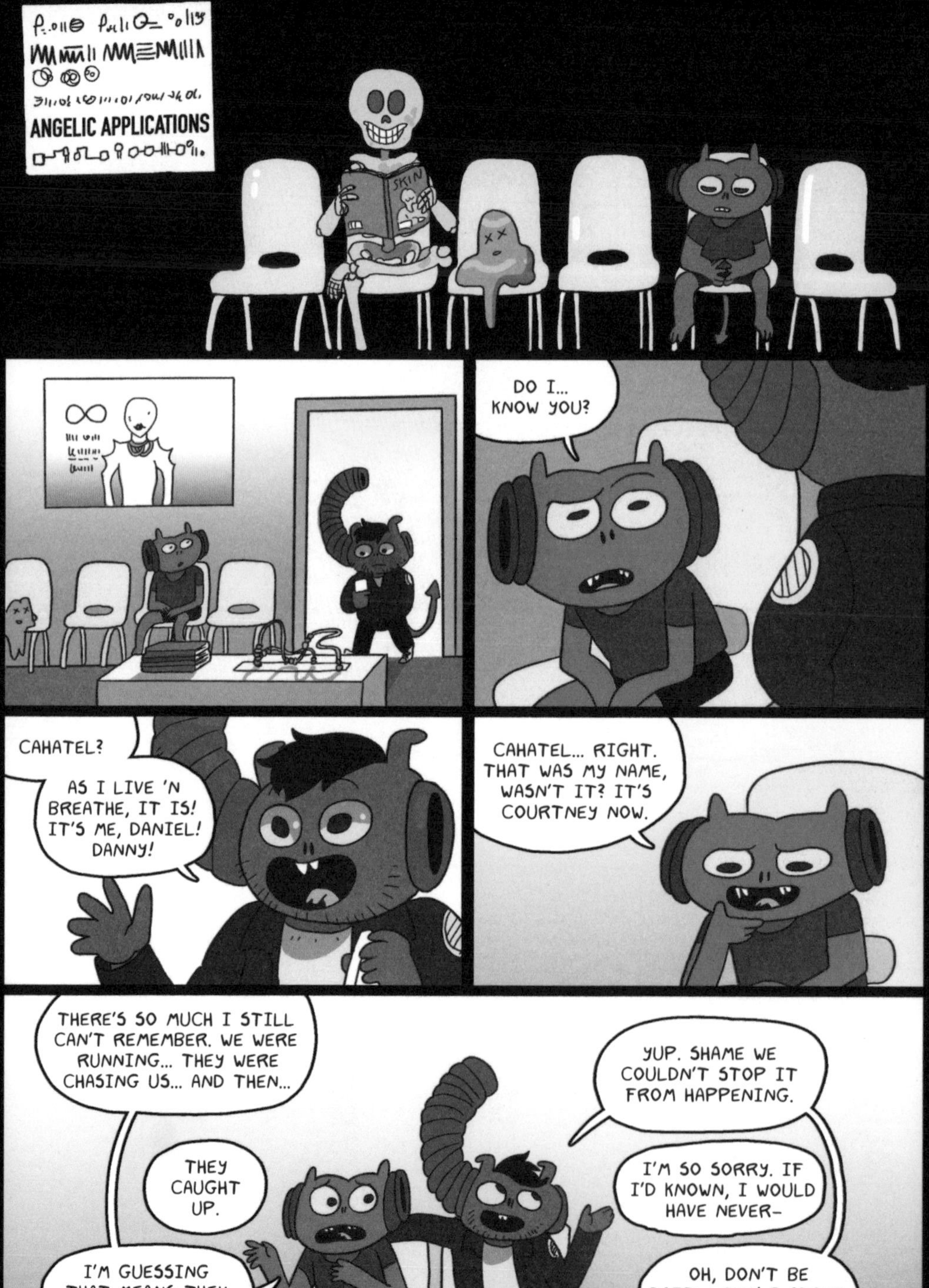
ANGELIC APPLICATIONS
SKIN
DO I... KNOW YOU?
CAHATEL?
AS I LIVE 'N BREATHE, IT IS! IT'S ME, DANIEL! DANNY!
CAHATEL... RIGHT. THAT WAS MY NAME, WASN'T IT? IT'S COURTNEY NOW.
THERE'S SO MUCH I STILL CAN'T REMEMBER. WE WERE RUNNING... THEY WERE CHASING US... AND THEN...
THEY CAUGHT UP.
I'M GUESSING THAT MEANS THEY BROKE YOU TOO.
YUP. SHAME WE COULDN'T STOP IT FROM HAPPENING.
I'M SO SORRY. IF I'D KNOWN, I WOULD HAVE NEVER–
OH, DON'T BE DAFT, LOVE! I STAND BY MY CHOICE. **OUR CHOICE**.

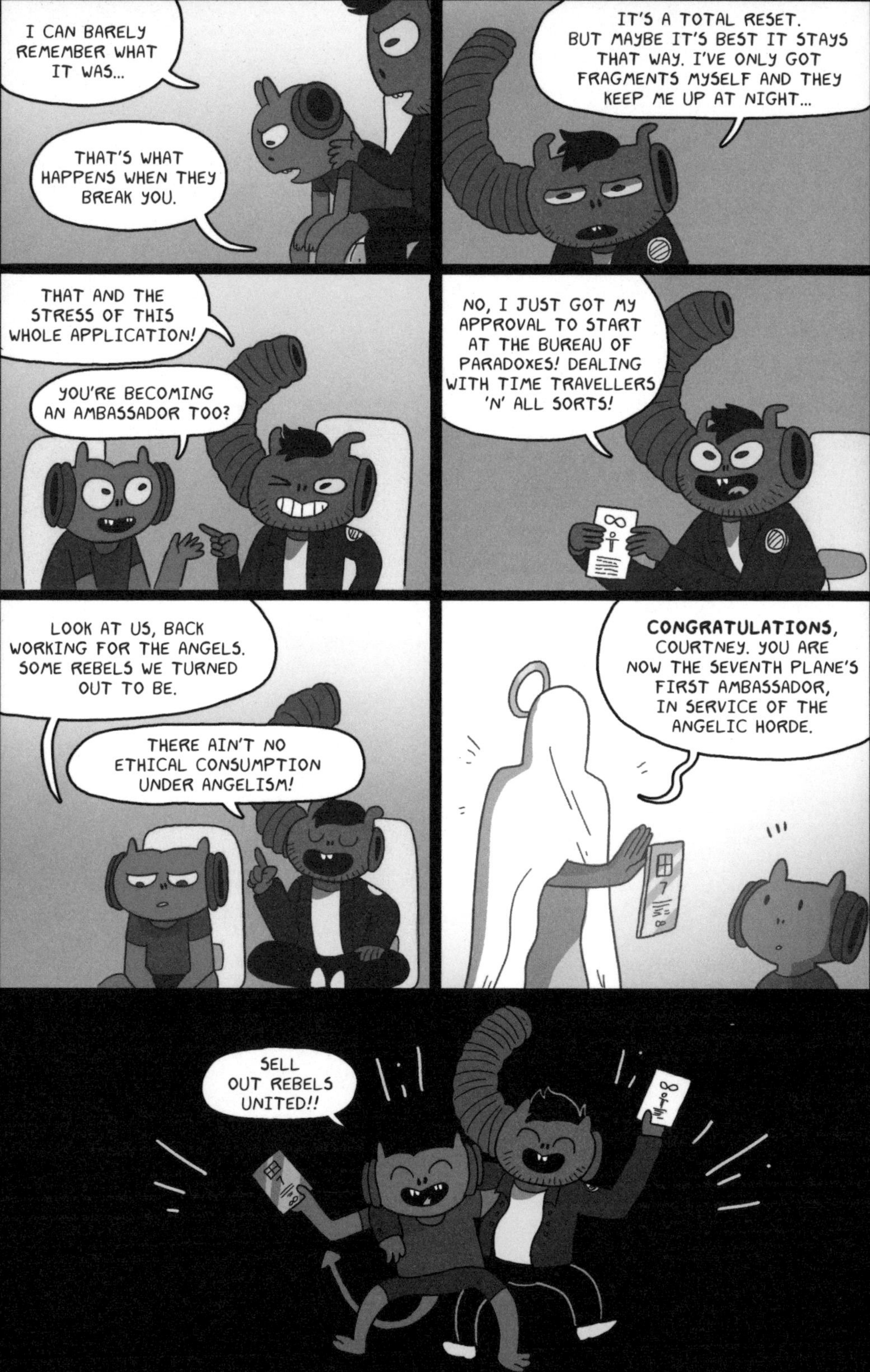
I CAN BARELY REMEMBER WHAT IT WAS...
THAT'S WHAT HAPPENS WHEN THEY BREAK YOU.
IT'S A TOTAL RESET. BUT MAYBE IT'S BEST IT STAYS THAT WAY. I'VE ONLY GOT FRAGMENTS MYSELF AND THEY KEEP ME UP AT NIGHT...
THAT AND THE STRESS OF THIS WHOLE APPLICATION!
YOU'RE BECOMING AN AMBASSADOR TOO?
NO, I JUST GOT MY APPROVAL TO START AT THE BUREAU OF PARADOXES! DEALING WITH TIME TRAVELLERS 'N' ALL SORTS!
LOOK AT US, BACK WORKING FOR THE ANGELS. SOME REBELS WE TURNED OUT TO BE.
THERE AIN'T NO ETHICAL CONSUMPTION UNDER ANGELISM!
CONGRATULATIONS, COURTNEY. YOU ARE NOW THE SEVENTH PLANE'S FIRST AMBASSADOR, IN SERVICE OF THE ANGELIC HORDE.
SELL OUT REBELS UNITED!!

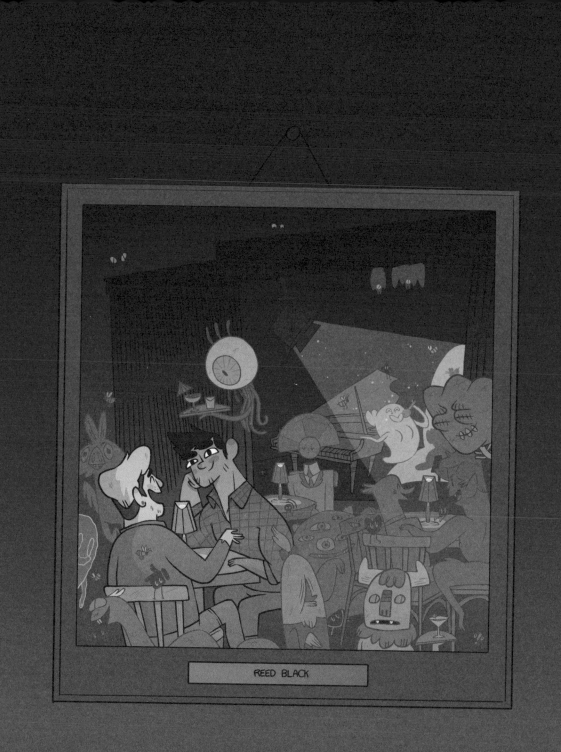

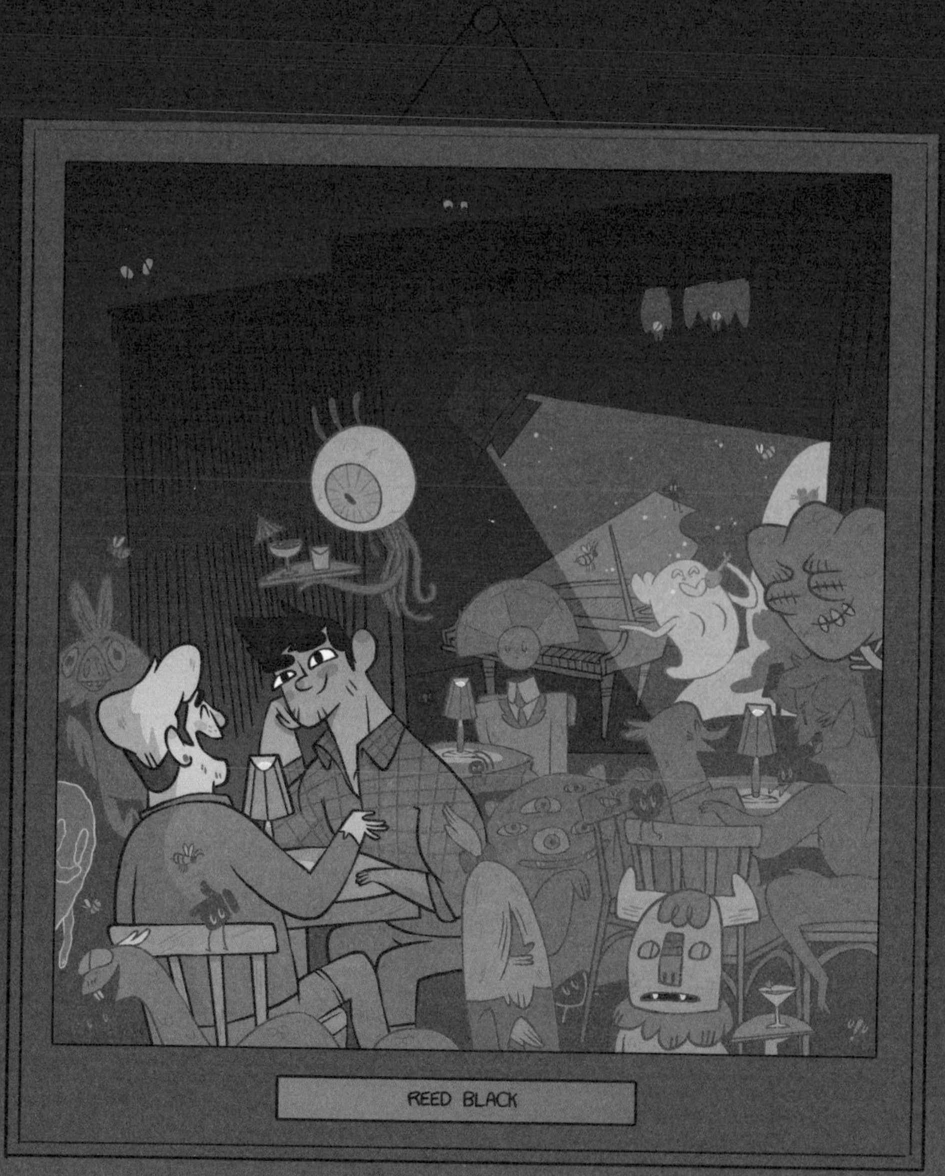
REED BLACK

CHAPTER 4
THE ESCAPE

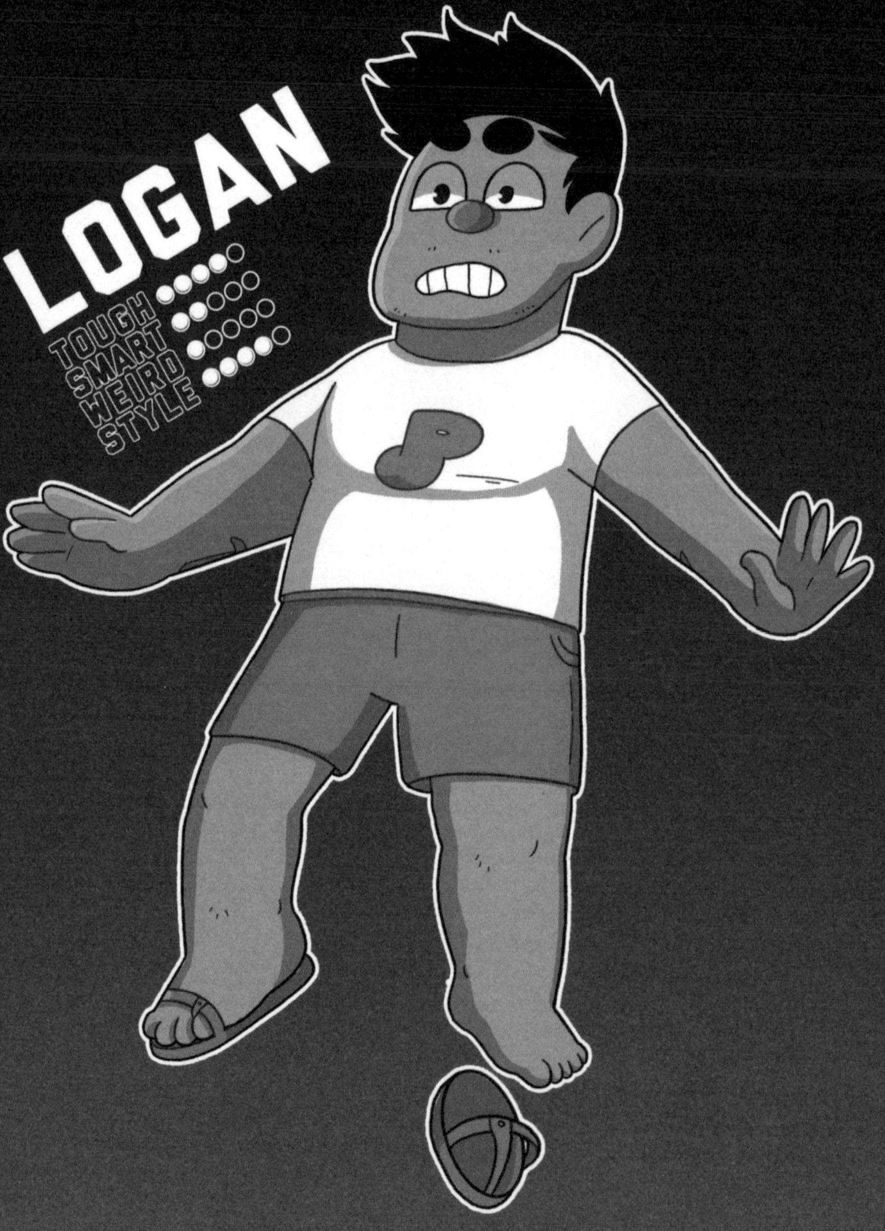
LOGAN
TOUGH
SMART
WEIRD
STYLE

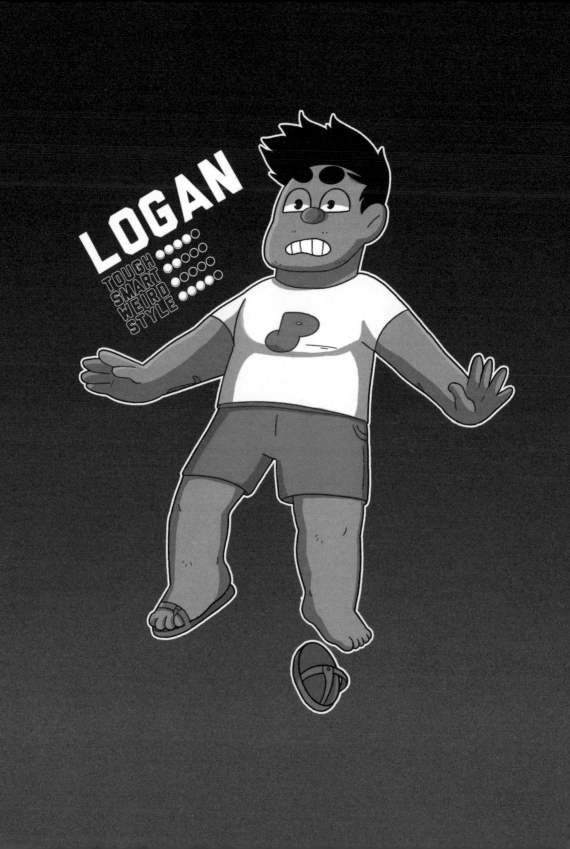

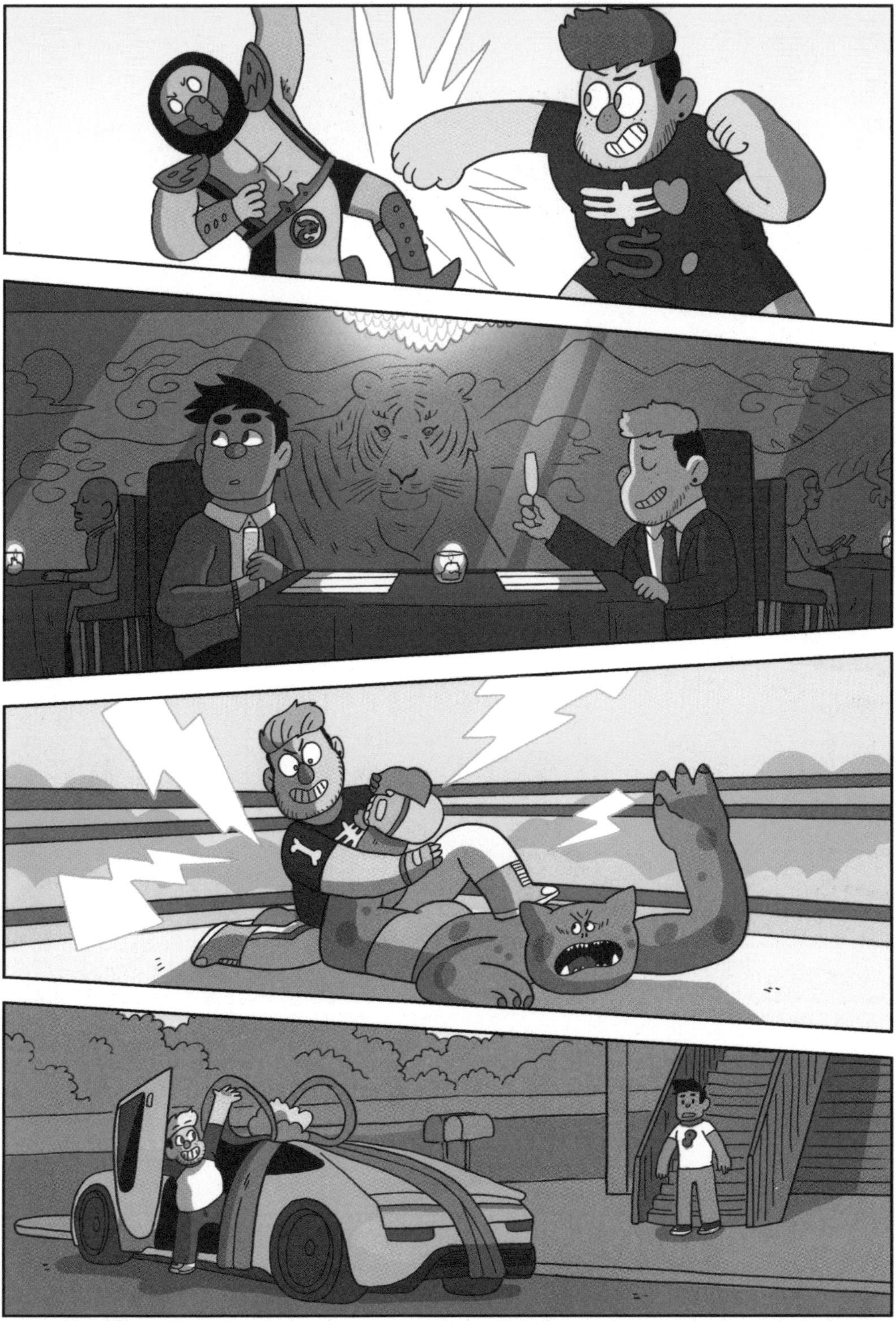

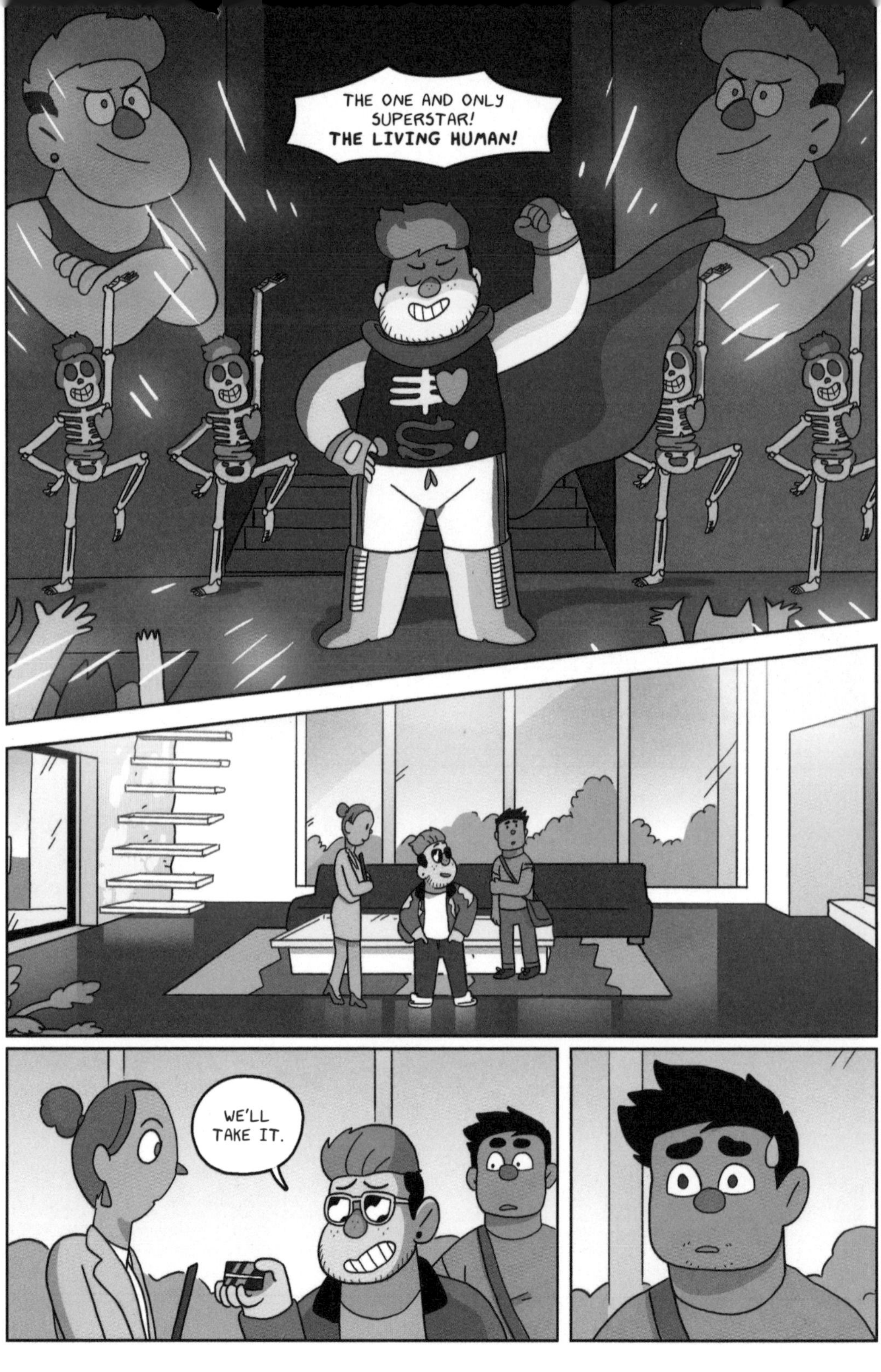
THE ONE AND ONLY
SUPERSTAR!
THE LIVING HUMAN!
WE'LL
TAKE IT.

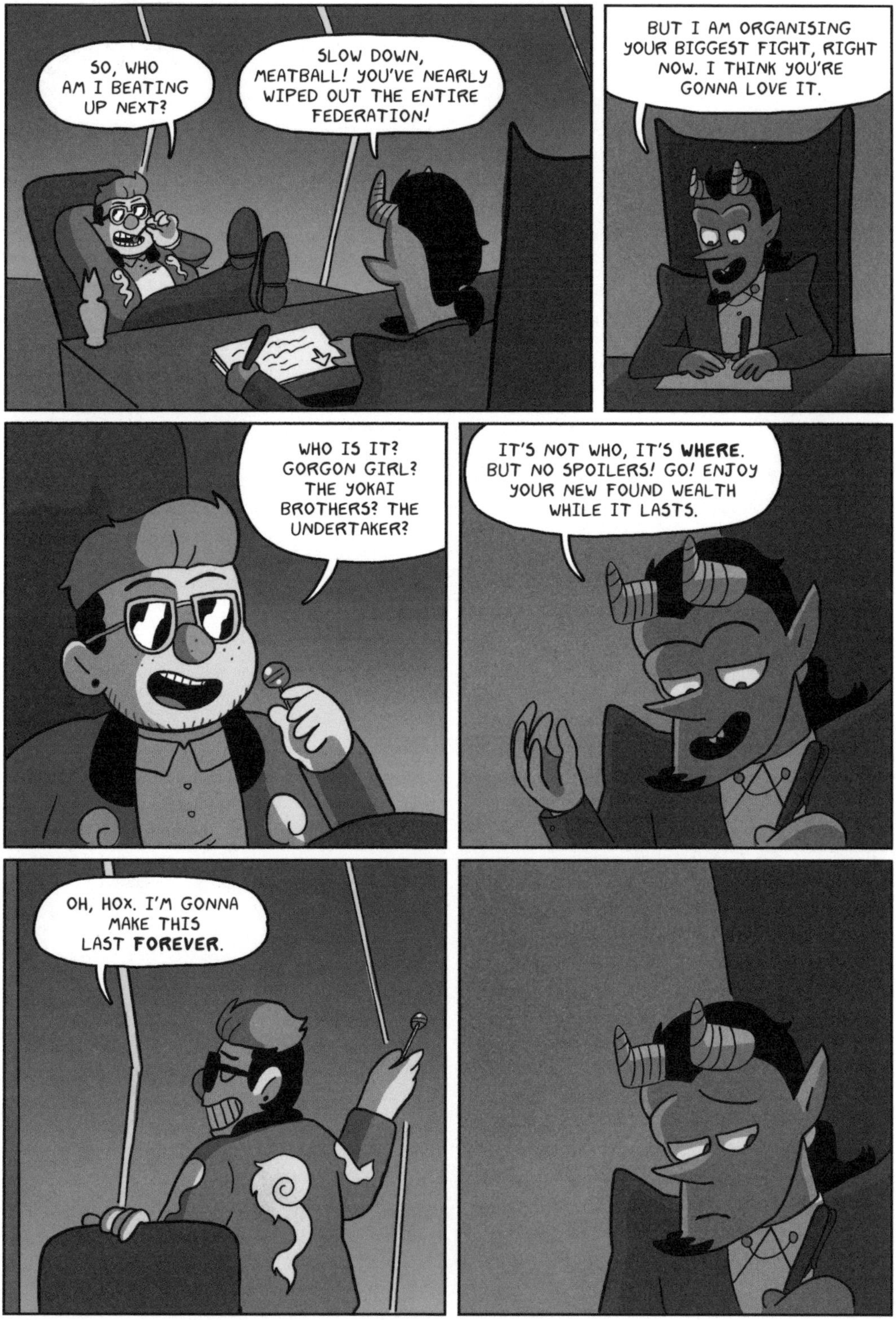
SO, WHO AM I BEATING UP NEXT?
SLOW DOWN, MEATBALL! YOU'VE NEARLY WIPED OUT THE ENTIRE FEDERATION!
BUT I AM ORGANISING YOUR BIGGEST FIGHT, RIGHT NOW. I THINK YOU'RE GONNA LOVE IT.
WHO IS IT? GORGON GIRL? THE YOKAI BROTHERS? THE UNDERTAKER?
IT'S NOT WHO, IT'S **WHERE**. BUT NO SPOILERS! GO! ENJOY YOUR NEW FOUND WEALTH WHILE IT LASTS.
OH, HOX. I'M GONNA MAKE THIS LAST **FOREVER**.

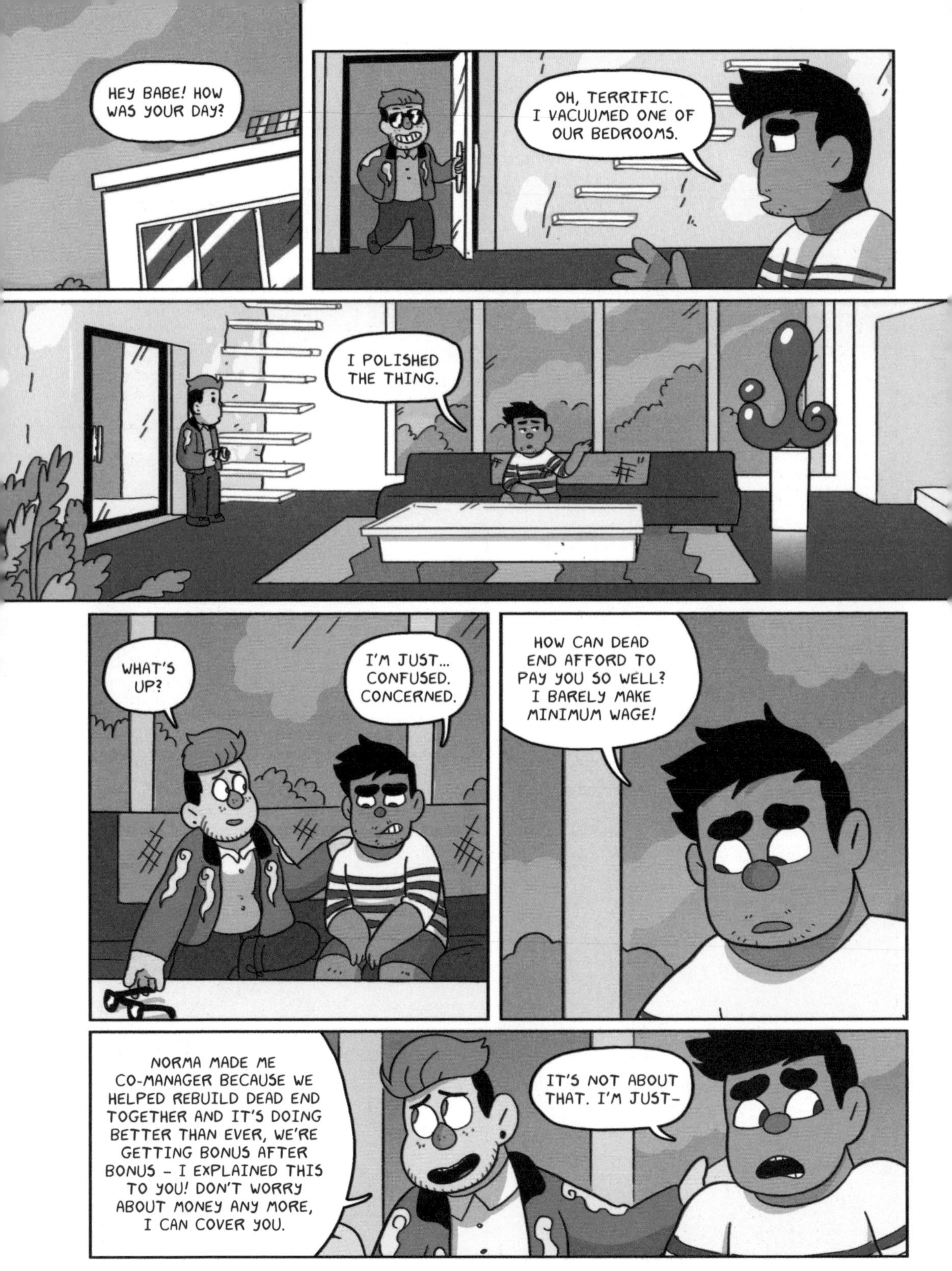
HEY BABE! HOW WAS YOUR DAY?
OH, TERRIFIC. I VACUUMED ONE OF OUR BEDROOMS.
I POLISHED THE THING.
WHAT'S UP?
I'M JUST... CONFUSED. CONCERNED.
HOW CAN DEAD END AFFORD TO PAY YOU SO WELL? I BARELY MAKE MINIMUM WAGE!
NORMA MADE ME CO-MANAGER BECAUSE WE HELPED REBUILD DEAD END TOGETHER AND IT'S DOING BETTER THAN EVER, WE'RE GETTING BONUS AFTER BONUS – I EXPLAINED THIS TO YOU! DON'T WORRY ABOUT MONEY ANY MORE, I CAN COVER YOU.
IT'S NOT ABOUT THAT. I'M JUST-

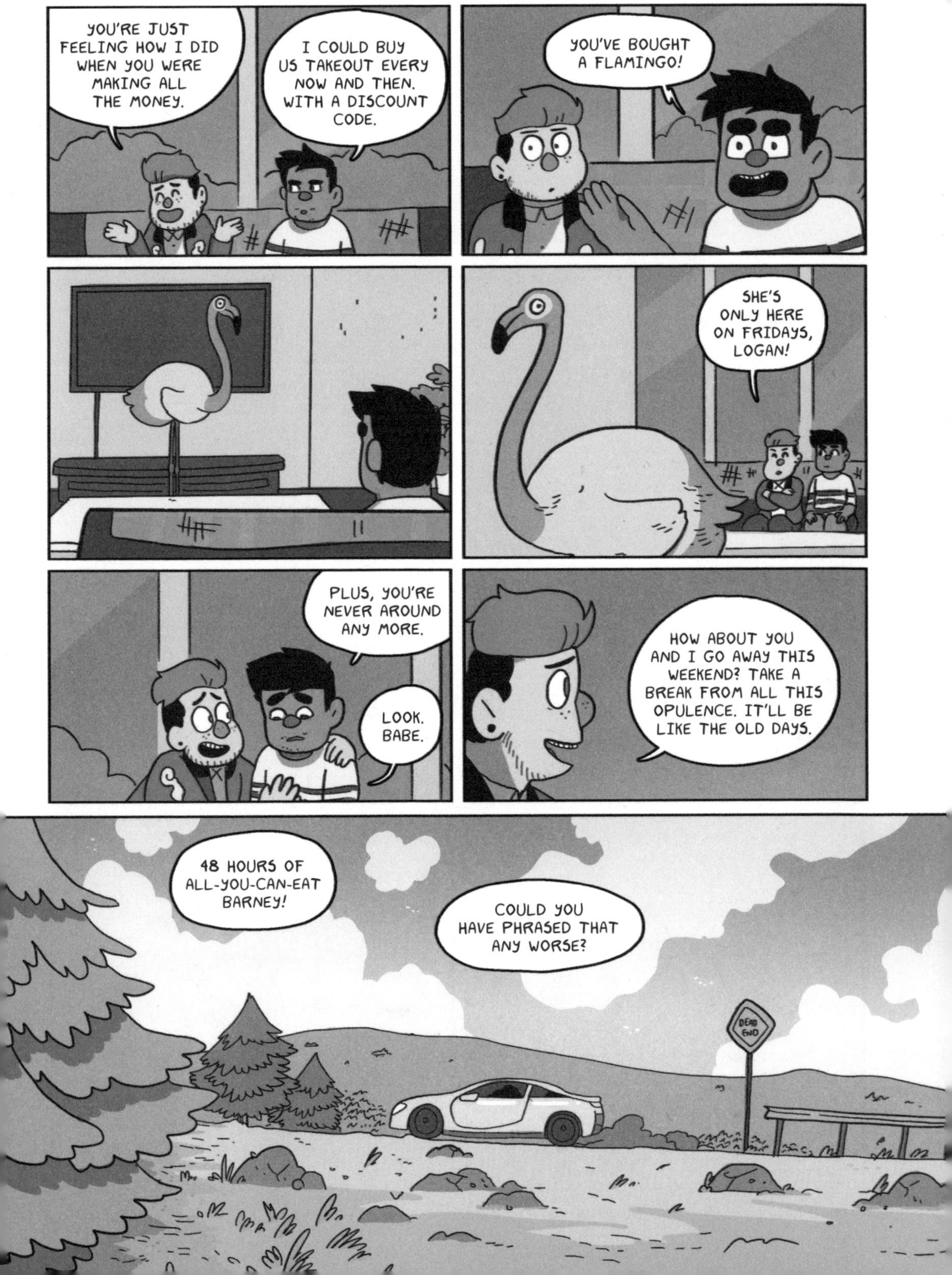
YOU'RE JUST FEELING HOW I DID WHEN YOU WERE MAKING ALL THE MONEY.
I COULD BUY US TAKEOUT EVERY NOW AND THEN. WITH A DISCOUNT CODE.
YOU'VE BOUGHT A FLAMINGO!
SHE'S ONLY HERE ON FRIDAYS, LOGAN!
PLUS, YOU'RE NEVER AROUND ANY MORE.
LOOK. BABE.
HOW ABOUT YOU AND I GO AWAY THIS WEEKEND? TAKE A BREAK FROM ALL THIS OPULENCE. IT'LL BE LIKE THE OLD DAYS.
48 HOURS OF ALL-YOU-CAN-EAT BARNEY!
COULD YOU HAVE PHRASED THAT ANY WORSE?
DEAD END

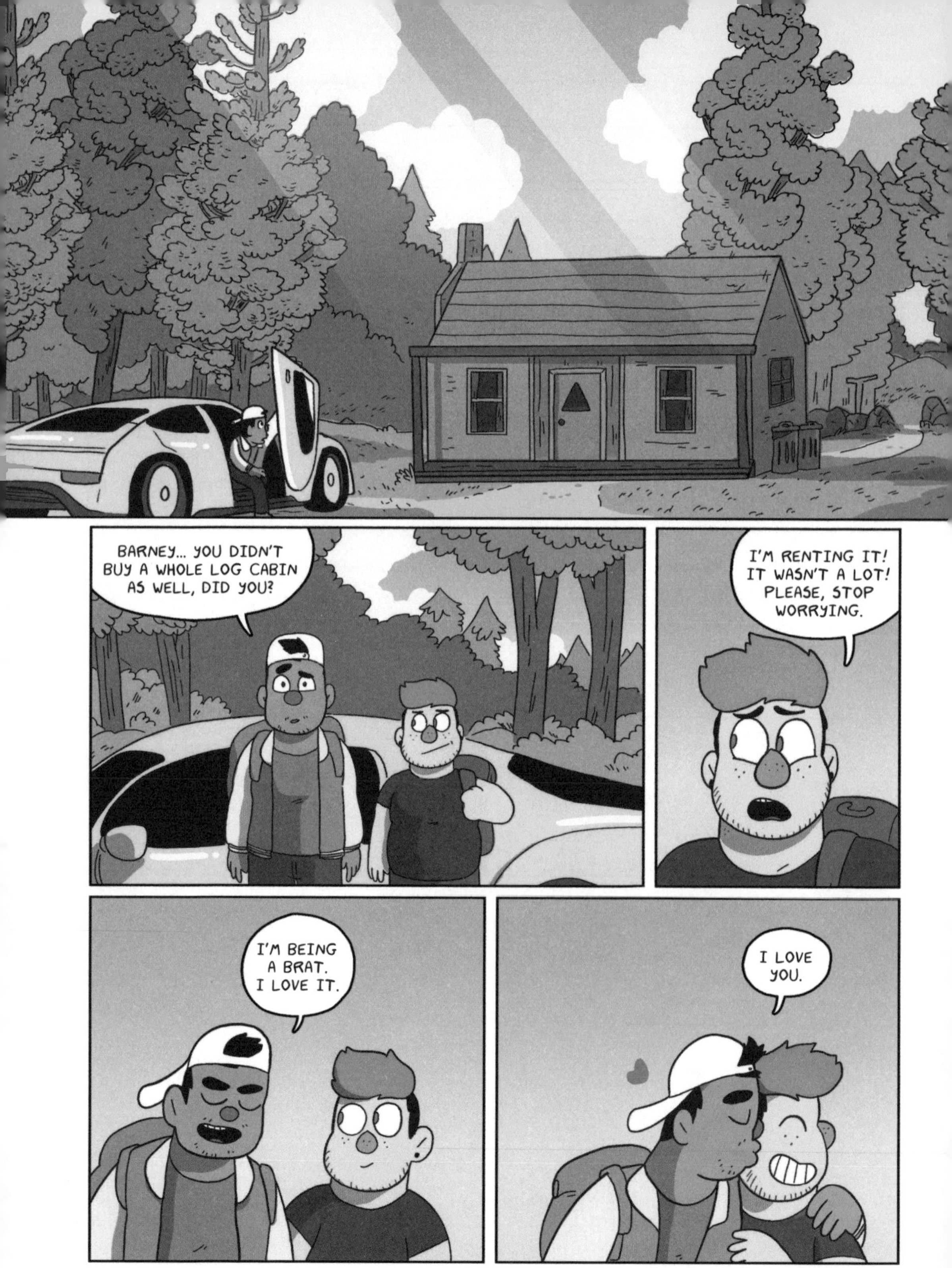
BARNEY... YOU DIDN'T BUY A WHOLE LOG CABIN AS WELL, DID YOU?
I'M RENTING IT! IT WASN'T A LOT! PLEASE, STOP WORRYING.
I'M BEING A BRAT. I LOVE IT.
I LOVE YOU.

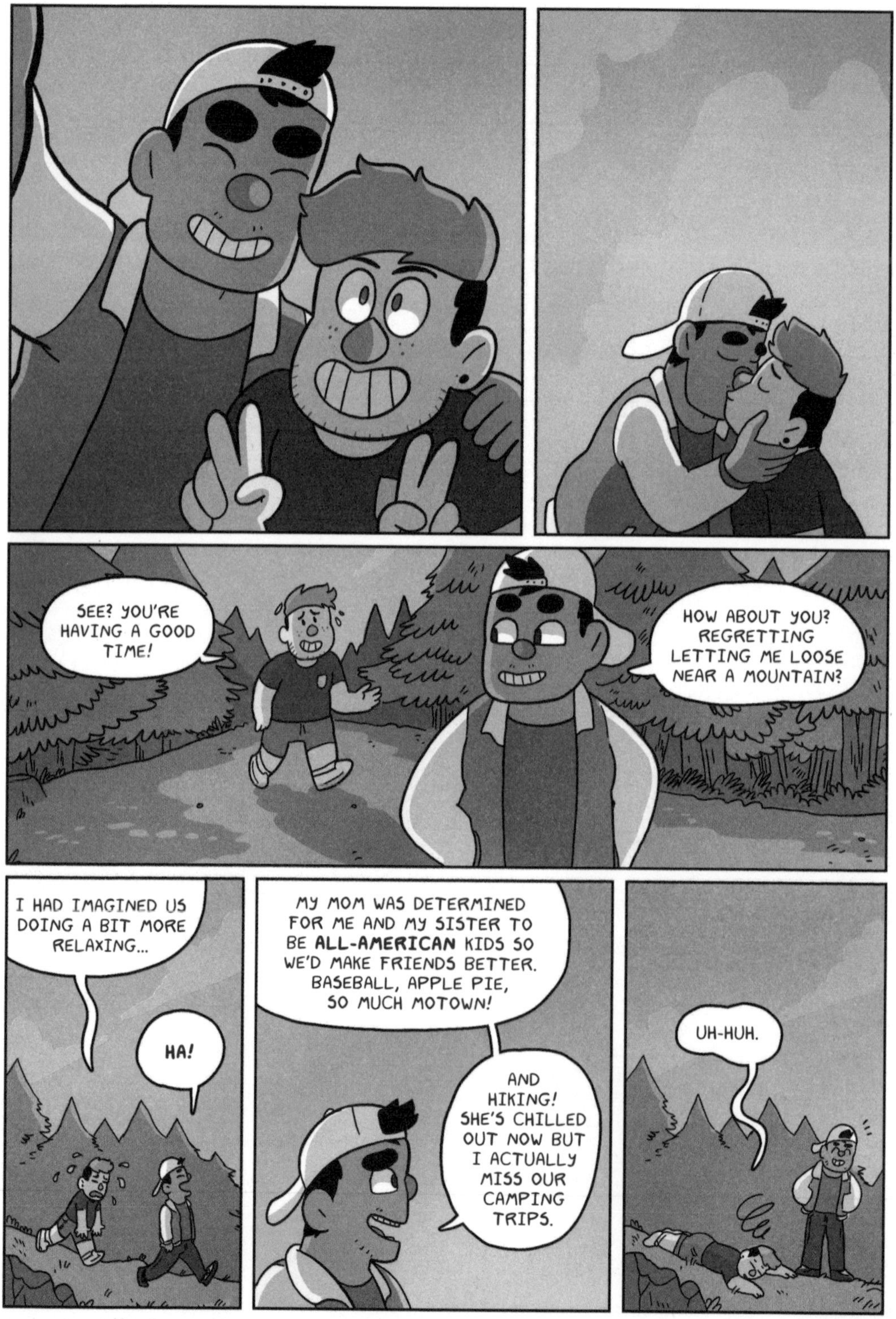
SEE? YOU'RE HAVING A GOOD TIME!
HOW ABOUT YOU? REGRETTING LETTING ME LOOSE NEAR A MOUNTAIN?
I HAD IMAGINED US DOING A BIT MORE RELAXING...
HA!
MY MOM WAS DETERMINED FOR ME AND MY SISTER TO BE **ALL-AMERICAN** KIDS SO WE'D MAKE FRIENDS BETTER. BASEBALL, APPLE PIE, SO MUCH MOTOWN!
AND HIKING! SHE'S CHILLED OUT NOW BUT I ACTUALLY MISS OUR CAMPING TRIPS.
UH-HUH.

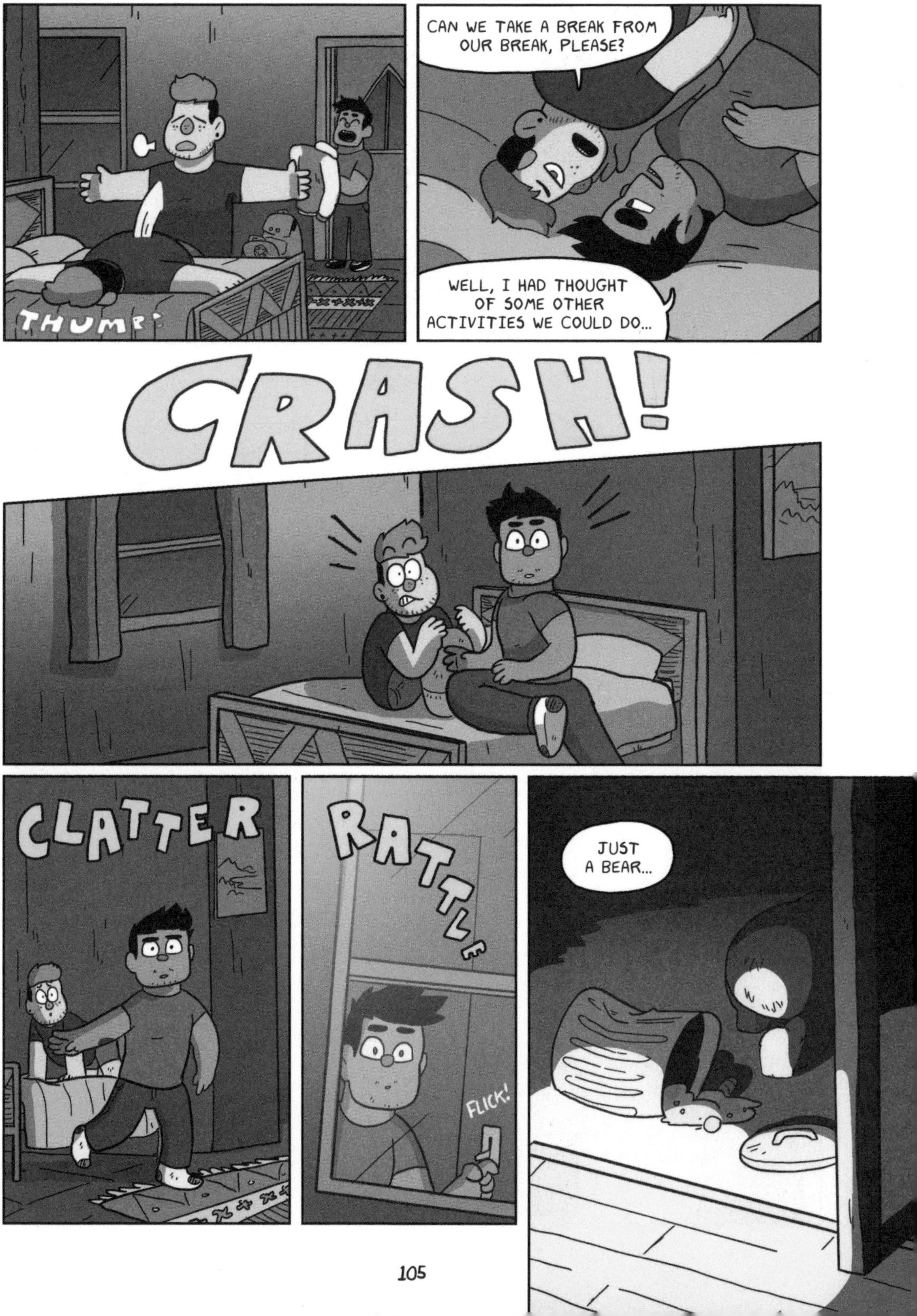
THUMP!
CAN WE TAKE A BREAK FROM OUR BREAK, PLEASE?
WELL, I HAD THOUGHT OF SOME OTHER ACTIVITIES WE COULD DO...
CRASH!
CLATTER
RATTLE
FLICK!
JUST A BEAR...

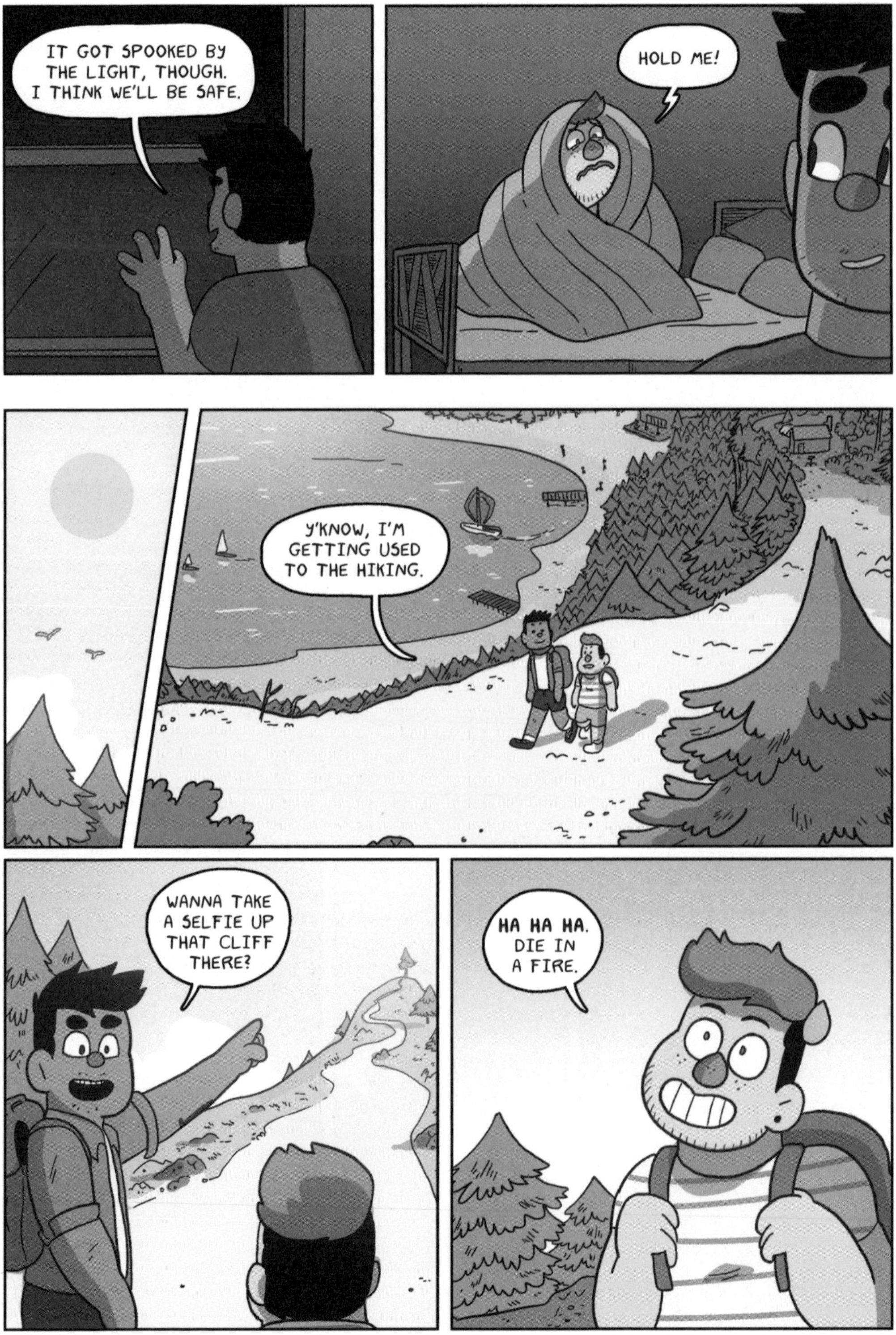
IT GOT SPOOKED BY THE LIGHT, THOUGH. I THINK WE'LL BE SAFE.
HOLD ME!
Y'KNOW, I'M GETTING USED TO THE HIKING.
WANNA TAKE A SELFIE UP THAT CLIFF THERE?
HA HA HA. DIE IN A FIRE.

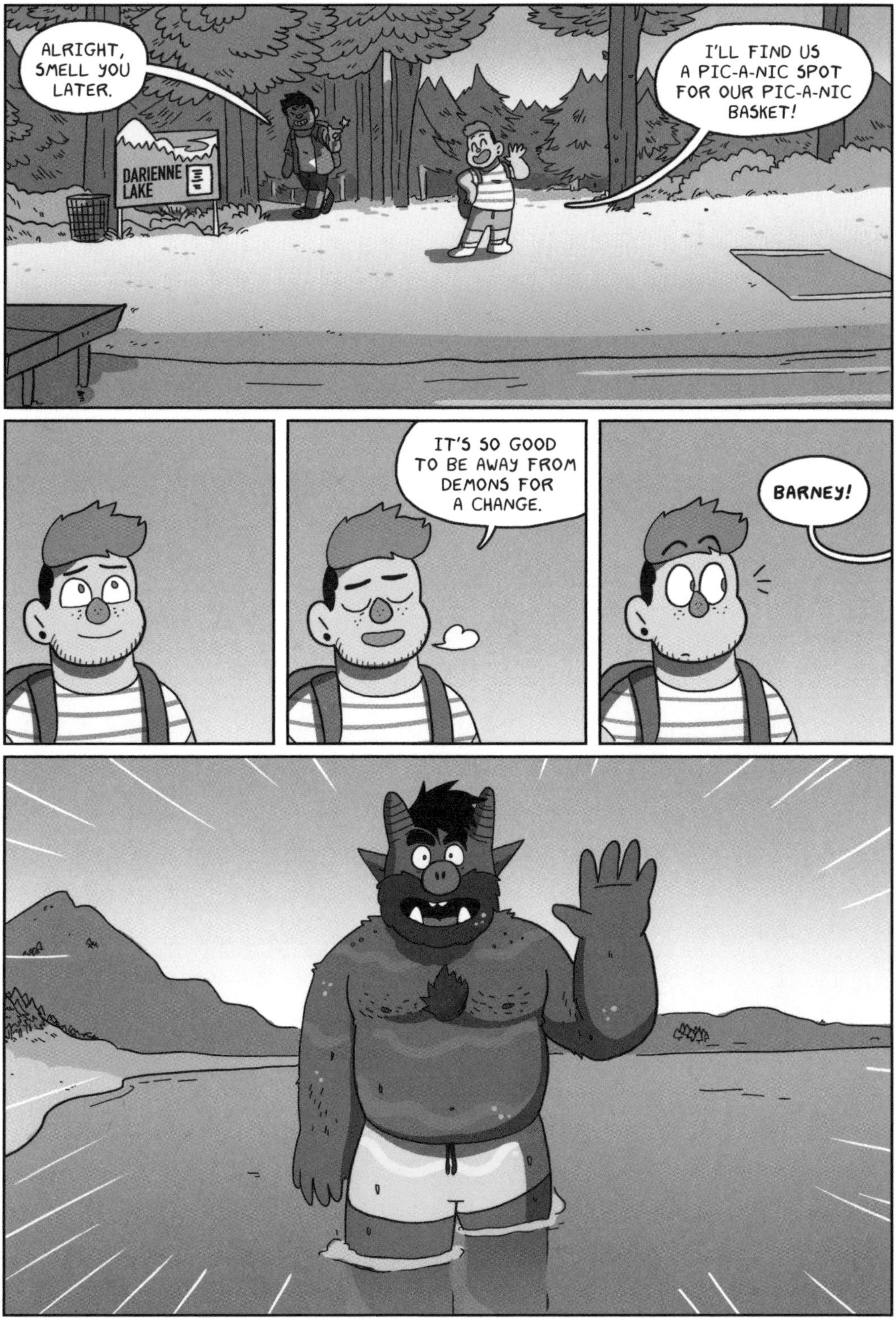
ALRIGHT, SMELL YOU LATER.
DARIENNE LAKE
I'LL FIND US A PIC-A-NIC SPOT FOR OUR PIC-A-NIC BASKET!
IT'S SO GOOD TO BE AWAY FROM DEMONS FOR A CHANGE.
BARNEY!

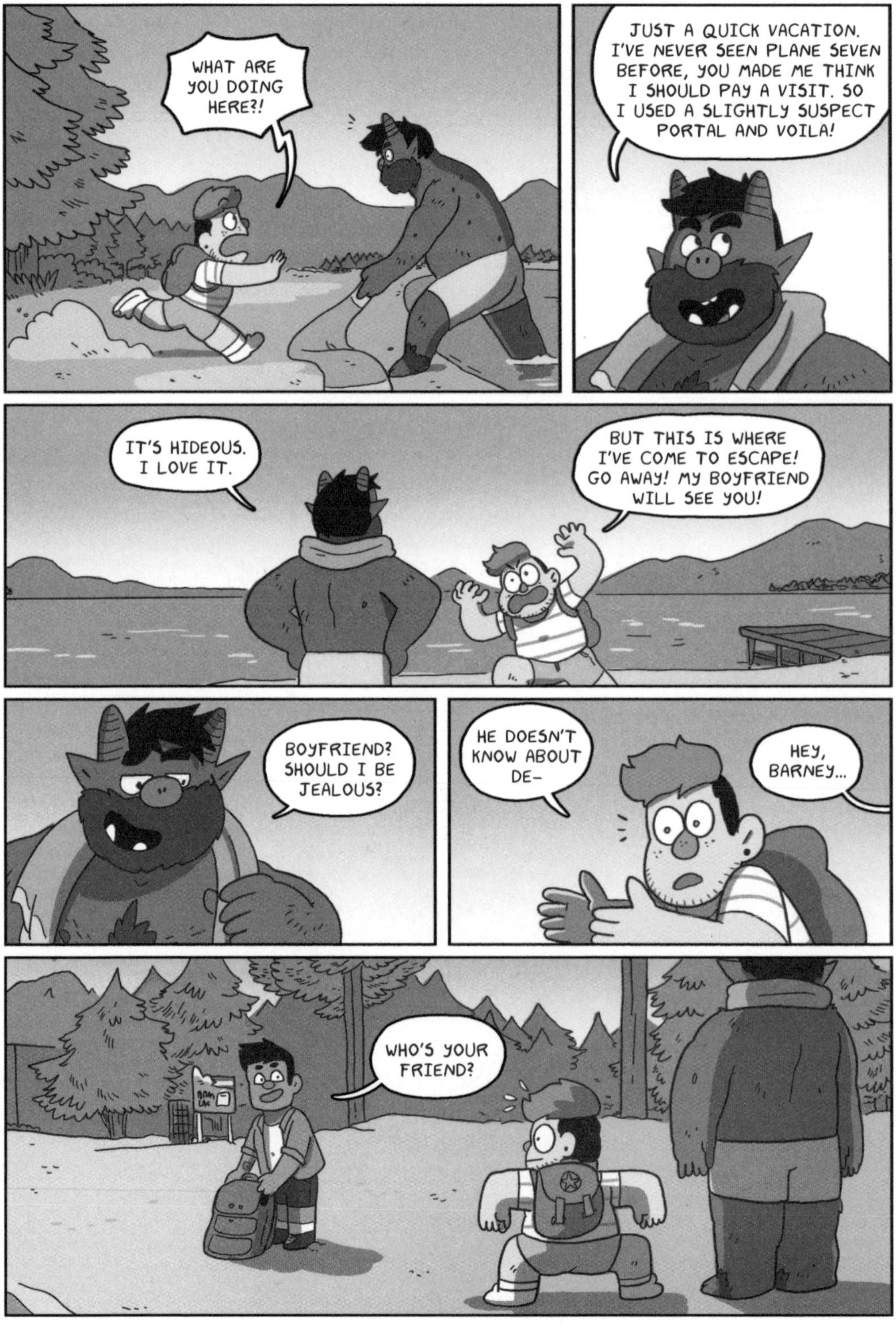
WHAT ARE YOU DOING HERE?!
JUST A QUICK VACATION. I'VE NEVER SEEN PLANE SEVEN BEFORE, YOU MADE ME THINK I SHOULD PAY A VISIT. SO I USED A SLIGHTLY SUSPECT PORTAL AND VOILA!
IT'S HIDEOUS. I LOVE IT.
BUT THIS IS WHERE I'VE COME TO ESCAPE! GO AWAY! MY BOYFRIEND WILL SEE YOU!
BOYFRIEND? SHOULD I BE JEALOUS?
HE DOESN'T KNOW ABOUT DE–
HEY, BARNEY...
WHO'S YOUR FRIEND?

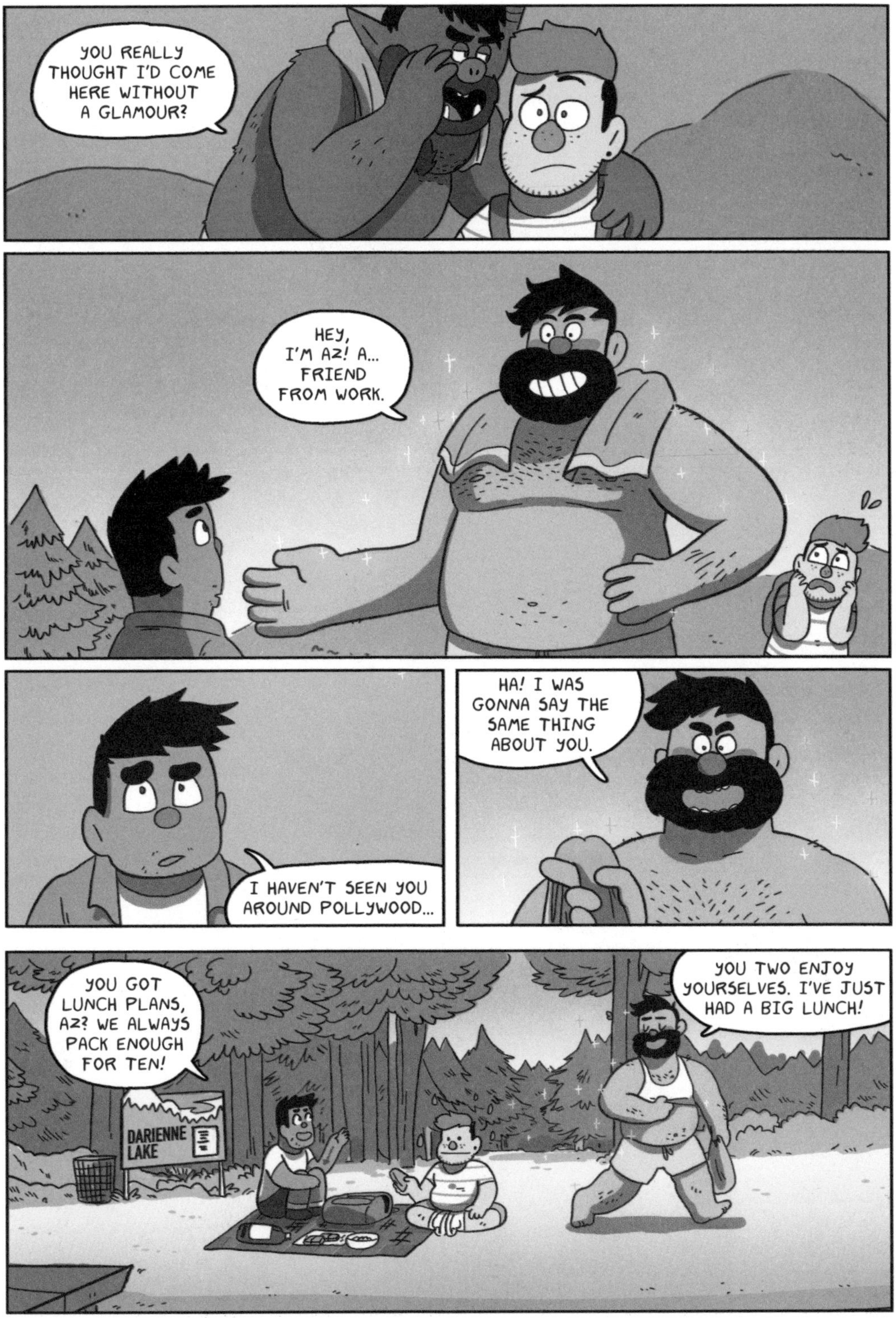

YOU REALLY THOUGHT I'D COME HERE WITHOUT A GLAMOUR?
HEY, I'M AZ! A... FRIEND FROM WORK.
I HAVEN'T SEEN YOU AROUND POLLYWOOD...
HA! I WAS GONNA SAY THE SAME THING ABOUT YOU.
YOU GOT LUNCH PLANS, AZ? WE ALWAYS PACK ENOUGH FOR TEN!
YOU TWO ENJOY YOURSELVES. I'VE JUST HAD A BIG LUNCH!
DARIENNE LAKE

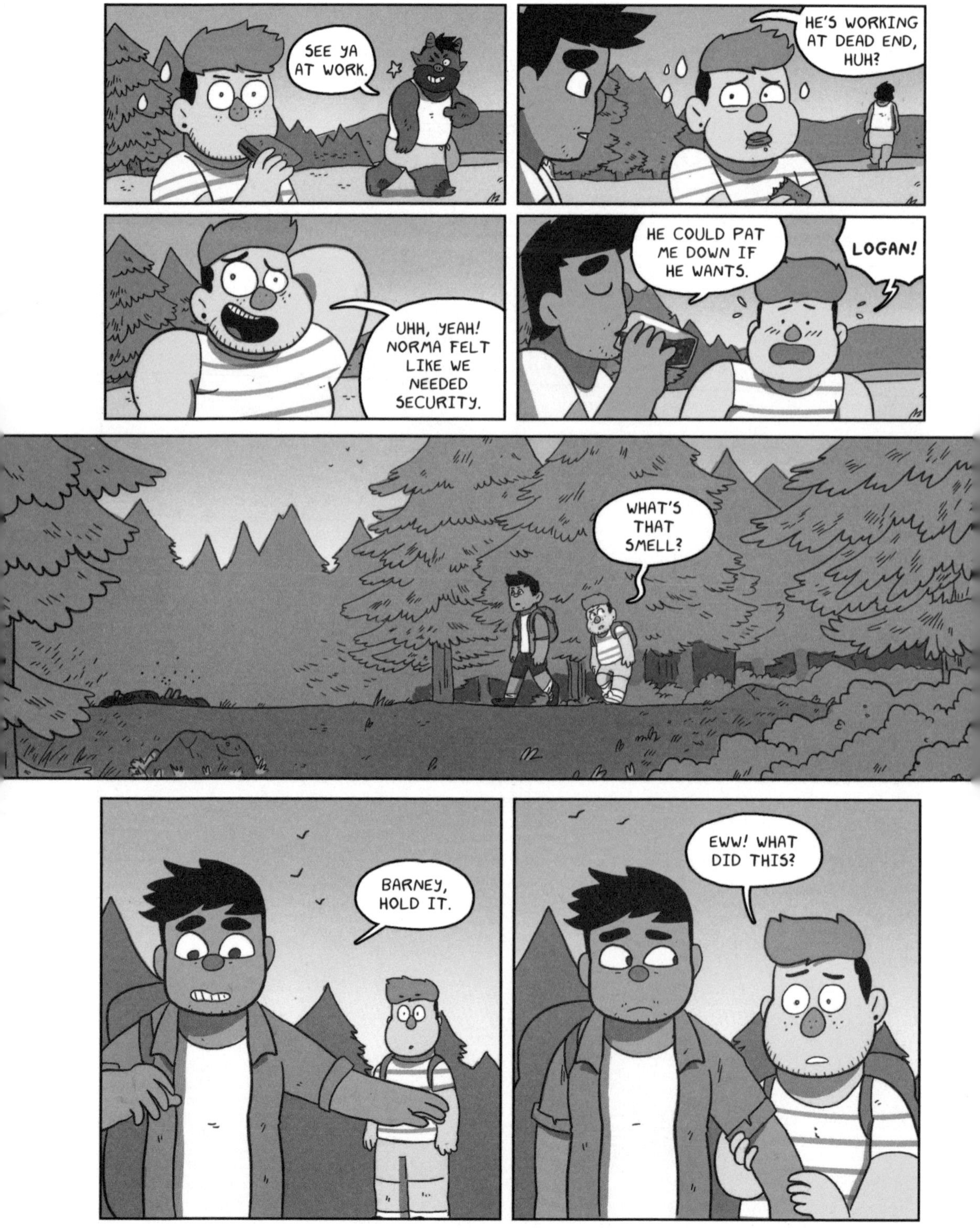
SEE YA AT WORK.
HE'S WORKING AT DEAD END, HUH?
UHH, YEAH! NORMA FELT LIKE WE NEEDED SECURITY.
HE COULD PAT ME DOWN IF HE WANTS.
LOGAN!
WHAT'S THAT SMELL?
BARNEY, HOLD IT.
EWW! WHAT DID THIS?

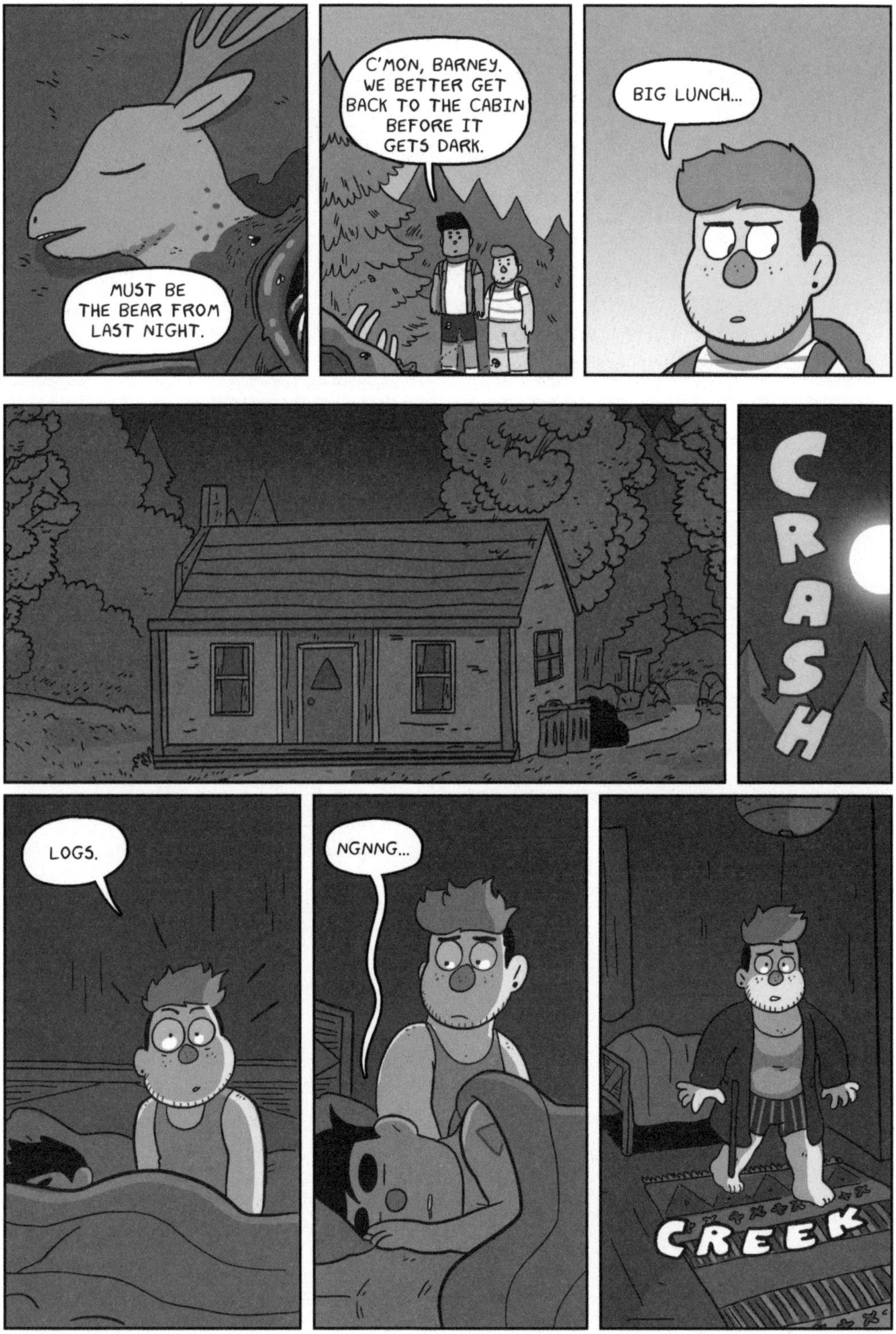
MUST BE THE BEAR FROM LAST NIGHT.
C'MON, BARNEY. WE BETTER GET BACK TO THE CABIN BEFORE IT GETS DARK.
BIG LUNCH...
CRASH
LOGS.
NGNNG...
CREEK

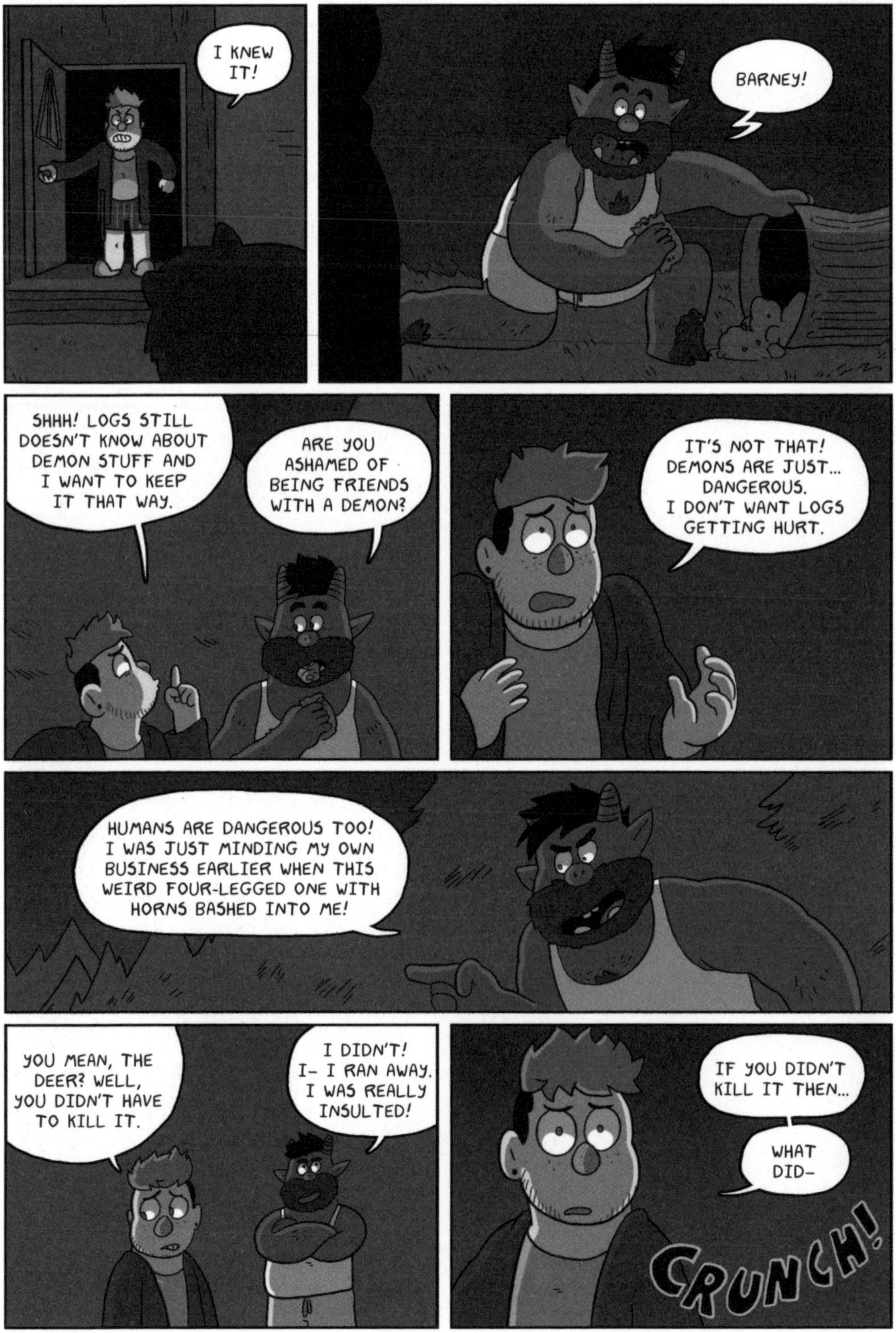
I KNEW IT!
BARNEY!
SHHH! LOGS STILL DOESN'T KNOW ABOUT DEMON STUFF AND I WANT TO KEEP IT THAT WAY.
ARE YOU ASHAMED OF BEING FRIENDS WITH A DEMON?
IT'S NOT THAT! DEMONS ARE JUST... DANGEROUS. I DON'T WANT LOGS GETTING HURT.
HUMANS ARE DANGEROUS TOO! I WAS JUST MINDING MY OWN BUSINESS EARLIER WHEN THIS WEIRD FOUR-LEGGED ONE WITH HORNS BASHED INTO ME!
YOU MEAN, THE DEER? WELL, YOU DIDN'T HAVE TO KILL IT.
I DIDN'T! I- I RAN AWAY. I WAS REALLY INSULTED!
IF YOU DIDN'T KILL IT THEN...
WHAT DID-
CRUNCH!

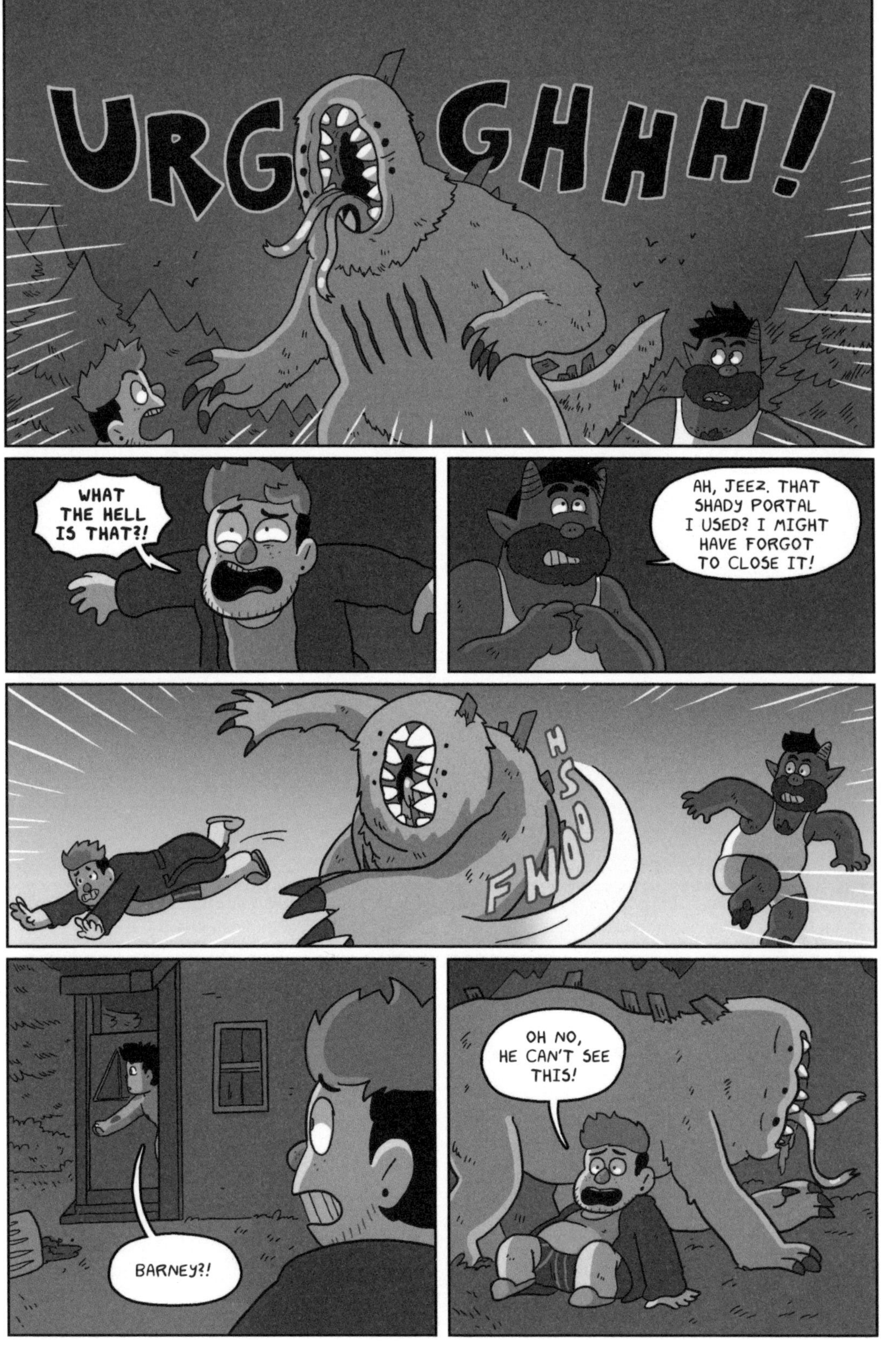
URGGHHH!
WHAT THE HELL IS THAT?!
AH, JEEZ. THAT SHADY PORTAL I USED? I MIGHT HAVE FORGOT TO CLOSE IT!
FWOOSH
BARNEY?!
OH NO, HE CAN'T SEE THIS!

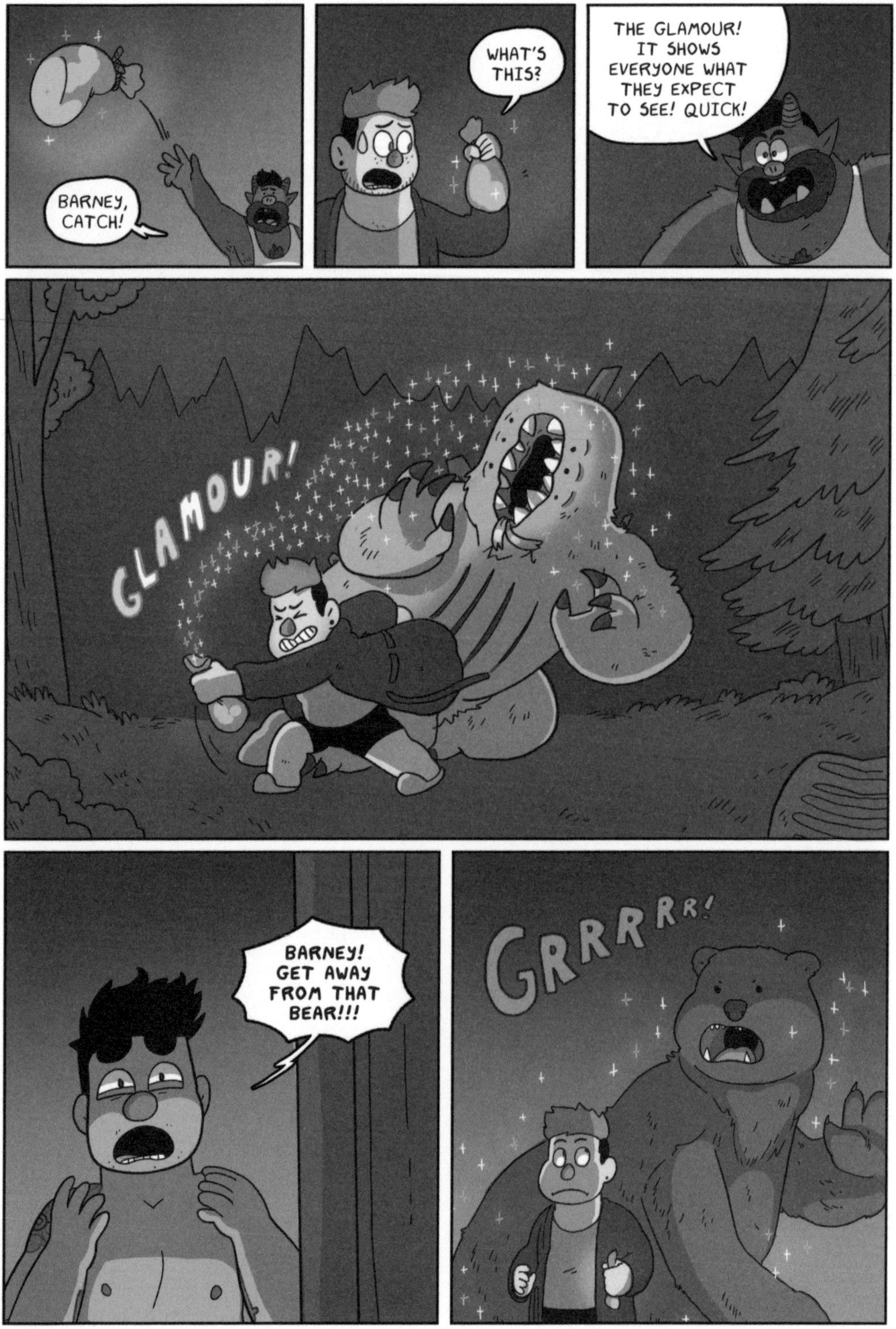
BARNEY, CATCH!
WHAT'S THIS?
THE GLAMOUR! IT SHOWS EVERYONE WHAT THEY EXPECT TO SEE! QUICK!
GLAMOUR!
BARNEY! GET AWAY FROM THAT BEAR!!!
GRRRRR!

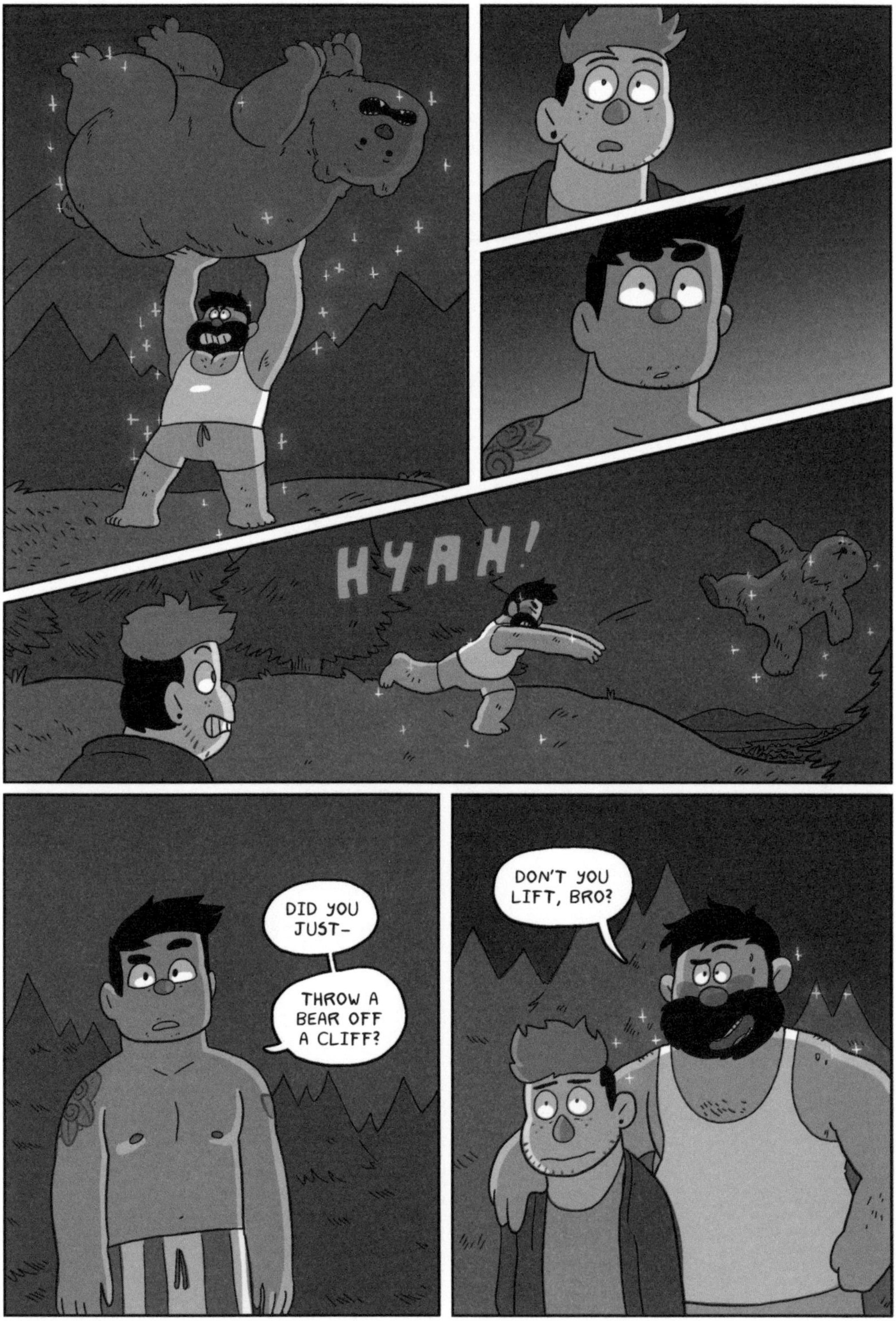
HYAH!
DID YOU JUST-
THROW A BEAR OFF A CLIFF?
DON'T YOU LIFT, BRO?

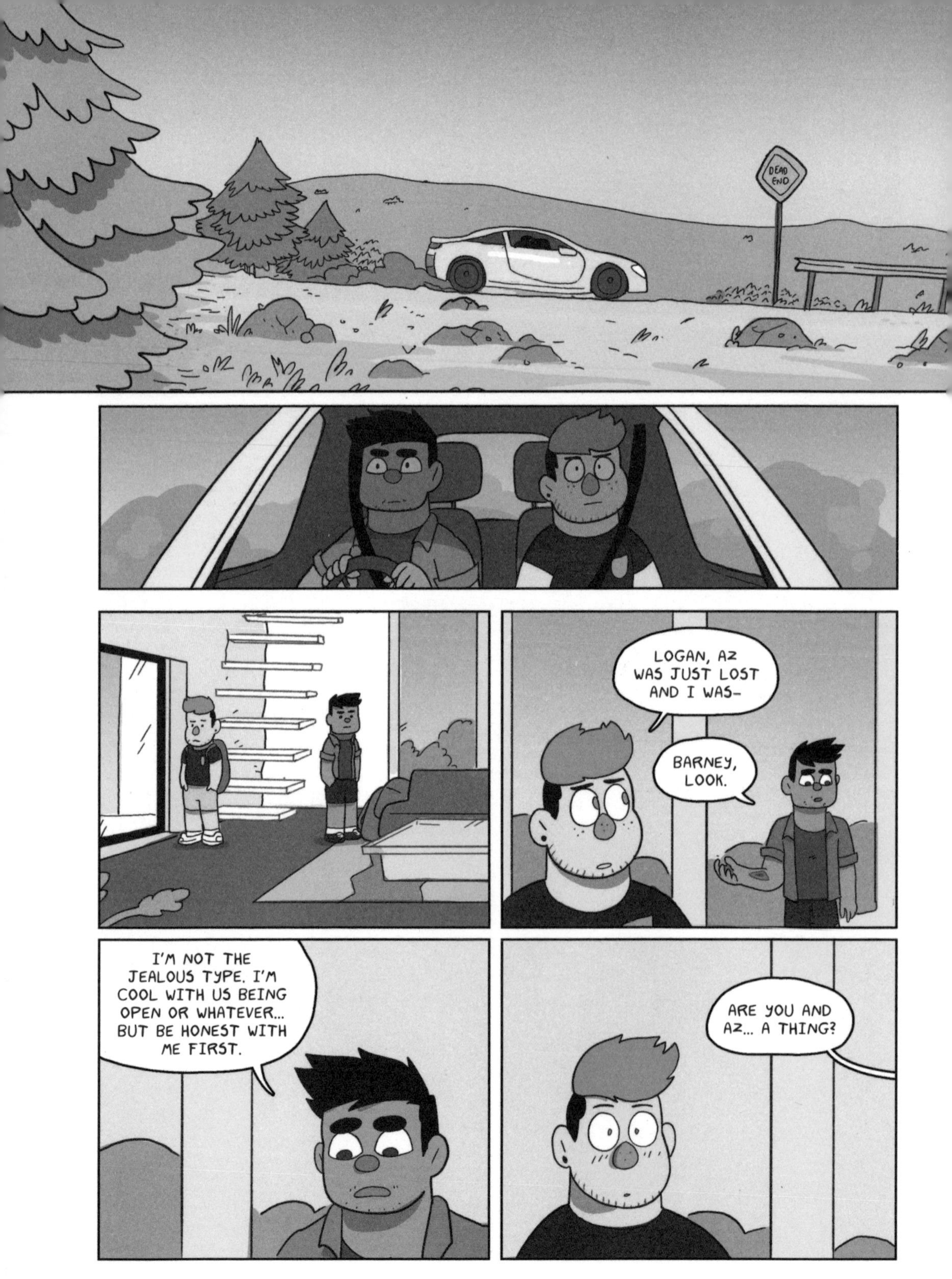
DEAD END
LOGAN, AZ WAS JUST LOST AND I WAS–
BARNEY, LOOK.
I'M NOT THE JEALOUS TYPE. I'M COOL WITH US BEING OPEN OR WHATEVER... BUT BE HONEST WITH ME FIRST.
ARE YOU AND AZ... A THING?

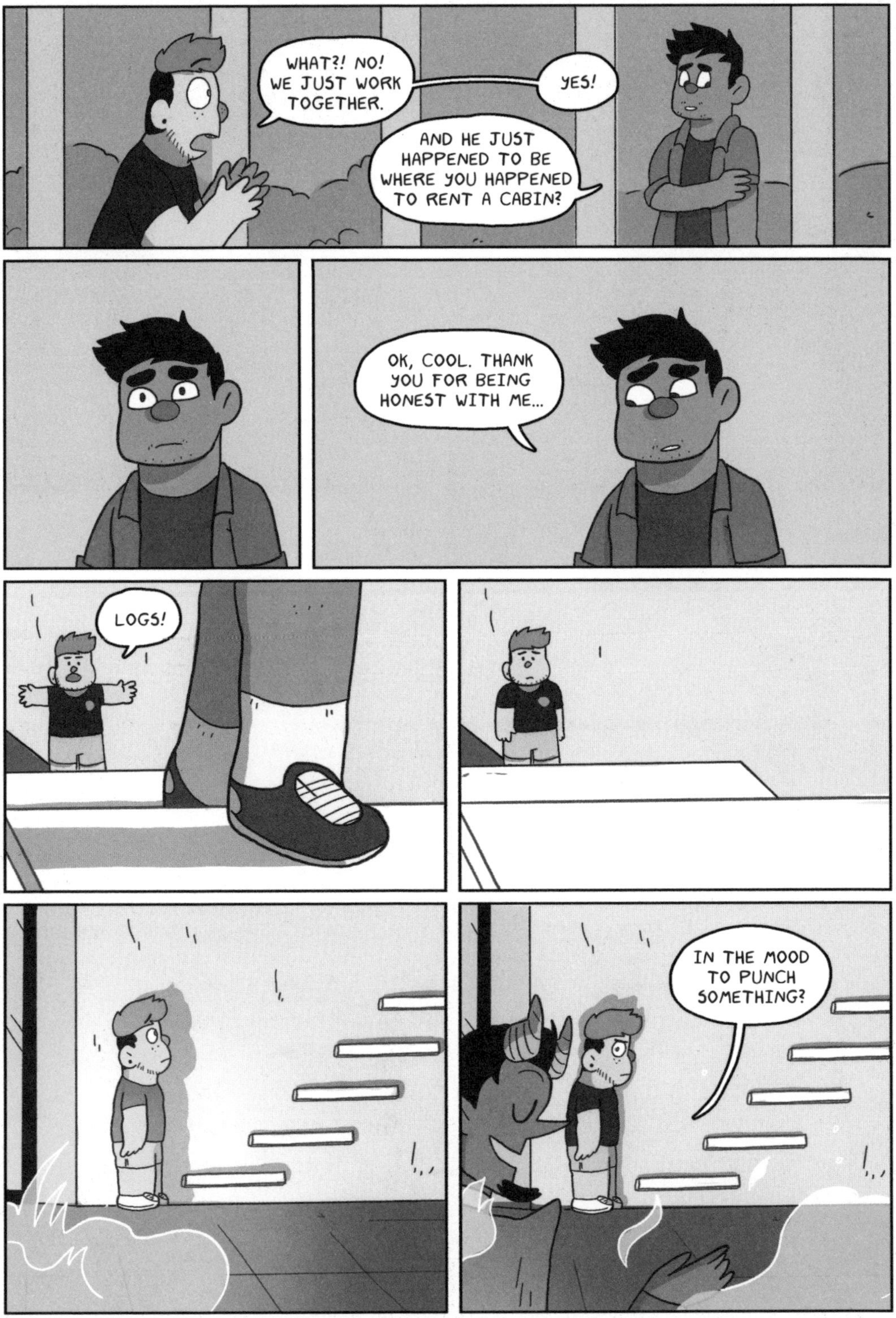
WHAT?! NO! WE JUST WORK TOGETHER.
YES!
AND HE JUST HAPPENED TO BE WHERE YOU HAPPENED TO RENT A CABIN?
OK, COOL. THANK YOU FOR BEING HONEST WITH ME...
LOGS!
IN THE MOOD TO PUNCH SOMETHING?

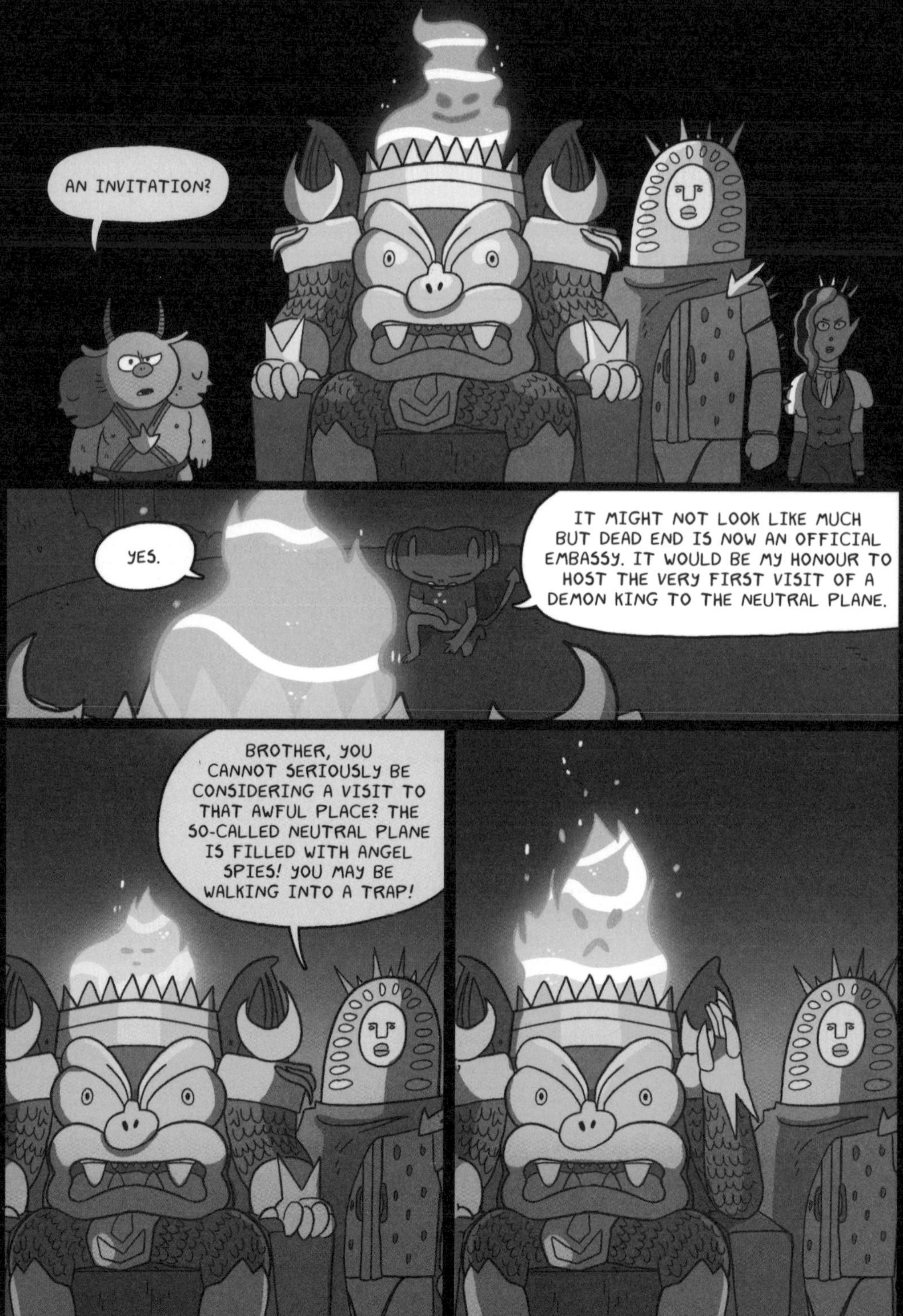
AN INVITATION?
YES.
IT MIGHT NOT LOOK LIKE MUCH BUT DEAD END IS NOW AN OFFICIAL EMBASSY. IT WOULD BE MY HONOUR TO HOST THE VERY FIRST VISIT OF A DEMON KING TO THE NEUTRAL PLANE.
BROTHER, YOU CANNOT SERIOUSLY BE CONSIDERING A VISIT TO THAT AWFUL PLACE? THE SO-CALLED NEUTRAL PLANE IS FILLED WITH ANGEL SPIES! YOU MAY BE WALKING INTO A TRAP!

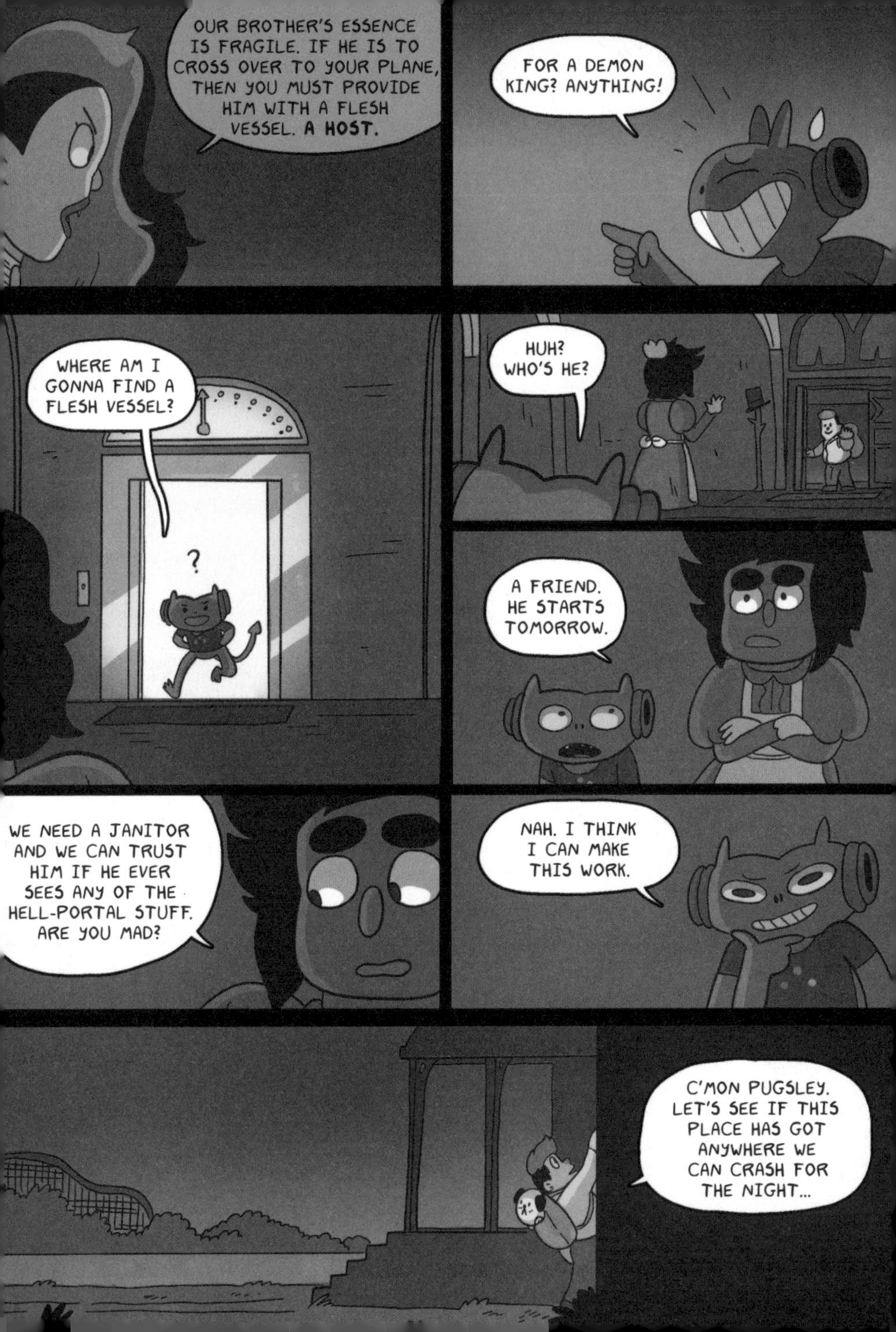
OUR BROTHER'S ESSENCE IS FRAGILE. IF HE IS TO CROSS OVER TO YOUR PLANE, THEN YOU MUST PROVIDE HIM WITH A FLESH VESSEL. A HOST.
FOR A DEMON KING? ANYTHING!
WHERE AM I GONNA FIND A FLESH VESSEL?
?
HUH? WHO'S HE?
A FRIEND. HE STARTS TOMORROW.
WE NEED A JANITOR AND WE CAN TRUST HIM IF HE EVER SEES ANY OF THE HELL-PORTAL STUFF. ARE YOU MAD?
NAH. I THINK I CAN MAKE THIS WORK.
C'MON PUGSLEY. LET'S SEE IF THIS PLACE HAS GOT ANYWHERE WE CAN CRASH FOR THE NIGHT...

MARIE CALLUM

CHAPTER 5
SMOKE AND MIRRORS

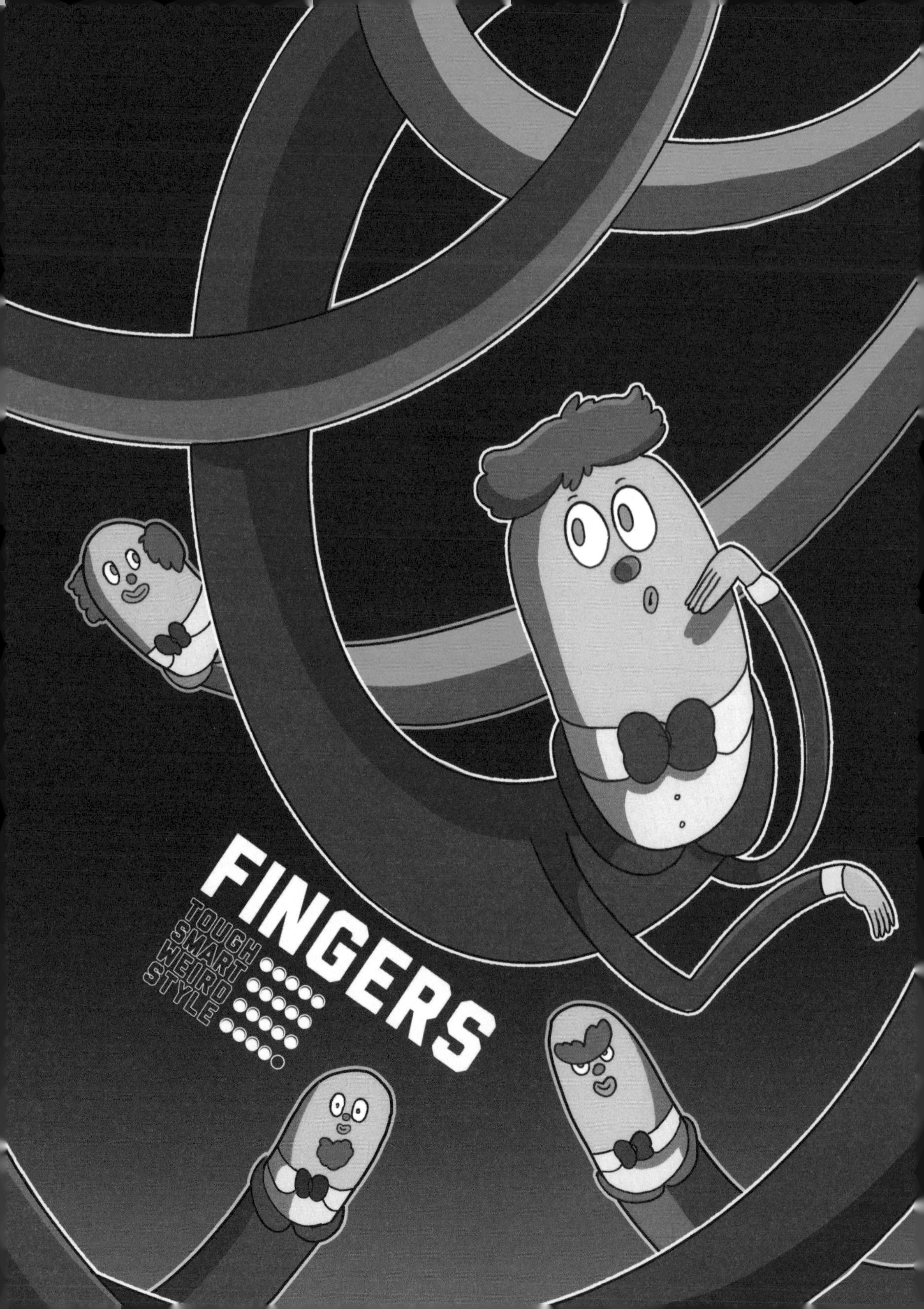

FINGERS
TOUGH
SMART
WEIRD
STYLE

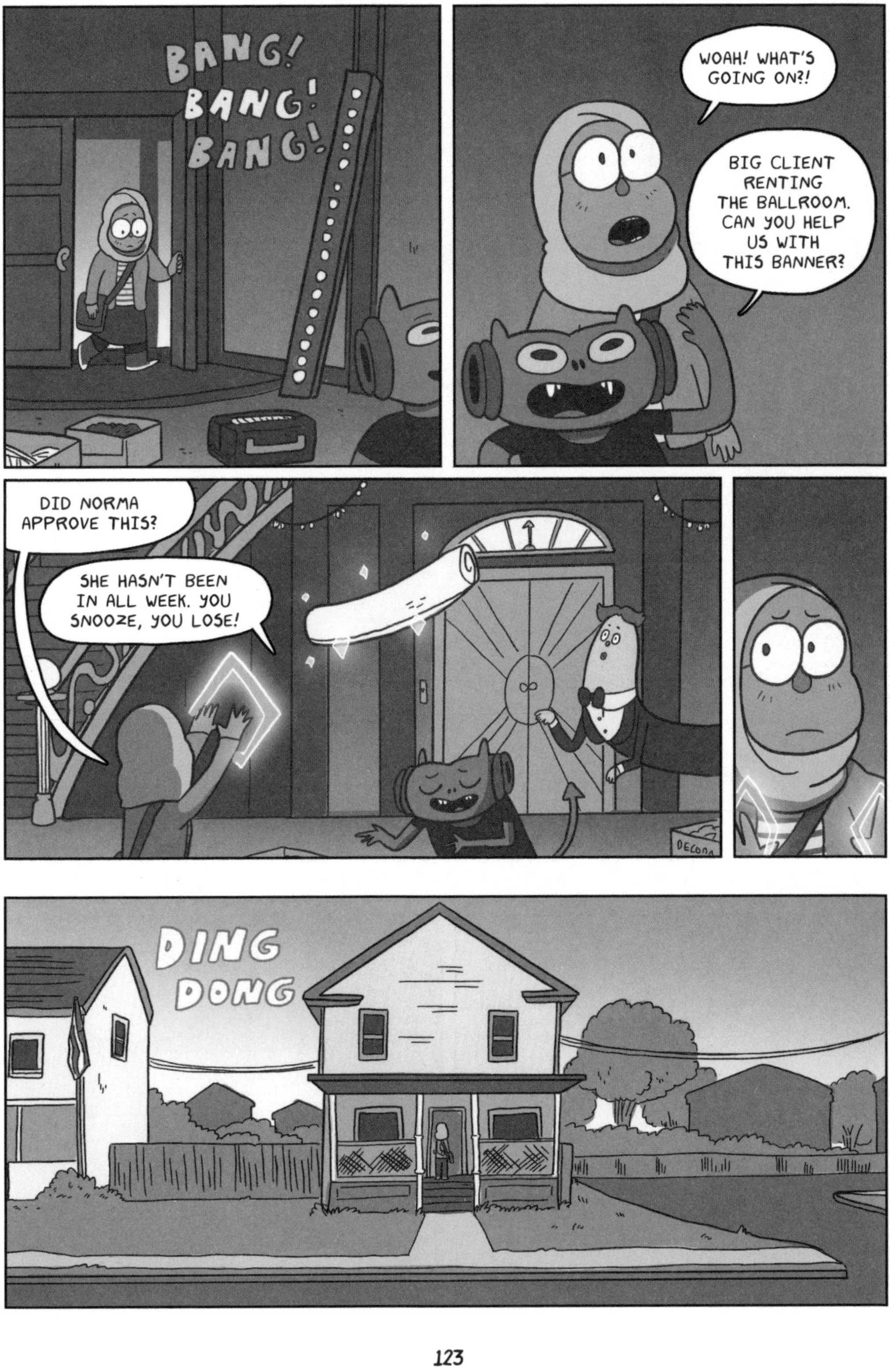
BANG!
BANG!
BANG!
WOAH! WHAT'S GOING ON?!
BIG CLIENT RENTING THE BALLROOM. CAN YOU HELP US WITH THIS BANNER?
DID NORMA APPROVE THIS?
SHE HASN'T BEEN IN ALL WEEK. YOU SNOOZE, YOU LOSE!
DING
DONG

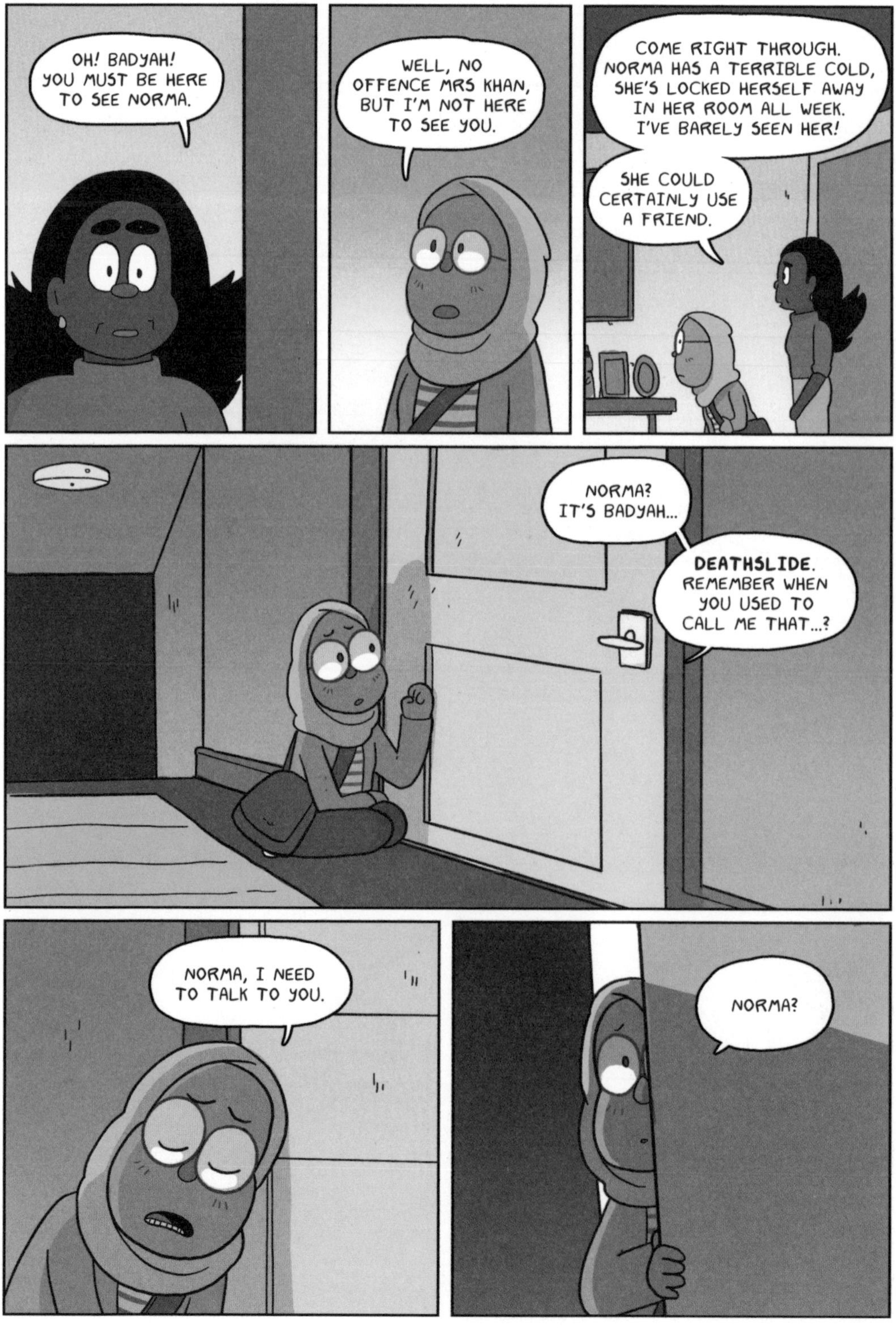
OH! BADYAH! YOU MUST BE HERE TO SEE NORMA.
WELL, NO OFFENCE MRS KHAN, BUT I'M NOT HERE TO SEE YOU.
COME RIGHT THROUGH. NORMA HAS A TERRIBLE COLD, SHE'S LOCKED HERSELF AWAY IN HER ROOM ALL WEEK. I'VE BARELY SEEN HER!
SHE COULD CERTAINLY USE A FRIEND.
NORMA? IT'S BADYAH...
DEATHSLIDE. REMEMBER WHEN YOU USED TO CALL ME THAT...?
NORMA, I NEED TO TALK TO YOU.
NORMA?

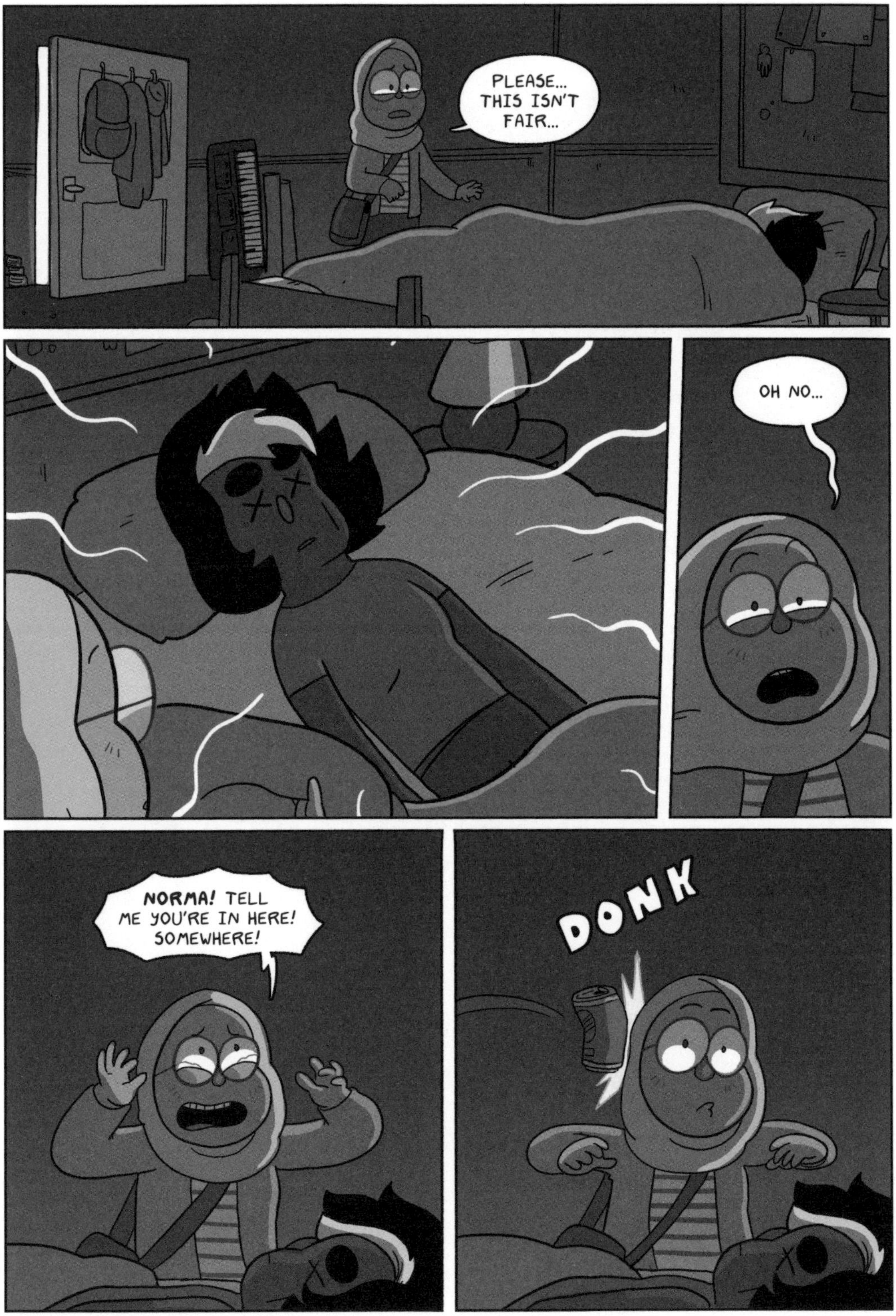
PLEASE... THIS ISN'T FAIR...
OH NO...
NORMA! TELL ME YOU'RE IN HERE! SOMEWHERE!
DONK

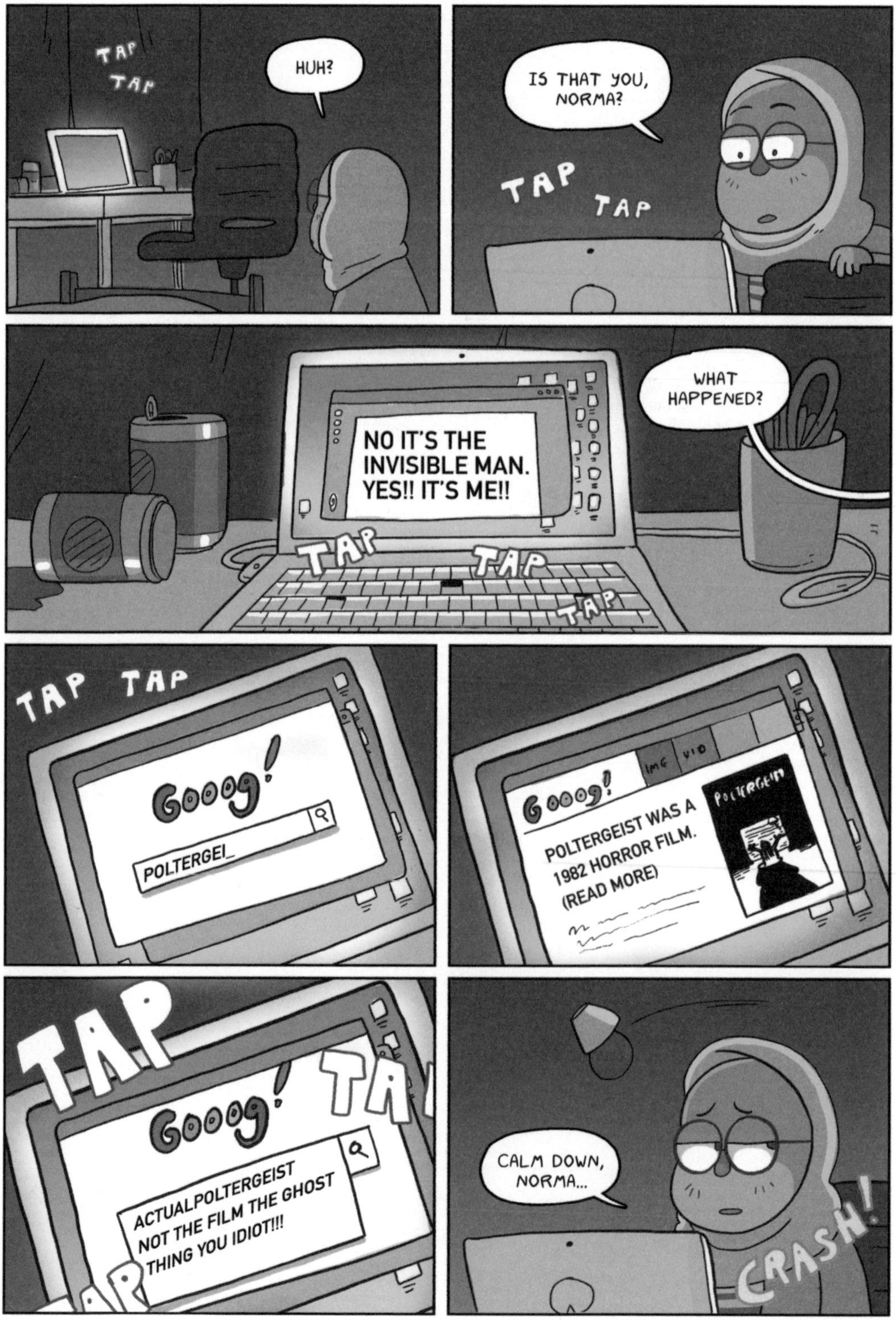
TAP
TAP
HUH?
IS THAT YOU, NORMA?
TAP
TAP
NO IT'S THE INVISIBLE MAN. YES!! IT'S ME!!
WHAT HAPPENED?
TAP
TAP
TAP
TAP TAP
Gooog!
POLTERGEI_
Gooog!
IMG
VID
POLTERGEIST WAS A 1982 HORROR FILM. (READ MORE)
TAP
TA
Gooog!
ACTUALPOLTERGEIST NOT THE FILM THE GHOST THING YOU IDIOT!!!
AP
CALM DOWN, NORMA...
CRASH!

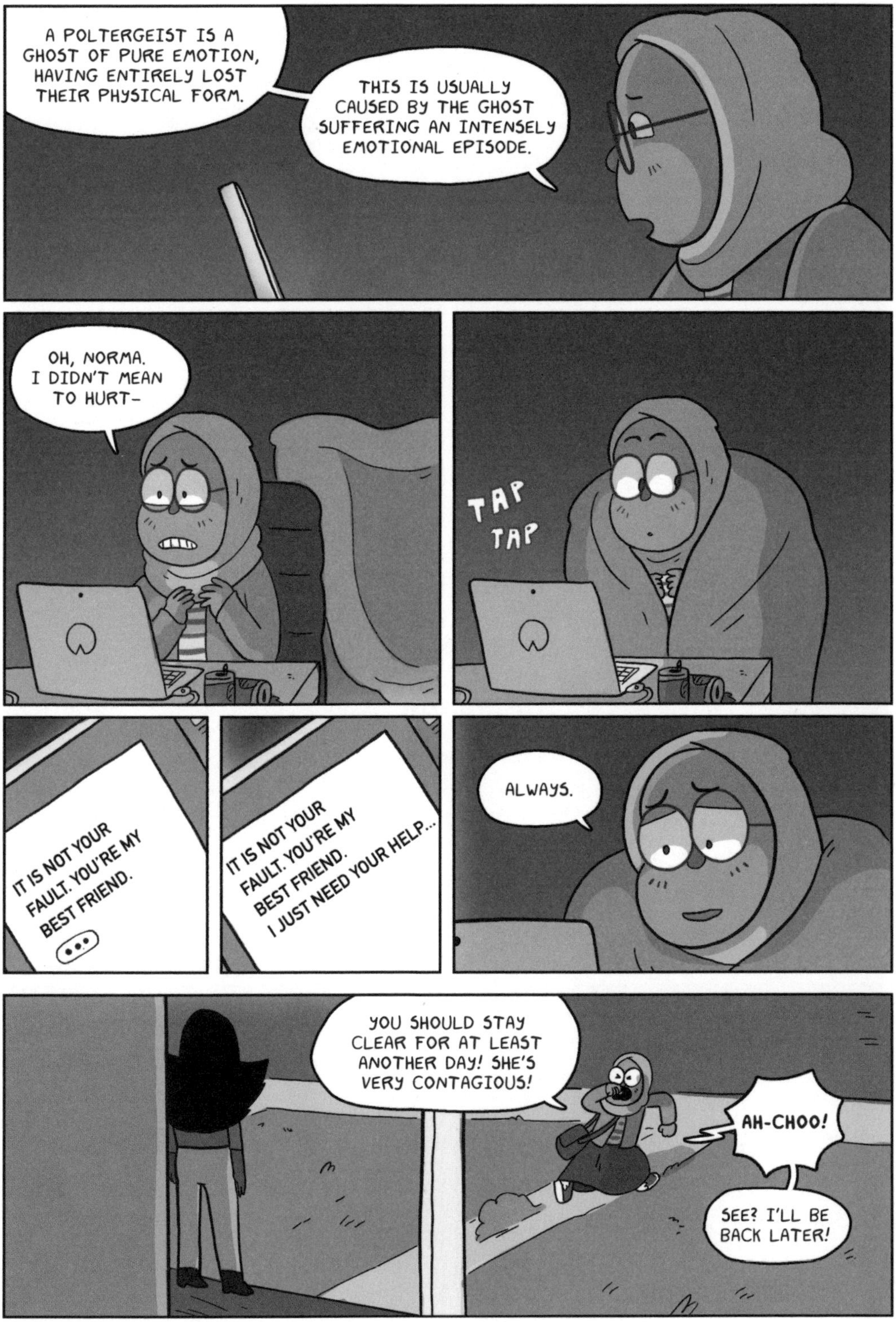
A POLTERGEIST IS A GHOST OF PURE EMOTION, HAVING ENTIRELY LOST THEIR PHYSICAL FORM.
THIS IS USUALLY CAUSED BY THE GHOST SUFFERING AN INTENSELY EMOTIONAL EPISODE.
OH, NORMA. I DIDN'T MEAN TO HURT-
TAP
TAP
IT IS NOT YOUR FAULT. YOU'RE MY BEST FRIEND.
IT IS NOT YOUR FAULT. YOU'RE MY BEST FRIEND. I JUST NEED YOUR HELP...
ALWAYS.
YOU SHOULD STAY CLEAR FOR AT LEAST ANOTHER DAY! SHE'S VERY CONTAGIOUS!
AH-CHOO!
SEE? I'LL BE BACK LATER!

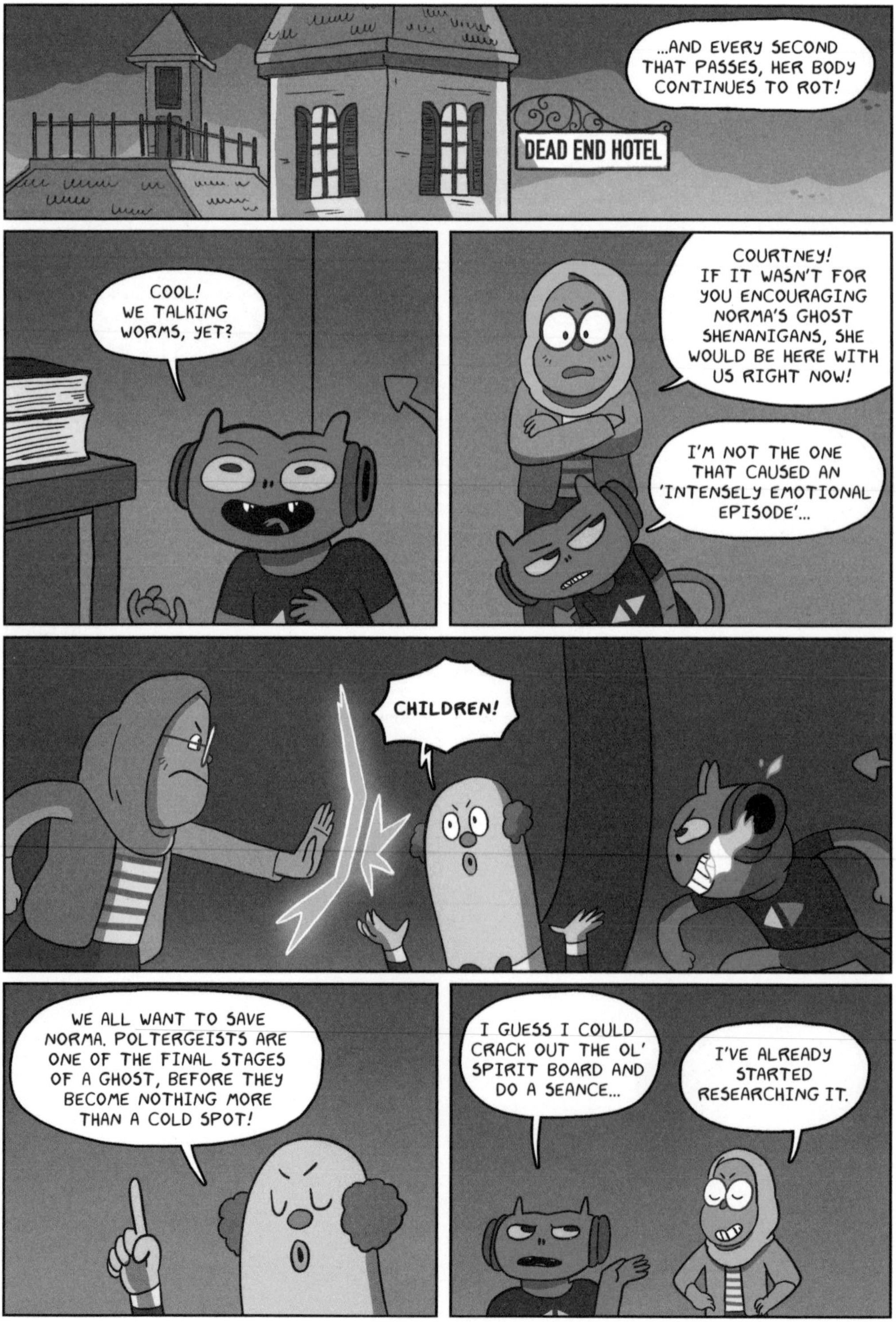
...AND EVERY SECOND THAT PASSES, HER BODY CONTINUES TO ROT!
DEAD END HOTEL
COOL! WE TALKING WORMS, YET?
COURTNEY! IF IT WASN'T FOR YOU ENCOURAGING NORMA'S GHOST SHENANIGANS, SHE WOULD BE HERE WITH US RIGHT NOW!
I'M NOT THE ONE THAT CAUSED AN 'INTENSELY EMOTIONAL EPISODE'...
CHILDREN!
WE ALL WANT TO SAVE NORMA. POLTERGEISTS ARE ONE OF THE FINAL STAGES OF A GHOST, BEFORE THEY BECOME NOTHING MORE THAN A COLD SPOT!
I GUESS I COULD CRACK OUT THE OL' SPIRIT BOARD AND DO A SEANCE...
I'VE ALREADY STARTED RESEARCHING IT.

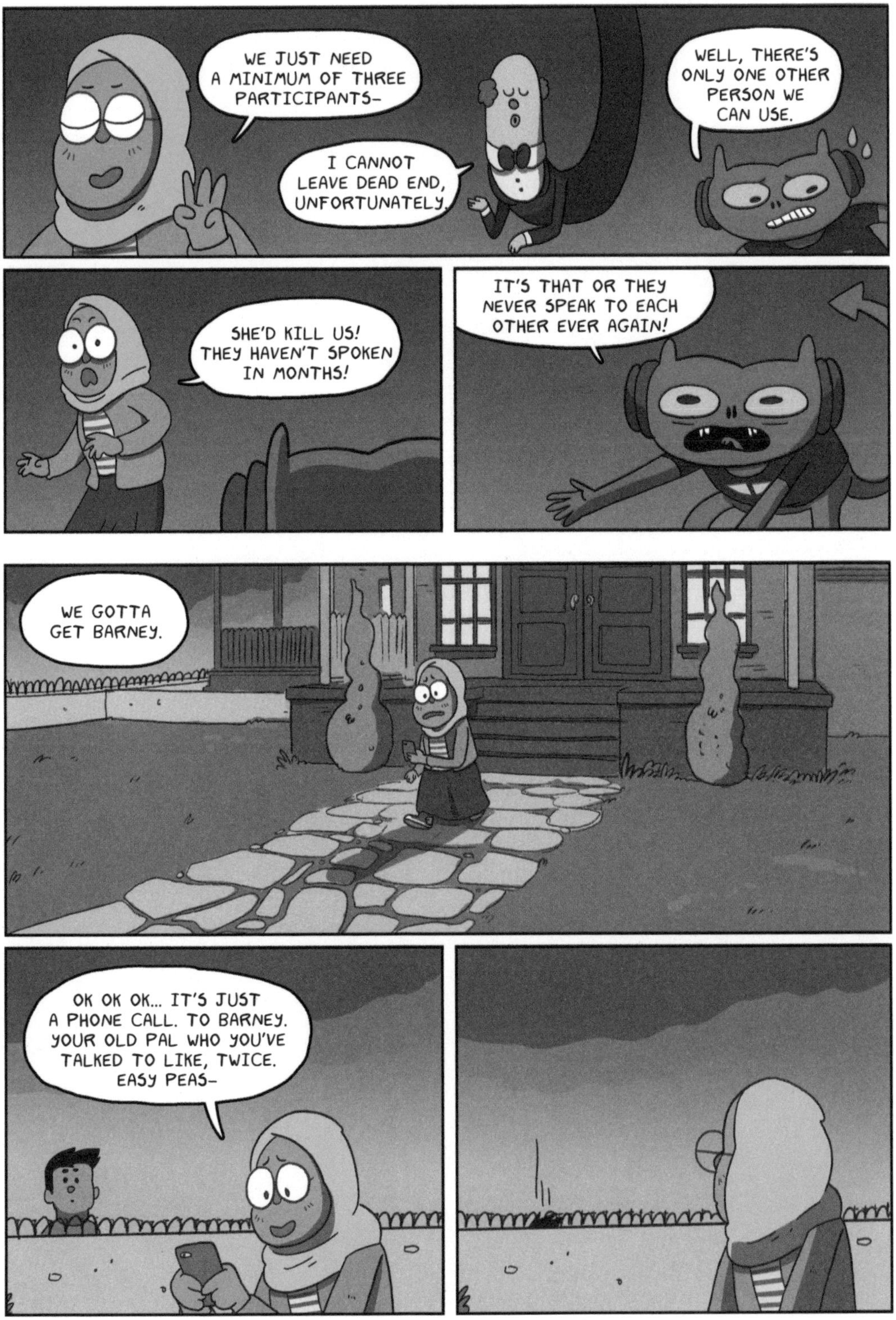
WE JUST NEED A MINIMUM OF THREE PARTICIPANTS-
I CANNOT LEAVE DEAD END, UNFORTUNATELY.
WELL, THERE'S ONLY ONE OTHER PERSON WE CAN USE.
SHE'D KILL US! THEY HAVEN'T SPOKEN IN MONTHS!
IT'S THAT OR THEY NEVER SPEAK TO EACH OTHER EVER AGAIN!
WE GOTTA GET BARNEY.
OK OK OK... IT'S JUST A PHONE CALL. TO BARNEY. YOUR OLD PAL WHO YOU'VE TALKED TO LIKE, TWICE. EASY PEAS-

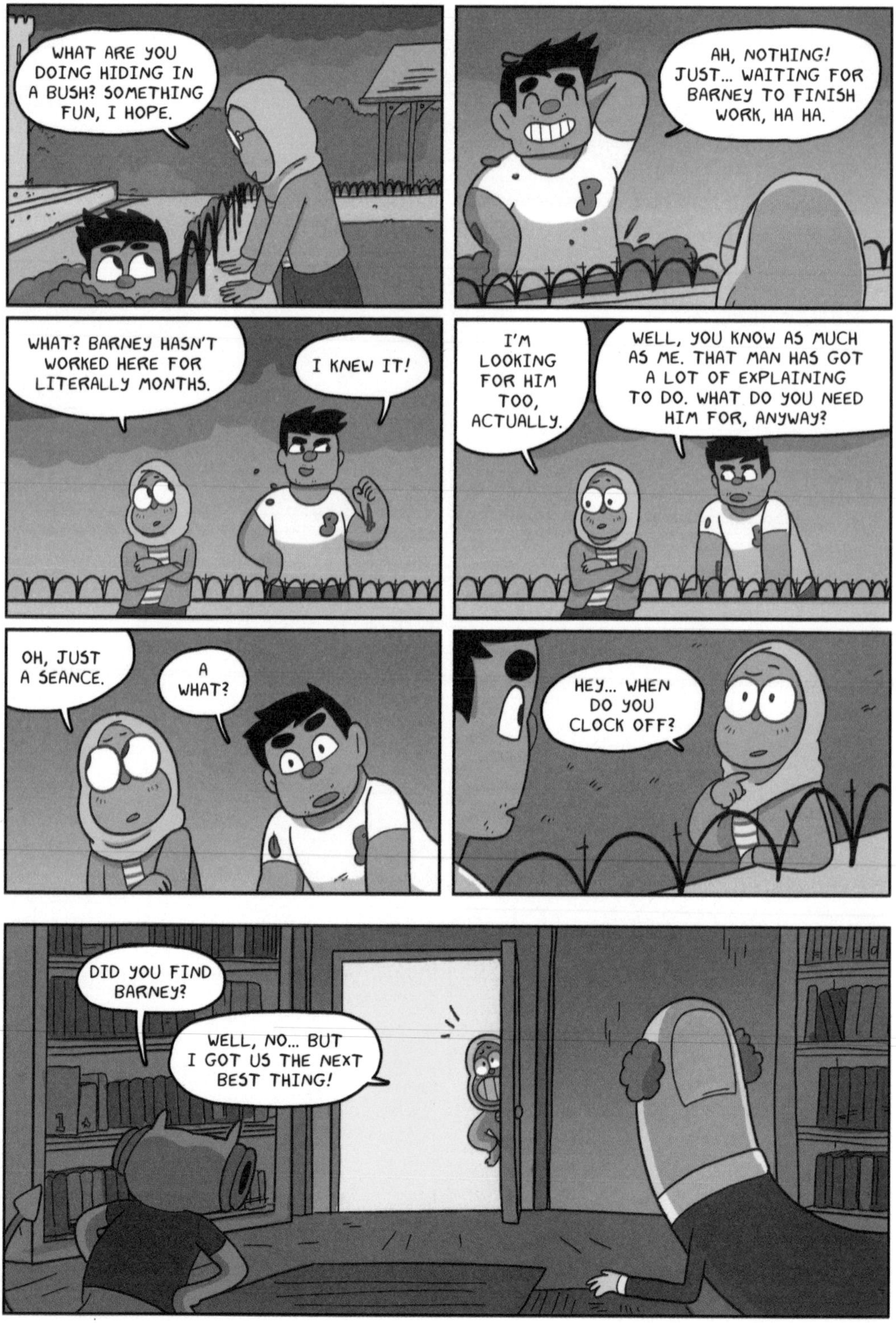
WHAT ARE YOU DOING HIDING IN A BUSH? SOMETHING FUN, I HOPE.
AH, NOTHING! JUST... WAITING FOR BARNEY TO FINISH WORK, HA HA.
WHAT? BARNEY HASN'T WORKED HERE FOR LITERALLY MONTHS.
I KNEW IT!
I'M LOOKING FOR HIM TOO, ACTUALLY.
WELL, YOU KNOW AS MUCH AS ME. THAT MAN HAS GOT A LOT OF EXPLAINING TO DO. WHAT DO YOU NEED HIM FOR, ANYWAY?
OH, JUST A SEANCE.
A WHAT?
HEY... WHEN DO YOU CLOCK OFF?
DID YOU FIND BARNEY?
WELL, NO... BUT I GOT US THE NEXT BEST THING!

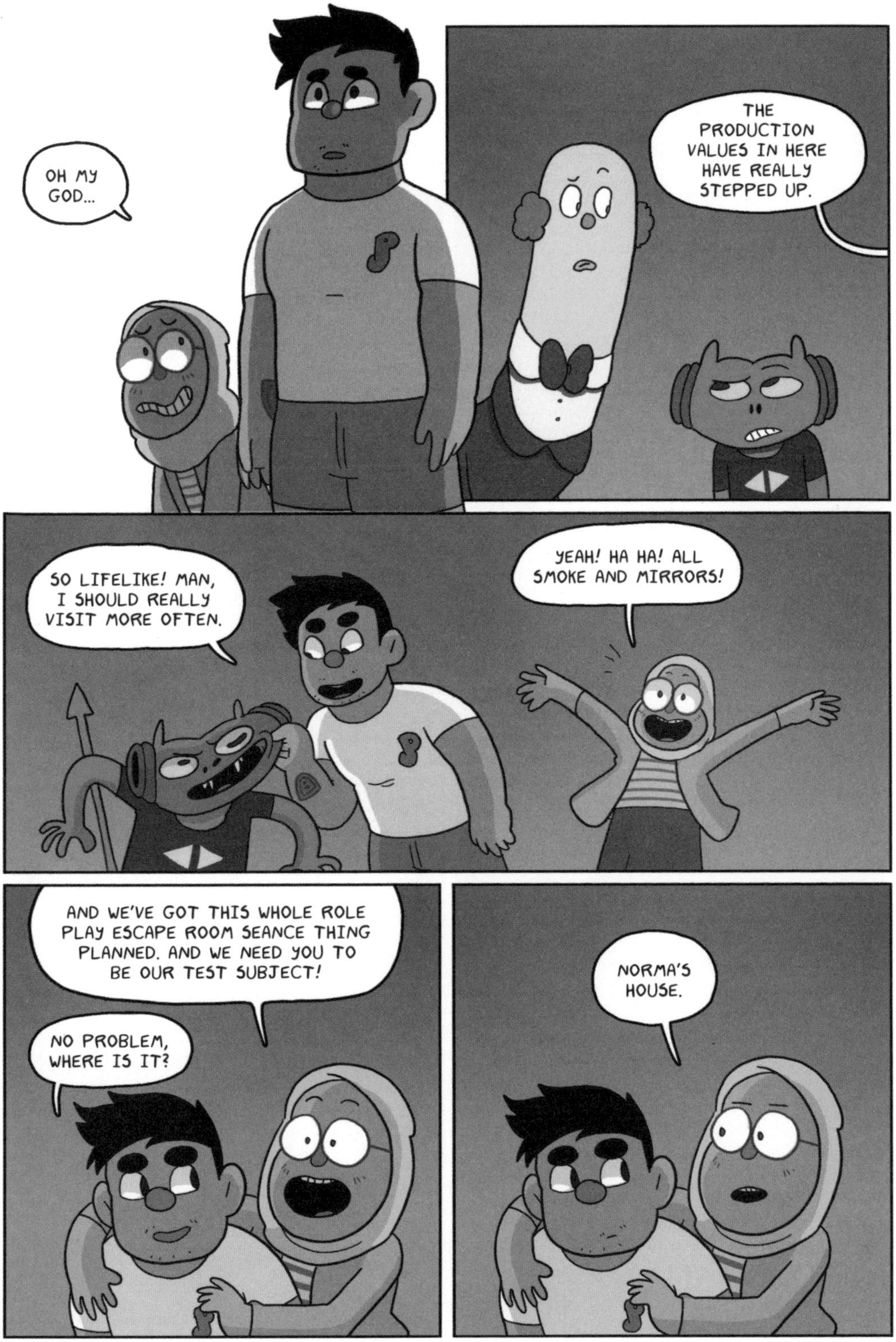
OH MY GOD...
THE PRODUCTION VALUES IN HERE HAVE REALLY STEPPED UP.
SO LIFELIKE! MAN, I SHOULD REALLY VISIT MORE OFTEN.
YEAH! HA HA! ALL SMOKE AND MIRRORS!
AND WE'VE GOT THIS WHOLE ROLE PLAY ESCAPE ROOM SEANCE THING PLANNED. AND WE NEED YOU TO BE OUR TEST SUBJECT!
NO PROBLEM, WHERE IS IT?
NORMA'S HOUSE.

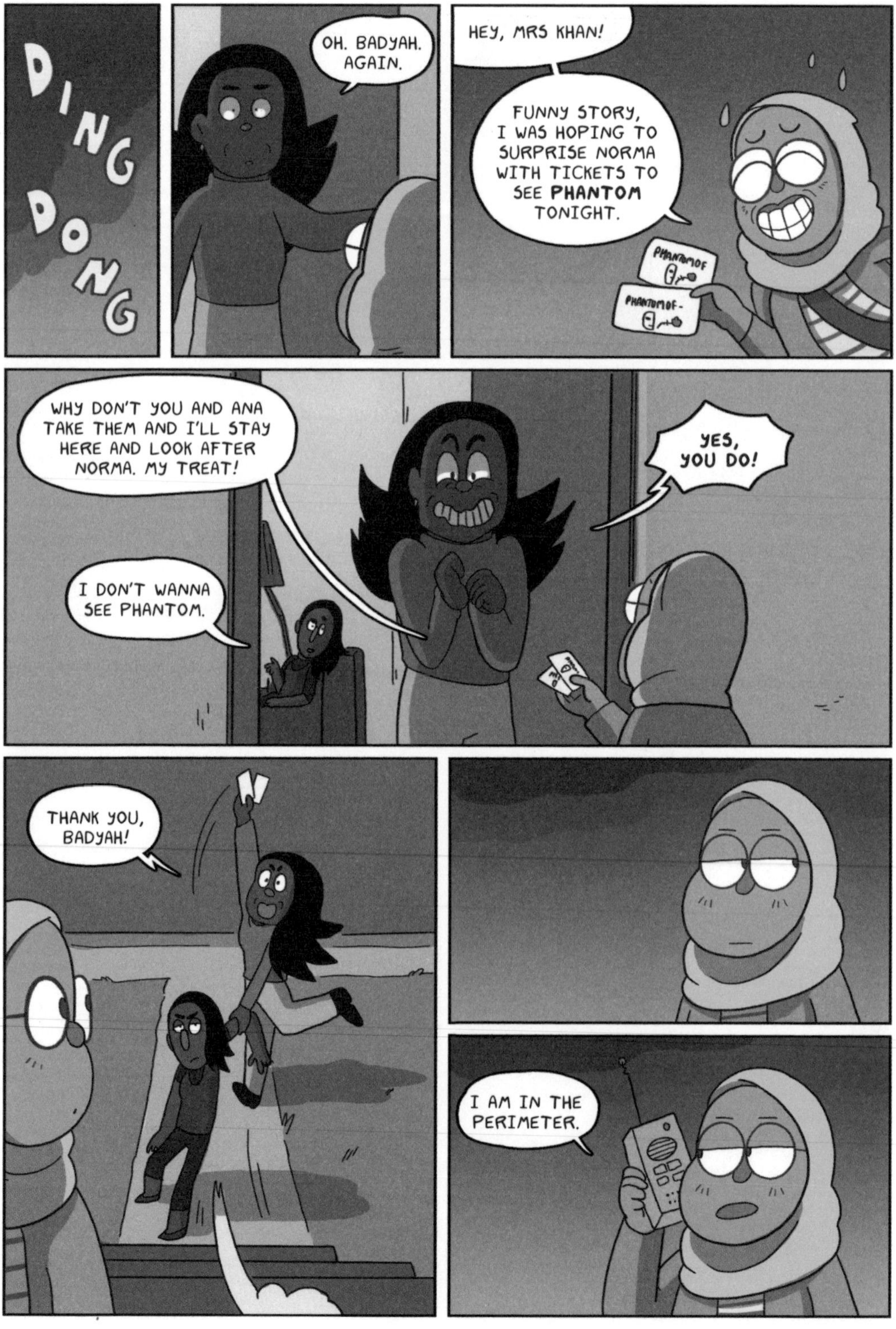
DING DONG
OH. BADYAH. AGAIN.
HEY, MRS KHAN!
FUNNY STORY, I WAS HOPING TO SURPRISE NORMA WITH TICKETS TO SEE **PHANTOM** TONIGHT.
PHANTOM OF
PHANTOM OF-
WHY DON'T YOU AND ANA TAKE THEM AND I'LL STAY HERE AND LOOK AFTER NORMA. MY TREAT!
YES, YOU DO!
I DON'T WANNA SEE PHANTOM.
THANK YOU, BADYAH!
I AM IN THE PERIMETER.

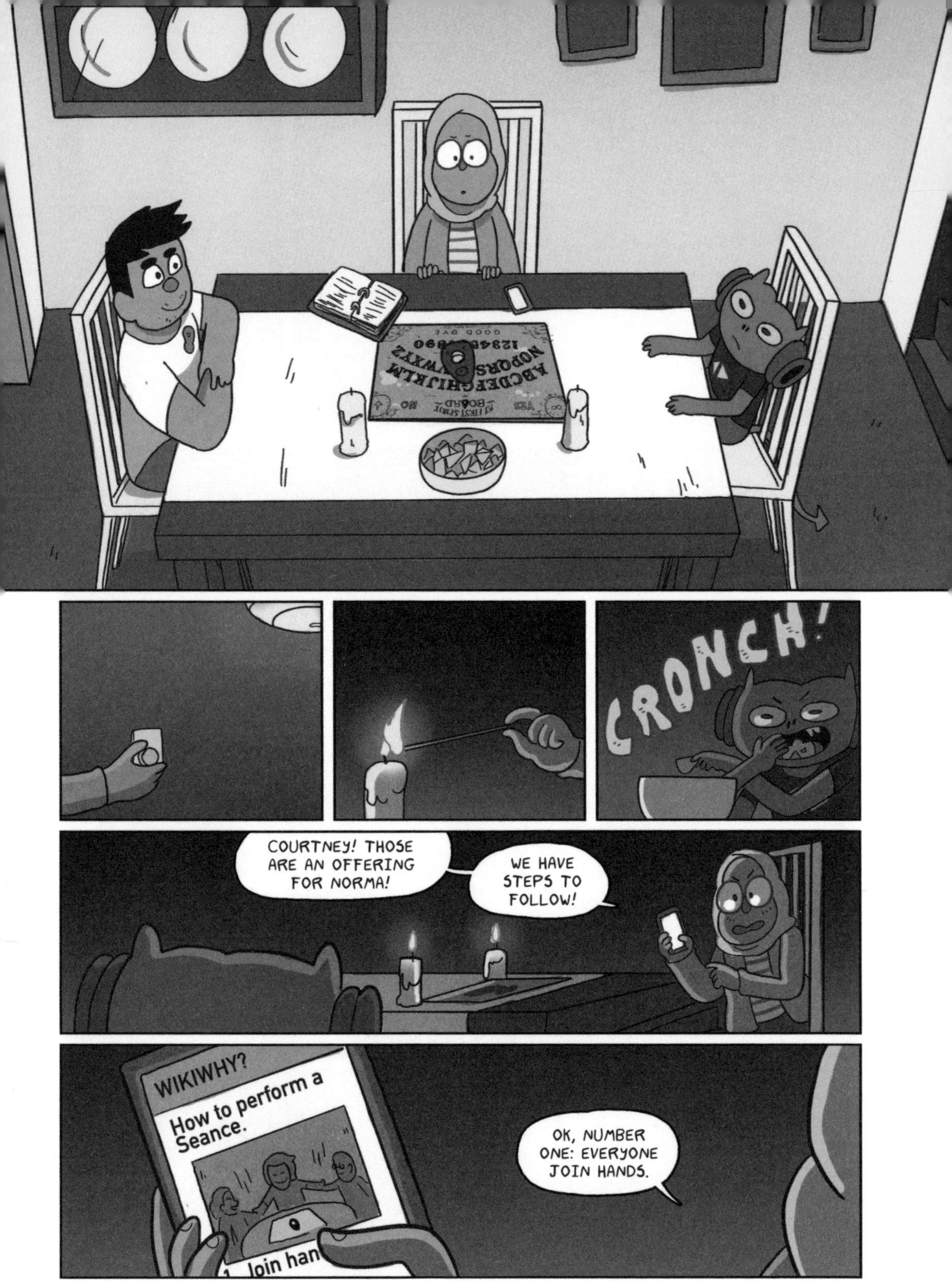
CRONCH!
COURTNEY! THOSE ARE AN OFFERING FOR NORMA!
WE HAVE STEPS TO FOLLOW!
WIKIWHY?
How to perform a Seance.
1. Join han
OK, NUMBER ONE: EVERYONE JOIN HANDS.

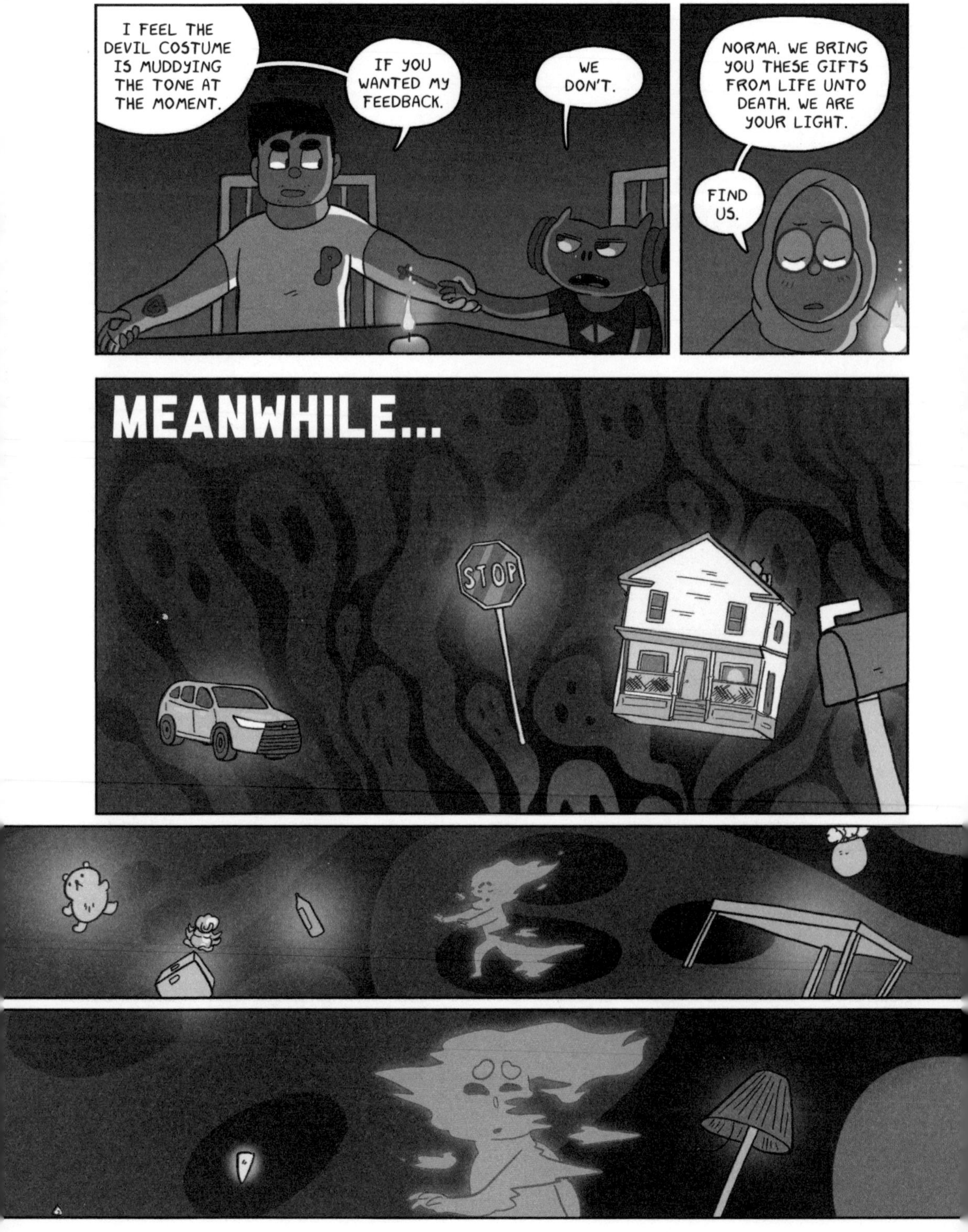
I FEEL THE DEVIL COSTUME IS MUDDYING THE TONE AT THE MOMENT.
IF YOU WANTED MY FEEDBACK.
WE DON'T.
NORMA. WE BRING YOU THESE GIFTS FROM LIFE UNTO DEATH. WE ARE YOUR LIGHT.
FIND US.
MEANWHILE...
STOP

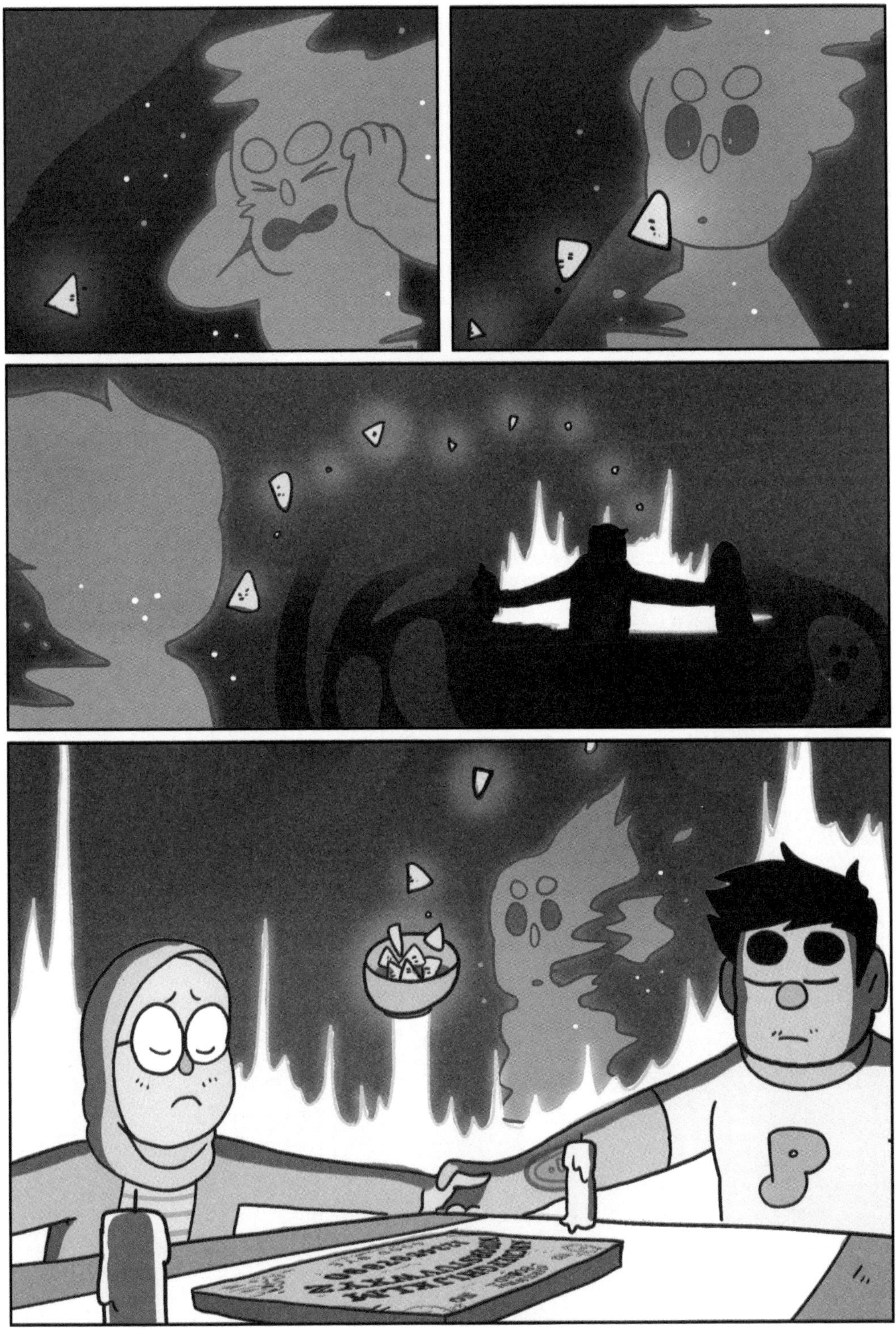

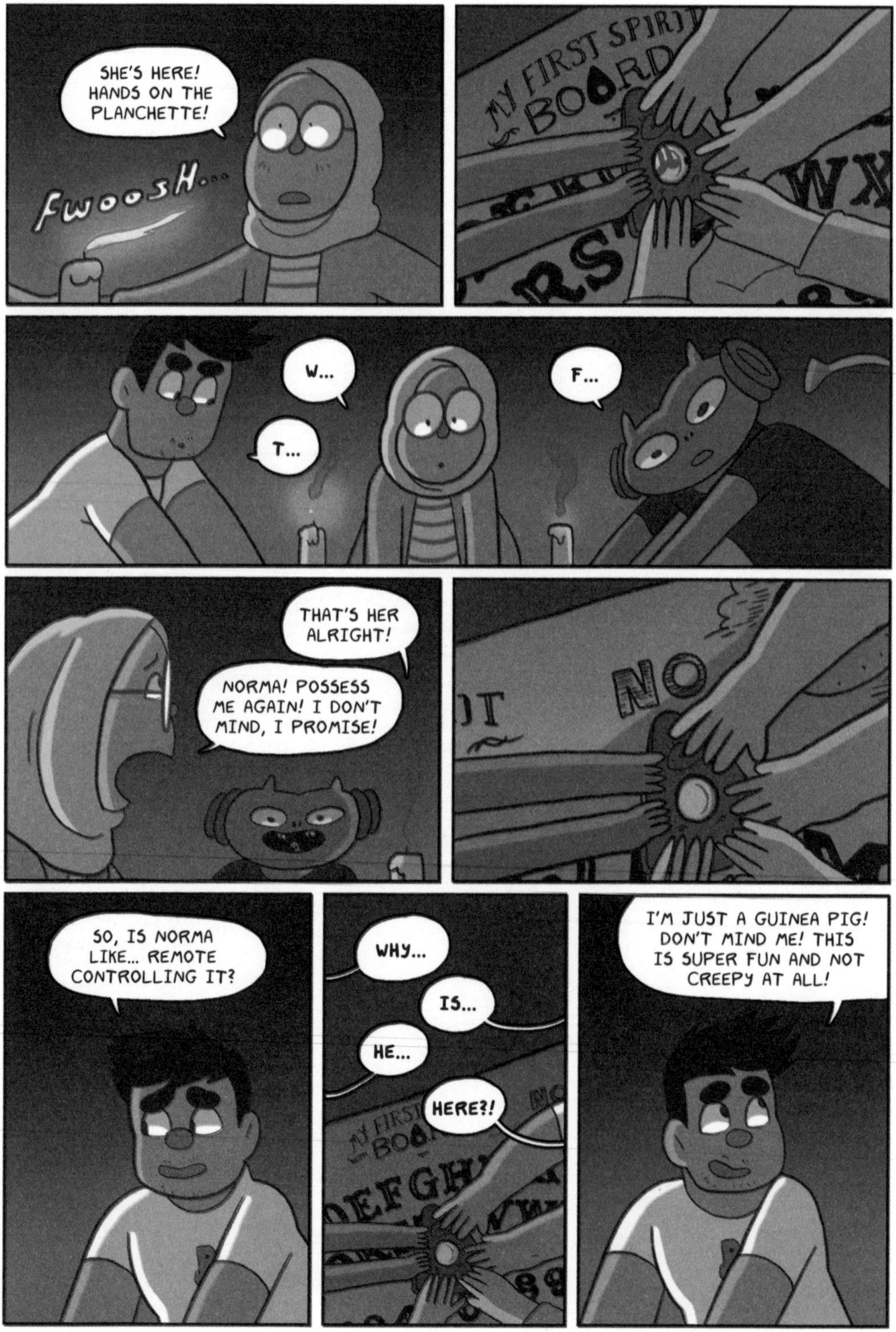
SHE'S HERE! HANDS ON THE PLANCHETTE!
FWOOSH...
MY FIRST SPIRIT BOARD
W...
T...
F...
THAT'S HER ALRIGHT!
NORMA! POSSESS ME AGAIN! I DON'T MIND, I PROMISE!
NO
SO, IS NORMA LIKE... REMOTE CONTROLLING IT?
WHY...
IS...
HE...
HERE?!
I'M JUST A GUINEA PIG! DON'T MIND ME! THIS IS SUPER FUN AND NOT CREEPY AT ALL!

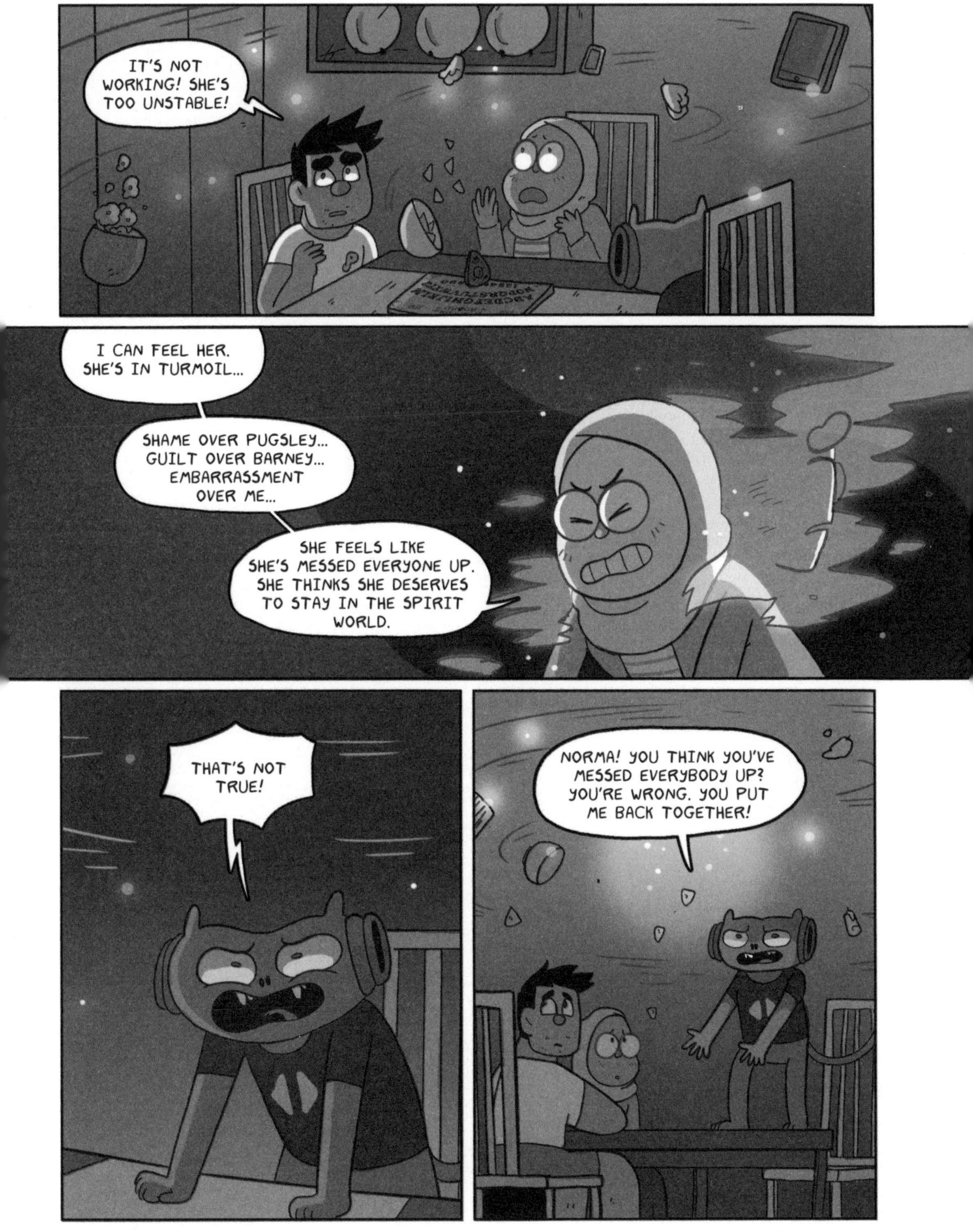
IT'S NOT WORKING! SHE'S TOO UNSTABLE!
I CAN FEEL HER. SHE'S IN TURMOIL...
SHAME OVER PUGSLEY... GUILT OVER BARNEY... EMBARRASSMENT OVER ME...
SHE FEELS LIKE SHE'S MESSED EVERYONE UP. SHE THINKS SHE DESERVES TO STAY IN THE SPIRIT WORLD.
THAT'S NOT TRUE!
NORMA! YOU THINK YOU'VE MESSED EVERYBODY UP? YOU'RE WRONG. YOU PUT ME BACK TOGETHER!

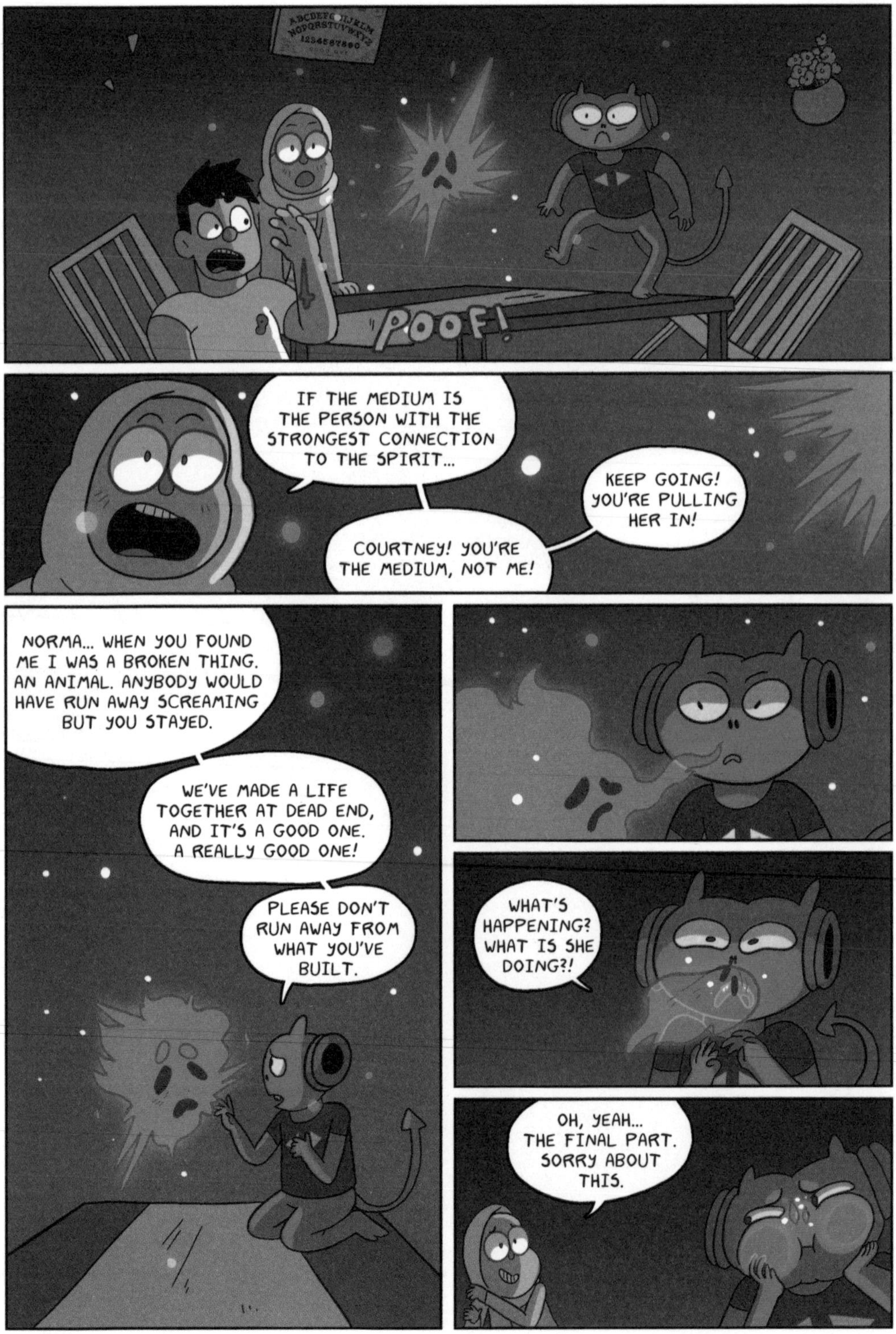
POOF!
IF THE MEDIUM IS THE PERSON WITH THE STRONGEST CONNECTION TO THE SPIRIT...
COURTNEY! YOU'RE THE MEDIUM, NOT ME!
KEEP GOING! YOU'RE PULLING HER IN!
NORMA... WHEN YOU FOUND ME I WAS A BROKEN THING. AN ANIMAL. ANYBODY WOULD HAVE RUN AWAY SCREAMING BUT YOU STAYED.
WE'VE MADE A LIFE TOGETHER AT DEAD END, AND IT'S A GOOD ONE. A REALLY GOOD ONE!
PLEASE DON'T RUN AWAY FROM WHAT YOU'VE BUILT.
WHAT'S HAPPENING? WHAT IS SHE DOING?!
OH, YEAH... THE FINAL PART. SORRY ABOUT THIS.

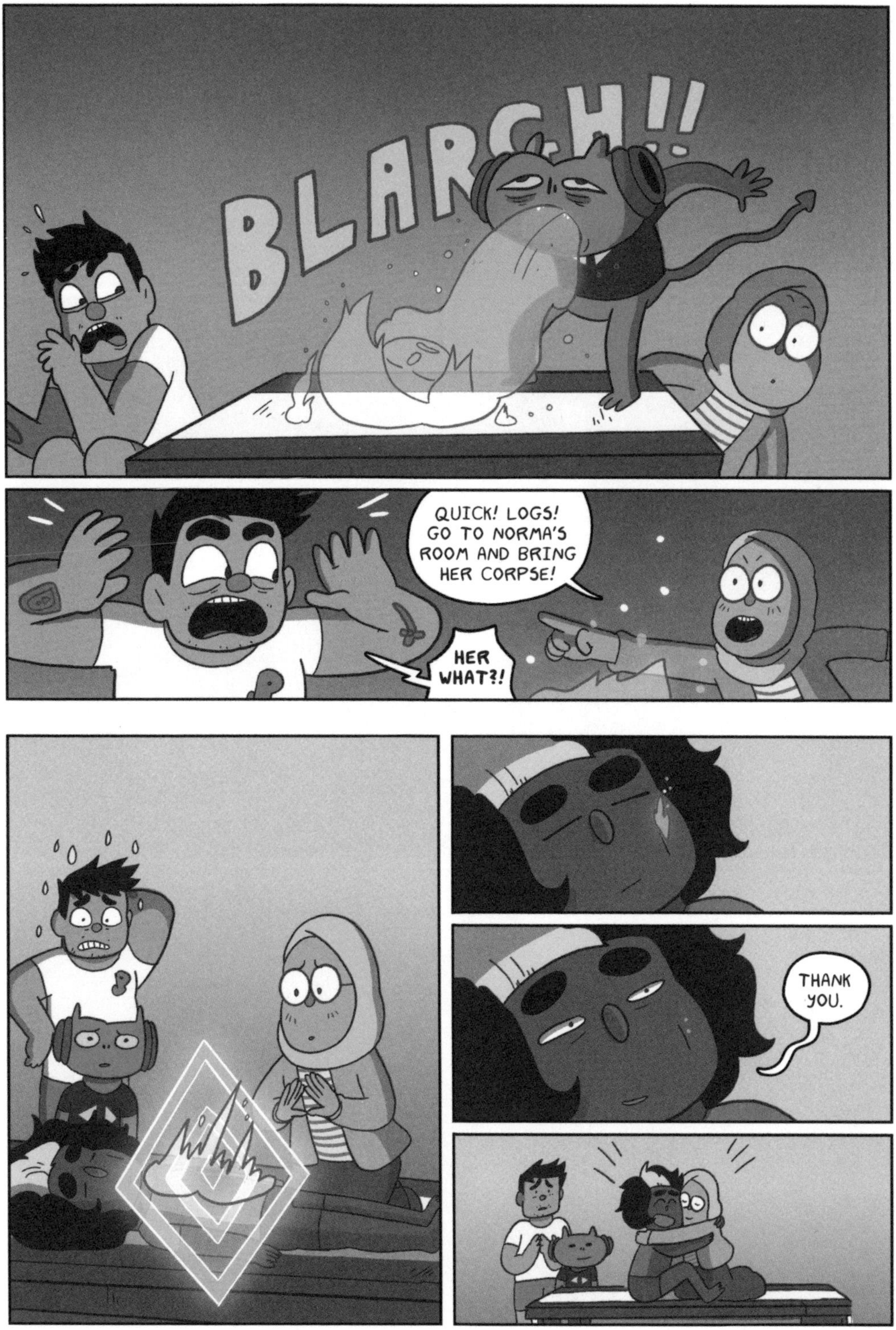
BLARGH!!
QUICK! LOGS! GO TO NORMA'S ROOM AND BRING HER CORPSE!
HER WHAT?!
THANK YOU.

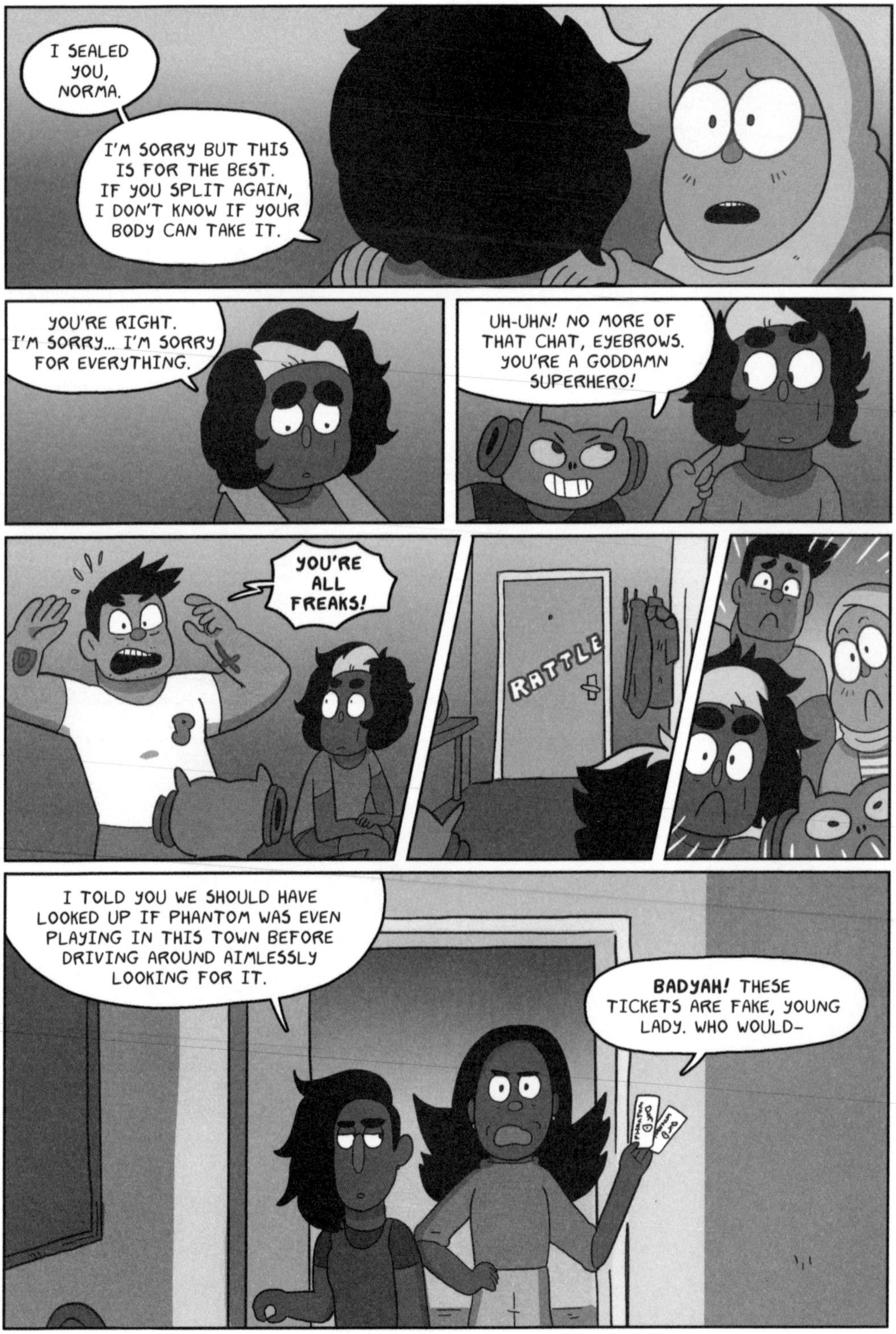
I SEALED YOU, NORMA.
I'M SORRY BUT THIS IS FOR THE BEST. IF YOU SPLIT AGAIN, I DON'T KNOW IF YOUR BODY CAN TAKE IT.
YOU'RE RIGHT. I'M SORRY... I'M SORRY FOR EVERYTHING.
UH-UHN! NO MORE OF THAT CHAT, EYEBROWS. YOU'RE A GODDAMN SUPERHERO!
YOU'RE ALL FREAKS!
RATTLE
I TOLD YOU WE SHOULD HAVE LOOKED UP IF PHANTOM WAS EVEN PLAYING IN THIS TOWN BEFORE DRIVING AROUND AIMLESSLY LOOKING FOR IT.
BADYAH! THESE TICKETS ARE FAKE, YOUNG LADY. WHO WOULD-

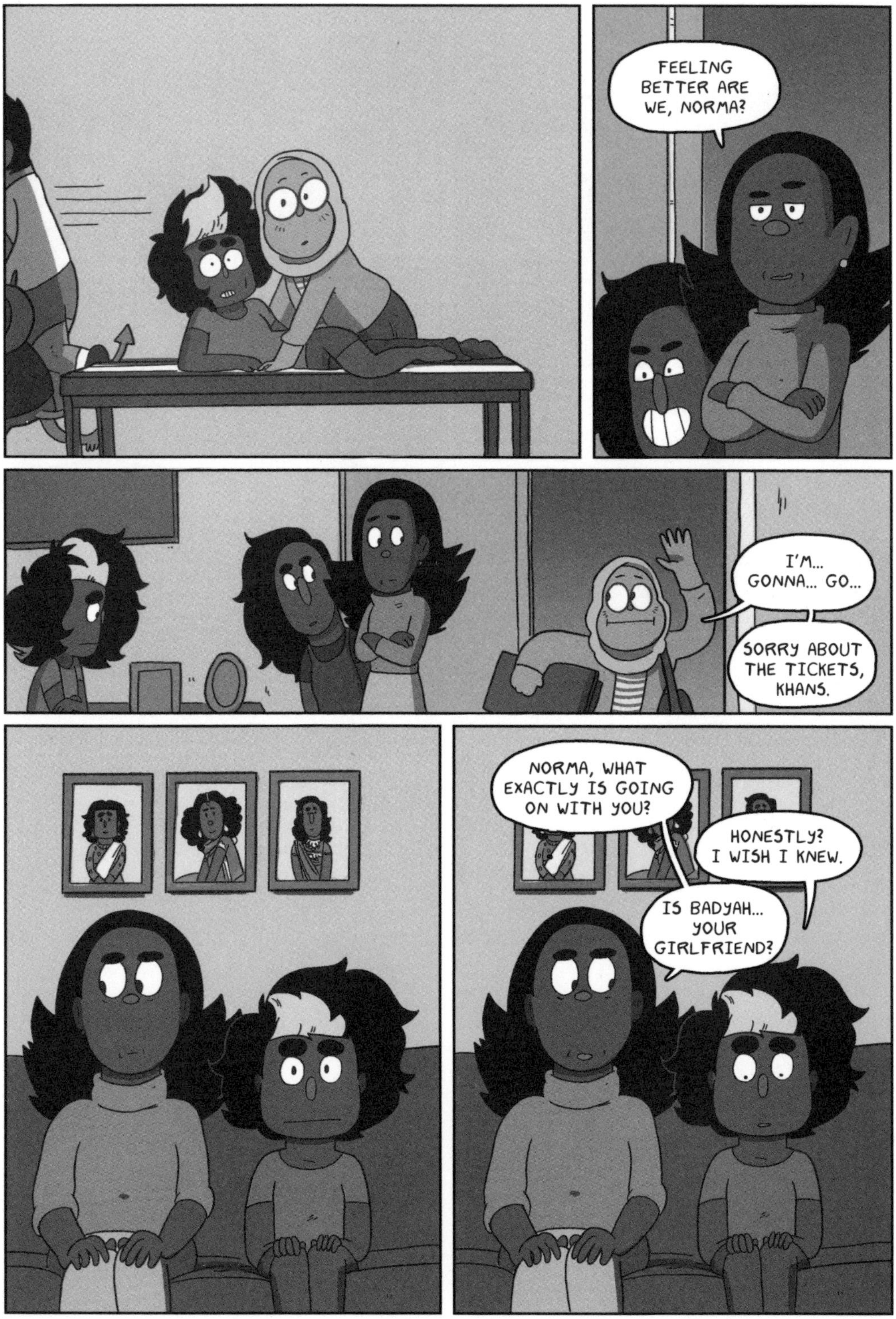
FEELING BETTER ARE WE, NORMA?
I'M... GONNA... GO...
SORRY ABOUT THE TICKETS, KHANS.
NORMA, WHAT EXACTLY IS GOING ON WITH YOU?
HONESTLY? I WISH I KNEW.
IS BADYAH... YOUR GIRLFRIEND?

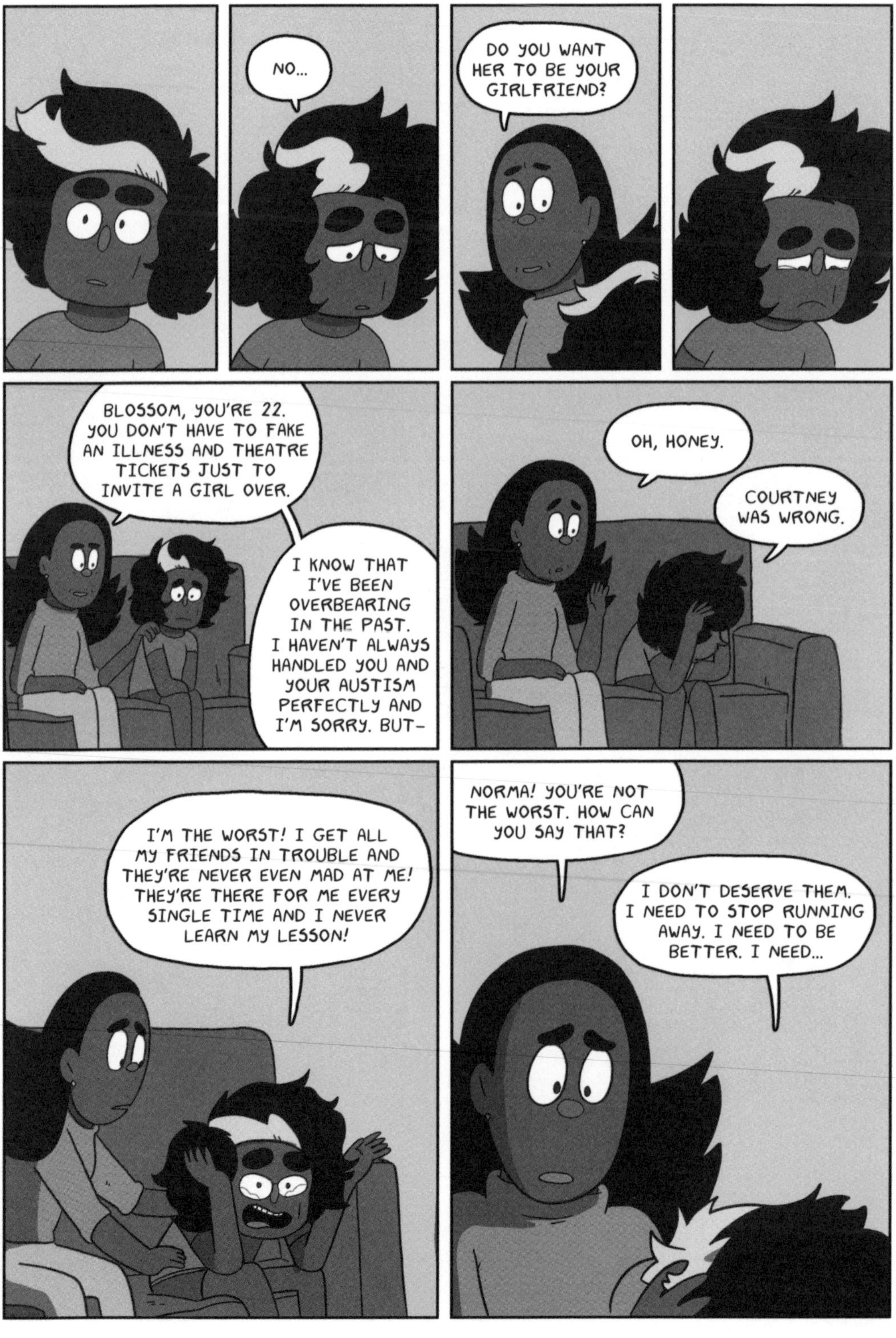
NO...
DO YOU WANT HER TO BE YOUR GIRLFRIEND?
BLOSSOM, YOU'RE 22. YOU DON'T HAVE TO FAKE AN ILLNESS AND THEATRE TICKETS JUST TO INVITE A GIRL OVER.
I KNOW THAT I'VE BEEN OVERBEARING IN THE PAST. I HAVEN'T ALWAYS HANDLED YOU AND YOUR AUSTISM PERFECTLY AND I'M SORRY. BUT-
OH, HONEY.
COURTNEY WAS WRONG.
I'M THE WORST! I GET ALL MY FRIENDS IN TROUBLE AND THEY'RE NEVER EVEN MAD AT ME! THEY'RE THERE FOR ME EVERY SINGLE TIME AND I NEVER LEARN MY LESSON!
NORMA! YOU'RE NOT THE WORST. HOW CAN YOU SAY THAT?
I DON'T DESERVE THEM. I NEED TO STOP RUNNING AWAY. I NEED TO BE BETTER. I NEED...

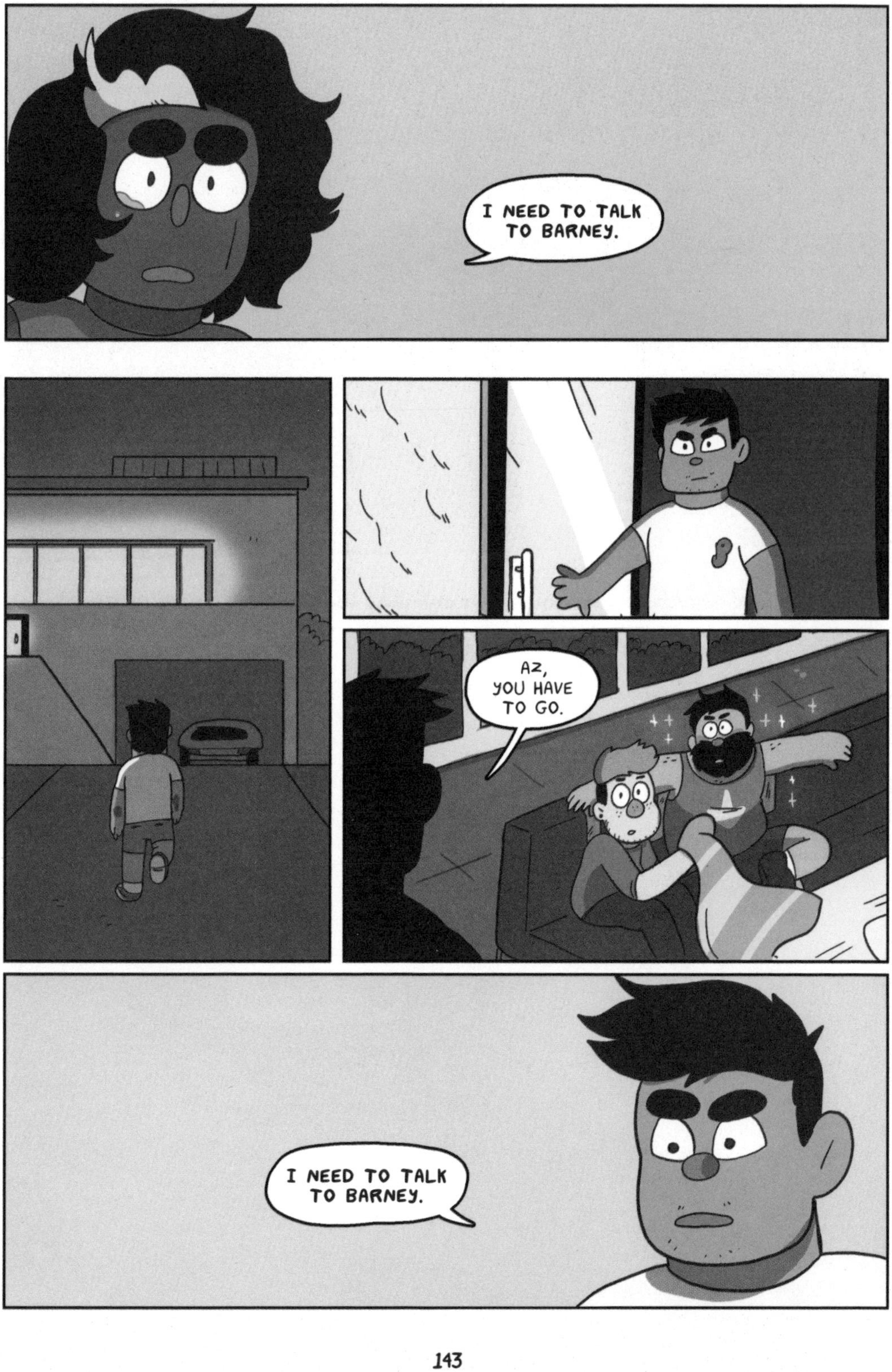
I NEED TO TALK TO BARNEY.
AZ, YOU HAVE TO GO.
I NEED TO TALK TO BARNEY.

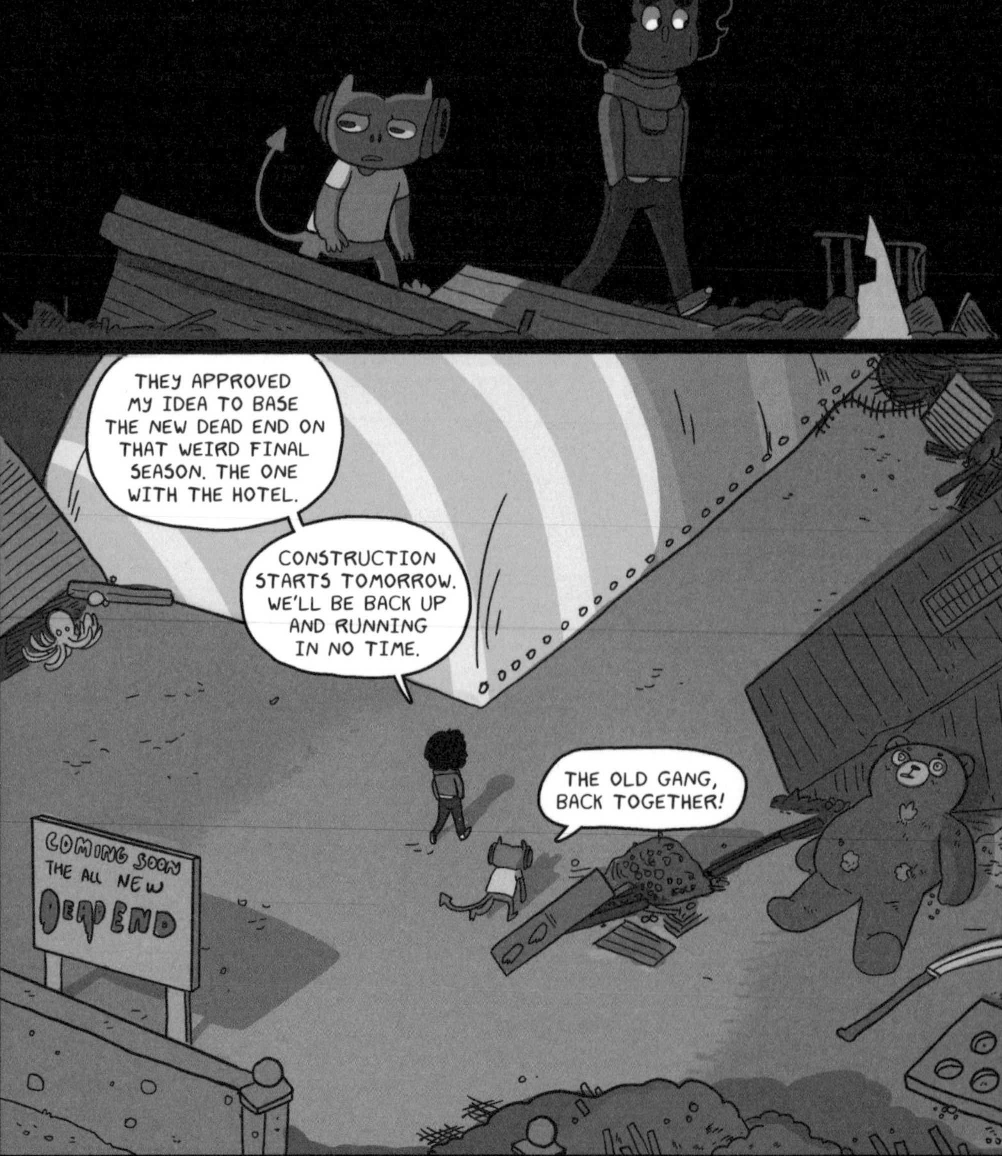
THEY APPROVED MY IDEA TO BASE THE NEW DEAD END ON THAT WEIRD FINAL SEASON. THE ONE WITH THE HOTEL.
CONSTRUCTION STARTS TOMORROW. WE'LL BE BACK UP AND RUNNING IN NO TIME.
THE OLD GANG, BACK TOGETHER!
COMING SOON THE ALL NEW DEAD END

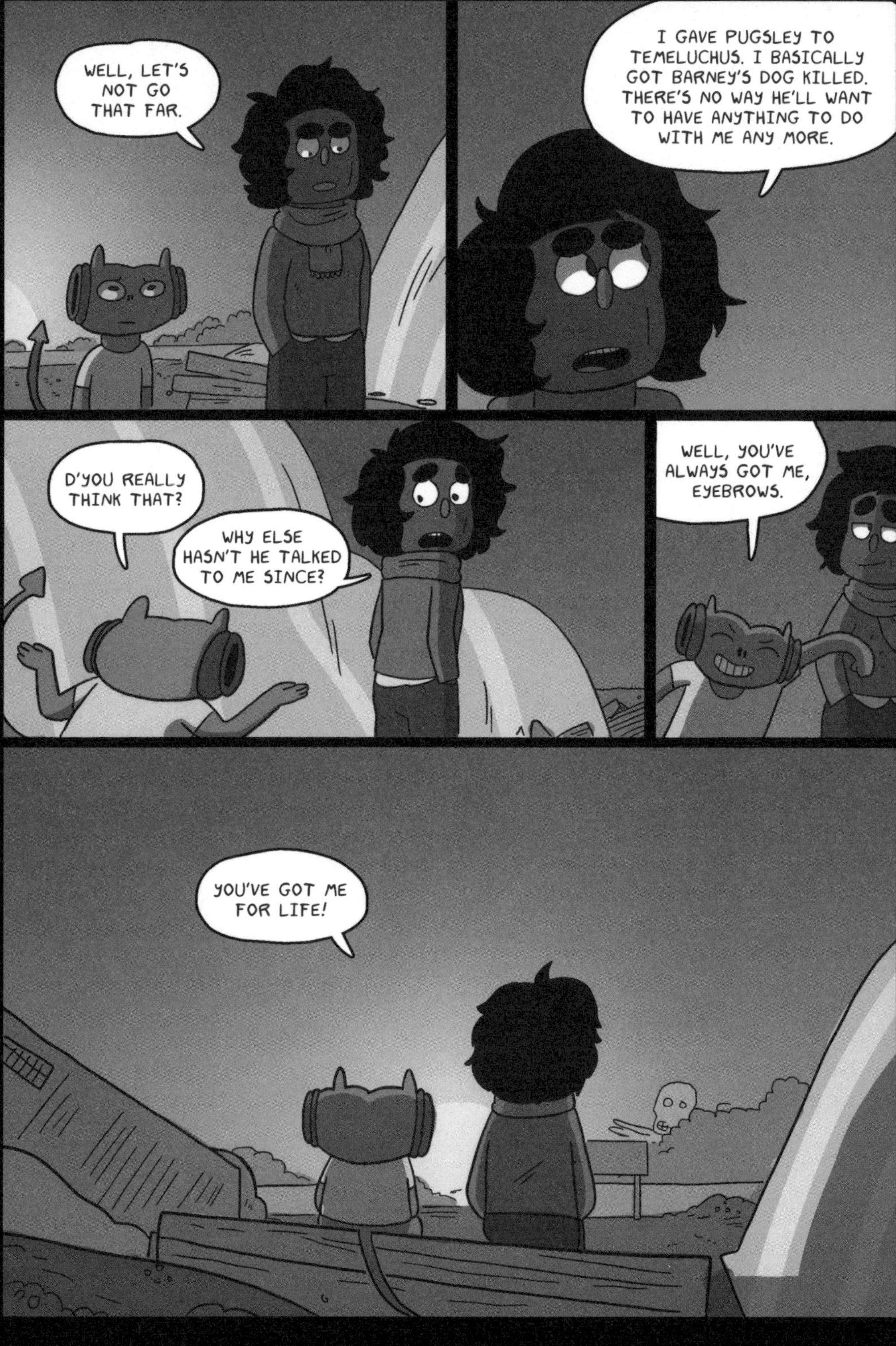
WELL, LET'S NOT GO THAT FAR.
I GAVE PUGSLEY TO TEMELUCHUS. I BASICALLY GOT BARNEY'S DOG KILLED. THERE'S NO WAY HE'LL WANT TO HAVE ANYTHING TO DO WITH ME ANY MORE.
D'YOU REALLY THINK THAT?
WHY ELSE HASN'T HE TALKED TO ME SINCE?
WELL, YOU'VE ALWAYS GOT ME, EYEBROWS.
YOU'VE GOT ME FOR LIFE!

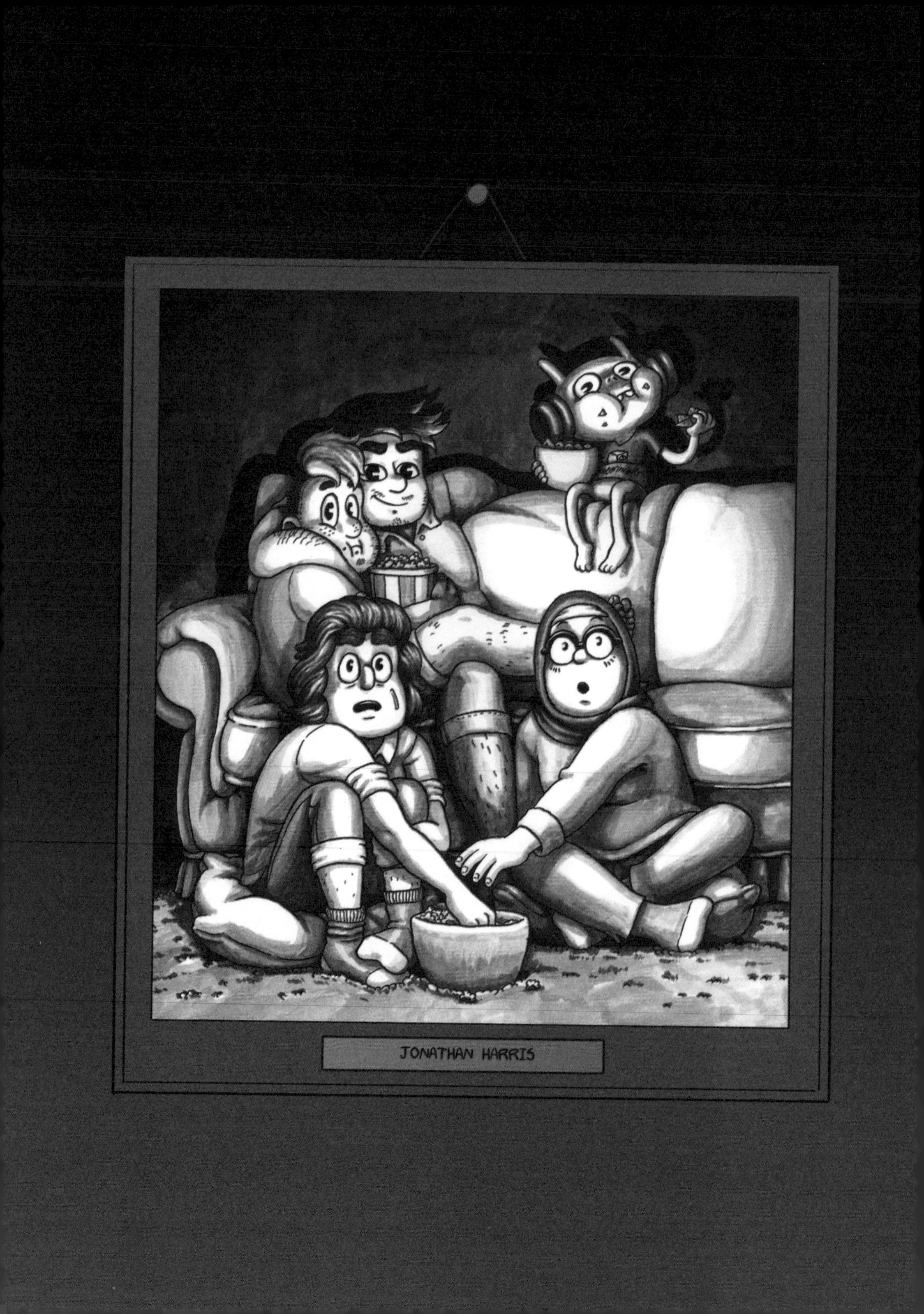
JONATHAN HARRIS

CHAPTER 6
HEEL TURN

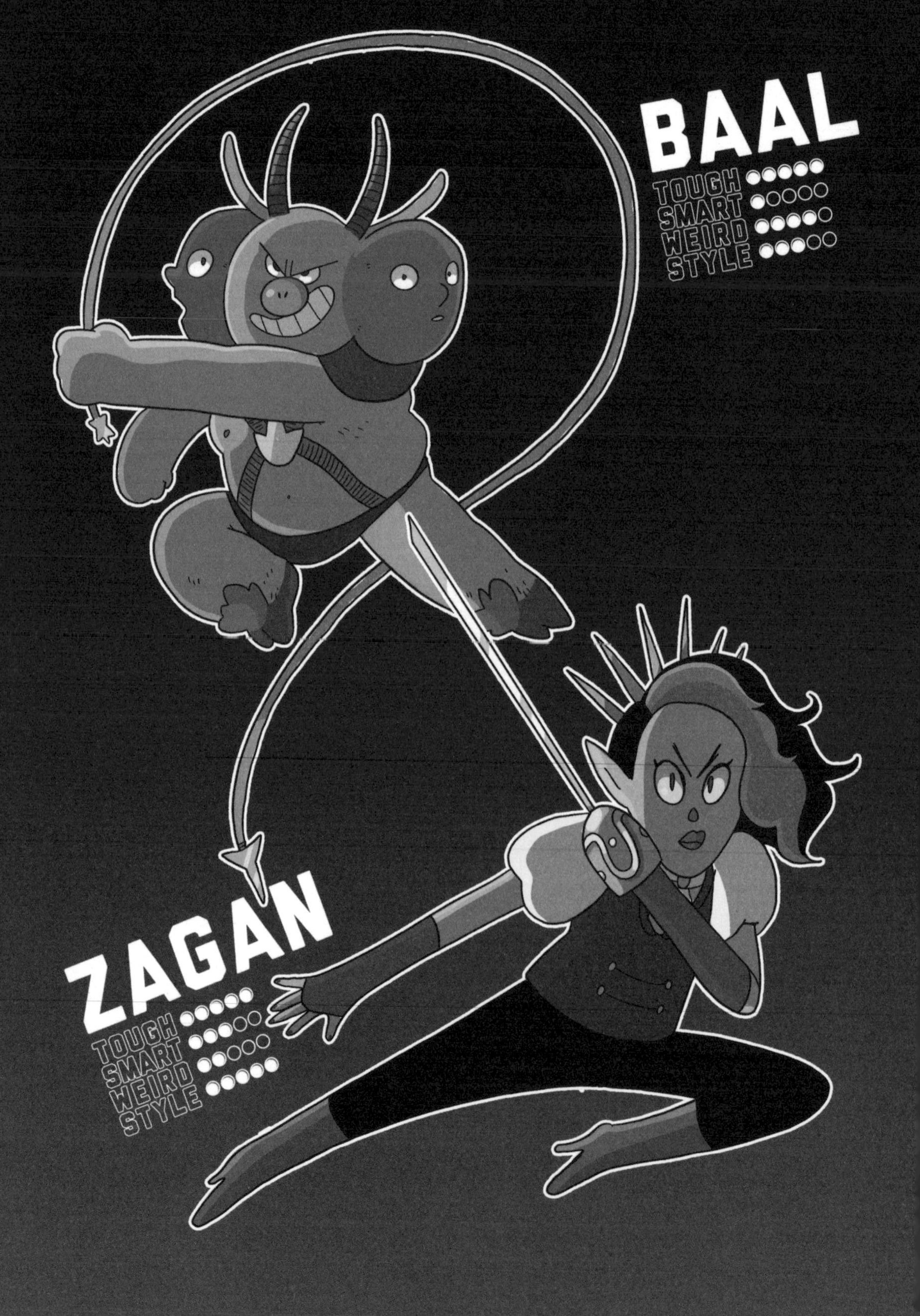
BAAL
TOUGH
SMART
WEIRD
STYLE
ZAGAN
TOUGH
SMART
WEIRD
STYLE

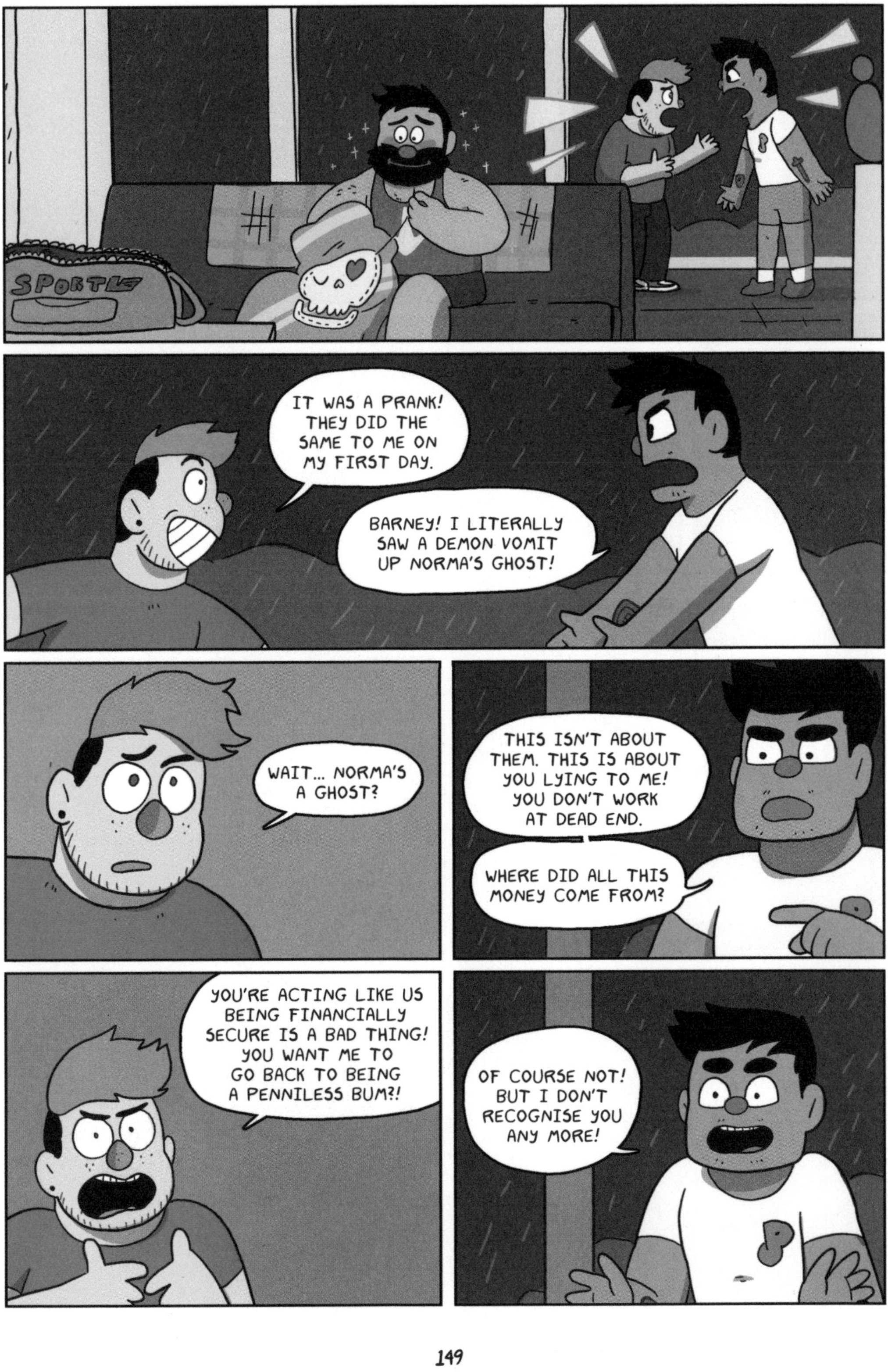

IT WAS A PRANK! THEY DID THE SAME TO ME ON MY FIRST DAY.
BARNEY! I LITERALLY SAW A DEMON VOMIT UP NORMA'S GHOST!
WAIT... NORMA'S A GHOST?
THIS ISN'T ABOUT THEM. THIS IS ABOUT YOU LYING TO ME! YOU DON'T WORK AT DEAD END.
WHERE DID ALL THIS MONEY COME FROM?
YOU'RE ACTING LIKE US BEING FINANCIALLY SECURE IS A BAD THING! YOU WANT ME TO GO BACK TO BEING A PENNILESS BUM?!
OF COURSE NOT! BUT I DON'T RECOGNISE YOU ANY MORE!

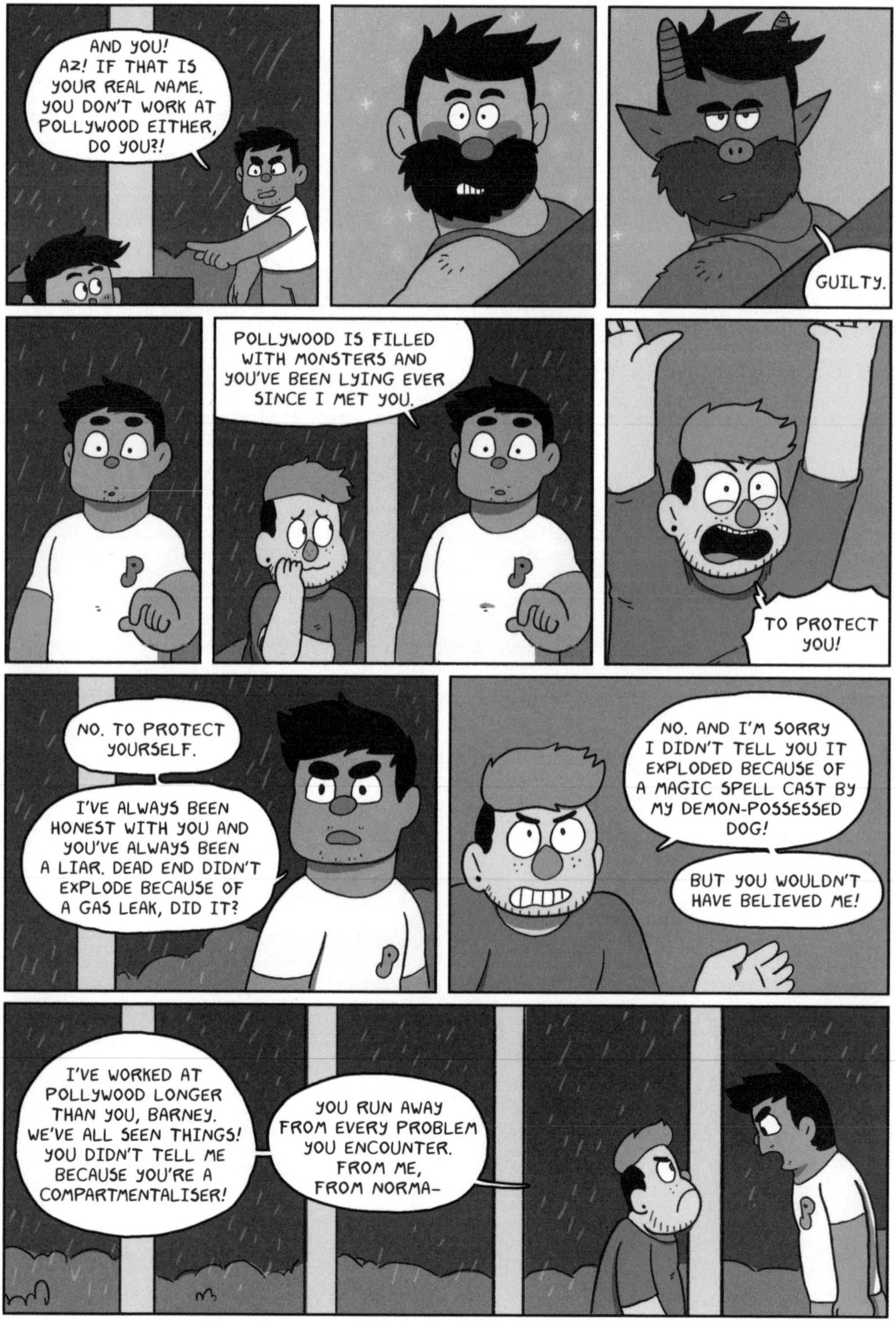
AND YOU! AZ! IF THAT IS YOUR REAL NAME. YOU DON'T WORK AT POLLYWOOD EITHER, DO YOU?!
GUILTY.
POLLYWOOD IS FILLED WITH MONSTERS AND YOU'VE BEEN LYING EVER SINCE I MET YOU.
TO PROTECT YOU!
NO. TO PROTECT YOURSELF.
I'VE ALWAYS BEEN HONEST WITH YOU AND YOU'VE ALWAYS BEEN A LIAR. DEAD END DIDN'T EXPLODE BECAUSE OF A GAS LEAK, DID IT?
NO. AND I'M SORRY I DIDN'T TELL YOU IT EXPLODED BECAUSE OF A MAGIC SPELL CAST BY MY DEMON-POSSESSED DOG!
BUT YOU WOULDN'T HAVE BELIEVED ME!
I'VE WORKED AT POLLYWOOD LONGER THAN YOU, BARNEY. WE'VE ALL SEEN THINGS! YOU DIDN'T TELL ME BECAUSE YOU'RE A COMPARTMENTALISER!
YOU RUN AWAY FROM EVERY PROBLEM YOU ENCOUNTER. FROM ME, FROM NORMA-

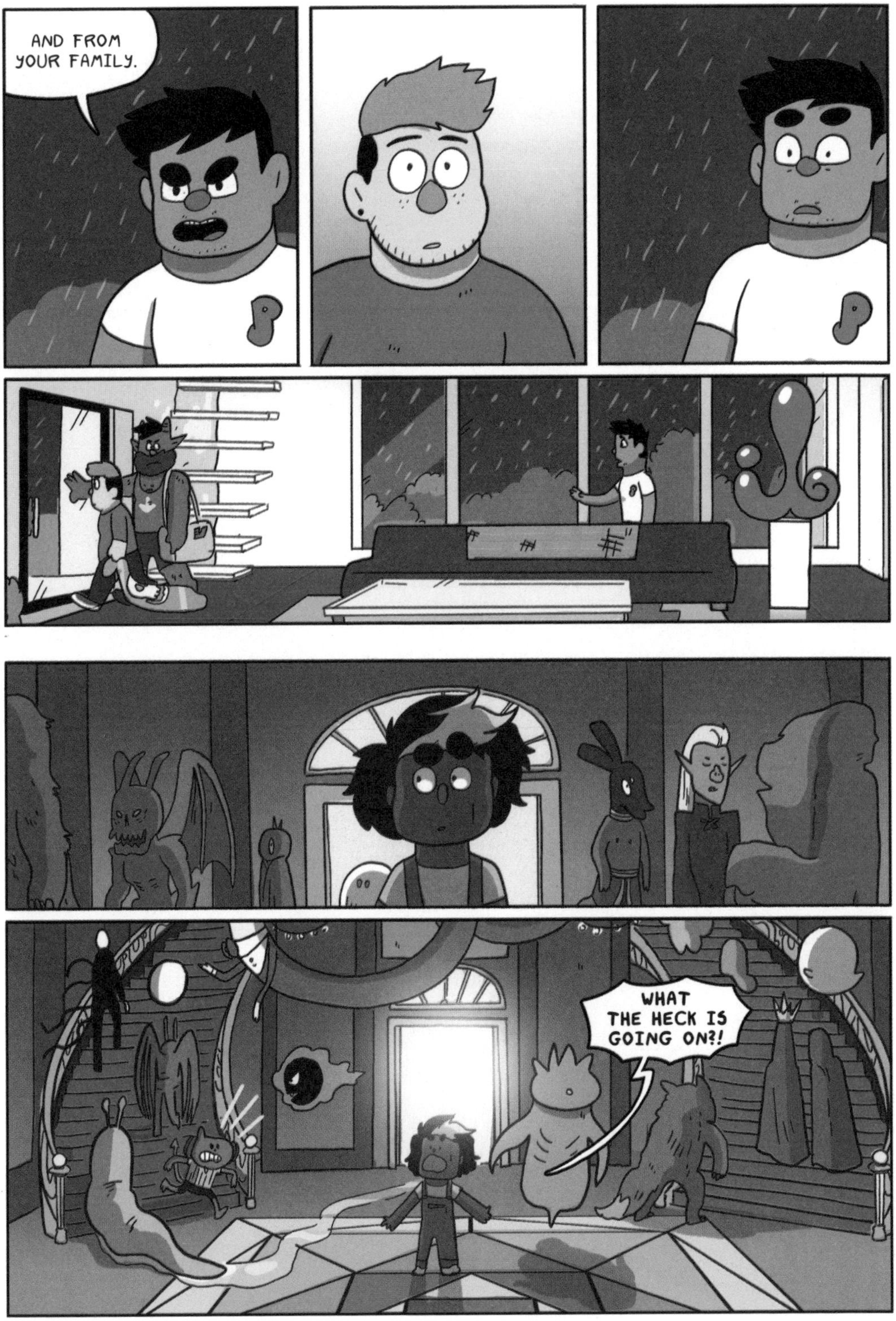
AND FROM YOUR FAMILY.
WHAT THE HECK IS GOING ON?!

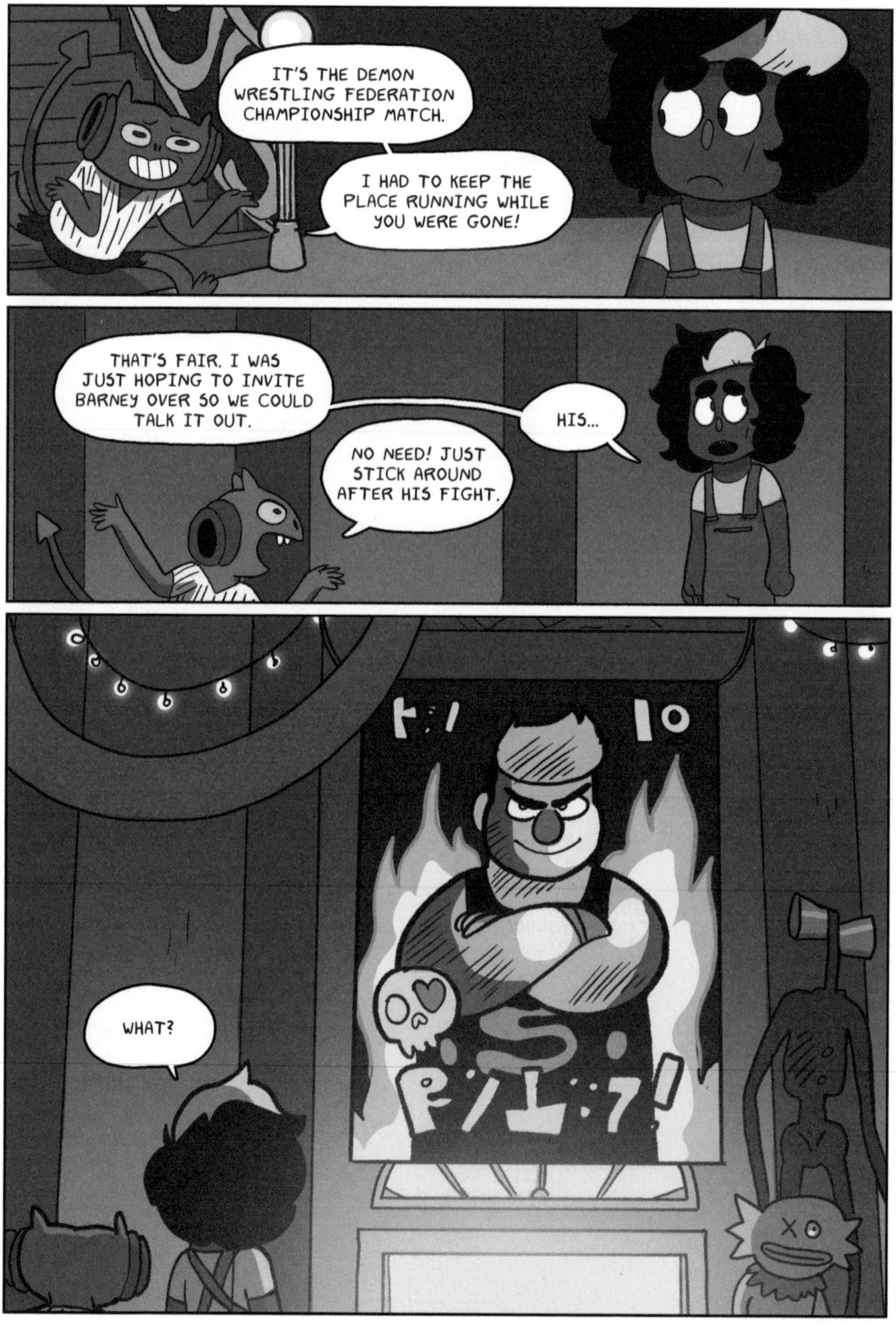
IT'S THE DEMON WRESTLING FEDERATION CHAMPIONSHIP MATCH.
I HAD TO KEEP THE PLACE RUNNING WHILE YOU WERE GONE!
THAT'S FAIR. I WAS JUST HOPING TO INVITE BARNEY OVER SO WE COULD TALK IT OUT.
NO NEED! JUST STICK AROUND AFTER HIS FIGHT.
HIS...
WHAT?

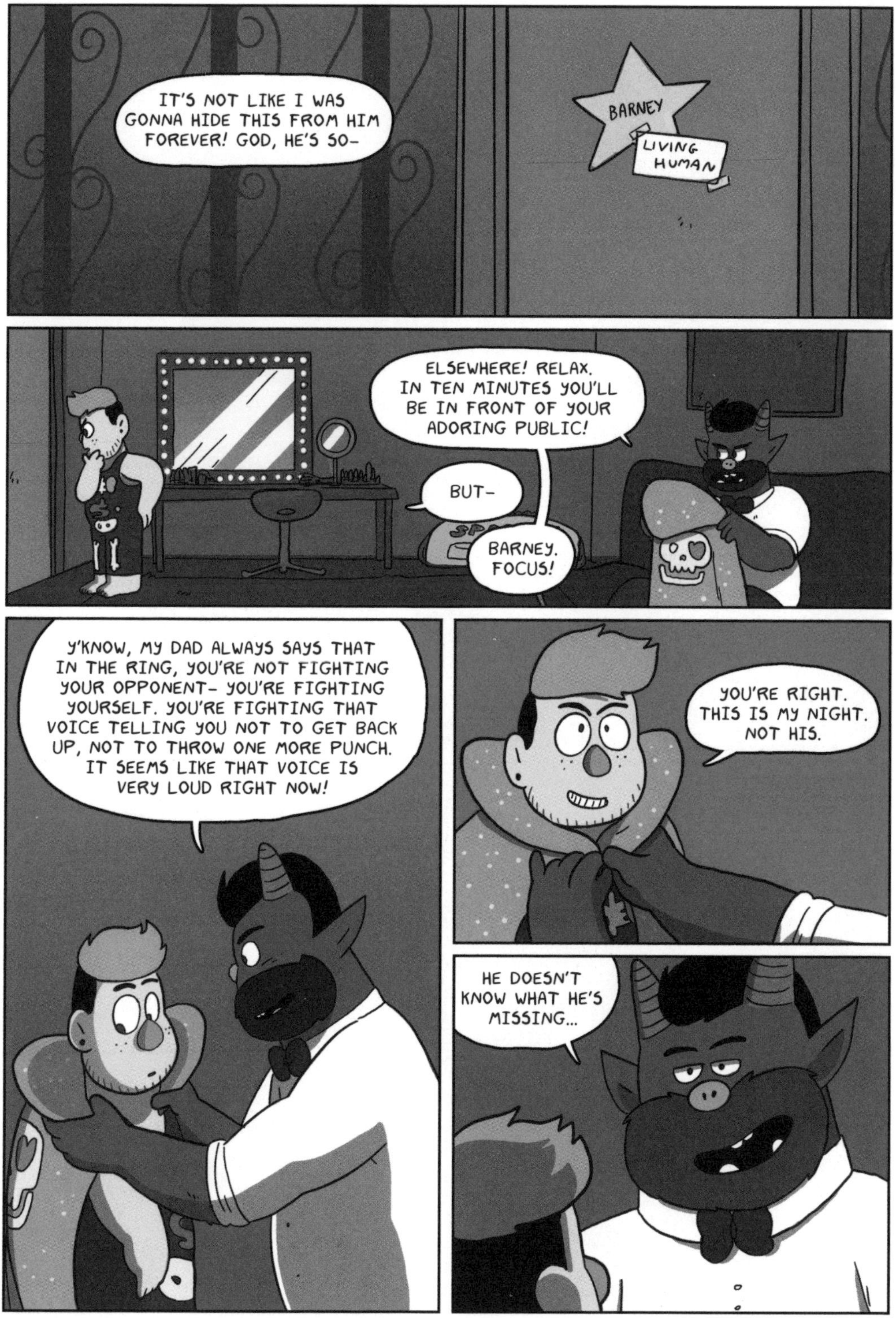
IT'S NOT LIKE I WAS GONNA HIDE THIS FROM HIM FOREVER! GOD, HE'S SO-
BARNEY
LIVING HUMAN
ELSEWHERE! RELAX. IN TEN MINUTES YOU'LL BE IN FRONT OF YOUR ADORING PUBLIC!
BUT-
BARNEY. FOCUS!
Y'KNOW, MY DAD ALWAYS SAYS THAT IN THE RING, YOU'RE NOT FIGHTING YOUR OPPONENT- YOU'RE FIGHTING YOURSELF. YOU'RE FIGHTING THAT VOICE TELLING YOU NOT TO GET BACK UP, NOT TO THROW ONE MORE PUNCH. IT SEEMS LIKE THAT VOICE IS VERY LOUD RIGHT NOW!
YOU'RE RIGHT. THIS IS MY NIGHT. NOT HIS.
HE DOESN'T KNOW WHAT HE'S MISSING...

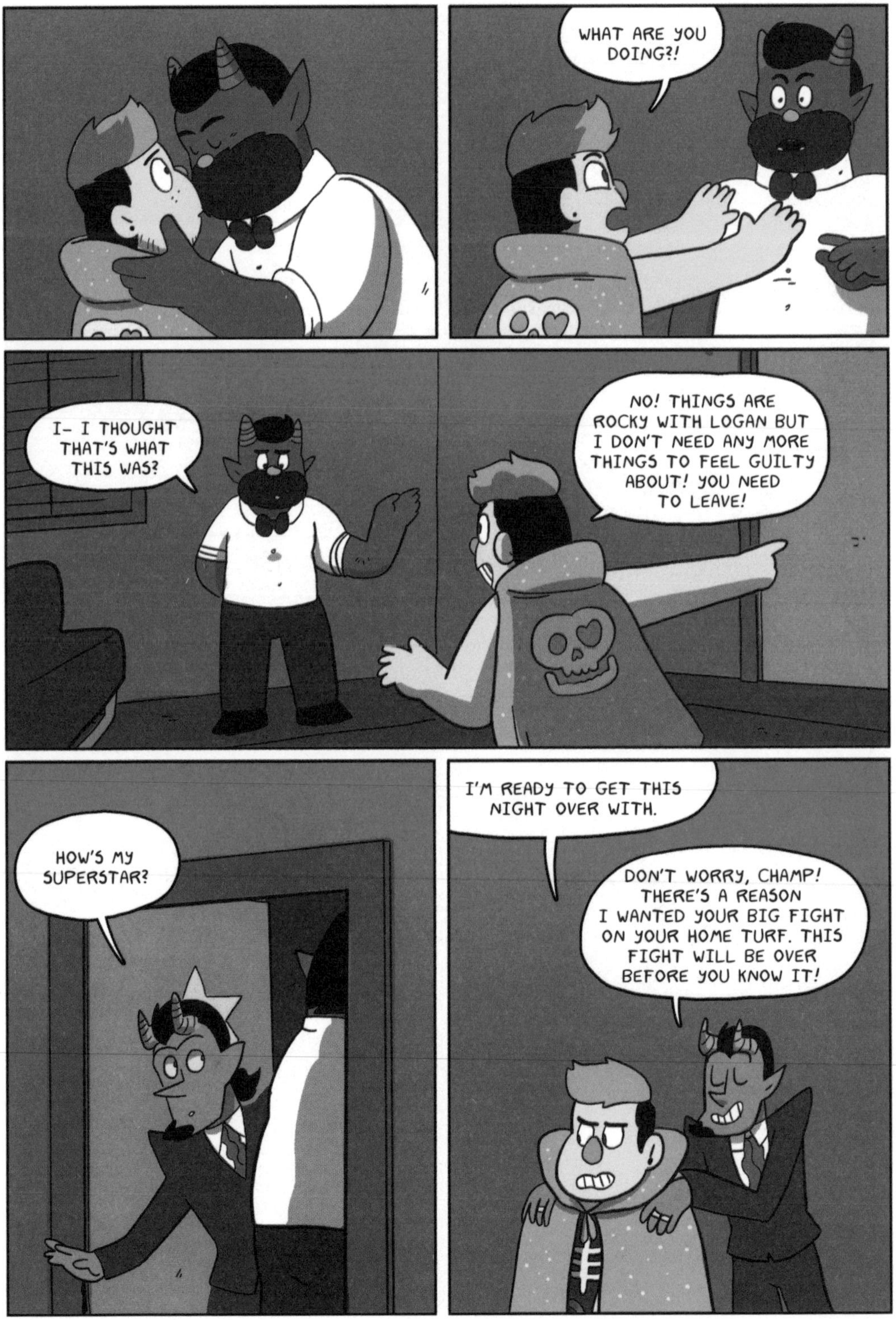

WHAT ARE YOU DOING?!
I- I THOUGHT THAT'S WHAT THIS WAS?
NO! THINGS ARE ROCKY WITH LOGAN BUT I DON'T NEED ANY MORE THINGS TO FEEL GUILTY ABOUT! YOU NEED TO LEAVE!
HOW'S MY SUPERSTAR?
I'M READY TO GET THIS NIGHT OVER WITH.
DON'T WORRY, CHAMP! THERE'S A REASON I WANTED YOUR BIG FIGHT ON YOUR HOME TURF. THIS FIGHT WILL BE OVER BEFORE YOU KNOW IT!

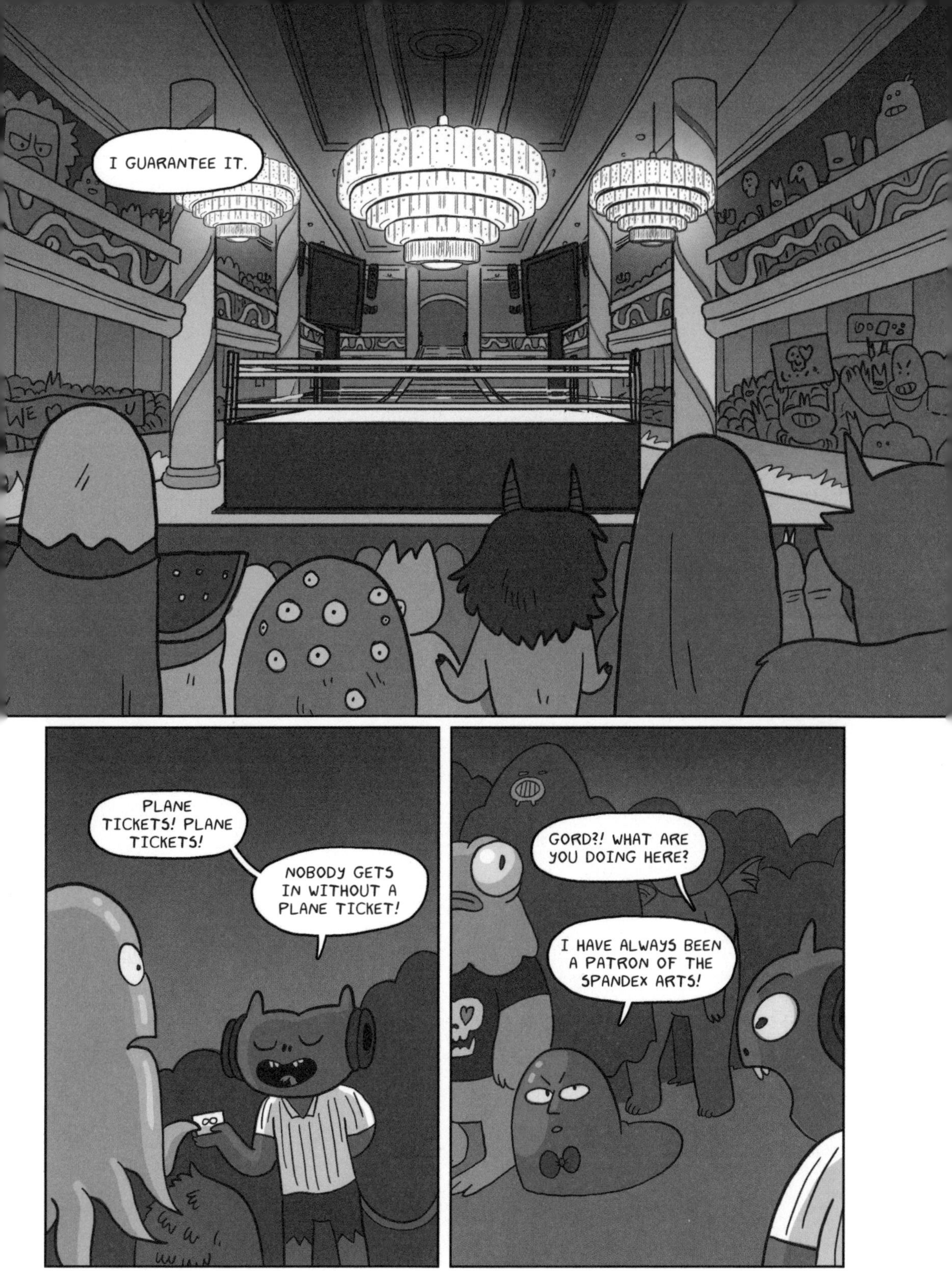
I GUARANTEE IT.
PLANE TICKETS! PLANE TICKETS!
NOBODY GETS IN WITHOUT A PLANE TICKET!
GORD?! WHAT ARE YOU DOING HERE?
I HAVE ALWAYS BEEN A PATRON OF THE SPANDEX ARTS!

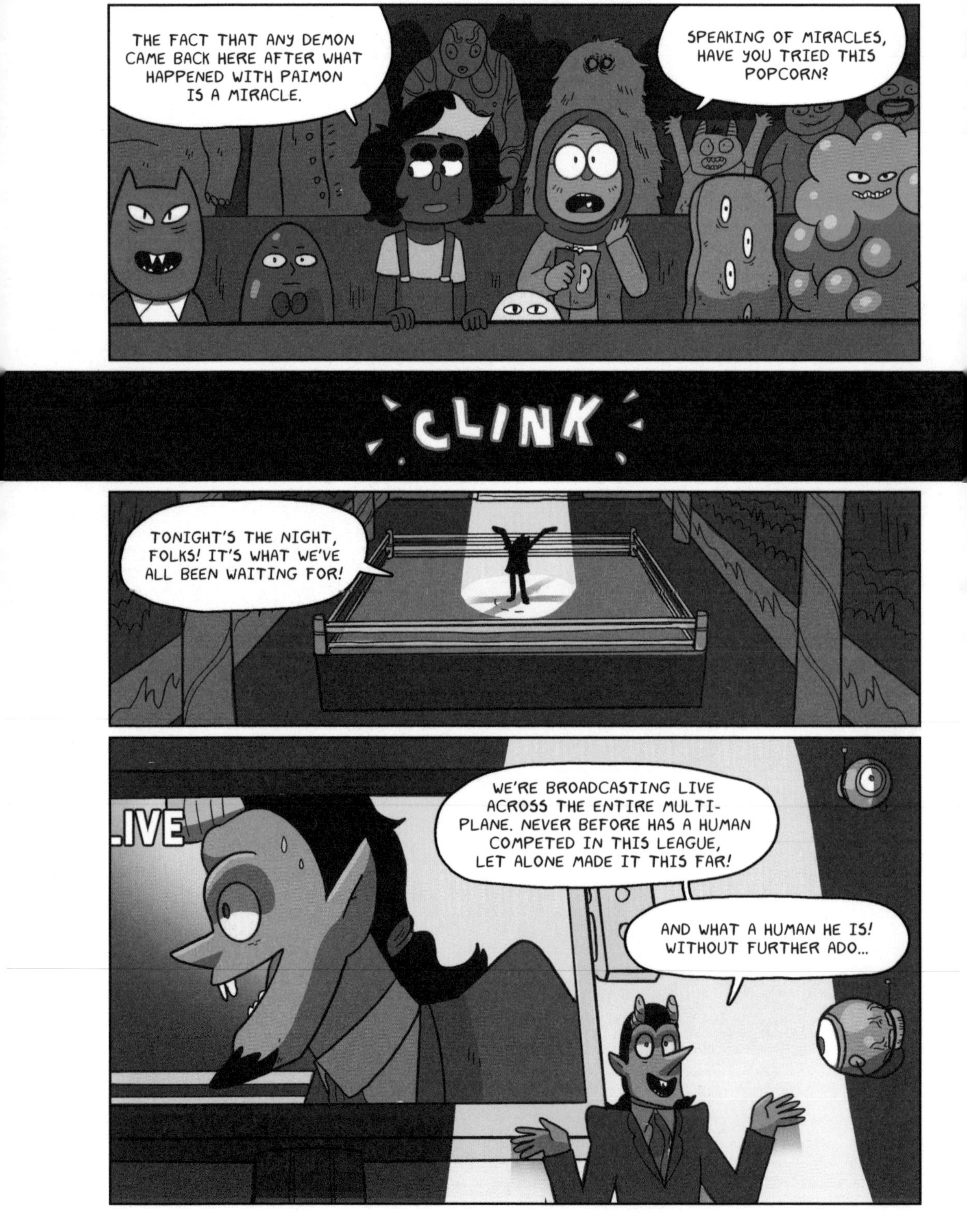
THE FACT THAT ANY DEMON CAME BACK HERE AFTER WHAT HAPPENED WITH PAIMON IS A MIRACLE.
SPEAKING OF MIRACLES, HAVE YOU TRIED THIS POPCORN?
CLINK
TONIGHT'S THE NIGHT, FOLKS! IT'S WHAT WE'VE ALL BEEN WAITING FOR!
LIVE
WE'RE BROADCASTING LIVE ACROSS THE ENTIRE MULTI-PLANE. NEVER BEFORE HAS A HUMAN COMPETED IN THIS LEAGUE, LET ALONE MADE IT THIS FAR!
AND WHAT A HUMAN HE IS! WITHOUT FURTHER ADO...

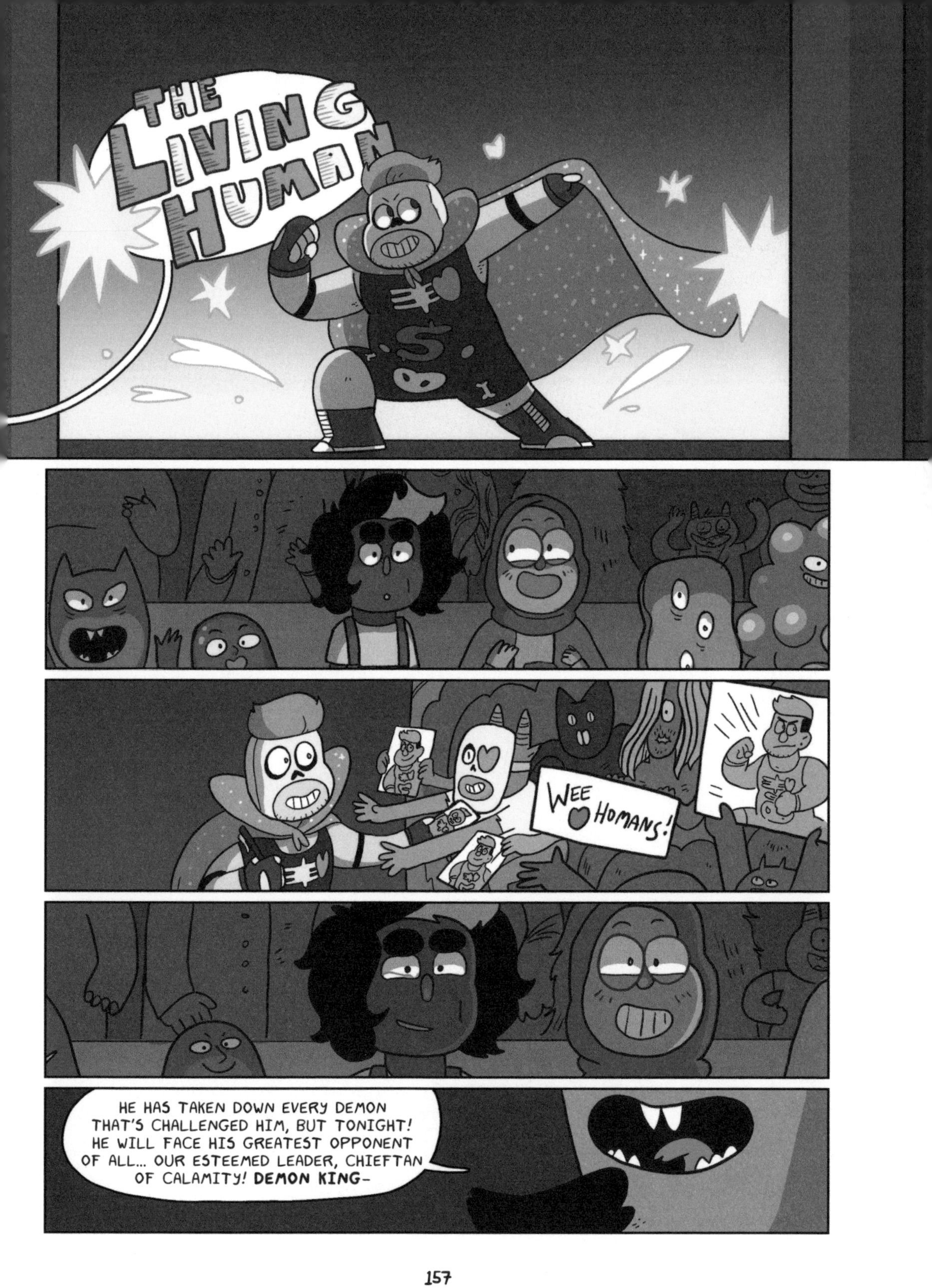
THE LIVING HUMAN
WEE HOMANS!
HE HAS TAKEN DOWN EVERY DEMON THAT'S CHALLENGED HIM, BUT TONIGHT! HE WILL FACE HIS GREATEST OPPONENT OF ALL... OUR ESTEEMED LEADER, CHIEFTAN OF CALAMITY! DEMON KING-

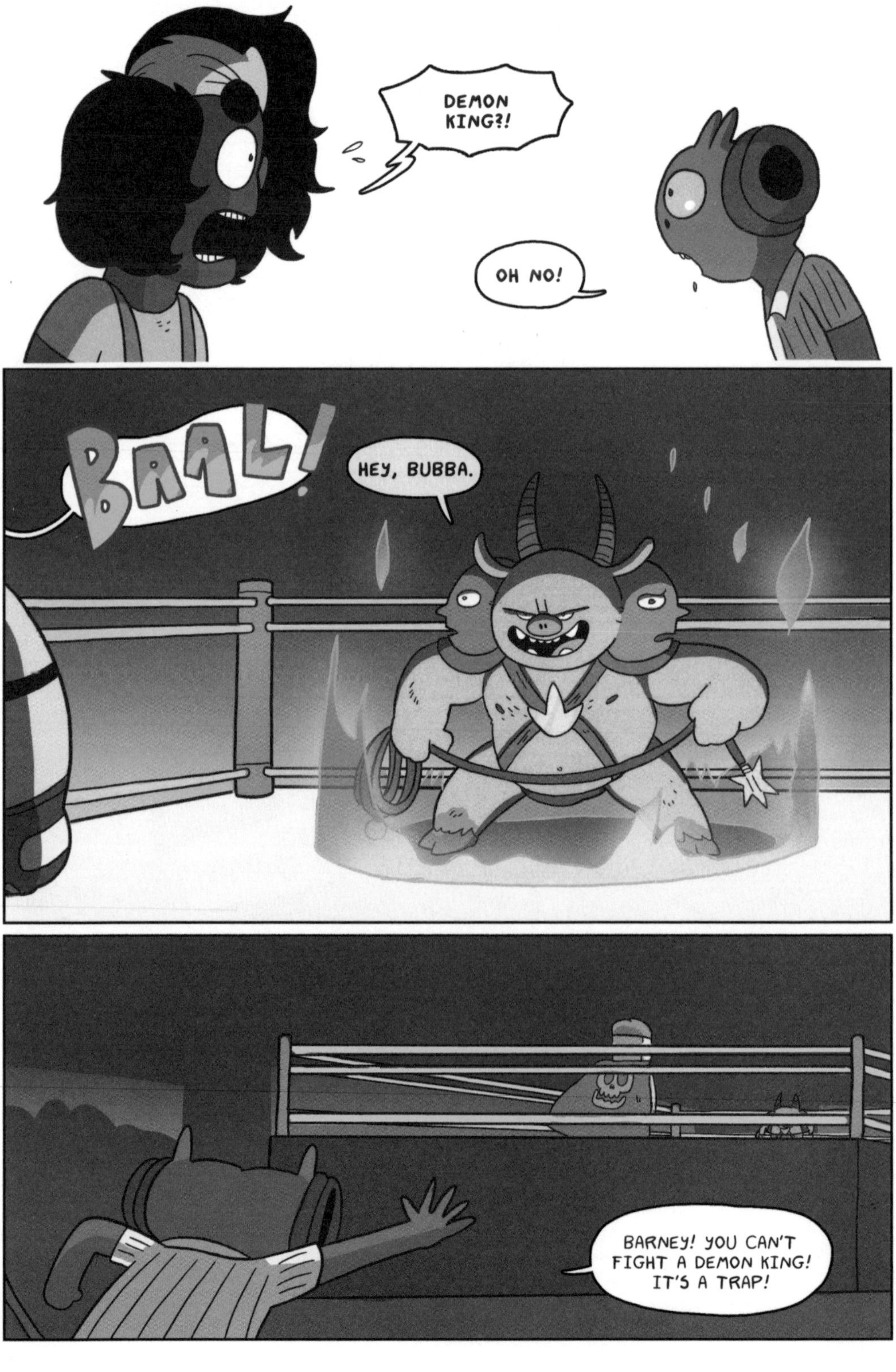
DEMON KING?!
OH NO!
BAAL!
HEY, BUBBA.
BARNEY! YOU CAN'T FIGHT A DEMON KING! IT'S A TRAP!

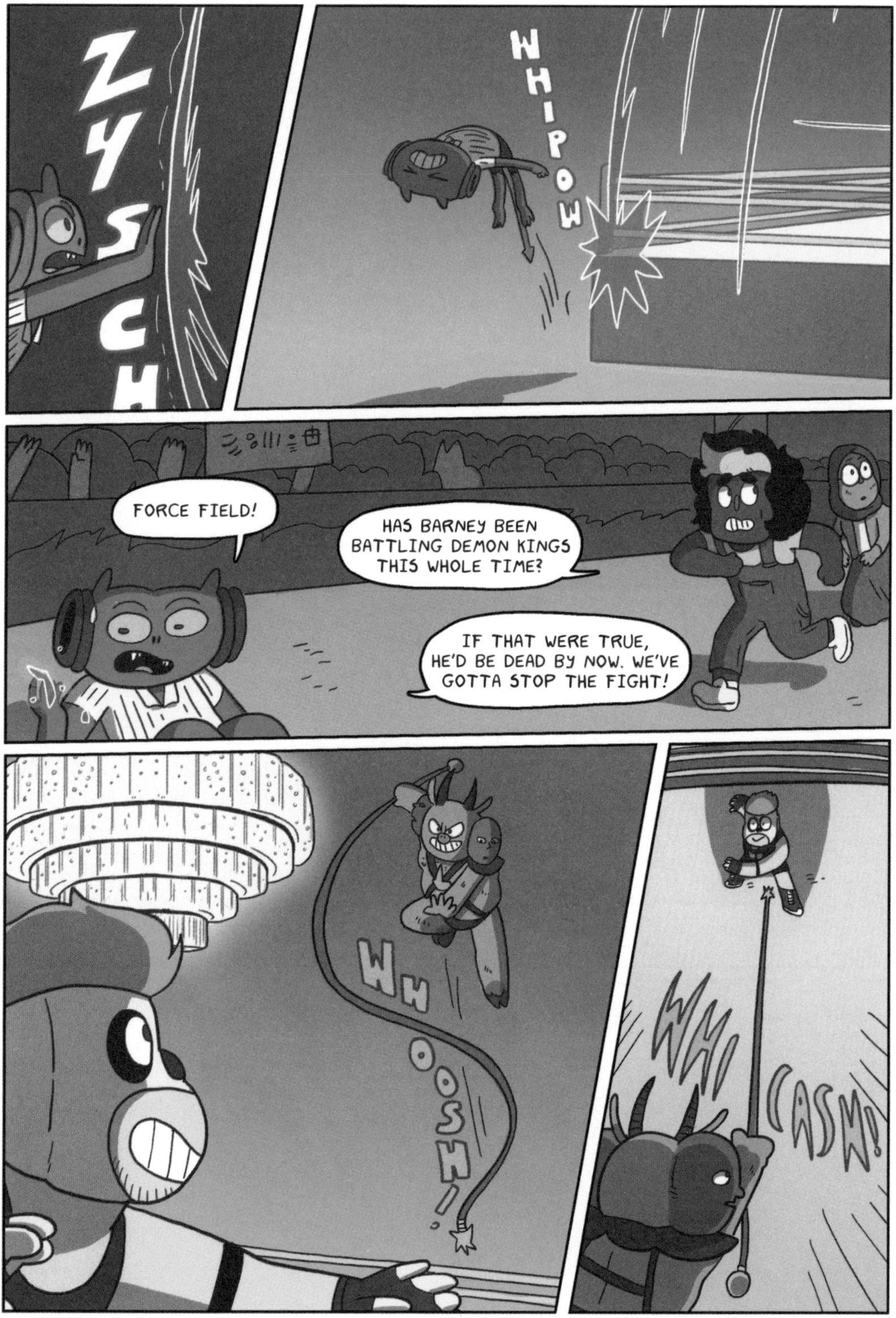
ZYSCH
WHIPOW
FORCE FIELD!
HAS BARNEY BEEN BATTLING DEMON KINGS THIS WHOLE TIME?
IF THAT WERE TRUE, HE'D BE DEAD BY NOW. WE'VE GOTTA STOP THE FIGHT!
WHOOOSH!
WHI
CASH!

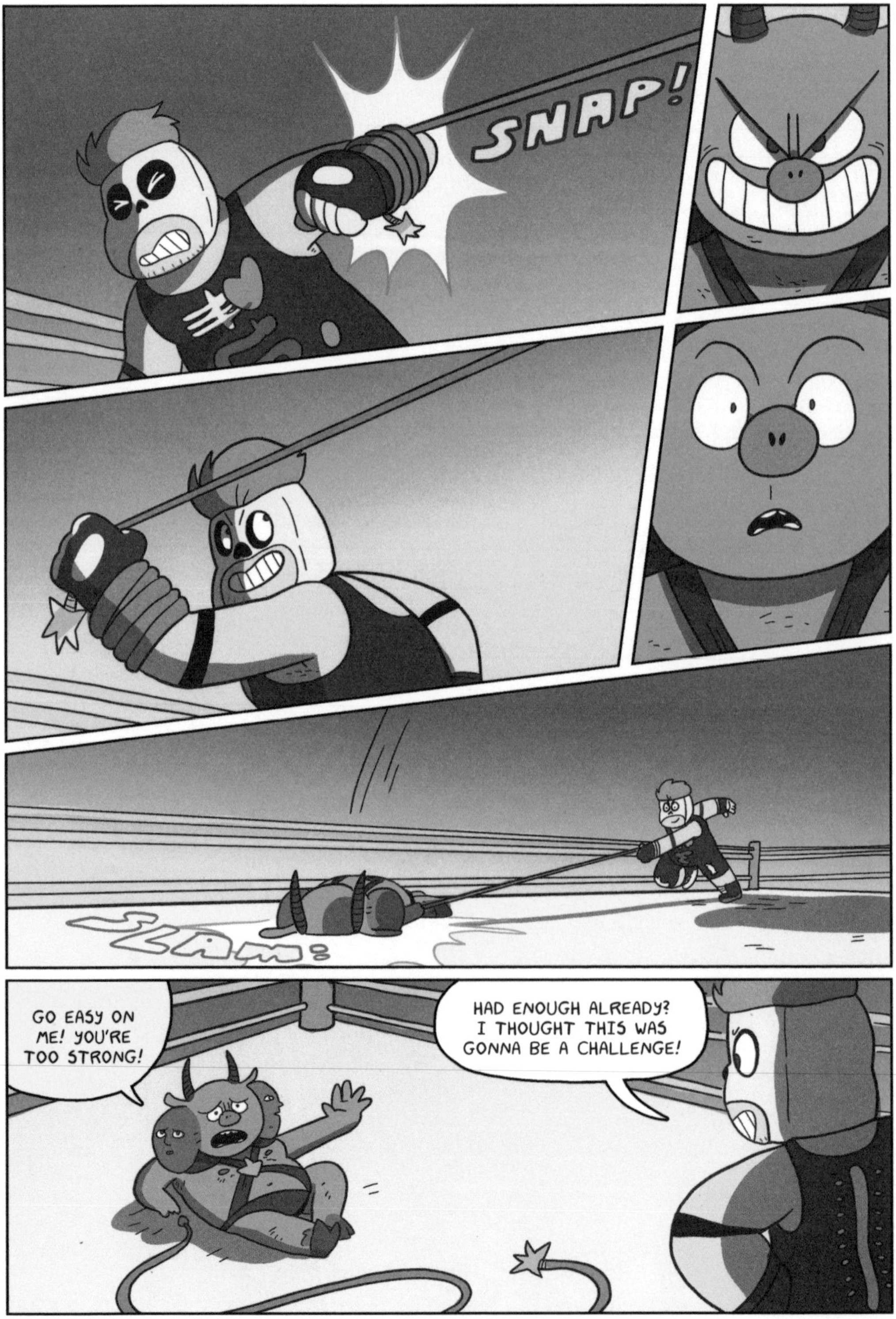
SNAP!
SLAM!
GO EASY ON ME! YOU'RE TOO STRONG!
HAD ENOUGH ALREADY? I THOUGHT THIS WAS GONNA BE A CHALLENGE!

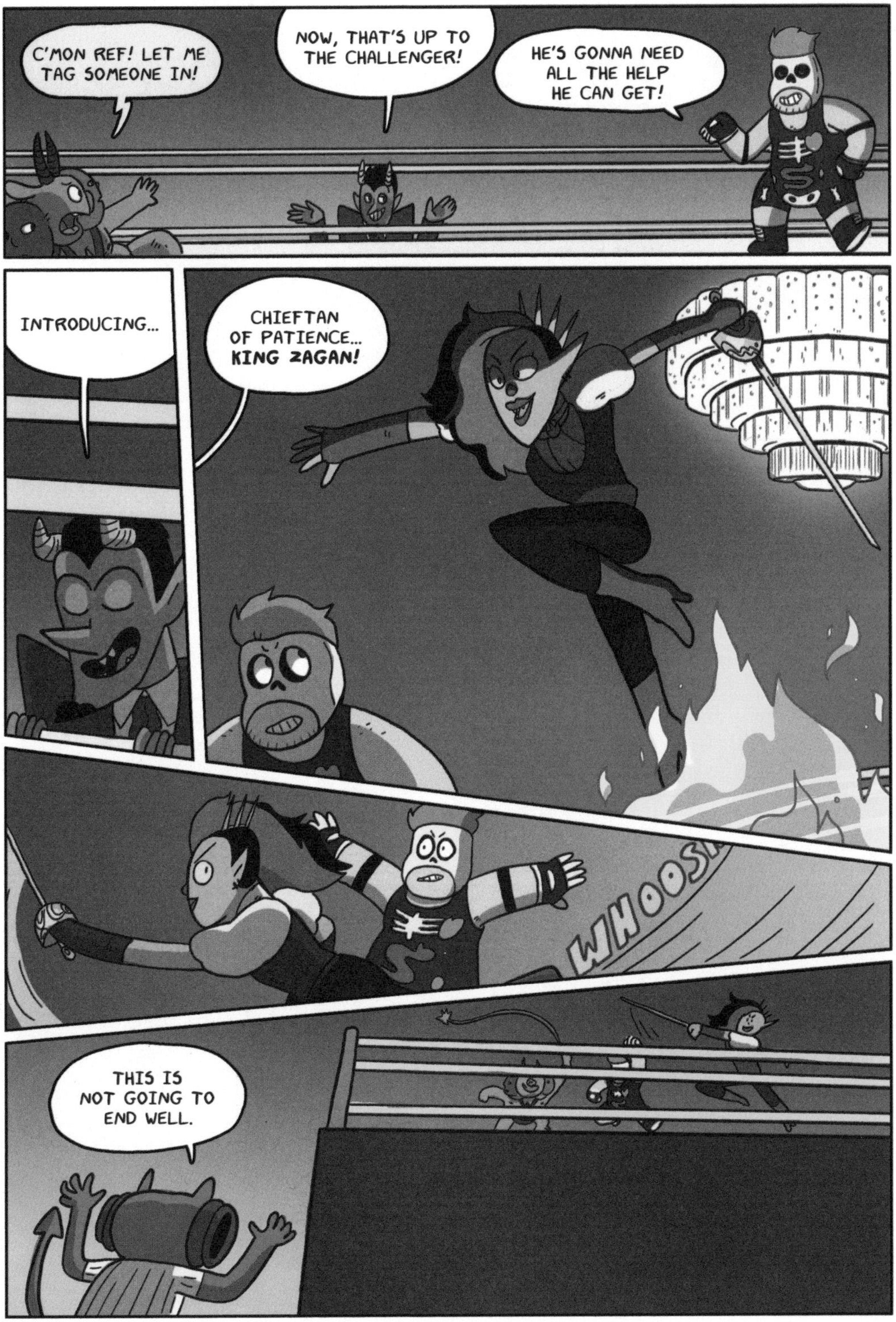
C'MON REF! LET ME TAG SOMEONE IN!
NOW, THAT'S UP TO THE CHALLENGER!
HE'S GONNA NEED ALL THE HELP HE CAN GET!
INTRODUCING...
CHIEFTAN OF PATIENCE... KING ZAGAN!
THIS IS NOT GOING TO END WELL.

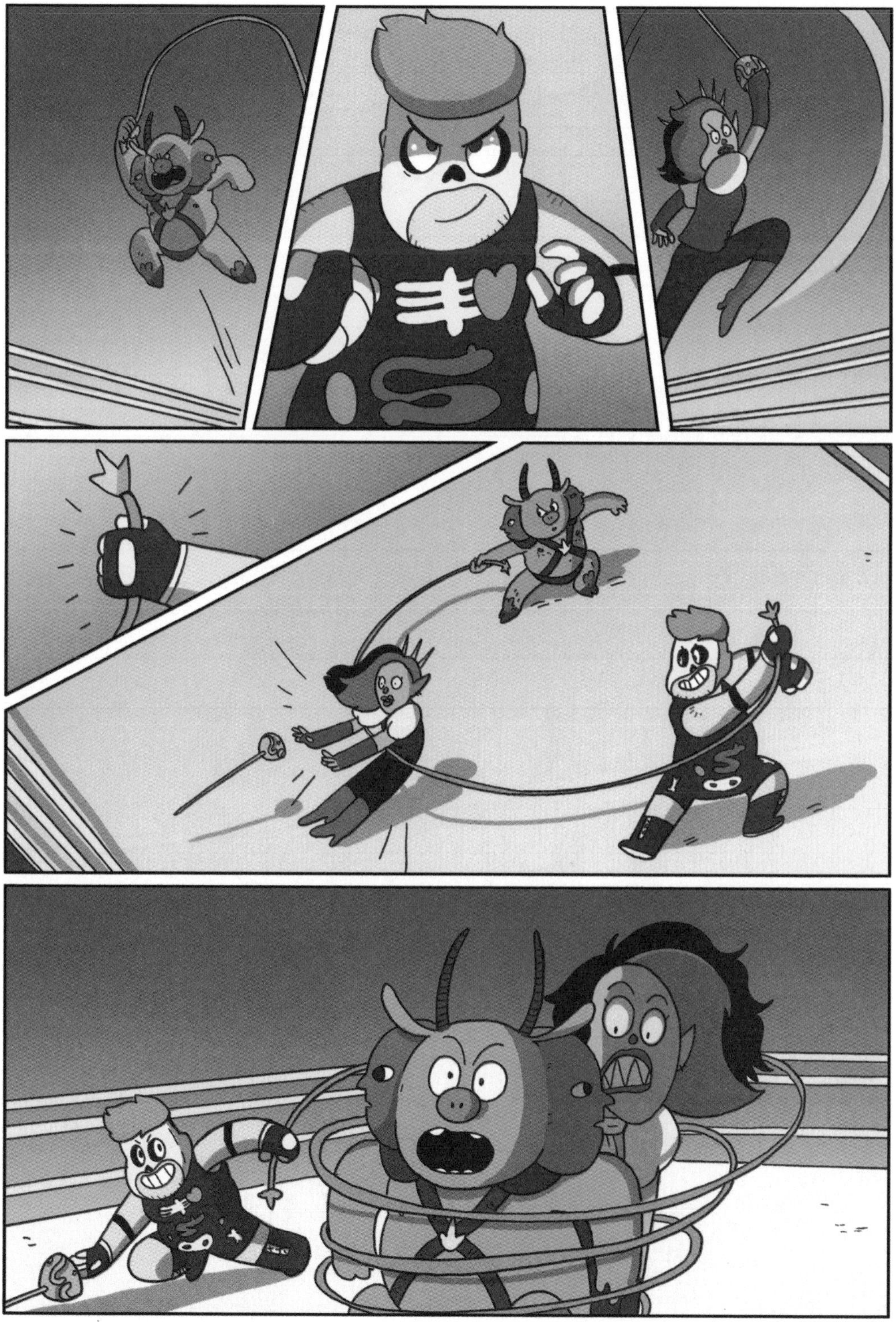

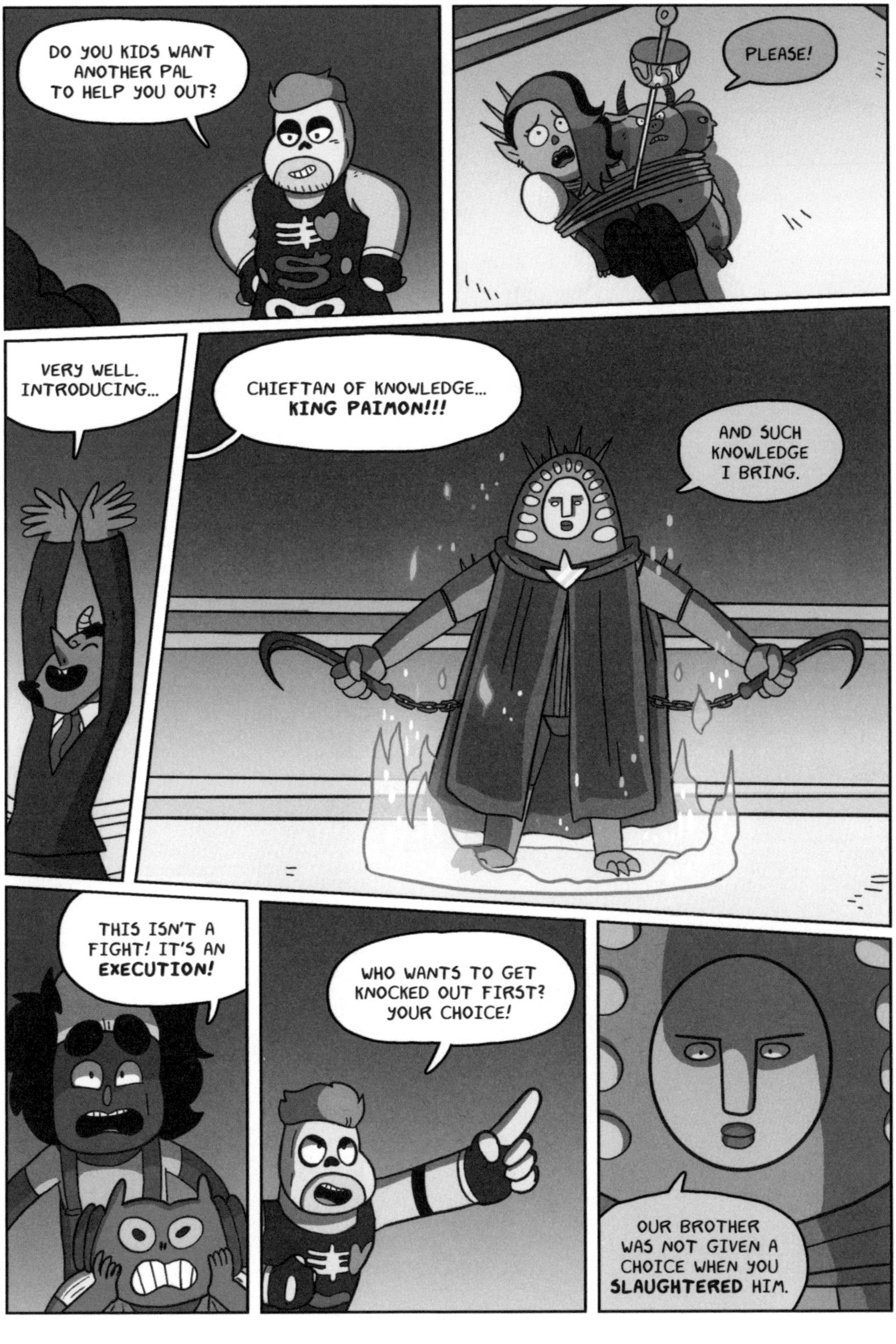

DO YOU KIDS WANT ANOTHER PAL TO HELP YOU OUT?
PLEASE!
VERY WELL. INTRODUCING...
CHIEFTAN OF KNOWLEDGE... **KING PAIMON!!!**
AND SUCH KNOWLEDGE I BRING.
THIS ISN'T A FIGHT! IT'S AN **EXECUTION!**
WHO WANTS TO GET KNOCKED OUT FIRST? YOUR CHOICE!
OUR BROTHER WAS NOT GIVEN A CHOICE WHEN YOU **SLAUGHTERED** HIM.

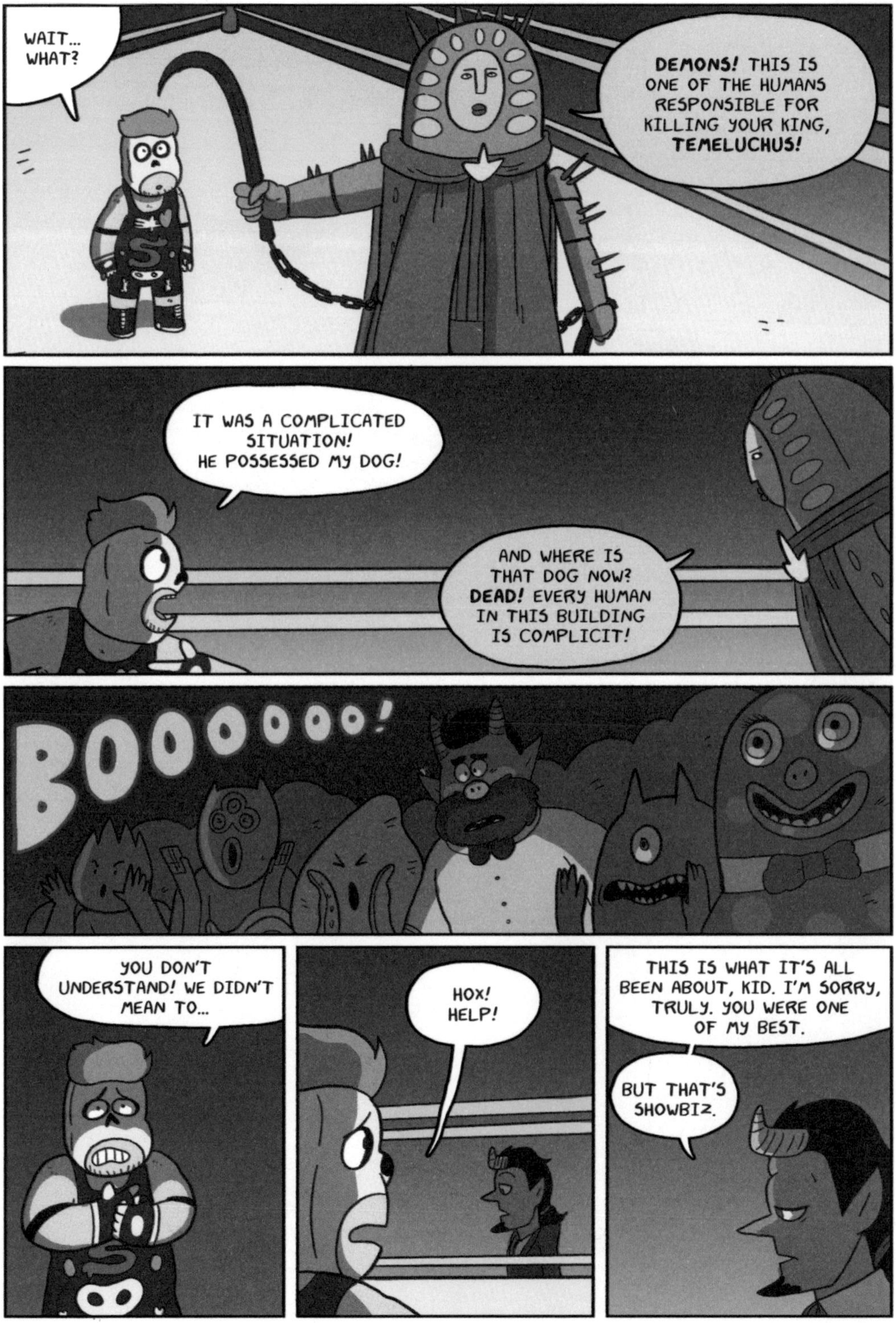
WAIT... WHAT?
DEMONS! THIS IS ONE OF THE HUMANS RESPONSIBLE FOR KILLING YOUR KING, TEMELUCHUS!
IT WAS A COMPLICATED SITUATION! HE POSSESSED MY DOG!
AND WHERE IS THAT DOG NOW? DEAD! EVERY HUMAN IN THIS BUILDING IS COMPLICIT!
BOOOOOO!
YOU DON'T UNDERSTAND! WE DIDN'T MEAN TO...
HOX! HELP!
THIS IS WHAT IT'S ALL BEEN ABOUT, KID. I'M SORRY, TRULY. YOU WERE ONE OF MY BEST.
BUT THAT'S SHOWBIZ.

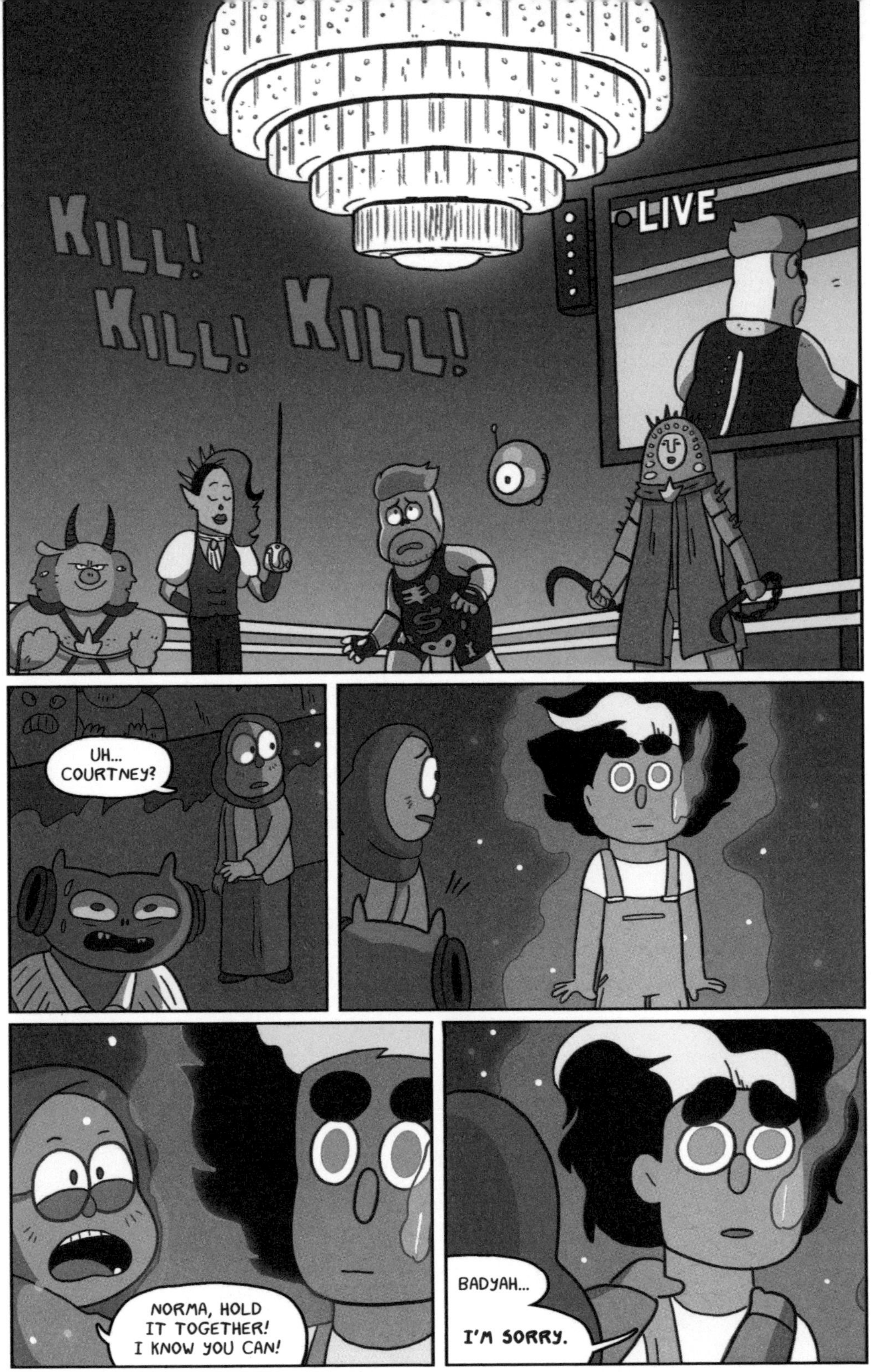
KILL! KILL! KILL!
LIVE
UH... COURTNEY?
NORMA, HOLD IT TOGETHER! I KNOW YOU CAN!
BADYAH...
I'M SORRY.

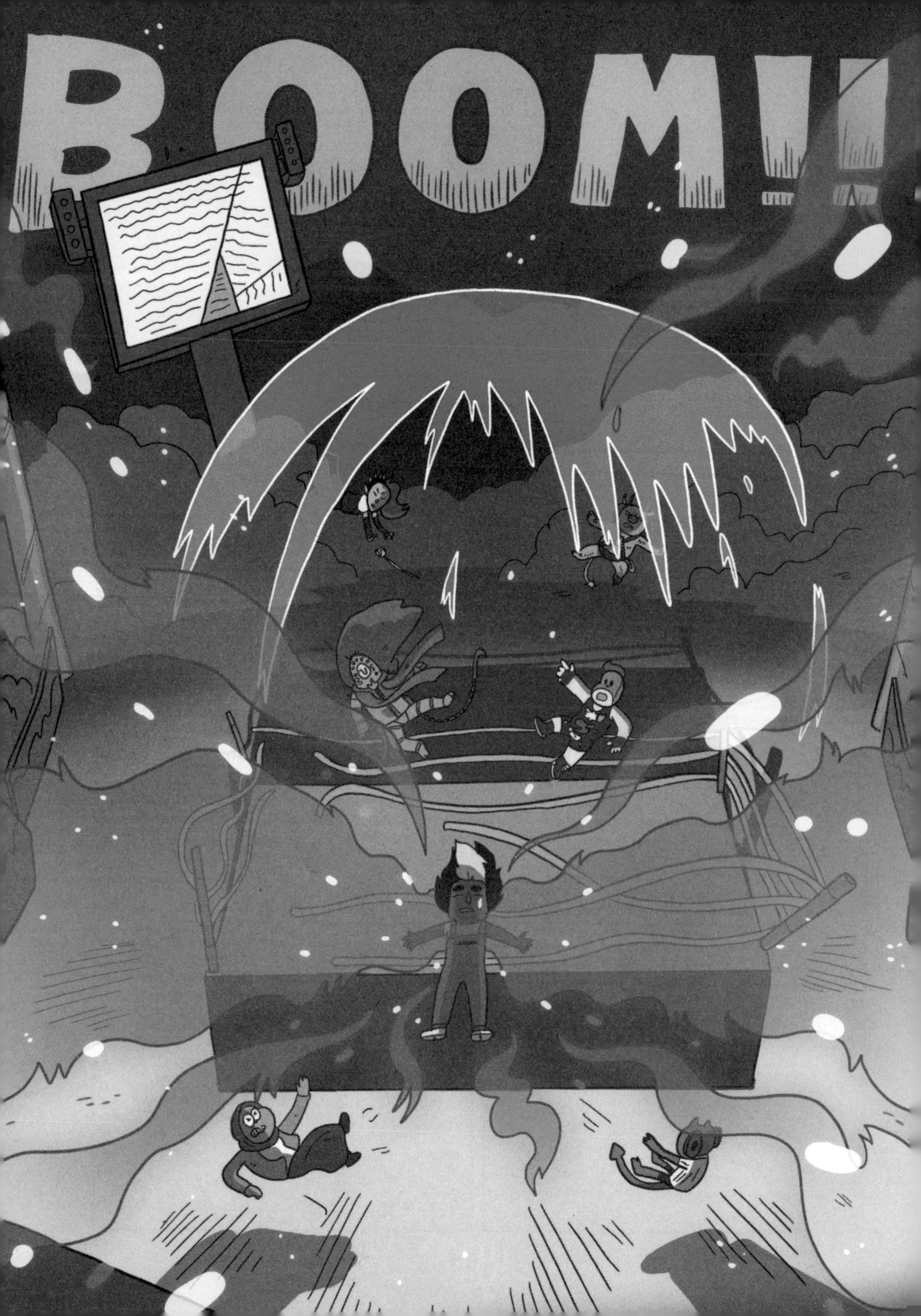
BOOM!!

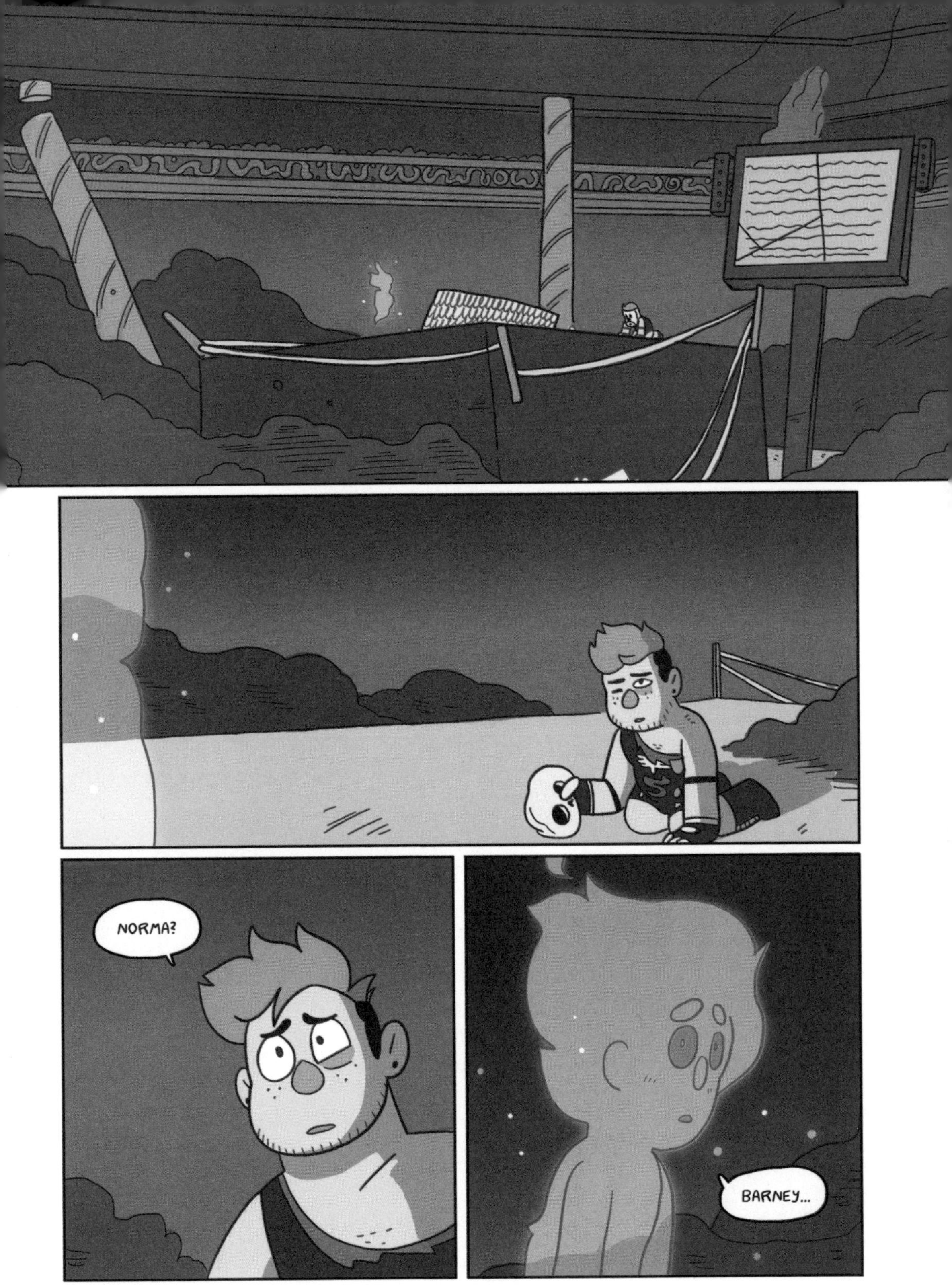
NORMA?
BARNEY...

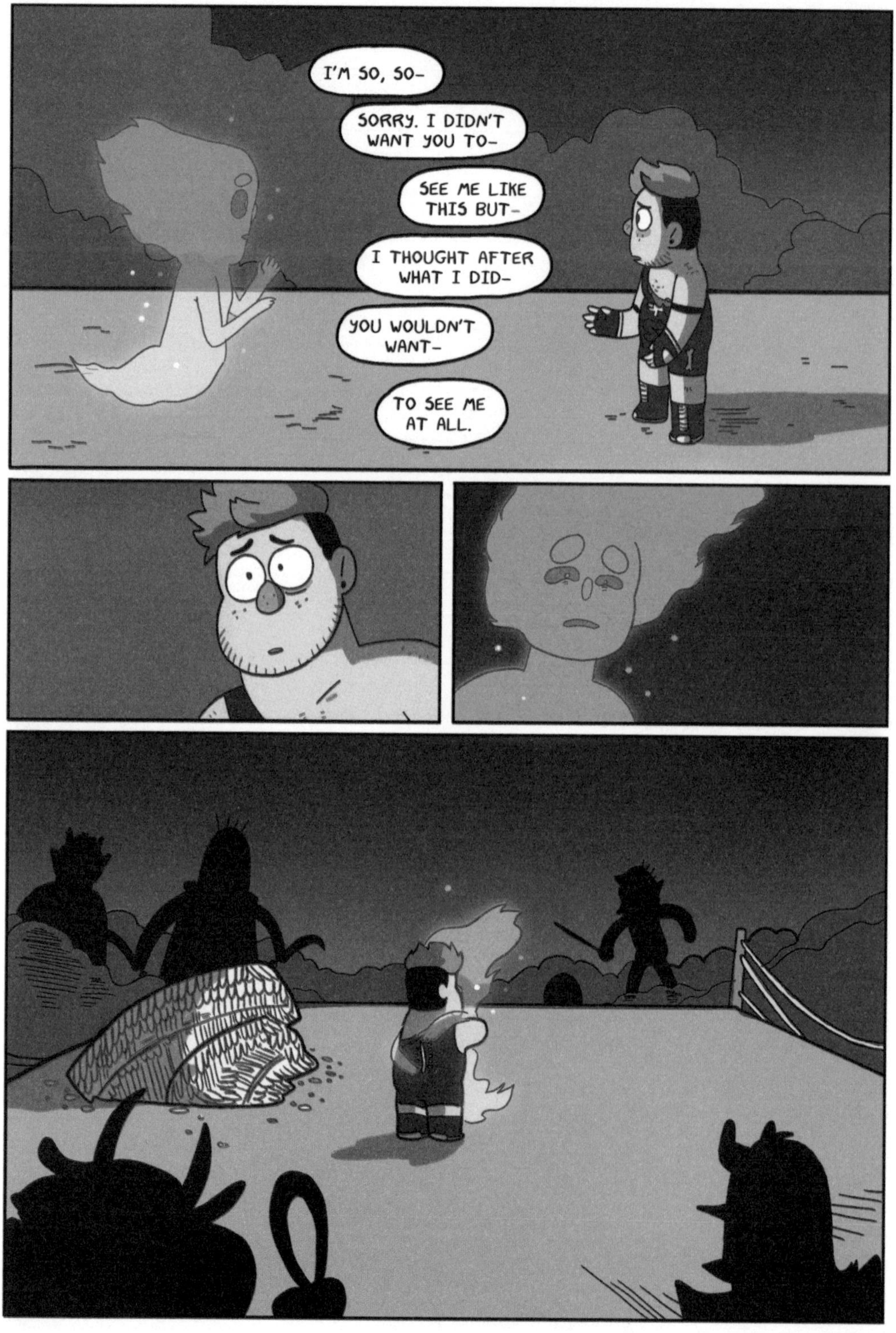
I'M SO, SO-
SORRY. I DIDN'T WANT YOU TO-
SEE ME LIKE THIS BUT-
I THOUGHT AFTER WHAT I DID-
YOU WOULDN'T WANT-
TO SEE ME AT ALL.

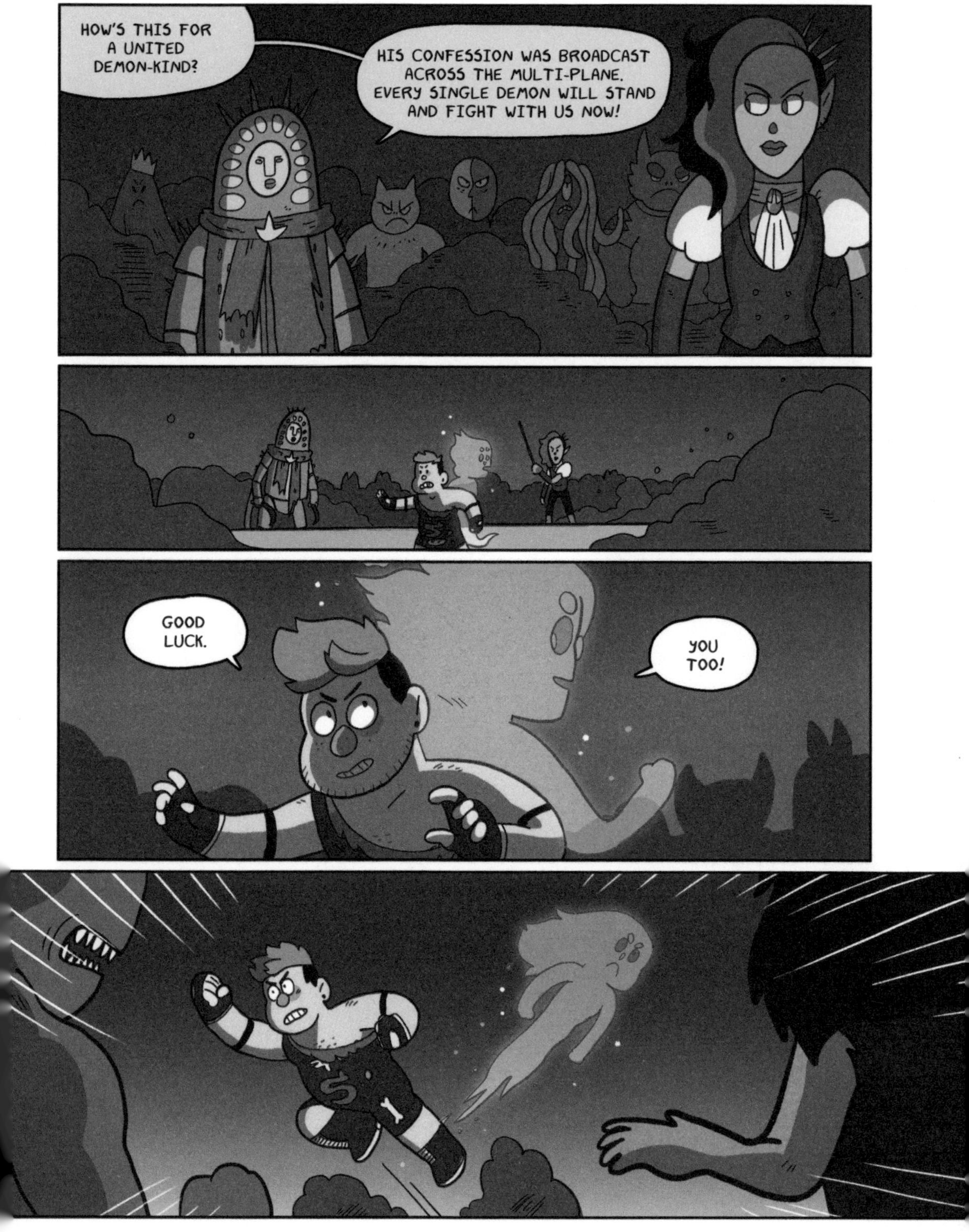
HOW'S THIS FOR A UNITED DEMON-KIND?
HIS CONFESSION WAS BROADCAST ACROSS THE MULTI-PLANE. EVERY SINGLE DEMON WILL STAND AND FIGHT WITH US NOW!
GOOD LUCK.
YOU TOO!

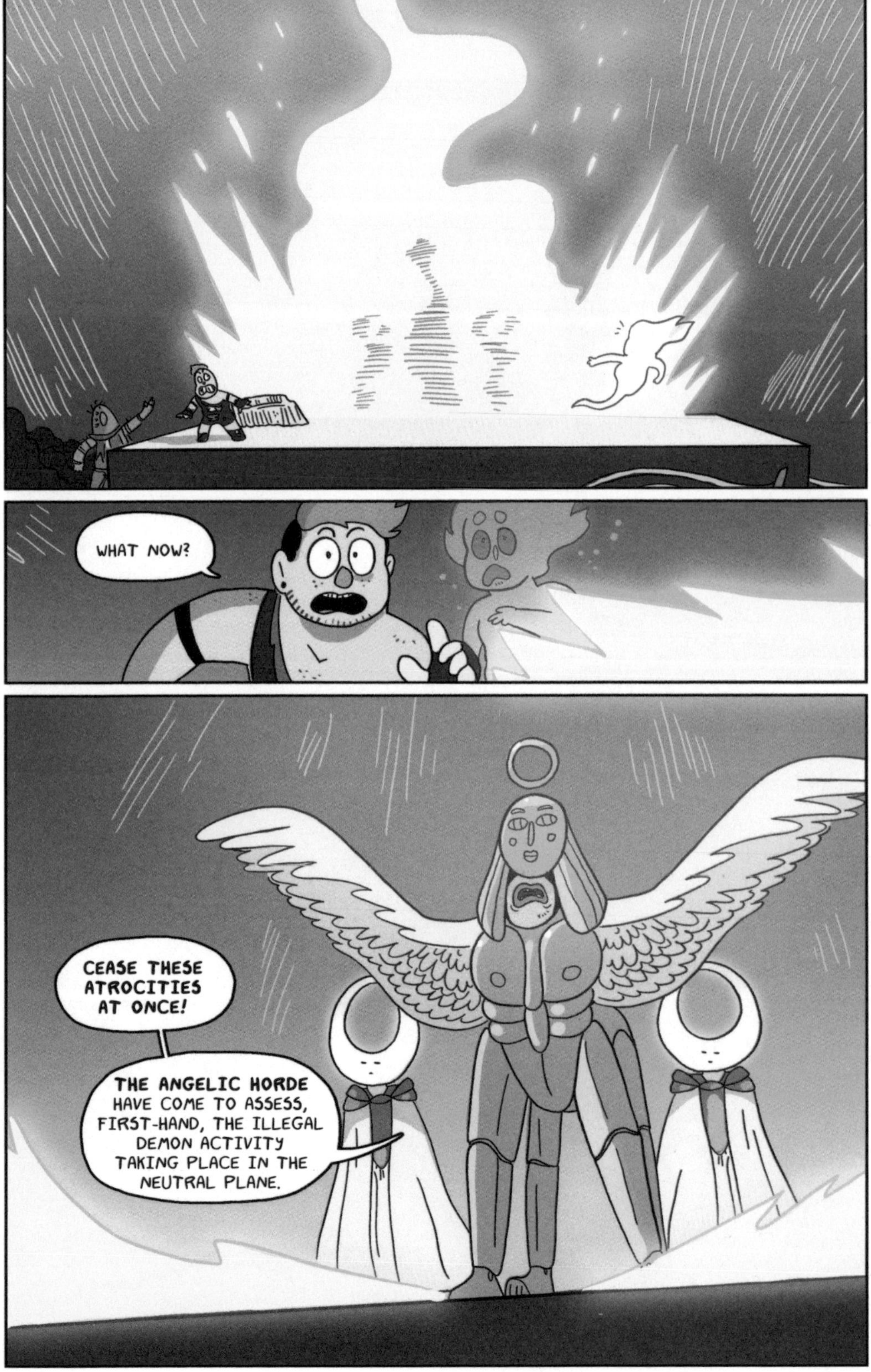
WHAT NOW?
CEASE THESE ATROCITIES AT ONCE!
THE ANGELIC HORDE HAVE COME TO ASSESS, FIRST-HAND, THE ILLEGAL DEMON ACTIVITY TAKING PLACE IN THE NEUTRAL PLANE.

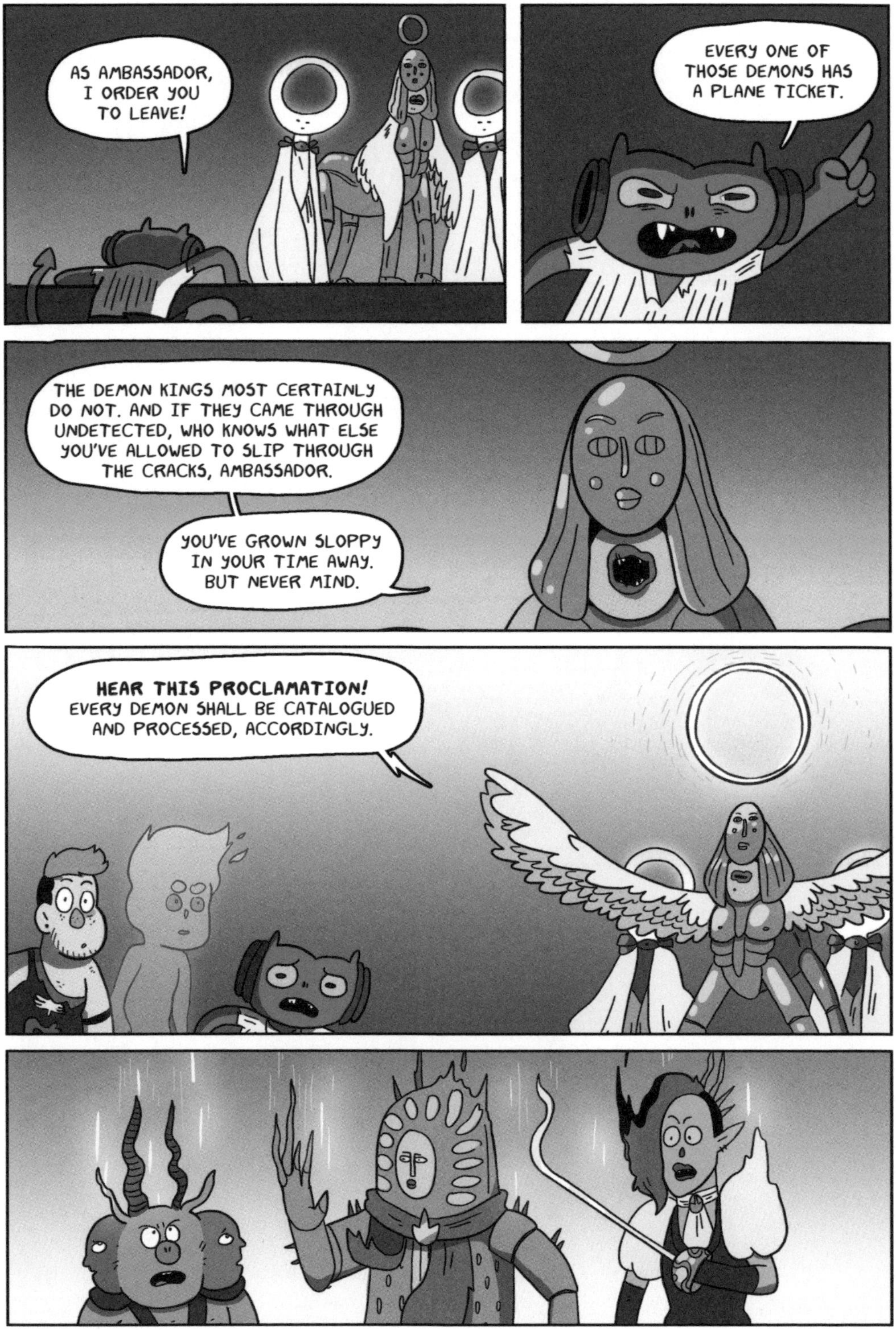
AS AMBASSADOR, I ORDER YOU TO LEAVE!
EVERY ONE OF THOSE DEMONS HAS A PLANE TICKET.
THE DEMON KINGS MOST CERTAINLY DO NOT. AND IF THEY CAME THROUGH UNDETECTED, WHO KNOWS WHAT ELSE YOU'VE ALLOWED TO SLIP THROUGH THE CRACKS, AMBASSADOR.
YOU'VE GROWN SLOPPY IN YOUR TIME AWAY. BUT NEVER MIND.
HEAR THIS PROCLAMATION! EVERY DEMON SHALL BE CATALOGUED AND PROCESSED, ACCORDINGLY.

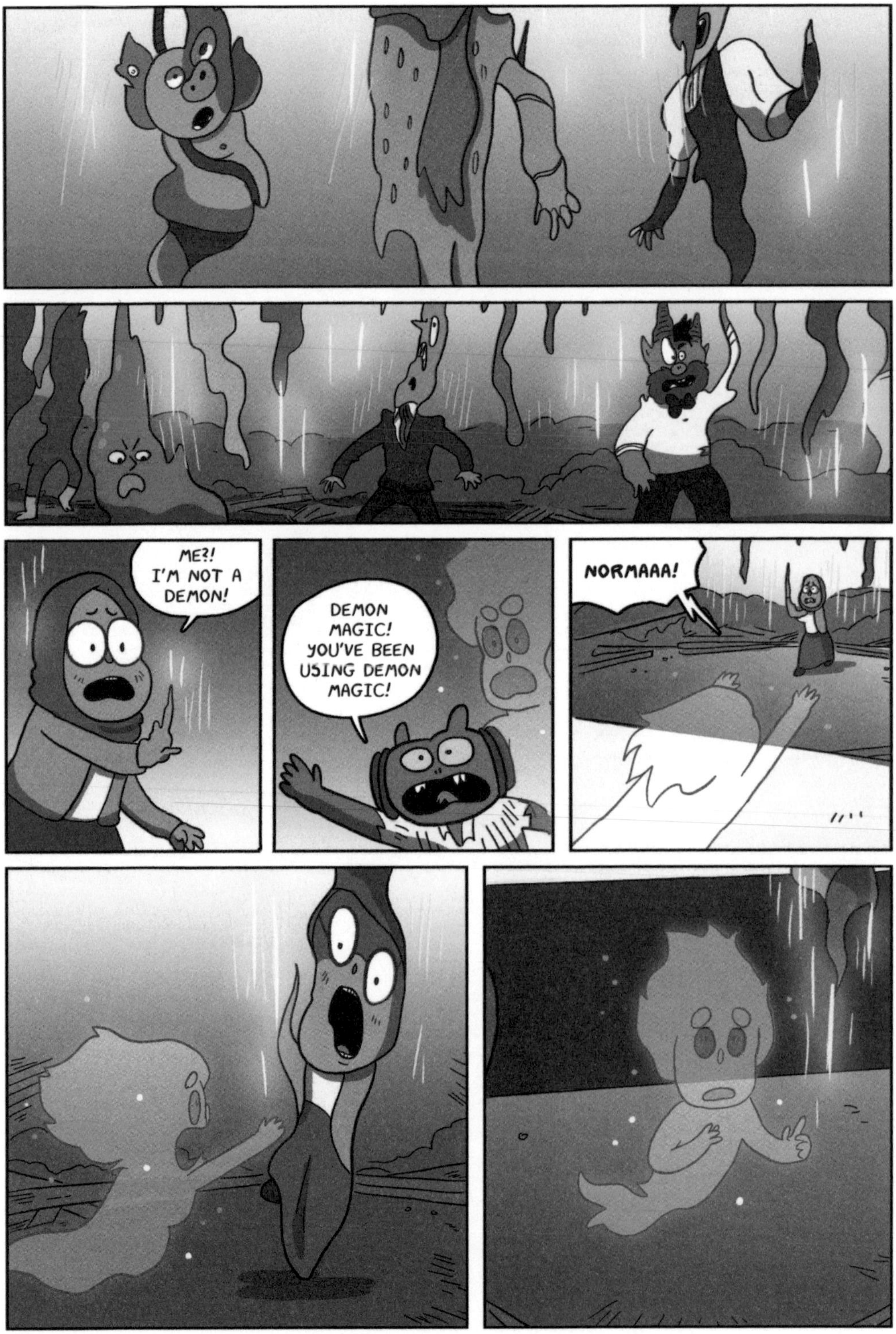
ME?!
I'M NOT A
DEMON!
DEMON
MAGIC!
YOU'VE BEEN
USING DEMON
MAGIC!
NORMAAA!

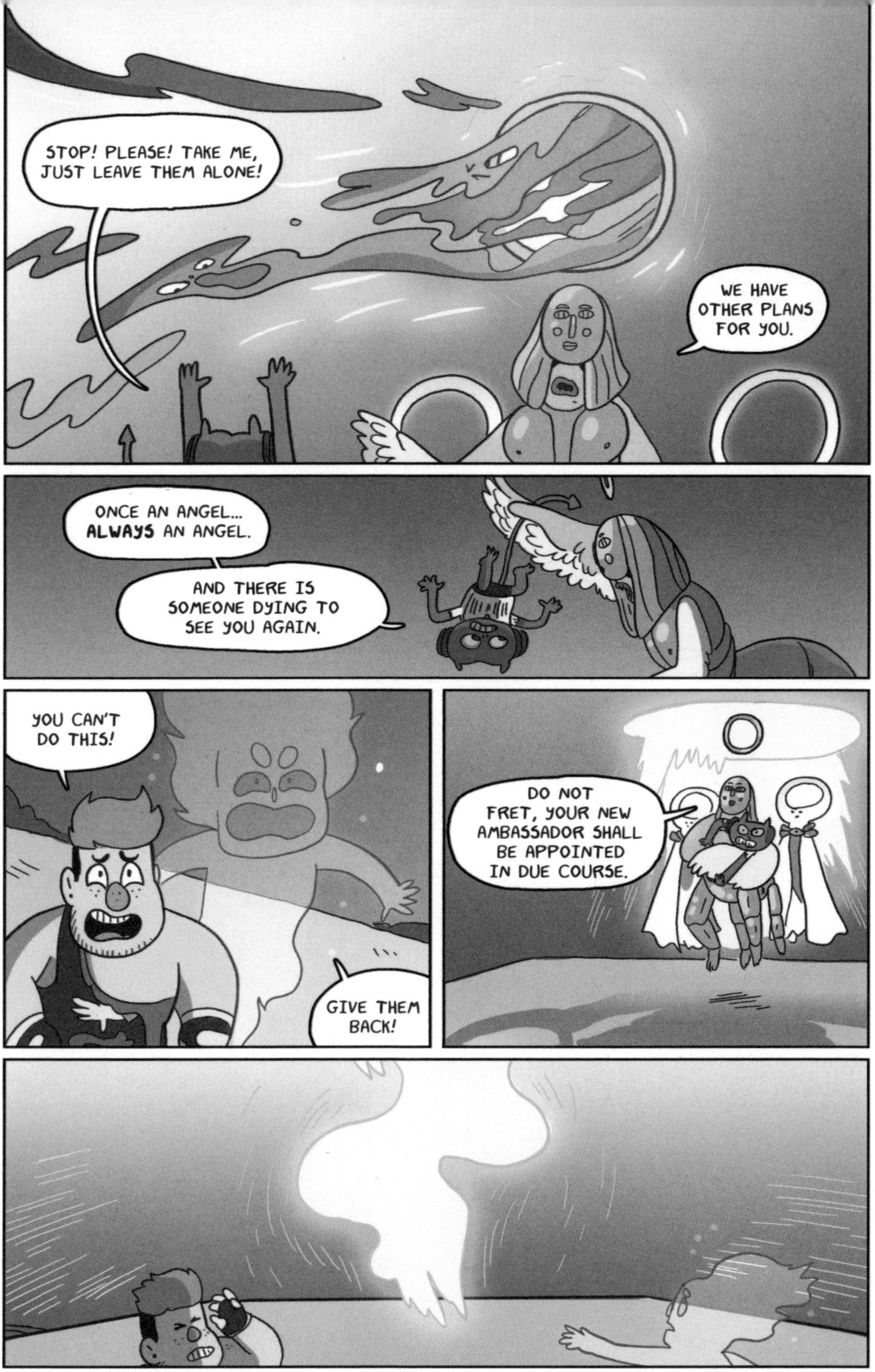
STOP! PLEASE! TAKE ME, JUST LEAVE THEM ALONE!
WE HAVE OTHER PLANS FOR YOU.
ONCE AN ANGEL... **ALWAYS** AN ANGEL.
AND THERE IS SOMEONE DYING TO SEE YOU AGAIN.
YOU CAN'T DO THIS!
GIVE THEM BACK!
DO NOT FRET, YOUR NEW AMBASSADOR SHALL BE APPOINTED IN DUE COURSE.

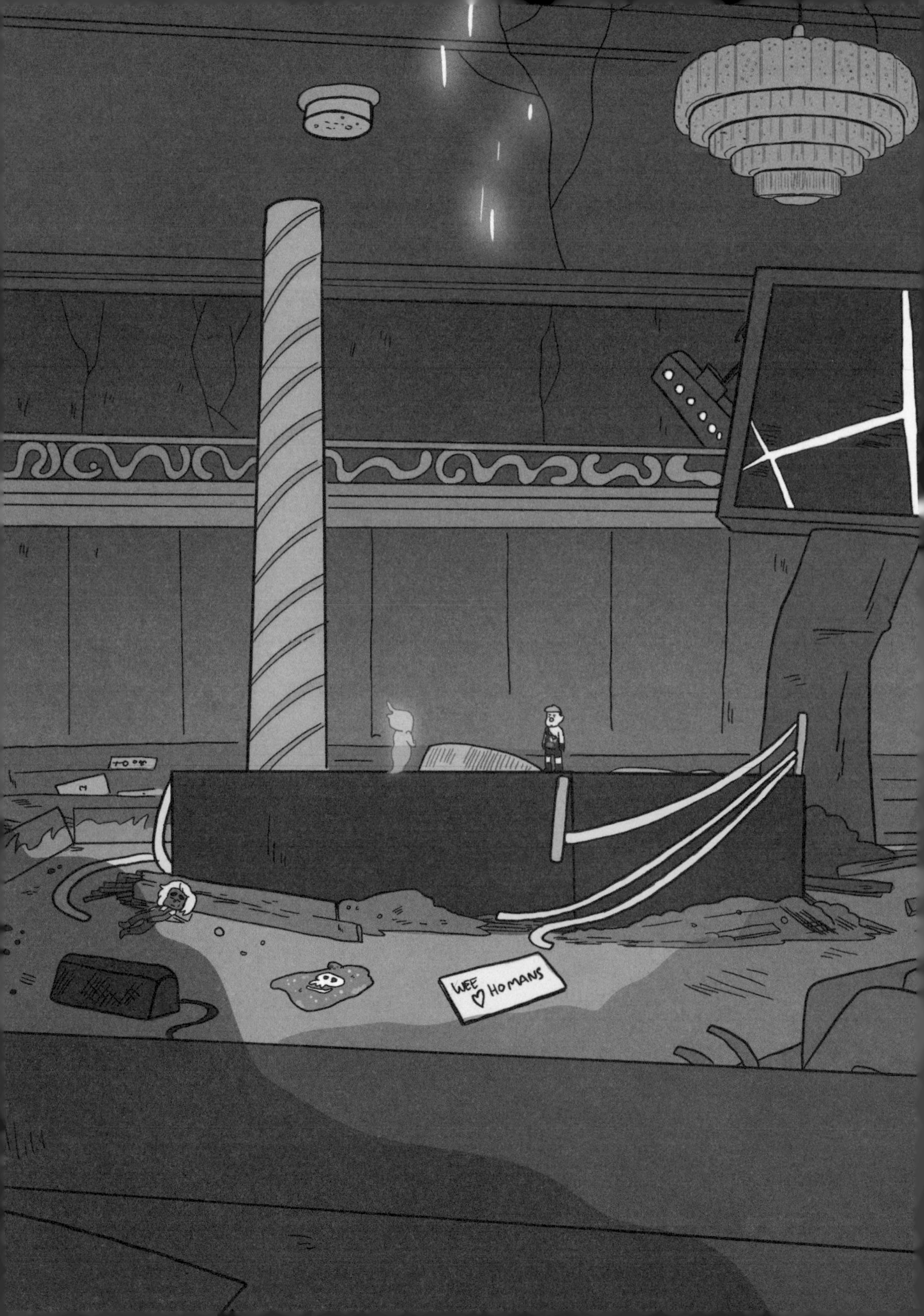
WEE ♡ HOMANS

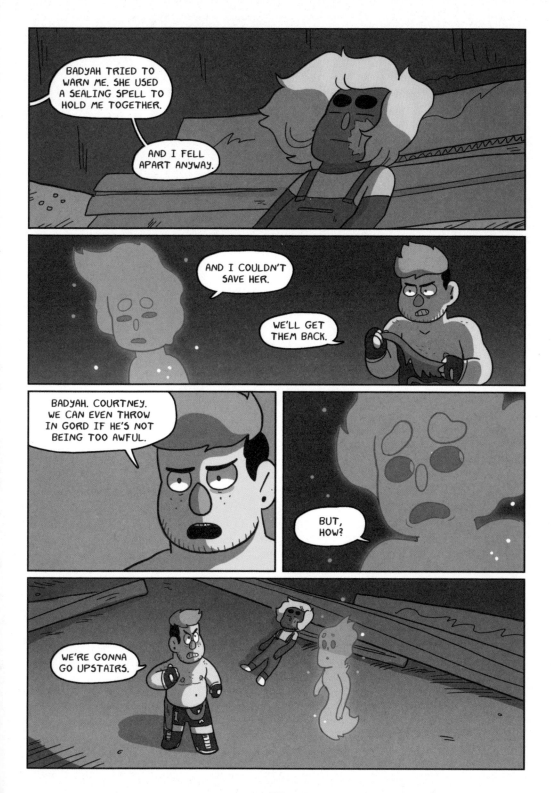

BADYAH TRIED TO WARN ME. SHE USED A SEALING SPELL TO HOLD ME TOGETHER.

AND I FELL APART ANYWAY.

AND I COULDN'T SAVE HER.

WE'LL GET THEM BACK.

BADYAH. COURTNEY. WE CAN EVEN THROW IN GORD IF HE'S NOT BEING TOO AWFUL.

BUT, HOW?

WE'RE GONNA GO UPSTAIRS.

A VERY, VERY LONG TIME AGO

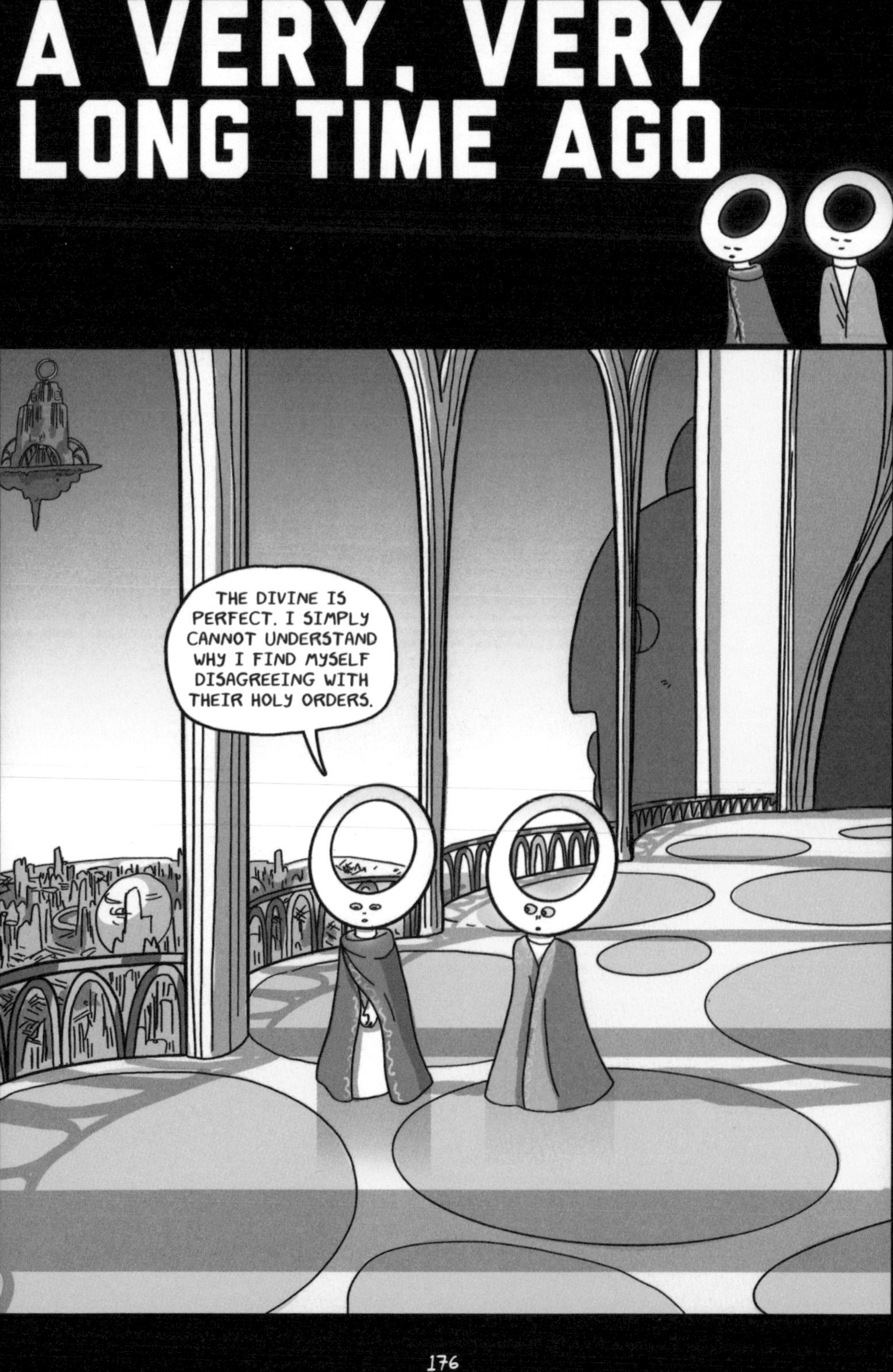
THE DIVINE IS PERFECT. I SIMPLY CANNOT UNDERSTAND WHY I FIND MYSELF DISAGREEING WITH THEIR HOLY ORDERS.

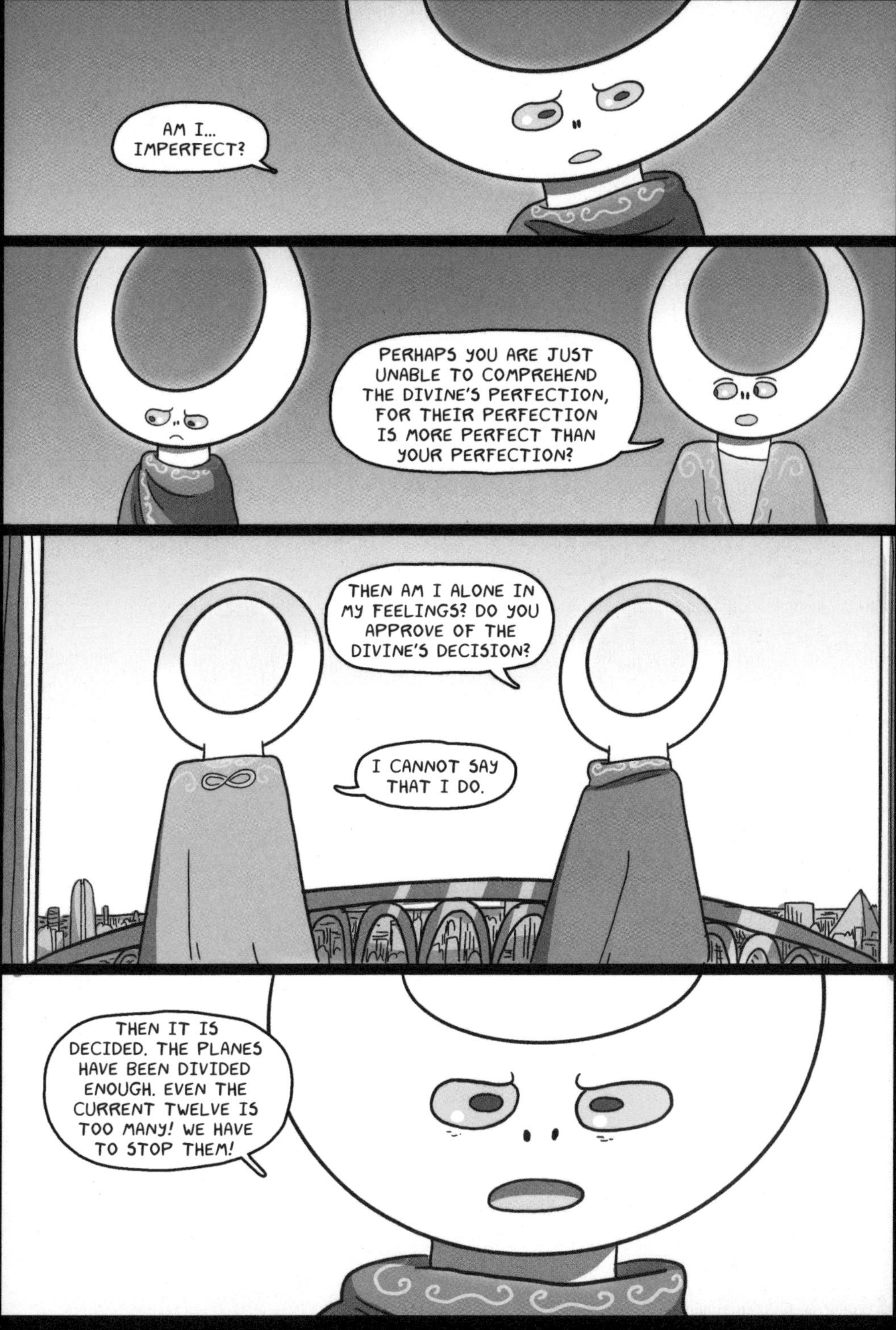
AM I... IMPERFECT?
PERHAPS YOU ARE JUST UNABLE TO COMPREHEND THE DIVINE'S PERFECTION, FOR THEIR PERFECTION IS MORE PERFECT THAN YOUR PERFECTION?
THEN AM I ALONE IN MY FEELINGS? DO YOU APPROVE OF THE DIVINE'S DECISION?
I CANNOT SAY THAT I DO.
THEN IT IS DECIDED. THE PLANES HAVE BEEN DIVIDED ENOUGH. EVEN THE CURRENT TWELVE IS TOO MANY! WE HAVE TO STOP THEM!

DASHIELL SILVA

CHAPTER 7
GOING UP

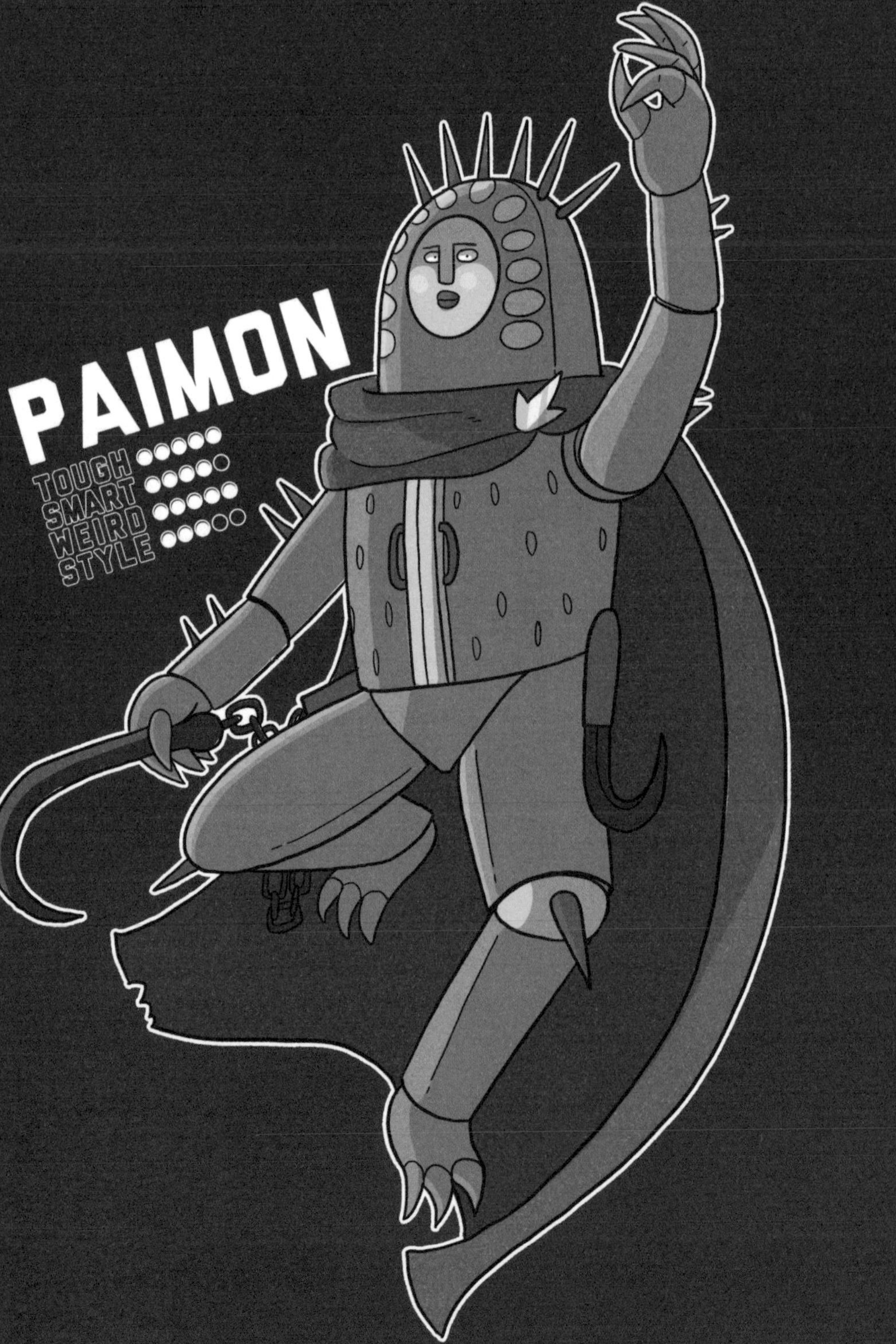
PAIMON
TOUGH
SMART
WEIRD
STYLE

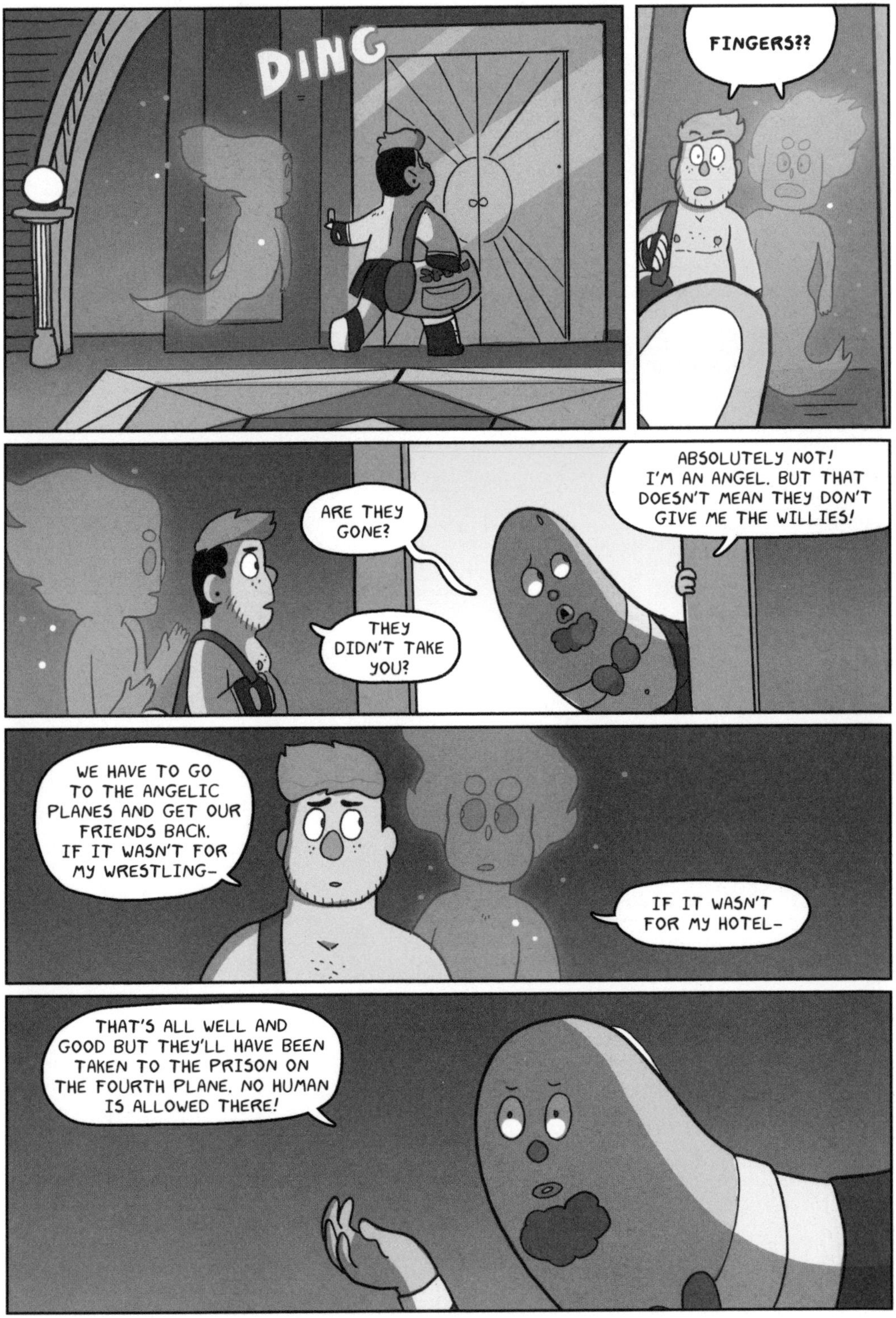
DING
FINGERS??
ARE THEY GONE?
THEY DIDN'T TAKE YOU?
ABSOLUTELY NOT! I'M AN ANGEL. BUT THAT DOESN'T MEAN THEY DON'T GIVE ME THE WILLIES!
WE HAVE TO GO TO THE ANGELIC PLANES AND GET OUR FRIENDS BACK. IF IT WASN'T FOR MY WRESTLING-
IF IT WASN'T FOR MY HOTEL-
THAT'S ALL WELL AND GOOD BUT THEY'LL HAVE BEEN TAKEN TO THE PRISON ON THE FOURTH PLANE. NO HUMAN IS ALLOWED THERE!

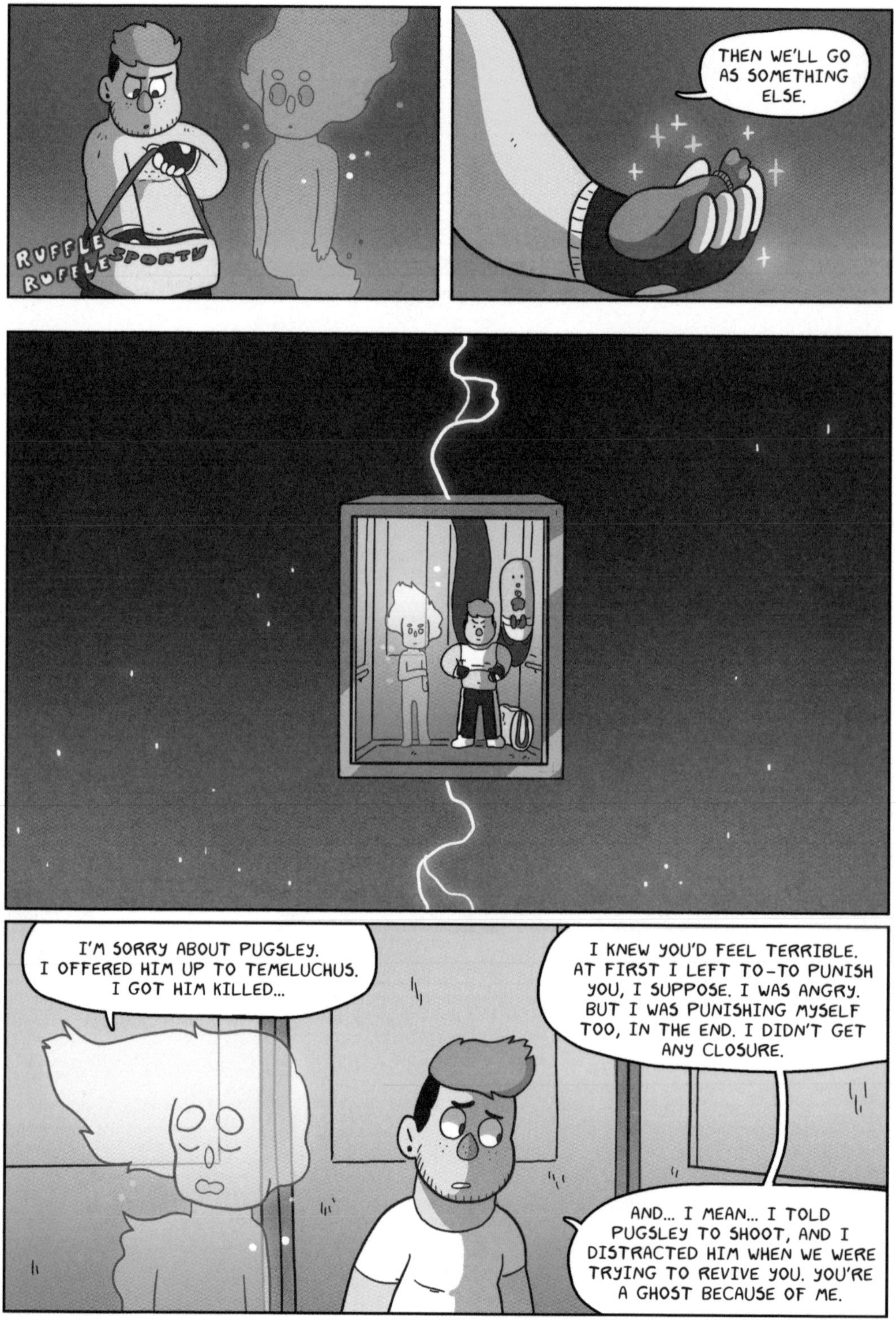
RUFFLE RUFFLE
SPORTY
THEN WE'LL GO AS SOMETHING ELSE.
I'M SORRY ABOUT PUGSLEY. I OFFERED HIM UP TO TEMELUCHUS. I GOT HIM KILLED...
I KNEW YOU'D FEEL TERRIBLE. AT FIRST I LEFT TO-TO PUNISH YOU, I SUPPOSE. I WAS ANGRY. BUT I WAS PUNISHING MYSELF TOO, IN THE END. I DIDN'T GET ANY CLOSURE.
AND... I MEAN... I TOLD PUGSLEY TO SHOOT, AND I DISTRACTED HIM WHEN WE WERE TRYING TO REVIVE YOU. YOU'RE A GHOST BECAUSE OF ME.

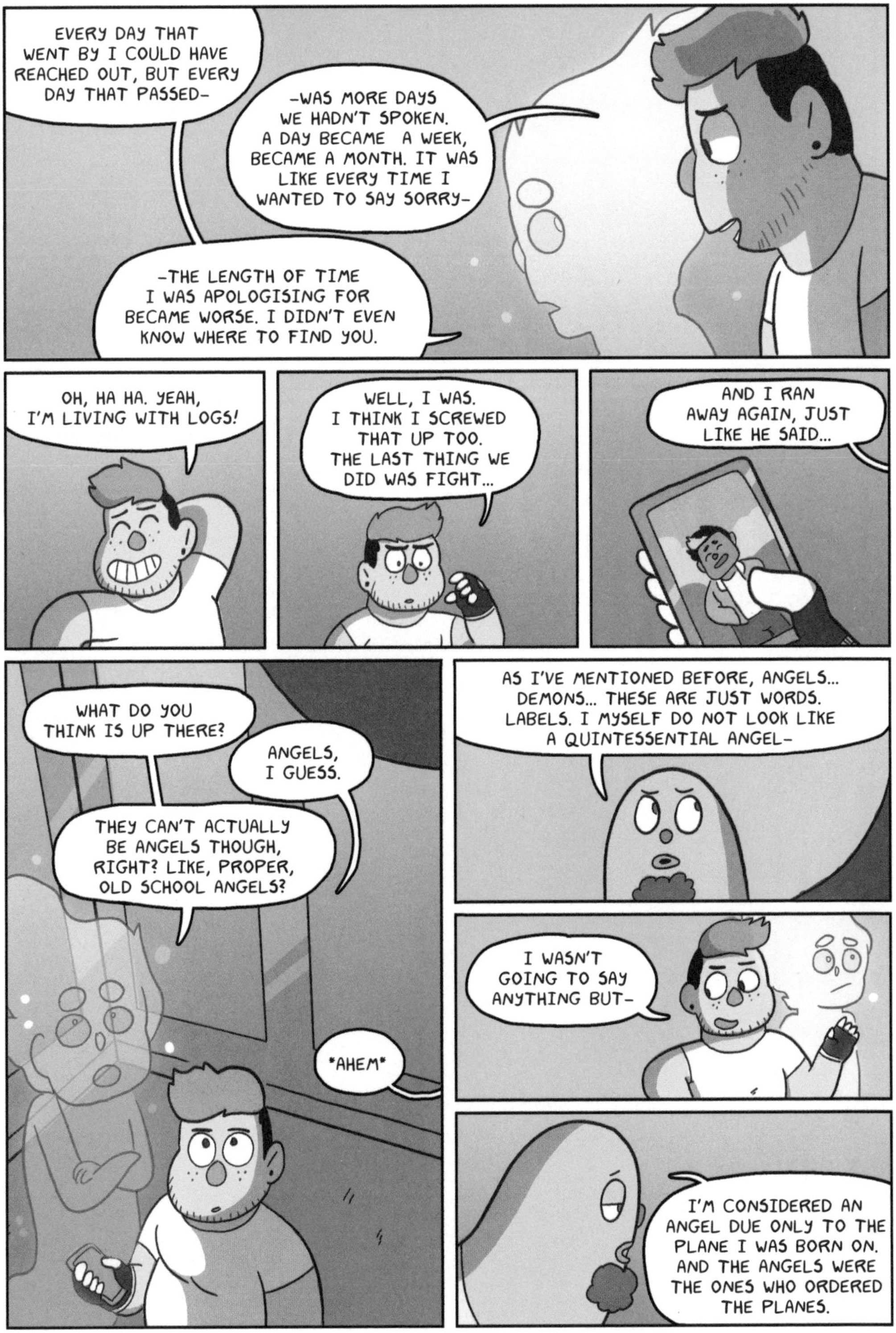
EVERY DAY THAT WENT BY I COULD HAVE REACHED OUT, BUT EVERY DAY THAT PASSED-
-WAS MORE DAYS WE HADN'T SPOKEN. A DAY BECAME A WEEK, BECAME A MONTH. IT WAS LIKE EVERY TIME I WANTED TO SAY SORRY-
-THE LENGTH OF TIME I WAS APOLOGISING FOR BECAME WORSE. I DIDN'T EVEN KNOW WHERE TO FIND YOU.
OH, HA HA. YEAH, I'M LIVING WITH LOGS!
WELL, I WAS. I THINK I SCREWED THAT UP TOO. THE LAST THING WE DID WAS FIGHT...
AND I RAN AWAY AGAIN, JUST LIKE HE SAID...
WHAT DO YOU THINK IS UP THERE?
ANGELS, I GUESS.
THEY CAN'T ACTUALLY BE ANGELS THOUGH, RIGHT? LIKE, PROPER, OLD SCHOOL ANGELS?
AHEM
AS I'VE MENTIONED BEFORE, ANGELS... DEMONS... THESE ARE JUST WORDS. LABELS. I MYSELF DO NOT LOOK LIKE A QUINTESSENTIAL ANGEL-
I WASN'T GOING TO SAY ANYTHING BUT-
I'M CONSIDERED AN ANGEL DUE ONLY TO THE PLANE I WAS BORN ON. AND THE ANGELS WERE THE ONES WHO ORDERED THE PLANES.

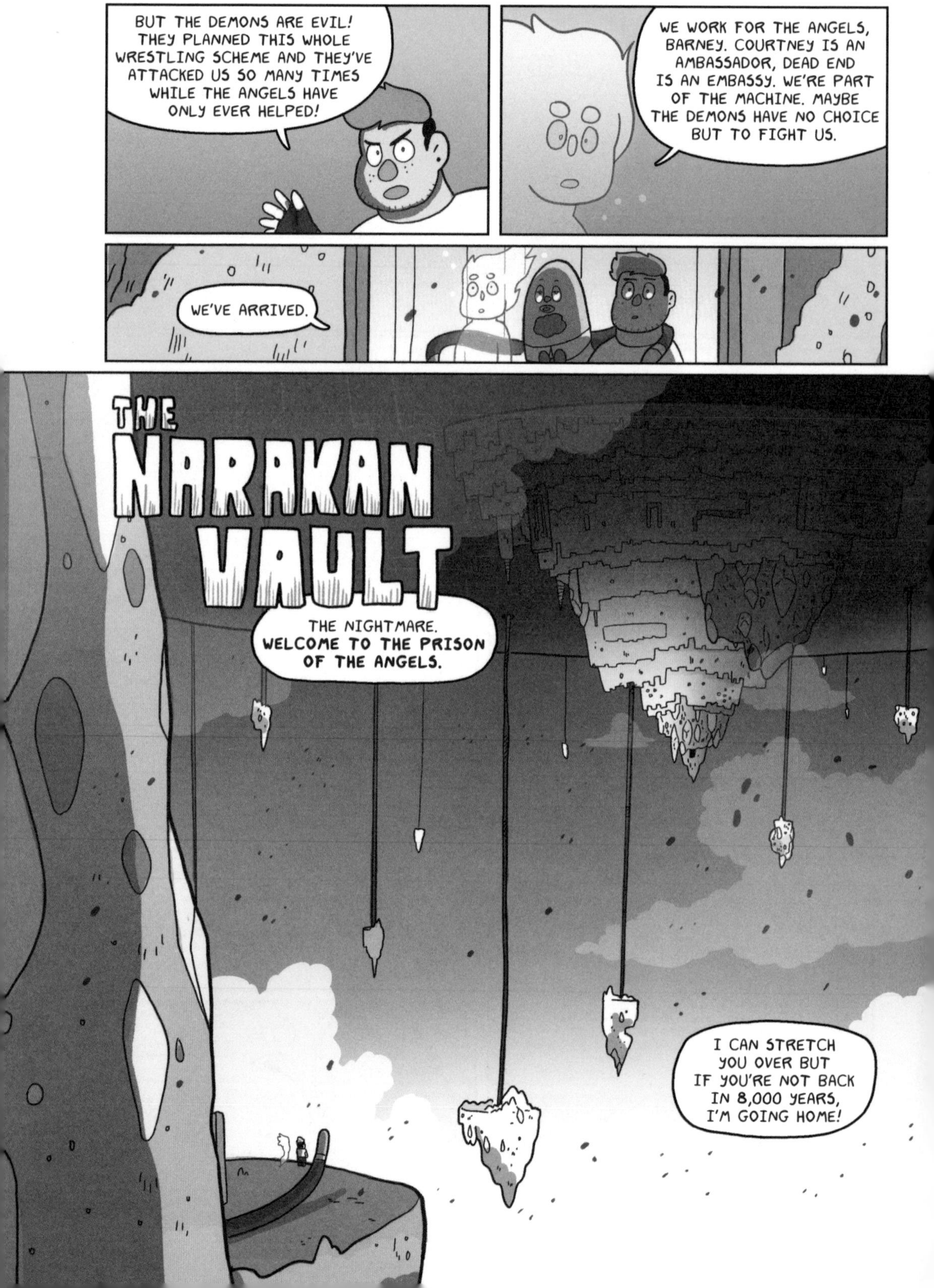
BUT THE DEMONS ARE EVIL! THEY PLANNED THIS WHOLE WRESTLING SCHEME AND THEY'VE ATTACKED US SO MANY TIMES WHILE THE ANGELS HAVE ONLY EVER HELPED!
WE WORK FOR THE ANGELS, BARNEY. COURTNEY IS AN AMBASSADOR, DEAD END IS AN EMBASSY. WE'RE PART OF THE MACHINE. MAYBE THE DEMONS HAVE NO CHOICE BUT TO FIGHT US.
WE'VE ARRIVED.
THE NARAKAN VAULT
THE NIGHTMARE. WELCOME TO THE PRISON OF THE ANGELS.
I CAN STRETCH YOU OVER BUT IF YOU'RE NOT BACK IN 8,000 YEARS, I'M GOING HOME!

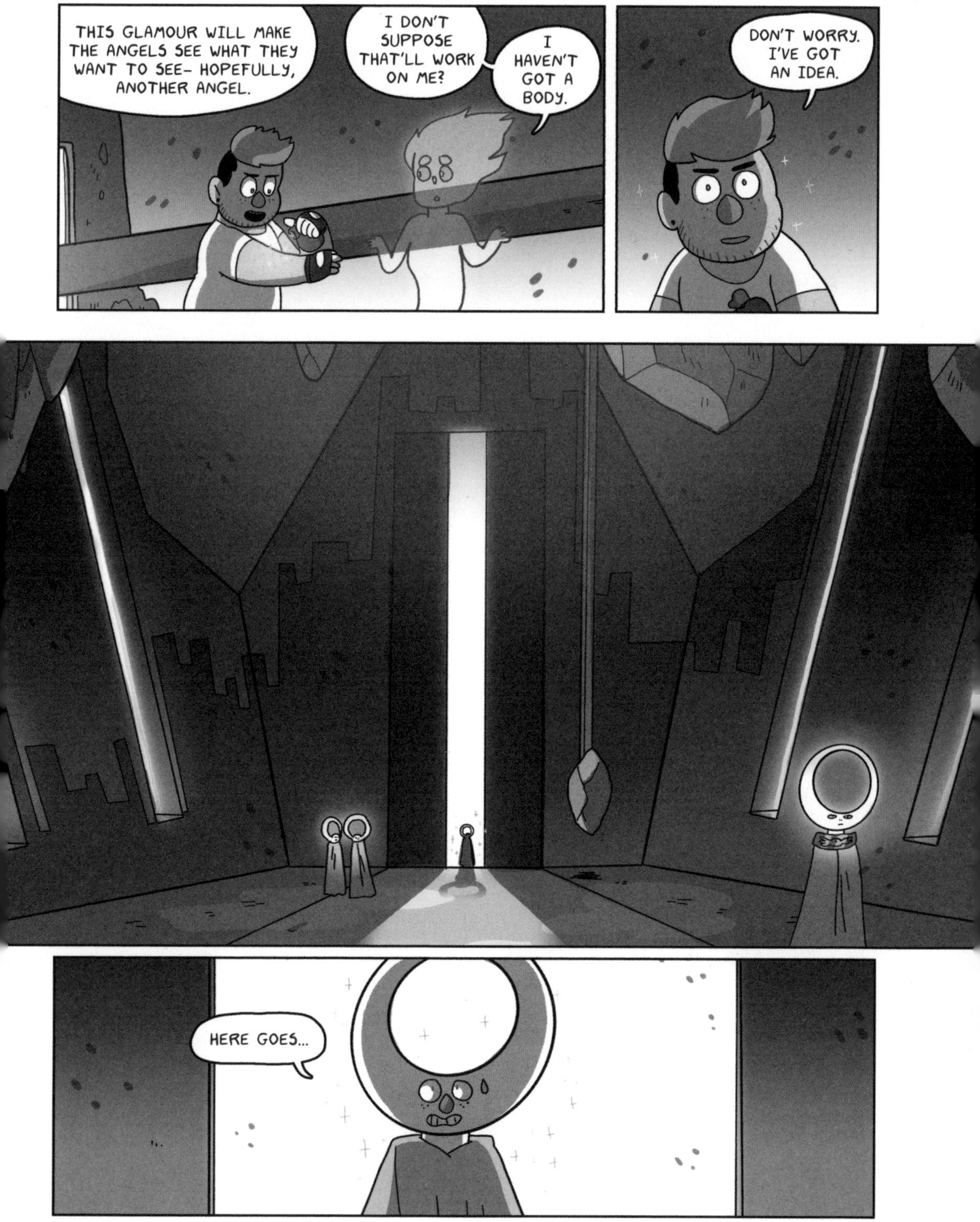
THIS GLAMOUR WILL MAKE THE ANGELS SEE WHAT THEY WANT TO SEE- HOPEFULLY, ANOTHER ANGEL.
I DON'T SUPPOSE THAT'LL WORK ON ME?
I HAVEN'T GOT A BODY.
DON'T WORRY. I'VE GOT AN IDEA.
HERE GOES...

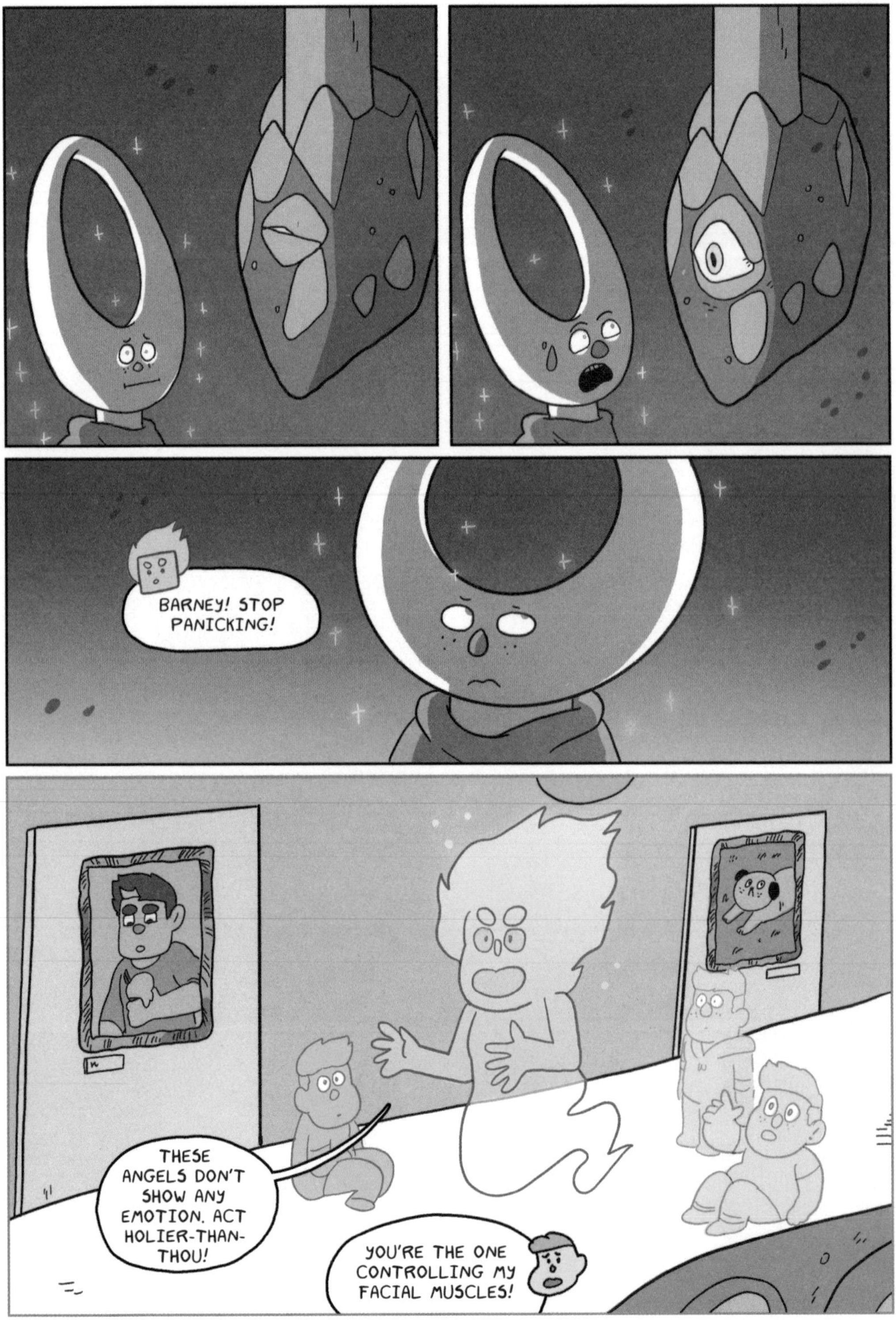

BARNEY! STOP PANICKING!
THESE ANGELS DON'T SHOW ANY EMOTION. ACT HOLIER-THAN-THOU!
YOU'RE THE ONE CONTROLLING MY FACIAL MUSCLES!

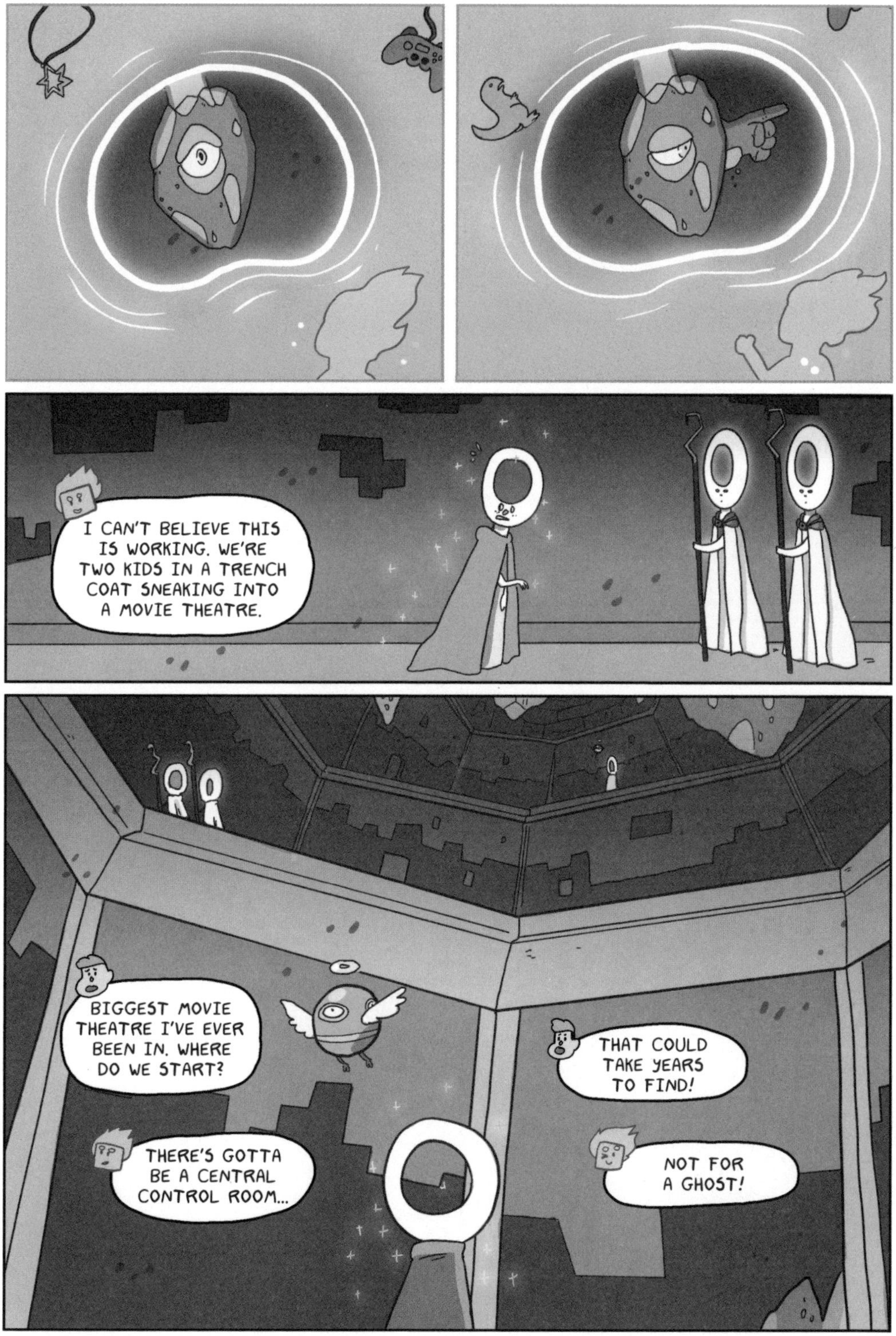
I CAN'T BELIEVE THIS IS WORKING. WE'RE TWO KIDS IN A TRENCH COAT SNEAKING INTO A MOVIE THEATRE.
BIGGEST MOVIE THEATRE I'VE EVER BEEN IN. WHERE DO WE START?
THERE'S GOTTA BE A CENTRAL CONTROL ROOM...
THAT COULD TAKE YEARS TO FIND!
NOT FOR A GHOST!

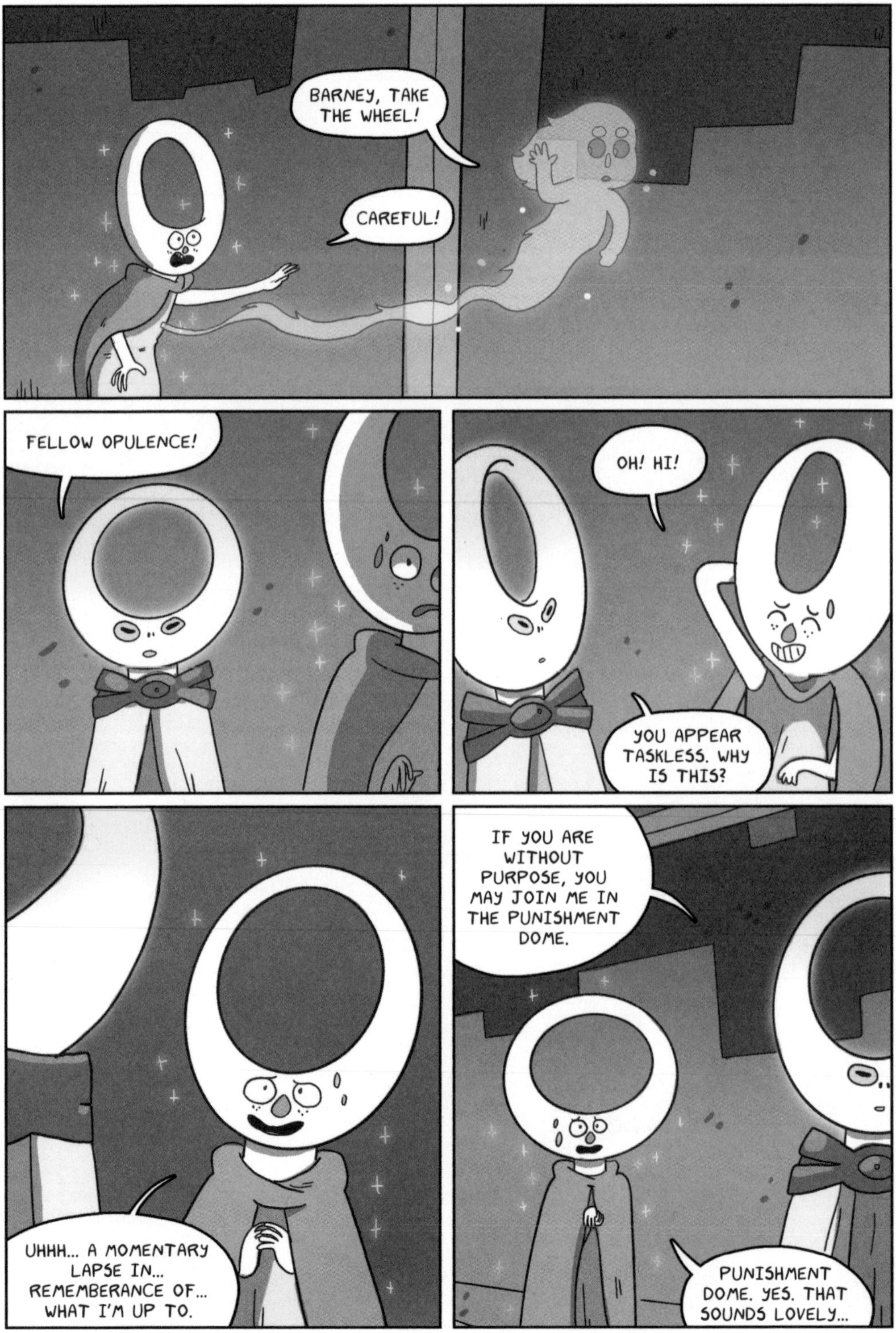

BARNEY, TAKE THE WHEEL!
CAREFUL!
FELLOW OPULENCE!
OH! HI!
YOU APPEAR TASKLESS. WHY IS THIS?
UHHH... A MOMENTARY LAPSE IN... REMEMBERANCE OF... WHAT I'M UP TO.
IF YOU ARE WITHOUT PURPOSE, YOU MAY JOIN ME IN THE PUNISHMENT DOME.
PUNISHMENT DOME. YES. THAT SOUNDS LOVELY...

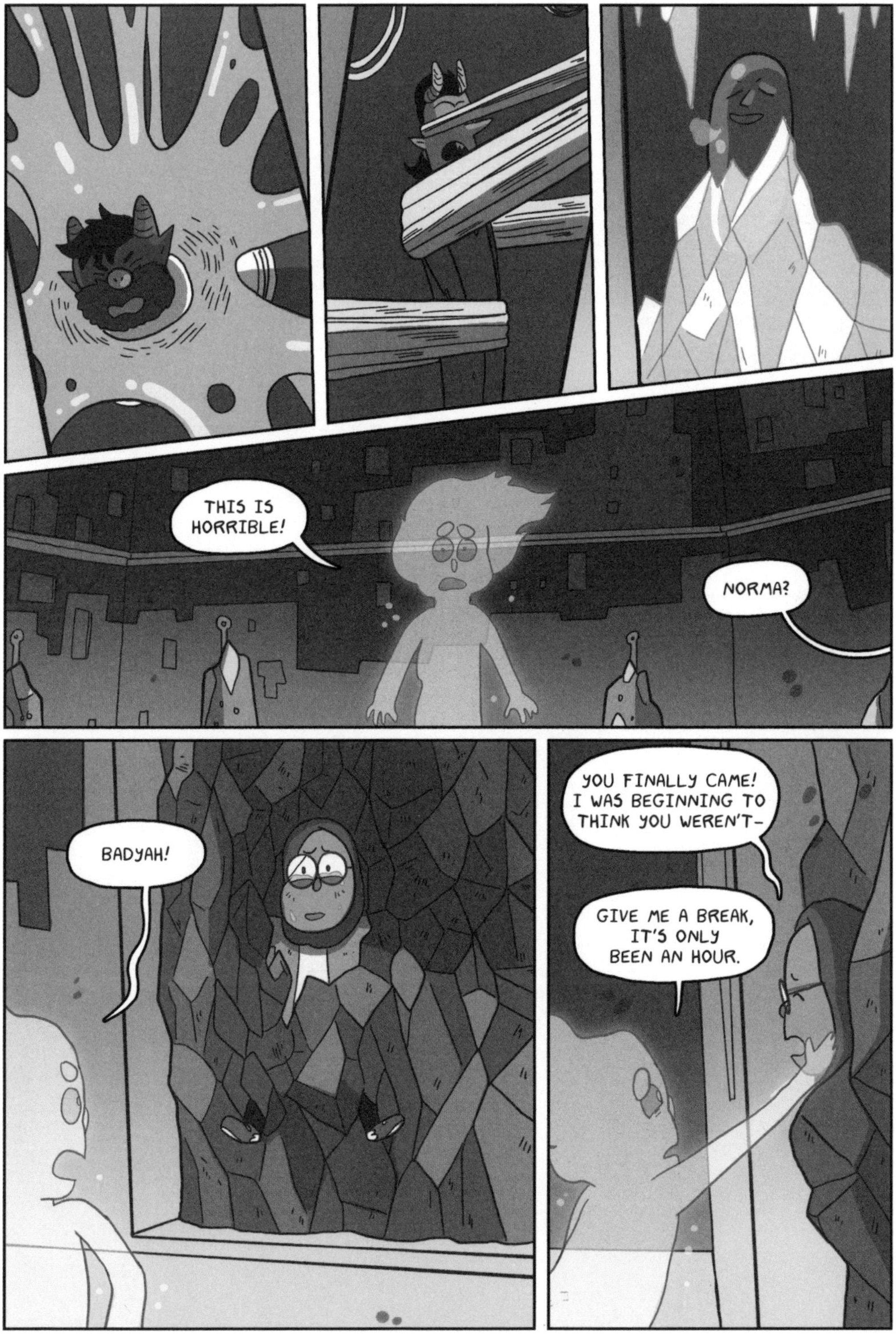
THIS IS HORRIBLE!
NORMA?
BADYAH!
YOU FINALLY CAME! I WAS BEGINNING TO THINK YOU WEREN'T-
GIVE ME A BREAK, IT'S ONLY BEEN AN HOUR.

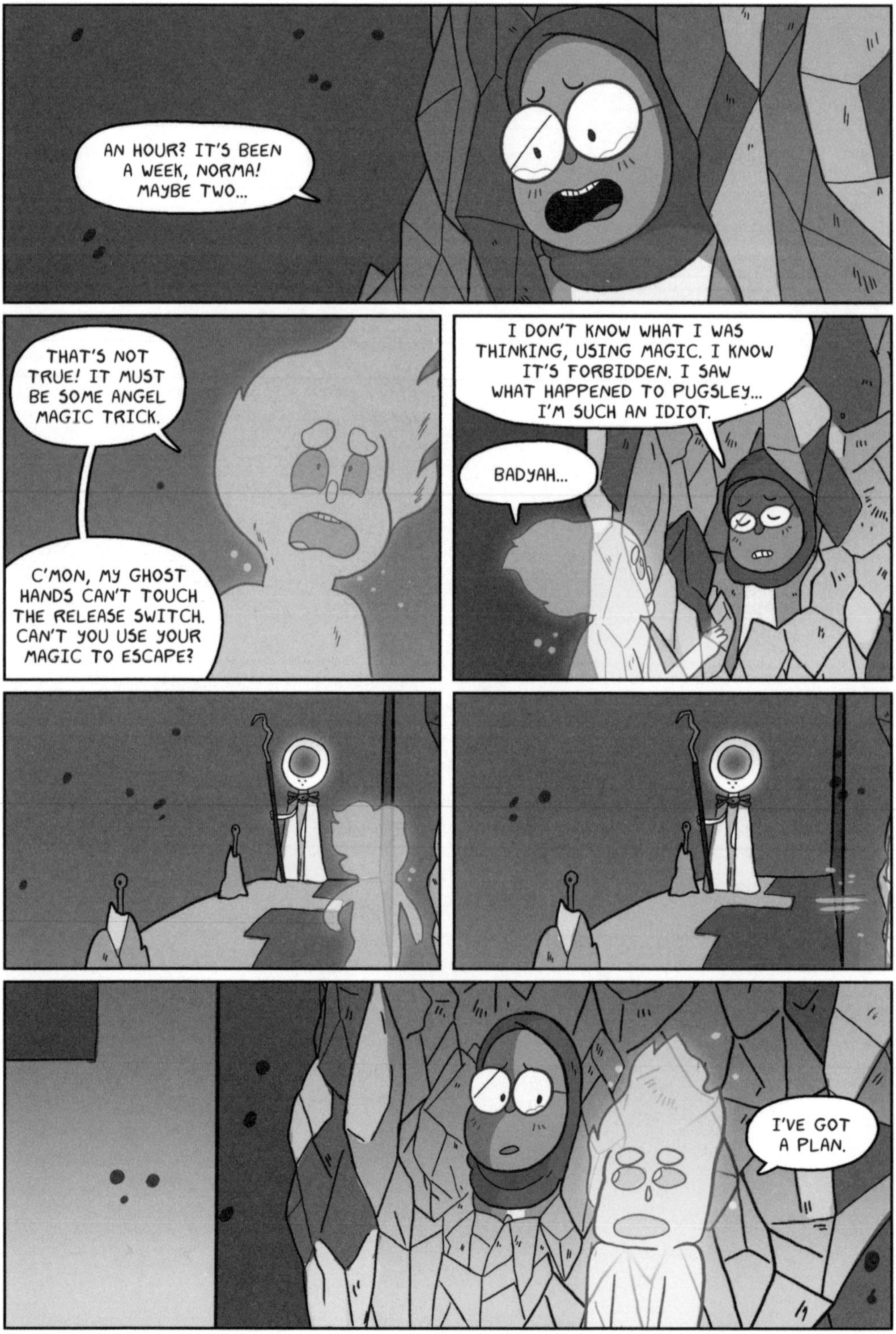
AN HOUR? IT'S BEEN A WEEK, NORMA! MAYBE TWO...
THAT'S NOT TRUE! IT MUST BE SOME ANGEL MAGIC TRICK.
C'MON, MY GHOST HANDS CAN'T TOUCH THE RELEASE SWITCH. CAN'T YOU USE YOUR MAGIC TO ESCAPE?
I DON'T KNOW WHAT I WAS THINKING, USING MAGIC. I KNOW IT'S FORBIDDEN. I SAW WHAT HAPPENED TO PUGSLEY... I'M SUCH AN IDIOT.
BADYAH...
I'VE GOT A PLAN.

ANGEL-
POSSESSION
A GO-GO!

WAIT... WHERE IS EVERYTHING? THE MEMORIES? EMOTIONS?

AND WHAT THE HELL IS THAT?!

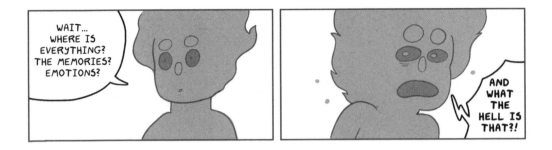

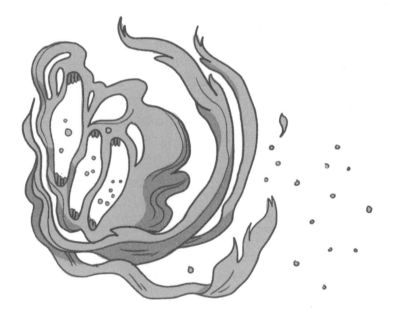

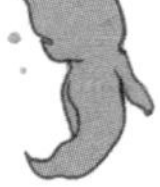

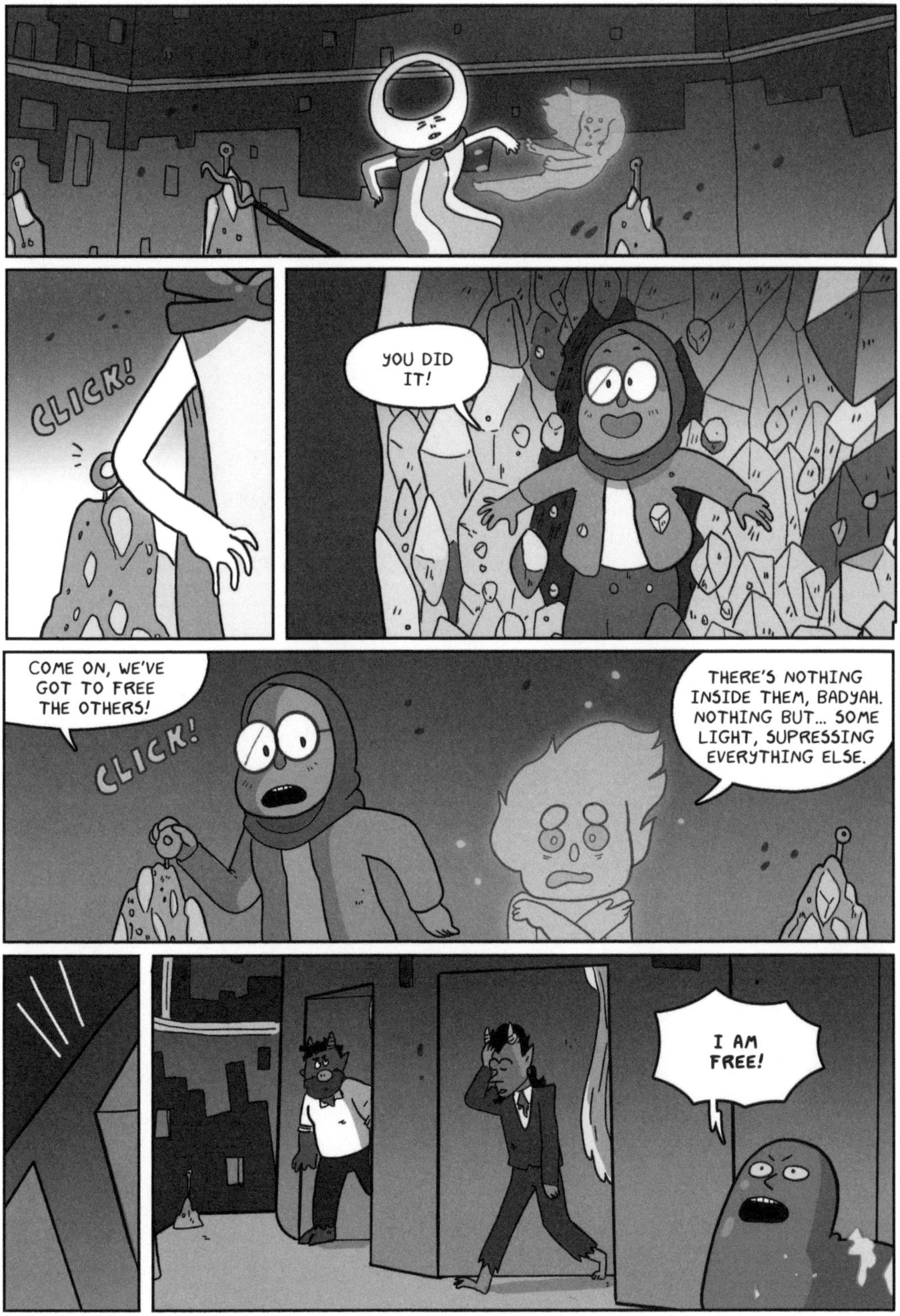
CLICK!
YOU DID IT!
COME ON, WE'VE GOT TO FREE THE OTHERS!
CLICK!
THERE'S NOTHING INSIDE THEM, BADYAH. NOTHING BUT... SOME LIGHT, SUPRESSING EVERYTHING ELSE.
I AM FREE!

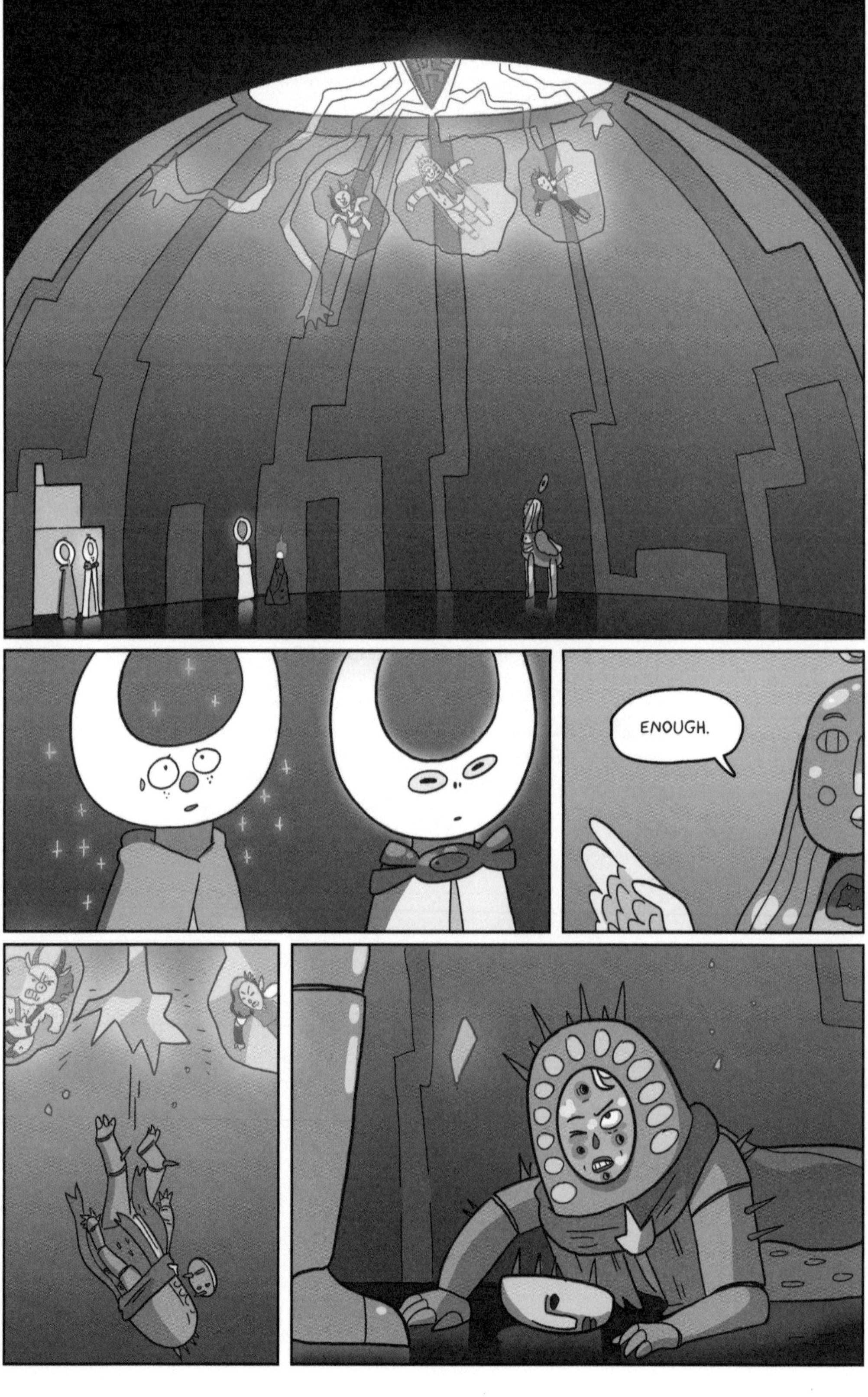
ENOUGH.

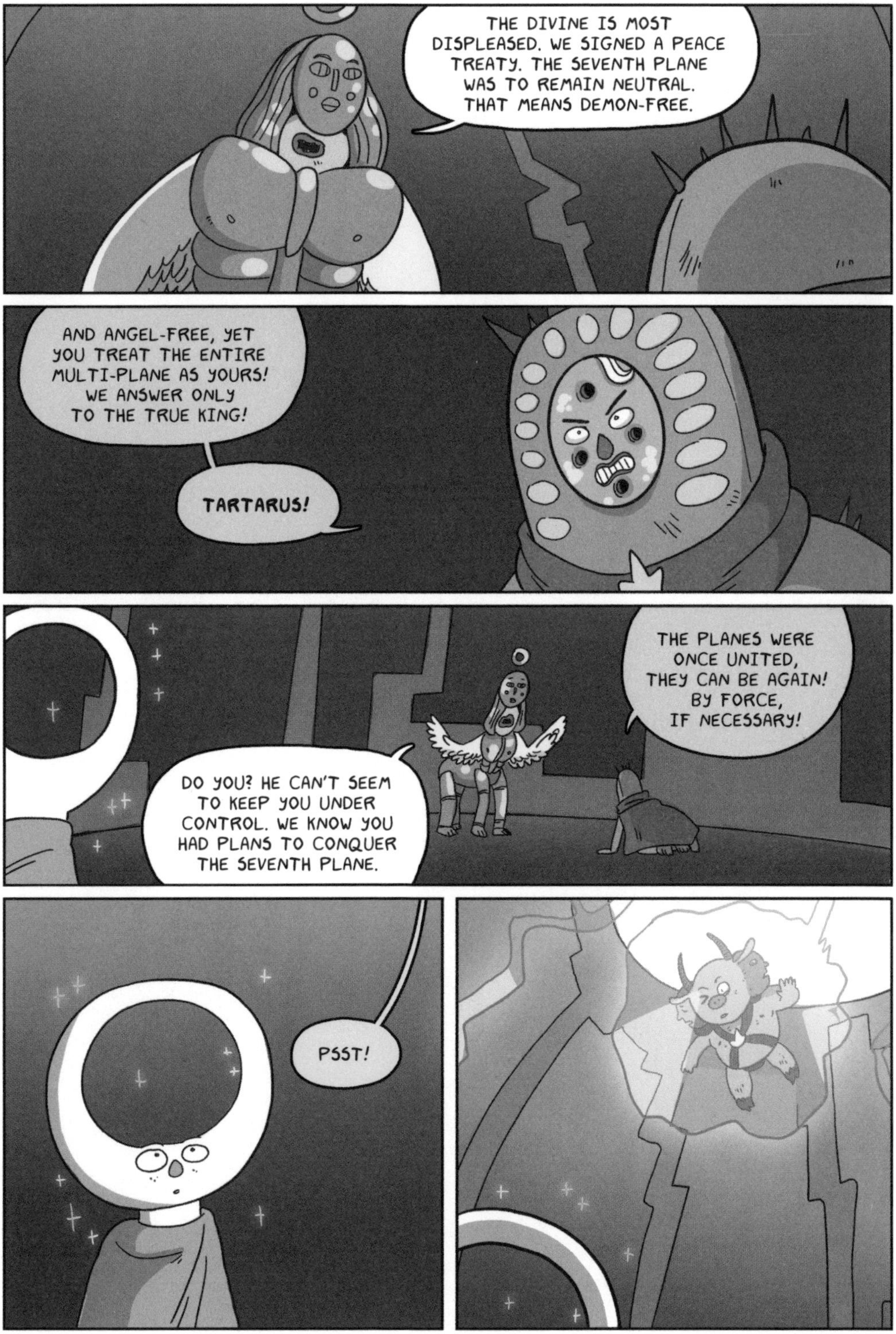
THE DIVINE IS MOST DISPLEASED. WE SIGNED A PEACE TREATY. THE SEVENTH PLANE WAS TO REMAIN NEUTRAL. THAT MEANS DEMON-FREE.
AND ANGEL-FREE, YET YOU TREAT THE ENTIRE MULTI-PLANE AS YOURS! WE ANSWER ONLY TO THE TRUE KING!
TARTARUS!
DO YOU? HE CAN'T SEEM TO KEEP YOU UNDER CONTROL. WE KNOW YOU HAD PLANS TO CONQUER THE SEVENTH PLANE.
THE PLANES WERE ONCE UNITED, THEY CAN BE AGAIN! BY FORCE, IF NECESSARY!
PSST!

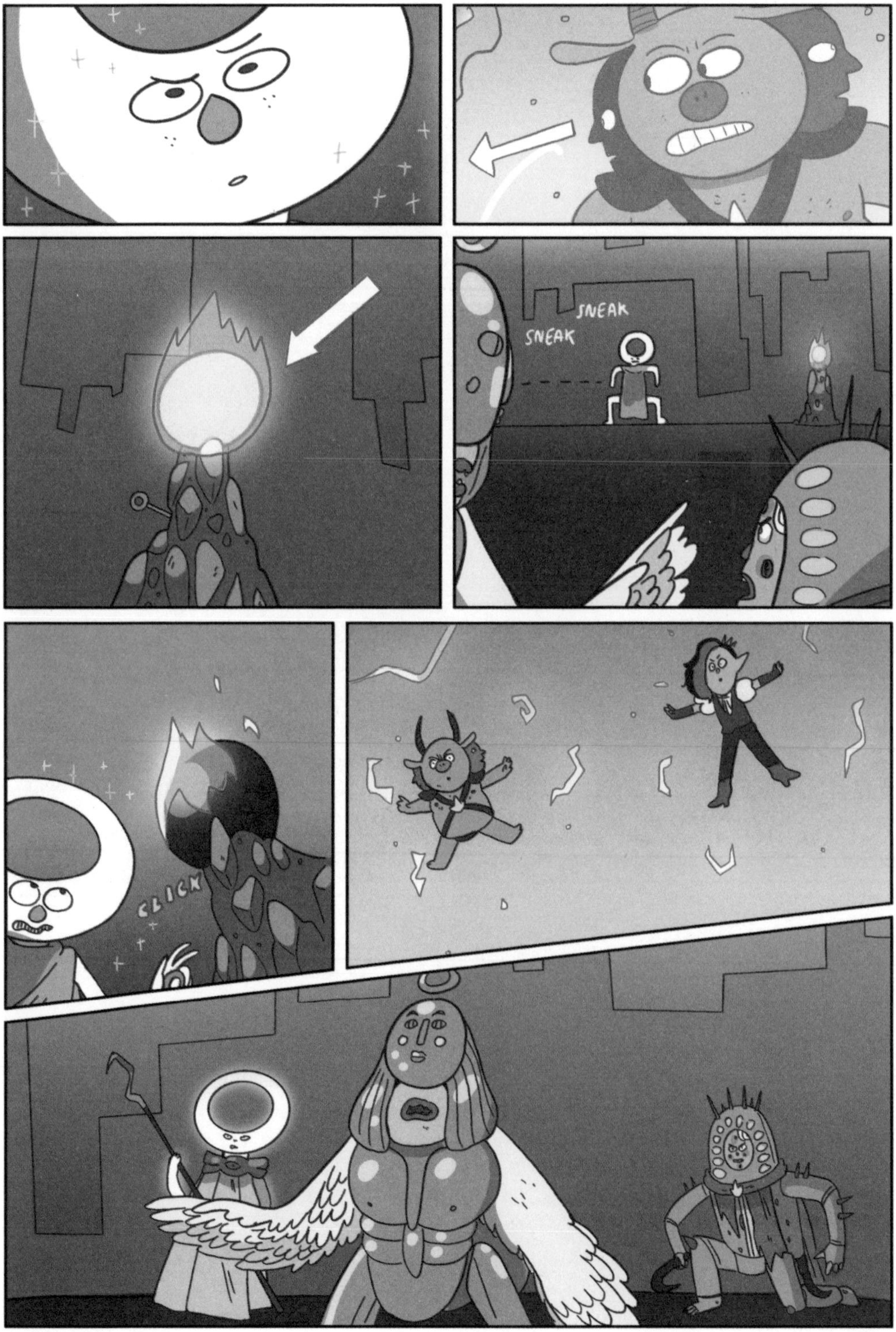
SNEAK
SNEAK
CLICK

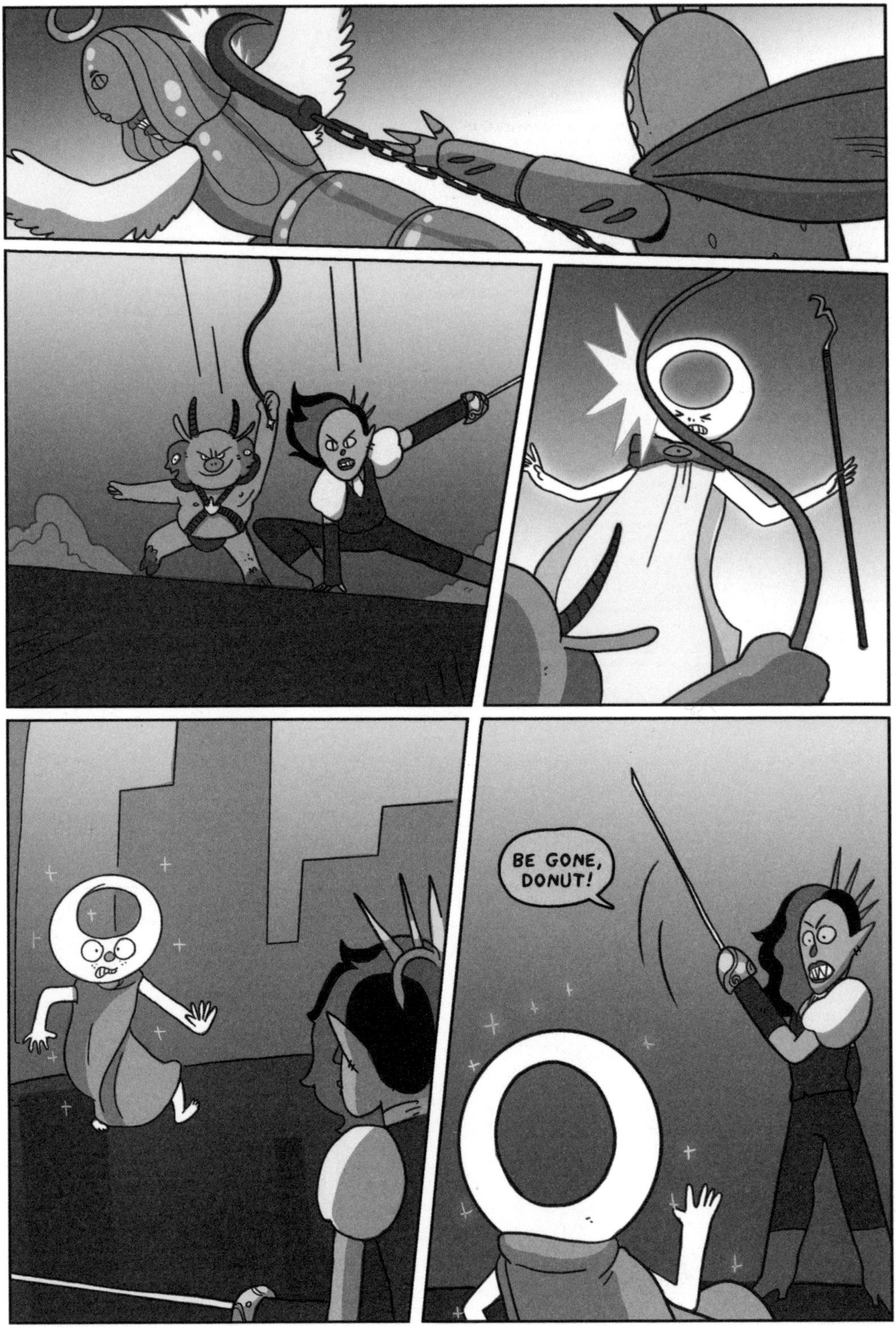
BE GONE, DONUT!

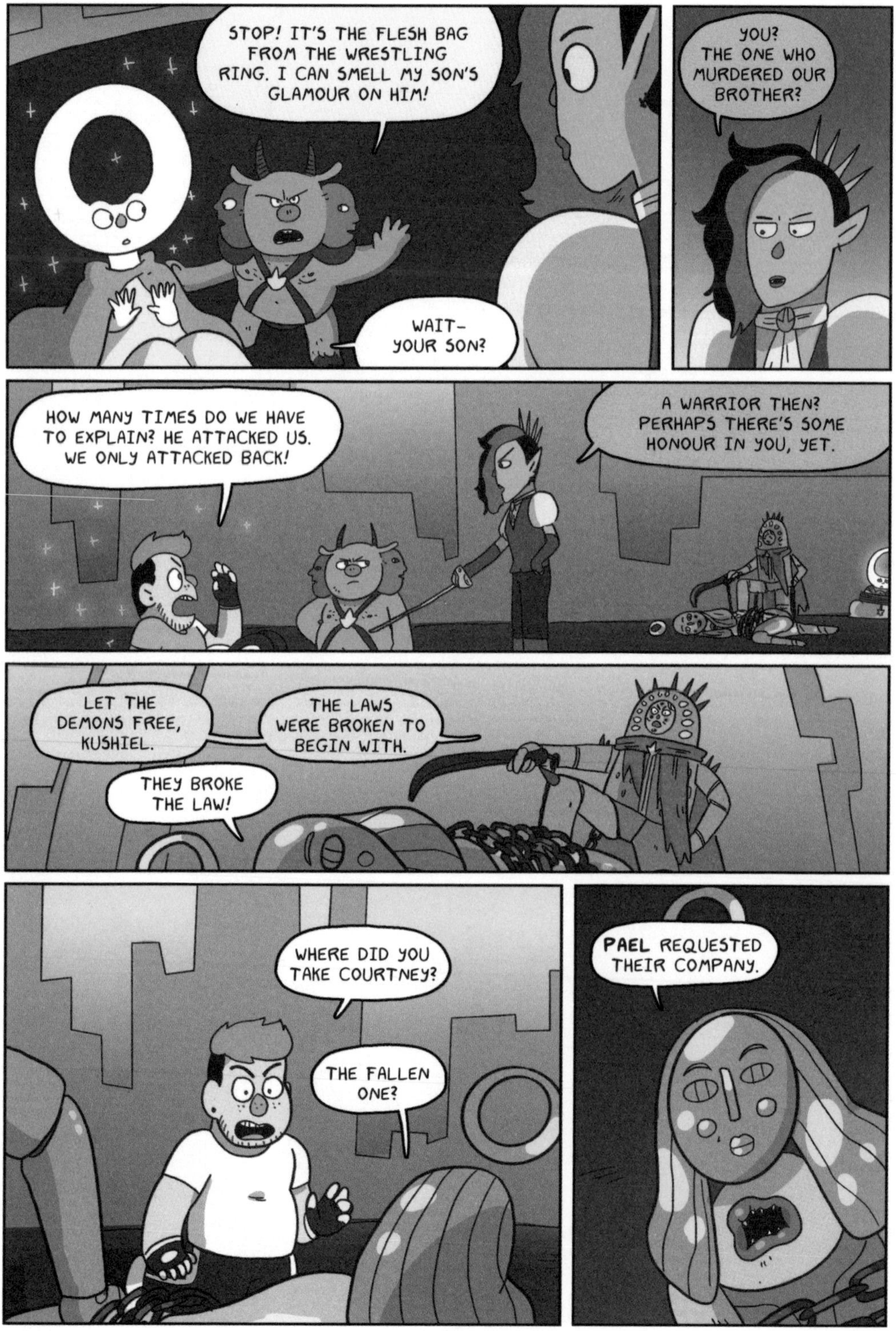

STOP! IT'S THE FLESH BAG FROM THE WRESTLING RING. I CAN SMELL MY SON'S GLAMOUR ON HIM!
WAIT- YOUR SON?
YOU? THE ONE WHO MURDERED OUR BROTHER?
HOW MANY TIMES DO WE HAVE TO EXPLAIN? HE ATTACKED US. WE ONLY ATTACKED BACK!
A WARRIOR THEN? PERHAPS THERE'S SOME HONOUR IN YOU, YET.
LET THE DEMONS FREE, KUSHIEL.
THE LAWS WERE BROKEN TO BEGIN WITH.
THEY BROKE THE LAW!
WHERE DID YOU TAKE COURTNEY?
THE FALLEN ONE?
PAEL REQUESTED THEIR COMPANY.

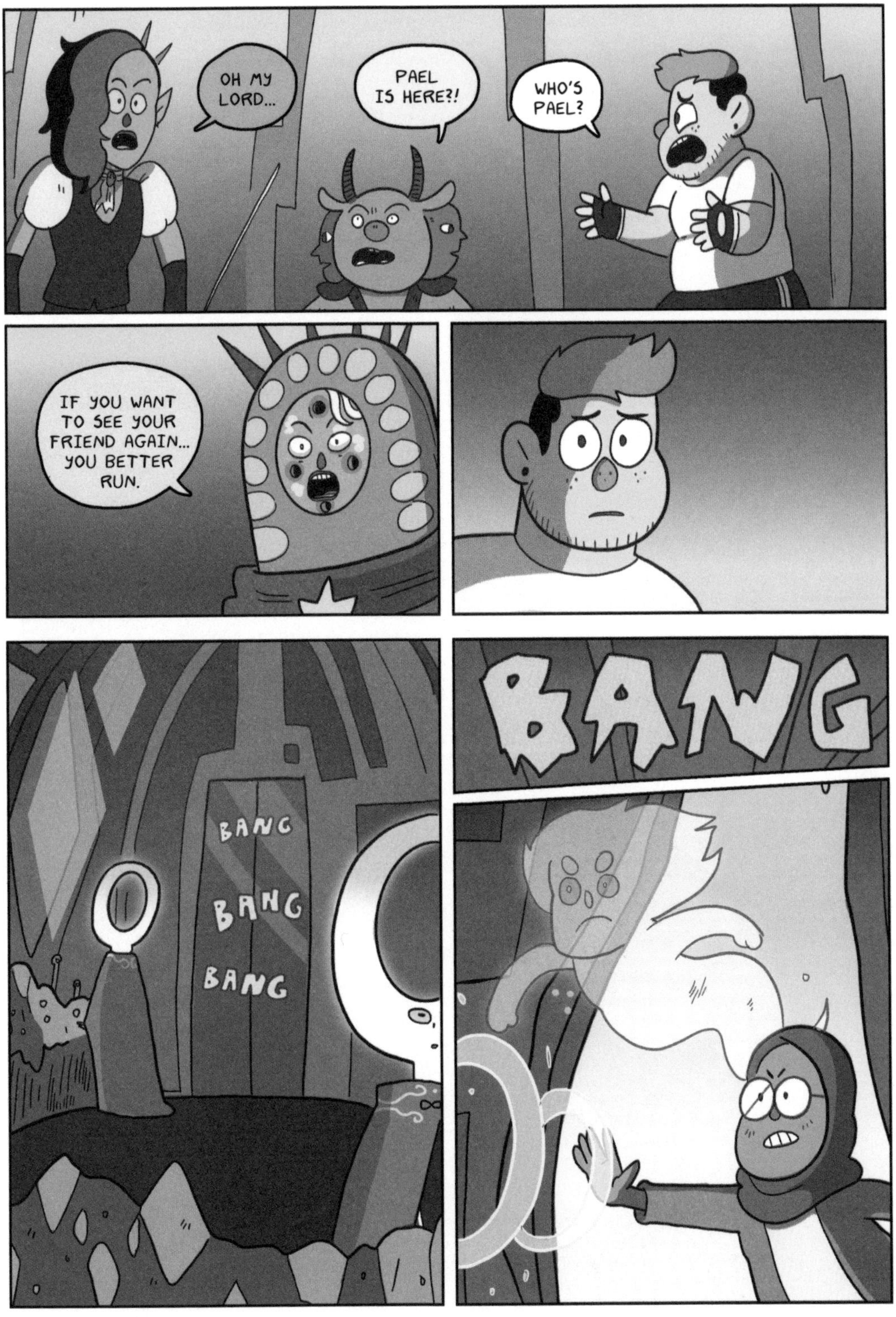
OH MY LORD...
PAEL IS HERE?!
WHO'S PAEL?
IF YOU WANT TO SEE YOUR FRIEND AGAIN... YOU BETTER RUN.
BANG
BANG
BANG
BANG

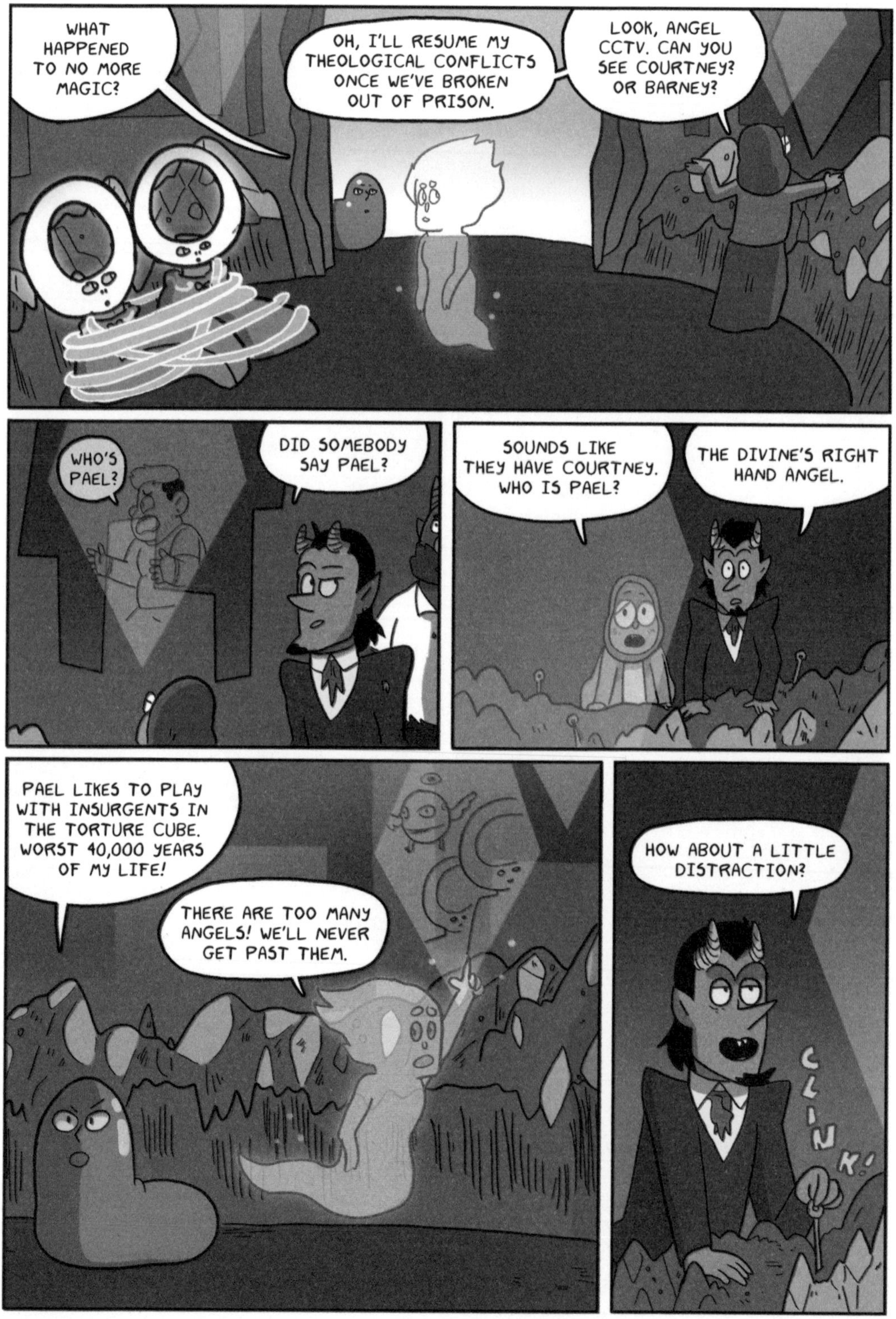
WHAT HAPPENED TO NO MORE MAGIC?
OH, I'LL RESUME MY THEOLOGICAL CONFLICTS ONCE WE'VE BROKEN OUT OF PRISON.
LOOK, ANGEL CCTV. CAN YOU SEE COURTNEY? OR BARNEY?
WHO'S PAEL?
DID SOMEBODY SAY PAEL?
SOUNDS LIKE THEY HAVE COURTNEY. WHO IS PAEL?
THE DIVINE'S RIGHT HAND ANGEL.
PAEL LIKES TO PLAY WITH INSURGENTS IN THE TORTURE CUBE. WORST 40,000 YEARS OF MY LIFE!
THERE ARE TOO MANY ANGELS! WE'LL NEVER GET PAST THEM.
HOW ABOUT A LITTLE DISTRACTION?
CLINK!

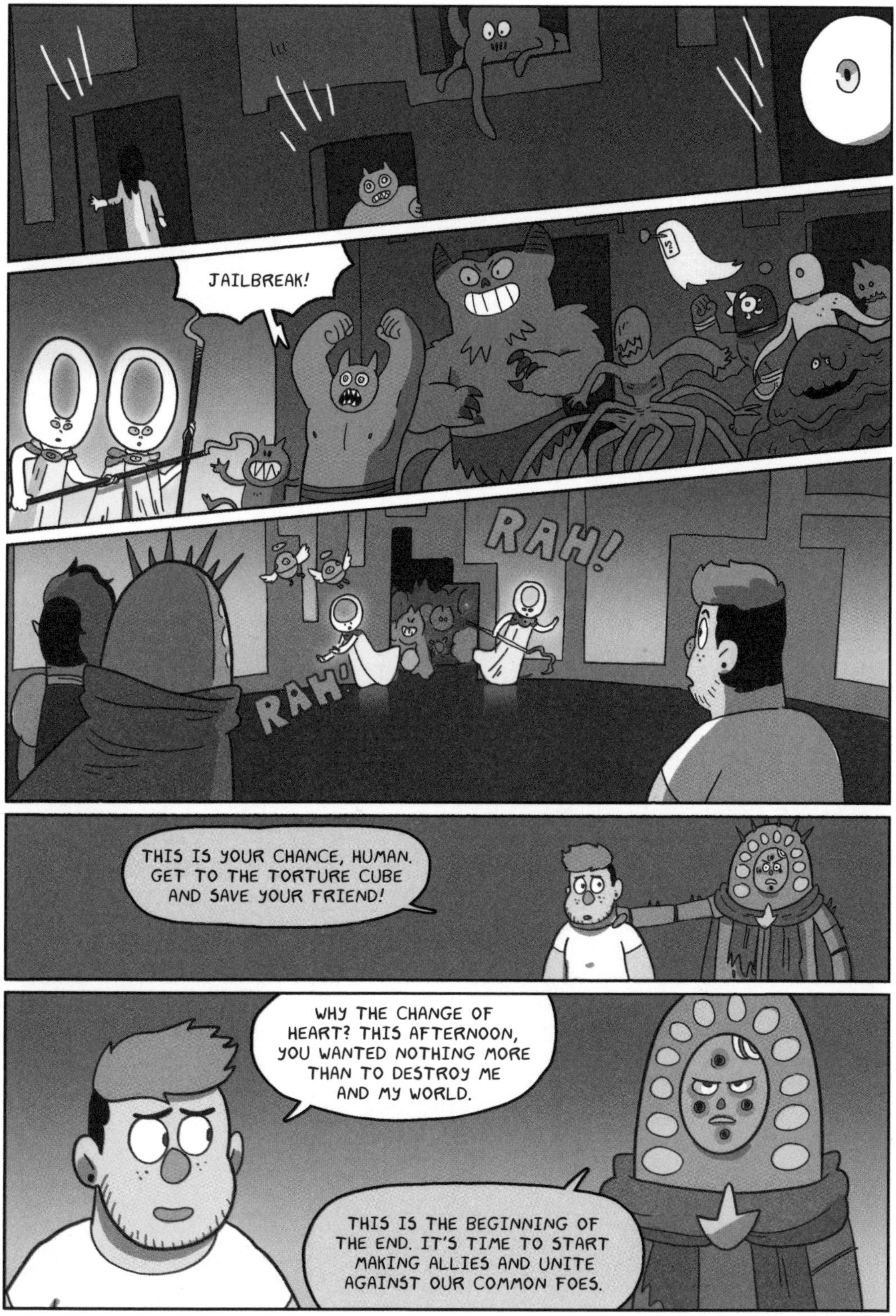

JAILBREAK!
RAH!
RAH!
THIS IS YOUR CHANCE, HUMAN. GET TO THE TORTURE CUBE AND SAVE YOUR FRIEND!
WHY THE CHANGE OF HEART? THIS AFTERNOON, YOU WANTED NOTHING MORE THAN TO DESTROY ME AND MY WORLD.
THIS IS THE BEGINNING OF THE END. IT'S TIME TO START MAKING ALLIES AND UNITE AGAINST OUR COMMON FOES.

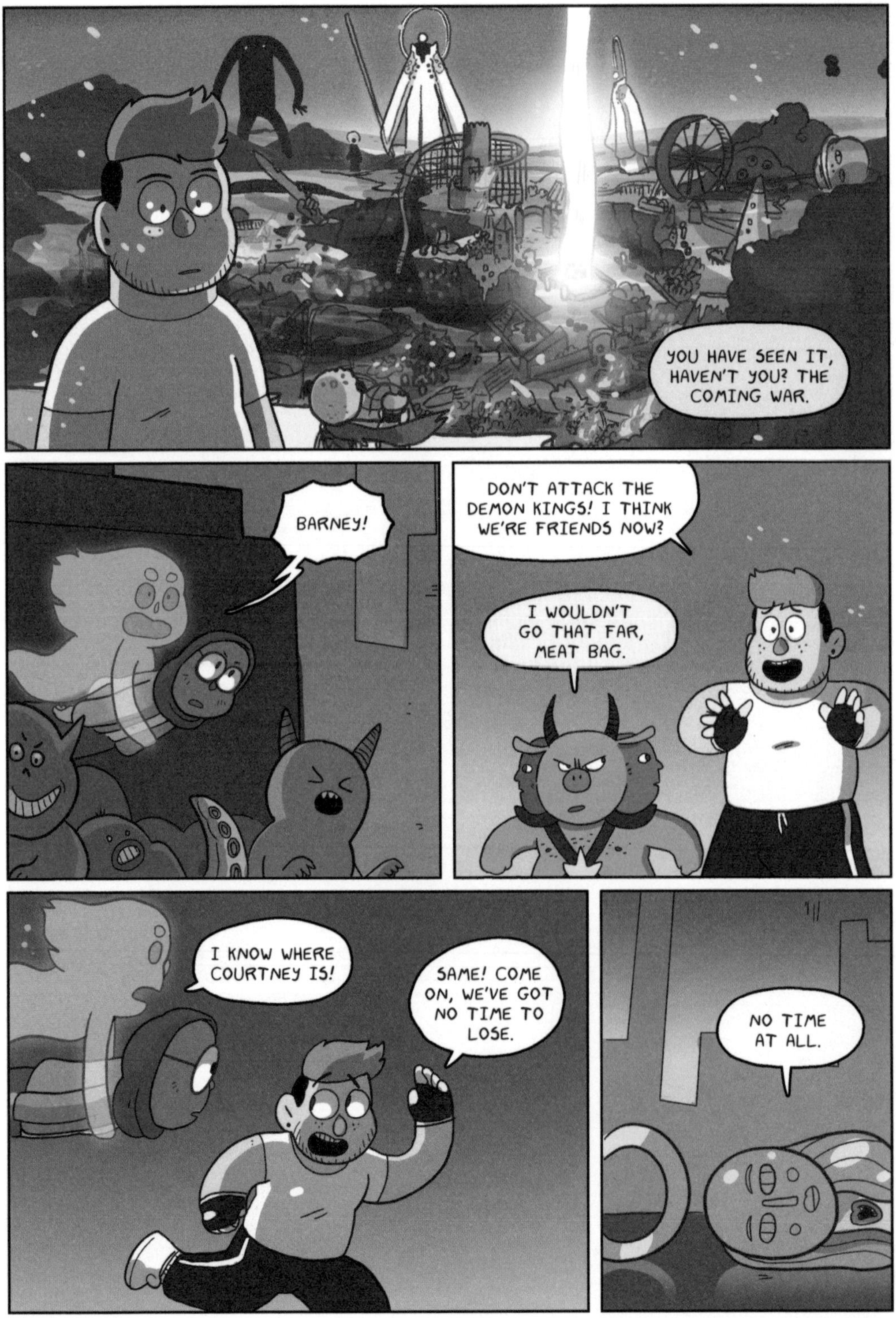

YOU HAVE SEEN IT, HAVEN'T YOU? THE COMING WAR.
BARNEY!
DON'T ATTACK THE DEMON KINGS! I THINK WE'RE FRIENDS NOW?
I WOULDN'T GO THAT FAR, MEAT BAG.
I KNOW WHERE COURTNEY IS!
SAME! COME ON, WE'VE GOT NO TIME TO LOSE.
NO TIME AT ALL.

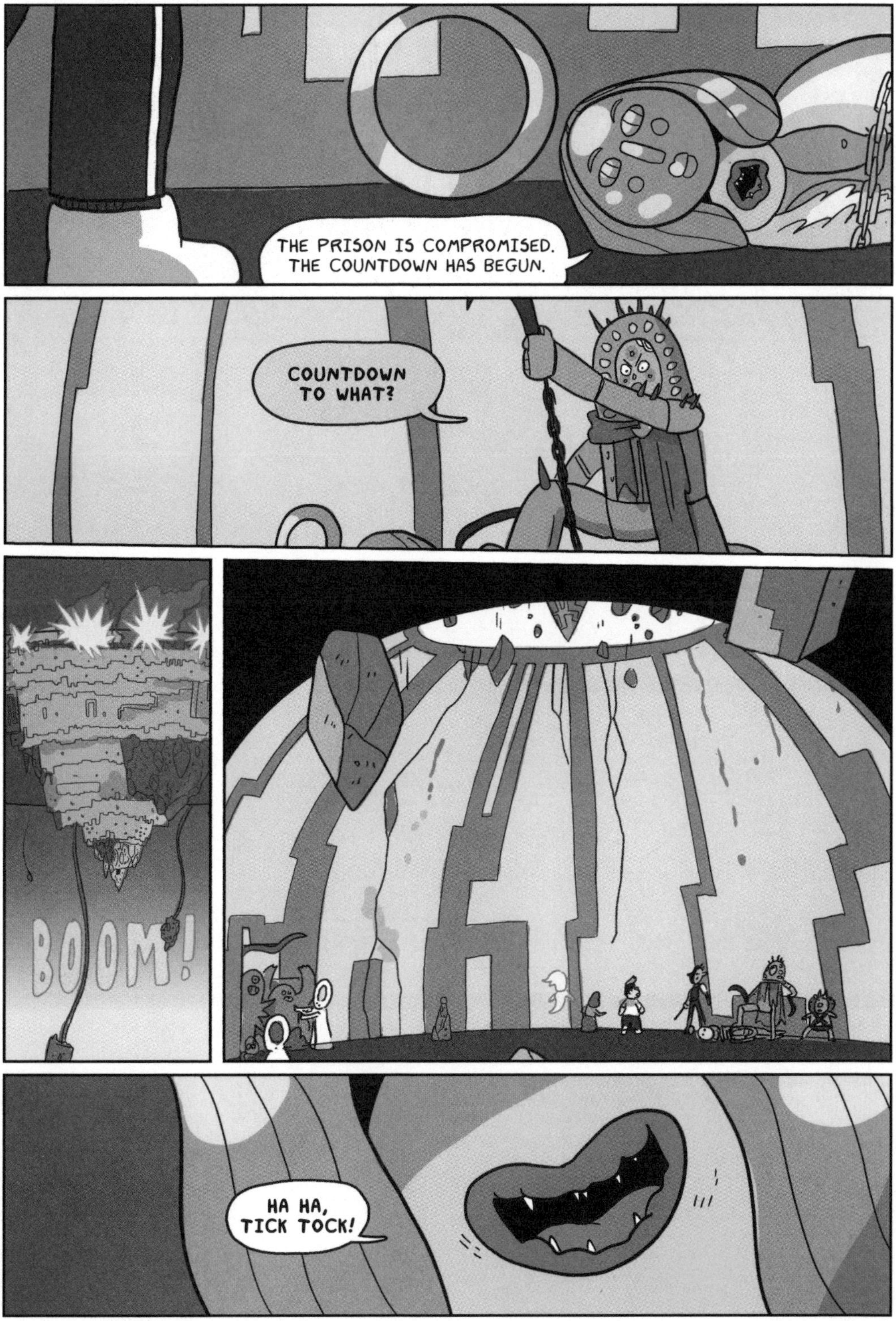
THE PRISON IS COMPROMISED. THE COUNTDOWN HAS BEGUN.
COUNTDOWN TO WHAT?
BOOM!
HA HA, TICK TOCK!

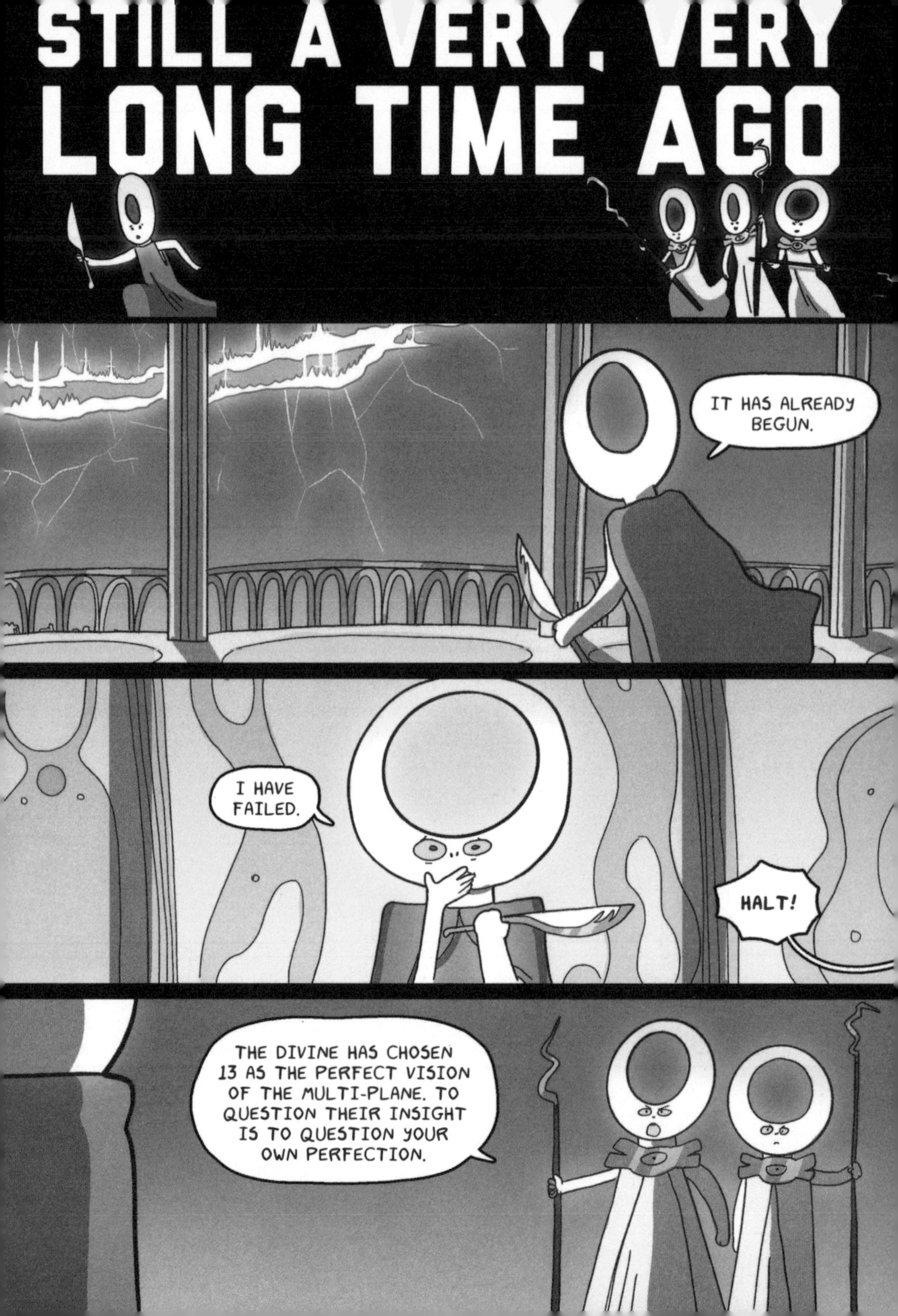
STILL A VERY, VERY LONG TIME AGO
IT HAS ALREADY BEGUN.
I HAVE FAILED.
HALT!
THE DIVINE HAS CHOSEN 13 AS THE PERFECT VISION OF THE MULTI-PLANE. TO QUESTION THEIR INSIGHT IS TO QUESTION YOUR OWN PERFECTION.

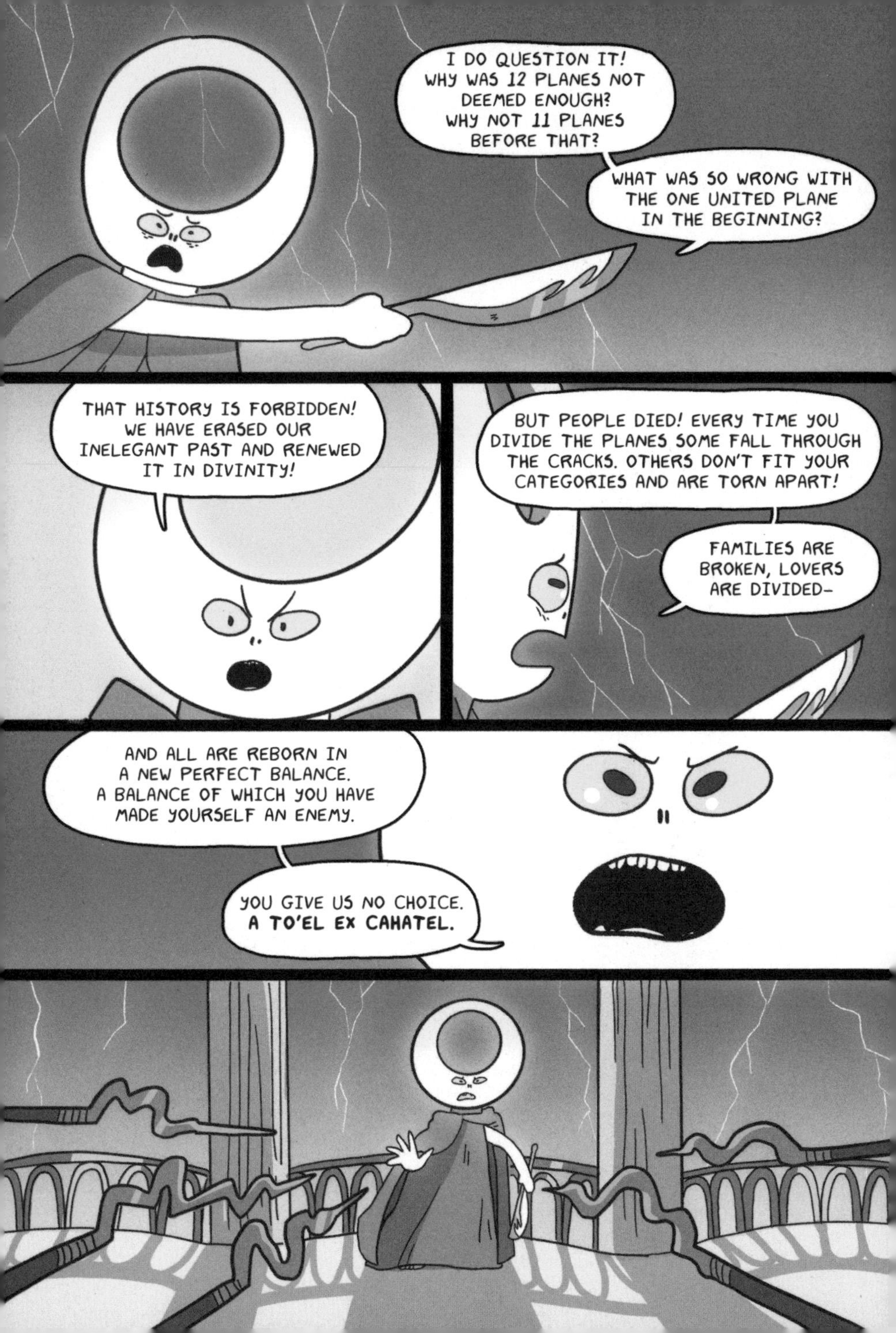
I DO QUESTION IT! WHY WAS 12 PLANES NOT DEEMED ENOUGH? WHY NOT 11 PLANES BEFORE THAT?
WHAT WAS SO WRONG WITH THE ONE UNITED PLANE IN THE BEGINNING?
THAT HISTORY IS FORBIDDEN! WE HAVE ERASED OUR INELEGANT PAST AND RENEWED IT IN DIVINITY!
BUT PEOPLE DIED! EVERY TIME YOU DIVIDE THE PLANES SOME FALL THROUGH THE CRACKS. OTHERS DON'T FIT YOUR CATEGORIES AND ARE TORN APART!
FAMILIES ARE BROKEN, LOVERS ARE DIVIDED–
AND ALL ARE REBORN IN A NEW PERFECT BALANCE. A BALANCE OF WHICH YOU HAVE MADE YOURSELF AN ENEMY.
YOU GIVE US NO CHOICE. **A TO'EL EX CAHATEL.**

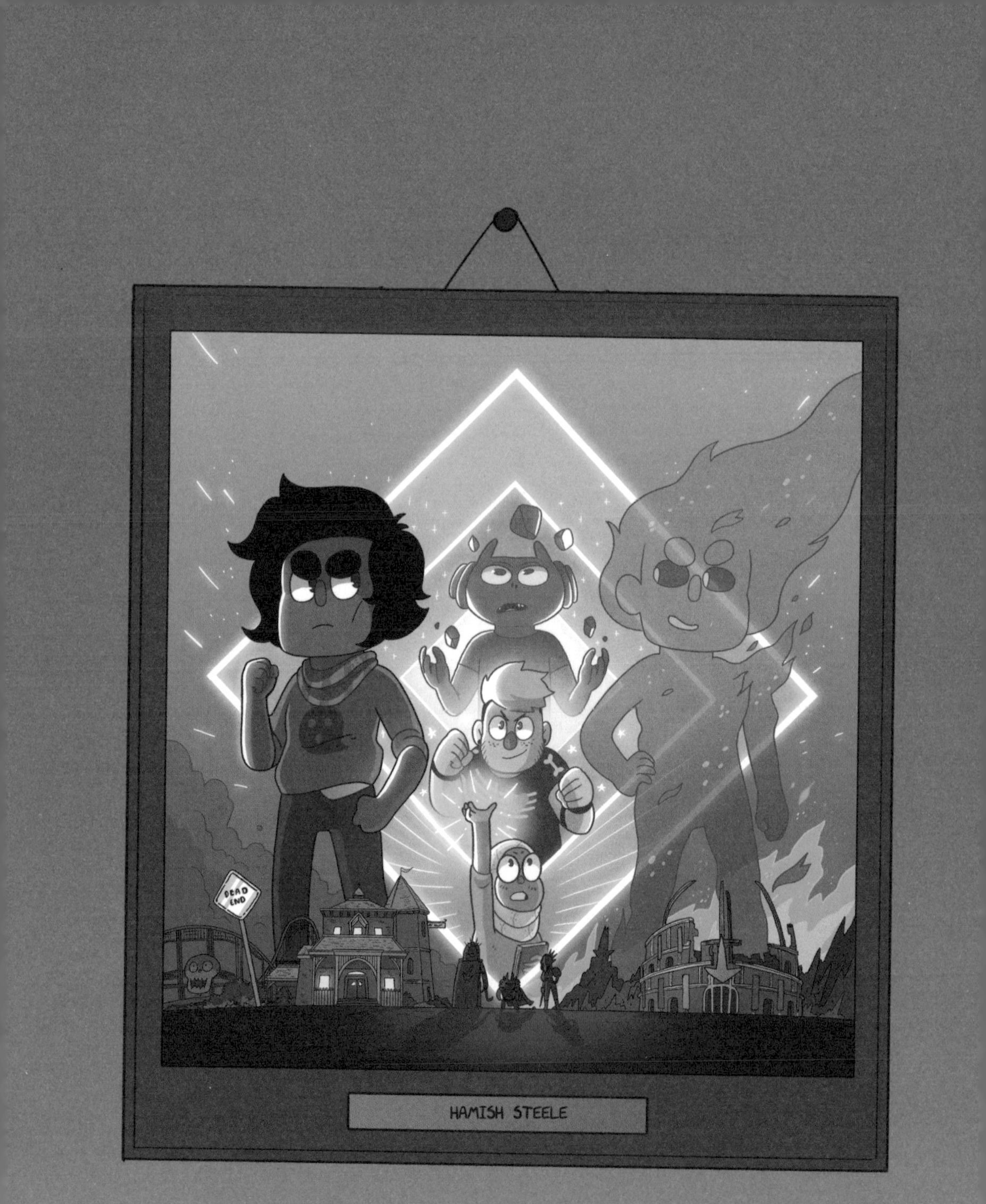
DEAD END
HAMISH STEELE

CHAPTER 8
THE BROKEN HALO

COURTNEY

TOUGH ●●●○○
SMART ●●●●○
WEIRD ●●●●●
STYLE ●●○○○

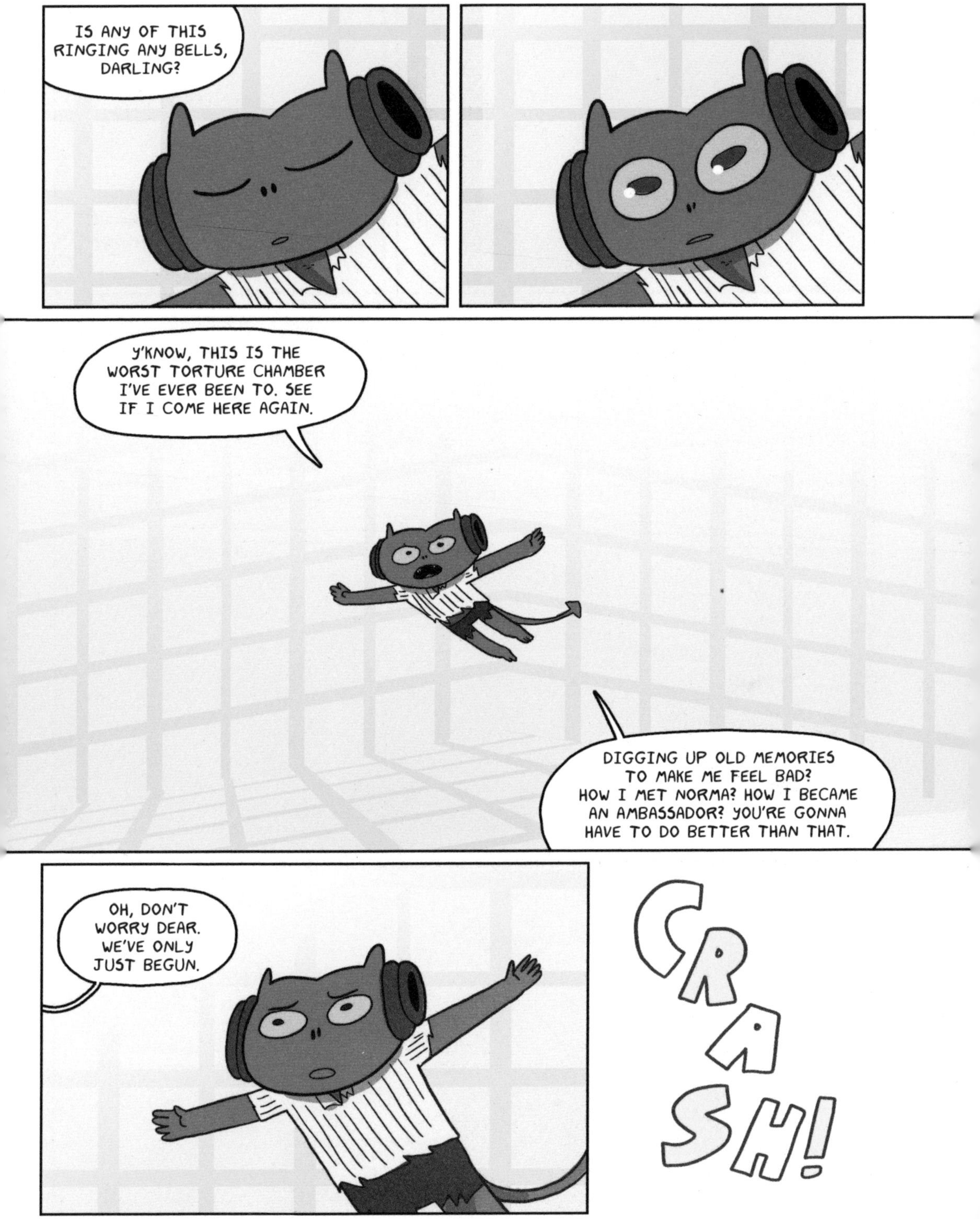
IS ANY OF THIS RINGING ANY BELLS, DARLING?
Y'KNOW, THIS IS THE WORST TORTURE CHAMBER I'VE EVER BEEN TO. SEE IF I COME HERE AGAIN.
DIGGING UP OLD MEMORIES TO MAKE ME FEEL BAD? HOW I MET NORMA? HOW I BECAME AN AMBASSADOR? YOU'RE GONNA HAVE TO DO BETTER THAN THAT.
OH, DON'T WORRY DEAR. WE'VE ONLY JUST BEGUN.
CRASH!

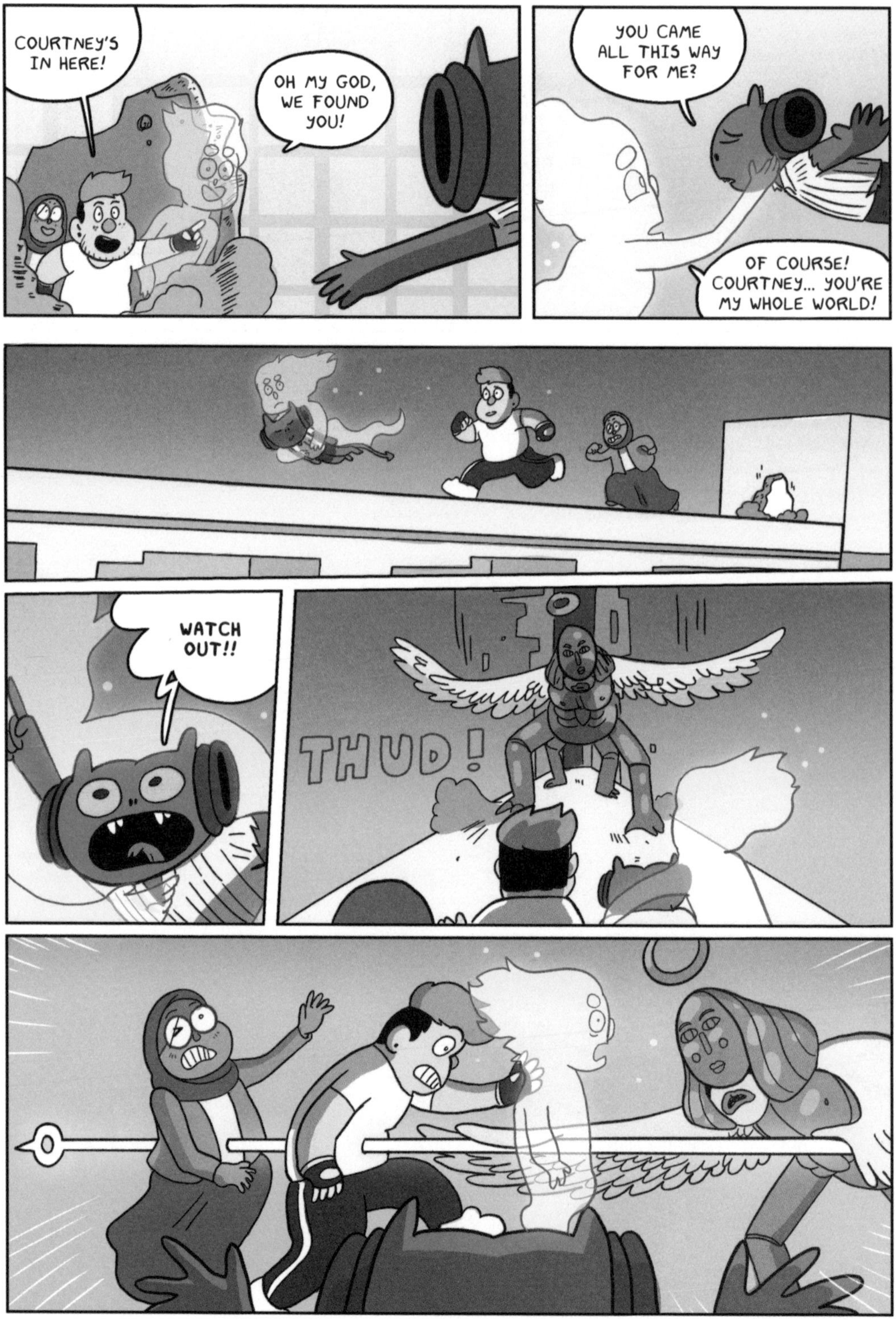
COURTNEY'S IN HERE!
OH MY GOD, WE FOUND YOU!
YOU CAME ALL THIS WAY FOR ME?
OF COURSE! COURTNEY... YOU'RE MY WHOLE WORLD!
WATCH OUT!!
THUD!

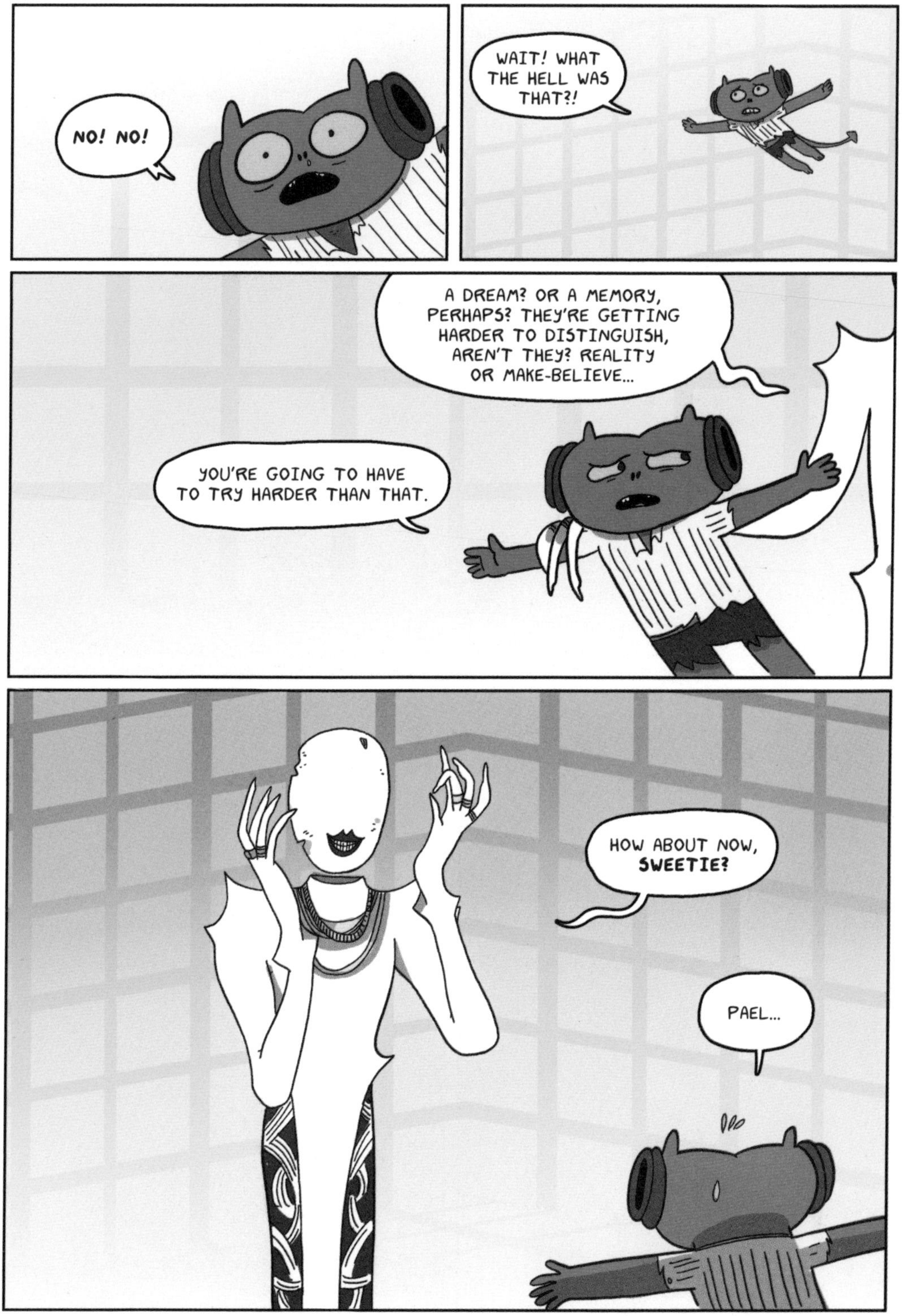
NO! NO!
WAIT! WHAT THE HELL WAS THAT?!
A DREAM? OR A MEMORY, PERHAPS? THEY'RE GETTING HARDER TO DISTINGUISH, AREN'T THEY? REALITY OR MAKE-BELIEVE...
YOU'RE GOING TO HAVE TO TRY HARDER THAN THAT.
HOW ABOUT NOW, **SWEETIE?**
PAEL...

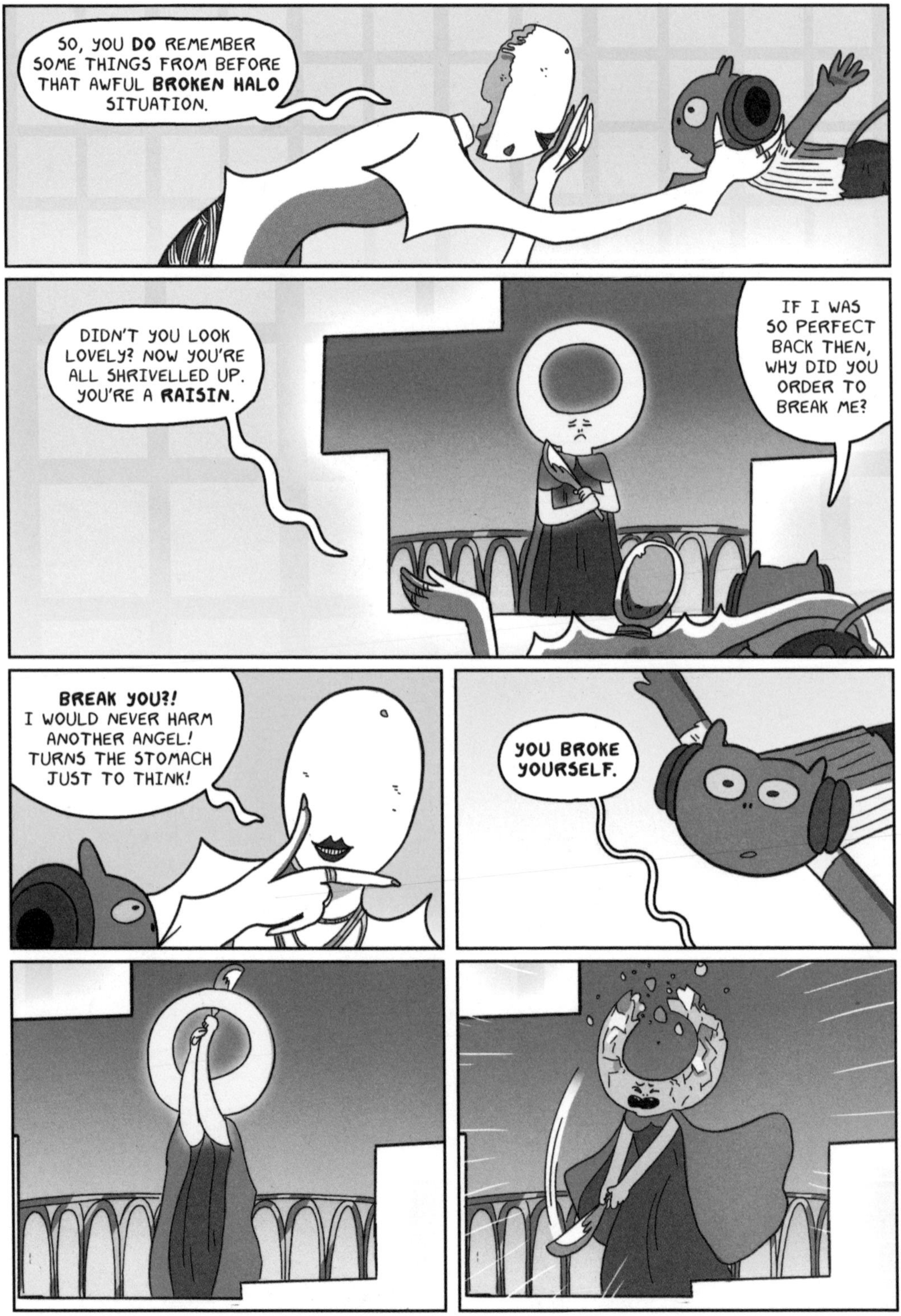
SO, YOU DO REMEMBER SOME THINGS FROM BEFORE THAT AWFUL BROKEN HALO SITUATION.
DIDN'T YOU LOOK LOVELY? NOW YOU'RE ALL SHRIVELLED UP. YOU'RE A RAISIN.
IF I WAS SO PERFECT BACK THEN, WHY DID YOU ORDER TO BREAK ME?
BREAK YOU?! I WOULD NEVER HARM ANOTHER ANGEL! TURNS THE STOMACH JUST TO THINK!
YOU BROKE YOURSELF.

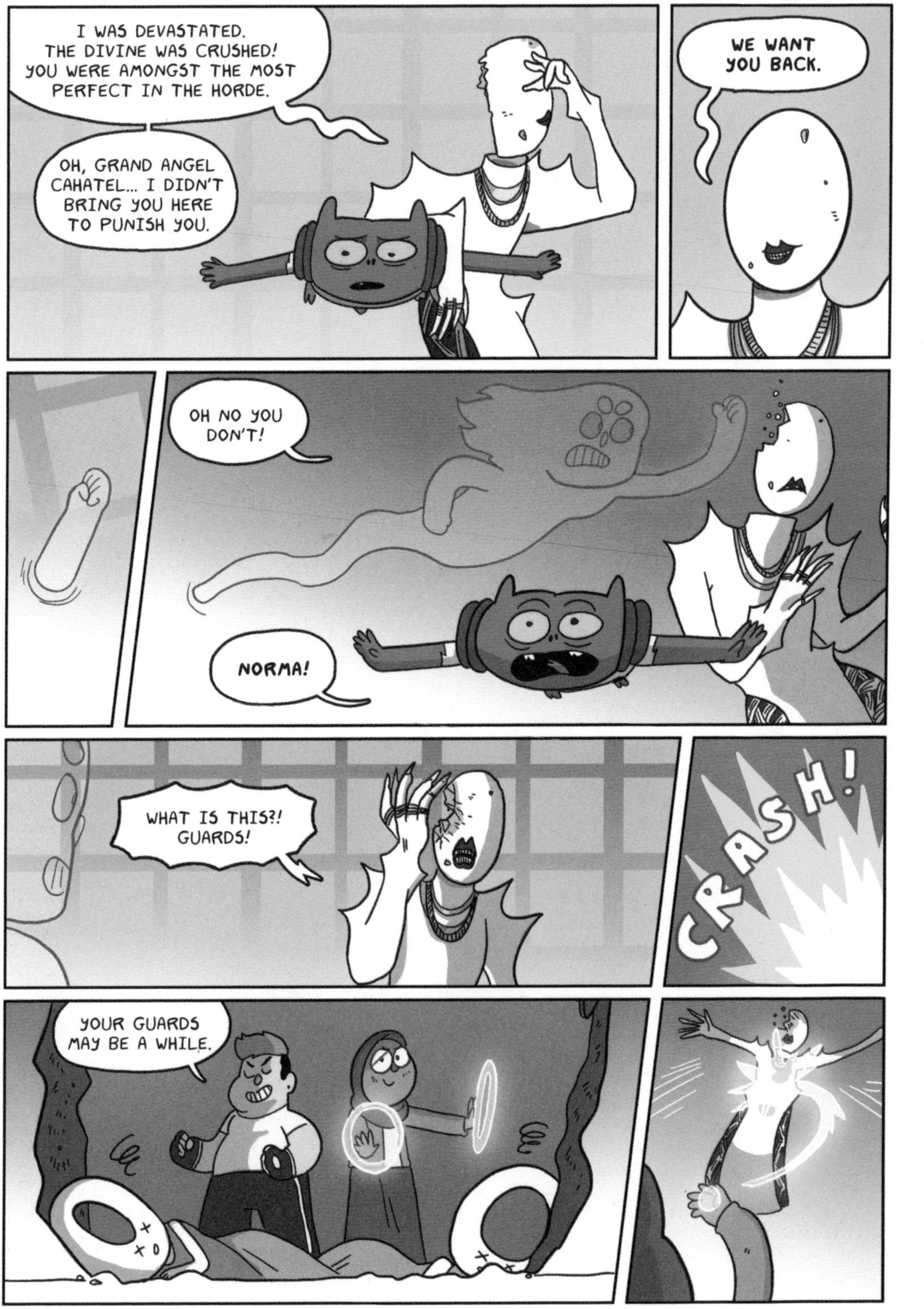
I WAS DEVASTATED. THE DIVINE WAS CRUSHED! YOU WERE AMONGST THE MOST PERFECT IN THE HORDE.
OH, GRAND ANGEL CAHATEL... I DIDN'T BRING YOU HERE TO PUNISH YOU.
WE WANT YOU BACK.
OH NO YOU DON'T!
NORMA!
WHAT IS THIS?! GUARDS!
CRASH!
YOUR GUARDS MAY BE A WHILE.

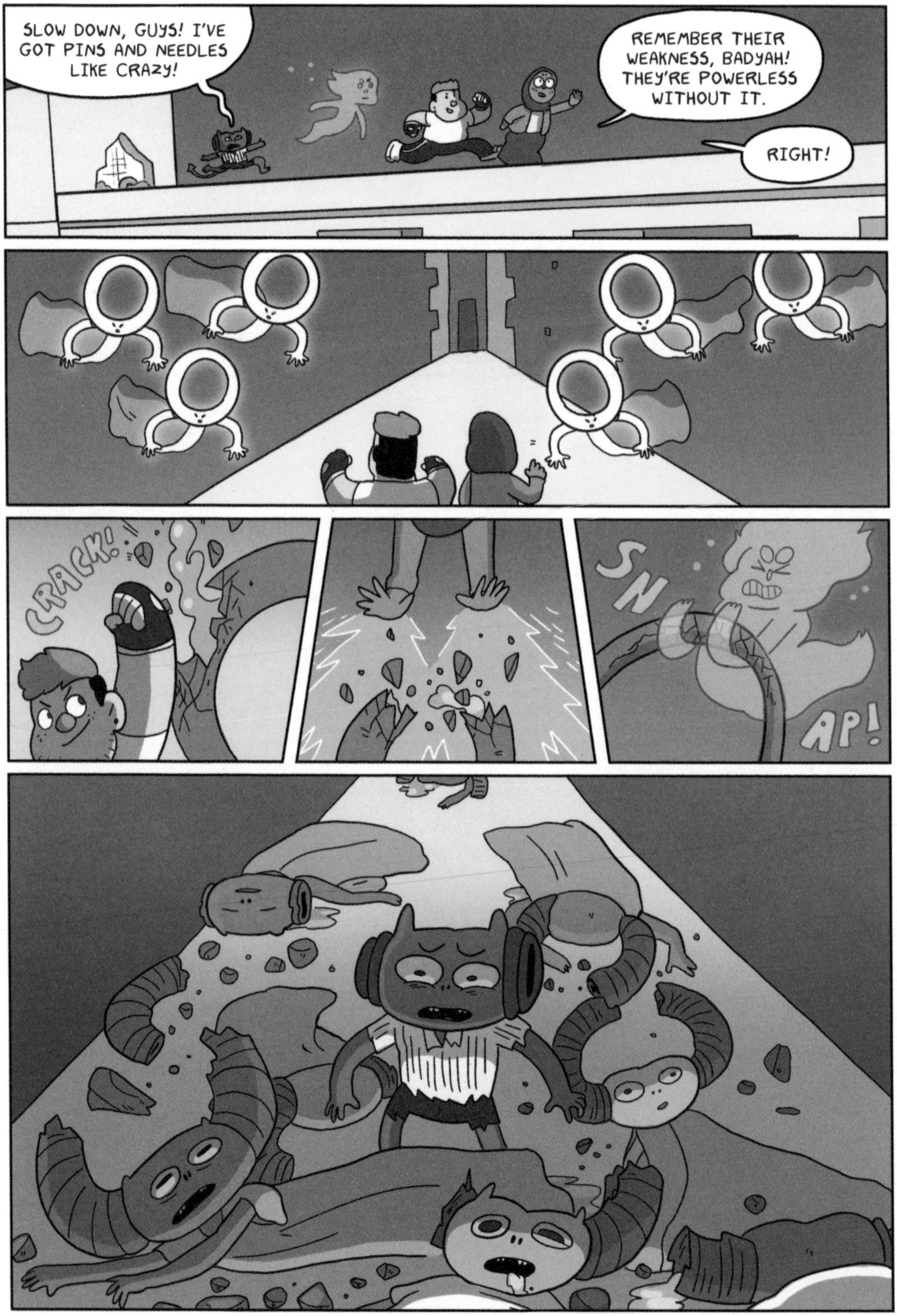
SLOW DOWN, GUYS! I'VE GOT PINS AND NEEDLES LIKE CRAZY!
REMEMBER THEIR WEAKNESS, BADYAH! THEY'RE POWERLESS WITHOUT IT.
RIGHT!
CRACK!
SN
AP!

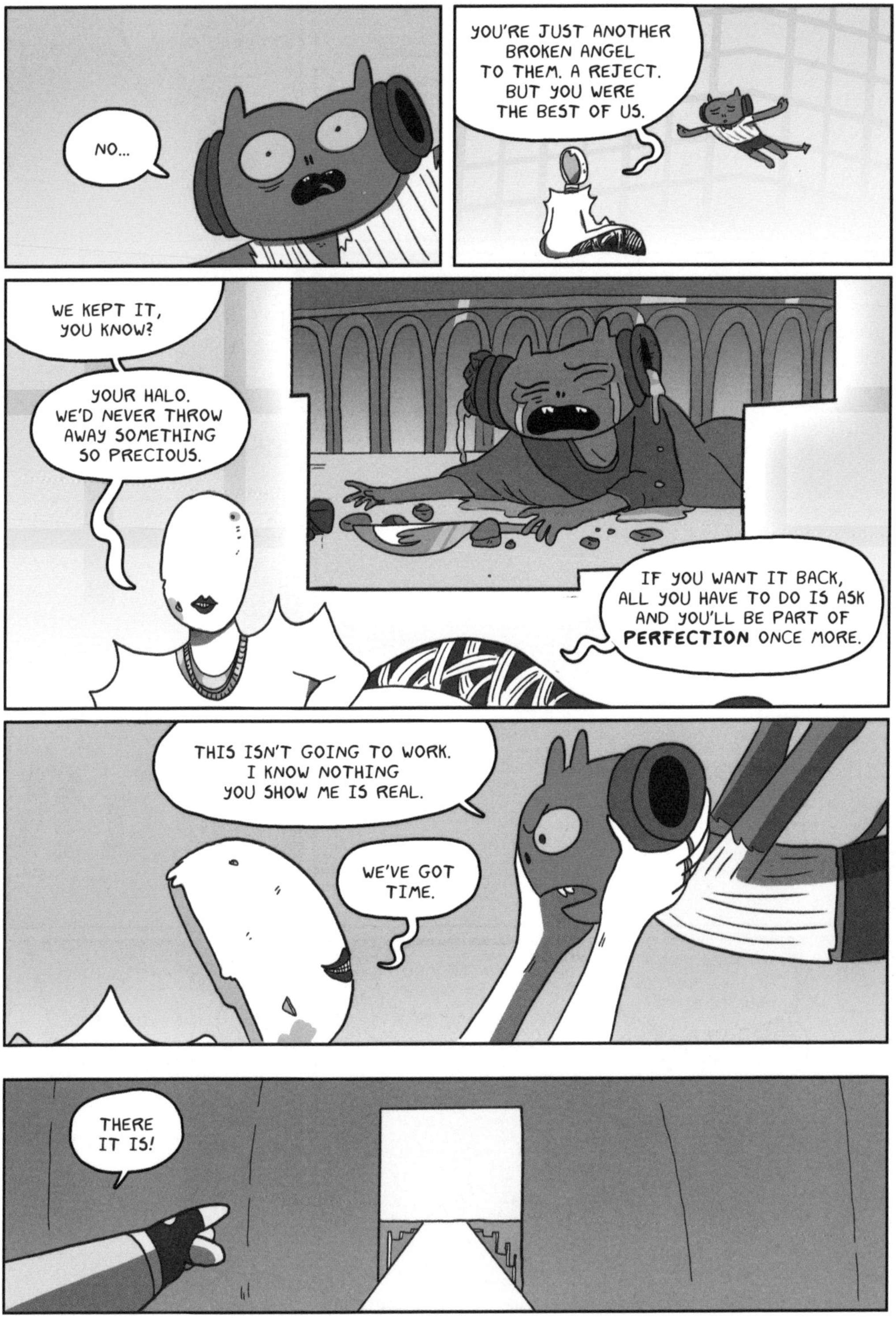
NO...
YOU'RE JUST ANOTHER BROKEN ANGEL TO THEM. A REJECT. BUT YOU WERE THE BEST OF US.
WE KEPT IT, YOU KNOW?
YOUR HALO. WE'D NEVER THROW AWAY SOMETHING SO PRECIOUS.
IF YOU WANT IT BACK, ALL YOU HAVE TO DO IS ASK AND YOU'LL BE PART OF **PERFECTION** ONCE MORE.
THIS ISN'T GOING TO WORK. I KNOW NOTHING YOU SHOW ME IS REAL.
WE'VE GOT TIME.
THERE IT IS!

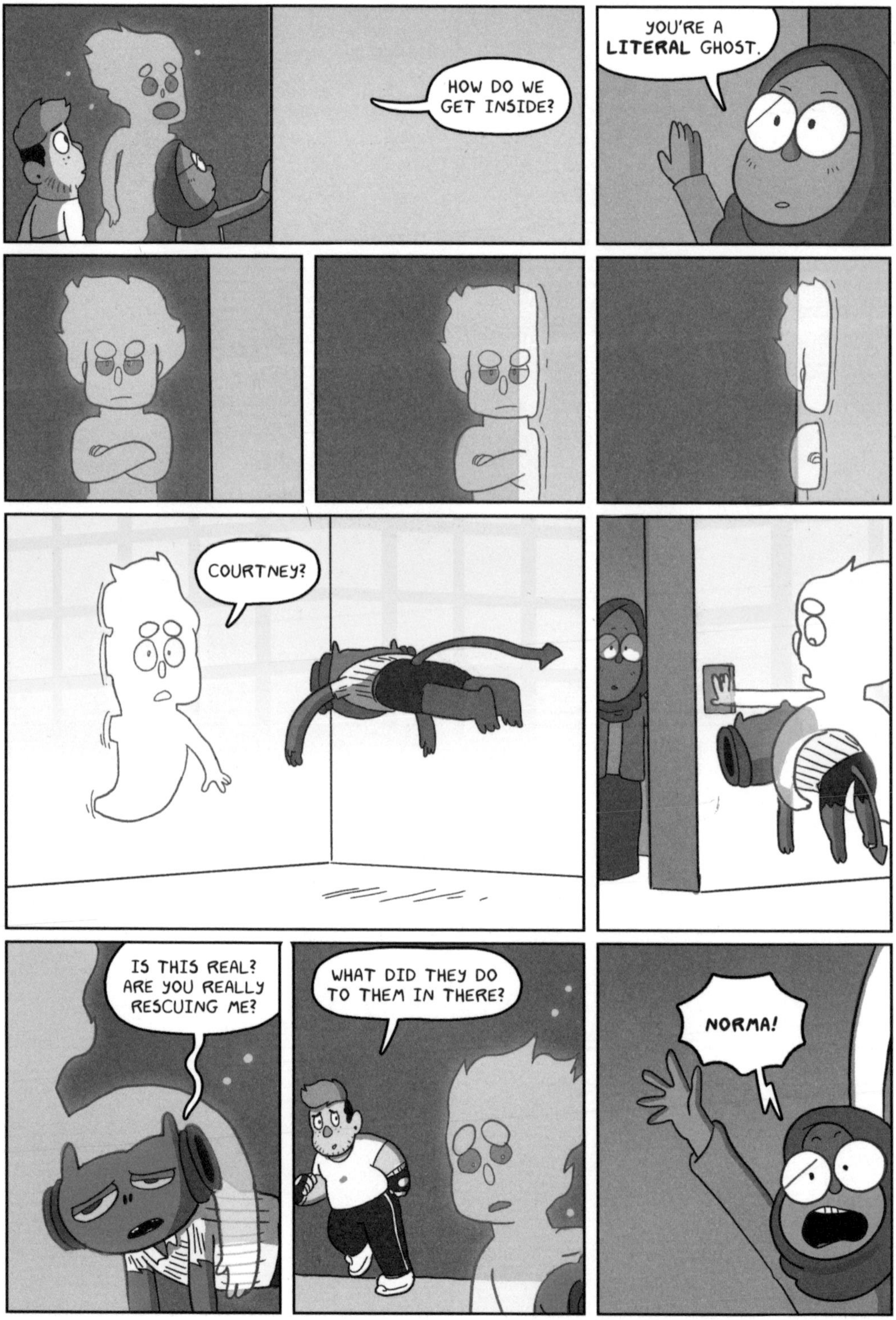
HOW DO WE GET INSIDE?
YOU'RE A LITERAL GHOST.
COURTNEY?
IS THIS REAL? ARE YOU REALLY RESCUING ME?
WHAT DID THEY DO TO THEM IN THERE?
NORMA!

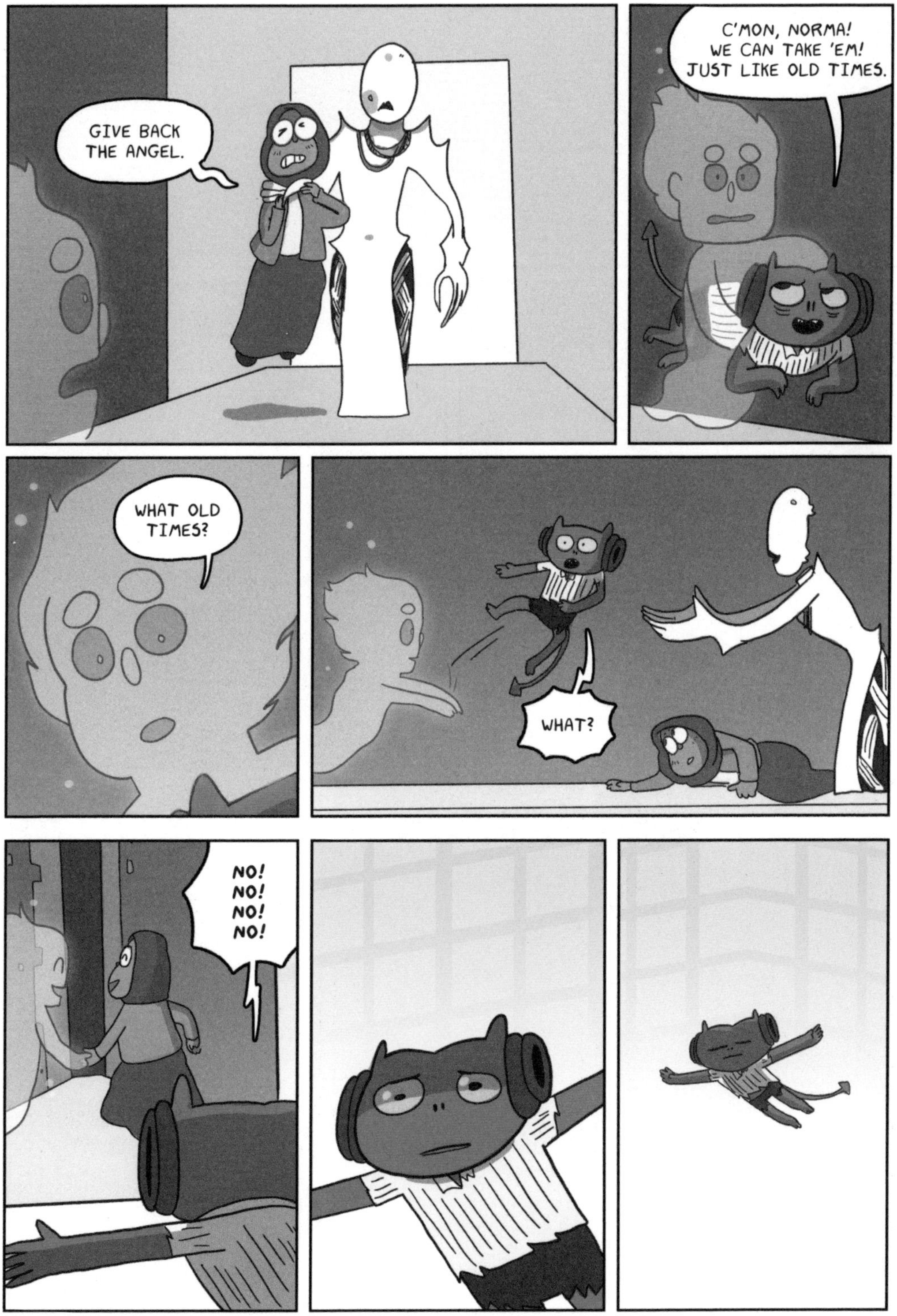
GIVE BACK THE ANGEL.
C'MON, NORMA! WE CAN TAKE 'EM! JUST LIKE OLD TIMES.
WHAT OLD TIMES?
WHAT?
NO! NO! NO! NO!

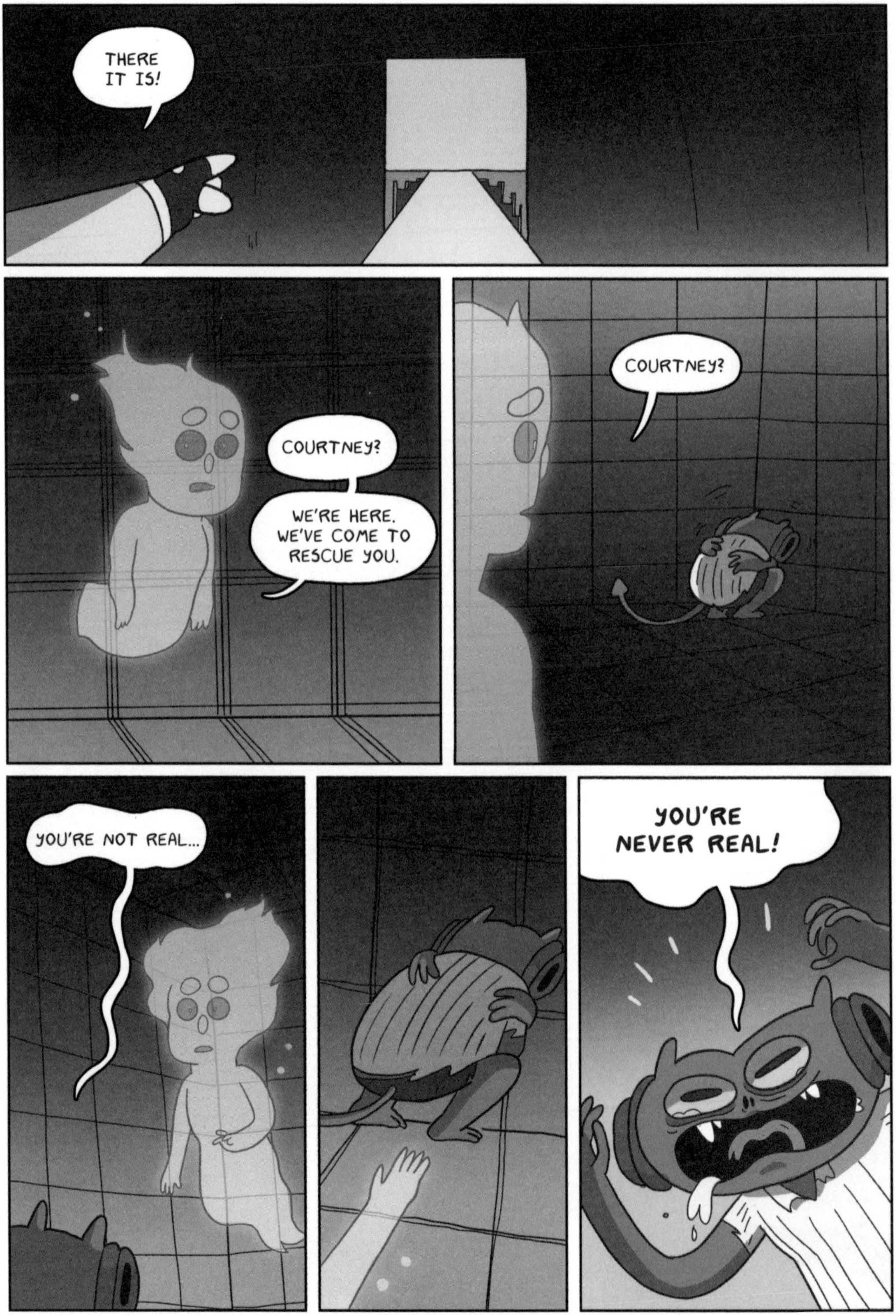
THERE IT IS!
COURTNEY?
WE'RE HERE. WE'VE COME TO RESCUE YOU.
COURTNEY?
YOU'RE NOT REAL...
YOU'RE NEVER REAL!

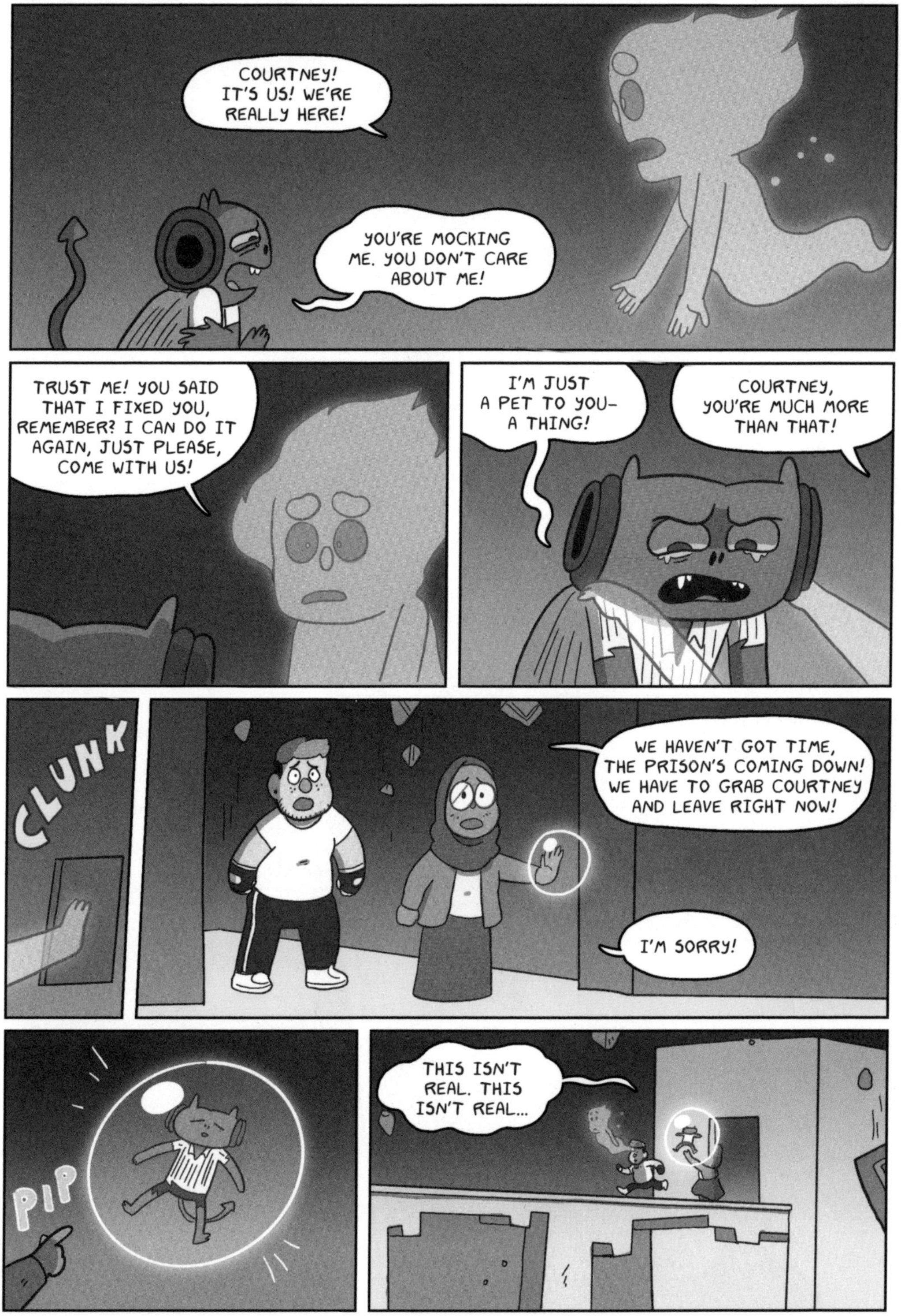
COURTNEY! IT'S US! WE'RE REALLY HERE!
YOU'RE MOCKING ME. YOU DON'T CARE ABOUT ME!
TRUST ME! YOU SAID THAT I FIXED YOU, REMEMBER? I CAN DO IT AGAIN, JUST PLEASE, COME WITH US!
I'M JUST A PET TO YOU– A THING!
COURTNEY, YOU'RE MUCH MORE THAN THAT!
CLUNK
WE HAVEN'T GOT TIME, THE PRISON'S COMING DOWN! WE HAVE TO GRAB COURTNEY AND LEAVE RIGHT NOW!
I'M SORRY!
PIP
THIS ISN'T REAL. THIS ISN'T REAL...

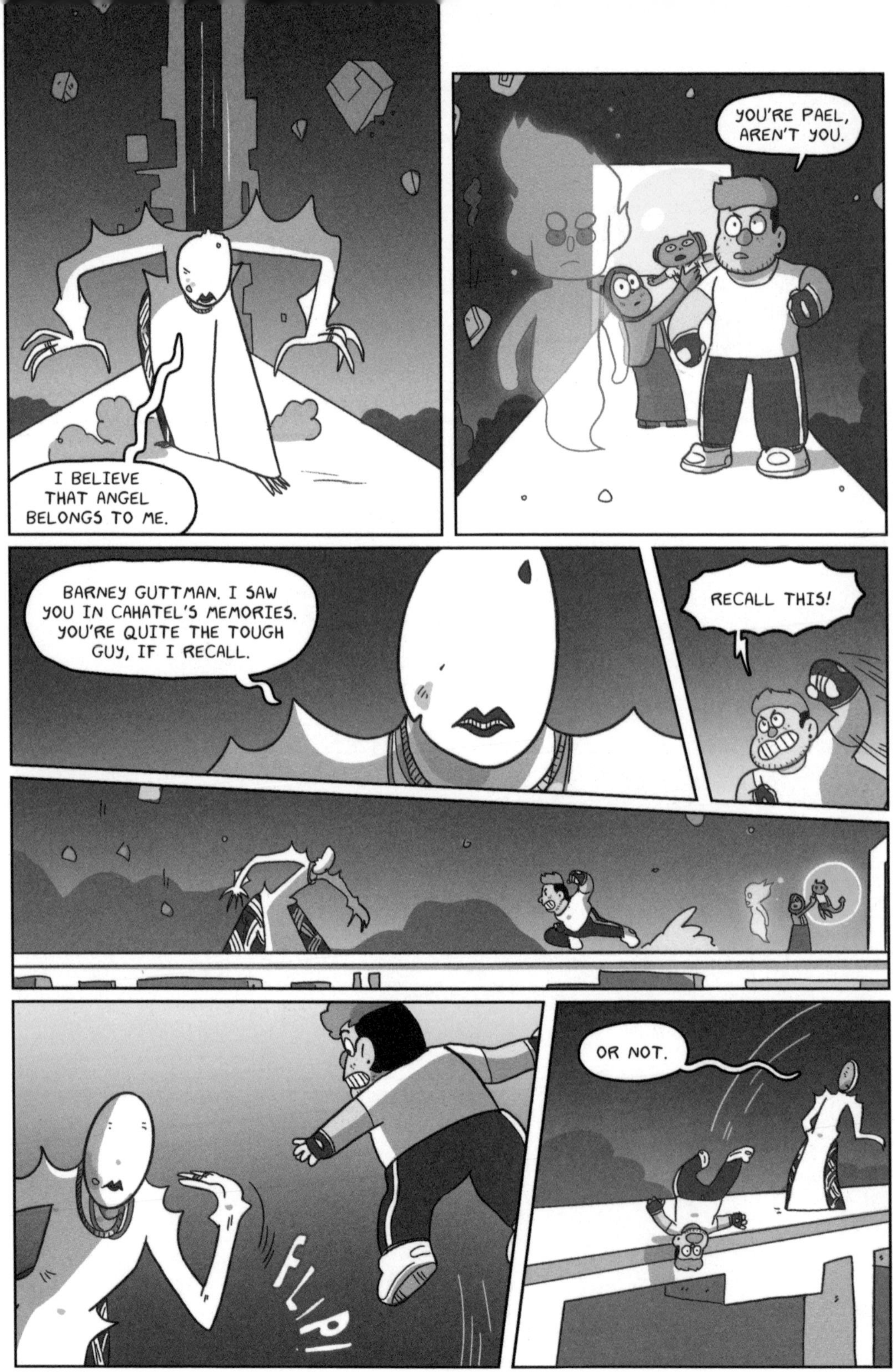
I BELIEVE THAT ANGEL BELONGS TO ME.
YOU'RE PAEL, AREN'T YOU.
BARNEY GUTTMAN. I SAW YOU IN CAHATEL'S MEMORIES. YOU'RE QUITE THE TOUGH GUY, IF I RECALL.
RECALL THIS!
FLIP!
OR NOT.

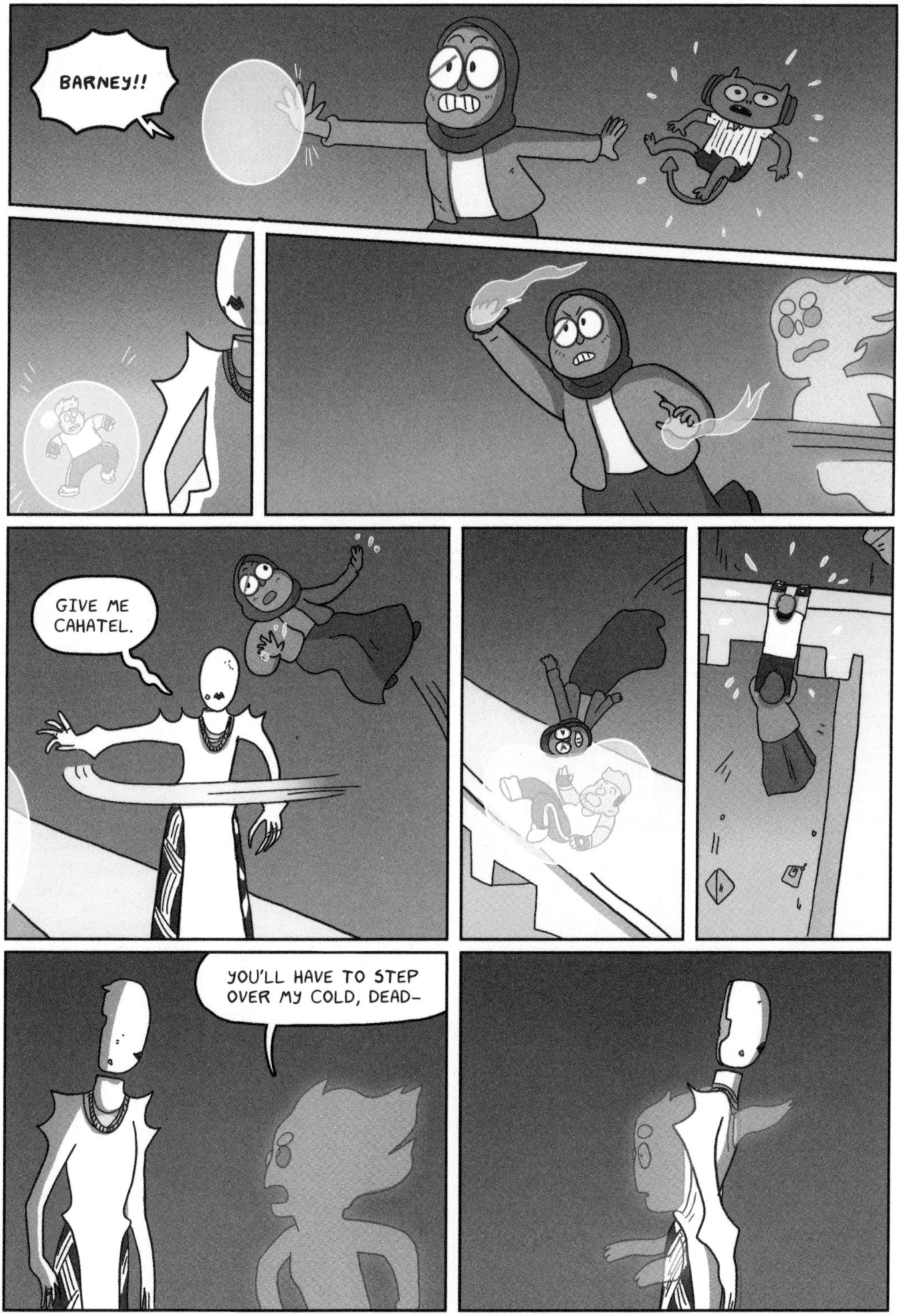
BARNEY!!
GIVE ME CAHATEL.
YOU'LL HAVE TO STEP OVER MY COLD, DEAD-

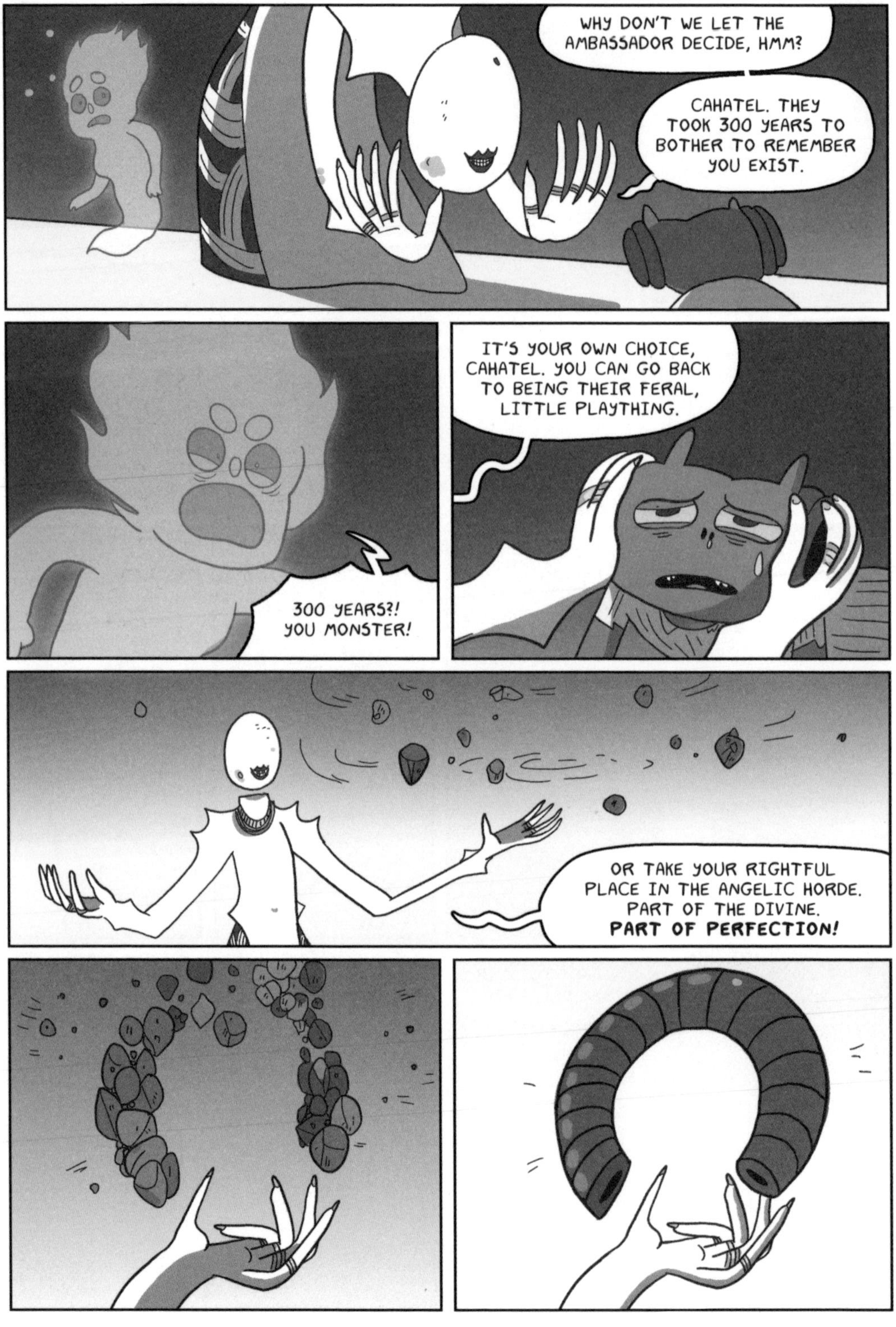
WHY DON'T WE LET THE AMBASSADOR DECIDE, HMM?
CAHATEL. THEY TOOK 300 YEARS TO BOTHER TO REMEMBER YOU EXIST.
300 YEARS?! YOU MONSTER!
IT'S YOUR OWN CHOICE, CAHATEL. YOU CAN GO BACK TO BEING THEIR FERAL, LITTLE PLAYTHING.
OR TAKE YOUR RIGHTFUL PLACE IN THE ANGELIC HORDE. PART OF THE DIVINE. PART OF PERFECTION!

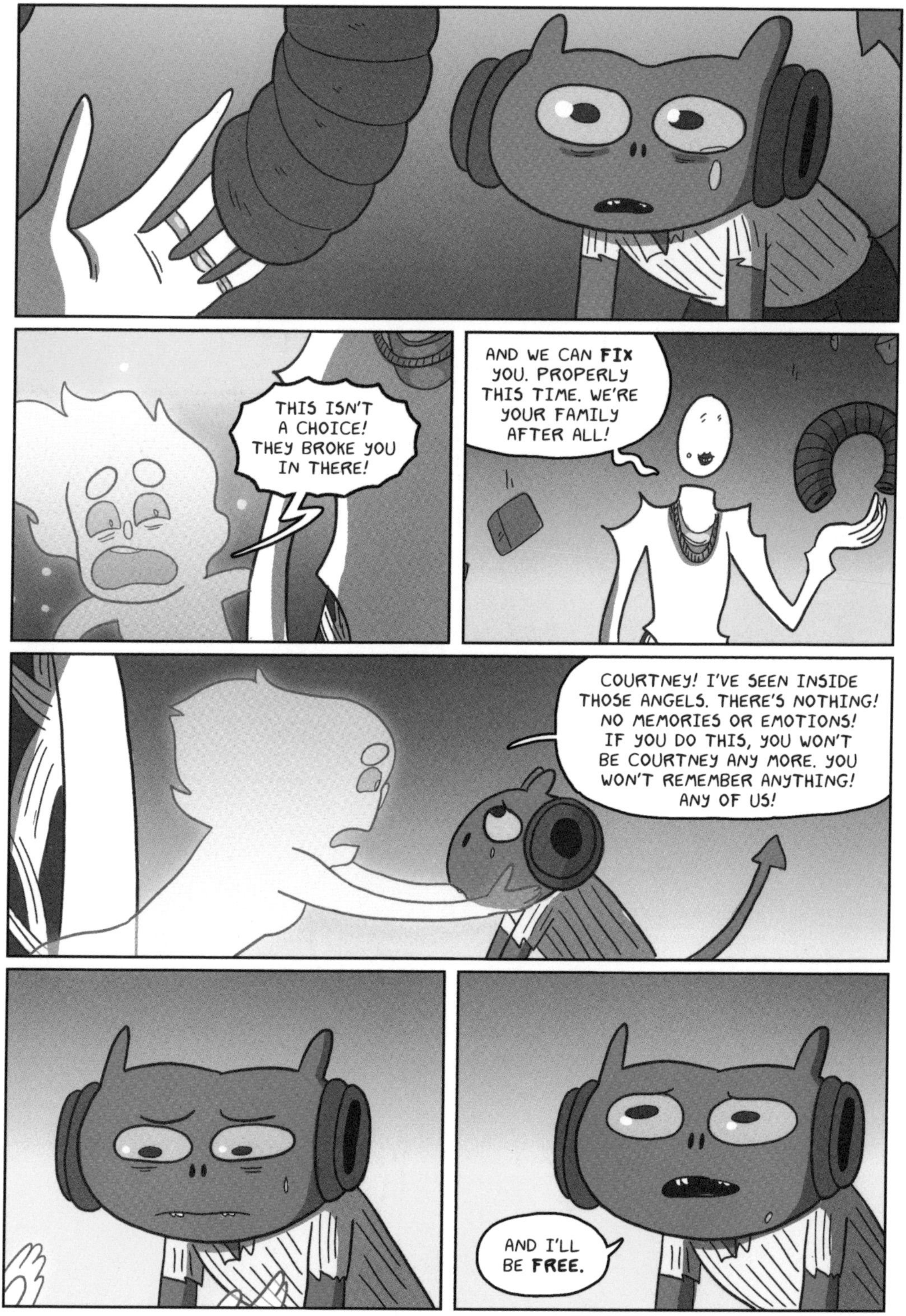

THIS ISN'T A CHOICE! THEY BROKE YOU IN THERE!
AND WE CAN FIX YOU. PROPERLY THIS TIME. WE'RE YOUR FAMILY AFTER ALL!
COURTNEY! I'VE SEEN INSIDE THOSE ANGELS. THERE'S NOTHING! NO MEMORIES OR EMOTIONS! IF YOU DO THIS, YOU WON'T BE COURTNEY ANY MORE. YOU WON'T REMEMBER ANYTHING! ANY OF US!
AND I'LL BE FREE.

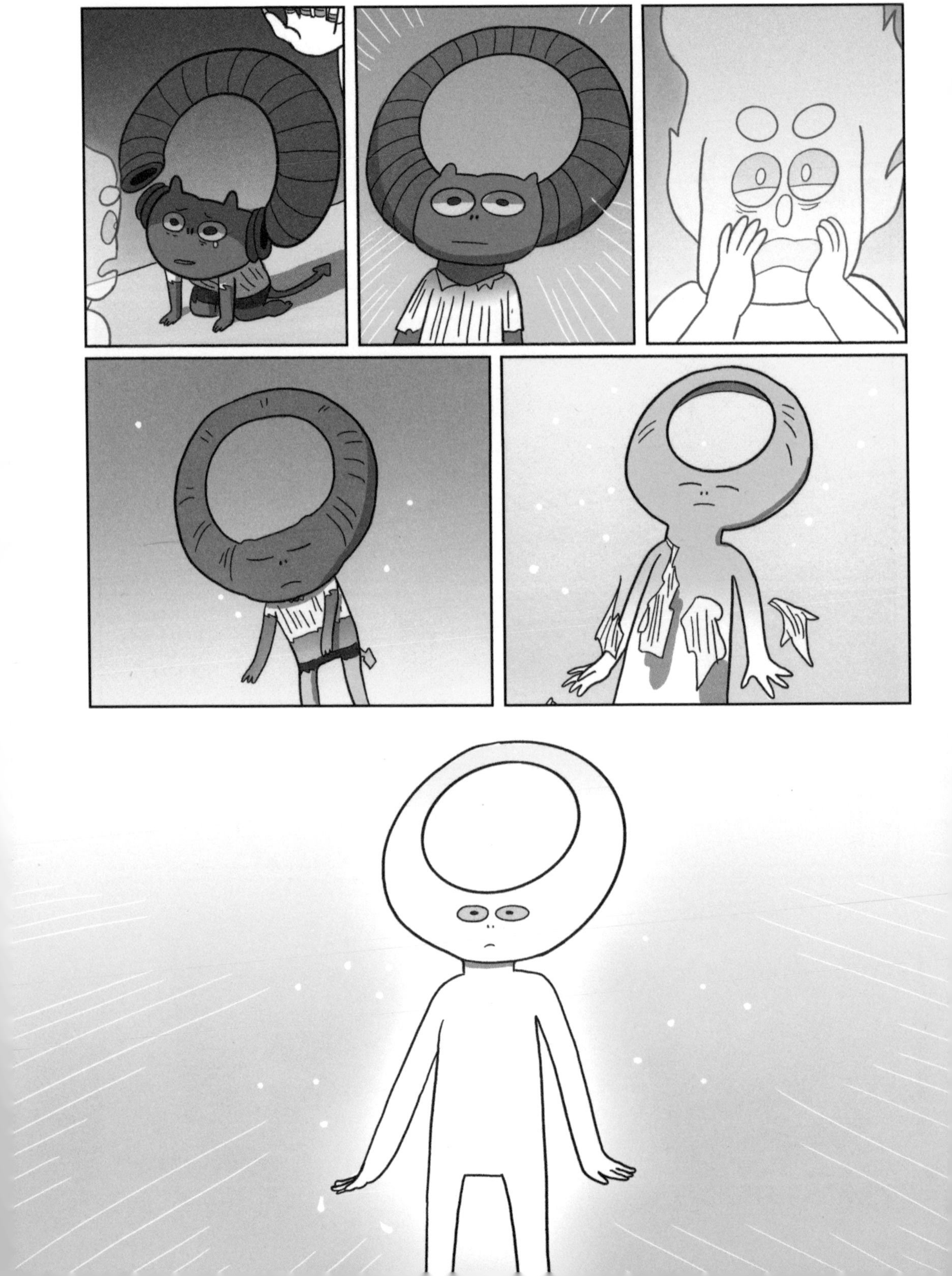

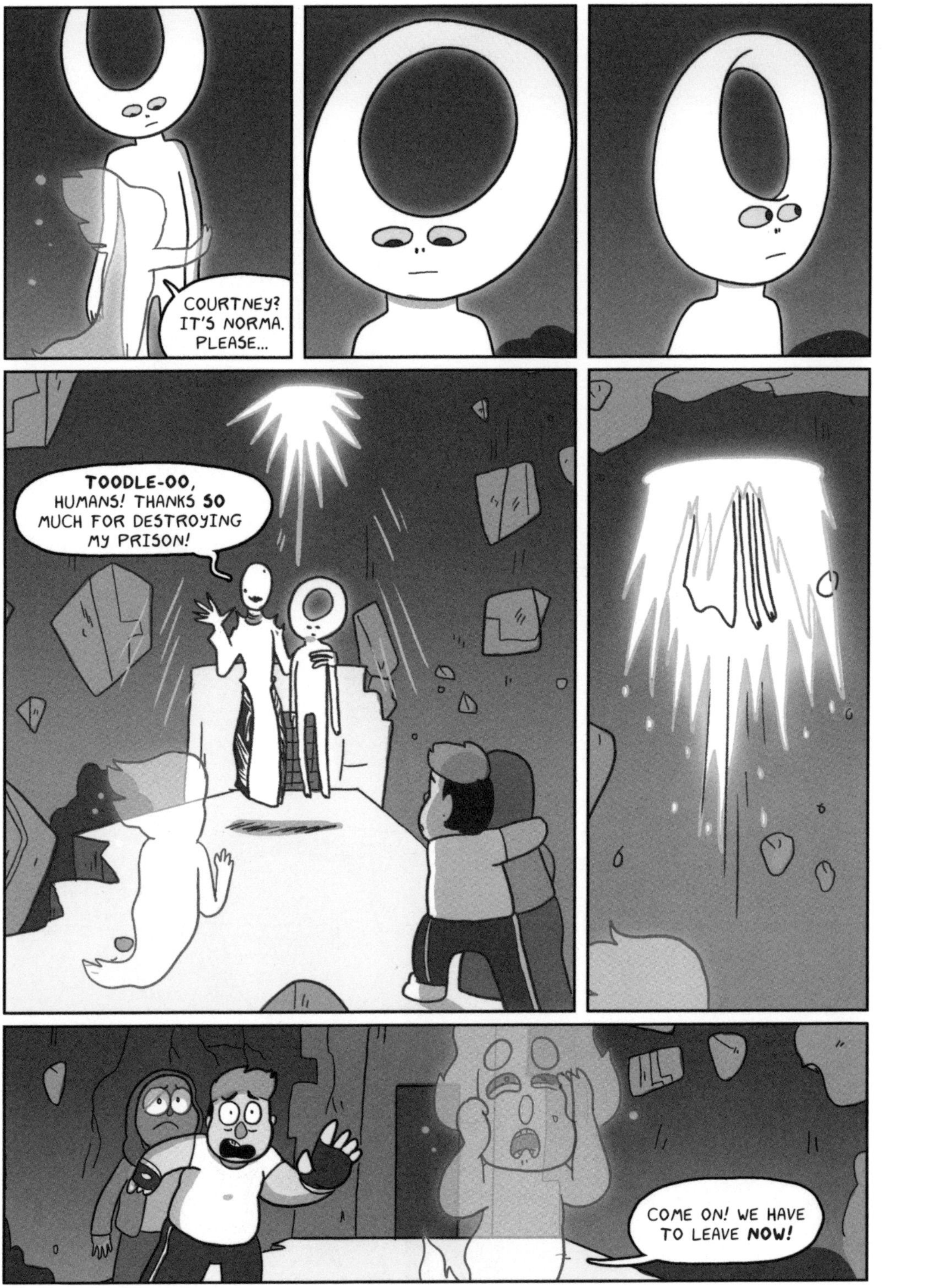
COURTNEY? IT'S NORMA. PLEASE...
TOODLE-OO, HUMANS! THANKS SO MUCH FOR DESTROYING MY PRISON!
COME ON! WE HAVE TO LEAVE NOW!

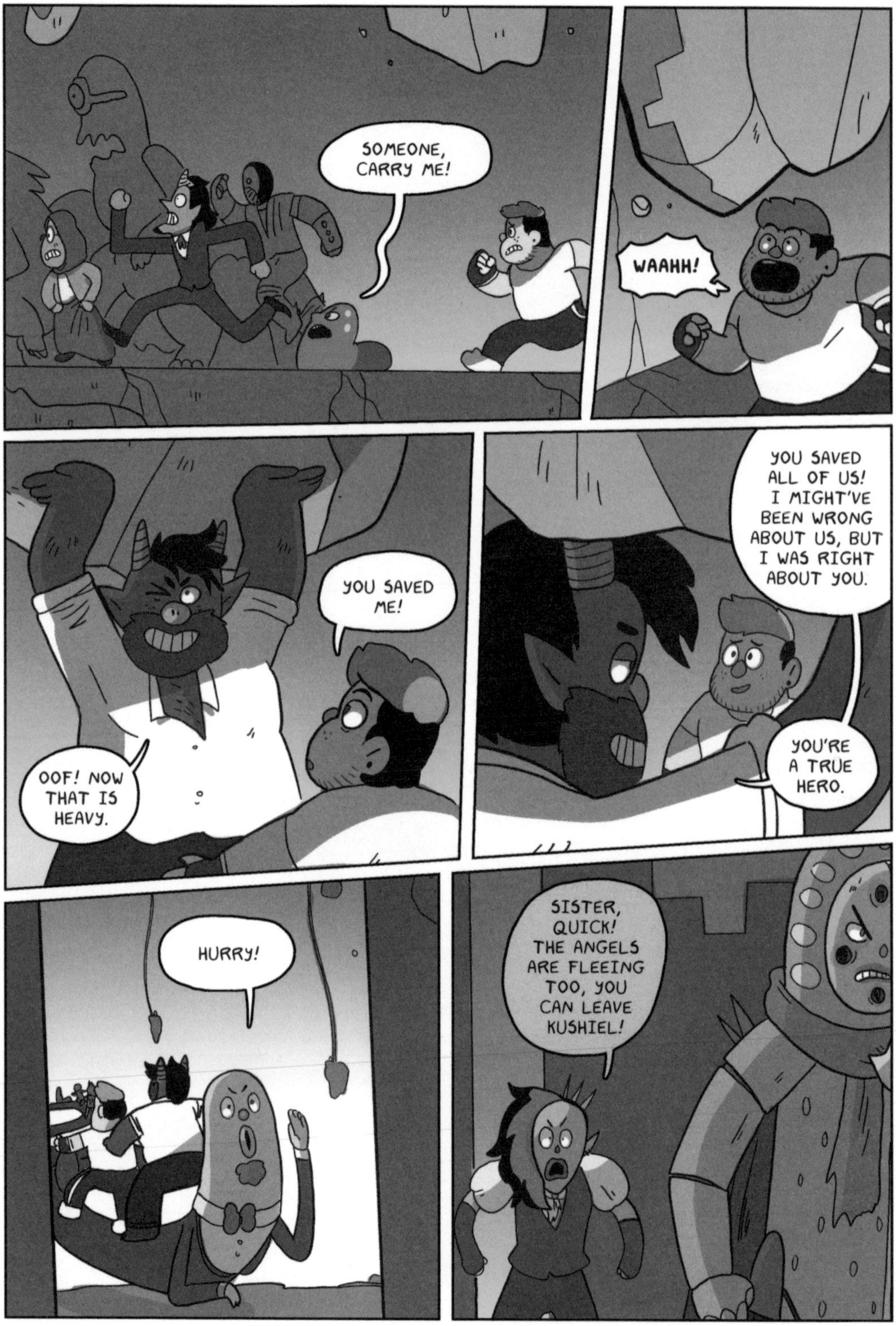
SOMEONE, CARRY ME!
WAAHH!
YOU SAVED ME!
OOF! NOW THAT IS HEAVY.
YOU SAVED ALL OF US! I MIGHT'VE BEEN WRONG ABOUT US, BUT I WAS RIGHT ABOUT YOU.
YOU'RE A TRUE HERO.
HURRY!
SISTER, QUICK! THE ANGELS ARE FLEEING TOO, YOU CAN LEAVE KUSHIEL!

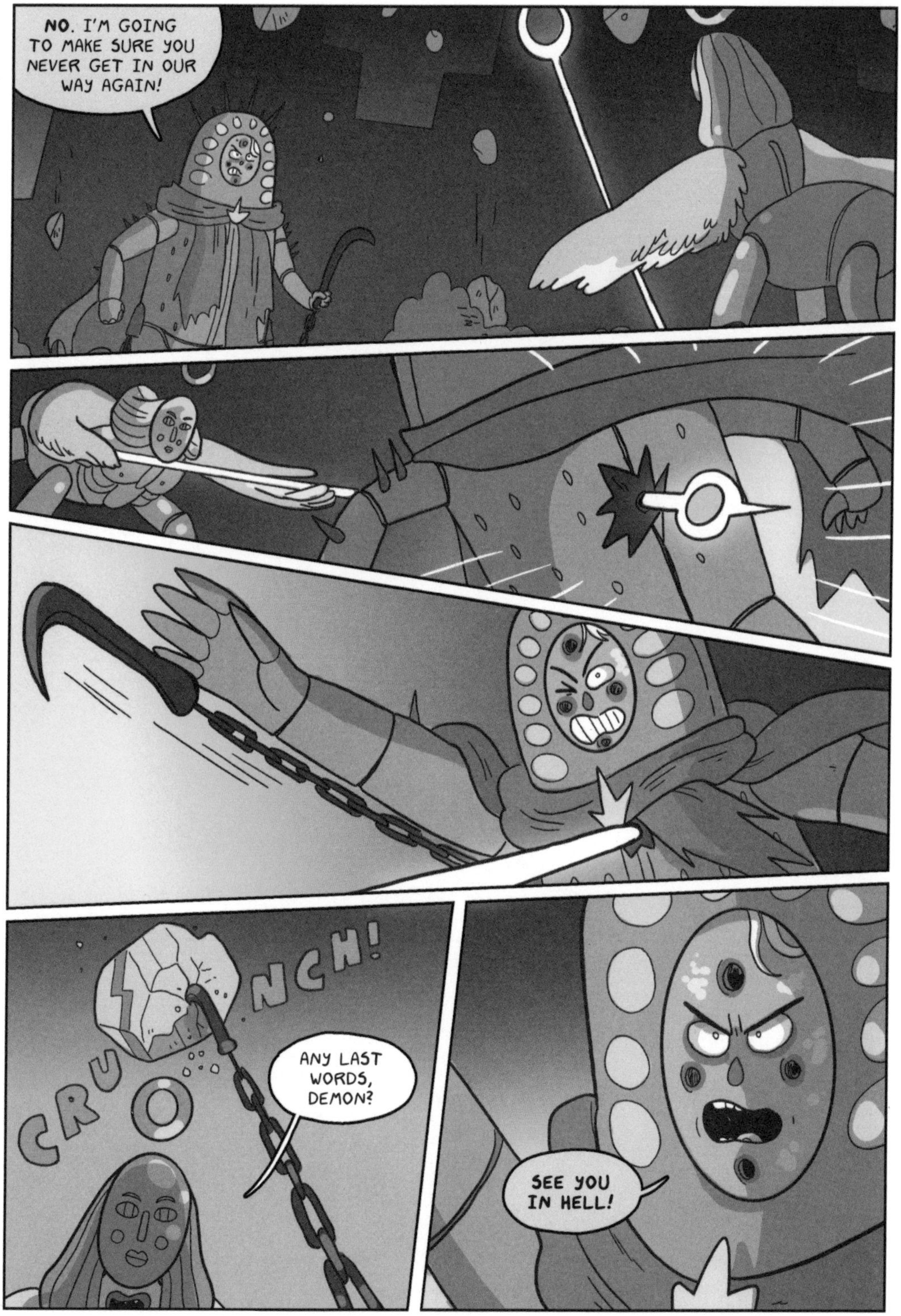
NO. I'M GOING TO MAKE SURE YOU NEVER GET IN OUR WAY AGAIN!
CRUNCH!
ANY LAST WORDS, DEMON?
SEE YOU IN HELL!

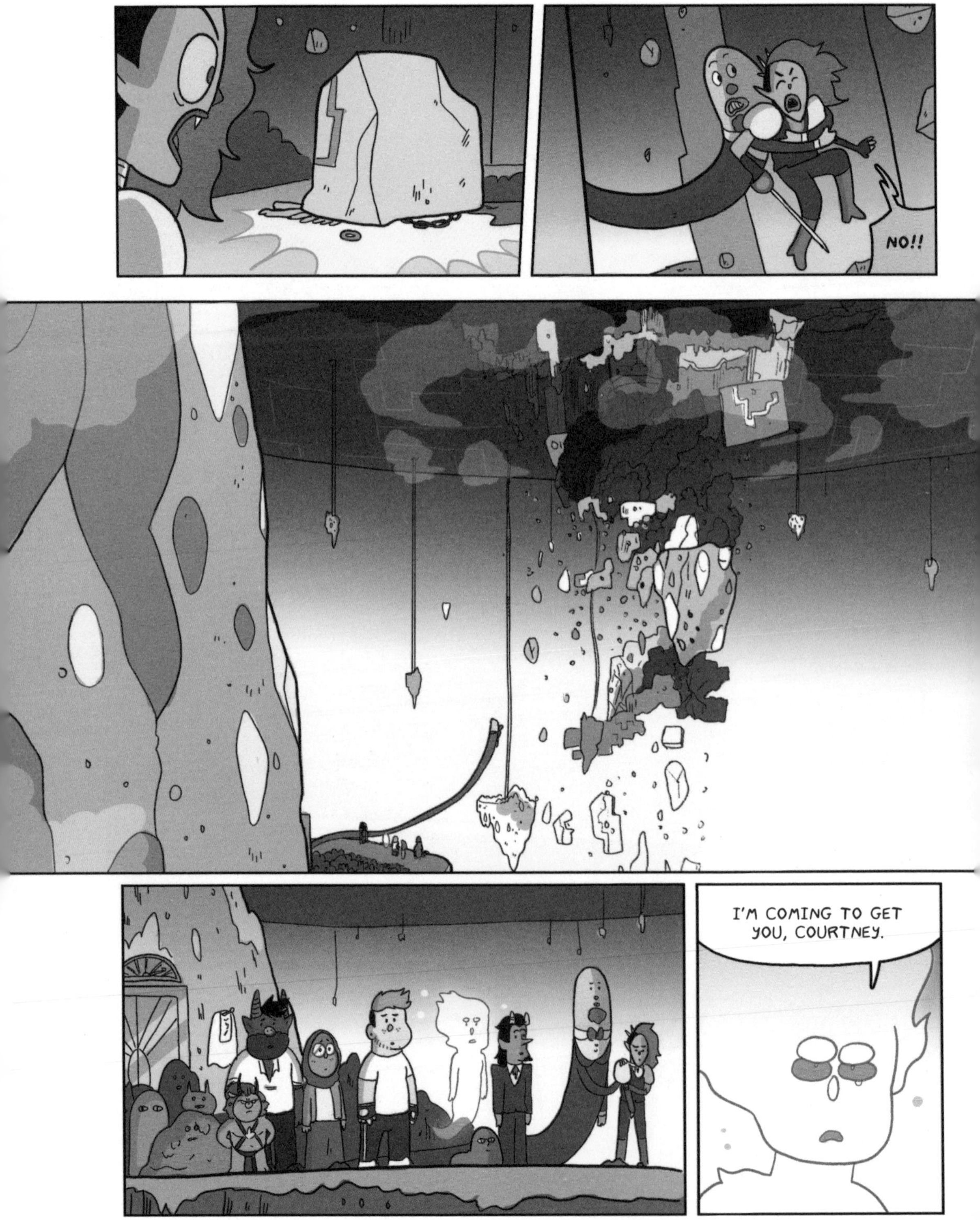
NO!!
I'M COMING TO GET YOU, COURTNEY.

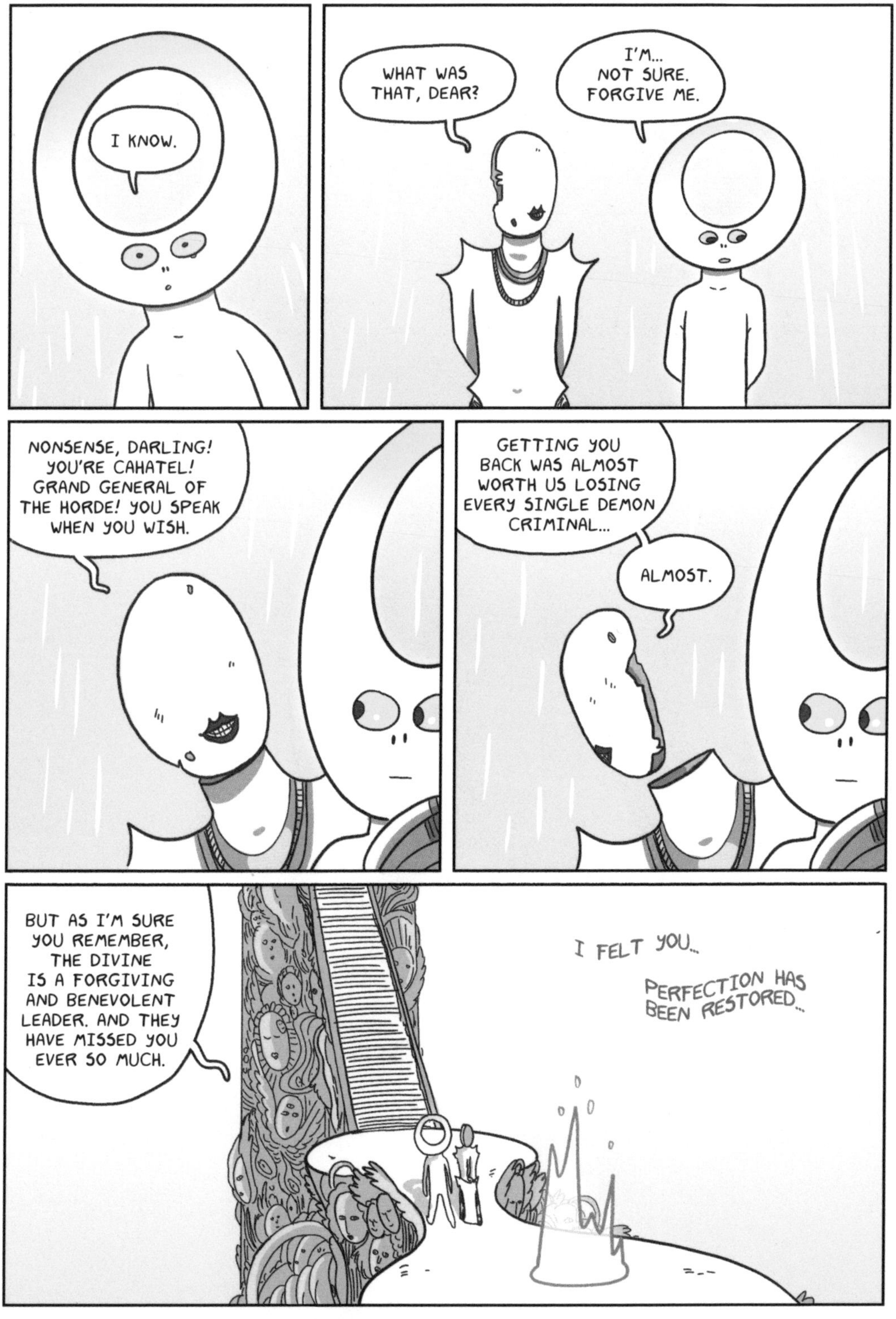
I KNOW.
WHAT WAS THAT, DEAR?
I'M... NOT SURE. FORGIVE ME.
NONSENSE, DARLING! YOU'RE CAHATEL! GRAND GENERAL OF THE HORDE! YOU SPEAK WHEN YOU WISH.
GETTING YOU BACK WAS ALMOST WORTH US LOSING EVERY SINGLE DEMON CRIMINAL...
ALMOST.
BUT AS I'M SURE YOU REMEMBER, THE DIVINE IS A FORGIVING AND BENEVOLENT LEADER. AND THEY HAVE MISSED YOU EVER SO MUCH.
I FELT YOU...
PERFECTION HAS BEEN RESTORED...

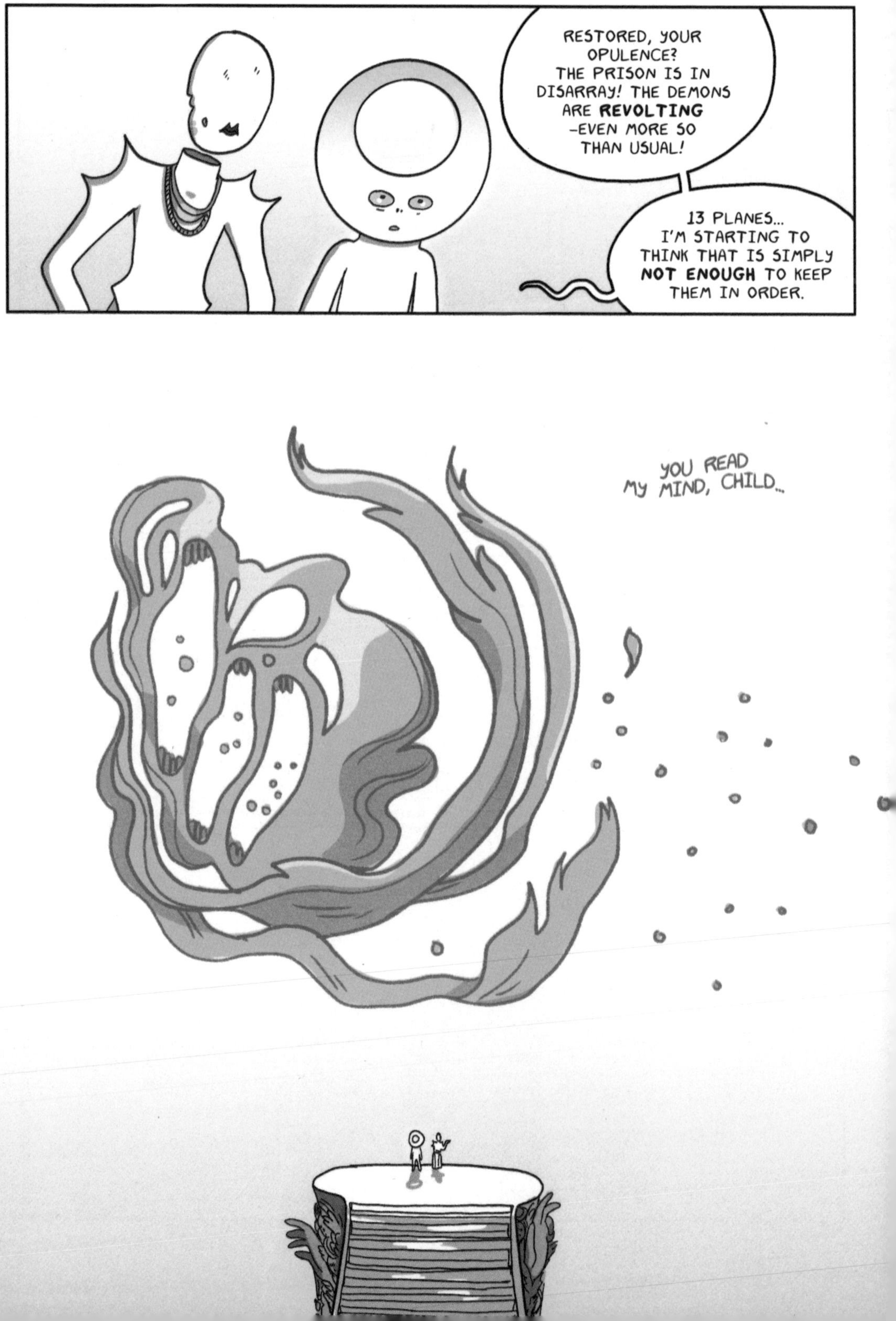
RESTORED, YOUR OPULENCE? THE PRISON IS IN DISARRAY! THE DEMONS ARE **REVOLTING** -EVEN MORE SO THAN USUAL!
13 PLANES... I'M STARTING TO THINK THAT IS SIMPLY **NOT ENOUGH** TO KEEP THEM IN ORDER.
YOU READ MY MIND, CHILD...

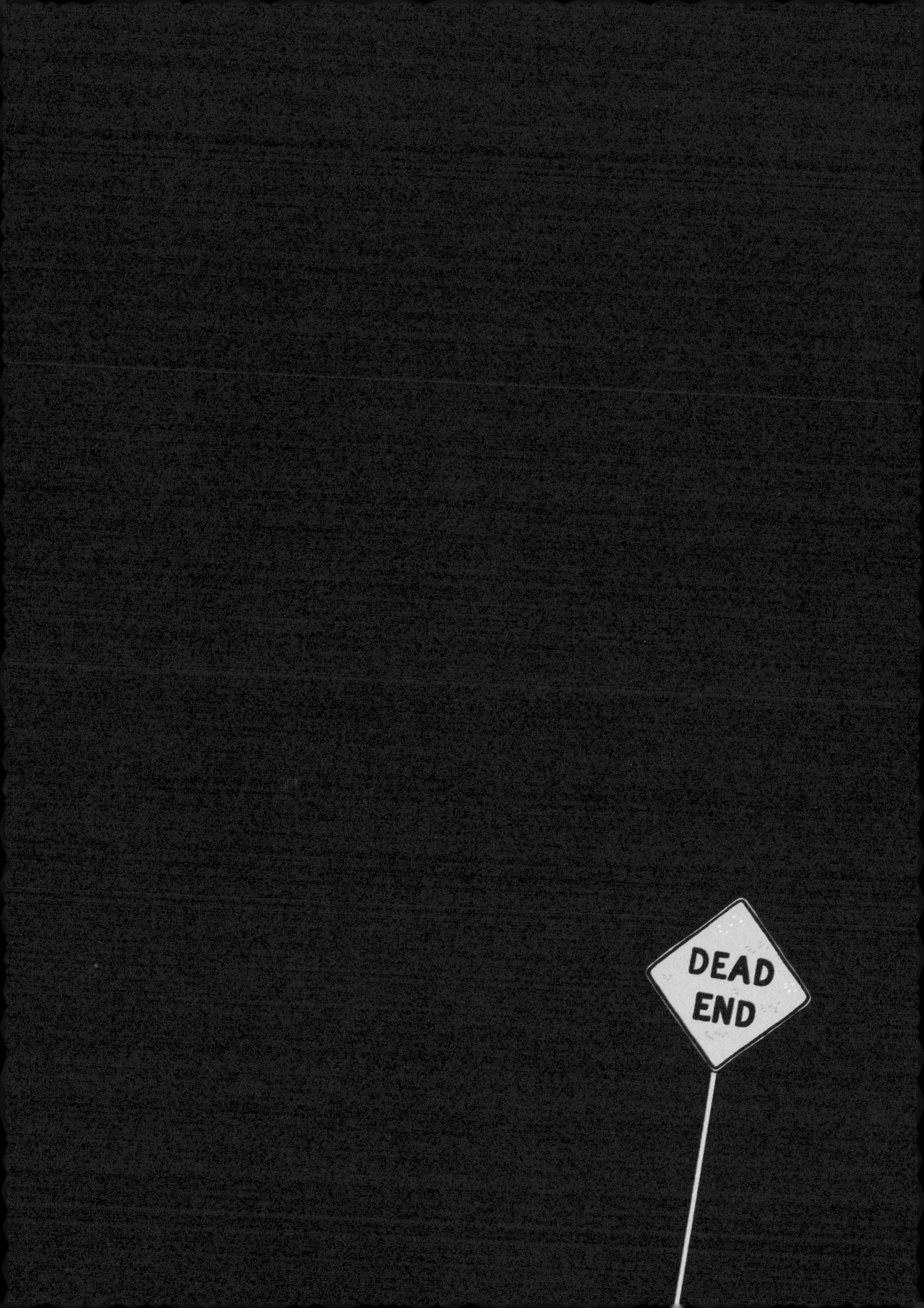
DEAD
END

AMBASSADOR'S LOG... DAY ONE.

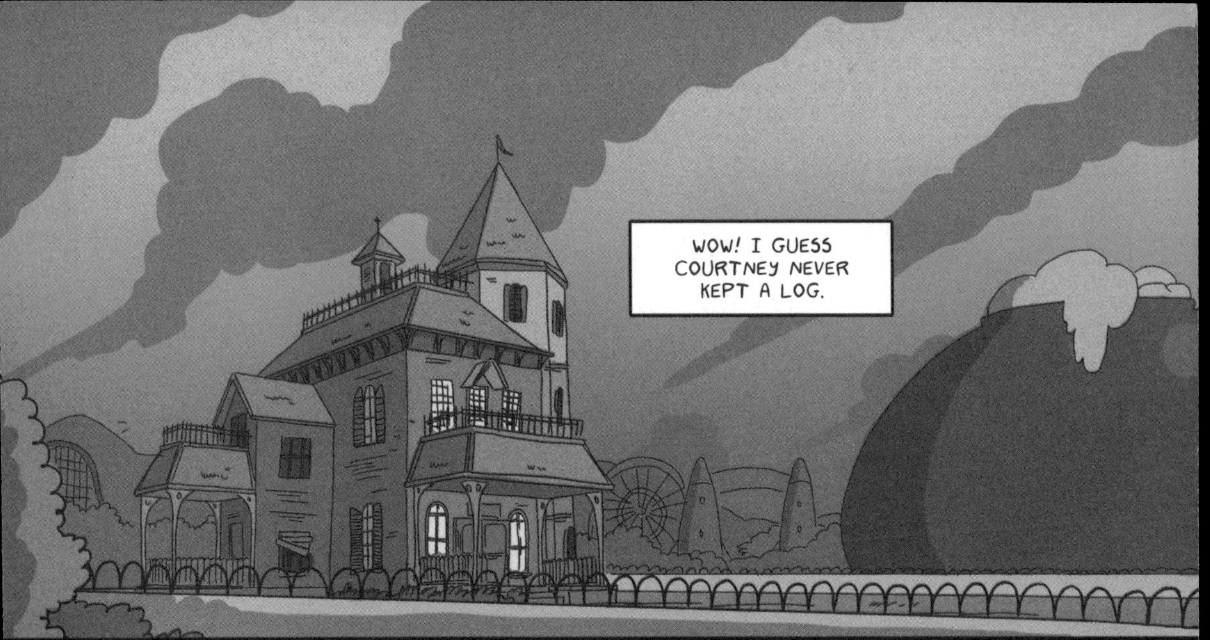
WOW! I GUESS COURTNEY NEVER KEPT A LOG.

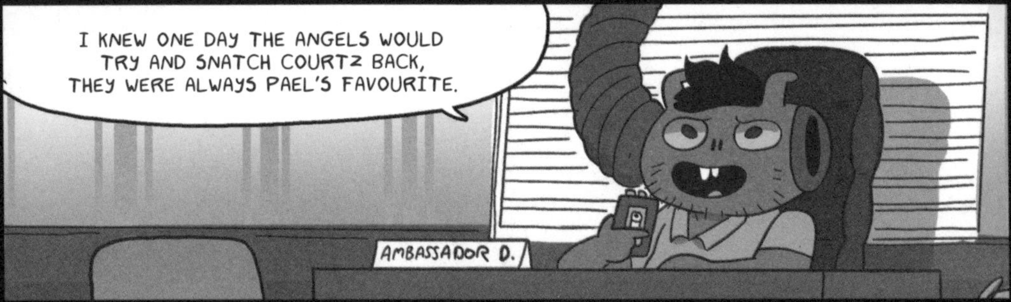
I KNEW ONE DAY THE ANGELS WOULD TRY AND SNATCH COURTZ BACK, THEY WERE ALWAYS PAEL'S FAVOURITE.
AMBASSADOR D.

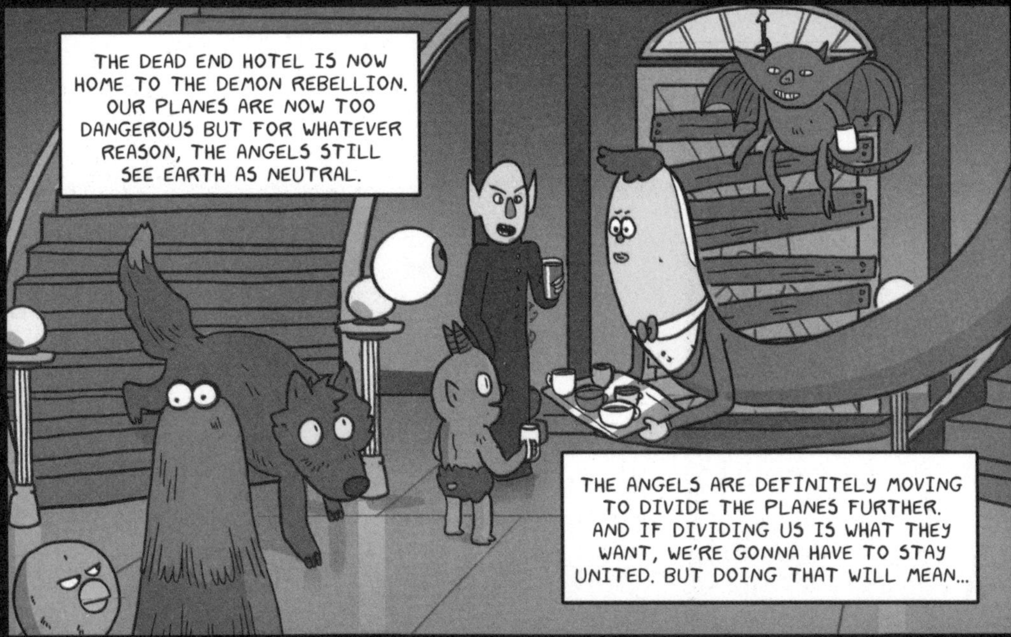
THE DEAD END HOTEL IS NOW HOME TO THE DEMON REBELLION. OUR PLANES ARE NOW TOO DANGEROUS BUT FOR WHATEVER REASON, THE ANGELS STILL SEE EARTH AS NEUTRAL.
THE ANGELS ARE DEFINITELY MOVING TO DIVIDE THE PLANES FURTHER. AND IF DIVIDING US IS WHAT THEY WANT, WE'RE GONNA HAVE TO STAY UNITED. BUT DOING THAT WILL MEAN...

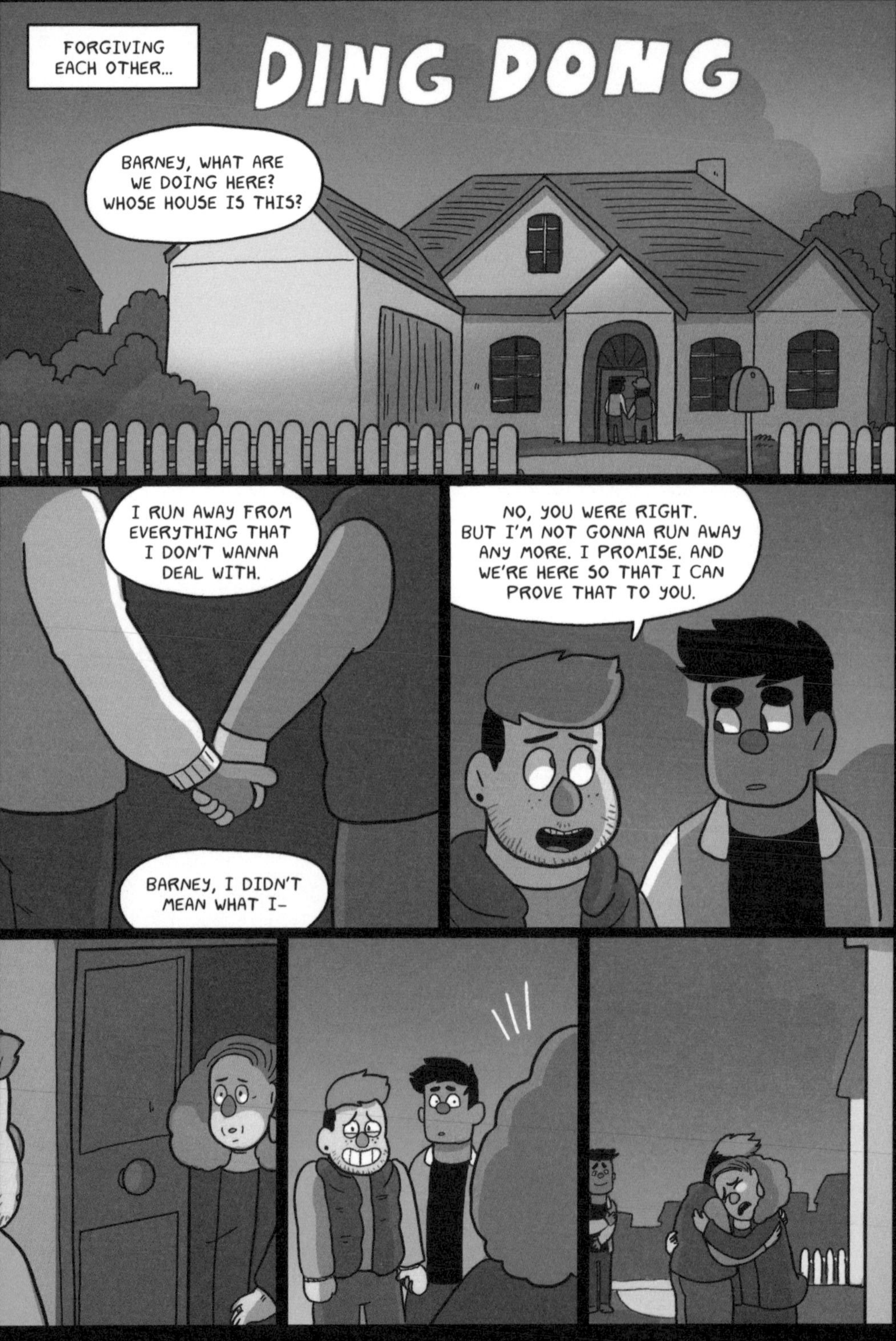
FORGIVING EACH OTHER...
DING DONG
BARNEY, WHAT ARE WE DOING HERE? WHOSE HOUSE IS THIS?
I RUN AWAY FROM EVERYTHING THAT I DON'T WANNA DEAL WITH.
BARNEY, I DIDN'T MEAN WHAT I-
NO, YOU WERE RIGHT. BUT I'M NOT GONNA RUN AWAY ANY MORE. I PROMISE. AND WE'RE HERE SO THAT I CAN PROVE THAT TO YOU.

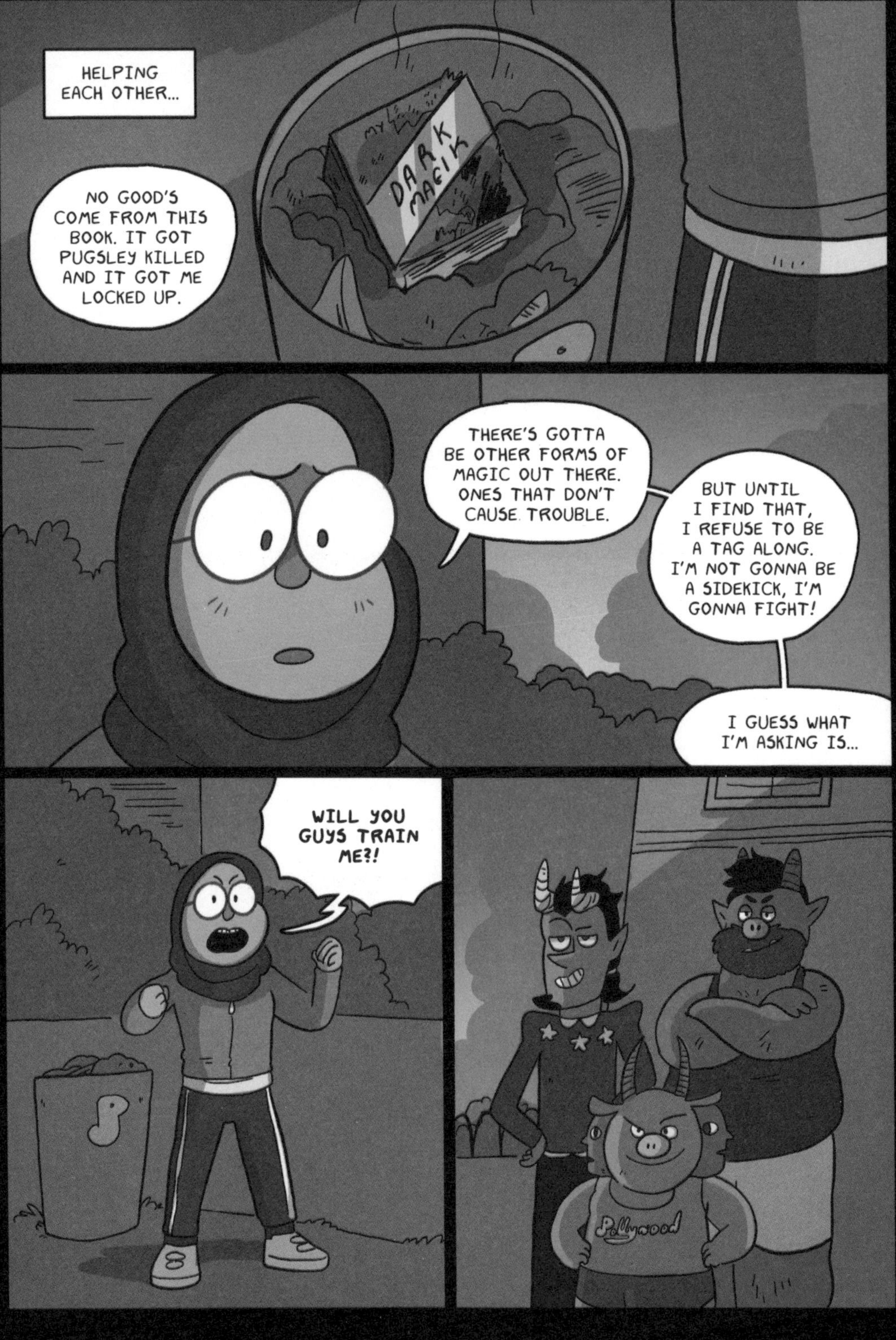
HELPING EACH OTHER...
NO GOOD'S COME FROM THIS BOOK. IT GOT PUGSLEY KILLED AND IT GOT ME LOCKED UP.
MY DARK MAGIK
THERE'S GOTTA BE OTHER FORMS OF MAGIC OUT THERE. ONES THAT DON'T CAUSE TROUBLE.
BUT UNTIL I FIND THAT, I REFUSE TO BE A TAG ALONG. I'M NOT GONNA BE A SIDEKICK, I'M GONNA FIGHT!
I GUESS WHAT I'M ASKING IS...
WILL YOU GUYS TRAIN ME?!
Pollywood

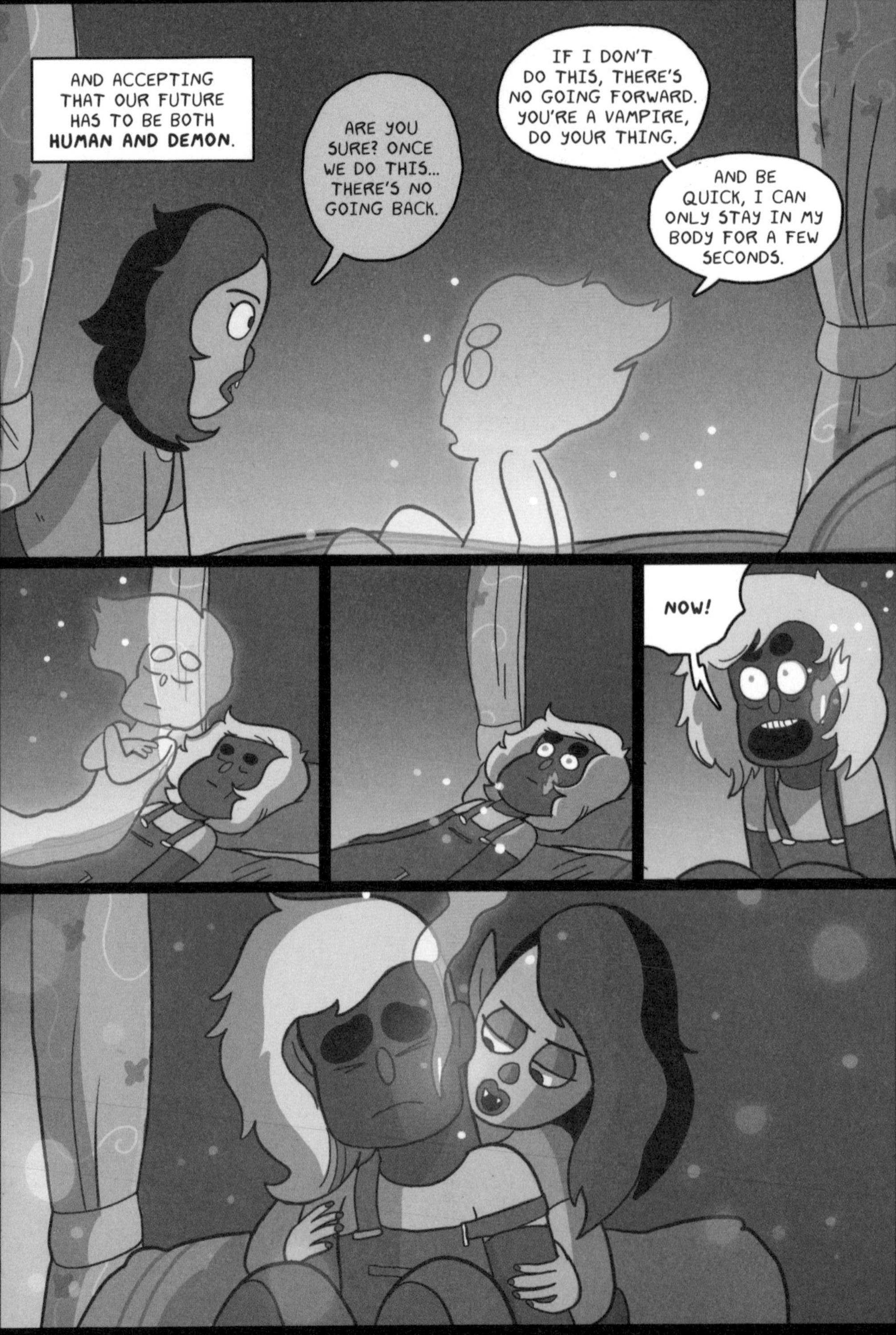
AND ACCEPTING THAT OUR FUTURE HAS TO BE BOTH **HUMAN AND DEMON**.
ARE YOU SURE? ONCE WE DO THIS... THERE'S NO GOING BACK.
IF I DON'T DO THIS, THERE'S NO GOING FORWARD. YOU'RE A VAMPIRE, DO YOUR THING.
AND BE QUICK, I CAN ONLY STAY IN MY BODY FOR A FEW SECONDS.
NOW!

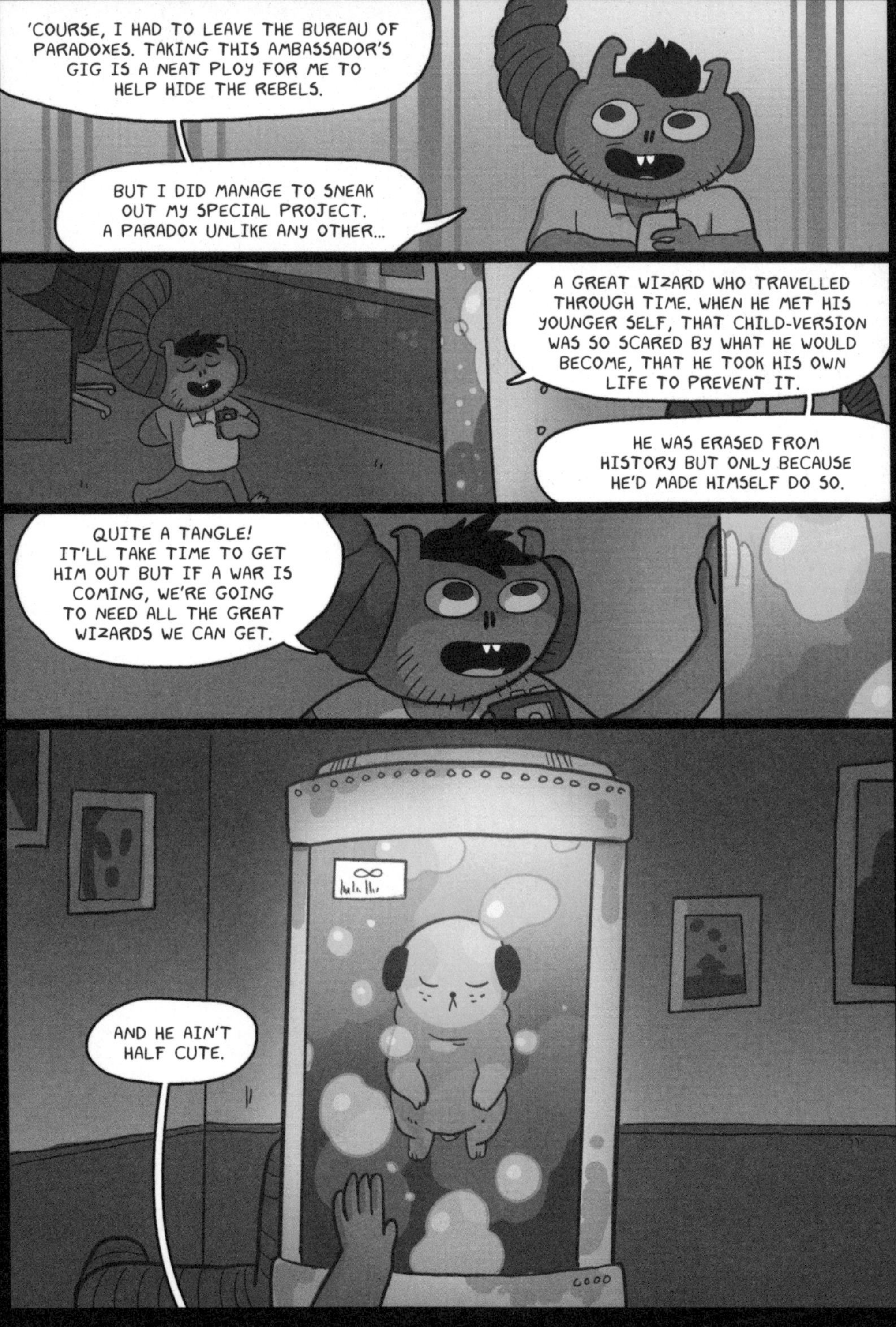
'COURSE, I HAD TO LEAVE THE BUREAU OF PARADOXES. TAKING THIS AMBASSADOR'S GIG IS A NEAT PLOY FOR ME TO HELP HIDE THE REBELS.
BUT I DID MANAGE TO SNEAK OUT MY SPECIAL PROJECT. A PARADOX UNLIKE ANY OTHER...
A GREAT WIZARD WHO TRAVELLED THROUGH TIME. WHEN HE MET HIS YOUNGER SELF, THAT CHILD-VERSION WAS SO SCARED BY WHAT HE WOULD BECOME, THAT HE TOOK HIS OWN LIFE TO PREVENT IT.
HE WAS ERASED FROM HISTORY BUT ONLY BECAUSE HE'D MADE HIMSELF DO SO.
QUITE A TANGLE! IT'LL TAKE TIME TO GET HIM OUT BUT IF A WAR IS COMING, WE'RE GOING TO NEED ALL THE GREAT WIZARDS WE CAN GET.
AND HE AIN'T HALF CUTE.

HAMISH

TOUGH
SMART
WEIRD
STYLE

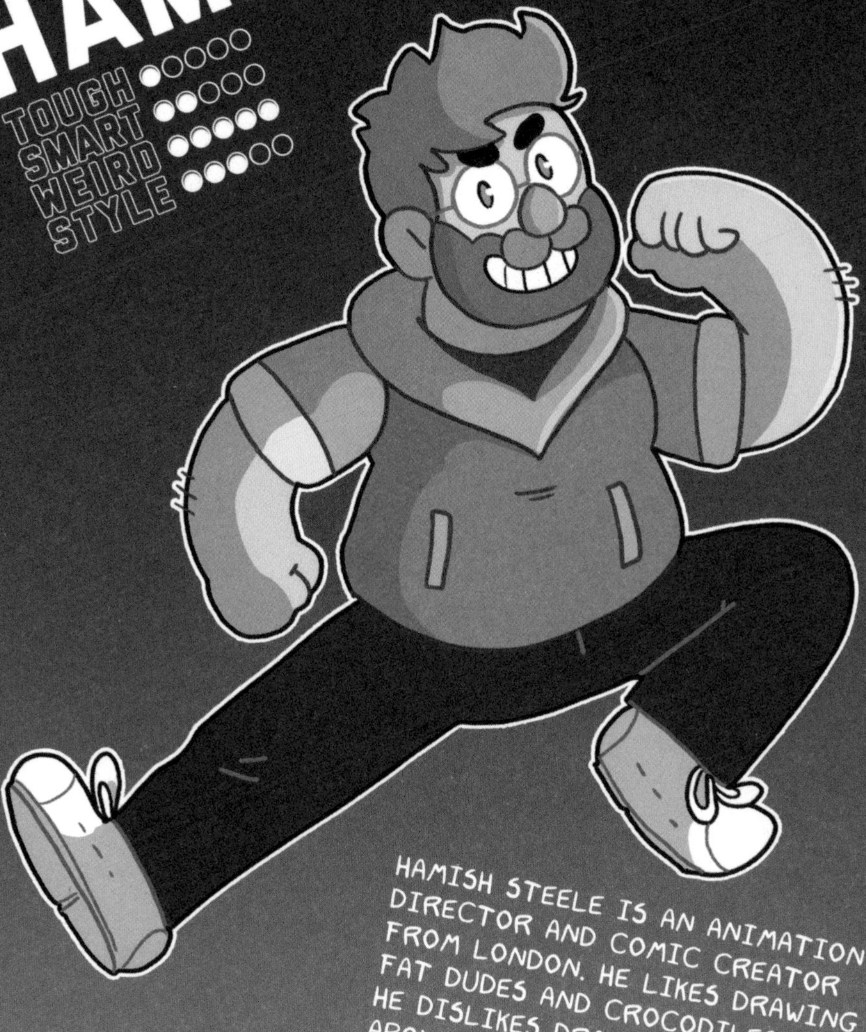

HAMISH STEELE IS AN ANIMATION DIRECTOR AND COMIC CREATOR FROM LONDON. HE LIKES DRAWING FAT DUDES AND CROCODILES. HE DISLIKES DRAWING SHOES. ABOVE IS A DRAWING OF HIM WEARING HIS DREAM HOODIE.

ALSO IN THE SERIES :

HAMISH STEELE
DEAD ENDIA
THE WATCHER'S TEST
NOBROW

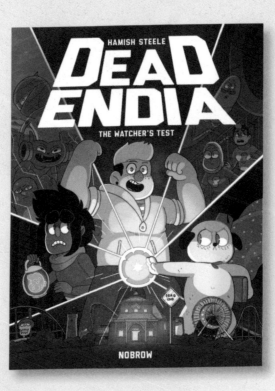

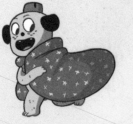

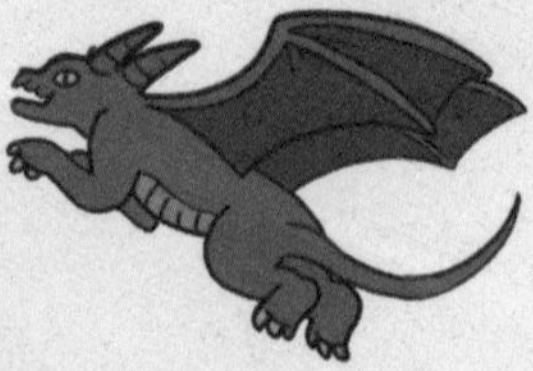

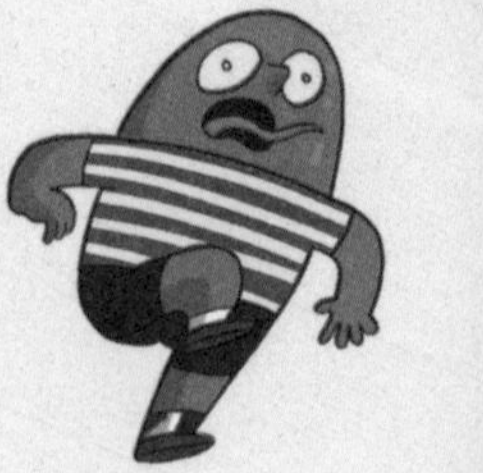

DEADENDIA:

THE WATCHER'S TEST

ISBN: 978-1-910620-47-2

★★★

"*DEADENDIA* IS IMMEDIATELY APPEALING WITH ITS COLORFUL ART, UNIQUE SETTING, AND FUNNY JOKES, BUT I ESPECIALLY LOVED THE COMPLICATED EMOTIONAL ARCS OF THE CHARACTERS AND THE WEIRD, SPOOKY MAGIC UNDERLYING EVERYTHING!"

~ MOLLY KNOX OSTERTAG, CREATOR OF *THE WITCH BOY*

★★★

MORE BY HAMISH STEELE:

HAMISH STEELE
PANTHEON
THE TRUE STORY OF THE EGYPTIAN DEITIES
NOBROW

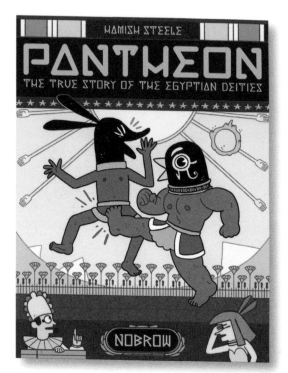

PANTHEON:

THE TRUE STORY OF THE

EGYPTIAN DEITIES

ISBN: 978-1-910620-20-5

16+

***

"SAVAGE, BAWDY, IRREVERENT AND UPROARIOUSLY FUNNY"

~ *THE GUARDIAN*

***

SPECIAL THANKS TO:

LYDIA BUTZ, YASMINA CHOWDHURY, ANGY EL-KHATIB,
GALACTIC JONAH, AMMAR KHALID, ZAHIRA KHARSANY,
JACK PETCH, JUSTIN RIDLEY, JAMES STEVENSON
BRETTON, TOM STUART AND MELISSA TRENDER.

FIRST PUBLISHED IN 2019 BY NOBROW LTD.
27 WESTGATE STREET, LONDON E8 3RL.

1 3 5 7 9 10 8 6 4 2

PUBLISHED IN THE US BY NOBROW (US) INC.
PRINTED IN POLAND ON FSC® CERTIFIED PAPER.

MIX
Paper from responsible sources
FSC® C001693
www.fsc.org

ISBN: 978-1-910620-62-5
WWW.NOBROW.NET